Elizabeth George's first novel, *A Great Deliverance*, was honoured with the Anthony and Agatha Best First Novel awards in America and received the Grand Prix de Littérature Policière in France. The critically acclaimed *Payment in Blood* followed, and *Well-Schooled in Murder*, which was awarded the prestigious German prize for international mystery fiction, the MIMI, in 1990. *A Suitable Vengeance, For the Sake of Elena, Missing Joseph, Playing for the Ashes, In the Presence of the Enemy, Deception on his Mind, In Pursuit of the Proper Sinner, A Traitor to Memory, A Place of Hiding, With No One as Witness, Careless in Red, This Body of Death* and most recently *Believing the Lie* were also highly acclaimed by critics. Her novels have now been adapted for television by BBC TV. Elizabeth George lives on Whidbey Island, in the state of Washington. Visit her website at www.elizabethgeorgeonline.com

Praise for Elizabeth George:

'Absolutely remarkable and a great achievement'
Boyd Hilton on *BBC Radio FiveLive*

'It shifts the way you look at things – I was completely drawn into this world I knew nothing about and I'm full of admiration' Sarah Harrison

'A very powerful novel' Kate Mosse

'Why haven't I read Elizabeth George before? Maybe because someone told me she was a serious crime writer, and I listen to thrillers to escape, not to think. All this will change; she's brilliant' Sue Arnold, *Guardian*

'With *What Came Before He Shot Her*, I think she's taken her writing to a new level. Of ⸺ i but boy, the j

D1498710

Also by Elizabeth George

FICTION

A Great Deliverance
Payment in Blood
Well-Schooled in Murder
A Suitable Vengeance
For the Sake of Elena
Missing Joseph
Playing for the Ashes
In the Presence of the Enemy
Deception on his Mind
In Pursuit of the Proper Sinner
A Traitor to Memory
A Place of Hiding
With No One as Witness
Careless in Red
This Body of Death
Believing the Lie

SHORT STORIES

The Evidence Exposed
I, Richard

ANTHOLOGY

Crime From the Mind of A Woman (Ed.)
Two of the Deadliest (Ed.)

NON-FICTION

Write Away: One Novelist's Approach to Fiction and the
Writing Life

FOR YOUNG ADULTS

The Edge of Nowhere

ELIZABETH GEORGE

What Came Before
He Shot Her

HODDER

First published in Great Britain in 2007 by Hodder & Stoughton

This edition published by Hodder & Stoughton in 2012
An Hachette UK company

2

Copyright © Susan Elizabeth George 2007

The right of Elizabeth George to be identified as the Author
of the Work has been asserted by her in accordance with the
Copyright, Designs and Patents Act 1988.

All rights reserved. No part of this publication may be
reproduced, stored in a retrieval system, or transmitted, in any form
or by any means without the prior written permission of the publisher,
nor be otherwise circulated in any form of binding or cover other than
that in which it is published and without a similar condition
being imposed on the subsequent purchaser.

All characters in this publication are fictitious and any resemblance
to real persons, living or dead is purely coincidental.

A CIP catalogue record for this title is
available from the British Library

ISBN 978 1444 73837 7

Printed and bound by CPI Group (UK) Ltd, Croydon CRO 4YY

Hodder & Stoughton policy is to use papers that are natural,
renewable and recyclable products and made from wood
grown in sustainable forests. The logging and manufacturing
processes are expected to conform to the environmental
regulations of the country of origin.

Hodder & Stoughton Ltd
338 Euston Road
London NW1 3BH

www.hodder.co.uk

For Grace Tsukiyama
Political liberal
Creative spirit
Mom

Better authentic mammon than a bogus god.

Louis MacNeice, *Autumn Journal*

I

Joel Campbell, eleven years old at the time, began his descent towards murder with a bus ride. It was a newish bus, a single-decker. It was numbered 70, on the London route that trundles along Du Cane Road in East Acton.

There is not much notable on the northern section of this particular route, of which Du Cane Road is but a brief part. The southern section is pleasant enough, cruising near the V & A and past the stately white edifices of Queen's Gate in South Kensington. But the northern part has a list of destinations that reads like a where's where of places in London not to frequent: the Swift Wash Laundry on North Pole Road; H. J. Bent Funeral Directors (cremations or burial) on Old Oak Common Lane; the dismal congeries of shops at the turbulent inter-section where Western Avenue becomes Western Way as cars and lorries tear towards the centre of town; and, looming over all of this like something designed by Dickens, Wormwood Scrubs. Not Wormwood Scrubs the tract of land circumscribed by railway lines, but Wormwood Scrubs the prison, part fortress and part asylum in appearance, place of unremitting grim reality in fact.

On this particular January day, though, Joel Campbell took note of none of these features of the journey upon which he was embarking. He was in the company of three other individuals, and he was cautiously anticipating a positive change in his life. Prior to this moment, East Acton and a small terrace house in Henchman Street had represented his circumstances: a grubby sitting-room and grubbier kitchen below, three bedrooms above, and a patchy green at the front, round which the terrace of little homes horseshoe'd like a collection of war widows along three sides of a grave. It was a place that might have been pleasant fifty years ago, but successive generations of inhabitants had put their mark upon it, and the current generation's mark was given largely to rubbish on doorsteps, broken toys discarded on the single path that followed the U of the terrace, plastic snowmen and rotund Santas and reindeer toppling over on the jutting roofs of bay windows from November till May, and a sinkhole of a mud puddle in the middle of the green that stood there eight months of the year, breeding insects like someone's entomology project. Joel was glad to be leaving this place, even if leaving meant a long plane ride and a new life on an island very different from the only island he'd so far known.

'Ja-*mai*-ca.' His gran didn't so much say as intone the word. Glory Campbell drew out the *mai* till it sounded the way a warm breeze felt, welcome and soft, with promise gilding its breath. 'What you t'ink 'bout *dat*, you t'ree kids? Ja-*mai*-ca.'

You t'ree kids were the Campbell children, victims of a tragedy played out on Old Oak Common Lane on a Saturday afternoon. They were progeny of Glory's elder son, dead like her second son although in entirely different circumstances. Joel, Ness, and Toby, they were called. Or 'poor lit'l t'ings', as Glory had taken to referring to them once her man George Gilbert had received his deportation papers and she'd seen which way the wind of George's life was likely to blow.

This use of language on Glory's part was something new. In the time the Campbell children had been living with her – which was more than three years and counting this time around and looking to be a permanent arrangement – she'd been a stickler for correct pronunciation. She herself had been taught the Queen's English long ago at her Catholic girls' school in Kingston and, while it hadn't served her as well as she'd hoped when she'd immigrated to England, she could still trot it out when a shop assistant needed sorting, and she intended her grandkids to be able to do some proper sorting as well, should they ever have the need.

But all that altered with the advent of George's deportation papers. When the buff envelope had been opened and its contents perused, digested, and understood, and when all the legal manoeuvring had been engaged in to prolong if not to thwart the inevitable, Glory had shed over forty years of God-save-the-current-monarch in an instant. If her George was heading for Ja-*mai*-ca, so was she. And the Queen's English wasn't necessary there. Indeed, it could be an impediment.

So the linguistic tone, melody, and syntax morphed from Glory's rather charmingly antique version of Received Pronunciation to the pleasant honey of Caribbean English. She was going native, her neighbours called it.

George Gilbert had left London first, escorted to Heathrow by Immigration Officials keeping the current prime minister's promise to do something about the problem of visitors overstaying their visas. They came for him in a private car and glanced at their watches while he bade Glory a farewell thoroughly lubricated by Red Stripe, which he'd begun to drink in anticipation of the return to his roots. They said, 'Come along, Mr Gilbert,' and took him by the arms. One of them reached into his pocket as if in search of handcuffs should George not cooperate.

But George was happy to go along with them. Things hadn't really been the same at Glory's since the grandkids had dropped on them like three human meteors from a galaxy he'd never quite understood. 'Look damn *odd*, Glor,' he'd say when he thought they weren't listening. 'Least, the boys do. S'pose the girl's all right.'

'You hush up 'bout them,' was Glory's reply. Her own children's blood was thoroughly mixed – although less so than the blood of her grandkids – and she wasn't about to have anyone comment on what was as obvious as burnt toast on snow.

Mixed blood was not the disgrace it had been in centuries past. It no longer made anyone anathema.

But George blew out his lips. He sucked on his teeth. From the corners of his eyes, he watched the young Campbells. 'They not fitting good into Jamaica,' he pointed out.

This assessment didn't deter Glory. At least that was how it seemed to her grandchildren in the days leading up to their exodus from East Acton. Glory sold the furniture. She boxed up the kitchen. She sorted through clothes. She packed the suitcases and, when there were not enough to include everything that her granddaughter Ness wished to take to Jamaica, she folded those garments into her shopping trolley and declared that they'd pick up a suitcase on the way.

They made a ragtag parade weaving over to Du Cane Road. Glory led the way in a navy winter coat that hung to her ankles, with a green and orange turban tied round her head. Little Toby came second, tripping along on his tiptoes as was his habit, an inflated life-ring round his waist. Joel struggled to keep up third, the two suitcases he carried making his progress difficult. Ness brought up the rear, in jeans so tight it was hard to see how she was going to manage to sit without splitting them open, teetering along on four-inch heels with black boots climbing up her legs. She had the shopping trolley in her grip, and she wasn't happy about having to drag it along behind her. She wasn't happy about anything, in fact. Her face dripped scorn and her gait spoke contempt.

The day was cold the way only London can be cold in January. The air was heavy with damp, along with exhaust fumes and the soot of illegal fires. The frost of morning had never melted, instead turning into patches of ice that threatened the unwary pedestrian. Grey defined everything: from the sky to the trees to the roads to the buildings. The entire atmosphere was hopeless writ large. In the fading daylight, sun and spring were an empty promise.

On the bus, even in a place like London – where everything

that might possibly be seen had already been seen at one time or another – the Campbell children still garnered looks, each for a reason peculiar to the individual. In Toby it was the great bald patches across his head, where his half-grown hair was wispy and far too thin for a seven-year-old boy, as well as the life-ring, which took up too much space and from which he resolutely refused to be parted even so much as to remove it from his waist and 'bleeding *hold* it in front of you, for God's sake,' as Ness demanded. In Ness herself, it was the unnatural darkness of her skin, obviously enhanced by make-up, as if she were trying to be more of what she only partially was. Had she shed her jacket, it would also have been the rest of her clothing beyond her jeans: the sequinned top that left her midriff bare and put her voluptuous breasts on display. And in Joel it was, and would always be, his face covered by teacake-size splotches that could never be called freckles but were instead a physical expression of the ethnic and racial battle that his blood had gone through from the moment of his conception. Like Toby, it was his hair as well, in his case wild and unruly, springing from his head like a rusty scouring pad. Only Toby and Joel looked as if they *might* be related, and none of the Campbell children looked like someone who might belong to Glory.

So they were noticed. Not only did they block most of the aisle with their suitcases, shopping trolley, and the five additional Sainsbury bags that Glory had deposited around her feet, but they made a vignette that begged for consideration.

Of the four of them, only Joel and Ness were aware of the scrutiny of the other passengers, and they each reacted differently to the glances. For Joel, each look seemed to say *yellow-arse bastard*, and each hasty movement of a gaze away from him to the window seemed to be a dismissal of his right to walk the earth. For Ness, these same looks meant lewd evaluation, and when she felt them alight on her, she wanted to tear open her jacket and thrust out her breasts and shriek as she often did in the street: 'You wan' it, man? *This* wha' you want?'

Glory and Toby, however, were in worlds of their own. For Toby this was his natural state, a fact that no one in the family cared to dwell upon. For Glory this was a condition prompted by her current situation and what she intended to do about it.

The bus lurched along its route, splashing through puddles from the last rainfall. It swerved into the kerb and out again without regard for the safety of the passengers clinging to its poles within, and it became more crowded and more claustrophobic as the journey went on. As is always the state of public transport in the winter in London, the heat in the vehicle was on full force and since not a single window – aside from the driver's – was actually operational, the atmosphere was not only balmy but also thick with the sort of micro-organisms that spew forth from unguarded sneezes and coughs.

All of this gave Glory the excuse she was looking for. She'd been keeping a keen eye on where they were along the route anyway, sifting through all the possible reasons she could give for what she was about to do, but the atmosphere inside the vehicle was enough. When the bus ventured along Ladbroke Grove in the vicinity of Chesterton Road, she reached for the red button and thumbed it firmly. She said, 'Out, you lot,' to the kids, and they shoved their way down the aisle with all of their belongings and clambered into the blessedly cold air.

This place, of course, was nowhere near Jamaica. Nor was it within shouting distance of any airport where a plane could take them in a westerly direction. But before these facts could be pointed out to her, Glory adjusted her turban – pushed askew as she'd struggled down the aisle – and said to the children, 'Can't be heading off for Ja-*mai*-ca wit'out saying our goodbyes to your auntie, now can we?'

Auntie was Glory's only daughter, Kendra Osborne. Although she lived a single bus ride away from East Acton, the Campbell children had seen her only six times in the last three years, on the obligatory Christmas and Easter Sunday get-togethers. To say that she and Glory were estranged, though, would be to misrepresent the matter. The truth was that neither woman approved of the other, and their disapproval revolved around men. To be present in Henchman Street more than two days a year would have required Kendra to see George Gilbert lounging, unemployed and unemployable, around the house. To pay a call in North Kensington might have exposed Glory to any one of the string of Kendra's lovers – taken up, then quickly discarded. The two women considered their lack of physical contact a truce. The telephone served them well enough.

So the idea that they might be tripping over to bid farewell to their aunt Kendra was greeted with some confusion, surprise, and suspicion on the part of the children, depending upon which child's reaction to this unexpected announcement was being examined: Toby assumed they'd arrived in Jamaica, Joel tried to cope with an abrupt change in plans, and Ness muttered 'Oh, *right*,' under her breath, an unspoken notion of hers having just been confirmed.

Glory didn't deal with any of this. She merely led the way. Like a mother duck with her offspring, she assumed her grandchildren would follow her. What else were they to do in a part of London with which they were not altogether familiar?

Thankfully, it was not an overlong walk from Ladbroke Grove to Edenham Estate, and only on Golborne Road did they attract attention. It was market day, and while the number of stalls was not as impressive as it might have been had they been walking along Church Street or weaving through the environs of Brick Lane, at E. Price & Sons Fresh Fruit and Veg the two elderly gentlemen – father and son, although truth to tell they looked much more like brothers – remarked upon the untidy band of interlopers to the women they were serving. These ladies were themselves one-time interlopers into the area, but the Price father and son had learned to accept them.

They had little choice in the matter, for in the sixty years they'd operated E. Price & Sons Fresh Fruit and Veg, the Prices had seen the inhabitants of Golborne Ward – as the area was called – alter from English to Portuguese to Moroccan, and they knew the wisdom of embracing their paying customers.

But the little group trudging along the street was clearly not intent upon making any purchases from the stalls. Indeed, they had their sights fixed upon Portobello Bridge and soon enough they were across it. Here, a short distance along Elkstone Road and well within the unremitting roar of the Westway Flyover, Edenham Estate was plopped down next to a meandering park called Meanwhile Gardens. Central to this estate was Trellick Tower, and it presided over the landscape with unjustified pride, thirty floors of Grade II-listed concrete, with a west-facing aspect of balconies by the hundreds, sprouting upon them satellite dishes, motley windbreaks, and flapping lines of laundry. Its separated lift shaft – joined to the building by a system of bridges – gave the tower its single distinction. Otherwise, it was similar to most of the post-war high-density housing that encircled London: enormous, grey vertical scars on a landscape, well-meant intentions gone wrong. Spread out beneath this tower was the rest of the estate, comprising blocks of flats, a home for the elderly, and two lines of terrace houses that backed on to Meanwhile Gardens.

It was in one of these terrace houses that Kendra Osborne lived, and Glory shepherded her grandkids to this place, dropping her Sainsbury bags upon the top step with a sigh of relief. Joel set down his burden of suitcases and rubbed his sore hands along the sides of his jeans. Toby looked around and blinked as he fingered his life-ring spasmodically. Ness shoved her shopping trolley into the door of the garage, crossed her arms beneath her breasts and cast a baleful look upon her grandmother, one which clearly said, What's next, bitch?

Too clever by half was Glory's uneasy thought as she beheld

her granddaughter. Ness had always been several steps ahead of her siblings.

Glory turned from the girl and resolutely rang the bell. Daylight was fading and while time was not exactly of the essence, considering Glory's game plan, she was becoming anxious for the next part of their lives to begin. When there was no response, she rang a second time.

'Looks like we won't be saying any goodbyes here, *Gran*,' was Ness's acidulous comment. 'Guess we best keep on going to the *airport*, eh?'

Glory ignored her. She said, 'Le's jus' check round here,' and she led the children back towards the street and up a narrow path between the two lines of terraces. This path gave access to the back of the houses and to their tiny gardens, which were laid out behind a tall brick wall. She said to Joel, 'Hol' your bruvver up, luv. Toby, see is 'ere lights on inside.' And then to any of them who might be interested, 'Could be she up to it wiv one of her men. Dat Kendra's got a one-track mind.'

Joel cooperated and squatted so that Toby could climb on to his shoulders. Toby did so obediently although the process was made difficult by the life-ring. Once hoisted, Toby clung to the wall. He murmured, 'She got a barbecue, Joel,' and stared at this object with fascination.

''S 'ere lights on?' Glory asked the little boy. 'Toby, lookit de *house*, darlin.'

Toby shook his head, and Glory took this to mean no lights were shining from the lower floor of the house. There were no lights shining from the upper floors either, so she was faced with an unanticipated glitch in her plan. But Glory was nothing if not a woman who could improvise. She said, 'Well . . .' as she rubbed her hands together, and she was about to go on when Ness spoke sharply.

'Guess we'll just have to go on to Jamaica, won't we, *Gran*?' Ness had come no farther than the path itself, and she stood with her weight on one hip, her booted foot thrust out, and her arms akimbo. This posture spread open her jacket and put her bare midriff, her pierced navel, and her considerable cleavage on display.

Seductive came to Glory in a flutter, but she dismissed the thought as she often did, as she'd told herself she *had* to do, in the past few years of her granddaughter's constant company.

'Guess we jus' have to leave Aunt Ken a *note*.'

Glory said, 'You lot come wiv me,' and back around the building they went, to Kendra's front door, where the suitcases, shopping trolley, and Sainsbury bags all made a jumble from the steps down to the narrow street. She told the children to sit on the slab that went for the porch, although anyone could see there was little enough space to do so. Joel and Toby cooperated, hunkering down among the carrier bags, but Ness stood back, and her expression said that she was just waiting for the inevitable excuses to come pouring out of her grandmother's mouth.

Glory said, 'I make a place for you. An' it take time when you make a place. So I go ahead and I send for you when t'ings are ready in Ja-*mai*-ca.'

Ness blew out a derisive breath. She looked around to see if there was someone nearby who might bear witness to her grandmother's lies. She said, 'We staying with Aunt Kendra, then? She know that, Gran? She even round here? She on holiday? She move house? How you even know where she is?'

Glory cast Ness a look but gave her attention to the boys, who were so much more likely to bend their behaviour to her plan. At fifteen, Ness was too street wary. At eleven and seven, Joel and Toby still had a great deal ahead of them to learn.

'Talked to your auntie yesterday,' she said. 'She's out at de shops. She's laying on somet'ing special for your tea.'

Another derisive breath from Ness. A solemn nod from Joel. A restless shifting from one buttock to the other from Toby. He plucked at Joel's jeans. Joel put his arm around Toby's shoulders. This sight warmed the one or two cockles that actually existed in Glory's heart. They would all be fine, she told herself.

She said, 'I got to go, you lot. An' what I want is you kids stopping here. You wait for Auntie. She be back. She fetching your tea. You wait for her here. Don't go wanderin cos you don't know dis place and I don't want you lost. Y'unnerstan? Ness, you mind Joel. Joel, you mind Toby.'

'I ain't,' Ness began but Joel said, ''Kay.' It was all he could say, so tight was his throat. His life had so far taught him that there were some things it was pointless to fight, but he hadn't yet mastered not feeling about them.

Glory kissed the top of his head, saying, 'You a good lad, luv,' and she patted Toby diffidently. She picked up her suitcase and two of the carrier bags, and she backed away, drawing in a deep breath. She didn't actually *like* leaving them on their own like this, but she knew that Kendra would be home soon. Glory hadn't phoned her in advance, but aside from her little problem with men, Kendra lived by the book, responsibility incarnate. She had a job, and she was training for another, to get back on her feet after her last disastrous marriage. She was heading towards a real *career*. No way in hell was Kendra off anywhere unexpected. She'd be back soon. It was, after all, a bit past teatime.

'You lot don't move an inch,' Glory told the grandkids. 'You give your auntie a big kiss from me.'

That said, she turned to leave them. Ness stood in her way. Glory tried to give her a tender smile. 'I send for you, darlin,' she said to the girl. 'You don' b'lieve me. I c'n tell. But it's God's truth, Ness. I send for you. Me an' George, we make a house for you lot to come to an' when it's all ready for you—'

Ness turned. She began to walk off, not in the direction of Elkstone Road which would have been the same route as Glory's but in the direction of the path between the buildings, the path to Meanwhile Gardens and what lay beyond them.

Glory watched her go. Stalking, she was, and her high-heeled boots made a sound like whip-cracks in the cold air. And just like whip-cracks, the sound struck Glory's cheeks. She wasn't *meaning* to do wrong to the children. The way things were at the moment were simply the way they had to be.

She called after Ness, 'You got any message I give to our George? He setting up a house for you, Nessa.'

Ness's steps quickened. She stumbled on a bit of raised pavement, but she did not fall. In a moment, she'd vanished round the side of the building, and Glory listened in vain for some kind of words to float back to her on the late afternoon. She wanted something to reassure her, something to tell her that she had not failed.

She called out, 'Nessa? Vanessa Campbell?'

In return there came only an anguished cry. It was cousin to a sob, and Glory felt it like a blow to her chest. She looked to her grandsons for what their sister had been unwilling to give her.

'I send for you,' she said. 'Me an' George, when we got de house in order, we tell Aunt Ken to make de 'rangements. Ja-mai-ca.' She intoned the word. 'Ja-*mai*-ca.'

Toby's response was to move even closer to Joel. Joel's was to nod.

'You b'lieve me, den?' his grandmother asked.

Joel nodded. He couldn't see any other choice.

The tall overhead lights came on along the path as Ness circled around a low brick building on the edge of Meanwhile Gardens. This was a child drop-in centre – devoid of children at this time of day – and when Ness glanced at it, she saw a lone Asian woman within, who looked to be closing up for the evening. Beyond this place, the gardens fanned out, and a serpentine path wove through tree-studded hillocks, tracing the way to a staircase. This climbed in a metal spiral to an iron-railed bridge, and the bridge itself spanned the Paddington branch of what was the Grand Union Canal. The canal served as the northern boundary of Meanwhile Gardens, a division between Edenham Estate and a collection of housing where sleek, modern flats sat cheek by jowl with antique tenements in a declaration of the fact that life overlooking the water had not always been so desirable.

Ness took in some of this, but not all. She homed in on the steps, the iron-railed bridge above them, and where the road crossing that bridge might lead.

Inside, she burned, so much that the very heat of her made her want to fling her jacket to the ground and then stamp upon it. But she was acutely aware of the January cold beyond the heat inside her, touching her flesh where her flesh was bare. And she felt caught inextricably between both of them: the heat within and the cold without.

She reached the steps, unmindful of the eyes that watched her from beneath one of the adolescent oak trees that studded the hillocks in Meanwhile Gardens, unmindful of the eyes that watched her from beneath the bridge over the Grand Union Canal. She didn't yet know that as darkness fell – and some-times even when it was far from falling – transactions were made in Meanwhile Gardens. Cash was passed from one hand to another; it was counted furtively and, just as furtively, illegal substances were handed over. Indeed, as she reached the top of the steps and gained the bridge, the two individuals who'd been watching her melted out from their hiding places and met each other. They conducted their business in such a fluid manner that, had Ness been looking, she would have known that this was a regular encounter.

But she was intent upon her own purpose: an end to heat that burned from within. She had no money and no know-ledge of the area, but she knew what to look for.

She stepped on to the bridge and took her bearings. Across the road was a pub, and beyond this ran a stretch of terrace houses on either side of the street. Ness studied the pub but saw nothing promising within or without, so she headed in the direction of the houses. Experience taught her that somewhere nearby had to be shops, and experience did not lead her astray. She came upon them within fifty yards, with Tops Pizza offering the best of the possibilities.

A group of teenagers mingled in front of it: three boys and two girls. All of them were black, to one degree or another. The boys wore baggy jeans, sweatshirts with their hoods drawn up, and heavy anoraks. This was something of a uniform in this part of North Kensington. The kit as a piece told an onlooker where their loyalties lay. Ness knew this. She also knew what was required of her. Match rough with rough. It would not be a problem.

The two girls were already doing this. They lounged back against the front window of Tops Pizza, eyelids lowered, breasts thrust out, flicking ash from their cigarettes on to the pavement. When either of them spoke, they did so with a toss of the head while the boys sniffed around them and strutted like cocks.

'You a star, yeah. Come wiv me and I show you good times.'

'What you want wiv hanging 'bout here, darlin? You out here seeing the sights? Well, I got a real sight to show you.'

Laughter, laughter. Ness felt her toes curl inside her boots. It was always the same: a ritual whose outcome differed only in what came of its conclusion.

The girls played along. Their part was to act not only reluctant but scornful. The reluctance gave hope, and the scorn fed the fire. Nothing worthwhile should ever be easy.

Ness approached them. The group fell silent in that intimidating fashion adolescents adopt when an intruder appears in their midst. Ness knew the importance of speaking first. Words and not appearance produced the initial impression when more than one person was chanced upon in the street.

She jerked her head at them and shoved her hands into the

pockets of her jacket. She said, 'You lot know where to score?' She blew out a laugh and threw a look over her shoulder. 'Shit. I'm aching for it.'

'I got somet'ing you ache for, darlin.' It was the expected response. It was given by the tallest boy in the crew. Ness met his eyes squarely and looked him over top to toe before he could do the same to her. She could feel the two girls bristle at this, her invasion of their territory, and she knew the importance of her response.

She rolled her eyes and gave her attention to the girls. She said, 'Bet no one scores from *this* lot. Right?'

The bustier of the girls laughed. Like the boys, she eyed Ness but this was a different kind of evaluation. She was assessing Ness's potential for inclusion. To help things along, Ness said, 'Get a hit?' and indicated the cigarette the girl held.

'Ain't a spliff,' was the reply.

'Know that, don't I,' Ness said. 'But it's something anyways and, like I say, I fucking *need* something, I do.'

'Darlin, I tell you I *got* what you need. Jus' step round the corner and I show it to you.' The tallest boy again. The others grinned. They shuffled their feet, touched fists, and laughed.

Ness ignored them. The girl handed over her cigarette. Ness took a drag. She eyed the two girls as they eyed her.

No one said a name. That was part of the dance. An exchange of names meant a step was taken and no one wanted to be the first person to take it.

Ness handed the cigarette back to its owner. The girl took a drag. Her companion said, 'Wha' you want, den?' to Ness.

'Hell, it don't matter,' Ness replied. 'Jesus, I go for coke, weed, olly, E, anyt'ing. I'm jus' fucking *itchin*, you know.'

'I got a way to scratch—' the tallest boy began.

'Shut up,' the girl said. And then to Ness, 'Wha' you got on you? It ain't free round here.'

'I c'n pay,' Ness said. 'Long's cash i'n't wha's required.'

'Hey, den, baby—'

'Shut *up*,' the girl said to Tall Boy once again. 'I got to say it, Greve. You vexin me, man.'

'Now, Six, you gettin' 'bove yourself.'

'Dat your name?' Ness asked her. 'Six?'

'Yeah,' she said. 'Dis here's Natasha. Who might you be?'

'Ness.'

'Cool.'

'So where we score round this place?'

Six jerked her head at the boys and said, 'Not from this lot, you c'n be sure, innit. Dey is *not* producers, lemme tell you dat.'

'Where, den?'

Six looked at one of the other boys. He'd hung back, silent, observing. Six said to him, 'He deliverin any substance tonight?'

The boy shrugged, revealing nothing. He looked at Ness, but his eyes weren't friendly. He finally said, 'Depends. An' if he is, no saying he plan to skim. Anyways, he ain't givin it away, and he don't do deals wiv bitches he don't know.'

'Hey, come *on*, Dashell,' Six said impatiently. 'She cool, all right? Don' be nasty.'

'Dis ain't no one-time deal,' Ness told Dashell. 'I plan on being a reg'lar.' She shifted from foot to foot, then, from foot to foot, to foot to foot, a little dance that said she acknowledged him: his position in the group and his power over them.

Dashell looked from Ness to the other two girls. His relationship with them seemed to turn the tide. He said to Six, 'I ask him, den. Won't be before half eleven, though.'

Six said, 'Cool. Where he bring it?'

'If he goin to skim, don't worry bout it. He find you.' He jerked his head at the other two boys. They sauntered in the direction of the Harrow Road.

Ness watched them go. She said to Six, 'He c'n supply?'

'Oh yeah,' Six said. 'He know who to call. He real enough, i'n't he, Tash?'

Natasha nodded and gave a glance in the direction Dashell and his companions were taking. 'Oh, he take care of us,' she said. 'But cars going two ways down dat street.'

It was a warning, but Ness saw herself as a match for anyone. As she evaluated things in that moment, it didn't matter how she got the stuff. The point was oblivion for as long as oblivion could be prompted into lasting.

'Well, I c'n drive a car, can't I?' she said to Natasha. 'Where we stop, den? It's a long time till half eleven roll around.'

In the meantime, Joel and Toby continued to wait for their aunt, obediently sitting on the top step of the four that climbed to her front door. From this position they had two choices of vistas to contemplate: Trellick Tower with its balconies and windows, where lights had been shining for at least an hour: and the line of terrace houses across the lane. Neither prospect comprised much to occupy the minds or imaginations of an eleven-year-old boy and his seven-year-old brother.

The boys' senses, however, were fully occupied: by the cold, by the unremitting noise from the Westway Flyover traffic and from the Hammersmith and City line of the London underground which – at this section of the route – was not under the ground at all, and by a growing need, in Joel, at least, to find a toilet.

Neither of the boys had any knowledge of this place so, in the gloom that fast became the darkness, it began to take on disturbing qualities. The sound of male voices approaching meant they could be accosted by members of whatever gang of drug dealers, muggers, burglars, or bag-snatchers dominated life on this particular estate. The sound of raucous rap music from a car passing on Elkstone Road just to the west of them declared the arrival of that same gang's kingpin who would accost them and demand a tribute that they could not pay. Anyone entering Edenham Way – the little lane in which their aunt's terrace house sat – was someone who would notice them, who would question them sharply, and phone the police when they did not provide appropriate answers. The police would then come. Care would follow. And that word Care – which was always rendered with an upper case C, at least in Joel's mind – was something akin to the bogey-man. While other children's parents might have said in a fit of frustration or in a desperate attempt to garner cooperation from their recalcitrant offspring, 'Do what I say or I swear you're going to end up in care,' for the Campbell children the threat was real. Glory Campbell's departure had brought them one step closer. A phone call to the police would seal the deal.

So Joel wasn't sure what to do as he and Toby entered the second hour of the wait for their aunt. He needed a toilet terribly, but if he spoke to a passerby or knocked on a door and asked could he relieve himself inside, he ran the risk of attracting unwanted attention. So he squeezed his legs together and tried to concentrate on something else. The options were the unnerving noises already mentioned or his little brother. He chose his brother.

Next to him, Toby remained in a world where he had long spent most of his waking hours. He called it Sose, and it was a place inhabited by people who spoke gently to him, who were known for their kindness to children and animals, and for their embraces, which they gave freely whenever a little boy felt afraid. With his knees drawn up and his life-ring still around his waist, Toby had a place to rest his chin, and that was what he had been doing since he and Joel had situated themselves on the top step. For all that time, he had kept his eyes closed and had gone where he vastly preferred to be.

Toby's position exposed his head to his brother, the very last thing that – aside from the occasional unnerving inter-loper on the estate – Joel wished to see. For Toby's head, with its great gaps of hairlessness, spoke of a failure of duty. It made a declaration and an accusation, and both of them pointed in Joel's direction. Glue had been the cause of Toby's hair loss, which wasn't actually loss at all but rather a painful removal by scissors, the only way to free his scalp from what a ring of young bullies had dumped upon him. This ring of thugs-in-the-making and the torments they had foisted upon Toby whenever they had the chance were just two of the reasons Joel was not unhappy to leave East Acton. Because of bullies, no walk for sweets to Ankaran Food and Wine was safe for Toby to make alone and, on the rare occasion when Glory Campbell supplied money for lunch instead of cheese and pickle sandwiches, if Toby managed to keep the cash in his pocket until the appointed hour, it was only because the local miniature yobs had targeted someone else.

So Joel didn't want to look at his brother's head because it reminded him again that he had not been there the last time Toby had been set upon. Since he'd appointed himself his brother's protector in Toby's infancy, the sight of him wandering up Henchman Street with his anorak's hood pulled up and fixed to his head with glue had caused Joel's chest to burn so much that he couldn't breathe, had caused him to duck his head in shame when Glory, in her own guilt-driven fury, had demanded to know how he'd let this happen to his own little brother.

Joel roused Toby as much not to have to look at his head as in desperate need to find a place to empty his bladder. He knew his brother wasn't asleep, but getting him back to present time and place was like awakening a baby. When Toby finally looked around, Joel stood and said, with a bravado he didn't particularly feel, 'Let's check this place out, mon.' Since being called *man* was a source of pleasure to the little boy, Toby went along with the plan without questioning the wisdom of leaving their belongings in a place where someone might likely steal them.

They went in the direction Ness had taken, between the buildings and towards Meanwhile Gardens. But rather than pass the child drop-in centre, they followed the path along the walled back gardens of the terrace houses. This gave on to the eastern section of Meanwhile Gardens, which here narrowed to a mass of shrubbery beside a tarmac path and, beyond that, the canal once again.

The shrubbery was an invitation Joel did not decline. He said, 'Hang on, Tobe,' and while his brother blinked at him affably, Joel engaged in what the London male tends to do unashamedly whenever he's caught short: He peed on the bushes. He found the relief enormous. It gave him a new lease of life. Despite the fears he'd earlier harboured about the estate, he cocked his head at the tarmac path on the other side of the shrubbery. Toby was meant to follow him, and he did. They trotted along and, within thirty yards, they found themselves looking down at a pond.

This glimmered with black menace in the darkness, but that menace was vitiated by the waterfowl perched along the edge of the water and clucking in the reeds. What light there was shone on a little wooden landing. A path curved down to this, and the boys ran along it. They clomped across the wood and hunkered at the edge. To their sides, ducks plopped from the land and paddled away.

'Wicked this, innit, Joel?' Toby looked around and smiled. 'We c'n make a fort here. Can we do dat? If we build it over'n dem bushes, no one—'

'Shh.' Joel put his hand over his brother's mouth. He had heard what Toby in his excitement had not. A footpath accompanied the Grand Union Canal above them and just beyond Meanwhile Gardens. Several people were coming along it, young males by the sound of them.

'Gimme toke 'f dat spliff, blood. Don' hol'back on me now.'

'You c'n pay or wha' cos I not off'ring charity, man.'

'Come on, we know you deliverin weed an' bone all over dis place.'

'Hey, don' fuck wiv me. You know wha' you know.'

The voices faded as the boys passed on the path above

them. Joel stood when they had gone and made his way up the side of the bank. Toby whispered his name fearfully, but Joel waved him off. He wanted to see who the boys were because he wanted to know in advance what this place promised him. At the top, however, when he looked down the path in the direction that the voices had taken, all he could see was shapes, silhouetted where the towpath curved. There were four, all identically dressed: baggy jeans, sweatshirts with the hoods drawn up, anoraks over them. They shuffled along, impeded by the low crotches of their jeans. As such, they looked anything but threatening. But their conversation had indicated otherwise.

To Joel's right a shout went up, and he saw in the distance someone standing on a bridge that arched over the canal. To his left the boys turned to hear who'd called them. A Rasta by the look of him, Joel saw. He was dangling a sandwich bag in the air.

Joel had learned enough. He ducked and slid down the bank to Toby. He said, 'Le's go, man,' and pulled Toby to his feet.

Toby said, 'We c'n have the fort—'

'Not now,' Joel told him. He led him in the direction they'd come until they were back in the relative safety of their aunt's front porch.

2

Kendra Osborne returned to the Edenham Estate just after seven o'clock that evening, rattling around the corner from Elkstone Road in an old Fiat Punto made recognisable, to those who knew her, by its passenger door on which someone had spray-painted *take it in the mouth,* a dripping red imperative that Kendra had left, not because she couldn't afford to have the door repainted but because she couldn't find the time to do so. At this point in her life, she was working at one job and trying to develop a career in another. The first was behind the till in an AIDS charity shop in the Harrow Road. The second was massage. This latter field of employment was in its infancy in Kendra's life: she'd completed eighteen months of coursework at Kensington and Chelsea College, and in the last six weeks she'd been trying to establish herself as a masseuse.

She had a two-fold plan in mind as far as the massage business went. She would use the small spare room in her house for clients who wished to come to her; she would travel by car with her table and her essential oils stowed in the back for clients who wished her to go to them. She would, naturally, charge extra for this. In time, she'd save enough money to open a small massage salon of her own.

Massage and tanning – booths and beds – were what she actually intended, and in that she revealed a fairly good understanding of her white-skinned countrymen. Living in a climate where the weather often precludes the possibility of anyone's having the healthy glow of naturally bronzed skin, at least three generations of white people in England have fried themselves into first and sometimes second degree sunburns on a regular basis on those rare days when the sun puts in an appearance. Kendra's plan was to tap into those people's desire to expose themselves to ultra-violet carcinogens. She would lure them in with the idea of the tan they were seeking and then introduce them to therapeutic massage somewhere along the way. For those regular customers whose bodies she would have already been massaging at her own home or theirs, she would offer the dubious benefits of tanning. It seemed a plan destined for sure success.

Kendra knew all this would take enormous time and effort, but she had always been a woman unafraid of hard work. In this, she was nothing like her mother. But that was not the only way in which Kendra Osborne and Glory Campbell differed from each other.

Men comprised the other way. Glory was frightened and incomplete without one, no matter what he was like or how he treated her, which is why she was at that very moment sitting at an airport boarding gate, waiting to jet off to a broken-down alcoholic Jamaican with a disreputable past and absolutely no future. Kendra, on the other hand, stood on her own. She'd been married twice. Once a widow and now a divorcée, she liked to say that she'd done her time – with one winner and one utter loser – and now her second husband was doing his. She didn't *mind* men, but she'd learned to see them as good merely for relieving certain physical needs.

When those needs came upon her, Kendra had no difficulty finding a man happy to accommodate her. An evening out with her best girlfriend was sufficient to take care of this for, at forty years old, Kendra was tawny, exotic, and willing to use her looks to get what she wanted, which was a bit of fun with no strings attached. With her career plans in place, she had no room in her life for a love-struck male with anything more on his mind than sex with appropriate precautions taken.

At the point when Kendra swung her car right to the narrow garage in front of her house, Joel and Toby – having returned from their outing to the Meanwhile Gardens duck pond – had been sitting in the frigid cold for an additional hour, and both of them were numb around the bottom. Kendra didn't see her nephews on her top front step, largely because the street lamp in Edenham Way had been burnt out since the previous October with no sign of anyone's having a plan to replace it. Instead, what she saw was someone's discarded shopping trolley blocking access to her garage and filled to the brim with that person's belongings.

At first it seemed to Kendra that these were goods meant for the charity shop, and while she didn't appreciate her neighbours dropping off their discards in front of her house instead of carting them up to the Harrow Road, she wasn't one to turn goods away if there was a possibility that they might sell. So when she got out of the car to pull the trolley to one side, she was still in the good humour that sprang from having had a successful afternoon giving demonstration sports massages at a gym built under the Westway Flyover in the Portobello Green Arcade.

That was when she saw the boys, their suitcases, and the carrier bags. Instantly, Kendra felt dread surge up from her stomach, and realisation followed in a rush.

She unlocked the garage and shoved open the door without a word to her nephews. She understood what was about to happen, and the understanding prompted her to curse, her voice soft enough to ensure that the boys couldn't hear her, but loud enough to give herself at least a modicum of the satisfaction that comes with cursing in the first place. She chose the words *shit* and *that goddamn cow* and once she said them, she climbed back into the Fiat and pulled it into the garage, all the time thinking furiously of what she could possibly do to avoid having to deal with what her mother had just thrust upon her. She was able to come up with nothing.

By the time she'd parked the car and gone around to the back of it to drag her massage table from the boot, Joel and Toby had left their perch and come to join her. They hesitated at the corner of the house, Joel at the front and Toby his usual shadow.

Joel said to Kendra without hello or preamble, 'Gran say she got to fix up a house first, for us to come to live in in Jamaica. She sending for us when she got it fixed. She say we're meant to wait for her here.' And when Kendra didn't answer because, despite her dread, her nephew's words and his hopeful tone made her eyes smart at her mother's base cruelty, Joel went on even more eagerly, saying, 'How you been, Aunt Ken? C'n I help you wiv dat?'

Toby said nothing. He hung back and danced on his toes, looking solemn and like a bizarre ballerina doing a solo in a production involving the sea. 'Why the hell's he wearing that thing?' Kendra asked Joel with a nod at his brother.

'Th' life-ring? It's wha' he likes jus' now, innit. Gran gave it him for Christmas, remember? She said in Jamaica he c'n—'

'I know what she said,' Kendra cut in sharply, and the sudden anger she felt was directed not at her nephew but at herself as she abruptly realised she should have known right then, right on Christmas Day, what Glory Campbell intended. The moment Glory had made her airy announcement about following her no-good boyfriend back to the land of their births as if she were Dorothy setting off to see the wizard and things were going to be as simple as tripping down some yellow brick road . . . Kendra wanted to slap herself for wearing blinkers that day.

'Kids'll *love* Jamaica,' Glory had said. 'An' George'll rest easier there 'n here. Wiv dem, I mean. 'S been hard on him, y' know. T'ree kids an' us in dis tiny li'l place. We been living in each other knickers.'

Kendra had said, 'You can't take them off to Jamaica. What about their mum?'

To which Glory had replied, 'I 'spect Carole won't even know dey gone.'

No doubt, Kendra thought, as she hauled the massage table from the back of the car, Glory would now use that as an excuse in the letter that was surely to follow her departure at some point when she could no longer avoid writing it. *I've had a decent think about it,* she would declare, for Kendra knew her mother would use her erstwhile appropriate English and not the faux Jamaican she'd taken up in anticipation of her coming new life, *and I remember what you said about poor Carole. You're right, Ken. I can't take the kids so far away from her, can I?* That would be an end to the matter. Her mother wasn't evil but she'd always been someone who firmly believed in putting first things first. Since the first thing in Glory's mind had always been Glory, she was unlikely ever to do something that might be to her disadvantage. Three grandchildren in Jamaica living in a household with a useless, unemployed, card-playing, television-watching specimen of overweight and malodorous male whom Glory was determined to hang on to because she'd never once been able to cope for even a week without a man and she was at the age where men are hard to come by . . . That scenario would spell out *disadvantage* even to the base illiterate.

Kendra slammed home the lid of the boot. She grunted as she hoisted up the heavy folding table by its handle. Joel hurried to assist her. He said, 'Lemme take dat, Aunt Ken,' quite as if he believed he could handle its size and its weight. Because of this and although she didn't want to, Kendra softened a bit. She said to Joel, 'I've got it, but you can pull down that door. And you can fetch that trolley inside the house, along with everything else you've got with you.'

As Joel complied, Kendra looked at Toby. The brief moment of experiencing softness deserted her. What she saw was the puzzle everyone saw and the responsibility that no one wanted because the only answer that anyone had ever managed – or been willing – to glean about what was wrong with Toby was the useless label *lacking an appropriate social filter*, and in the family chaos that had become the norm shortly before his fourth birthday, no one had had the nerve to investigate further. Now Kendra – who knew no more about this child than what she could see before her – was faced with coping with him until she could come up with a plan to divest herself of the responsibility.

Looking at him standing there – that ridiculous life-ring, his head a chopped up mess, his jeans too long, his trainers duct-tape closed because he'd never learned to tie his shoes laces – Kendra wanted to run in the opposite direction.

She said shortly to Toby, 'So. What d'you have to say for yourself?'

Toby halted in his dance and looked to Joel, seeking a sign of what he was meant to do. When Joel didn't give him one, he said to his aunt, 'I got to pee. S'this Jamaica?'

'Tobe. You *know* it ain't,' Joel said.

'Isn't,' Kendra told him. 'Speak proper English when you're with me. You're perfectly capable of it.'

'Isn't,' Joel said cooperatively. 'Tobe, this isn't Jamaica.'

Kendra took the boys inside the house where she set about snapping on lights as Joel brought in two suitcases, the carrier bags, and the shopping trolley. He stood just inside the door and waited for some sort of direction. As he'd never been to his aunt's house before, he looked around curiously, and what he saw was a dwelling that was even smaller than the house in Henchman Street.

On the ground floor, there were only two rooms in a shotgun design, along with a tiny, hidden W.C. What went for an eating area lay just beyond the entry, and beyond that a kitchen offered a window that was black with night, reflecting Kendra's image when she flicked on the bright overhead light. Two doors set at right angles to each other made up the far left corner of the kitchen. One of them led to the back garden with the barbecue that Toby had seen, and the other stood open on a stairway. There were two floors above and, as Joel would later discover, one of these comprised a sitting-room while the top floor held a bathroom and bedrooms, of which there were two.

Kendra made for these stairs, dragging the massage table with her. Joel hurried over to help her with it, saying, 'You takin' this above, Aunt Ken? I c'n do it for you. I'm stronger'n I look.'

Kendra said, 'You see to Toby. Look at him. He's wanting the loo.'

Joel looked around for an indication of where a toilet might be, an action Kendra might have seen and interpreted had she been able to get beyond feeling that the walls of her house were about to close in on her. As it was, she headed up the stairs and Joel, not liking to ask questions that could make him seem ignorant, waited until his aunt had started upstairs where the continued banging suggested she was taking the massage table to the top floor of the house. That was when he worked the lock on the garden door and hurried his brother outside. Toby didn't question this. He just made his stream into a flowerbed.

When Kendra came back downstairs, the boys were once again by the suitcases and the shopping trolley, not knowing what else they were meant to do. Kendra had been standing in her bedroom trying to calm herself, trying to develop a plan of action and coming up with nothing that wasn't going to disrupt her life completely. She'd reached the point at which she had to ask the question whose answer she didn't particularly want to hear.

She said to Joel, 'Where's Vanessa, then? Has she gone with your gran?'

Joel shook his head. 'She's round,' he said. 'She got vex an'—'

'Angry,' Kendra said. 'Not vex. Angry. Irritated. Annoyed.'

'Annoyed,' Joel said. 'She got annoyed an' she ran off. But

I 'spect she'll be back soon enough.' He said this last as if he expected his aunt to be happy to hear the news. But if coping with Toby was the last thing Kendra wanted to do, coping with his unruly and unpleasant sister was a very close second to it.

A nurturing woman would perhaps at this point have begun bustling about, if not getting life organised for the two hapless waifs who'd happened to appear on her doorstep, at least getting them something to eat. She would have climbed those stairs a second time and made some sort of sleeping arrangements out of the two bedrooms that the house possessed. There wasn't adequate furniture for this – especially in the room set aside for massages – but there was bedding that could be put on the floor and extra towels that could be rolled into pillows. Food would follow that sleeping set-up. And then a search for Ness could begin. But all of this was foreign to Kendra's way of life, so instead she went to her bag and pulled out a packet of Benson and Hedges. She lit up, using a burner on the stove, and she began to consider what she was meant to do next. The phone rang and saved her.

What she thought was that Glory – in an uncharacteristic fit of conscience – was ringing to say she'd come to her senses about George Gilbert, Jamaica, and the desertion of three children who relied upon her. But the caller was Kendra's best girlfriend Cordie, and as soon as Kendra heard her voice, she remembered that they'd arranged a girls' night out. In a club called No Sorrow they'd planned to drink, smoke, talk, listen to the music, and dance: alone, together, or with a partner. They'd pull men to prove they still had their attractions and if Kendra decided to bed someone, Cordie – happily married – would live the encounter vicariously via mobile the next morning. It was what they always did when they went out together.

Cordie said, 'Got your dancing shoes on?' which introduced Kendra to a life-defining moment.

She became aware that she was not only feeling the physical

need for a man, but probably *had* been feeling that need for a day or so and had been sublimating it with attention to her work at the shop and her training in massage. The reference to dancing shoes, though, made the need go deep where it intensified until she realised that she couldn't actually remember when she'd last spread her legs for a man.

So she did some quick thinking. This involved the boys and what she could do with them so that she'd still have time to get to No Sorrow while the pickings were good. Mentally, she considered her fridge and her cupboards, for there had to be something she could rustle up to feed to them and, with the hour being what it was, they were probably hungry. A sorting out of the spare room would follow, to give them an area to sleep tonight. She could pass out towels and flannels and make a formal introduction between them and the bath. And bedtime would immediately follow bathtime. Certainly, she could accomplish everything and still be ready to accompany Cordie to No Sorrow by half-past nine.

Kendra said to Cordie in the style of language she adopted when speaking to her friend, 'I polishing them now, innit. If they shine good enough, I ain't wearing knickers, b'lieve it.'

Cordie laughed. 'Oooh, you one nasty slag. What time, den?'

Kendra looked to Joel. He and Toby were standing by the door to the garden, Toby partially unzipped but both boys still wearing their jackets done up to their chins. She said to Joel, 'What time d'you lot usually go to bed?'

Joel thought about this. There wasn't really a usual time. There had been so many changes in their lives over the years that establishing schedules had been the last thing on anyone's mind. He tried to make out what kind of answer his aunt wanted from him. Clearly, someone on the other end of the phone was waiting to hear good news, and good news seemed to equate with Toby and Joel being put to bed as soon as possible. He looked at the wall clock above the sink. It was a quarter past seven.

He said arbitrarily and falsely, 'Half-eight most nights, Aunt Ken. But we could go now, couldn't we, Tobe?'

Toby always agreed with other people, except when it came to the television. As this moment had no television attached to it, he nodded complacently.

That was Kendra Osborne's life-defining moment and, while she didn't like it in the least, she felt it present itself so strongly that she could not assign it a more convenient name. She felt the slightest crack in her heart followed by an odd sensation of sinking that seemed to go on in her spirit. These two things told her that smoking, dancing, pulling men, and shagging would have to wait till later. Her grip loosened on the phone, and she turned to the night-blackened kitchen window. She pressed her forehead against it and felt the pressure of cold smooth glass on her skin. She spoke not to Cordie or to the boys but to herself.

What she said was, 'Jesus. Jesus God.' She didn't intend it as a prayer.

The days that followed did not pass easily for reasons that were beyond Kendra's control. Having her world invaded by her young relations knotted up her already complicated life. The difficulty she had in organising just the *basics* like meals, clean clothes, and enough toilet paper for the bathroom was exacerbated by the necessity of contending with Ness.

Kendra's experience of dealing with fifteen-year-old girls was limited to the fact that she had once been one herself, a particular in a woman's background that doesn't necessarily give her the wherewithal to cope with another female in the midst of the worst part of her adolescence. And Ness's adolescence – which otherwise would already have been fraught with the typical challenges a girl faces in growing up: from peer pressure to nasty spots on the chin – had so far been much rockier than Kendra knew. So when Ness hadn't turned up in Edenham Way by midnight on the night that Glory Campbell had deposited the children on her daughter's doorstep, Kendra set out to look for her.

Her reason for this was a simple one: the Campbell children didn't know the area well enough to be wandering around it at night or even during the day. Not only could they quickly become lost in a part of town dominated by labyrinthine housing estates whose questionable inhabitants engaged in even more questionable activities, but as a young female out and about alone, she would have been putting herself at risk anywhere. Kendra herself never felt in danger, but that was due to her personal philosophy of walk-fast-and-look-mean, which had long served her well when it came to chance night-time encounters in the street.

After Joel and Toby were bedded down on the floor of the spare room, Kendra went by car to try to find the girl but had no success. She went south as far as Notting Hill Gate and north as far as Kilburn Lane. As the hour grew later, all she ended up seeing in her cruising up one street and down another were the gangs of boys and young men who, like bats, habitually emerged after dark to see what sort of action they could rustle up.

Ultimately, Kendra stopped at the police station in the Harrow Road, an impressive Victorian edifice of brick whose size, in comparison with what stands around it, telegraphs its intention of being in that spot for a long time to come. She made her enquiry of a special constable, a self-important white female who took her time about looking up from her paperwork. No, was the answer she received. No fifteen-year-old girls had been brought into the station for any reason . . . madam. At another time, Kendra might have felt the bristling under her skin that would have been her reaction to that pause between *reason* and *madam*. But she had greater worries than being on the receiving end of someone's disrespect that night, so she let the incident go, and she took one last circuit of the immediate area. But there was no Ness anywhere.

Nor did Ness appear that night. It wasn't until nine on the following morning that she knocked on Kendra's door.

The conversation they had was brief, and Kendra decided to allow it to be satisfactory. To her questions of where in God's name Vanessa had been all night because she'd been goddamn worried to *death* about her, Ness said she'd got lost and after wandering a bit, she'd found an unlocked community hall over in Wornington Estate. There she'd fallen asleep. Sorry, she said and went to the coffee maker where last night's brew had not yet been refreshed with the morning's. She poured herself a cup and spied her aunt's Benson and Hedges on the table, where Joel and Toby were dipping into bowls of breakfast cereal that Kendra had hastily borrowed from one of her neighbours. Could she have a fag, then, Aunt Ken? Ness wanted to know and What's *you*, gawping at? to Joel.

When Joel ducked his head and went back to his cereal, Kendra tried to take the temperature of the kitchen to sort out what was actually going on. She knew there was more here than met the eye, but she didn't know how to get to what it was.

'Why'd you run off?' Kendra asked her. 'Why'd you not wait for me to get home like your brothers?'

Ness shrugged – she was to do that so often that Kendra would grow to desire nailing her shoulders into place – and she picked up the packet of cigarettes.

'I didn't tell you to help yourself, Vanessa.'

Ness took her hand off the packet and replied, 'Whatever.' And then she said, 'Sorry.'

The apology prompted Kendra to ask her if she'd run off because of her gran. 'Her leaving you here. Jamaica. All that. You've a right to be—'

'Jamaica?' Ness said with a snort. 'Di'n't want to go to no bloody Jamaica, did I. Gettin' a job an' my own place, innit. I was tired of dat old cow anyways. C'n I get a smoke off you or wha'?'

Having spent her formative years with Glory and Glory's English Kendra wasn't about to listen to this version of their language. She said, 'Don't talk like that, Vanessa. You know how to speak properly.'

Ness rolled her eyes. 'Whatever,' she said. 'Can. I. Have. A. Cigarette. Then?' She enunciated each word precisely.

Kendra nodded. She let go any further questions about Ness's whereabouts and the reasons behind them as the girl lit up in the same manner Kendra had done on the previous night: on a burner of the stove. She inspected Ness as Ness inspected her. Each of them saw an opportunity on offer. For Kendra it was a fleeting moment of invitation to a form of motherhood previously denied her. For Ness it was an equally fleeting glimpse of a model of who she could become. The two of them dangled there for an instant in a limbo of possibility. Then Kendra remembered everything she was attempting to balance on the tray of her life, and Ness remembered everything she wanted so much to forget. They turned from each other. Kendra told the boys to hurry their breakfast. Ness took a hit from her cigarette and moved to the window to look at the grey winter day outside.

What followed was, first of all, disabusing Ness of the idea that she would be finding a job and a place of her own. At her age, no one was going to employ her, and the law required her to be in school. Ness took this news better than Kendra expected although in a manner that she also anticipated. The signature shrug. The signature statement: 'Whatever, Ken.'

'Aunt Kendra, Vanessa.'

'What*ever*.'

Then began the tedious process of getting all three of the children into school, a jumping through hoops made even more difficult by the fact that Kendra's place of employment – the charity shop in the Harrow Road – would give her only an hour off at the end of each day to tend to this problem and the myriad other problems that went with the advent of three children into her life. She had the choice of quitting the charity shop, which she could not afford to do, or coping with the restriction placed upon her, so she chose the latter. That she also had a third choice was a thought she dwelt on more than once as she struggled with everything from finding inexpensive but appropriate furniture for the spare bedroom to heaving four people's clothes to the launderette instead of having just her own to deal with.

Care was the other choice she had. Making the phone call. Declaring herself wildly out of her depth. Gavin was the reason Kendra couldn't do this. Gavin her brother, father to the children, and everything Gavin had put himself through. Not only that, but everything that *life* had put Gavin through, even to his untimely and unnecessary death.

Settling the kids into her home and seeing to their placement in school ate up ten days. During this time, they remained at home while she went to work, with Ness in charge and only the television for entertainment. Ness was under strict instructions to stay on the premises and, as far as Kendra knew, the girl cooperated since she was always there in the morning when Kendra left and there in the late afternoon when Kendra returned. The fact that Ness was not present in Edenham Way during the intervening hours escaped Kendra's notice, and the two boys made no mention of this. Joel said nothing because he knew what the outcome would be for him if he passed this information to his aunt. Toby said nothing because he did not notice. As long as the television was on, he could retreat into Sose, where he preferred to spend his time anyway.

Thus, Ness had ten days in which to meld into life in North Kensington, and she had no difficulty doing so. Six and Natasha being unrepentant truants from their own school, they made a threesome with Ness and they were only too happy to show her what was what in the area: from the quickest route down to Queensway where they could loiter in Whiteley's till they were run off, to the best spot where they could chat up boys. When the two girls weren't initiating her into those sorts of delights, they were passing along to her the various substances that would make her life more blissful. With this, however, Ness was careful. She knew the wisdom of being in possession of all of her faculties when her aunt returned from her day's work.

Joel watched all this and longed to say something. But he was caught between warring loyalties: to his sister whom he no longer quite recognised let alone understood, and to his aunt who had taken them into her home instead of delivering them elsewhere. So he said nothing. He just watched Ness leave and return – careful to wash herself, her hair, and if necessary her clothing prior to Kendra's arrival – and he waited for what was surely to come.

What came first was Holland Park School, the third of the comprehensives that Kendra contacted hoping for Joel and Ness to be admitted. If she couldn't get them into a school that was relatively local, they would be forced to return to East Acton each day, which wasn't what she wanted for them, nor for herself. She'd tried an RC comprehensive first, thinking that a quasi-religious and, one hoped, disciplined environment might be just the ticket to set Ness on the straight and narrow that she needed. There were no places available, so she'd gone on to an Anglican comprehensive next, with the same result. She moved on to Holland Park School third, and there she finally had success. There were several places, and all that would be necessary – aside from taking the admission's test – was purchasing the necessary uniforms.

Joel was easy to fit into the grey-upon-unrelieved-even-darker-grey of the required school kit. Ness was not so accommodating. She declared that she wasn't about to 'wear dat shit nowheres'. Kendra corrected her grammar, established a fine of fifty pence henceforth for linguistic crudities, and told her she most certainly was.

They could have embarked upon a battle of wills at that

point, but Ness gave in. Kendra allowed herself to be pleased and foolishly thought she had won a round with the girl, little knowing that Ness's plans for herself didn't include going to Holland Park School for love or money, so – reflecting on this fact – she'd quickly realised that it didn't matter whether her aunt purchased the uniform for her to wear or not.

With Joel and Ness taken care of, there remained the matter of Toby. Wherever he went to school, it had to be somewhere along the route Joel and Ness would follow to get to the number 52 bus, which would ferry them to Holland Park. Although none of them spoke of the subject openly, all of them knew that Toby could not be allowed to wander to school on his own, and Kendra could not hope to get back to her massage salon plans – which had been lying fallow since the night she'd arrived home to find the boys on her doorstep – while simultaneously keeping up her employment at the charity shop and either driving or walking Toby to and from school.

So for another ten days, she worked upon the problem. It should have been simple: there were primary schools in every direction from Edenham Estate and there were a number on the route that Toby's siblings were taking to get to their bus. But between there being no places and there being no suitable situation in these schools for someone with Toby's 'obvious special needs', as it was generally termed upon one minute's conversation with the boy, Kendra had no luck. She was beginning to think she would have to keep the child with her permanently rather than enrol him somewhere – a horrifying thought – when the headteacher at Middle Row School directed her to the Westminster Learning Centre in the Harrow Road, just up the street from the charity shop. Toby could attend Middle Row School, the headteacher told her, as long as he had special daily instruction at the learning centre as well. 'To sort out his difficulties,' the headteacher said, quite as if she believed an academic tutorial had a hope of curing what ailed him.

This all seemed meant. While it was a bit of a stretch to

think Middle Row was on the direct route to the bus for Ness and Joel, they could still get to a stop in Ladbroke Grove from Toby's school in a five-minute walk. And after school, having Toby nearby at the learning centre meant Kendra would be able to keep tabs on Joel and Ness as well, for his siblings would have to walk him there. Kendra's plan was that they would take turns doing it, stopping in to see her on the way.

In all of this, she failed to take Ness into account. Ness allowed her aunt to think and plan whatever she wished. She'd been growing quite adept at pulling the wool over her aunt's eyes and, like many adolescent girls who think themselves omnipotent as a result of successfully running wild for a period of time with no one the wiser, she'd started to assume she'd be able to do so indefinitely.

Naturally, she was wrong.

Holland Park School is an anomaly. It stands in the midst of one of the most fashionable neighbourhoods of London: a leafy, redbrick and white stucco area of individual mansions, historic conversions, and blocks of costly flats and exorbitantly priced maisonettes. Yet the vast majority of its pupils trek in to the school from some of the most disreputable housing estates north of the Thames, making the populace of the immediate area decidedly white and the populace of the school a gamut that is skewed to the colours brown and black.

Joel Campbell would have had to be blind or not in possession of his wits to think he belonged in the immediate environs of Holland Park School. Once he discovered that there were two distinct routes from the number 52 bus to the comprehensive, he chose the one that exposed him least to the blank and uninviting glances of cashmere-garbed women walking their Yorkshire terriers and children being transported to schools out of the area by au pairs driving the family Range Rovers. This was the route that took him to the corner of Notting Hill Gate. From there, he made his way west by foot to Campden Hill Road rather than ride the bus any farther, resulting in a walk that would have taken him down several streets in which he belonged about as comfortably as a Ginster's pasty nestled next to beef Wellington.

From the first day, he made this journey alone after leaving Toby at the gates to Middle Row School. Ness – cooperatively dressed in her drab grey uniform and carrying a rucksack on her back – went with them as far as Golborne Road. But there, she left her brothers to go on their way while she pocketed her bus money and went on hers.

She continued to say to Joel, 'Better not grass, y'unnerstan? You do an' I go af'er you, blood.'

Joel continued to nod and watched her walk off. He wanted to tell her that there was no need for her to threaten him. He wouldn't grass. When had he ever? First of all, she was his sister and, even if she hadn't been, he knew the most important rule of childhood and adolescence: no telling tales. So he and Ness operated on a strictly don't ask/don't tell policy. He had no idea what she was up to aside from playing truant, and she didn't reveal any details to him.

He would have preferred her company, though, not only in fulfilling their assigned duty to Toby each morning and afternoon but also in having to navigate the experience of being the new kid at Holland Park School. For the school seemed to Joel to be a place fraught with dangers. There were the academic dangers of being seen as stupid rather than shy. There were the social dangers of having no friends. There were the physical dangers of his appearance which, along with having no friends, could easily mark him as a target for bullying. Ness's presence would have made the going easier for him, Joel decided. She would have fitted in better than he. He could have ridden along on her coat-tails.

No matter that Ness – as she was now and not as she had been in her childhood – would not have allowed this. The way Joel still saw his sister, if only periodically, made him feel her absence at school acutely. So he sought to be a fly on the wall, attracting the attention of neither pupils nor teachers. To his PSHE teacher's hearty question of 'How're you getting on then, mate?' he always made the same reply. 'S'okay.'

'Any troubles? Problems? Homework going all right?'

'S'okay, yeah.'

'Made any friends, yet?'

''M doing all right.'

'Not being bullied by anyone, are you?'

A shake of the head, eyes directed to his feet.

'Because if you are, you report it to me at once. We don't tolerate that nonsense here at Holland Park.' A long pause in which Joel finally looked up to see the teacher – he was called Mr Eastbourne – intently assessing him. 'Wouldn't lie to me, would you, Joel?' Mr Eastbourne said. 'My job's to make your job easier, you know. D'you know what your job is at Holland Park?'

Joel shook his head.

'Getting on,' Eastbourne said. 'Getting ed-u-cated. You want that, don't you? Because you have to want it in order to succeed.'

'Okay.' Joel wished only to be dismissed, free from scrutiny once more. If studying eighteen hours a day would have allowed him to become invisible to Mr Eastbourne and to everyone else, he would have done that. He would have done anything.

Lunchtime was the worst. As in every school that has ever existed, boys and girls congregated in groups, and the groups themselves had special designations known only to the members. Those teens deemed popular – a label they gave to themselves, which everyone else apparently accepted without question – hung about at a distance from those considered clever. Those who were clever – and they always had the marks to prove it – kept away from those whose futures were obviously limited to working behind a till. Those with advanced social agendas stayed clear of those who were backward. Those who followed trends remained aloof from those who scorned such things. There were pockets of individuals, naturally, who didn't fit anywhere within these designations, but they were the social outcasts who didn't know how to welcome anyone into their midst anyway. So Joel spent his lunchtimes alone.

He'd done this for several weeks when he heard someone speak to him from nearby his regular eating spot, which was leaning out of sight against the far corner of the security guard's hut at the edge of the schoolyard near the gate. It was a girl's voice. She said, 'Why d'you eat over here, mon?' and when Joel looked up, realising that the question was directed at him, he saw an Asian girl in a navy headscarf standing on the route into the schoolyard, as if she'd just been admitted by the security guard. She wore a school uniform that was several sizes too large for her. It successfully obscured whatever feminine curves she might have had.

Since he'd managed to avoid being spoken to by anyone save his teachers, Joel didn't quite know what to do.

The girl said, 'Hey. Can't you talk or summick?'

Joel looked away because he could feel his face growing hot, and he knew what that did to his odd complexion. 'I c'n talk,' he said.

'So what you doing here, then?'

'Eating.'

'Well, I c'n see that, mon. But no one eats here. 'S not even allowed. How'd you never get told to eat where you s'posed to?'

He shrugged. 'I ain't hurtin no one, innit.'

She came around and stood in front of him. He looked at her shoes so that he wouldn't have to look at her. They were black and strappy, the sort of shoes one might find in a trendy shop on the high street. They were also out of place, and they made him wonder if she had trendy *other* things on beneath the over-large uniform she was wearing. It was something that his sister might have done, and thinking of this girl as a Ness-like figure allowed Joel to feel slightly more comfortable with her. At least she was a known commodity.

She bent and fixed him with her eyes. She said, 'I know you. You come on the bus. Number fifty-two like me. Where you live?'

He told her, snatching a glance at her face. It altered from curious to surprised. She said, 'Ede'ham Estate? *I* live there, innit. Up the tower. I never seen you round. An' where you catch the bus anyways? Not near me but I seen you inside.'

He told her about Toby: walking him to school. He didn't mention Ness.

She nodded then said, 'Oh. Hibah. Tha's who I am. Who you got for PSHE?'

'Mr Eastbourne.'

'Religious education?'

'Mrs Armstrong.'

'Maths?'

'Mr Pearce.'

'Oooh. He c'n be nasty, innit. You good at maths?'

He was, but he didn't like to admit it. He enjoyed maths. It was a subject with answers that were right or wrong. You knew what to expect from maths.

Hibah said, 'You got a name?'

'Joel,' he told her. And then he offered her something she hadn't asked. 'I'm new.'

'I *know* that,' she said and he grew hot again because it seemed to him that she sounded scornful. She explained, 'You hanging here, y'unnerstan. I reckoned you was new. And anyways, I saw you here b'fore.' She tilted her head in the direction of the gate that closed the school off from the rest of the world. She offered him something in exchange for the information he'd offered her. She said, 'My boyfriend comes lunchtimes most days. So I see you on my way to the gate to talk to him.'

'He don't go here?'

'He don't go anywheres. He s'posed to, innit. But he won't. I meet him here cos 'f my dad ever saw me wiv him, he beat me black 'n' blue, y'unnerstan. Muslim,' she added and looked embarrassed at the admission.

Joel didn't know what to say to this, so he said nothing. Hibah said, 'Year Nine,' after a moment. 'But we c'n be friends, you 'n me. Nothing more 'n that, y'unnerstan, cos like I say, I got a boyfriend. But we c'n be friends.'

This was so surprising an offer that Joel was stunned. He'd never actually had someone say such a thing to him and he couldn't begin to imagine why Hibah was doing so. Had she been questioned on the matter, Hibah herself could not have explained it. But having an unacceptable boyfriend and an attitude towards life that placed her squarely between two warring worlds, she knew what it was like to feel like a stranger everywhere, which made her more compassionate than her peers. Like water that seeks its own level, misfits recognise their brothers even when they do so unconsciously. Such was the case with Hibah.

She finally said, when Joel did not respond, 'Shit. Not like I got a disease or summick. Well anyways, we could say hi on the bus. Tha' won't kill you, innit.' And then she walked off.

The bell for class rang before Joel could catch up with her and offer friendship in return.

3

As far as friendship was concerned, things were developing differently for Ness, at least on a superficial level. When she parted ways with her brothers every morning, she did what she had been doing since her first night in North Kensington: she met up with her new mates Natasha and Six. She effected this regular engagement by detaching from Joel and Toby in the vicinity of Portobello Bridge, where she hung about till she was sure the boys would not know in which direction she was going to head. When they were out of sight, she walked quickly in the opposite direction, on a route that took her past Trellick Tower, setting her north towards West Kilburn.

It was crucial that she take care with all this, for to gain her destination she had to use a footbridge over the Grand Union Canal, which put her squarely on the Harrow Road, in the vicinity of the charity shop where her aunt was employed. No matter that Ness generally arrived in this area well in advance of the opening hours of that shop, there was always the possibility that Kendra might choose to go in early one day, and the one thing Ness didn't want to happen was being spotted by Kendra crossing over into Second Avenue.

In this, she didn't fear a run-in with her aunt, for Ness was still of the mistaken opinion that she was more than a match for anyone, Kendra Osborne included. She merely didn't want the annoyance of having to waste any time with Kendra. If she saw her, she would have to cook up an excuse for being decidedly in the wrong area of town at the wrong time of day, and while she believed she could do that with aplomb – after all, weeks into her removal from East Acton to this part of town and her aunt *still* didn't know what she was up to – she didn't want to expend the energy on that. It was taking energy enough for her to transform herself into the Ness Campbell she'd decided to become.

Once across the Harrow Road, Ness walked directly to the Jubilee Sports Centre, a low-slung building in nearby Caird Street that offered the inhabitants of the neighbourhood something else to do besides getting into or dodging trouble. Here, Ness ducked inside and near the weight room – from which the clanging of barbells and the groaning of power lifters emanated at most hours of the day – she used the ladies' toilet to change into the clothes and the shoes she'd stuffed into her rucksack. The hideous grey trousers she replaced with a skin of blue jeans. The equally hideous grey jumper she set aside for a lacy top or a thin T-shirt. With stiletto boots on her feet and her hair allowed to spring round her head the way she liked it, she added to her makeup – darker lipstick, more eyeliner, eye shadow that glittered – and stared in the mirror at the girl she'd created. If she liked what she saw – which she usually did – she left the sports centre and went round the corner into Lancefield Street.

It was here that Six lived, in the midst of the vast complex of buildings called the Mozart Estate, an endless maze of London brick: dozens of terraces and blocks of flats that extended all the way to Kilburn Lane. Intended like every other estate to relieve the overcrowding of the tenement buildings it replaced, over time the estate had become as unsavoury as its predecessors. By day, it looked relatively innocuous since few people were ever out and about save the elderly on their way to the local shop for a loaf of bread or a carton of milk. By night, however, it was a different matter, for the nocturnal denizens of the estate had long lived on the wrong side of the law, trading in drugs, weapons, and violence, dealing appropriately with anyone who tried to stop them, including the local police, whom villains of all shapes, forms, and ages had easily evaded from the time the estate first opened.

Six lived in one of the apartment blocks. It was called Farnaby House: three storeys tall, accessed through a thick wooden security door, possessed of balconies for lounging upon in the summertime, having lino floors in the corridors and yellow paint on the walls. From the outside, it didn't seem at all an unpleasant place to live, until further investigation revealed the security door hopelessly broken, the small windows next to it either cracked or boarded over, the scent of urine acrid inside the entry, and holes kicked into the corridor walls.

The flat that Six's family occupied was a place of odour and noise. The odour was predominantly of stale cigarette smoke and unwashed clothes, while the noise emanated both from the television and from the second-hand karaoke machine that Six's mother had given her for Christmas. It would, she'd told herself, advance her daughter's dream of pop stardom. It would also, she hoped but did not admit aloud, keep her off the streets. The fact that it was doing neither was something that Six's mother didn't know and would have turned a blind eye to had anything in Six's behaviour suggested it. The poor woman worked at two jobs to keep clothes on the backs of the four children – out of seven – whom she still had at home. She had neither the time nor the energy to wonder what her offspring were doing while she herself was cleaning rooms in the Hyde Park Hilton or ironing sheets and pillowcases in the laundry of the Dorchester Hotel. Like most mothers in her position, she wanted something better for her children. That three of them were already following in her footsteps – unmarried and regularly producing offspring by various worthless men – she put down to bloody-mindedness. That three of the other four were set to do the same, she simply didn't acknowledge. Only one of this latter group attended school with any regularity. As a result, 'the Professor' was his sobriquet.

When Ness arrived at Farnaby House and made her way through the broken security door and up one flight of stairs, she found Six entertaining Natasha in the bedroom she shared with her sisters. Natasha was sitting on the floor, applying a viscous coat of purple varnish to her already red and stubby fingernails while Six clutched the karaoke's microphone in the vicinity of her chest as she bumped and ground her way through the musical interlude of a vintage Madonna piece. As Ness entered, Six took Madonna to the next level. She jumped off the bed on which she'd been performing, and she pranced around Ness to the beat of the music before she accosted her and pulled her forward for a kiss with tongue.

Ness pushed her away and cursed in a manner that would have got her steeply fined had her aunt been listening. She wiped her mouth savagely on a pillow that she scooped from one of the three beds in the room. This left behind two smears of blood-red lipstick: one on the pillowcase and the other like a gash across her cheek.

On the floor, Natasha laughed lazily while Six – who never lost a beat – gyrated over to her. Natasha accepted the kiss quite willingly, her mouth opening to the size of a saucer to accommodate as much tongue as Six felt inclined to give her. They went at it for such a length of time that Ness's stomach curdled and she averted her eyes. In doing this, she looked around and found the source of her friends' lack of inhibition. A hand mirror lay, glass up, upon the chest of drawers, with the remains of white powder dusting it.

Ness said, 'Shit! You lot di'n't *wait*? You still holdin substance, or is dat it, Six?'

Six and Natasha broke off from each other. Six said, 'I *tol'* you to be here las' night, di'n't I?'

Ness said, 'You know I can't. 'F I ain't home by . . . Shit. *Shit*. How'd you score, den?'

'Tash did,' Six said. 'Dere's blow and dere's blow, innit.'

The two girls laughed companionably. As Ness had learned,

they had an arrangement with several of the delivery boys who cycled the routes from one of West Kilburn's main suppliers to those of the area's users who preferred indulging at home to visiting a crack house: a skimming off the top from six or seven bags in exchange for fellatio. Natasha and Six took turns administering it although they always shared the goods received in payment.

Ness scooped up the mirror, wet her finger, and cleaned off what little powder was left. This she rubbed on her gums, to little effect. At this, she felt a hard hot stone start to grow larger in the middle of her chest. She *hated* being on the outside looking in, and that was where she was standing at the moment. It was also where she would continue to stand if she couldn't join the girls in their high.

She turned to them. 'You got weed, den?'

Six shook her head. She danced over to the karaoke machine and shut it off. Natasha watched her with glowing eyes. It was no secret that, two years younger, Natasha worshipped everything about Six, but on this particular morning, Ness found such idolatry annoying, especially stacked up with the part Nastasha had played in getting herself and Six supplied on the previous night, with the exclusion of Ness.

She said to Natasha, 'Shit, you know wha' you look like, Tash? Lezzo, da's what. You wan' eat Six for *dinner*?'

Six narrowed her eyes at this, dropping down on the bed. She rooted through a pile of clothes on the floor, snagged a pair of jeans, and brought out a packet of cigarettes from one of the pockets. She lit up and said, 'Hey, watch'r mouf, den, Ness. Tash's all right.'

Ness said, 'Why? You like 't as well?'

This was the sort of remark that might have otherwise spurred Six to get into a brawl with Ness, but she was loath to do anything to disturb the pleasant sensation of being high. Besides, she knew the source of Ness's displeasure, and she wasn't about to be misdirected on to an unrelated topic because

Ness couldn't bring herself to say something directly. Six was a girl who didn't communicate with others by using half measures. She'd learned to be direct from toddlerhood. It was the only way to be heard in her family.

She said, 'You c'n be one of us wiv it or one of us wivout it. Don't matter to me. 'S up to you. Me 'n' Tash, we like you fine, innit, bu' we ain't changin' our ways to suit you, Ness.' And then to Natasha, 'You cool wiv dat, Tash?'

Natasha nodded although she hadn't the slightest idea what Six was talking about. She herself had long been a hanger-on, needing to be pulled through life by someone who knew where she was going so that she – Natasha – never had to think or make a decision on her own. Thus, she was 'cool' with just about anything going on around her as long as its source was the current object of her parasitic devotion.

Six's little speech put Ness in a bad position. She didn't want to be vulnerable – to them or to anyone – but she needed the other two girls for the companionship and escape they provided. She sought a way to reconnect with them.

She said, 'Give us a fag,' and attempted to sound bored with the entire topic. 'Too early for me anyways.'

'But you jus' said—'

Six cut off Natasha. She didn't feel like a row. 'Yeah,' she agreed, 'too fuckin early.' She threw the cigarettes and the plastic lighter to Ness, who shook one out, lit up, and passed the packet and lighter to Natasha. A form of peace came among them with this, which allowed them to plan the rest of their day.

For weeks, their days had followed a pattern. Morning found them at Six's flat where her mother was gone, her brother was at school and her two sisters were sometimes in bed and sometimes hanging about the flats of their three oldest siblings who, with their offspring, lived on two of the other estates in the area. Ness, Natasha, and Six would use this time to do each other's hair, nails, and makeup and listen to music on the radio.

Their day broadened after half past eleven, at which time they explored the possibilities up in Kilburn Lane, where they attempted to pinch cigarettes from the newsagent, gin from the off licence, used videos from Apollo Video, and anything they could get away with from Al Morooj Market. At all of this, they had limited success since their appearance on the scene heightened the suspicions of the owners of each of these establishments. These same owners frequently threatened the girls with the truant officer, a form of attempted intimidation that none of them took seriously.

When Kilburn Lane wasn't their destination of choice, it was Queensway in Bayswater, a bus ride from the Mozart Estate, where attractions aplenty abounded in the form of internet cafés, the shopping arcade in Whiteley's, the ice rink, a few boutiques, and – pollen for the bee-flight of their utmost desire – a mobile phone shop. For mobile phones comprised the single object without which an adolescent in London could not feel complete. So when the girls made the pilgrimage to Queensway, they always made the mobile phone shop the ultimate shrine they intended to visit.

There, they were regularly asked to leave. But that only whetted their appetite for possession. The price of a mobile was beyond their means – especially since they had no means – but that didn't put mobiles beyond their scheming.

'We c'd text each other,' Six pointed out. 'You c'd be one place and I c'd be 'nother, and all's we need is dat mobile, Tash.'

'Yeah,' Natasha sighed. 'We c'd text each other.'

'Plan where to meet.'

'Try to get shit when we need it from one 'f the boys.'

'Dat as well. We *got* to get a mobile. Your aunt got one, Ness?'

'Yeah, she got one.'

'Why'n't you pinch it for us?'

'Cos I do dat, she take notice of me. An' I like how it is wivout her notice.'

There was no lie in this. By having the sense and the discipline to restrict her nights out to the weekends, by being home in her school uniform when her aunt returned from the charity shop or a massage class, by pretending to do a modicum of schoolwork at the kitchen table while Joel did the real thing, Ness had successfully kept Kendra in the dark about her life. She took extraordinary care with all of this, and on the occasions when she drank too much and could not risk being seen at home, she religiously phoned her aunt and told her she'd be sleeping at her mate Six's flat.

'What kind of name is that?' Kendra wanted to know. 'Six? She's called Six?'

Her real name was Chinara Kahina, Ness told her. But her family and her friends always called her Six, after her birth order, second to the youngest child in the family.

The word *family* gave a legitimacy to Six that lulled Kendra into a false sense of both security and propriety. Had she seen what went for *family* in Six's home, had she seen the home itself, and had she seen what went on there, Kendra would not have been so quick to embrace gratitude at Ness's having found a friend in the neighbourhood. As it was, and with Ness giving her no cause for suspicion, Kendra allowed herself to believe all was well. This in turn gave her a chance to get back to her career plans in massage and to reestablish her friendship with Cordie Durelle.

This friendship had suffered in the weeks since the Campbell children had descended upon Kendra. Their girls' nights out had been postponed as regularly as they'd once been experienced, and the long phone chats that had been one of the hallmarks of their relationship had been cut shorter until they'd ultimately metamorphosed into promises to 'phone back soon, luv', except soon never came. Once life in Edenham Way developed what seemed to Kendra to be a pattern, however, she was able to inch carefully towards making her days and nights like what they'd been before the Campbells.

She began with work. No longer needing that wages-reducing one-hour-per-day of free time that she'd been given at the charity shop to see to the needs of her niece and nephews, she returned to full-time employment. She re-engaged with a class at Kensington and Chelsea College as well as with demonstration massages down at the sports centre in Portobello Green. She felt confident enough of how the Campbells were doing to extend her demonstration massages to two of the other gyms in the area, and when from this she cultivated her first three regular clients, she began to feel that life was sorting itself out. So on the day that Cordie popped into the charity shop on a rainy afternoon not too long after Ness's experience of tongue-kissing Six, Kendra was pleased to see her.

She was expecting Joel and Toby since it was near the time when the boys were setting off for home from the learning centre up the street. As the bell on the shop door chimed, she looked up from what she was doing – trying to make an appealing display out of a dismal donation of 1970s costume jewellery – and when she saw Cordie lounging in the doorway instead of the boys, she smiled and said, 'Take me *away* from this, girl.'

'You must've got yourself one *helluva* man,' Cordie remarked. 'I been picturing him giving it to you three times a day, wiv you laying there moaning an' all your girl-brains wasted to nothing. Dat how it is, Miss Kendra?'

'You joking? Haven't had one in so long I forget what parts 'f them is different from us,' Kendra said.

'Well, thank God for that,' Cordie told her. 'Swear to God, I was starting to t'ink you been shagging my Gerald and avoidin' me cos you sure I'd see the truth on your face. Only lemme tell you, slag, I be that grateful you do Gerald. Save me from getting rode every night.'

Kendra chuckled sympathetically. Gerald Durelle's sex drive had long been the cross his wife Cordie was forced to bear. In combination with his determination to have a son from her – they already had two daughters – that drive made her willing presence in his bed the primary requirement for their marriage. As long as Cordie acted hungry in the beginning and sexually sated in the end, he didn't notice that the middle comprised her staring into space and wondering if he was ever going to realise she was secretly on the pill.

'He figure things out yet?' Kendra asked her friend.

'Hell no,' Cordie said. 'Man's ego enough to make him t'ink I just *dying* to keep popping out babies till he's got what he want.'

She sauntered over to the counter. She was, Kendra saw, still wearing the surgical mask that was part of the uniform of the manicurists at the Princess European and Afro Unisex Hair Salon just down the street. She had it slung around her neck, like the love-child of an Elizabethan ruff, completing her ensemble of purple polyester smock and quasi-medical shoes. Child of an Ethiopian father and a Kenyan mother, Cordie was deep black and majestic in appearance, with an elegant neck and a profile that looked like something one might find on a coin. But even possessing good genes, a perfectly symmetrical face, excellent skin, and a mannequin's body could not make her look like a fashion statement in the outfit that the hair salon required its employees to wear.

She went for Kendra's bag, which she knew Kendra kept in a cupboard beneath the till. She opened it and found herself a cigarette.

'How's your girls?' Kendra asked her.

Cordie shook the flame from a match. 'Manda says she wants makeup, her nose pierced, and a boyfriend. Patia wants a mobile.'

'How old they now?'

'Six and ten.'

'Shit. You got your work cut out.'

'Tell me,' Cordie said. 'I 'spect 'em both to be pregnant time they're twelve.'

'Wha's Gerald t'ink?'

She blew smoke out through her nose. 'They got him running, those girls. Manda crook her finger, he melt to a puddle. Patia show a few tears, he got the wallet out 'fore he got the handkerchief in his hand. I say no to summick, he say yes. "I wan' dem to have wha' I never got," he say. Tell you, Ken, having kids today is having a headache won't go away no matter wha' you use.'

'I hear you on that,' Kendra said. 'Thought I was safe from it, I did, and look wha' happen. I end up wiv three.'

'How you coping?'

'All right, considerin I got no clue wha' I'm doin.'

'So when I get to meet 'em? You hiding dem or summick?'

'Hiding? Why'd I want to do that?'

'Don't know, innit. Maybe one 'f 'em got two heads.'

'Yeah. Tha's it all right.'

Kendra chuckled, but the fact was that she *was* hiding the Campbells from her friend. Keeping them under wraps obviated the necessity of having to explain anything about them to anyone. And an explanation would be needed, of course. Not only for their appearance – Ness being the only one who looked remotely as if she might be a relation of Kendra's and she was doing most of that with makeup – but also for the oddities in their behaviour, particularly the boys. While Kendra might have made an excuse for Joel's persistent introversion, she knew she would be hard-pressed to come up with a reason why Toby was as he was. To try to do so ran the risk of getting into the subject of his mother, anyway. Cordie already knew about the fate of the children's father, but the whereabouts of Carole Campbell comprised a topic of conversation they'd never embarked upon. Kendra wanted to keep it that way.

Circumstances made part of this impossible. Not a minute after she'd spoken, the shop door opened once again. Joel and Toby scuttled in out of the rain, Joel with his school uniform soaked on the shoulders, Toby with his life-ring inflated as if he expected a flood of Biblical proportions.

There was nothing for it but to introduce them to Cordie, which Kendra accomplished quickly by saying, 'Here's two of 'em anyways. This's Joel. This's Toby. How 'bout a pepperoni slice from Tops, you two? You needin' a snack?'

Her use of a style of language was nearly as confusing to the boys as was the unexpected offer of pizza. Joel didn't know what to say, and since Toby always followed Joel's lead, neither of the boys offered a word in reply. Joel merely ducked his head while Toby rose to his toes and danced to the counter where he scooped up several beaded necklaces and decked himself out like a time traveller from the summer of love.

'Cat gotcher tongue, den?' Cordie said in a friendly fashion. 'You lot feelin shy? Hell, I wish my girls take a page out of dis book for 'n hour or so. Where's dat sister of yours? I got to meet her, too.'

Joel looked up. Anyone adept at reading faces would have known he was searching for an excuse for Ness. Rarely did someone ask after her directly, so he had nothing prepared in reply. 'Wiv 'er mates,' he finally said, but he spoke to his aunt and not to Cordie. 'They working on a project f'r school.'

'Real scholar, is she?' Cordie asked. 'Wha' 'bout you lot? You scholars, too?'

Toby chose this moment to speak. 'I got a Twix for not weeing in my trousers today. I wanted to, but I d'in't, Aunt Ken. So I got a Twix cos I asked could I use the toilet.' At the conclusion of this, he executed a little pirouette.

Cordie looked at Kendra. She started to speak. Kendra said expansively to Joel, 'How 'bout that pepperoni slice?'

Joel accepted with an alacrity that declared he wanted to be gone as much as Kendra wanted him and his brother to vanish. He took the three pounds she handed to him. He ushered Toby out of the shop and in the direction of Great Western Road.

They left behind them one of those moments in which things get glossed over, things get addressed, or things get altogether ignored. Exactly how it was going to be was something that rested in Cordie's hands, and Kendra decided not to help her out in the matter.

Social courtesy dictated a polite change of subject. Friendship demanded an honest appraisal of the situation. There was also middle ground between these two extremes, and that was where Cordie found a safe footing. She said, 'You been having a time of it,' as she crushed out her cigarette in a second-hand ashtray which she found on one of the display shelves. 'Di'n't 'spect motherhood to be like this, innit.'

'Didn't 'spect motherhood at all,' Kendra told her. 'I'm coping good enough, I s'pose.'

Cordie nodded. She looked thoughtfully towards the door. She said, 'Their mum goin' to take dem off you, Ken?'

Kendra shook her head and to keep Cordie far away from the subject of Carole Campbell, she said, 'Ness's a help to me. Big one. Joel's good, 's well.' She waited for Cordie to bring up the subject of Toby.

Cordie did so, but in a way that made Kendra love her all the more. She said, 'You need help, you give me a bell, Ken. And when you ready for dancin', I ready, too.'

'I do that, girl,' Kendra said. 'Right now, though, things's good wiv us all.'

The admissions officer from Holland Park School put an abrupt end to Kendra's delusion. Although this individual – who identified herself as Mrs Harper when she finally phoned – took nearly two months to make the call that was to shatter life as it had been bumping along at No 84 Edenham Way, there was a reason for this. By never turning up for so much as an hour at the school, indeed by never showing her face at all save on the day she took the entrance test, Ness had successfully fallen through the cracks. Since the school's population was given to an itinerancy caused by the government's continual placement and displacement of the country's asylum seeker immigrants, the fact that a Vanessa Campbell showed up on a teacher's class register but not in the class itself was taken by many of her instructors to mean that her family had merely moved on or been moved to other housing. Thus, they made no report of Ness being among the missing, and it was seven weeks after her enrolment in the school before Kendra received the phone call about her lack of attendance.

This call came not to the house but to the charity shop. As Kendra was there alone – a common enough occurrence – she couldn't leave. She wanted to. She wanted to climb inside her Punto and drive up and down the streets looking for her niece, much as she'd done on the night of the Campbells' arrival in North Kensington. Because she couldn't do that, she paced the floor instead. She walked up a row of second-hand blue jeans and down a row of worn wool coats and tried not to think of lies: the lies Ness had been telling her for weeks and the ones she herself had just mouthed to Mrs Harper.

With her heart pounding so fiercely in her ears that she could barely hear the woman on the other end of the line, she'd said to the admissions officer, 'I *am* so sorry about the confusion. Directly I enrolled Ness and her brother, she had to help care for her mum in Bradford.' Where on earth Bradford came from, she wouldn't have been able to say. She wasn't even sure she could find it quickly on a map, but she knew it had a large ethnic population because they'd been rioting during the finer weather: Asians, blacks, and the local skinheads, all set to kill each other to prove whatever they apparently felt needed proving.

'Is she at school in Bradford, then?' Mrs Harper enquired.

'Private tutoring,' Kendra said. 'She'll be back tomorrow, as it happens.'

'I see. Mrs Osborne, you really ought to have phoned . . .'

'Of course. Somehow, I just . . . Her mum's been unwell.

It's a strange situation. She's had to live apart from the kids . . . the children . . .'

'I see.'

But of course, she didn't see and couldn't see and Kendra had no intention of lifting the veil of obscurity for her. She just needed Mrs Harper to believe her lies because she needed Ness to have a place at Holland Park School.

'So you say she'll be back tomorrow?' Mrs Harper asked.

'I'm picking her up at the station tonight.'

'I thought you said tomorrow?'

'I meant in school tomorrow. Unless she falls ill. If that happens, I'll phone you at once . . .' Kendra let her voice drift off and waited for the other woman's reply. In a moment, she thanked her stars that Glory Campbell had forced an acceptable form of the English language upon all her children. In this circumstance being able to produce grammatically correct speech in an acceptable accent served Kendra well. She knew that it made her more believable than she would have been had she fallen into the dialect that Mrs Harper had no doubt expected to hear on the other end of the phone when she'd placed her call.

'I'll let her teachers know, then,' Mrs Harper said. 'And please do next time keep us informed, Mrs Osborne.'

Kendra refused to be offended by the admission officer's imperative. So thankful was she that the woman had accepted her unlikely tale of Ness caring for Carole Campbell that, short of a direct insult, she would have found any comment from Mrs Harper tolerable. She felt relieved that she'd been able to concoct a story on the spur of the moment but shortly after she'd ended the call, the very fact that she'd been *forced* to concoct such a story sent her pacing. She was still doing that when Joel and Toby stopped by on their way home from the learning centre.

Toby was carrying a workbook on whose individual pages colourful stickers had been fixed, celebrating his successful completion of the phonetic drills meant to help him with his reading. He had more stickers on his life-ring, declaring *Well done! Excellent!* and *Good Work* in bright blue, red, and yellow. Kendra saw these but did not remark upon them. She said to Joel, 'Where's she been going every day?'

Joel wasn't stupid, but he was bound by the rule about telling tales. He frowned and played dumb. 'Who?'

'Don't pretend you don't know what I'm talking about. The admissions officer rang me. Where's Ness been going? Is she with this girl . . . What's her name? Six? And why the hell haven't I met her?'

Joel dropped his head to avoid replying. Toby said, 'Lookit my stickers, Aunt Ken. I got to make a purchase from the comic books cos I got enough stickers now. I chose Spiderman. Joel got it in his rucksack.'

The mention of rucksack put Kendra in the picture about what Ness had been doing, and she cursed herself for being a fool. So when she got back to the estate that evening – keeping Joel and Toby with her until it was time to close the shop so that Joel would not have the chance to warn his sister about the game being up – the first thing she did was scoop Ness's rucksack off the back of the chair on which she'd hung it. Kendra opened it unceremoniously and dumped its contents on the kitchen table where Ness had been chatting to someone on the phone while she idly leafed through the most recent prospectus from Kensington and Chelsea College every bit as if she actually intended to make something of her life.

Ness's glance went from the prospectus to the pile of her belongings, from there to her aunt's face. She said into the phone, 'I got to go,' and rang off, watching Kendra with an expression that might have been called wary had it not also been so calculating.

Kendra sorted through the contents of the rucksack. Ness looked beyond her to where Joel hung in the doorway. Her eyes narrowed as she evaluated her brother and his potential as a grass. She rejected this. Joel was all right. The information, she decided, must have come from another source. Toby? That, she told herself, was not bloody likely. Toby was generally with the cuckoos.

Kendra tried to read the contents of Ness's rucksack like a priest practising divination. She unrolled the blue jeans and unfolded the black T-shirt whose golden inscription *Tight Pussy* resulted in its being deposited directly into the bin. She fingered through makeup, nail varnish, hair spray, hair clips, matches, and cigarettes, and she stuffed her hands into the high-heeled boots to see if there was anything hidden inside them. Finally she went through the pockets of the jeans, where she found one packet of Wrigley's spearmint and one of rolling papers. These she clutched in the hapless triumph of someone who sees the incarnation of the worst of her fears.

She said, '*So*.'

Ness said nothing.

'What have you got to say?'

Above them in the sitting-room, the television went on, its sound turned to an irritating volume that told everyone within two hundred yards that someone in 84 Edenham Way was watching *Toy Story II* for the twelfth time. Kendra shot a look to Joel. He interpreted it and ducked up the stairs to deal with Toby and the television volume. He remained there, knowing the wisdom of keeping clear of explosive situations.

Kendra repeated her question to Ness. Ness reached for her packet of cigarettes and picked the book of matches from among the other contents of the rucksack now spread across the table.

Kendra snatched them from her and threw them into the kitchen sink. She followed them with the cigarettes. Gesturing with the rolling papers, she said, 'My God, what about your dad? He *started* with weed. You know that. He told you, didn't he? He wouldn't have pretended. Not with you. He said, "They'll see me like I am or they won't see me at all." You even went with him to St Aidan's and waited for him in the crèche. During his meetings. He told me that, Ness. So what d'you think it was all about? Answer me. Tell me the truth. Do you think you're immune?'

Ness had only one way to survive a reference to her father, and that way was retreat: a distancing that she effected by allowing that hot stone always within her to grow in size until she could feel it climbing a burning path to reach the back of her tongue. Contempt was what she experienced when anger did its work upon her. Contempt for her father – which was the only safe emotion she could harbour towards him – and even more contempt for her aunt. She said, 'What're you twisted 'bout? I make rollies, innit. Shit, you the sort always t'ink the worse.'

'Speak English like you were taught, Vanessa. And don't tell me you've been making rollies when you've got a packet of cigarettes big as life inside that rucksack. Whatever else you think, I am *not* stupid. You're smoking weed. You're running round truant. What else are you doing?'

Ness said, 'I tol' you I wa'n't wearing that bloody kit.'

'You mean me to think this is all a reaction to having to wear a school uniform you don't like? What sort of fool do you think I am? Who've you been with all these weeks? What've you been doing?'

Ness reached for the packet of Wrigley's. She used it to gesture at her aunt, a movement that asked – with no little sarcastic intent – if she could chew a piece of gum since she wasn't, apparently, going to be allowed to smoke. She said, 'Nuffink.'

'Nothing,' Kendra corrected her. 'No-thing. *Nothing.* Say it.'

'Nothing,' Ness said. She folded a piece of gum into her mouth. She played with its wrapper, rolling the foil around her index finger and keeping her gaze fixed on it.

'Nothing with who, then?'

Ness made no reply.

'I asked you—'

'Six an' Tash,' she cut in. 'All right? Six an' Tash. We hang at her house. We listen to music. Tha's it, innit.'

'She's your source? This Six?'

'Come *on*. She's my mate.'

'So why haven't I met her? Because she's supplying you and you know I'll twig it. Isn't that right?'

'Fuck it. I *tol'* you wha' the papers 's for. You goin' t' believe wha' you want to believe. 'Sides, not like you *wanted* to meet anyone, innit.'

Kendra saw that Ness was trying to turn the tables, but she wasn't going to allow that to happen. Instead she resorted to an anguished, 'I can't have this. What's *happened* to you, Vanessa?' in that age-old parental cry of despair, which is generally followed by the internal query of What did I do wrong?

But Kendra didn't follow up her first question with that silent and self-directed second one, for at the last moment, she told herself that these were not her children and technically none of them should even be her problem. Since they had an impact on her life, however, she tried another tack, without knowing her words formed the single query least likely to produce a positive result. She said, 'What would your mum say, Vanessa, if she saw how you're acting now?'

Ness crossed her arms beneath her breasts. She would *not* be touched in this way, not by reference to the past or prognostication of the future.

Although Kendra didn't know exactly what Ness was up to, she concluded that whatever it was, it had to do with drugs and most likely, because of her age, with boys as well. This added up to news that wasn't good. But beyond that, Kendra knew nothing aside from what went on on the estates round North Kensington, and she knew plenty about that. Drug deals. Contraband exchanging hands. Muggings. Break-ins. The occasional assault. Gangs of boys looking for trouble. Gangs of girls doing much the same. The best way to avoid putting yourself into harm's way was to walk a narrow path defined by school, home, and nothing else. This, apparently, was not what Ness had been doing.

She said to her, 'You can't do this, Ness. You're going to get hurt.'

'I c'n take care of myself,' Ness said.

That, of course, was the real issue. For Kendra and Ness each had an entirely different definition of what taking care of oneself actually meant. Rough times, disease, disappointment, and death had taught Kendra she had to stand alone. The same and more had taught Ness to run, as fast and as far as her mind and her will would take her.

So Kendra asked the only question left to ask, the one she hoped would get through to her niece and mould her behaviour henceforth. She said, 'Vanessa, d'you want your mum to know how you're behaving?'

Ness raised her gaze from the study she was making of her chewing gum wrapper. She cocked her head. 'Oh yeah, Aunt Ken,' she finally replied, 'like you're really going to tell her that.'

It was a direct challenge, nothing less. Kendra decided the time had come to accept it.

4

While Kendra could have taken them by car, she opted instead for the bus and the train. Unlike Glory who in the past had always accompanied the Campbell children to visit their mother because she wasn't otherwise employed, Kendra had a job to go to and a career to develop, so the children were going to have to make the journey to Carole Campbell by themselves after this. To do that, they'd need to know how to get there and back on their own.

Crucial to Kendra's plan for the day was that Ness should not know where they were going initially. If she knew, she would bolt and Kendra needed her cooperation even if Ness didn't realise she was giving it. She wanted Ness to see her mother – for reasons that Kendra could not express either to herself or to the girl – and she also wanted Carole Campbell to see Ness. For mother and daughter had had a bond at one time, even through Carole's terrible periods.

They began their journey on the number 23 bus to Paddington station. As it was a Saturday, the bus was overly crowded since the route would take them to the top of Queensway where, at the weekends, hordes of kids hung about the shops, cafés, restaurants, and cinemas. This, indeed, was where Ness thought that they were going, and when they approached the appropriate stop in Westbourne Grove, the fact that Ness automatically stood and began to head for the stairs – for they'd crammed themselves into the upper deck of the bus – told Kendra a great deal about where her niece had been spending her time during the days when she was meant to be at school.

Kendra caught the back of Ness's jacket as the girl started to negotiate her way down the aisle. She said, 'Not here, Vanessa,' and she held on until the bus was moving again.

Ness looked from her aunt to the fast disappearing vista that was the corner of Queensway. Then she looked at her aunt again. She realised she'd been had in some way, but she didn't know in what way it was since, always with Six and Natasha as her companions, she'd never ridden the number 23 bus any farther than Queensway.

'Wha's this, then?' she said to Kendra.

Kendra made no reply. Instead, she adjusted the collar of Toby's jacket and said to Joel, 'You all right there, luv?'

Joel nodded. He'd been assigned the job of seeing to Toby, and he was making the best of it that he could. But he felt agonised down to the roots of his hair about the responsibility. For on this day, Toby had been in a state from the minute he'd awakened, as if he'd had preternatural knowledge of where they'd be going and what would happen when they got there. Because of this he had insisted on bringing his life-ring with him, fully inflated, and he'd made a spectacle of himself, tiptoeing along, muttering, and fluttering his hands around his head as if he were being attacked by flies. It was even worse inside the bus, where he wouldn't take off the ring for love or money. Neither would he deflate it in order to make more room for his family or the other passengers. At Kendra's suggestion that he do so, he'd said *No* and *No!* louder and louder and he'd started crying that he *had* to keep it on cos Gran was coming for them and anyway Maydarc *told* him it was helping him *breathe* and he would *suff'cate* if anyone took it from him. Ness had said, 'Shit, give it *here*, then,' and had taken matters into her own hands, which only exacerbated a bad situation that was already causing everyone's attention to fall upon them. Toby began to shriek, Ness began to snarl, 'I am narked now, mon. You got that, Toby?' and Joel cringed and wanted more than anything just to disappear.

'Vanessa,' Kendra said firmly to her, in part to diffuse the situation but also in part because Ness would be required to remember the route in the future, 'this is the number twenty-three bus. You've got that, right?'

'You are startin to vex me as well, Aunt Ken,' was Ness's reply. 'Why I need gettin' it anyways?' She didn't add *bitch*, but it was in her tone.

'You need *gettin' it* because I'm telling you to get it,' Kendra told her. 'Number twenty-three bus. Westbourne Park to . . . Ah yes. Here we are. To Paddington station.'

Ness's eyes narrowed. She knew very well what debarkation at Paddington station likely presaged. Along with her siblings, she'd been to this place many times over the years. She said, 'Hey. I *ain't*—'

Kendra grabbed her arm. 'You are,' she said. 'And if I know you, the last thing you really want is to make a scene like a five-year-old right here in front of strangers. Joel, Toby? Come along with us.'

Ness could have run off when they alighted, but in the past few years she'd become a girl who liked to plan her defiance for a moment when the other party least suspected that defiance was on her mind. Running off as they made their way into the cavernous railway station was the *expected* response, so Ness adopted a different strategy.

She tried to shake off her aunt's grip. She said, 'All right. All *right*,' and she even attempted to speak what was, to her, her aunt's excessively irritating Lady Muck English. 'You can let go now,' she went on. 'I'm not doing a bloody runner, okay? I'll go, I'll go. But it won't make a diff'rence to anything, cos it never does. Gran ain't told you that? Well, you'll see fast enough.'

Kendra didn't bother to correct either her lapses in grammar or her pronunciation. Instead, she rooted twelve pounds from her bag and gave the money to Joel and not to Ness, whom she didn't trust, no matter the girl's ostensible cooperation.

She said, 'While I do the tickets, you lot go over to WH Smith.
Buy her the magazine she likes and her sweets, and get something for yourselves. Joel?'

He looked up. His face was solemn. He was just turned
twelve years old – one week into it – with the weight of the
world settling on his shoulders. Kendra could see this, and
while she regretted it, she knew there was also no help for the
matter. 'I'm depending on you. You keep that money from
your sister, all right?'

'I don't want your bleeding money, *Ken*dra,' Ness snapped.
'Come *on*.' This last she said to her brothers, leading them
towards the station's WH Smith. She grabbed Toby by the
hand and tried, by pressing down on his shoulders, to force
him into walking on the flat of his feet instead of on his toes.
He protested and squirmed to get away from her. She gave
up the effort.

In the meantime, Kendra watched to make sure they were
heading towards WH Smith. She went to fetch their tickets.
The machines were out of order as usual, so she was forced
to join the queue in the ticket hall.

The three Campbells negotiated the surging crowd, most
of whom were jockeying for position to stand with their gazes
fixed on the departures board as if they'd just received word
of the imminent Second Coming. Joel guided Toby through
the travellers, in Ness's wake, pointing out sights like a
demented tour guide to keep his brother moving forward:
'Lookit dat surfboard, Tobe. Where you 'spect dat bloke is
going?' and 'You see dat, Tobe? They were triplets in dat
pushchair.' In this way, he got his brother into WH Smith,
where he looked around for Ness and finally caught sight of
her at the magazines. She'd selected *Elle* and *Hello!* and she
was heading for the display of sweets and other snacks when
Joel caught up with her.

If anything, it was even more crowded in WH Smith than
it had been on the concourse. Toby's life-ring made things

worse for them in the shop, but this difficulty was ameliorated by the fact that he stuck to Joel's side like a foxtail in fur.

He said, 'I don' want crisps wiv flavours dis time. Jus' the reg'lar kind. C'n I get a Ribena 's well?'

'Aunt Ken didn't say about drinks,' Joel replied. 'We'll see wha' kind of money we got left.' It would be little enough, and Joel saw this when the boys joined their sister. He said to Ness, 'Aunt Ken di'n't say two magazines. We got to have enough money for her chocolate, Ness. For the snack 's well.'

'Well, sod Aunt Kendra with a broomstick, Joel,' was Ness's reply. 'Gi' me the money to pay for these.' She gestured with *Hello!* On its cover, an antique rock 'n' roller posed toothily, displaying his twentysomething wife and an infant young enough to be a great-grandchild.

'C'n I get a Milky Way?' Toby asked. 'Crisps, Milky Way, and Ribena, Joel?'

'I don't think we got enough to—'

'*Gi'* me that money,' Ness said to Joel.

'Aunt Ken said—'

'I got to bloody *pay*, don't I?'

At this, several people turned in their direction, including the Asian boy who was working the till. Joel flushed, but he didn't give in to his sister. He knew he'd get hell from her later on, but for now, he decided he'd do as he'd been told and damn whatever consequences Ness would force him to face.

He said to Toby, 'So what kind of crisps you want, Tobe?'

Ness said, 'Shit. You are one pathetic—'

'Kettle Crisps okay?' Joel persisted. 'These here don't got flavours on them. These do you okay?'

It would have been a simple matter for Toby just to nod so that they could get out of the shop. But as usual, he went his own way. In this case, he decided he had to look at each bag of crisps on display, and he refused to be contented until he'd touched every one of them as if they were possessed of magical properties. Ultimately, he chose the one Joel had been holding out to him all along, making this choice based not on nutritional value – of which as a seven-year-old he knew nothing at all and cared even less – but rather on the colour of the bag. He said, 'Dat one's real pretty. Green's my favourite. Di' you know dat, Joel?'

'Would you stop him being so bloody lame and hand over the money?' Ness demanded.

Joel ignored her and, having made his own snack selection from among the chocolate bars, he picked up an Aero for their mother. At the till, he handed over the money, and he made certain his was the palm the change got dropped into, and not his sister's.

Kendra was waiting for them outside of the shop. She took the bag of their purchases and inspected them, pocketing the change that Joel handed over. In a moment of concession, she gave Ness the bag to carry. Then she made all three of the children stand still and look at the departures board above them. She said, 'Now. How d'you tell which train we take?'

Ness rolled her eyes. 'Aunt Ken,' she said, ''xactly how stupid you think—'

'Look at the destination?' Joel said helpfully. 'Look at the stops between here and there?'

Kendra smiled. 'Think you can work it out for us, then?'

'Platform fucking nine,' Ness said.

'You watch your mouth,' Kendra said. 'Joel, platform nine is right. You take us there?'

He did so.

Once they were underway, Kendra resumed her quiz about the trip to make certain they could find their way in the future. She directed the questions to all three of the Campbells, but only one of them answered.

How many stops till they were to get off? she wanted to know. What d'you give the conductor when he passes through the carriage? What if you forgot to buy a ticket? What do you do if you have to pee?

Joel replied cooperatively to each question. Ness sulked and flipped through *Hello!*. Toby bounced his legs against the seat, watched the scenery, and asked Joel was he going to eat his chocolate. Joel nearly said yes, but then he registered the hope on his brother's shiny face. He handed his chocolate to Toby, and he continued to field his aunt Kendra's questions.

What's the name of the stop? she asked. Where d'they go once they reach the right station? What do they say? To who? If it's outside, where do they go? What about if it's inside?

Joel knew some of the answers, but he didn't know them all. When he faltered, Kendra asked Ness, whose reply was consistent: 'Don't care, do I?' to which Kendra would say, 'Don't think I won't sort you later on, Miss Vanessa.'

In this manner, they travelled west, miles and miles from anything resembling London. Even so, the three Campbells couldn't help being familiar with this place, since for years they'd been making this journey, alighting in Wiltshire and walking the mile and a half to the tall brick walls and the green iron gates, either in the company of their grandmother or, before that, with their father leading them along the verge to a spot where it was safe to cross the road.

'I ain't going farther 'n this.' As the train pulled off, Ness made her declaration from inside the station, a tiny brick building about the size of a public toilet, identified near the tracks only by a white sign pitted with rust. There was no platform to speak of, nor was there a taxi rank out here in the middle of nowhere. Indeed, the station itself – surrounded by hedges beyond which fields lay fallow for the winter – was unmanned.

There was a single bench in front of the station, faded green with large patches of grey where the paint had worn away over the years. Ness plopped herself down on to this. 'I ain't going with you.'

Kendra said, 'Hang on. You won't be—'

But Ness cut in with, 'And you can't drag me there. Oh

you c'n try, but I c'n fight you, and I bloody well will. I mean it.'

'You *got* to go,' Joel told his sister. 'Wha's she going to say when you 'n't there? She gonna ask. Wha' m'I sposed to tell her?'

'Tell her I'm dead or summick,' Ness replied. 'Tell her I run off to join the fucking circus. Tell her wha' you want to tell her. Only I ain't going to see her again. I came this far, innit, but now I'm going back to London.'

'With what ticket?' Kendra asked. 'With what money to buy yourself one?'

'Oh I got money if turns out I need it,' Ness informed her. 'And plenty more where it came from 's well.'

'Money from where? From what?' Kendra asked her.

'Money I work for,' Ness replied.

'Now you telling me you have a *job*?'

'I s'pose it depends on what you call work.' Ness unbuttoned her jacket, revealing her breasts in their plunging blouse. She smirked and said, 'Don' you know, Aunt Ken? I dress to get money. I *always* dress to get money.'

In the end, Kendra knew argument was useless. So she extracted a promise from Ness. She then gave one in turn, although both of them knew their words were largely worthless. For Kendra's part, she simply had too much to contend with already without also having to engage Ness in a battle over how she was getting money or whether she was going to accompany her aunt and her little brothers to see their mother. For Ness, promises had long ago become idle words of the sound and fury variety. People had been making them to her and breaking them consistently over her back as long as she could remember, so she was able both to promise and to renege on that promise with complete impunity, and she told herself that she didn't care when others did the same.

The promises given in this case were simple. Kendra would

not insist that Ness accompany them a step farther on their route to see Carole Campbell. In return, Ness would wait for their reappearance at the station some two hours hence. This deal hammered out between them, Kendra and the boys left Ness on the ancient wooden bench, between a notice board that hadn't been unlocked and updated in a decade and a rubbish bin that looked as if it hadn't been emptied in just about as long.

Ness watched them go. For a moment altogether too brief, so relieved was she at having escaped another excruciating visit to her mother that she actually considered keeping her promise to her aunt. Deep inside her, there still existed the child who recognised an act of love when it was truly an act of love, and that child intuitively understood that what Kendra had in mind for her – both through the now aborted trip to see Carole Campbell and through her promise to wait and not wander off on her own – was actually in her best interest. But when it came to her best interest, Ness's problem was twofold: first, the part of her that *wasn't* a child was a fifteen-year-old girl-woman at that point in her life where parental directives seemed akin to torture by enemy forces. And second, that fifteen-year-old girl-woman had long ago lost the ability to transform the words of any adult into anything she could understand as having benefit to her. Instead, she saw only what other people demanded from her and what she could gain from them in turn, through acquiescence in or refusal of their requests.

In this case and upon reflection, acquiescence meant a nice long sit in the cold. It meant a numb backside pressed God only knew how long into the splintery wood of the station bench, followed by an interminable train ride back to London during which Toby would annoy her to such a degree that she'd want to throw him on to the railway tracks. Worse, acquiescence meant missing out on whatever Six and Natasha had planned for the afternoon and the evening, and that meant being on the outside looking in the next time she got together with her friends.

So, at the end of the day, there really was no choice to be made between remaining at the station and heading back into London. There was only the waiting for an eastbound train. When one chugged to a halt some twenty-eight minutes after Kendra's departure with Joel and Toby, Ness climbed aboard without a backward glance.

The other three made an odd sight walking up to the guard gate: Toby wearing his seaside life-ring, Joel in his ill-fitting Oxfam clothes, and Kendra dressed in cream and navy blue, as if she intended this visit as a substitute for afternoon tea at a country hotel.

When she had admittance past the guard gate, Kendra led her nephews along a curving driveway. This skirted a broad expanse of lawn on which oak trees stood – bare of leaves – near flowerbeds that were colourless in the winter weather. In the distance sprawled their ultimate destination: the body, wings, spires, and turrets of an unwashed Gothic revival building, its facing stones streaked with mould and grime, the nooks and crannies of its exterior a nesting place for birds.

Crows cawed and hurtled upward into the sky as Kendra and the boys reached the wide front steps. There the building's windows looked blankly out at them, hung outside with vertical iron bars, inside with crooked Venetian blinds. Before the massive front door, Toby faltered. Armed with his life-ring, he'd trotted along so easily from the time they'd left the railway station that his sudden hesitation took Kendra by surprise.

Joel said to her hastily, "'S okay, Aunt Ken. He don't know where we are 'xactly. But he'll be fine once he sees Mum.'

Kendra avoided asking the obvious question: how could Toby *not* know where they were? He'd been coming here for most of his life. And Joel avoided giving her the obvious answer: Toby had already retreated to Sose. Instead, Joel pushed open the front door and held it for his aunt. He urged Toby to follow her inside.

Reception was to the left of the entrance, black and white lino squares over which lay a doormat that was tattered at the edges. An umbrella stand and a wooden bench were the only furniture in the foyer. A small lobby with a wide wooden staircase opened off this. The staircase made sharp turns as it climbed to the first and second floors of the building.

Joel went to Reception, Toby's hand in his and their aunt following. The woman at the desk was someone he recognised from his earlier visits although he didn't know her name. But he remembered her face, which was yellow and lined. She smelled quite strongly of smoked cigarettes.

She handed passes over automatically. She said, 'Mind you keep them pinned to your clothes.'

Joel said, 'Cheers. She in her room?'

Reception waved him off with a gesture towards the stairs. 'You'll have to ask upstairs. Go on with you, then. Doesn't do anyone any good with you lolling round here.'

That wasn't supposed to be the case, however. Not in the broader sense. People came to this place – or were put here by their families, by magistrates, by judges, or by their GPs – because it would do them good, which was another way of saying that it would cure them, making them normal and able to cope.

On the second floor, Joel stopped at another desk. A male nurse looked up from a computer terminal. He said, 'Telly room, Joel,' and went back to work.

They walked along a lino-floored corridor, where rooms opened to the left and windows ran along the right. Like those on the floors below, the windows were covered with bars. They had the same Venetian blinds as well, the sort that declared *institution* by their width, their lopsided angles of repose, and the amount of dust gathered on them.

Kendra took in everything as she followed her nephew.

She'd never been inside this place. On the rare occasions when she'd come to see Carole, she'd met her outside because the weather had been fine. She wished the weather had been fine today: unseasonably warm and a good excuse for further avoidance.

The television room was at the end of the corridor. When Joel opened the door, the smells assailed them. Someone had been playing with the radiators, and the blazing heat that resulted from this was melding the odours of unwashed bodies, soiled nappies, and collective bad breath. Toby stopped just beyond the threshold, then his body stiffened as he backed into Kendra. The rank odour was acting like smelling salts on him, pulling him from the safety of his mind back to reality. It was present time and present place for him now, and Toby looked over his shoulder as if considering flight.

Kendra pushed him gently into the room. ''S okay,' she told him. But she couldn't blame him for his hesitation. She wanted to hesitate herself.

No one looked their way. A golf tournament was on the television, and several people sat in a circle before it, eyes glued to the limited action provided by that sport. At one card table, four others worked upon a large jigsaw puzzle while at another, two ancient ladies were hanging over what looked like an old wedding album. Three other people – two men and one women – were doing nothing more than shuffling along the wall while in a corner a wheelchair-bound person of indeterminate sex was calling out weakly, 'Gotta have a piss, God damn it,' and going ignored. On the wall above the wheelchair a poster hung, printed with 'When life gives you lemons, make lemonade.' On the floor next to it sat a long-haired girl, silently weeping.

One person in the room was given to industry, on her hands and knees, scrubbing the floor. She was just beyond the jigsaw puzzle table, working from the corner of the room. She had no bucket, no broom, no mop, no sponge to assist her in her endeavour, just her bare knuckles which she swept repeatedly in an arc on the lino.

Joel recognised their mother from the ginger of her hair which was similar to his own. He said to his aunt, 'There she is,' and he tugged Toby in her direction.

'She's Cleanin' Caro today,' one of the jigsaw ladies said as they approached. 'Going to make things nice 'n' tidy, she is. Caro! You got company, luv.'

One of the jigsaw companions put in, 'Wearing out the bloomin floor's more like it. And tell her to do summick about your brother's nose.'

Joel inspected Toby. Kendra did the same. The little boy's upper lip was slick and shiny. Kendra searched in her bag for the tissue or handkerchief that she did not have while Joel looked round the room for something to clean Toby up with. There was nothing to hand, so he was reduced to using his shirt tail, which he then tucked into his jeans.

Kendra went to the kneeling figure of Carole Campbell and tried to remember when last she'd seen her. Months and months ago, it had to be. Or perhaps even longer, in spring the previous year because of the flowers, the weather, and the fact that they had met out of doors. Since then, Kendra had always been too busy. Scores of projects and dozens of obligations had sufficed to keep her away from this place.

Joel squatted down next to his mother. He said, 'Mum? Brought you a magazine t'day. Me and Toby and Aunt Ken here. Mum?'

Carole Campbell continued her useless swiping, making large semi-circles against the dull green floor. Joel eased forward and laid the copy of *Elle* before her. 'Brought you this,' he said. 'It's brand new, Mum.'

It was also a little worse for wear, rolled up while they were walking from the station. Its edges curled upward as they headed towards dog-eared, and a handprint marred the cover girl's face. But it was enough to make Carole stop her cleaning.

She gazed at the magazine and her fingers went to her own face, touching those features that made her what she was: a mixture of Japanese, Irish, and Egyptian. She compared herself – uncared for, unclean – to the flawless creature who was pictured. Then she looked at Joel and from him to Kendra. Toby, sheltered at Joel's side, tried to make himself small.

'Where's my Aero?' Carole asked. 'I'm meant to have an orange Aero, Joel.'

'Here it is, Carole.' Hastily, Kendra brought it out of the bag. 'The boys got it for you at WH Smith when they picked out the *Elle*.'

Carole ignored her, the chocolate forgotten, lost in another thought. 'Where's Ness?' she asked, and she looked around the room. Her eyes were grey-green and they appeared un-focused. She seemed caught somewhere in the nether land, between complete sedation and incurable ennui.

'She di'n't want to come,' Toby said. 'She bought a *Hello!* with Aunt Ken's money, so I di'n't get a chocolate bar, Mum. If you don' want the Aero, c'n—'

'They keep asking me,' Carole cut in. 'But I won't.'

'Won't what?' Joel asked.

'Do their bloody puzzles.' She jerked her head at the table where the jigsaw puzzle was being assembled, and she added slyly, 'It's a test. They think I don't realise that, but I do. They want to know what's going on in my sub . . . my sub*con*scious and that's how they intend to find out, so I won't work on the puzzles. I say that if they want to know what's in my head, why don't they ask me directly? Why don't I get to see a doctor? Joel, I'm meant to see the doctor once a week. Why don't I get to *see* him?' Her voice had grown louder and she clutched her magazine to her chest. Next to him, Joel felt Toby start to tremble. He looked to Kendra for some sort of rescue, but she was gazing at his mother as if she were a laboratory specimen.

'I want to see the doctor,' Carole cried. 'I'm *meant* to see him. I know my rights.'

'You saw him yesterday, Caro,' the first jigsaw lady informed her. 'Just like you always do. Twice a week.'

Carole's face clouded. On it flickered an expression so like Toby's when he was gone from them that both Kendra and Joel drew an unsteady breath. Carole said, 'Then I want to go home. Joel, I want you to speak to your father. You must do it straightaway. He'll listen to you and you must tell him—'

'Gavin's dead, Carole,' Kendra told her sister-in-law. 'You understand that, don't you? He's been dead four years.'

'Ask him may I come home, Joel. It won't happen again. I understand things now. I didn't then. There was just too much . . . up here . . . Too much . . . Too much . . . Too much . . .' She took the magazine and tapped it against her forehead. Once, twice. And then harder each time she said 'Too much.'

Joel looked to Kendra for some kind of rescue, but Kendra was out too far beyond her depth. The only rescue she could come up with was getting clear of this place as soon as possible before irreparable damage was done. Not that irreparable damage hadn't already been done. But she suddenly wanted no more of it, no further visitation on either her or the children from fate, Karma, predestination, or whatever else you wanted to call it

Although he couldn't have expressed it in words, Joel understood from his aunt's expression, her posture, and her silence that he would have to go this visit with his mother alone. There wasn't a single nurse or orderly in the room to come to their aid, and even if there had been, Carole wasn't harming herself. And it had been made clear from the very first time she'd ended up in this place that, unless a patient meant to do harm to her body, there was no one to save her from the worst of herself.

He sought a distraction. 'Toby's birthday's coming, Mum. He'll be eight years old. I haven't worked out what to get him yet cos I don't have much money, but I got a little. Summick like eight quid dat I been saving. I was thinking maybe Gran would send money, an' I'd be able to—'

His mother grabbed his arm. 'Speak to your father,' she hissed. 'Swear you'll speak to your father. I'm meant to come home. Do you understand me?' She pulled Joel closer to her and he caught her smell: unwashed woman and unwashed hair. He tried very hard not to jerk away.

Toby, on the other hand, felt no such compunction. He backed away from Joel and into his aunt, saying, 'C'n we go home? Joel, can we go?'

Carole seemed to rouse from some waking sleep at this. Suddenly she noticed Toby cowering and Kendra standing above him. She said in a voice growing ever louder, 'Who's this? Who are these people, Joel? Who've you brought with you? Where's Nessa, then? Where's Ness? What've you done with Ness?'

Joel said, 'Ness wouldn't . . . she couldn't . . . Mum, this here's Toby and Aunt Kendra. You know them. Course Toby's getting big now. Near eight years old. But Aunt Ken—'

'Toby?' Carole Campbell went inward as she said the name, attempting to sort through the train crash of her memories to find the relevant one. She rocked back on her heels and considered the little boy before her, then Kendra, trying to make sense of who these people were and, more important, trying to understand what they wanted of her. 'Toby,' she murmured. 'Toby. Toby.' Suddenly her face filled with light as she managed to attach *Toby* to an image in her mind. For his part, Joel felt an answering relief and Kendra felt the passing of a potential crisis.

But then, as if on the edge of a coin, Carole's comprehension slipped, and her expression crumpled. She looked directly at Toby and put her hands up – palms outward – as if she would fend him off in some way. 'Toby!' she cried out, his name no longer a name to her but an accusation.

'Tha's right, Mum,' Joel said. 'This's Toby. Tha's who this is, innit.'

'I should have dropped you,' Carole cried in reply. 'When I heard the train. I should have dropped you but someone stopped me. Who? Who stopped me from dropping you?'

'No, Mum, you can't—'

She clutched her head, fingers deep in her ginger hair. 'I must go home now. Straightaway, Joel. Ring your father and tell him I must come home and God, God, *God*, why can't I remember anything any more?'

5

Since part of his job was to know when the pupils in his PSHE group were floundering in one area or another – after all, the class wasn't called Personal Social Health Education for nothing – Mr Eastbourne eventually noticed that Joel Campbell needed a bit of special attention. This became apparent to him when a colleague routed Joel from his lunchtime hiding place for the third time, delivering him to Mr Eastbourne for an intimate colloquy that was supposed to reveal the nature of the boy's problems. Anyone with eyes could see the nature of the boy's problems, of course: he kept to himself, had no friends, spoke only when spoken to and not always then, and spent his free time attempting to blend into the notice boards, the furniture, or whatever else comprised the environment in which he found himself. What remained to be excavated from Joel's psyche were the reasons for the problems.

Mr Eastbourne possessed one quality above all others that made him an exceptional instructor in PSHE: he knew his limitations. He disliked faux bonhomie, and he understood that spurious attempts to be matey with a troubled adolescent were unlikely to produce a positive result. So he availed himself of a member of the school's mentoring programme, a human inventory of community members who were willing to assist pupils with everything from reading to relieving anxiety. Thus, not long after the visit to his mother, Joel found himself being ushered into the presence of an odd-looking Englishman.

He was called Ivan Weatherall, a white man on the far side

of fifty who favoured hunting jackets with tatty leather in all the appropriate places as well as baggy tweed trousers worn too high on the waist and held there with both braces and a belt. He had appalling teeth but exceptionally nice breath, chronic dandruff but freshly washed hair. Manicured, closely shaven, and polished where polish was called for, Ivan Weatherall knew what it was to be an outsider, having endured both fagging and bullying at boarding school, as well as possessing a libido so low as to make him a misfit from his thirteenth birthday right into his dawning old age.

He had a most peculiar way of speaking. So anomalous was it to what Joel was used to – even from his aunt – that at first he concluded Ivan Weatherall was having a monumental joke at Joel's own expense. He used terms like *Righto, I dare say, Spot on,* and *Cheerio,* and behind his wire-rimmed spectacles, his blue eyes locked on Joel's and never looked away, as if he were waiting for a reaction. This forced Joel into either giving him one, meeting his gaze, or looking elsewhere. Most of the time he chose to look elsewhere.

He and Ivan met twice a week, tucked away in an office made available for the mentoring programme. Ivan began their relationship with a formal bow from the waist, and, 'Ivan Weatherall, at your service. I haven't seen you hereabouts. How pleasant to meet you. Shall we perambulate or is remaining stationary your preference?'

To this bizarre opening, Joel made no reply since he thought the man was having him on.

Ivan said, 'Then I shall make the decision. As rain appears imminent, I suggest we avail ourselves of what seating accommodation is on offer.' Then he ushered Joel into the little office, where he deposited his gangly frame into a red plastic chair and hooked his ankles round its front legs.

'You're a relative newcomer to our little corner of the world, I understand,' he said. 'Your habitation is . . . where? One of the estates, I believe? Which one?'

Joel told him, managing to do so without looking up from his hands which played with the buckle on his belt.

'Ah, the location of Mr Goldfinger's grand building,' was Ivan's reply. 'Do you live inside that curious structure, then?'

Joel correctly assumed that Ivan was referring to Trellick Tower, so he shook his head.

'Pity,' Ivan Weatherall said. 'I live in that general area myself, and I've wanted to explore that building for ever. I consider it all a bit grim – well, what *can* one do with concrete *besides* make it look like a minimum security prison, don't you agree? – and yet those bridges . . . floor after floor of them . . . They do make a statement. I dare say one still wishes that London's post-war housing problems could have been solved in a more visually pleasing manner.'

Joel raised his head and ventured a look at Ivan, still trying to work out if he was being made fun of. Ivan was watching him, head cocked to one side. He'd altered his position during his prefatory remarks, leaning back so that his chair rested on its two back legs. When Joel's eyes met his, Ivan gave him a little friendly salute. '*Entre nous*, Joel,' he said in a confidential tone, 'I'm a type one generally refers to as an English eccentric. Quite harmless and engaging to have at a dinner party where Americans are present and declaring themselves desperate to meet a *real* Englishman.' They were hard enough to come by in this part of town, he went on to tell Joel, especially in his own neighbourhood, where the small houses were mostly occupied by large Algerian, Asian, Portuguese, Greek, and Chinese families. He himself lived alone – 'Not even a budgerigar to keep me company' – but he liked it that way as it gave him time and space to pursue his hobbies. Every man, he explained, needed a hobby, a creative outlet through which one's soul earned expression. 'Have you one yourself?' he enquired.

Joel ventured a reply. The question seemed harmless enough. 'One what?'

'A hobby, a soul-enriching extra-curricular endeavour of one form or another?'

Joel shook his head.

'I see. Well, perhaps we can find you one. This will, naturally, involve a minor bit of probing with which I will ask you to cooperate to the best of your ability. You see, Joel, we are creatures of parts. Physical, mental, spiritual, emotional, and psychological parts. We are akin to machines, if it comes down to it, and every mechanism that makes us what we are needs to be attended to if we are to function both efficiently and to our utmost capacity. You, for instance. What do you intend to do with your life?'

Joel had never been asked such a question. He knew, of course, but he was embarrassed to admit it to this man.

'Well, then, that is part of what we'll search for,' Ivan said. 'Your intentions. Your path to the future. I myself, you see, longed to be a film producer. Not an actor, mind you, because at the end of the day I could never abide people ordering me about and telling me how to act. And not a director because I could also never abide being the one *doing* the ordering. But producing . . . Ah, that was my love. Making it *happen* for others, giving their dreams life.'

'Did you?'

'Produce films? Oh yes. Twenty of them as it happens. And then I came here.'

'Whyn't you in Hollywood, then?'

'With a starlet hanging from my every appendage?' Ivan shuddered dramatically then smiled, revealing his tortured teeth. 'Why, I'd made my point. But that's a conversation for another time.'

Over the ensuing weeks, they had many such conversations, although Joel kept his darkest secrets to himself. So while Ivan knew that Joel and his siblings lived with their aunt, he didn't know precisely why. And while he knew that Joel's responsibility was to stop by Middle Row School for Toby so that the little boy did not have to walk anywhere alone, where Joel actually *took* Toby and why he did so were topics that never came up between him and his assigned mentor. As for Ness, Ivan knew that she was a chronic truant whose attendance problems had not been resolved by the single phone call made from the admissions officer to Kendra Osborne.

Other than that, Ivan did most of the talking. Joel, listening, grew used to the eccentricities of the older man's speech. He actually found himself liking Ivan Weatherall, as well as looking forward to their meetings. But this factor in their relationship – the liking part of it – made Joel even more reluctant to speak honestly with him. Should he do so, which he assumed was the purpose of their visits, he believed that he would be seen as 'cured' of whatever the school had decided ailed him. Cured, he would no longer need to meet with Ivan, and he didn't wish that to happen.

It was Hibah who revealed a way that Joel might keep Ivan chatting in his life even if the school decided that was no longer necessary. Near the fourth week of their meetings, she saw Joel emerging from the library with the Englishman, and she plopped down next to Joel on the number 52 bus later that afternoon to put him into the picture.

She began with, 'You seeing that mad English bloke, eh? You watch out f'r him.'

Joel, working on a maths problem he'd been given for homework, didn't at first take note of the menace behind her words. He said, 'Wha'?'

'Tha' Ivan bloke. Hangs round *kids*, he does.'

''S his job, innit.'

'Not talking 'bout school,' she said. 'Other places is where. You been over to Paddington Arts?'

Joel shook his head. He didn't even know what Paddington Arts was, let alone where it was.

Hibah told him. Paddington Arts was a centre for creative works, not far from the Grand Union Canal and just off Great

Western Road. Classes were offered there – yet another stab at giving the area's youth something to do besides head into trouble – and Ivan Weatherall was one of the instructors.

'So he *says*,' Hibah told Joel. 'I hear otherwise.'

'From who?' Joel asked.

'My boyfriend's who. *He* say Ivan got a thing for boys. Boys just like you, Joel, innit. Mixed boys, he likes, an' my boyfriend oughta know.'

'Why?'

She rolled her large eyes expressively. 'You can *figger*. You not thick or summick, are you? Anyways, more'n jus' my boyfriend say it. Older blokes's grew up in the area. Tha' bloke Ivan, he been round here for*ever*, an' it's always been the same wiv him. You watch yourself's what I'm saying.'

'He never do nothing but talk wiv me,' Joel told her.

Again the eye roll. 'Don' you know nuffink? Tha's how it always begin,' she said.

Kendra's lie to the admissions officer at Holland Park School comprised the reason that it took several weeks for the next level of educational concern to be triggered regarding Ness's lack of attendance. During this time, Ness carried on much as before with only a slight variation, leaving the house with her brothers and parting from them in the vicinity of Portobello Bridge. What made it look to her aunt as if she were actually attending school this time around was the fact that she no longer carried a change of clothes in her rucksack but rather two notebooks and a geography text pinched from Six's brother, the Professor. Her change of clothes she merely left at Six's.

Kendra chose to be soothed into belief by this. It was the path of least resistance. It was also, unfortunately, only a matter of time before that path went from bumpy to impassable.

It was late March and in the midst of a classic English downpour when several occasions conspired against her. The first of these occurred when a lithe and well-dressed black man entered the charity shop, shook off a tan umbrella, and asked to speak to Mrs Osborne. He was Nathan Burke, he said, the education officer from Holland Park School.

Cordie Durelle was in the shop with Kendra, on her break from the Princess European and Afro Unisex Hair Salon. As before, she was smoking. As before, she wore her purple smock, with her surgical mask slung around her neck. She and Kendra had been discussing Gerald Durelle's recent inebriated and destructive hunt through the house for what he assumed – correctly – had to be the birth control pills, which he believed were keeping his wife from becoming pregnant with the son he desired, and Cordie had just reached the climax of her tale when the shop door opened and its bell rang.

Their conversation ceased as if by telepathic agreement, largely because Nathan Burke was breathtaking and both of the women needed to take that breath. He spoke politely and precisely, and he moved across the shop to the counter with the confidence of man who'd had a decent upbringing, a decent education, and a life spent largely outside England and in an environment where he'd been treated as equal to everyone else.

Burke asked which one of the ladies was Mrs Osborne and could he speak to her on a private matter. Kendra idenitifed herself cautiously and told him he could speak in front of her best friend Cordie Durelle. Cordie shot her a grateful glance at this, for she always appreciated being in the presence of an attractive man. She lowered her eyelids and attempted to look as sultry as a woman in a purple smock and surgical mask can look.

Nathan Burke didn't have the time to notice her, however. He'd been paying visits to the parents of Holland Park's truant pupils since nine o'clock that morning, and he had five more to get through before he could end his day and finally go home to the sympathetic ministrations of his life partner. Because of this, he got directly to the point. He brought out the relevant attendance records and broke the news to Kendra.

Kendra looked at the records, feeling the pounding of dread begin in her head. Cordie glanced at the records as well. She said the obvious, 'Shit, Ken. She ain't ever gone to school, innit.' And then to Nathan Burke, 'Wha' kinda school you got over there? She get bullied or summick dat she don' want to go?'

Kendra said, 'She could hardly get bullied if she never went in the first place,' her voice matched to Burke's and not to her friend's.

Cordie showed mercy and eschewed her usual acerbic comment, ignoring Kendra's choice of dialect. She said, 'She getting up to trouble, den. Only question's what kind: boys, drugs, drink, street crime.'

'We've got to get her in school,' Nathan Burke said, 'no matter what she's been doing while she's been truant. The question is how to do this.'

'She ever felt the belt?' Cordie said.

'Fifteen. She's too old for that. And anyway, I won't beat those children. What they've faced already . . . They've had enough.'

Mr Burke appeared to be all ears at this, but Kendra wasn't about to give him the bible on her family's history. Instead she asked him what he recommended, short of beating a girl who would probably be only too happy to beat her aunt in response.

'Establishing consequences usually does the trick,' he said. 'Do you object to discussing a few you might try?'

He went over them and their various outcomes: driving Ness to school and walking her to her first scheduled class in front of all the other pupils to cause her an embarrassment she wouldn't want to endure a second time; removing privileges like use of the phone and the television; gating the girl; sending her to boarding school; arranging for private counselling to get to the root of the matter; telling her that she –

Kendra – would accompany her to each of her classes if she continued to avoid them . . .

Kendra couldn't imagine a single one of those listed conse-quences that her niece wouldn't shrug at. And short of hand-cuffing Ness to her wrist in an attempt to control her behaviour, Kendra couldn't come up with an outcome of her truancy that might impress upon her niece the importance of attending school. Too much had been taken away from the girl over the years with nothing to replace those elements of a normal life that she had lost. One could hardly tell her that education was important when no one was giving her a similar message about having a stable mother, a living father, and a dependable home life.

Kendra saw all this, but she had no idea what to do about any of it. She put her elbows on the counter and drove her fingers into her hair.

This prompted Nathan Burke to offer a final suggestion. The problem of Vanessa, he said, might be something that required a group home. Such things existed, if Mrs Osborne felt unequal to the task of coping with the girl. In Care—

'They *ain't* . . .' She raised her head and corrected herself. 'These children are *not* going into care.'

'Does that mean we'll see Vanessa at school, then?' Mr Burke asked.

'I don't know,' Kendra said, opting for honesty.

'I'll have to refer her onward, then. Social Services will need to become involved. If you can't get her to attend school, that's the next step. Explain this to her, please. It might help matters.'

He sounded compassionate, but compassion was the last thing Kendra wanted. To get him to leave – which was what she *did* want – she nodded. He departed soon after, although not before choosing a piece of Bakelite jewellery to take home to his partner.

Cordie went for Kendra's cigarettes, having long finished her own. She lit up two of them, handing one to her friend.

She said, 'Okay. I got to say it.' She inhaled as if for courage and went on in a rush. 'Maybe, Ken, jus' maybe you in over your head wiv dis sort of t'ing.'

'What sort of thing?'

'Mothering sort of t'ing.' Cordie went on hastily, 'Look, you ain't never . . . I mean, how c'n you 'spect to know wha' to do wiv this lot when you never done it before? Anyways, did you ever even *wan'* to? I mean, maybe puttin' dem some place else . . . I *know* you don' wan' to do dat, but could be real families could be found . . .'

Kendra stared at her. She wondered at the fact that her friend knew her so little, but she was honest enough with herself to accept her own responsibility for Cordie's ignorance. What else could Cordie assume when she herself had never told her the truth? And she didn't know *why* she'd never told her except that it seemed so much more modern and liberated and I-am-woman to allow her friend to believe she'd actually had a choice in the matter. She said simply, 'Those kids're staying, Cordie, least till Glory sends for them.'

Not that Glory Campbell had ever had any intention of doing so, a supposition of Kendra's that became fact just a few days later when she picked up the post to find the first letter that Glory had sent from Jamaica in the months since she'd been gone. There was nothing surprising in its contents: she'd had a serious think about the situation, Kendra, and she'd come to realise that she *couldn't* remove the grandkids from England. Taking them so far from dear Carole would probably put the final nail in the coffin of the woman's precarious sanity, what was left of it. Glory didn't want to be responsible for that. But she *would* send for Joel and Nessa for a little visit sometime in the future when she had the money put together for their tickets.

There was, unsurprisingly, no mention of Toby.

So that was that. Kendra had known it would come. But she couldn't spend time dwelling on the matter. There was

Ness to contend with and the future hanging over her if she did not agree to go to school.

As far as consequences were concerned, nothing worked because to Ness, there was simply nothing worthwhile to lose. And what she was after, she couldn't find anyway, not in school and certainly not in her aunt's tiny house in Edenham Estate. For her part, Kendra lectured Ness. She shouted at her. She drove her to the school and walked her to the first class on her schedule as Nathan Burke had suggested. She tried gating her, which, naturally, was impossible without either Ness's agreement to be gated or chains and locks to make sure she stayed put. But nothing worked. Ness's response was unchanging. She *wasn't* wearing those 'disgustin rags', she *wasn't* sitting in 'some stupid-ass classroom', and she *wasn't* about to waste her time 'workin fucking sums and such' when she could be out and about with her mates.

'You need a break,' Cordie told Kendra the afternoon Nathan Burke phoned the charity shop to inform Kendra that Ness had been assigned a social worker as a last resort before the magistrate became involved. 'We ain't had our girls' night in however long. Le's take one, Ken. You need it. So do I.'

That was how Kendra found herself in No Sorrow on a Friday night.

Kendra prepared for her girls' night out by informing Ness that she would be left in charge of Toby and Joel for the evening, which meant that she would remain at home despite what her other plans might be. The instructions were to keep the boys happy and occupied, which meant that Ness was to interact with them in some way to make sure they were both distracted and safe. As this wasn't something Ness was likely to do even when ordered, Kendra honeyed her directives and ensured compliance by adding that there would be money in it for Ness if she cooperated.

Joel protested, saying that he didn't *need* minding. He wasn't a baby. He could cope on his own.

But Kendra wasn't to be talked out of the arrangement. For God only knew what might happen if someone streetwise wasn't in charge of refusing to open the front door to a knock after dark. And, despite all the trouble she was causing, it could not be denied that Ness was streetwise. So 'There's money in it for you, Nessa,' she repeated to her niece. 'What's your decision? Can you be trusted to stay home with the boys?'

Ness did some quick calculations in her head, only some of which had to do with money and what she could do with it once she got it. She decided that, having nothing on for the night but the usual, which was hanging with Six and Natasha over at Mozart Estate, she'd opt for the money. She said 'Whatever' to her aunt, which Kendra mistakenly embraced as an acquiescence that would not be dislodged by any tempting vagaries of the coming evening.

It had been Cordie's turn to choose their outing, and she'd selected clubbing. They began their night with dinner, and they prefaced the dinner with drinks. They went for Portuguese in Golborne Road, and they washed down their starters with a Bombay Sapphire martini each and their main courses with several glasses of wine. Neither of the women drank much on a regular basis, so they were more than a little inebriated when they staggered back across Portobello Bridge where, beyond Trellick Tower, No Sorrow was coming to life for the evening.

They'd pull a couple of men, Cordie said. She needed an extra-marital snogging diversion and, as for Kendra: it was high time for Kendra to get a length.

No Sorrow announced itself in neon script across translucent front windows, just those two green words done in a classy Art Deco style. The club was a complete anomaly in the neighbourhood, with owners who were banking on this part of North Kensington lurching towards gentrification. Five years earlier, no one in his right mind would have invested ten pounds in the property. But that was the nature of London in a nutshell: one might call a neighbourhood or even an entire borough down for the count at any time, but only a fool would ever label it out.

The club was the last of a strip of disreputable looking shops: from launderette to library to locksmith. Its door was angled away from these establishments, as if it couldn't bear to see the company it was forced to keep. Beyond that door, No Sorrow existed on two floors of the building. The ground level offered a crescent-shaped bar, tables for chatting at, dim lighting, and walls and ceiling made grubby by the cigarette smoke that perpetually thickened the air. The first floor offered music and drinks, a dj spinning discs at head-splitting volume, and strobe lights making the entire environment look like something out of a bad acid trip.

Kendra and Cordie started out on the ground floor. This would constitute their reconnaissance of the place. They secured drinks and took a few minutes to 'scope out the man flesh', as Cordie put it.

To Kendra, it looked like a case of the odds being good but the goods being odd: men – most of whom were advanced middle-aged and showing it – outnumbered women on the ground floor, but when she looked them over, Kendra told herself that not a single one of them interested her. This was the safest conclusion for her to draw since it was fairly obvious that she interested none of them either. The handful of young women in the place had captured all the attention. Kendra felt every one of her forty years.

She would have insisted upon leaving had Cordie not already determined that Kendra needed some fun. To her suggestion that they depart, Cordie said, 'In a bit, but le's go upstairs first,' and she headed in the direction of the stairs. To her way of thinking, if there were no men available up there, at least she and Kendra could get in a few dances: by themselves or with one another.

On the first floor, they found that the noise was deafening, and the light came from only three sources – a small anglepoise lamp shining on the dj's equipment, two dim bulbs above the bar, and the strobe. Because of this, at the top of the stairs, Kendra and Cordie paused to get used to the murk. They also had to get used to the temperature, which was very nearly tropical. London in early spring meant no one would dare think to open a window, even to be rid of some of the cigarette smoke which – lit by the strobe – made the room look like a tableau demonstrating the perils of yellow fog.

There were no tables up here, just a chest-high shelf running round the room, on which a dancer could place a glass for safekeeping while experiencing the joys of the music. This was currently rap, all lyrics, all beat and no tune, but no one was finding that a problem. It seemed as if two hundred people were mashed together in the dancing area. It seemed as if another hundred or so were vying for the attention of the three bartenders, who were mixing drinks and pouring pints as fast as they could.

With a whoop, Cordie plunged directly into the action, handing over her drink to Kendra and shimmying between two young men who appeared happy to have her company. Watching them, Kendra began to feel worse than she'd felt downstairs – her age and more – which illustrated how different life was for her now. Prior to the Campbells' arrival, she'd been living primarily with the knowledge – fuelled by both of her brothers' deaths – that life was fleeting. She'd been experiencing things rather than reacting to them. She *made* things; they did not make her. But in the months since her mother had foisted an unexpected form of parenthood upon her, she'd managed to do very little that even resembled her old life. It seemed to her that she'd ceased being who she was, in fact, and what was worse, she'd ceased being who she'd long ago intended to be.

Time and experience – and especially two marriages – had

taught Kendra that she had only herself to blame if she didn't like the way her bed was made. If she was feeling her age and feeling burdened by responsibilities that she did not want, it was up to her to do something about it. It was for this reason and because at that precise moment the *something* appeared to be dancing in a crowd of perspiring twenty-year-olds that Kendra decided to join them. But fuelled by that chemical depressant – the alcohol she'd consumed that evening – she found that the activity did not uplift her. It did not bring about the desired secondary result, either, which was finding someone to shag at the end of the evening.

Cordie was all apologies for this as they walked home later. She herself had managed a very nice fifteen minutes snogging with a nineteen-year-old boy in the corridor leading to the toilets, and she couldn't believe that Kendra – whom she declared to be 'dead-on-any-bloke's-feet *gorgeous*, girl' – had not managed at least as much.

Kendra tried to be philosophical about this. Her life was too complicated to accommodate a man, even temporarily, she said.

'Jus' don' start t'inking you ain't got it no more, Ken,' Cordie warned her. 'Sides, men being wha' dey are, you c'n always get one, you lower your standards enough.'

Kendra chuckled. It *didn't* matter, she told her friend. Stepping out for the evening had been enough. In fact, they needed to do this more often, and she intended to turn over a new leaf in the matter, if Cordie was in agreement.

Cordie said, 'Jus' tell me where t'sign up,' and Kendra was about to reply when they emerged from the gloom of the path that passed in front of Trellick Tower into Edenham Way. There she caught a glimpse of the front of her house. A car was parked to block her garage door, a car she couldn't identify.

She said, '*Shit*,' and quickened her pace, determined to see what Ness had got up to in the hours they'd been gone.

She had her answer before she reached either the car or

her front door, for it soon became apparent that the car was occupied, and one of the two people inside it was unmistakably her niece. Kendra could tell this from the shape of Ness's head and the texture of her hair, from the curve of her neck as the man she was with lifted his head from the region of her breasts.

He reached across her to open her door, much like a kerb crawler dismissing a common whore. When Ness didn't remove herself, he gave her a little push, and when that didn't work, he got out of the vehicle himself and walked around to her door. He pulled her out, and her head lolled back. She was either drugged or exceedingly drunk.

Kendra needed no further invitation. She shouted, 'You bloody well hang on right there!' and she charged forward to accost the man. 'You take your hands off that girl!'

He blinked at her. He was much younger than she'd thought, despite being entirely bald. He was black, bulky, and pleasant-featured. He wore odd harem trousers like an exotic dancer, white trainers, and a black leather jacket zipped to his throat. He had Ness's bag slung across his back and Ness herself under one arm.

'You hear me? Let her *go*.'

'I do that, she crack her head on the steps,' he said reasonably. 'She bleeding drunk. I found her up in—'

'You found her, you found her,' Kendra scoffed. 'I don' fuckin *care* where you found her. Get your bloody hands off her, and do it now. You know how old she is? Fifteen, *fifteen*.'

The man looked at Ness. 'Lemme tell you, she don' act—'

'Give her here.' Kendra reached the car and grabbed Ness by the arm. The girl stumbled against her and raised her head. She looked like a ruin; she smelled like an illegal distillery. She said to the man, 'You wan' t' stick it in me or wha? I *tol*' you I ain't doin no free shots, innit.'

Kendra glared at him. 'Get out of here,' she said. 'Give me that bag and just get out. I get your number plates. I phone the cops.' And to Cordie, 'You take down his number plates, girl.'

He said in protest, 'Hey, I jus' bringing her home. She up at the pub. It clear she going to get herself into a bad situation 'f she stays there, so I get her out of th' place.'

'Like Sir Bloody Lancelot, eh? Get those numbers, Cordie.'

As Cordie began to go through her bag for something to write on, the young man said, 'Fuck it, den.' He shook Ness's bag from his shoulder and dropped it on the ground. He bent to look her in the face, and he told her to tell the truth.

Ness said cooperatively, 'You wanted me to suck is the truth, innit. You wanted it *bad*.'

He said, 'Shit,' and slammed the passenger door. He went back to the driver's side and said over the roof of the car to Kendra, 'You better deal with her, 'fore someone else does,' which resulted in Kendra taking note that the term *seeing red* was an accurate description of what happened to one's vision when anger's heat reached a certain degree. He drove off before she could reply: a stranger standing in judgement of her failure.

She felt utterly exposed. She felt enraged. She felt used and foolish. So when Ness giggled and said, 'Tell you, Ken, dat one got a prong like a fuckin *mule*,' Kendra slapped her so hard that her palm sent pain up the length of her arm.

Ness toppled. She fell against the house. She dropped to her knees. Kendra surged forward to hit her again and drew her arm back. Cordie caught it. She said, 'Hey, Ken. Don't,' and that was enough.

It was also enough to sober Ness up, at least partially. So when Kendra finally spoke to her, she was more than ready to make a reply.

'You want the world to know you as a slag?' Kendra cried. ''S that what you want for yourself, Vanessa?'

Ness struggled to her feet and backed away from her aunt. 'Like I bloody fuckin care,' she said.

*   *   *

She stumbled towards the path between the terraces of houses and from there into Meanwhile Gardens. Behind her, she heard Kendra call out her name, she heard her shout 'You get back home,' and she felt a harsh bubble of laughter force its way up into her throat. For Ness, there was no home any longer. There was just a place where she shared a bed with her aunt while her little brothers slept on hastily purchased camp beds in the room next door. Under those beds, Joel and Toby had persisted in keeping their suitcases neatly packed for more than two months. No matter the time that had passed since her departure, the boys still believed what they wanted to believe about their grandmother and her promise of a life of eternal sunshine in the land of her birth.

Ness hadn't once tried to make them see the truth of the matter. She hadn't once pointed out the significance of the fact that the kids hadn't heard a word from Glory Campbell since the day she'd left them on Kendra's doorstep. As far as Ness was concerned, Glory Campbell's disappearance from their lives was a case of good riddance. If Glory didn't need or want her grandchildren, then her grandchildren certainly didn't need or want her. But telling herself that week after week hadn't done much to ease Ness's feelings in the matter.

When she left her aunt in front of No 84 Edenham Way, Ness gave no real thought to where she was going. She just knew that she didn't want to be in her aunt's presence a moment longer. She was sobering up more quickly than she would have thought possible, and with that sobriety came the nausea she otherwise would have felt the next morning. This propelled her towards water in which she might bathe her sweating face, depositing her on the footpath that ran along the canal at the top of the garden.

Despite her condition, she knew the danger of falling into the canal, so she took some care. She lowered herself to the foot-path and lay on her stomach. She bathed her face in the greasy water, felt its oiliness cling to her cheeks, caught the scent of it – not unlike that of a stagnant pool – and promptly vomited. Afterwards, she lay there weakly and listened to the sound of her aunt searching for her in Meanwhile Gardens. Kendra's voice told Ness that her aunt was working her way past the child drop-in centre and into the heart of the gardens, a direction that would take her along the path winding between the hillocks and ultimately to the foot of the spiral staircase. She staggered to her feet, knowing the way she herself had to go. She headed for the duck pond at the east border of the gardens and then beyond it and through the wildlife garden with its boardwalk path that curved into a darkness that was at once sinister and welcoming. She was beyond the point of caring about danger, so she didn't flinch at the sudden movement of a cat dodging across her path, nor was she bothered by the crack and crunch of twigs that suggested she was being followed. She just kept going, plunging into the darkness till she came upon the last of Meanwhile Gardens, which was the scent garden, and she registered the looming shape of its potting shed that marked the end of the path she'd taken.

She came to her senses there and saw she'd come around the back side of Trellick Tower, which rose to her left like the neighbourhood sentry and told her she was close to Golborne Road. She didn't so much make a decision about where to go as she accepted the simple logic of where she would go. Her feet took her to Mozart Estate.

She knew Six was at home, having rung her earlier upon Kendra's departure. She'd learned her friend had been entertaining Natasha along with two boys from the neighbourhood. That meant being a fifth wheel on a vehicle trundling to nowhere, so Ness had set out into the night alone. But now, Six was necessary to her.

Ness found the group – Six, Natasha, and the boys – gathered in the sitting-room of the family's flat. The boys were Greve and Dashell – one black and the other yellow-skinned – and they were both as drunk as football hooligans on the winning side. The girls were in much the same condition. And everyone was semi-dressed. Six and Natasha wore what went for knickers and bras but actually looked like three cough drops apiece, while the boys were draped in towels inexpertly wrapped around their waists. Six's siblings were nowhere to be seen.

Music was issuing forth at a stupendous volume from two refrigerator size speakers on either side of a broken down sofa. On this Dashell was sprawled, and he'd apparently and recently been receiving the affectionate ministrations of Natasha, who was retching into a tea towel as Ness came into the room. An open carton from Ali Baba Homemade Pizza lay discarded at one end of the sofa with an empty Jack Daniels bottle lolling lazily nearby.

The sexual aspect of the goings-on didn't bother Ness. The Jack Daniels aspect did. She hadn't gone to the Mozart Estate to seek out drink, and the fact that the teenagers had resorted to whiskey when they might have chosen something else suggested that what she wanted wasn't to be had tonight in this location.

Nonetheless, she turned to Six and said, 'You holdin substance?'

Six's eyes were bloodshot, and her tongue wasn't working well, but her brain was functioning at least moderately. She said. 'I look like I holdin substance, Moonbeam? Wha' you need? An' shi', Ness, why you coming here now? I up to get mine from dis bred, y'unnerstan?'

Ness understood. Only a mental case from an alien planet would have failed to understand. She said, 'Look, I got to have something, Six. Gimme and I'm out 'f here. A ziggy'll do.'

Natasha said, 'This one here'll give you a mouthful and tha's the troof, lemme tell you.'

Dashell laughed lazily as Greve sank into a three-legged chair.

Six said, 'You t'ink we'd be doing Mr Jack 'f we *had* a ziggy? I hate this shit, Nessa. Goddamn bu' you know it.'

'Fine. Great. Come on an' we'll find something better, yeah?'

'She got somet'ing better right here,' Greve said, and he indicated the gift he had for Six beneath the towel he was wearing.

All four of them laughed. Ness felt like smacking each of them in turn. She walked back towards the door and jerked her head meaningfully, the message being that Six was to follow. Six staggered in her direction. Behind them, Natasha collapsed on to the floor, where Dashell ran his left foot through her hair. Greve lolled with his head hanging forward as if the effort to hold it upright defeated him.

Ness said to Six, 'Jus' make the call. I do everything else.' She felt agitated. Since her first night in North Kensington she'd been relying on Six for substance, but now she saw she was going to need a more direct route to the source.

Six hesitated. She looked over her shoulder. She said sharply to Greve, 'Hey, you ain't passin out, bred, no *way.*'

Greve made no answer. Six said, 'Fuck,' and then to Ness, 'Come on wiv you, den.'

The telephone was in the bedroom shared by the household's female siblings. There, next to one of the three unmade beds, a shadeless lamp shone a meagre cone of light on a grimy plate, upon it a half-eaten sandwich curling in on itself. The phone was next to this, and Six picked it up and punched in a number.

Whoever was on the other end answered immediately Six said, 'Where you? Who the hell you *t'ink* it is, bred? Yeah. Right. So . . . *Where?* Shit, den, how many you got to do? Hell, forget it. We be dead 'f we wait dat long . . . Nah. I ring Cal . . . Hah. Ask me 'f I care 'bout dat.' She punched the phone off and said, 'This ain't goin' be easy, Moonbeam.'

'Who's Cal?' Ness asked. 'An' who'd you call?'

'Don't matter to you.' She punched in another number. This time there was a wait before she said, 'Cal, dat you? Where's he at? I got someone looking for –' a questioning glance at Ness. What did she want? Crank, olly, tranks, skag? What?

Ness couldn't come up with a reply as quickly as either Six or the recipient of her phone call wanted. Weed would have done well. Pressed to it in desperation, even the Jack Daniels would have been acceptable had there been any left in the bottle. She just, at the moment, wanted out.

Into the phone, Six said, 'Blow? Yeah, but where's he operatin'? No shit. No *shit* . . . They ain't goin' to – Oh yeah, I bet he got one or two tricks up his sleeve, dat bred.'

She ended the conversation after that, with a 'Someone 'sides your mum love you, bred.' She replaced the phone and turned to Ness. 'Straight to the top, Moonbeam,' she said. 'The source.'

'Where?'

She grinned. 'Harrow Road police station.'

That was the extent of what Six was willing to do for Ness. Going with her to the station was out of the question since Greve was waiting for her in the sitting-room. She told Ness that she was going to have to acquaint herself with the Blade if she needed to get loaded and couldn't wait for some other means of sending herself into oblivion. And the Blade – according to his right-hand man, Cal – was at that moment being questioned at the Harrow Road police station on some matter involving the burglarising of a video shop in Kilburn Lane.

'How'm I s'posed to know who dis bred is?' Ness asked when given this information.

'Oh b'lieve it, Moonbeam, you know when you see him.'

'An' how I s'posed to know he even goin' to get released, den, Six?'

Her girlfriend laughed at the naïveté of the question. 'Moonbeam, he the *Blade*,' she said. 'Cops ain't planning to mess wiv him.' She waggled her hand at Ness and returned to Greve. She straddled his chair, lifted his head, and lowered the scraps that went for her bra. 'Come *on*,' she said. 'I's time now, mon.'

Ness shuddered at the sight. She turned away quickly and left the flat.

She could have gone home at that point, but she was on a mission that demanded completion. So she left the estate for the short walk down Bravington Road. It finished at the Harrow Road, which was peopled at this time of night with the un-desirables of the area: drunks in doorways, crews of boys in hoodies and baggy jeans, and older men of ambiguous inten-tions. She walked fast and kept her expression surly. Soon enough she saw the police station dominating the south side of the street, its blue lamp glowing on steps that climbed to an impressive front door.

Ness didn't expect to recognise the man Six had sent her to meet. At this time of night, there were comings and goings aplenty at the station, but as far as she could tell, the Blade might have been any of them. She tried to think what a burglar might look like, but all she came up with was someone dressed in black. Because of this, she nearly missed the Blade al-together when at last he came out of the door, took a beret from his pocket, and slipped it on to his hairless head. He was slender and short – not much taller than Ness herself – and had he not stopped under the light to apply a match to a cigar-ette, Ness would have dismissed him as just another half-caste from the neighbourhood.

Under the light, however, and despite its blue glow, she saw the tattoo that curled from beneath the beret and permanently disfigured his cheek: a cobra, fangs bared. She also saw the line of gold hoops hanging from his earlobes and the casual way he balled up the empty cigarette packet and tossed it to land at the threshold of the door. She heard him clear his throat, then spit. He pulled out a mobile and flipped it open.

This was her moment. Because the night had unfolded as it had, Ness went for that moment and all it would bring. She crossed the street and walked up to the man, who looked to her to be somewhere in his twenties.

He was saying into the mobile, 'Where the fuck *are* you, mon?' when Ness touched him on the arm, giving a toss of her head as he turned to her, wary. She said, 'You the Blade, innit? I got to score t'night, bred, and I need substance bad so jus' say yes or no.'

He didn't respond and for a moment Ness thought she'd chosen wrong: either the person or the approach. Then he said impatiently into the phone, 'Jus' get over here, Cal,' after which he snapped it closed and regarded Ness. 'Who the fuck're you?' he demanded.

'Someone wantin to score and dat's all you need to know, mon.'

'Dat right, eh? An' just' wha' is it you wishing to score?'

'Weed or blow do me jus fine, innit.'

'How old're you, anyway? Twelve? Thirteen?'

'Hey, I'm legal 'n' I can pay.'

'Bet you can, woe-man. Wiv what, den? You got twenty quid in dat bag 'f yours?'

She didn't, of course. She had less than five pounds. But the fact that he'd pegged her as twelve or thirteen and the fact that he was so ready to dismiss her spurred her on and made her want more than ever what he had to provide. She shifted her weight so one hip jutted out. She cocked her head to one side and regarded him. She said, 'Mon, I c'n pay wiv wha'ever you want. More'n 'at I c'n pay wiv what you need.'

He sucked on his teeth in a way that made her go cold inside, but Ness dismissed this and what it suggested. Instead she told herself she had exactly what she wanted when he said, 'Now dat's one very in'ersting turn of events.'

6

A few weeks ahead of his eighth birthday, Toby showed Joel the lava lamp. It sat in the window of a shop near the top of Portobello Road, far north of the area for which the thoroughfare is famous: that sprawl of markets which burst like the weeds of commerce they are, in the vicinity of Notting Hill Gate.

The shop in which the lava lamp gave its oozing performance did its business between a halal butcher and an eatery called Cockney's Traditional Pie Mash and Eels. Toby had caught a glimpse of it when, in a crocodile of the smaller pupils from Middle Row School, he'd tripped along Portobello Road for an enlightening fieldtrip to the local post office, where the children were to practise buying stamps in a respectful manner that their teacher intended would be remembered for the rest of the purchases they would make in their lives. It was an exercise involving common maths and social interaction. Toby did not excel in either.

But he did take note of the lava lamp. In fact, the mesmerising rise and fall of the material within it that constituted the 'lava' drew him out of the crocodile and to the window where he immediately took a journey to Sose. He was roused from this by his crocodile partner's shouting out and attracting the attention of the teacher at the head of the line. The volunteer parent accompanying the group at the back of the line saw to the problem. She wrested Toby from the window and put him back into place. But the memory of the lava lamp lingered in Toby's mind. He began talking about it that very night over their fried scampi, chips, and peas. Dousing everything with brown sauce, he called the lamp *wicked*, and he continued to bring it up until Joel consented to be introduced to its visual pleasures.

The liquid in it was purple. The 'lava' was orange. Toby pressed his face to the window, sighed, and promptly fogged up the glass. He said, 'Innit *wicked*, Joel?' and he flattened his palm on the window as if he'd push right through it and become as one with the object of his fascination. 'C'n I have it, you think?'

Joel searched for the price, which he found displayed on a small card at the black plastic base of the lamp. £15.99 was scrawled in red. This was eight pounds more than he currently possessed. He said, 'No way, Tobe. Where's the money goin' to come from?'

Toby looked from the lava lamp to his brother. He'd been talked out of the inflated life-ring on this day, wearing it deflated beneath his clothing, but his fingers plucked at it anyway, spasmodically fingering the air at his waist. His face was crestfallen. He said, 'Wha' 'bout my birthday?'

'I c'n talk to Aunt Ken. Maybe Ness 's well.'

Toby's shoulders dropped. He wasn't so oblivious of the state of things in No 84 Edenham Way as to think Joel was promising anything but disappointment.

Joel hated to see Toby with lowered spirits. He told his brother not to worry. If the lava lamp was what he wanted for his special day, then somehow the lava lamp would be his.

Joel knew that he couldn't get the funds from his sister. Ness wasn't to be talked to for love and certainly not for money these days. In the time since they'd left Henchman Street, she'd become increasingly unapproachable. Who she'd once been was like a daguerreotype now: tilted this way or that he could almost see the girl from East Acton, Angel Gabriel in the Christmas pageant with white wings like clouds and a golden halo over her head, ballet shoes and a pink tutu, leaning from the window in Weedon House and spitting to the ground far below. She made no pretence of attending school any longer. No one knew how she spent her days.

That something profound had occurred to Ness somewhere along the line Joel understood. He simply didn't know what it was so, in his innocence and ignorance, he concluded it was something to do with the night she'd left them on their own while Kendra went out clubbing. He knew Ness hadn't returned that night, and he knew there had been a violent argument between his aunt and his sister. But what went before that argument he did not know.

He did know that his aunt had finally washed her hands of Ness and Ness seemed to like things this way. She came and went at all hours and in all conditions and, while Kendra watched her with narrowed eyes and an expression of disgust, she seemed to be playing a waiting game with Ness although what she was waiting for was not clear. In the meantime, Ness pushed the envelope of objectionable behaviour as if daring Kendra to take a stand. The tension was palpable when the two of them were in the house together. Something sometime was going to give way, and a landslide was going to follow.

What Kendra was actually waiting for was the inevitable: those ineluctable consequences of the way her niece was choosing to live. She knew this was going to involve a youth offending team, magistrates, possibly the police, and likely an alternative living situation for the girl, and the truth of the matter was that she had reached the point of welcoming all this. She recognised the fact that Ness's life had been a difficult one from the moment of her father's untimely death. But thousands of children had difficult lives, she reckoned, without throwing what remained of those lives into the toilet. So when Ness stumbled home every once in a while and did so drunk or loaded, she told her to have a bath, to sleep on the sofa, and to otherwise keep out of her sight. And when she reeked

of sex, Kendra told her she was on her own to sort things out
should she become pregnant or diseased.

'Like I care,' was Ness's response to everything. It prompted
Kendra to care in equal measure.

'You want to be an adult, be an adult,' she told Ness. But
most of the time, she said nothing.

So Joel was reluctant to ask Kendra for help in acquiring
a lava lamp for Toby. Indeed, he was reluctant to remind his
aunt of Toby's birthday at all. He thought fleetingly of how it
all had been in a past that was receding from his memory:
birthday dinners consumed from a special birthday plate, a
lopsided Happy Birthday sign strung up at the kitchen window,
a second-hand and unworking tin carousel in the centre of the
table, and his dad producing a birthday cake as if from
nowhere, always the appropriate number of candles lit, singing
a birthday song he'd created himself. No mere 'Happy Birthday
to You' for *his* children, he would say.

When Joel thought about this, he felt driven to do something about the life that had been thrust upon his siblings and
himself. But at his age, he could see nothing in front of him
to mitigate the uncertainty with which they were living, so
what was left to him was trying to make the life they had now
as much like the life they had before as possible.

Toby's birthday gave Joel an opportunity to do that. This
was why he finally made the decision to ask his aunt for help.
He chose a day when Toby had an extra session at the learning
centre after school. Rather than hang about waiting, he scurried over to the charity shop where he found Kendra ironing
blouses in the back room but visible to the door should anyone
enter.

He said, ''Lo, Aunt Ken,' and decided not to be put off
when she merely nodded sharply in reply.

She said, 'Where've you left Toby, then?'

He explained about the extra lesson. He'd told her before,
but she'd forgotten. He assumed she'd forgotten Toby's

birthday as well, since she'd made no mention of the coming day. He said in a rush lest he lose his courage, 'Toby's due to be eight, Aunt Ken. I wan' get him a lava lamp over Portobello Road he likes. Bu' I need more money, so c'n I work for you?'

Kendra took this all in. The tone of Joel's voice – so hopeful despite the expression on his face which he tried to keep blank – made her think about the lengths he went to in order to keep himself and Toby out of her way. She wasn't a fool. She knew how little welcome she'd been projecting towards the children.

She said, 'Tell me how much you need, then.' And when he told her, she stood there thinking for a moment, a line deepening between her eyebrows. Finally, she went to the till. From the counter beneath it she brought out a stack of papers in a rainbow of colours, and she gestured him to join her and to look them over at her side.

Private Massage made a straight line at the top of each of them. Beneath these words a silhouetted scene had been rendered, a figure lying face down on a table and another figure hovering over him, hands apparently kneading his back. Beneath this, a list of massages and their prices ran to the bottom of the page where Kendra's home phone number and mobile number were printed.

'I want these handed out,' she told Joel. 'You'd have to talk shop owners into putting them in their windows. I want them to go to gyms as well. Pubs, too. Inside phone boxes. Everywhere you can think of. You do that for me, I'll pay you enough to buy Toby that lamp.'

Joel's heart lightened. He could do that. He mistakenly thought it would be easier than anything. He mistakenly thought it would lead to nothing but the money he needed to make his little brother happy on his birthday.

Toby tagged along on the days when Joel delivered Kendra's advertisements. He couldn't be left at home, he couldn't be left at the learning centre to wait for Joel, and he certainly couldn't be taken to the charity shop where he'd get under Kendra's feet. There was no question that Ness might look after him, so he wandered along in Joel's wake and obediently waited outside the shops in whose windows the advertisements were put up.

Toby followed Joel inside the area's gyms, though, because there was no trouble he could get into in the vestibules where the reception counters and the notice boards were. He did the same in the police station and the libraries, as well as the entry porches of the churches. He understood that this activity was all about the lava lamp, and since that lava lamp dominated his thoughts, he was happy enough to cooperate.

Kendra had given Joel several hundred massage leaflets, and the truth of the matter is that Joel could have easily dumped the lot of them into the canal and his aunt would have been none the wiser. But Joel wasn't moulded to be dishonest, so day after day he trudged from Ladbroke Grove to Kilburn Lane, down the length of Portobello Road and Golborne Road, and to all points in between in an effort to shrink the size of the pile of handouts he'd been assigned. Once he'd exhausted all the shops, eateries, and pubs, he had to get more creative.

This involved – among other things – trying to decide who might want a massage from his aunt. Aside from individuals sore from over-working their muscles in the gyms, he came up with drivers forced to sit in buses all day or all night. This took him to the Westbourne Park garage, an enormous brick structure tucked under the A40 where city buses were housed and serviced and from which they departed on their rounds. While Toby squatted outside on the steps, Joel talked to a dispatcher who took the path of least resistance and told him distractedly that, yes, he could leave a pile of handouts right there on the countertop. Joel did so, turned to leave, and saw Hibah coming in.

She was carrying a lunch box, and she was garbed traditionally in headscarf and a long coat that dangled down to her ankles. She had her head lowered in a way entirely unusual for her, and when she raised it and caught sight of Joel, she grinned in spite of the performance of self-effacement she'd been giving.

She said, 'Wha' *you* doin here?'

Joel showed her the handouts and then asked the same question of her. She gestured to the lunch box.

'Bringin' this for m' dad. He drive the number twenty-three route.'

Joel smiled. 'Hey, we been on that.'

'Yeah?'

'To Paddington station.'

'Cool.'

She handed the lunch box to the dispatcher. He nodded, took it, and went back to his work. This was a regular errand Hibah ran, and she explained as much to Joel as they went outside to where Toby was waiting.

''S a way my dad keeps his finger on me,' she confided. 'He t'inks he get me to make and bring'm his lunch, I got to dress right an' I can't mess round wiv anyone I not s'posed to mess round wiv.' She winked. 'I got a niece, see, more like my age than lit'ler cos my bruvver – tha's her dad – 's sixteen years older 'n me. Anyways, she seeing an English boy, an' the world comin' to an *end* cos of that, innit. My dad swear I ain't ever seeing no English boys an' he's goin' to make sure tha' never happen even 'f he have to send me to Pakistan.' She shook her head. 'Tell you, Joel, I cannot *wait* t' be old 'nough t' be out on my own cos tha's what I am planning to do. Who's this?'

She was referring to Toby who, on this day, had not been talked out of his life-ring. He'd been sitting on the step where Joel had left him, and he'd popped up and come to join them as soon as they left the Westbourne Park garage. Joel told her who Toby was, without adding anything to the information.

She said, 'I di'n't know you had a bruvver.'

He said, 'He in Middle Row School.'

'He helpin you wiv the handouts?'

'Nah. I jus' takin him wiv me cos he can't stay on his own.'

'How many you got left?' she asked.

For a moment, Joel didn't know what Hibah meant. But then she flipped her thumb at the advertisements and she told him he could easily get rid of the rest of them by shoving them under the doors of all the flats in Trellick Tower. It would, she said, be easier than anything. She would help him do it.

'Come on,' she told him. ''S where I live. I get you in.'

A walk to the tower comprised no great distance. They trotted across Great Western Road and ducked into Meanwhile Gardens, with Toby dawdling along behind them. Hibah chatted away in her usual fashion as they took one of the serpentine paths. It was a fine spring Saturday – crisp but sunny – so the gardens were peopled with families and youths. Smaller children ran about the playground behind the chain link fence of the drop-in centre, and older boys zipped about a graffiti-decorated skate bowl that abutted it. They used skateboards, inline skates, and bicycles for their activity, and they attracted Toby's attention at once. His mouth opened into an O, his steps faltered, and he paused to watch, unmindful as always of the odd sight he presented: a little boy wearing too large jeans, a life-ring round his waist, and trainers that were closed with duct-tape.

The skate bowl comprised three levels ascending one of the hillocks, the easiest level being on the top and the most difficult and steepest on the bottom. These levels were accessed by means of concrete steps, and a wide lip around the entire bowl offered a waiting area for those who wished to use it. Toby climbed to this. He called out to Joel.

'Lookit!' he cried. 'I c'n do it, too, innit.'

Toby's presence among the riders and the spectators was greeted with 'Wha' the *hell*' and 'G't out 'f the *way*, stupid git!'

Joel, flushing, hurried up the steps to grab his brother by

the hand. He got him out without making eye contact with anyone, but he wasn't able to carry off the rescue nonchalantly when it came to Hibah.

She waited at the foot of the steps. When he dragged Toby, protesting, back to the path, she said, 'He simple or summick? Why's he got that tape round his shoes?' She made no mention of the life-ring.

'He's jus' differ'nt,' Joel told her.

'Well, I c'n see *that*, innit,' was her reply. She gave Toby a curious look and then looked at Joel. 'He get bullied, I reckon.'

'Sometimes.'

'Makes you feel bad, I 'spect.'

Joel looked away from her, blinked hard, and shrugged.

She nodded thoughtfully. 'Come on, then,' she said. 'You too, Toby. You been up the tower? I show you the view. You c'n see all the way to the river, mon. You c'n see the Eye. It's wicked, innit.'

Inside Trellick Tower, a security guard kept a position within a windowed office. He nodded at Hibah as she made for the lift. She punched for the thirtieth floor and the views it offered, which were – despite the grimy condition of the windows – as 'wicked' as she had promised. It was a spectacular eyrie, reducing cars and lorries to matchbox vehicles, vast tracts of houses and estates to mere toys.

'Lookit! Lookit!' Toby kept calling as he dashed from one window to the next.

Hibah watched him and smiled. She laughed as well, but there was no meanness in it. She was unlike others, Joel concluded. He thought perhaps she could be a friend.

She and Joel divided the remaining stack of Kendra's massage advertisements. Odd floors, even floors, they had soon dispensed with them all. They met at the lifts on the ground when they had finished their job. They walked outside and Joel wondered how he could thank or pay Hibah for her help.

While Toby moved off to gaze into the window of a

newsagent's – one of the shops that constituted the ground floor of the tower itself – Joel shuffled his feet. He felt hot and sticky, in spite of the breeze coming up Golborne Road. He was trying to develop a way to tell Hibah he had no money to purchase a Coke, a bar of chocolate, a Cornetto, or anything else she might fancy as a sign of his gratitude when he heard her name called and turned to see a boy approaching them on a bicycle.

He came upon them quickly, pedalling from the direction of the Grand Union Canal to the north. He wore the signature gear of baggy jeans, tattered trainers, a hoodie, and a baseball cap. He was clearly a mixed-race boy like Joel, yellow-skinned but otherwise featured like a black. The right side of his face was dragged down as if by an unseen force and glued into position permanently, giving him a sinister expression despite his adolescent spots.

He braked, hopped off, and threw his bike to the ground. He came at them swiftly, and Joel felt his intestines squeeze pain into his groin. The rule of the street meant that he had to stand his ground when accosted or be marked for ever as having the bottle for nothing but peeing his pants.

Hibah said, 'Neal! Wha' you doin' here? I thought you said you was going to—'

'Who dis? I been lookin for you. You say you headin f'r the bus garage an' you ain't dere. Wha's *dat* mean, den?'

He sounded threatening, but Hibah wasn't the sort of girl who responded well to threats. She said, 'You checkin' *up* on me? I don' like tha' much.'

'Why? You 'fraid to be checked up on?'

With some surprise, it came to Joel that this was the boyfriend Hibah had mentioned. He was the one she talked to through the school gates during their lunch period, the one who didn't attend school as he was meant to do but rather spent his days doing . . . Joel didn't know, and he didn't want to know. He merely wanted to make it clear to the boy that he had no interest in his property, which was what he obviously felt Hibah was.

He said to Hibah, 'Thanks for helping wiv the handouts,' and he started to move towards Toby, who was bouncing rhythmically against the glass of the newsagent's by means of his life-ring.

She said, 'Hey. Hang on.' And then to Neal, 'This is Joel, innit. He goes to school wiv me over Holland Park.' The tone of her voice made it clear enough: she wasn't happy about making the introduction because she wasn't happy about Neal's attempt to claim ownership of her. She said to Joel, 'This here is Neal.'

Neal looked Joel over, disgust making his lips go thin and his nostrils flare. He said, not to Joel but to Hibah, 'Why you wiv him in the tower, den? Saw you come out, di'n't I.'

'Oh, cos we making babies, Neal,' Hibah said. 'Wha' else we be doing in the tower in the middle of th' bloody day?'

Joel thought she was mad to speak in this way. Neal took a step towards her and for a moment Joel thought he'd be put in the position of having to brawl with Neal in order to keep Hibah safe from his wrath. That was far down on the list of things he wished to do with his afternoon, and he was relieved when Hibah diffused the situation by saying with a laugh, 'He just *twelve* years *old*, Neal. I showed him and his bruvver the view is all. Tha's his bruvver over there.'

Neal searched out Toby. '*Dat?*' he said and then to Joel, 'Wha's he, a freak or summick?'

Joel said nothing. Hibah said, 'Shut *up*. Tha's dead stupid, Neal. He's a lit'le kid, innit.'

Neal's yellow face went red as he turned back to her. Something within him was going to need to be released, and Joel braced himself to be on the receiving end of it.

Toby's call supervened. 'Joel, I got to poo. C'n we go home?'

Neal muttered, 'Shit.'

Hibah said, 'You got tha' right, at least.' And then she

laughed at her own joke, which made Joel smile although he tried to suppress it.

Neal, who couldn't track the humour, said to Joel, 'Wha' you laughing at, yellow-arse?'

Joel said, 'Nuffink.' And then to Toby, 'Come on, Tobe. We ain't far. Le's go.'

Neal said, 'Di'n't say you could go anywheres, did I?' as Toby came to join them.

Joel said, 'Won't answer f'r the smell 'f you mean us to stay.'

Hibah laughed again. She shook Neal by the arm. 'Come *on*,' she said. 'We got time 'fore my mum wonders where I am. Le's stop using it up like this.'

Neal came around at that reminder. He allowed himself to be led in the direction of the scent garden and its shrouded path. But he looked over his shoulder as he walked away. He was marking Joel. It would be for a future encounter of some sort. Joel knew it.

Kendra's intensity of purpose paid off sooner than she expected. The day after Joel set out with her massage advertisements, she received her first phone call. A man requested a sports massage as soon as possible. He lived in a flat above a pub called the Falcon, where Kilburn Lane became Carlton Vale. She made home visits, didn't she, because that's what he needed.

He sounded polite. He was soft-spoken. The fact that he lived above a pub seemed to make it safe. Kendra logged an appointment for him and loaded her table into the Punto. She threw Cumberland pie into the oven for Joel and Toby and produced some Maltesers and fig rolls for their pudding. She gave Joel an extra pound for having placed the advertisements so wisely, and she went on her way to find the Falcon, which turned out to be sitting on what was nearly a roundabout, with a modern church opposite and traffic shooting by from the three roads that met in front of it.

It was no easy feat to find somewhere to park and, as a result, Kendra had to lug the massage table some hundred yards from a lane that veered away from the main roads and provided space for two schools. She also had to cross over Kilburn Lane, so by the time she struggled inside the pub to enquire how to get to the flats above, she was out of breath and sweating.

She ignored the stares of the regular patrons gathered at the bar and hoisting pints at the tables. She followed the direction, which had her return to the pavement, go around the building, and find a door with four buzzers lined up on one side. She rang, banged her way up the stairs, and paused at the top to regain her breath.

One of the doors opened abruptly, silhouetting a well-built man in the light from within. He was obviously the one who'd phoned for the massage, for he hurried forward in the gloom of the corridor, saying, 'Lemme help you wiv dat.' He took the massage table from her and carried it easily into the flat. This turned out to be little more than a large bed-sit, possessing several beds, a basin, an electric fire, and a single ring for cooking whatever could be cooked on a single ring.

Kendra was taking all this in as the man set up the table. For this reason, she didn't take much note of him nor he of her until he had the table unfolded with its legs extended, and she had unpacked most of the accoutrements of massage.

He set the table upright and turned to face her. She shook out the table's cover and glanced his way. They both said, 'Damn,' at the same moment. It was the man who, on Kendra's disastrous girls' night out, had brought Ness home drunk and eager to do whatever he wished her to do to him.

Kendra was at a momentary loss. She was holding the table's covering, her arms extended, and she dropped them at once.

He said, 'Well, *dis* is a bloody awkward moment, innit.'

Kendra reached a quick decision about the matter. Business

was business, and this was business. She said, 'You said a sports massage?' in her most Lady Muck of voices.

He said, 'Yeah. Dat's what I said. Dix.'

'What?'

'My name. It's Dix.' He waited until Kendra had the table covered, the soft terry cushioning for his head in place. Then he said, 'She ever tell you what really happened dat night? It was like I said, y'know.'

Kendra smoothed her hand over the cover. She opened her bag and brought out her oils. She said, 'We didn't talk about it, Mr Dix. Now what scent oil would you like? I recommend lavender. It's most relaxing.'

A smile played around his lips. 'Not Mr Dix,' he said. 'Dix D'Court. You're called Kendra what?'

'Osborne,' she said. 'Mrs.'

His glance went from her face to her hands. 'You got no ring, Mrs Osborne. You divorced? Widowed?'

She could have told him it was none of his business. Instead she said, 'Yes,' and left it at that. 'You said you wanted a sports massage?'

'What I do first?' he asked.

'Strip down.' She handed him a sheet and turned her back. 'Keep your shorts on,' she told him. 'This's a real massage, by the way. I hope that's what you wanted when you phoned me, Mr D'Court. This is a legitimate business I'm running.'

'Wha' else would I want, Mrs Osborne?' he asked, and she could hear the laughter in his voice. In a moment, he said, 'I'm ready, den.' She turned to see him supine on the table, the sheet pulled up discreetly and tucked around his waist.

She thought a single word: *shit*. He had an exquisite body. Weight-lifting had defined his muscles. Over them stretched skin as smooth as a baby's. He had no hair that Kendra could see, save for eyebrows and lashes. Not a mark was on him. The sight of him reminded her at the worst possible time of the ages it had been since she'd had a man. This, she told herself, was not what she was supposed to be feeling in her line of work. A body was a body. Her hands upon it were the tools of her trade.

He was watching her. He repeated his question. 'She tell you?'

Kendra had forgotten the reference. She drew her eyebrows together, saying, 'What?'

'Your daughter. She tell you wha' happened b'tween us dat night?'

'I don't got . . . I don't have a daughter.'

'Den who . . . ?' For a moment it seemed he thought he was mistaken about who Kendra was. He said, 'Over Edenham Estate.'

'She's my niece,' Kendra said. 'She lives with me. You'll need to turn over. I'll begin with your back and shoulders.'

He waited for a moment, watching her. He said, 'You don' look old 'nough to have a daughter *or* a niece like dat.'

'I'm old,' Kendra said, 'just well-preserved.'

He chuckled and then cooperatively turned over. He did what most people do at first when being given a massage: he cradled his head with his arms. She changed his position, bringing his arms down to his sides and turning his head so he was lying face down. She poured the oil into her palms and warmed it, realising at that moment that she'd left her soothing music in the car. The result of this was that the massage would have to be given to the accompanying noise from the pub below, which came up through the floor steadily, impossible to ignore. She looked around for a radio, a stereo, a CD player, anything to make a difference to the ambience. There was virtually nothing in the bed-sit, save for the beds, which were difficult to ignore. She wondered why the man had three of them.

She began the massage. He had extraordinary skin: dark as black coffee with the feel of a newborn infant's palm, while just beneath it the muscles were perfectly defined. He had a body that indicated hard manual labour, but what encased it suggested he hadn't held a tool in his life. She wanted to ask him what he did for a living, that he should be fashioned so magnificently. But this, she felt, would betray an interest that she wasn't supposed to feel towards a client, so she said nothing.

She remembered her massage instructor explaining something that, at the time, had seemed rather mad. 'You must get into the Zen of the massage. The warmth of your intentions for the client's comfort should transmit itself to your hands until the you of you disappears, so there is nothing left but tissue, muscles, pressure, and movement.'

She'd thought What bollocks, but she attempted to go there. She closed her eyes and aimed herself towards the Zen of it all. 'Feels bloody good,' Dix D'Court murmured.

In silence, she did his neck, his shoulders, his back, his arms, his hands, his thighs, his legs, his feet. She knew every inch of him, and not a centimetre of his body was different in condition from any other. Even his feet were smooth, not a callus anywhere. When she finished this part of the massage, she concluded he'd spent his life floating in a vat of baby oil.

She asked him to turn over. She made him more comfortable with a towel she rolled up and placed beneath his neck. She picked up the bottle of oil to continue but he stopped her by reaching out and grasping her wrist, at the same time saying, 'Where'd you learn dis, anyway?'

She said automatically, 'Go to school, mon. Wha' else you t'ink?' And then, the correction because she'd spoken almost out of a dream state, matching his dialect simply because – she told herself – she'd achieved the Zen that her instructor had spoken of, 'I've taken a course at the college.'

'Give you high marks.' He grinned, showing teeth that were straight and white and as perfect as the rest of him. He closed his eyes and settled in for the second half of the massage.

Because she'd inadvertently slipped from Lady Muck,

Kendra felt found out. Her discomfort propelled her through the rest of the massage. She wanted to finish and be gone from this place. When she'd completed her work on his body, she stepped away and wiped her hands on a towel. The procedure was to give the client a few minutes at the end of the massage to lie on the table and to savour the experience. But in this instance, Kendra just wanted to be out of the bed-sit. She turned from the table and began to pack up.

She heard him move behind her, and when she turned it was to find him sitting up on the table, his legs dangling over the side, watching her, his body still lightly glistening from the oil she'd used upon him.

He said, 'She tell you the truth, Mrs Osborne? You never said and I can't le' you out 'f here till I know. The sort you t'ink I am? Not the truth, innit. She 'as down below—' by this he meant the pub – 'an' I go in cos I get a glass 'f tomato juice from the bar. She dead drunk, and she letting two blokes dance wiv her in a corner and feel her up. She got her blouse open. She hiking her skirt like she means—'

'All *right*,' Kendra said. All she could think was *fifteen years old, fifteen years old.*

He said, 'No. You got to hear cos you t'ink—'

'If I say I believe you . . .'

He shook his head. 'Too late for dat, Mrs Osborne. Too late. I get her out 'f the pub but she t'inks dat means wha' it don't. She offer it all, wha'ever I want her to do to me. I say fine, she can blow me—'

Kendra flashed her eyes at him. He held up a hand.

'—but we got to get to *her* place to do it, I tell her. The only way, see, I c'n get her to say where she lives. I drive her there. Dat's when you show up.'

Kendra shook her head. 'You was . . . No. You were—' She didn't know how to express it. She gestured to her breasts. She said, 'I saw you. Raising up.'

He turned his head, but she could see he was doing it to

think back to that night. He finally said, 'Her bag was on the floor. I *fetching* it. Woman, I do *not* do kids, an' one t'ing I c'n see is she's a kid.' He added, 'Not like you, not like you at all. Mrs Osborne. Kendra. C'n you walk over here?' He gestured to the table, to himself.

She said, 'Why?'

'Cos you a beauty, an' I want to kiss you.' He smiled. 'See? I don't lie 'bout nuffink. Not 'bout your niece. Not 'bout me. Not 'bout you.'

'I told you. This's my business. 'F you think I—'

'I *know*. I phone you up cos I see the handout in the gym, dat's all. I don't know who shows up an' I don't care. I got a competition to get ready for, an' I need my muscles seen to. Dat's it.'

'What sort of competition?'

'Body-building.' He paused, waiting for her to comment. When she didn't, he said, 'Working towards Mr Universe. I been lifting since I was thirteen years old.'

'How long's that, then?'

'Ten years,' he told her.

'You're *twenty-three*.'

'Problem wiv dat?'

'I'm *forty*, man.'

'Problem wiv dat?'

'Can't you do maths?'

'Maths don't make me wan' to kiss you less.'

Kendra stood her ground, without really knowing why she was doing so. She wanted his kiss, no mistake about that. She wanted more as well. The seventeen years between them meant there would be no strings, which was how she liked things. But there was something about him that made her hesitate: He seemed twenty-three in years only. In mind-set and behaviour, he seemed much older, and that spelled danger of a kind she'd avoided for a very long time.

He slid off the table, then. The sheet he'd been wearing

slipped to the floor. He came to her and put his hand on her arm. It slid to her wrist and he said, 'Truth is truth, Mrs Osborne. I phoned up f'r a massage. Money's over on th' table. Wiv a tip 's well. I di'n't 'spect anyt'ing else. Bu' I still want it. Question is, do you? Anyways, jus' a kiss.'

Kendra wanted to say no because she knew saying yes meant going to a place she ought to avoid. But she didn't reply. Nor did she walk away.

He said, 'I don' jus' take. You're meant to answer, Mrs Osborne.'

Someone else inside her did the talking. 'Yes,' she said.

He kissed her. He urged her mouth open, one hand on the back of her neck. She put her hand on his waist and then slid it over his buttocks, which were tight like the rest of him. And like the rest of him, they filled her with wanting.

She broke away. 'I don't do this,' she said.

He knew what she meant. 'I c'n tell dat,' he murmured. He drew back and looked at her. 'I don't 'spect nuffink. You c'n leave if you want.' With his fingers, he traced the curve of her cheek. With his other hand, he grazed across her breasts.

The caress finished off what resistance she had. She stepped back to him and lifted her mouth to his as her hands reached for his waist again, this time to remove the only article of clothing that he had on.

He said, 'My.' And then, 'Dat's my bed. Come 'ere.' He led her to the bed nearest the window and lowered her to it. 'You a goddess,' he said.

He unbuttoned her blouse. He freed her breasts. He gazed on them then upon her face before he lowered her to the mattress and lowered his mouth to her nipples.

She gasped because it had been so long, and she needed to have a man's worship of her body, feigned or not. She wanted him and in this moment, the fact of the wanting was the only thing that—

'Fuck it, Dix. Wha' the hell you *doing*? We had a bloody 'greement!'

They separated in a rush, scrambling for sheets, for clothing, for anything at all to cover themselves. It came to Kendra that there was a distinct reason for the room's three beds. Dix D'Court shared his accommodation, and one of his flatmates had just walked into the room.

7

On the night Ness saw the Blade come out of the Harrow Road police station, she made a decision. To her it was a simple one, meant to be, but it put her on a path that would for ever alter the lives of people she would never meet.

The Blade was not a pleasant man to look upon. He radiated danger in a manner so pellucid that he might have been wearing flashing lights around his neck instead of what he *was* wearing, which was a gold Italian charm meant to ward off the evil eye. He also radiated power. The power drew people to him; the danger kept them where he preferred them to be, which was subservient, tentative, and eager. He'd learned to cultivate behaviour most apt to intimidate, both because of his size and because of his physical attributes: at only five feet five inches tall, he could have been marked as someone easy to take down; completely hairless and with a face so sharply pulled back from his nose that the front of his skull looked more like a beak than anything else, he'd also learned early that there were only two ways to survive the environment into which he'd been born. He'd chosen the route of mastery rather than the route of escape. It was easier and he liked things easy.

Close to him, Ness had felt both the power and the danger, but she was in no state to be affected by either. Her encounter with her aunt followed by her visit to Six on the Mozart Estate had put her in a place where the last thing she cared about was self-preservation. So when she took in the details of the Blade – from the cowboy boots that gave him additional height to the cobra tattoo that made a statement by curling down from his head and on to his cheek – she saw just what she was looking for, which was someone capable of altering her state of mind.

What the Blade saw was what she offered superficially, and he was ready for that. He'd spent four hours in the police station – which was two hours more than he had agreed to – and while there had never been any question about whether he'd be back on the street as soon as he'd done the song and dance required of him, he hadn't produced for the police in a manner they liked, so he'd been at their mercy. He hated that, and hate set him on edge. He wanted to remove the sharpness of that edge. There were several ways to do this, and Ness was standing there blatantly promising one of them.

When his ride arrived, he didn't therefore climb into the passenger seat and tell the driver – one Calvin Hancock whose copious dreadlocks were carefully capped in deference to the manner that a hairless man might be suspected of preferring to see them – to take him to Portnall Road, where a seventeen-year-old girl called Arissa was waiting to service him. Instead, he jerked his head at the back seat for Ness to get into the car and he climbed in after her, leaving Calvin Hancock in the position of chauffeur.

He said to Calvin, 'Up Willesden Lane.'

Cal – as he was called – looked into the rear view mirror. This was a change of plan, and he didn't like plan changes. Having taken on the responsibility of protecting the Blade, having successfully done so for five years, and having received the questionable rewards of this success – which were the Blade's companionship and a place to sleep at night – Cal knew the risk of impulsive decisions and he knew what his own life would be like if something happened to the other man.

He said, 'Mon, I t'ought you wanted Rissa. Portnall's clean. She been keeping it dat way. We go up to Willesden, no way in hell we c'n tell who be dere you walk in.'

The Blade said, 'Fuck. You questioning me?'

Cal put the car into gear as answer.

Ness listened and admired. When the Blade said to Cal, 'Give us a ziggy,' she felt a frisson of wonder and excitement when the other man obediently pulled the car to the kerb, flicked open the glove box, and rolled the spliff. He lit it, took a hit, and handed it back to the Blade. His glance met Ness's in the rear view mirror as he moved the car back into the night-time traffic.

Next to her, the Blade leaned back. He ignored her, which made him seem even more appealing. He smoked his cannabis and offered Ness none of it. She ached and put her hand on his thigh. She slid it to his crotch. He knocked her away. He did it without a glance at her. She wanted to be his slave.

She said in a murmur that came to her from the countless films she'd seen and the bizarre image of successful human contact they provided, 'Baby, I *do* you. I do you in ways make your head feel like it goin' to 'splode. Dat what you want? Dat how you like it?'

The Blade tossed an indifferent glance her way. He said, 'I do *you*, slag. When and where. It don't happen opposite and you best remember that from the start.'

What Ness heard was only *from the start*. She felt the warm wet thrill of what the words implied.

Calvin drove them north, away from the Harrow Road and beyond Kilburn Lane. Fixed upon the Blade as she was, Ness made no note of where they were going. When they finally came upon an estate of low brick terraces sprawling through a system of narrow streets, with most of the lamps and all of the security lights long ago shot out, they might have been anywhere from Hackney to hell. Ness couldn't have said.

Cal parked and opened the passenger door on Ness's side. She slid out. The Blade followed. He handed the roach to Cal, said, 'Check it out, den,' and leaned against the side of the car as Cal disappeared along a path and between two buildings.

Ness shivered, not with the cold but with a kind of anticipation she'd never felt before. She tried to appear indifferent,
a *type*, as it were. But she couldn't take her eyes off the Blade.
Everything she wanted. That was how she thought of him. It
seemed to her that a miracle had come about on an evening
that had earlier appeared disastrous.

Cal returned in a few minutes. He said, 'Clean.'

The Blade said, 'You carrying?'

Cal said, 'Shit, mon. What else you t'ink?' He patted the
pocket of the tattered leather jacket he wore. 'Who love you
more'n your gran, baby? You safe long 's Cal Hancock
watching.'

The Blade gave no response to this. He jerked his head
towards the path through the buildings. Cal led the way.

Ness made up a third, like an afterthought. She kept close
to the Blade, intent upon looking as if – wherever they were
going – they would arrive together.

The estate they were on was a place of noise, acrid with
smells that combined rotting rubbish, cooking odours, and
burning rubber. They passed two drunken girls vomiting into
a dead shrub and a gang of young boys accosting an old-age
pensioner who'd foolishly decided to take his rubbish to the
bins after dark. They came upon a vicious, ear-splitting cat
fight and a lone, broom-thin woman plunging a hypodermic
needle into her arm in the shelter of a discarded mattress that
balanced against a leafless tree.

Their destination was a house in the middle of a terrace.
To Ness, it looked either unoccupied or asleep for the night.
But when Cal knocked on the door, a spy-hole opened.
Someone checked them out, found them acceptable, and
opened up. The Blade stepped past Cal and entered. Ness
followed. Cal remained outside.

Inside, there was no actual furniture. Instead, there were
old mattresses piled three high in several locations, and large
upended cardboard boxes scattered nearby to serve as tables.

What light there was came from two lopsided floor lamps that cast their glow on the walls and the ceiling so that the floor with its tattered maroon carpet squares was mostly in shadow. Aside from graffiti depicting a wild-haired man and a nude woman riding a hypodermic needle into the stratosphere, there was nothing on the walls and, taken as a whole, the house didn't appear to be a place where anyone actually lived.

It *was* occupied, however. One might have thought that a party was even going on, because there was scratchy music coming low from a radio that needed to have its station adjusted. But what one normally expects to see at a party – people engaged in conversation or some other activity with one another – was not a feature of this place. Instead, the activity was confined to smoking and where there *was* conversation, it was limited to comments about the quality of the crack and what it was providing in the way of mental and physical diversion.

Other smoking was going on as well, cannabis and tobacco, and substances were being bought and sold, with transactions completed by a middle-aged black woman in a purple negligée, which displayed the unfortunate, pendulous condition of her large breasts. She seemed to be the responsible party, aided by the doorman who, by means of the spy-hole, inspected individuals wishing to enter.

There was no question in anyone's mind about whether this place was a safe-house in which to engage in their chosen pursuit. Across the neighbourhood and spreading out in all directions, these sorts of dens popped up like toadstools in a moist woodland. The police couldn't keep track of them and on the off-chance that a neighbour developed the courage to report such a place and to request an arrest of its proprietor, the police had too many other irons in the fire to deal with the problem.

Purple Negligée supplied the Blade with what he'd come for, a request from him being unnecessary. Since she existed because he existed, she wanted to make him welcome. This house was his first incursion into territory controlled by an Albanian gang, and she owed him not only the roof over her head but also the form of livelihood that this business provided.

She said to him, 'How your gran, darlin?' as he lit up the pipe she'd given him. It was small, disappearing into the hollow of his hand, and a thread of smoke issued from it. 'She still in hospital? Dat's so rough innit. Your mum still keepin' you 'way from the rest of the kids 's well? Bloody slag. Wha' else I get you, darlin? Who dis anyway? She with you?'

The *she* was Ness, the Blade's shadow, who stood one step behind him like a royal consort. She was waiting for an indication of what she was meant to do, her expression a best attempt to hide uncertainty through a display of indifference. The Blade reached around and put his hand on the back of her neck. He pinched his thumb and forefinger beneath her ear and through this means brought her forward. He put the pipe in her mouth and watched as she sucked. He smiled and said to Purple Negligée, 'Who else she be with, gash, if she not wiv me?'

'Looks young, man. Dat not like you.'

'You t'inking dat cos you want me f'r yourself.'

She laughed. 'Oooh. You way too much man f'r me, baby.' She patted his cheek. 'Give a shout can Melia get you anyt'ing else.' She took herself down the darkened corridor, where the only couple in the place who were engaged with each other were having an inexpert knee trembler up against the wall.

Ness felt the effect of the drug quickly. Everything that was her life receded into the background, leaving her open to the present moment. The fact that she was in danger from any number of sources didn't occur to her. How could it when her rational mind had departed, leaving in its place what *seemed* not only rational but superior to any mind she'd ever possessed? The only thought she had was that she wanted more of what made her feel like this.

The Blade watched her and smiled. 'You liking dis, innit.'

''S *you*,' she said, for to her he was the source of all experience and sensation. He was what could make her whole. She said, 'Lemme suck you, mon. You won' b'lieve how you goin' to feel.'

'Expert, are you?'

'Only one way to know.'

'Your mum know you talk to blokes like dis?'

That cut through the pleasure. She turned and walked into the sitting area, leaving him behind. She lowered herself to one of the piles of mattresses, putting herself squarely between two young men. Until her arrival they'd been concentrating on their individual highs, but Ness made that difficult by saying to one of them, 'Wha' I got t' do get a hit of dat stuff?' and nodding at the pipe he held as she put her hand on the other's thigh and rode it up to his crotch in the same manner she'd tried on the Blade in the back seat of the car.

Across from her, the Blade saw what she was doing and knew why she was doing it, but he was not a man who let women run his show. The little slag, he thought, could do what she wanted. He went in search of Melia, leaving Ness in the sitting-room. She'd soon enough learn the price of playing men like puppets in a place like this.

The learning did not take long. Ness got the pipe for a hit, but it was a hit with a cost determined by what she appeared to be offering. She quickly found that the attention she was attracting came from more than the two men she'd placed herself between. Several others had taken note of her and, when her hand went to the crotch of her companion on the mattress, he was not the only one to feel the corresponding arousal.

There were other women present, but with more experience: they knew the wisdom of keeping to themselves and just enjoying the high they'd come for. And since none of the men wanted to waste the energy either coaxing or coercing when the same delights could be savoured with no effort whatsoever on their part, they gravitated to Ness.

They could see she was young, but it didn't matter. These were gentlemen who'd had perfectly willing eleven-year-old girls when they themselves had been thirteen and younger. In a world in which there was little to live for and less to hope for, most of the time they didn't even need to practise their clumsy arts of seduction.

Ness was therefore surrounded before she realised what was happening. The *fact* of the surrounding rather than what the surrounding meant began the process of clearing her head. A pipe was thrust at her for a hit but she no longer wanted it. Someone said, 'Ge' her down here, den,' and from behind she was lowered to the mattress. Hot breath was what she thought of, then: the feel of it and the smell of it. Two sets of hands pulling off her tights as another set spread her legs. A fourth set held her arms imprisoned. She cried out, which was taken for delight.

She began to writhe. The escape she wanted was seen instead as hot anticipation. She cried out again as zips were lowered, and she squeezed her eyes shut rather than have to see what she would otherwise see. A body fell upon her and she felt the heat of it and then the bulging throbbing head, which was when she screamed.

It was over quickly. Not how she feared it would be over, but how she dreamed. She heard a curse first and then immediately the body pulled away from her as if lifted by a force of nature. Then *he* was there, raising her from the mattress: not to carry her out of the horrible place in his arms, in the manner of a troubadour-sung hero, but to jerk her to her feet and curse her as an idiot fool slag who, if she needed to be taught a lesson, was fucking well going to be taught it by him and not by this scum.

It felt like being wooed. Ness knew that the Blade would not have come to her rescue had he not cared about her. He was one man among many. The many were bigger, tougher, and far more menacing. He'd risked *himself* to make her safe. So when he shoved her in front of him in the direction of the door, Ness felt the pressure against her scapula as a form of caress, and she went without protest into the night, where Cal Hancock was waiting, to whom the Blade said, 'Melia got t'ings handled. Le's go to Lancefield, mon.'

'Wha' 'bout her?' Cal said with a nod at Ness.

'She coming wiv us,' the Blade told him. 'Can't leave the slag here.'

Thus it was that some thirty minutes later, Ness found herself not in the decently appointed flat she imagined but rather in a squat just off Kilburn Lane, where a block of flats destined for the wrecking ball had been taken over in the meantime by those homeless individuals with the nerve to live in the same vicinity as the Blade. There, on a scratchy blanket that covered a futon on the floor, the Blade did to Ness what the men in the crack house had anticipated doing. Unlike inside the crack house, though, Ness eagerly accepted this attention.

She had an agenda of her own, and she decided as she spread her legs for him that the Blade was the only man on earth she wished to fulfil it.

When Kendra heard Dix tell the story of taking Ness from the Falcon and driving her home, she decided to believe him. Soft-spoken and ostensibly gentle-hearted, he seemed sincere. So, although she'd washed her hands of Ness on the same night that Ness had met the Blade and throughout the weeks that followed, Kendra came to realise that she needed to set her relationship with her niece back on course. How to do this was the question, however, since Ness was rarely at home.

The benefit of her absence was that Kendra was able to pursue her career without any familial disruptions, something that she was happy enough to do since it helped take her mind off what had nearly come to pass between Dix D'Court and herself post-massage in the bed-sit above the Falcon. And Kendra definitely needed to take her mind off that. She wanted to think of herself as a professional.

The downside of Ness's absence, however, was that the same conscience requiring Kendra to be professional in the area of massage also required her to reach out to the girl. This was not so much because Kendra hoped that a decent aunt-and-niece friendship might develop between them but because she'd been wrong in what she'd assumed had happened between Dix and Ness, and she needed to make amends for that. Kendra believed she owed that much to a brother who'd turned his life around: Gavin Campell, drug-addled for years until the birth and the near death of Toby.

'Woke me up, that did,' Gavin had told her. 'Showed me I can't leave these kids to Carole's minding them, and tha's the truth.'

What was also the truth was that none of the Campbell children had ever been struck by an adult. Thus, Kendra's encounter with Ness in front of her house that night – culminating as it had done with a blow to the face – comprised something that had to be smoothed over, explained in some way, or apologised for: whatever would work to get Ness back home where she belonged and where her father would have wanted her.

Kendra's need to do this was heightened by a phone call she received from Social Services not long after the sports massage at the Falcon. A woman called Fabia Bender of the Youth Offending Team was making an attempt to set up an appointment with Vanessa Campbell and whatever adult stood *in loco parentis* in Ness's life. The fact that Social Services were now actively engaged in the situation gave Kendra a wild card to play in her dealings with Ness. If she could find her.

Questioning Joel wasn't helpful. While he saw his sister on occasion, he told Kendra that there was nothing regular in her comings and goings. He didn't add that Ness was a stranger to him now. He merely said that she was sometimes there when he and Toby returned from the learning centre. She'd be having a bath, rooting through clothing, pinching packets of cigarettes from Kendra's carton of Benson and Hedges, eating left-over curry, or dipping crisps into a container of Mexican salsa as she watched a chat show on the television. When he spoke to her, she largely ignored him. It was always evident that she wasn't intending to stay for very long. He couldn't add anything more.

Kendra knew that Ness had mates among the adolescents in the area. She knew two of them were called Six and Natasha. But that was the limit of what she knew, although she assumed a great deal more. Alcohol, drugs, and sex topped the list. She reckoned that theft, prostitution, sexually transmitted diseases, and gang-related activities were not far behind.

For weeks, and despite her every effort, she didn't get an opportunity to have with Ness the conversation that she wanted to have. She looked for the girl but could not find her, and it was only when she had resigned herself to not locating Ness until Ness was ready to be located that she actually saw her, quite by chance, in Queensway, heading into Whiteley's. She was in the company of two girls. One was plump and one was gaunt, but they both were uniformed in the style of the streets. Tight jeans that sculpted everything from their buttocks to their pubic bones, stiletto heels, sheer tops tied at the waist over tiny colourful T-shirts. Ness was dressed in a similar fashion. Kendra recognised one of her own scarves wound through the girl's thick hair.

She followed them into Whiteley's and found them fingering costume jewellery in Accessorize. She said Ness's name, and the girl turned around, her hand going to the scarf in her hair as if she believed Kendra intended to take it from her.

'I need to talk to you,' Kendra said. 'I've been trying to find you for weeks.'

'I ain't hiding from you,' was Ness's reply. The plump girl

sniggered, as if Kendra had somehow been put in her place, if not by Ness's words then by her tone, which was churlish.

Kendra looked at the girl who'd sniggered. 'Who are you, then?' she asked.

The girl didn't reply. She produced instead a surly expression meant to put Kendra off, which it failed to do. The gaunt girl said, 'I'm Tash innit,' and was silenced for this show of marginal affability with a look from the other.

'Well, Tash,' Kendra said, 'I've a need to speak to Vanessa alone. I'd like you and this other person – are you Six, by the way? – to give us that opportunity.'

Natasha had never heard a black woman speak such a form of English aside from on the television, so her response was to gawp at Kendra. Six's response was to shift her weight from one hip to the other, to cross her arms beneath her breasts, and to give Kendra a head-to-toe look that was designed to make her feel like a marked woman destined for a street mugging or worse.

'Well?' Kendra said when neither of the girls moved.

'They ain't going nowheres,' Ness said. 'And I ain't talking to you cos I got nothing to say.'

'But I do,' Kendra said. 'I was wrong and I want to talk to you about that.'

Ness's eyes narrowed. It had been some time since the incident in front of Kendra's house, so she wasn't sure what to make of the word *wrong*. But she'd never before had an adult admit to wrongdoing – aside from her father – so she felt a corresponding confusion that made her hesitate and robbed her of a quick reply.

Kendra took the opportunity that Ness's silence provided. 'Come with me for a coffee. You can meet your friends afterwards if you want to do that.' She took two steps towards the shop door to indicate her departure.

Ness hesitated for a moment before saying to the other girls, 'Le' me see what the cow wants. I catch you up front of the cinema.'

They agreed to this, and Kendra led Ness to a café not far from Whiteley's. She wanted her out of the shopping centre, where the noise level was high and the gangs of kids wandering around provided too many distractions. The café was crowded, but it was mostly populated by shoppers taking a break and not by kids waiting for action. Kendra bought drinks at the counter and, while she was waiting, she took the time to rehearse what she wanted to say.

She made it brief and to the point. 'I was dead wrong to hit you, Nessa,' she said to her niece. 'I was angry that you'd not stayed home with Joel and Toby like you'd said you would. Top of that, I thought something was going on that wasn't going on, and I . . .' She looked for a way to explain it. 'I slipped over the edge.' She didn't add the rest of it, the two parts that completed the tale: the ache of encroaching middle age that she'd felt that night in No Sorrow when she hadn't managed to pull even one man, and the encounter with Dix D'Court in which he'd explained what had happened between Ness and himself. Both of these parts of the tale revealed much more about Kendra than she wanted to reveal. All Ness needed to know was that her aunt had been wrong, she knew she'd been wrong, and she'd come to make things right.

'I want you to come home, Nessa,' she said. 'I want to start again with you.'

Ness looked away from her. She dug her cigarettes – Kendra's pinched Benson and Hedges – from her shoulder bag and lit one. She and her aunt were sitting on stools at a counter that ran along the front window of the café, and a group of boys were passing. Their steps slowed when they saw Ness in the window and they spoke among themselves. Ness nodded at them. It was a movement that seemed almost regal. In reply, they gave head jerks that appeared oddly respectful, and kept moving.

Kendra noted this. The brief contact between Ness and the boys, even though it was only visual, sent a chill of intuition down Kendra's spine. She couldn't say what it all meant – the nod, the boys, the chill she felt – except that it didn't seem good.

She said, 'Toby and Joel, Ness. They want you home as well. Toby's birthday's coming. With all the changes been happening in your lives over these months, if you were there—'

'You wanting me to mind dem, innit,' was Ness's conclusion. 'Dat's why you here. Toby 'n' Joel finally getting in your way. Wha' else you want, den?'

'I'm here because I did wrong to you and I want you to know that I *know* I did wrong. I want to say sorry. I want us to be family to each other.'

'I ain't got fam'ly.'

'That isn't true. You have Toby and Joel. You have me. You have your mum.'

Ness spluttered a laugh. She said, 'Yeah. My *mum*,' and drew in deeply on her cigarette. She hadn't touched her coffee. Kendra hadn't touched her own.

'Things don't have to be this way,' she told Ness. 'Things can change. You and I can start over.'

'T"ings end up way dey end up,' Ness said. 'Ever'body want somet'ing. You no different.' She gathered up her belongings.

Kendra saw that she intended to leave. She played her wild card. 'Social Services phoned,' she said. 'Woman called Fabia Bender wants to meet with you. With me 's well. We have to see her, Ness, because if we don't—'

'Wha'? Like she going to send me somewheres? Like I even care?' Ness adjusted her shoulder bag and tweaked the scarf in her hair. 'I got people watching out f'r me now. I got no worries 'bout Social Services, 'bout you, 'bout anyt'ing. An' dat's how it is.'

That said, she was gone, out of the café and heading back in the direction of Whiteley's. In the sunlight of late spring, she teetered along the pavement on her high heels, leaving her aunt to wonder how much worse things could get between them.

When the day came for Joel to make his purchase of the lava lamp for Toby's birthday, the first thing he had to sort out was what to do with his little brother while he made that purchase since Kendra was at work in the charity shop, and there was consequently no help from that quarter. Had Ness been at home, he would have asked her to look after him. It wasn't an errand that would take terribly long since it comprised a jaunt to Portobello Road, a quick exchange of money in the shop, and then another jaunt back to Edenham Way. Even Ness in her present state might have been prevailed upon to remain with Toby, making sure he didn't answer the door should a stranger knock upon it. But since she wasn't there, Joel faced several choices. He could take Toby with him and spoil the birthday surprise; he could leave him at home and hope for the best; he could stow him in a spot where something in the place might possess an inherent interest designed to keep him occupied.

He thought of the duck pond in Meanwhile Gardens and the toast left over from breakfast. He decided that if he made a hiding place among the reeds – something akin to the fort Toby had spoken about fashioning there months ago – and he armed his brother with the toast for duck food, he could keep him safe and occupied long enough to buy the lava lamp and return.

So he gathered up the toast, added some extra bread just in case his errand took longer than he expected, and waited for his brother to blow up his life-ring. That done, he made sure Toby wore a windbreaker against a potentially cool day, and they set off around the side of the houses to join the path that led along their back gardens. The sun was out, and the sun brought with it people wanting to enjoy the fair weather. Joel could hear them just beyond the child drop-in centre in the form of the whoosh of skateboard action in the skate bowl and children's babble in the playing area of the drop-in centre itself. He worried at first that the pleasant weather might also mean people at the duck pond, but when he and Toby worked their way through the shrubbery and hopped on the secondary path that curved down to the water, he was relieved to see that no one was on the little dock. There were ducks aplenty, however. They paddled sublimely, occasionally bottom-upping themselves as they searched beneath them for something to eat.

Along the edges of the pond, the reeds grew thickly. Although Toby complained that he wanted to be on the dock above the birds, Joel explained to him the benefits of secreting himself among the reeds instead. These were the duck houses, he told him. If he remained quiet and still in the reeds, there was a very good chance that the ducks would come to him and eat the bread right from his hand. Wouldn't that be better than throwing it at them from the dock and hoping they'd notice?

Toby had little experience of ducks and consequently didn't know that bread tossed into the water would attract any duck worth his feathers within a good fifty yards. The plan as Joel explained it sounded reasonable to him, so he was happy enough to be ensconced in a roughly fashioned duck blind in the reeds, from which he could watch the birds and patiently wait for them to discover him.

'You got to stay here,' Joel told him when he had Toby in place. 'You got dat innit? I'll be back direc'ly I get somet'ing over Portobello Road. You wait right here. You do dat for me, Tobe?'

Toby had positioned himself on his stomach with his chin on the life-ring that he'd wriggled higher on his body. He nodded and fastened his eyes on the water, just through the reeds. 'Gimme the toast, den,' he said. 'I bet th' ducks's hungry.'

Joel made sure the toast and the bread were within reach.

He backed out of the blind, and climbed to the path. He was relieved to see that, from above the pond, Toby was out of sight. He only hoped his brother would remain there, hidden. He didn't intend to be gone for more than twenty minutes.

Heading for the shop in which Toby had shown him the lava lamp required him to make for Portobello Bridge, the viaduct that would take him over the railway tracks and into what remained of the open air market of Golborne Road. He made the first part of the journey at a trot and as he went, he wondered how much his little brother remembered about how their birthdays had once been celebrated. If it had been a good spell for their mother, there would have been five of them cramped around the little kitchen table. If it had been one of their mother's bad times, there would have been only four, but their father would have made up for the absence of their mother by singing the special birthday song deliberately loud and deliberately out of tune, after which he would hand over a birthday present, like a pocket knife or a cosmetic bag, like in-line skates that were second-hand but cleaned up nicely or a special pair of trainers that a child longed for but never mentioned.

But all that had been before the Campbell children had been relocated to Henchman Street, where Glory did her best to create a celebration – as long as one of them reminded her that a birthday was coming up – but where George Gilbert usually threw a spanner in the works by coming home drunk, or using the birthday as an excuse to become drunk, or otherwise insinuating himself into the centre of what went for the festivities. Joel didn't know what a birthday would be like at Kendra Osborne's house, but he intended to make it as special as he could.

The massive estate of Wornington Green marked one of the turns Joel needed to make, but just along Wornington Road a sunken tarmac football pitch caught his attention. This pitch was lined in brick and fenced in on all four sides with chain link, and an angled top to this boundary was supposed to discourage anyone from using the area when it was not intended to be used. But a set of steps on the west side of the pitch allowed access to it since the gate at the top had long ago been destroyed, and the purpose of the pitch itself – offering a playing area for the children of Wornington Green – had been altered shortly afterwards. Below him, Joel could see one of the neighbourhood's many graffiti artists in one midst of a project, applying his craft to the filthy brick walls in a rainbow of colours.

He was a Rasta, although his dreadlocks were secured beneath a large knitted cap that drooped with the weight of the hair inside it. The scent of weed drifted upward from him, and Joel could see that a spliff dangled between his lips. He appeared to be putting the finishing touches on a masterwork consisting of words and a cartoon-like figure. The words were red, high-lighted with white and orange. They said *Question Not* and they served as the base of the figure who rose out of them like a phoenix from the ashes: a black man wielding knives in each hand, offering a suitably fierce snarl from a tattooed face. This finished piece was one of many already decorating the pitch: buxom cartoon women, cigarette- or dope-smoking men in various poses, menacing cops with pistols drawn, guitarists bent backwards as they sent their music heavenward. Where there weren't graffiti of this nature, there was tagging. Initials, names, sobriquets of the streets . . . It was difficult to imagine any child able to play football on the pitch with so many distractions.

'So wha' you gawping at, mon? You never seen artis' at work?'

The question came from the Rasta, who'd taken note of Joel peering down through the chain link fence. Joel took it at face value and not as the challenge it might have been, coming from another sort of man. This bloke looked harmless, a conclusion Joel reached based upon the somnolent expression on his face, as if he were being escorted to dreamland by the weed he was smoking.

'Dis ain't art,' Joel said. 'Art's in museums.'

'Yeah? T'ink you could do dis, den? I hand over the paint and you make something nice 's dis?' He gestured with the spliff, pointing out his nearly finished piece.

'Who is it anyway?' Joel asked the Rasta. 'Wha's it mean "question not"?'

The Rasta approached him, leaving his spray paint behind. He came to the side of the pitch, his head cocked. He said, 'You joking, innit? You playing Cal Hancock for a fool.'

Joel frowned. 'Wha' you mean?'

'Askin' who dis is? Mean to tell me, you don' know? How long you been round here, mon?'

'January.'

'An' you don' know?' Cal shook his head in wonder. He took the spliff from his mouth and generously handed it up to Joel for a toke. Joel put his hands behind his back, the universal sign of refusal.

'You clean, den?' Cal Hancock asked him. 'Dat's good, mon. Give yourself a future. You got a name?'

Joel told him.

Cal said, 'Campbell? Got a sister?'

'Ness, yeah.'

Cal whistled and took a deep drag on the spliff. 'See,' he said. His nod was thoughtful.

'You know her or summick?'

'Me, mon? No. I don' mess with women got mental shit goin on, y'unnerstan.'

'My sister *ain't* . . .' What *mental* implied, the inescapable connection it offered to Carole Campbell, the future it promised: these were topics Joel dared not veer towards, not even to deny them. He kicked his trainer-shod toe against the low brick wall of the pitch.

'Maybe she ain't, bred,' Cal said affably. 'But she a bad piece of action, have a man raging long before she rage, lemme tell you dat. She shell-shock a bred, she want to, y'unnerstan?

She suck a bred dry 's a dog's bone and leave him to wonder what hit him and how in hell he goin to manage getting hit again.'

'You *sure* you ain't her man?' Joel asked.

Cal chuckled. 'Oh las' time I checked my bollocks in place, so I pretty sure, blood.' He gave a wink and sauntered back to his artwork.

'So who is it anyways?' Joel called after him, gesturing to the figure he was working on.

Cal waved lazily in reply. 'You know when it's time,' he told him.

Joel watched him for a moment, saw how he expertly laid on a curve of shading to the *Q* in *Question*. Then he moved off.

Some considerable time had passed since Toby had shown Joel the lava lamp he wanted but, when Joel reached the shop in Portobello Road, he was relieved to see that the lamp was still burbling away in the window.

Joel stepped inside. An automatic buzzer signaled his entry and, within three seconds, an Asian man came through a door at the back. He took one look at Joel and his eyes narrowed suspiciously.

He said, 'Where is your mum, boy? What do you want in my shop, please? Have you someone with you?' The man looked about as he spoke. Joel knew he wasn't looking for his mother but for the crew of boys he assumed were lurking nearby, ready to do mischief. It was a reflex reaction in this area of town: one part paranoia and two parts experience.

Joel said, 'I want one of the those lava lamps.' He made his English as proper as he could.

'So you do, boy, but you must pay for it.'

'I know that, don't I. I got the money.'

'You have fifteen pounds and ninety-nine pence?' the man said. 'I must see it, please.'

Joel approached the counter. Swiftly, the man put his hands

beneath it. He never put his gaze anywhere but on Joel, and when Joel reached into his pockets and brought out his crumpled five pound note plus all of his coins, the shop owner counted it with his eyes not his fingers, keeping his hands on whatever it was beneath the counter that was apparently making him feel secure. Joel imagined a big Arab kind of knife, one with a curved blade that could take off someone's head.

He said in reference to the money, 'Here it is. C'n I get one, then?'

'One?'

'Lava lamp. Dat's what I come for, innit.'

The Asian jerked his head towards the window display, saying, 'You may have your choice,' and as Joel moved off to pick the lamp he wanted, the man whisked the money off the counter and into the till, slamming the drawer like someone afraid of a secret being seen.

Joel picked out the purple and orange lamp that Toby had admired. He unplugged its flex and carried it back to the counter. The lamp wore a patina of dust from the length of time it had been in the window, but that was no matter. Dust could be dealt with easily enough.

Joel placed the lamp carefully on the counter. He waited politely for the man to package it. The man did nothing save stare at him until Joel finally said, 'C'n you put it in a box or summick? It's got a box, innit?'

'There is no box for the lamp,' the Asian man told him, his voice rising as if he were being accused of something. 'If you want it, take it. Take it and go at once. If you do not want it, then leave the shop. I have no boxes to give you.'

'You got a carrier bag, though?' Joel said. 'A newspaper or summick to wrap this in?'

The man's voice went higher as he saw a plot hatching: this strange-looking boy the vanguard of a crew who meant to raze his shop to the ground. 'You are giving me trouble, boy. You and your sort always do. Now I say this to you: Do you want the lamp because if you do not, you must leave at once or I shall ring the police straightaway.'

Despite his young age, Joel recognised fear when he saw it, and he knew what fear could prompt people to do. So he said, 'I don't mean you no trouble, y'unnerstan. Just asking for a bag to carry this home.' He saw a stack of carrier bags just beyond the till and he dipped his head at them. 'One of them'll do.'

With his eyes fastened on Joel, the shopkeeper snaked his arm over to the carrier bags and plucked one. He shoved it across the counter and watched like a cat ready to pounce as Joel shook the bag open and put the lamp inside.

Joel said, 'Cheers,' and retreated from the counter. He was as reluctant to turn his back on the Asian as the Asian was to turn his back on Joel. It was a relief to get back outside.

When he retraced his steps to Meanwhile Gardens and the duck pond, Joel saw that Cal Hancock had completed his project. His place had been taken by another Rasta wearing a light blanket around his shoulders, squatting in a corner of the football pitch, where he was lighting up. In another corner huddled three sweatshirt-wearing men who looked to be in their twenties. One of them was in the process of removing a handful of small plastic bags from the pouch of his shirt.

Joel gave them a glance and hurried off. Some things were better left unseen.

He went the back way to the duck pond, around Trellick Tower and through the scent garden instead of weaving through Edenham Estate to reach the spot via the path he and Toby had used earlier. Because of this, his view of the pond was altered, but the spot where he had placed the duck blind was as hidden as it had been from the other angle from which he'd seen it. This was all to the good. He decided he would use it again to tuck Toby away in safety if he needed to do so.

He scurried down towards the dock and worked his way

to the hiding spot, calling his brother's name softly. There was no reply, which caused him to pause for a moment and make sure he was in the right place, something he discovered soon enough when he saw the flattened reeds marking the spot where Toby had been lying. The bread was gone and so was Toby.

Joel murmured, '*Shit.*' He looked around and called his brother's name more loudly. He tried to think of all the places Toby might have taken himself to, and he worked his way out of the reeds and up to the main path. It was then that the noise from the skate bowl captured his attention: not only the whooshing of the boards against the concrete sides of the bowl but also the whoops of the riders who were enjoying it.

He picked up speed and made for the skate bowl. Because of the weather, all three of the bowls' levels were in heavy use and, in addition to the riders and the cyclists in the immediate area, there were a few spectators pausing in their walks on the upper path along the canal to watch the action and others who were lounging on the benches that dotted the garden's little hills.

Toby was with neither of these groups. Instead, he was sitting on the edge of the middle skate bowl, his feet dangling and his jeans rucked up so that the duct tape was clearly visible wrapped around his trainers. He was slapping his hands against his life-ring as four boys whipped back and forth and up the sides of the bowl on skateboards brightly decorated with transfers. They wore baggy trousers cut to their calves and riding low beneath their crotches. They had on dingy T-shirts with faded band logos and wore knitted ski caps on their heads.

Toby was squirming back and forth on his bottom as he watched the boys zooming across the bowl and soaring up the sides, expertly turning their boards in mid-air and swooping back down and across the bowl where they repeated the movement on the other side. So far they seemed intent upon ignoring

Toby, but he wasn't making it easy for them. He was crying out, 'C'n I do it? C'n I try? Can I? Can I?' as he bounced his feet on the bowl.

Joel approached. But as he did so, he caught sight of a second group of boys up on the bridge that carried Great Western Road across the Grand Union Canal. They had paused in the midst of crossing the bridge, and they were looking down at the gardens. After exchanging a few words, they made for the spiral stairs. Joel could hear them clumping on the metal steps. He couldn't yet tell who they were. Still, the size of them, their numbers, and their manner of dress . . . All of this suggested they were a crew, and he didn't want to be in the vicinity when they made their way to the skate bowl if, indeed, that was where they were heading.

He hurried to the middle bowl on whose edge Toby was crying out to be part of the action. He said to his brother, 'Tobe, whyn't you wait where the ducks are? You s'posed to wait. Di'n't you hear me tell you to wait?'

Toby's sole response was a breathy, 'Look at 'em, Joel. I 'spect I could do it. If they let me. I been askin' 'em to let me. Don' you reckon I could do it?'

Joel cast a glance to the spiral steps. He saw that the crew of boys had reached the bottom. He made a fleeting wish that they would take their business – whatever it was – somewhere along the canal. There was an abandoned barge beneath the bridge, and he fervently hoped they were using it as their lair. It had been there for week, just waiting for someone to take it over. But, instead of making for the barge, they came directly towards the skate bowl, sweatshirts with the hoods up over baseball caps, unzipped anoraks despite the mild weather, baggy jeans riding low on their hips.

Joel said, 'Come on, Tobe. We got to sort out our room, 'member? Aunt Ken said we got to keep it neater an' stuff's everywhere jus' now, y'unnerstan?'

'Lookit!' Toby cried, pointing to the boys still whipping

around the skate bowl. 'Hey, c'n I do it? I could do it 'f you lemme.'

Joel bent and took his brother's arm. 'We gotta go,' he said. 'An' I'm that vex you di'n't wait where you was 'posed to wait. Come on.'

Toby resisted standing. 'No. I could do it. C'n I do it, you lot? I could 'f you lemme.'

'"I could 'f you lemme. I could 'f you lemme."' The voice mimicked Toby's, and Joel did not need to turn around to know that he and his brother had become the focus of the boys who'd come down from the bridge. 'I could do it 'f you lemme, Joelly Joel. Only I got to wipe my arse first cos I forgot to do it when I crapped my pants dis morning.'

Joel frowned when he heard his own name spoken, but he still didn't turn to see who the boys were. He said in a fierce whisper, 'Tobe, we got to *go.*'

But that was overheard. 'I bet you got to go, yellow-arse. Bes' run while you c'n still find your way. You an' the li'l tosser wiv you. An' Jesus, wha's he doin wiv dat life-ring?'

Toby finally noticed the other boys, which is to say that the nastiness of the speaker's tone, not to mention his proximity, managed to wrest his attention from the skate bowl. He looked to Joel for guidance as to whether he was meant to reply, while in the skate bowl the pace suddenly slowed as if with the expectation of more fascinating action.

'Oh, I know why he got dat life-ring, innit?' the same taunting voice said. 'He goin' for a swim. Greve, why'n't you help him out wiv dat?'

Joel knew what that meant. Aside from the duck pond, there was only one source of water close at hand. He felt Toby's fingers close over the frayed bottom of his blue jeans. He still hadn't risen from his position on the edge of the bowl, but his face had altered. The joy of watching the boys in the bowl had become the fear of seeing the boys behind Joel. He didn't know them, but he could hear the menace in their voices, even if he didn't know why that menace was directed at himself.

'Who's he, Joel?' Toby asked his brother.

It was time for Joel to find out. He turned. The boys formed a rough crescent. At its centre was the droopy-faced, mixed-race boy whom Hibah had claimed as her boyfriend. She'd called him Neal. If there had been a surname, Joel couldn't remember what it was. What he did remember was his only run-in with Neal and the little joke he'd made at Neal's expense, just the sort of remark a boy like Neal was unlikely to forget. In the presence of his crew, over whom Neal was doubtless always eager to maintain suzerainty, Joel knew that the other boy might well take the opportunity to demonstrate his power, if not over a helpless child like Toby then over his brother, the defeat of whom would score him many points.

Joel spoke to the boy called Greve, who'd taken several steps forward to put his hands on Toby. 'Leave him be,' he said. 'He ain't hurting you. Come on, Tobe. We got to get home.'

'Dey got to get *home*,' Neal said. 'Dat's where dey swimming. You got a nice pool in your garden, *Tobe*. An' what th' hell kind of name is dat, anyways?'

'Toby,' Toby muttered, although his head was lowered.

'Toe-bee. Dat's sweet innit. Well, Toe-bee, lemme jus step out of y'r way so you c'n run 'long home.'

Toby started to rise, but Joel knew the game. One step in their direction and Neal and his crew would be all over both of them, just for the fun of it. Joel reckoned he could survive an encounter with these boys because there were enough people in Meanwhile Gardens at this time of day that either someone would come to his rescue or would pull out a mobile and phone nine-nine-nine. But he didn't want to let Toby fall into the clutches of this group of boys. To them, Toby was like a three-legged dog, something to humiliate, to taunt, and to hurt.

He said to Neal in perfect friendliness, 'Why, you c'n stay

jus' there, mon. Where we going ain't in dat direction anyways, so you no trouble to us just like you are.'

One of the crew with Neal sniggered at this reply, so casually had Joel managed to speak it and so clearly had he communicated an utterly inappropriate lack of fear. Neal shot a look at the group of boys, seeking the source of this disrespect. When he didn't find it, he turned back to Joel.

'Real yellow arse you are, Joe-ell. Get out 'f dis place. An' don't let me see you—'

'No more yellower'n you,' Joel pointed out, although the truth was that only two ethnicities had gone into Neal's making while Joel's had involved at least four that anyone had been willing to identify for him. 'So I wouldn't be talkin' bout who got wha' colour to his skin, bred.'

'Don' *bred* me, Joe-ell, like summick you ain't. I squish bugs your size fer breakfast, innit.'

Titters came from the group of boys. Spurred by this, Neal took a step forward. He nodded at Greve, a motion that indicated the boy was to take Toby as he'd been instructed and then he directed his attention to the bag Joel was carrying.

'Give dat over,' he said as Greve approached and Toby shrank away from him. 'Le's just have a look wha' you got.'

Joel was perfectly caught at this point, with only one way out, which had very little hope of success. He could see what was going to happen if he didn't act, so he acted quickly. He jerked Toby fully to his feet, thrust the bag with the lava lamp into his arms, and said, 'Run. Run! Now, Tobe, run!'

For once, Toby didn't question instruction. He slid into the skate bowl and took off across the bottom of it. Someone shouted, 'Get 'im,' and the pack of boys made a move as one unit, but Joel flung himself into their way.

He said to Neal, 'You fucking horse turd. You stick it in a pig's arse, innit. You play at bein' a real hot speck when you half pig and dat's why you stick it where you stick it.'

This was, as it was intended to be, a suicide speech. But it got Neal's attention. It also got the attention of Neal's crew because they always did whatever Neal did, having very little in the way of brainpower of their own. Neal's face went the colour of brick, and the spots upon it went purple. His fists balled up. He lunged. His crew moved in for the kill, but he shouted, 'I wan' it!' and descended on Joel like a rabid dog.

Joel took the force of Neal's flying body in his mid-section. Both of the boys crashed to the ground with their arms swinging. A delighted shout went up from Neal's crew, and they pressed forward to watch. The boys in the skate bowl joined them, until what Joel saw beyond Neal's looming rage-ensanguined face was a mass of legs and feet.

Joel wasn't a fighter. His breath had always come short whenever he was ignited to action, and the only time he'd ever been in an actual dust-up, he'd not been able to catch his breath and he'd ended up in casualty with a plastic mask over his nose and mouth. So what he knew about fighting came from what he saw on television, which consisted of ineffectively swinging his fists and hoping they made contact with some part of Neal's body. He did manage to land a blow on the other boy's collar-bone, but Neal countered with one that hit Joel squarely on the temple and made his brain start singing.

Joel shook his head to clear it. Neal shifted position and sprawled across Joel's chest. He put the full force of his weight on Joel's body, and he used his knees to pin Joel's arms to the ground. He began punching in earnest. Joel squirmed in an attempt to get him off. He threw his body right and left, but he couldn't loose the other boy from him.

'Half-breed li'tle bastard,' Neal snarled through his crooked teeth and his drooping mouth. 'Teach *you* to disrespeck . . .' He grabbed Joel's neck and began to squeeze.

All around him, Joel heard grunting and breathing: not only his own and Neal's but the other boys' as well although theirs was excited and hot with anticipation. Not a film this time. Not a television show. But the real thing. Neal was their man.

'*Get* 'im,' someone muttered fiercely.

Someone else said, '*Yeah*. Go f'r it, mon.'

And then someone said, 'Got to finish dis, bred. *Take* it, take it,' and Joel realised that something had been passed to Neal from one of the boys at the edge of the crowd.

He saw the silver streak of it against Neal's palm: a pocket knife and nicely honed. No one was coming to his rescue as Joel had hoped, and he knew he was finished. But the certainty of this knowledge swept power into him, born of the human instinct to live. Neal had leaned to take the knife from his cohort; this put him off balance and gave Joel a chance.

He flung his body in the direction of the lean, which threw Neal off him. Joel fell upon him, then, landing blows, pounding against bone and flesh with all the strength he had. He fought like a girl: grabbing Neal's hair, scratching at his unfortunate face, doing anything he could to stay one step ahead of the other boy's intention and two steps ahead of his rage. He was fighting not to punish Neal, not to prove something to him, not to establish himself as bigger, better, or more adept. He was fighting simply to stay alive because he understood with the perfect clarity that comes with terror that the other boy intended to kill him.

He no longer knew where the knife was. He was unable to tell if Neal had it or if it had been knocked from his hands. He *did* know that this was a fight to the death, though, and so did the other boys, for they had fallen into a tense silence although not one of them had backed away from the brawl.

It was because of this silence that Joel heard a voice, a man calling out, 'What's going on here?' And then, 'Get back. Step *out* of my way. You heard me, Greve Johnson. And you, Dashell Patricks. What are you boys doing?' And immediately after that, 'For the love of God!' which heralded Joel's being jerked off Neal, hauled to his feet, and thrust to one side.

Joel saw it was Ivan Weatherall, of all people, his mentor from Holland Park School. Ivan said, 'Is that a *knife* over there? Are you out of your minds? Is that yours, Joel Campbell?' and without waiting for a reply, he shouted at the rest of them to clear off.

Despite the fact that Ivan was one and they were many, he exuded such confidence that the boys obeyed, surprised and unused to being troubled when they were in the midst of one of their pursuits. This included Neal, who was nursing a cut lip. As his mates began to pull him from the site, he shouted, 'Don' you *fuck* with me,' an imperative obviously intended for Joel. 'I'll *have* you, arse-wipe. Yellow-arse road kill. You and your bruddah. You eat your muddah's pussy.'

At this, Joel made a move to go after Neal, but Ivan grabbed his arm. To Joel's surprise, he said under his breath, 'Fight me, boy. Fight to get away. Go on. Do it, for the love of God. I've got a grip . . . Good. Right- o . . . Kick me as well . . . Yes, yes. Spot on, that. . . . Now I'll get you in a lovely half-nelson—' with a quick movement that imprisoned Joel under his arm – 'and we'll make our way to this bench. Keep fighting me, Joel . . . I'll throw you down here . . . try not to hurt you . . . Ready? Here we go.'

Joel found himself on the bench as promised, and when he looked around, Neal and his crew had retreated to the spiral stairs, heading up to the Great Western Road. The skate-boarders had also dispersed, and he was left with Ivan Weatherall. He couldn't understand how the miracle had been effected.

'They think I've sorted you, which suffices for the moment,' Ivan said in explanation. 'It appears I came along just in time, though. What on earth were you thinking, taking on Neal Wyatt?'

Joel said nothing in reply. He was breathing hard. He didn't want to end up in casualty again, so he thought it best not to waste effort on speech. Beyond that, he wanted to be away from Ivan. He needed to find Toby. He needed to get both of them safely home.

'It just happened, did it?' Ivan asked. 'Well, that shouldn't surprise me, and I suppose it doesn't. Neal Wyatt has issues with most of the planet, I'm afraid, which is what comes from having a father in prison and a mother possessing a deadly predilection for crack cocaine. There is, of course, a way out for what ails him, a cure if you will. But he won't take it. More's the pity because he's actually quite talented at the piano.'

Joel started at this, surprised at this altered vision of Neal Wyatt.

Ivan nodded in understanding. 'Shame, isn't it?' He looked over his shoulder to the bridge, across which the boys had shuffled on their way to whatever was the next piece of trouble they had in mind. 'Well, then, have you caught your breath? Are you ready to go?'

''M okay.'

'Really? You don't quite seem it, but I shall take you at your word. I recall you live somewhere nearby but not in Trellick Tower. I shall walk you home.'

'I don't need—'

'Nonsense. Don't be foolish. We all need something, and the first step on the path to maturity – not to mention peace of mind – is admitting that. Come along.' He smiled, showing his terrible teeth. 'I shall not require you to hold my hand.'

He fetched a parcel from beneath the bench on which they'd been sitting, tucked it under his arm and affably explained that it contained parts for a clock that he was assembling. He nodded towards Elkstone Road a short distance away and led Joel in its direction while, beyond and around them, Meanwhile Gardens continued to get back to normal.

Ivan chatted amiably, confining his conversation to clocks. Their assembly, he informed Joel, was his hobby and his passion. Did Joel recall the conversation they'd had about creative outlets on the day they'd met? No? Yes? Had he thought about what he wished to do so that his soul could earn its expression?

'Remember,' Ivan said, 'we are like machines in this, Joel. Every part of us needs to be oiled and cared for if we are to function to our utmost capacity. So where are you in the decision-making process? What is it you intend to do with your life? Beyond brawling with the Neal Wyatts of our world.'

Joel wasn't sure that Ivan was serious. Instead of replying, he scanned the area for Toby and said, 'I got to fetch my bruvver. He ran when Neal came.'

Ivan hesitated. 'Ah yes. Of course. Your little brother. That does at least explain . . . Well. Never mind. Where might he have gone? I shall help you find him and then act as your escort home.'

Joel didn't want this but, short of being rude, he didn't know how to tell Ivan he felt best left alone. So he followed the pavement along Elkstone Road, Ivan tagging along, and he checked to see if Toby had run to their aunt's house. Failing to find him there, he set off between the buildings towards the duck pond, and there he discovered Toby crouched in the duck blind with his hands over his head.

He'd somehow punctured his life-ring. It hung around his waist still, but it was now only partially inflated. He hadn't lost the bag that Joel had thrust at him, though. It was at his side and, when Joel reached him through the reeds, he saw that the lava lamp had escaped damage. He was thankful for this. At least Toby's birthday would not be ruined.

He said, 'Hey, Tobe. 'S okay now. Le's go home. This here's Ivan. He wants to meet you.'

Toby looked up. He'd been crying, and his nose was dripping. He said to Joel, 'I di'n't wee in my pants. I have to go, but I di'n't wee my pants, Joel.'

'Tha's real good.' Joel lifted Toby to his feet. He said to Ivan, who remained above them on the path to the pond, 'This's Toby.'

'Delighted,' Ivan said. 'And impressed with the wisdom of your apparel as well, Toby. Is that short for Tobias, by the way?'

Joel looked at his brother, dwelling on the word *apparel*. Then he realised Ivan was talking about the life-ring in conjunction with the vicinity of water. The man thought they'd possessed forethought when it came to Toby's safety.

'It's jus' Toby,' Joel informed Ivan. 'I 'spect my mum and dad di'n't know Toby was short for anything.'

They climbed the bank to join Ivan who, taking a long look at Toby, removed a white handkerchief from his pocket. Rather than see to Toby's face on his own, though, he wordlessly handed the linen to Joel. Joel nodded a thank you and wiped down his brother. Toby kept his gaze fixed on Ivan, as if he were seeing a creature from another solar system.

When Toby was cleaned up, Ivan smiled. He said, 'Shall we, then?' and indicated the direction of the terrace houses. He said, 'As I've learned from school, you young gentlemen live with your aunt. Would today be an appropriate time to make her acquaintance?'

'She's off at the charity shop,' Joel said. 'Up the Harrow Road. Where she works.'

'The AIDS shop, is it?' Ivan asked. 'Why, I'm quite familiar with that place. It's noble work, she does, then. Ghastly disease.'

'M'uncle died of it,' Joel said. 'Aunt Ken's bruvver. My dad's her older bruvver. Gavin. Her younger bruvver, he was Cary.'

'Quite a loss she's experienced.'

'Her husband died, too. Her first, tha' is. Her second husband's . . .' Joel realised he was saying too much. But he had felt compelled to share something, in gratitude for Ivan's being there when he was needed and saying nothing about the oddity of Toby when they'd come upon him.

The fact that they'd reached his aunt's house again allowed him to let the rest of what he'd almost told Ivan go unsaid, and Ivan didn't comment upon this as Joel and Toby mounted the steps. Instead he said, 'Well, I should like to meet your aunt at a later date. Perhaps I'll call in at the charity shop and introduce myself, with your permission of course.'

Joel thought fleetingly of Hibah's words of warning about this man. But nothing untoward had happened between them on any of the occasions when they'd met for their mentoring sessions. Ivan *felt* safe to be around, and Joel wanted to trust that feeling.

He said, 'You can if you want.'

'Excellent,' Ivan said and extended his hand. Joel shook it and then prodded Toby to do the same.

Ivan reached into his jacket pocket and brought out a card, which he handed to Joel. He said, 'This is where you can find me outside school hours. There's my address. My phone number as well. I don't have a mobile – I cannot abide those wretched things – but if you phone my home and I'm not there, an answer machine will take your message.'

Joel turned the card over in his hands. He couldn't imagine why he would ever use it. He didn't say as much but Ivan seemed to know what he was thinking.

He said, 'You might want to tell me your plans and dreams. When you're ready, that is.' He stepped away from the building and tipped his finger at Joel and then at Toby. 'Until later, then, gentlemen,' he said and went on his way.

Joel watched him for a moment before he turned to the door and opened it for Toby. Ivan Weatherall, he decided, was the oddest man he'd ever met. He knew things about everyone – personal and otherwise – and yet he still seemed to manage to take people as they came. Joel never felt a misfit in his presence because Ivan never acted as if there was anything unusual in his mongrel features. Indeed, Ivan acted as if the whole world were made of people who'd been taken from a shaken bag of races, ethnicities, beliefs, and religions. How peculiar he was in the world where Joel lived.

Still, Joel ran his fingers over the embossed print on the

face of the card. Thirty-two Sixth Avenue, he read, with a clock below Ivan Weatherall's name. He said to the air what he'd so far kept to himself.

'Psychiatrist,' he whispered. 'That's what, Ivan.'

8

'So when I get home from work,' Kendra said, 'I c'n see the boy's been in a fight. But he i'n't talking, is he, and neither is Toby. Not that I'd expect Toby to grass. Not on Joel of all people.' She removed her gaze from the soles of Cordie's feet, and studied the reflexology chart that lay on the kitchen table, next to which she and her friend were sitting. She moved her thumbs slightly to the left on Cordie's right foot. She said, 'How's this, then? Wha's it do for you?'

Cordie was playing willing guinea pig. She'd removed her wedge-soled shoes, had allowed her feet to be washed, patted dry, and rubbed with lotion, and had provided Kendra with a running commentary about the myriad effects that reflexology was having on the rest of her body.

She said, 'Hmmm. Makes me think of chocolate cake, Ken.' She held up a finger, frowned, said, 'Nah. Nah, dat ain't it . . . Keep on . . . Li'tle more . . . Oh yeah. I got it now. More like . . . handsome man kissing the back of my neck.'

Kendra slapped her lightly on the calf. 'Get serious,' she said. 'This's important, Cordie.'

'Hell, so's a handsome man kissing the back of my neck. When we having 'nother girls' night out? I want one of dem twenty-year-olds from the college dis time, Ken. Someone wiv big muscles in his thighs, y'unnerstan what I mean?'

'You been reading too many ladies' sex magazines. Wha's muscles in his thighs got to do wiv anyt'ing?'

'Give him strength to hold me like I want to be held. Up against the wall wiv my legs wrapped round him. Hmm. Dat's what I want next, innit.'

'Like I almost b'lieve you, Cordie,' Kendra informed her. 'You want dat, you know where to get it and you know who more 'n willing to give it to you. How's dis now?' She applied new pressure.

Cordie sighed. 'You bloody good, Ken.' She leaned back in the chair as well as she could, considering it was a kitchen chair. She lolled her head against the back of it and said to the ceiling, 'How'd you know, den? 'Bout the fight.'

'Bruises on his face where someone hit him,' Kendra said. 'I get home from work and find him in the bathroom trying to make it all disappear. I ask him what happened, and he say he fell on the steps of the skate bowl. Over the gardens.'

'Could've,' Cordie pointed out.

'Not wiv Toby afraid to leave his side. Somet'ing happened, Cordie. I can't sort it why he won't tell me.'

''Fraid of you, maybe? You Lady Mucking him too much, Ken? Dat . . . When you talk proper, it c'n keep a distance, y'unnerstan. Between you and . . . well, anyone.'

Kendra said, 'I 'spect it's more he's 'fraid of causing me trouble. He sees Ness's doin' enough of dat.'

'An' where is Miss Vanessa Campbell dese days?' Cordie asked sardonically.

'In an' out like always.'

Kendra went on to explain her attempt to apologise to Ness for what had gone on between them. She hadn't yet mentioned any of this to Cordie, because she knew her friend would ask the logical question about the apology: the why question that she didn't particularly want to answer. But in this instance, and because of Joel's fight, Kendra felt the need of a girlfriend's counsel. So when Cordie asked her why the hell *she* was apologising to a girl who had disrupted life at 84 Edenham Way from the moment of her arrival, Kendra told her the truth: she'd run into the man who'd been with Ness in the car that night when Kendra had accosted the girl. He'd told an entirely different story from the one she'd assumed. He was . . . Kendra tried to come up with a way to explain that wouldn't lead to Cordie's questioning her further. She said at last that the man had been so sincere in what he'd told her that she knew at the level of her heart that he was telling the truth: Ness had been drunk at the Falcon pub, and he'd brought her home before trouble could befall her.

Cordie homed in on the detail she felt most salient. Kendra *ran into* him? How'd that come about? Who was he, anyway? What made him even bother to explain what had happened with Vanessa Campbell on the night in question?

Kendra grew uncomfortable. She knew that Cordie would scent a lie the way a hound scents a fox, so she didn't bother. She told her friend about the phone call for the sports massage, about ending up in the bed-sit above the Falcon pub, about coming face to face with the man who'd been with Ness that night.

'He's called Dix D'Court,' Kendra added. 'I only saw him that one time.'

'And dat was 'nough to b'lieve him?' Cordie asked shrewdly. 'Oooh. You ain't telling me ever't'ing, Ken. No lyin' to me now cos I c'n read it all over you. Summick happened. You get shagged at long last?'

'Cordie Durelle!'

'Cordie Durelle wha'? I don't 'member him real clear, mind, but if he want a sports massage, dat tells me he got a decent sports body.' She thought about this. 'Damn. *You* get muscular thighs? Dat is outrageously unfair.'

Kendra laughed. 'Di'n't get nothing,' she said.

'Not f'r want of his tryin's what I 'spect.'

'Cordie, he's twenty-three,' Kendra told her.

Cordie nodded. 'Gives him stamina.'

'Well, I wouldn't know. We jus' talked after the massage's done. Dat's all.'

'Don't b'lieve you f'r a second. But if it's the truth, den you sixteen ways a fool. Put me in a room with someone wants a sports massage and we ain't having stimulatin' conver*sa*tion 'bout the state of world affairs when it's over, innit.' Cordie removed her feet from Kendra's lap, the better to get into the conversation without distractions. She said, 'So. You find Ness and say sorry. What happen next?'

Nothing, Kendra said. Ness wouldn't hear *sorry* or anything else.

She kept her comments confined to her niece since allowing them to drift to Dix D'Court would mean revealing to Cordie that he'd phoned her again and again since the night of the massage. It wasn't about another sports massage that he'd rung her, either. He wanted to see her. She'd felt something that night, he said to her. He'd felt something as well. He didn't want to walk away from that. Did she?

After the first three calls, Kendra had let her mobile take his messages. She'd let her machine at home do the same. She didn't return his calls, assuming he'd finally go away. He hadn't done so.

It was shortly after this conversation with Cordie that Dix D'Court showed up at the charity shop in the Harrow Road. Kendra would have told herself that his appearance in the shop was a coincidence, but he disabused her of this notion immediately. His parents, he said, owned the Rainbow Café. Did she know where it was? Just down the street? He'd been on his way there when a display in the window of the charity shop caught his eye. ('Lady's coat wiv the big buttons,' he said later. It would be his mum's birthday soon.) He'd slowed to look at the coat and then, beyond it, he'd seen her in the shop. That's why he'd entered, he explained.

'Whyn't you phoning me back?' he asked. 'You not getting the messages I been leaving?'

'I've been getting them,' Kendra told him. 'I just didn't see a good reason to return them.' She watched her language. She needed formality and she clung to it.

'You 'voiding me, den.' A statement, not a question.

'I suppose I am.'

'Why?'

'I give massages, Mr D'Court. You weren't ringing me about arranging to have one. Least, if you were, you never said as much. Just "I want to see you", which didn't tell me it was business you were after.'

'We got b'yond business. Wiv you as ready 's me for what was 'bout to happen.' He held up a hand to stop her from replying, saying, 'An' I know it ain't gentlemanly to mention dat to you. Gen'rally I like being a gentleman. But I also like history being straight, y'unnerstan, not being rewritten for someone's convenience.'

She'd been in the midst of counting the money in the till when he'd walked in, so near to closing up for the day that in another ten minutes he would have missed her. Now, she removed the cash drawer and carried it to the back room where she stowed it in the safe and locked it up. He was meant to see this as rejection, but he refused to take it that way.

He followed her, but he didn't enter the back room. Rather, he stood at the door where the shop lights silhouetted him in a disturbing fashion. The body Kendra had seen that night above the Falcon pub was framed by the doorway. He was a tempting proposition.

But Kendra had other things in mind for life and one of them was not an entanglement with a twenty-three-year-old boy. *Boy*, she reminded herself. Not man. B-o-y, as in nearly two decades her junior.

Which made it all the better, didn't it? she then asked herself. The seventeen years between them declared there was no possibility for entanglements.

'Here's what I t'ink,' he said to her. 'You like most women, an' dat means you 'specting dis is just a quick shag I want. I ring you to finish what we started cos I don't like a woman getting away so easy. I like to put 'nother notch in my belt. Or wherever a bloke puts a notch cos I don't ackshully know.'

Kendra chuckled. 'Now that,' she told him, 'is just about exactly what I don't think, Mr D'Court. If I thought it was that – a quick shag and we're done – I would've rung you back and made the arrangements because I won't lie and there's no point to it, is there: you were in the room and a party to what happened between us. And what happened wasn't exactly me saying "Get your hands off me, blood." But I get the feeling that's not who you are or how you are, and, see, I don't want what you're after. And the way I look at it, two people – man and woman, I mean – need to be after the same thing when they hook up together or one of them's heading for trouble of the heart-breaking kind.'

He gazed at her, and what shone from his face was admiration, liking, and amusement all blended together. He said, 'Dix.' It was his only reply.

'What?'

'Dix. Not Mr D'Court. An' you're right wiv what you say, which makes it rougher, see. Makes me want you more cos, damn, you ain't like—' He smiled and shifted to her style of speaking – 'you are not like most women I meet. Believe it.'

'That,' she said tartly, 'is because I'm older. Seventeen years. I've been married twice.'

'Two fools to let you get away, den.'

'Not their intention.'

'What happened?'

'Death to one and car theft to the other. He's in Wandsworth. Told me he was in the spare parts business. I just didn't know where the parts were coming from.'

'Ouch. And the other? How'd he—'

She held up her hand. 'Not going there,' she said.

He didn't press her, merely saying, 'Rough. You had tough times wiv men. I ain't like dat.'

'Good for you. That doesn't change way things are with me.'

'An' how's dat?'

'Busy. A life. Three kids I'm trying to sort, and a career I'm trying to get off the ground. I've got no time for anything more than that.'

'An' when you need a man? For what a man c'n give you?'

'There are ways,' she said. 'Just think about it.'

He crossed his arms and was silent. He finally said, 'Lonely. Satisfaction, yeah. But how long it last?' And before she could answer, he went on to say, 'But if dat's the way you want it, I got to 'cept it and jus' move on. So . . .' He looked around the back room as if he were seeking some sort of employment. He said, 'You locking up, right? Come 'long an' meet my mum and dad. Rainbow Café, like I said. Mum's got my protein smoothie waitin for me, but I 'spect she do you a cup of tea.'

'Easy as that?' Kendra said.

'Easy as dat,' Dix told her. 'Fetch y'r bag. Le's go.' He grinned. 'Mum's only three years older'n you, so you'll like her, I 'spect. Have t'ings in common.'

That remark went straight to the bone, but Kendra had no intention of following it. She began to head back into the shop, where her bag was stowed under the counter. Dix didn't move, though. They were face to face.

He said, 'You one damn beautiful woman, Kendra.' He put his hand on the back of her neck. He used gentle pressure. She was meant to move into his arms, and she knew it.

She said, 'You jus' told me . . .'

'I lied. Not 'bout my mum, mind. But 'bout letting go. Dat is summick I got no intention of doing.'

He kissed her then. She didn't resist. When he moved her into the back room of the shop and away from the doorway, she didn't resist that either. She wanted to do so, but that desire

and all the cautions that went with it were bleating uselessly
from her intellect. In the meantime, her body was saying something else, telling a tale about how long it had been, about how
good it felt, about how insignificant it was, really, just to have
a quick shag with no strings attached. Her body told her that
everything he'd said about his intentions towards her were lies
anyway. He was twenty-three years old, and at that age men
only wanted the sex – hot penetration and satisfying orgasm
– and they'd do and say anything to make sure they got it. So
no matter what he'd said in agreement to her assessment of
the situation between them, what he really wanted was indeed
another notch on his belt, seduction brought to a satisfying
conclusion. All men were like that, and he was a man.

So she allowed the moment to reign, no past and no future.
She embraced the now.

She gasped, 'Oh my sweet Jesus,' when at last they
connected.

He was everything – muscular thighs and all – that his body
had promised he would be.

The fact that Six and Natasha were no closer to their dream
of possessing mobile phones than they'd been on the night
that Ness had met them was what caused the initial chink in
the relationship among the three girls. This chink was widened
when the Blade bestowed upon Ness the late twentieth-
century's most irritating electronic device. The mobile, he told
her, was for ringing him should anyone vex her when she
wasn't with him. No one, he said, was going to mess his woman
about and, if anyone did, they would hear from him in very
short order. He could get to her fast no matter where she was,
so she wasn't to be shy about giving him a bell if she needed
him.

To a fifteen-year-old girl like Ness, these declarations –
despite the fact of their being made on a questionably stained
futon in a filthy squat without electricity or running water –

sounded like certain proof of devotion and not what they really were, which was evidence of the Blade's intentions to keep tabs on her and to have her available when he wanted her. Six, who was far more experienced in the arena of unsatisfactory relationships and definitely better informed in the ways of the Blade – having grown up in the same part of North Kensington as he – greeted everything Ness said about the man with suspicion if not outright disdain. These reactions on her part were exacerbated when the mobile phone put in an appearance in Ness's life.

The girls had ventured farther than Whiteley's on this particular afternoon. They'd gone to Kensington High Street where they'd entertained themselves first by trying on clothes at Top Shop, rooting through racks of out-of-season jerseys in H & M, and ultimately finding their way to yet another branch of Accessorize where the general plan was to pinch a few pairs of earrings.

Six excelled at this activity, and Ness wasn't far behind her. Natasha, however, had very little talent in the sleight-of-hand department, being as clumsy as she was gawky. Usually, Natasha was in charge of diversion, but on this day she decided to join the action. Six hissed at her, 'Tash! Do what you s'posed! You vex me, slag,' but that did nothing to turn the tide of Natasha's intentions. Instead she went for the rack of earrings and knocked it over just as Six was attempting to shove three pairs of garish chandeliers into her pocket.

The result of this was the three girls being escorted from the premises. There, outside the shop and in full view of the passing throng on the High Street, two overweight security guards, who seemed to materialise out of the commercial ether of the precinct, stood them up against the wall and photographed them with an old Polaroid camera. The pictures, the girls were informed, would be put up by the till. If they *ever* entered this shop again . . . Nothing more needed to be said.

The entire enterprise set Six's teeth on edge. She wasn't used to such humiliating treatment because she wasn't used to being caught. And she wouldn't have been caught had not the maddening Natasha taken it into her head that she was going to nick something from the shop. Six said, 'Damn, Tash, you are one fucking stupid cow,' but making that declaration to Natasha didn't give Six the satisfaction she desired. She sought another focus for it. Ness was the logical target.

Six went at her obliquely. Like most people unable to assess their own emotional state, she displaced what she was feeling on to something less terrifying. The lack of cash was a suitable substitute for the lack of purpose in life.

She said, 'We got to get some dosh. We can't be relying on nicking shit an' passing it on. Dat's goin to take 's for ever, innit.'

'Yeah,' said Tash, maintaining her position of always agreeing with whatever Six said. She didn't question what they needed the cash for. Six had her reasons for everything. Cash was always useful, especially when the bicycle delivery boys weren't willing to risk scooping a bit of substance from the top of a sandwich bag for whatever sexual fantasy they had that might be fulfilled.

'So where we gettin' it?' Six excavated her shoulder bag and brought out a packet of Dunhills recently pinched from a tobacconist on the Harrow Road. She prised one out without offering the packet to the other two girls. She had no matches or lighter, so she stopped a white woman with a child in a pushchair and demanded something 'to fire up dis fag, innit'. The woman hesitated, mouth open but words blocked. Six said to her, 'You hear me, slag? I need a fuckin light an' I 'spect you got summick I could use in dat bag of yours.'

The woman looked around as if seeking rescue, but the way of life in London – defined by a better-you-than-me morality – declared that no one was going to come to her aid. Had she said, 'Step out of my way, you nasty piece of business, or I shall scream so loudly you'll not have eardrums when I'm through with you', Six would have been so astonished at the singularity of this reply that she would have done as the woman demanded. But instead, when the poor creature fumbled in her bag to accommodate the request, Six saw her purse within, clocked its bulge, felt the gratification that comes with gathering a few easy unearned pickings, and told her to hand over some cash as well.

'Jus' a loan,' she said to the woman, with a smile. 'Less you want to make it a gift or summick.'

Ness, seeing the interaction, said, 'Hey, Six,' and her voice was a caution. Nicking merchandise from shops was one thing; engaging in street muggings was another.

Six ignored her. 'Twenty pounds'll do,' she said. 'Take that Bic 's well, case I want 'nother fag later on.'

The fact that it didn't look like a mugging and didn't run the course of a typical mugging was what allowed the enterprise to conclude smoothly. The woman – with a child to care for and far more than twenty pounds in her possession – was relieved to be let off so lightly. She handed over her lighter, extricated a twenty pound note from her wallet without opening it fully to display how many more twenty pound notes she was carrying, and scurried on her way when Six stepped to one side.

'Yeah!' Six said, delighted at the conclusion of her engagement with the woman. And then she caught sight of Ness's face, which didn't bear the level of approval she was looking for. She said to her, 'Wha'? You too good for dis or summick?'

Ness didn't like what had just gone down, but she knew the wisdom of not making a comment. Instead she said, 'Give us a fag, den. I dying for one innit.'

Six wasn't persuaded by Ness's reply. Living as she did by her wits and by her ability to read her associates, she could sense disapproval. She said, 'Whyn't you get your own, Moonbeam? I been taking the risk. You been scoring the profit.'

Ness widened her eyes but otherwise kept her expression the same. 'Dat ain't true.'

'Tash?' Six said. 'True or not, slag?'

Natasha floundered around for a reply that would offend neither girl. She couldn't come up with one quickly enough to satisfy Six.

Six said to Ness, 'Sides, you don't need to risk nuffink, way I see it, Moonbeam. Gotcher *man* providing for you now. An' you ain't even sharing wiv no one. Not *money*, dat is. Not substance, neither. Bone *or* weed. As f'r other t'ings . . . well, I ain't saying.' She laughed and tried to light her cigarette. The Bic was dead. She said, '*Fuck* dat bitch!' and threw the lighter into the street.

What Six had said about the Blade struck Ness in a place she hadn't expected to be touched. She said, 'What you talking 'bout, Six?'

Six replied, 'Like I said. I ain't saying, Moonbeam.'

'You best say, slag,' Ness told her, speaking from a fear as deep as Six's own although having an entirely different source. 'You got summick to tell me, you tell me. Now.'

Possession of a mobile phone. Having a source of ready cash should she want it. Being chosen by someone of import. These were the stimuli to what Six next said. 'You t'ink you the *only* one, slag? He been fucking a bitch called Arissa same 's he fucking you. Fucking her *'fore* you, matter fack, and di'n't stop doing her when he started up wiv you. An' 'fore you two, he got some slag up the chute over'n Dickens estate an' he planted 'nother one in Adair Street, next door his mum. Ever'one knows it cos dat's what he does. I hope to hell you're taking precautions cos he setting up you and setting up Arissa just like the others and when he done, he walk away. Dat's how he like it. Ask round, you don't b'lieve me.'

Ness felt a coldness come over her, but she knew the importance of projecting indifference. She said, 'Like I care? He get me a baby, I like it good. Get myself my own place, den, and dat's just what I want.'

'You t'ink he come round afterwards? You t'ink he give you cash? Let you keep dat mobile? You pop out a kid, he finish wiv you. Dat's what he does, an' you so stupid you ain't seeing it yet.' She directed her next comments not to Ness but to Natasha, speaking as if Ness had disappeared. She said, 'Shit, Tash, wha' you t'ink? He must got a solid gold one, dat blood. So *obvious* wha' he got in mind, innit. Either women 's more fucking *stupider* 'n I ever thought or he got a dick make dem sing when he plug it in. Which you s'pose it is?'

This was far too much for Natasha to cope with. The conversation was obvious enough but the underlying causes were too subtle for her to understand. She didn't know whom to side with or even why she was supposed to take a side at all. Her eyes grew watery. She sucked on her lip.

Six said, 'Shit. I'm out of here, den.'

Ness said, 'Yeah. You take off, cunt.'

Tash made a noise akin to a whimper and looked from Six to Ness, waiting for the fight to begin. She hated the thought of it: screeching, kicking, shoving, pulling hair, and clawing at flesh. When women went after each other, it was worse than a cat fight, for brawls between women always *began* things that went on for ever. Brawls between men put an end to disputes.

What Tash didn't take into account in that moment was the influence of the Blade. Six, however, did. She knew that a fight with Ness would not end with a fight with Ness. And while she truly hated walking away from the sort of gauntlet that Ness had thrown before her, she also wasn't a fool.

She said, 'Le's go, Tash. Ness's got a man wiv *needs* she got to see to. Ness got a *baby* she desp'rate to produce. No time for slags like us, any more.' And to Ness, 'Have fun, bitch. You one sorry cunt.'

She spun on the spiked heel of her boot and took off in the direction of Kensington Church Street, where a ride on the number 52 bus would return her and Natasha to their own environment. Ness, she decided, could use her bloody mobile phone to ring the Blade and ask him to fetch her home. She'd find out soon enough just how willing he was to accommodate her.

Kendra found herself, in very short order, exactly where she had not wanted to be. She had long despised women who went soft inside at the thought of a man, but that was where she began heading. She ridiculed herself for feeling what she soon felt about Dix D'Court, but the thought of him became so dominant that the only way to put her mind at rest was to pray that the curse of her own sexuality be lifted in some way. Which it was not.

She wasn't so foolish as to call what she was feeling for the young man *love*, although another woman might have done so. She knew it was basic animal stuff: the ultimate trick a species plays upon its members to propagate itself. But that knowledge didn't mitigate the intensity of what was going on in her body. Desire planted its insidious seeds within her, desiccating the previously fertile plain of her ambition. She kept at it as best she could – giving massages, taking further classes – but the drive to do so was fast disappearing, overcome by the drive to experience Dix D'Court. Dix, with all the vigour of his youth compelling him, was happy to do what he could to please her since it pleased him so much as well.

It didn't take long, however, for Kendra to learn that Dix wasn't as ordinary a twenty-three-year-old as she'd thought the first time they coupled in the back room of the charity shop. While he eagerly embraced the carnality of their relationship, his background as the child of loving parents whose relationship had remained constant and devoted throughout his life demanded that he seek something similar for himself. This secondary desire was bound to come out sooner or later, especially since, because of his youth, Dix – unlike Kendra –

did associate much of what he was feeling with the idea of romantic love that permeates western civilisation.

What he said about this was, 'Where we headed, Ken?' They faced each other, naked in her bed while, below them in the sitting-room, Dix's favourite film was playing on the video machine, to entertain Toby and Joel and to keep them from interrupting what was going on when their aunt and her man had disappeared upstairs. The film was a pirated copy of *Pumping Iron*. Dix's god starred, his sculpted body and wily mind acting as metaphors for what one determined man could do.

Dix had chosen to ask his question in advance of their mating, which gave Kendra an opportunity to avoid answering in the manner she knew he wanted. He'd asked in the midst of mutual arousal, so she lowered herself – snakelike – down his body, her nipples tickling him on the way. Her reply was thus non-verbal. He groaned, said, 'Hey, baby. Oh shit, Ken,' and gave himself to pleasure in such a way that she thought she'd succeeded in diverting him.

After a few moments, though, he gently pushed her away. She said, 'No like?'

He said, 'You know dat ain't it. Come here. We got to talk.'

She said, 'Later,' and went back to him.

He said, 'Now,' and moved away from her. He tucked the sheet around himself as a further shield. She lay exposed, the better to keep him engaged.

This didn't work. He averted his eyes from where she wanted them – on her breasts – and showed himself determined to have his say. 'Where we heading, Ken? I got to know. Dis is good, but it ain't all dere is. I want more.'

She chose to misinterpret him, saying with a smile, 'How much more? We doing it so often I c'n hardly walk.'

He didn't return the smile. 'You know what I'm talking 'bout, Kendra.'

She flopped on her back and gazed at the ceiling, where a

crack from one side into the middle curved like the Thames around the Isle of Dogs. She reached without looking for a packet of Benson and Hedges. He hated her smoking – his own body was a temple undefiled by tobacco, alcohol, drugs, or processed food – but when he said her name in a fashion simultaneously impatient and minatory, she lit up anyway. He moved away from her. So be it, she thought.

She said, 'What, then? Marriage, babies? You don't want me for that, mon.'

'Don't be telling me what I want, Ken. I speak for myself.'

She drew on her cigarette and then coughed. She shot him a look that dared him to remonstrate, which he did not. She said, 'I walked that road twice. I'm not doing it—'

'Third time's the charm.'

'And I can't give you kids, which you're going to want. Not now maybe cause you're little more than a baby yourself, but you're going to want them and then what?'

'We sort dat out when we come to it. An' who knows wha' science'll be able to—'

'Cancer!' she said and she felt the anger. Unfair, unaccountable, a blow at eighteen that had not really affected her till she was thirty. 'I don't have the proper parts, Dix, not a single one. And there is no coming back from that, all right?'

Oddly enough, he wasn't put off by this knowledge. Instead, he reached out, took her cigarette from her, leaned past her to crush it out, and then kissed her. She knew he wouldn't like the taste of her – which was one reason she'd lit up in the first place – but that didn't deter him. The kiss went on. It led where she had wanted to go moments earlier, and when it did so, she thought she had prevailed. But when they were finished, he didn't separate from her. He gazed down at her face – his elbows holding his weight off her body – and he said, 'You never told me 'bout the cancer. Whyn't you never tell me, Ken? What else you not saying?'

She shook her head. She was feeling the loss for once, and

she didn't like what she was feeling. She knew it was merely a trick of biology: that ache of wanting which would fade soon enough, as her mind took over from her body once again.

He said, 'It's you anyways. I c'n live wivout the rest. An' we got Joel and Toby for our kids. Ness 's well.'

Kendra laughed weakly. 'Oh yeah. You want that kind of trouble.'

'*Stop* bloody telling me what I want.'

'Someone's got to, cause you sure as hell don't know.'

He rolled off her, then. He looked disgusted. He turned, sat up, and swung his legs over the side of the bed. His trousers – the same sort of harem trousers he'd been wearing that night at the Falcon – lay on the floor and he scooped them up. He stood, back to her, and stepped into them, drawing them up over the nicely muscled buttocks she so liked to admire.

She sighed, saying, 'Dix, I *been* there. It i'n't the paradise you're thinking it is. 'F you'd just believe me, we wouldn't even need to have this sort of conversation, baby.'

He turned back to her. 'Don't call me baby. Now I know how you mean it, I don't like how it sound.'

'I don't mean it—'

'Yeah, Ken. You do. He a baby, dat boy. Don't know what he wants. T''inks he's in *love* when all it is is sex. He come to his senses soon enough, he will.'

She sat up in the bed, resting against the wicker headboard. She said, 'Yeah well . . . ?' and looked at him meaningfully. It was a schoolmarm look. It said she knew him better than he knew himself because she'd lived life longer and experienced more. It was, in short, a maddening look, designed to set on edge the teeth of a man who had what he wanted in front of him, just out of reach.

He said, 'I can't help what it was like for you with the other two, Ken. I c'n only be who I am. I c'n only say it'd be different wiv us.'

She blinked the sudden, surprising pain from her eyes. She

said, 'We don't control that. You think we do, but we don't, Dix.'

'I got my life heading—'

'Well, so did he,' she cut in. 'Got murdered in the street. Got knifed cos he was walking home from work and two bloods di'n't think he showed 'em enough *respect*. Course they high, so whatever he showed wasn't going to matter much, but they cornered him and they knifed him anyway. And the cops . . . ? Just 'nother dead blood. Nig-nogs ridding the world of each other, according to them. And he, Dix, my husband Sean, he had intentions just like you. Property management.' She laughed shortly, bitterly, a laugh that said *The nerve of that man to have his dreams*. 'He wanted the ordin'ry things in life, too. Adopting the kids we can't have on our own. Setting up house. Buying things like furniture, a toaster, a door mat. Simple stuff like that. And he dies cos the knife punctures his spleen. It cuts all the way cross his stomach and he bleeds out, Dix. That's how he dies. He jus' bleeds out.'

He sat on the edge of the bed, her side of it, near but not touching. He raised his hand, his intention of caressing her an obvious one. She tilted her head away from him. He dropped his arm.

She said, 'And number two, Dix? He looks like he got his dream made, and it's humble enough. Car parts business wiv me helping by doing the books, a man and wife sort of thing, just like your mum and dad in their café. Only I don't get that he's stealing cars 's well. So damn good at it – moving 'em in and moving 'em out – you can't blink cos you miss the action. So we lose everything, he go to Wandsworth, and I just barely escape the same thing. So you see, I ain't . . .' She realised how badly her language was slipping at the same moment as she realised she'd begun to weep, and the combination of these two pieces of knowledge created within her a pool of humiliation so deep that she thought she might drown. She lowered her head to her upraised knees.

He said nothing because what, indeed, does a twenty-three-year-old male – so new to adulthood – say to assuage what looks like grief but is so much more? Dix still possessed that youthful vigour which declares that anything is possible in life. Untouched by tragedy, he could see but he could not relate to its depth, or its capacity to colour the future through fear.

He could love her back to wellbeing, he thought. To him, what they had was good, and its goodness possessed the strength to obliterate anything that had gone before. He knew this and felt it at a level so atavistic, however, that no words came to him to express himself. He felt reduced to nerve endings and desire, dominated by the intention of proving to her that things were different when it came to him. His inexperience limited him, though. Sex was the only metaphor he could grasp.

He reached for her, saying, 'Ken, baby, Ken.'

She jerked away and rolled on to her side. For Kendra, everything she was and everything she had tried to become was fast collapsing as the Kendra she presented to the world was crushed by the weight of the past, which she generally managed to hold at bay. Acknowledging, admitting, speaking about . . . She had no reason to do any of this when she was living out her daily life and simply pursuing her ambitions. To have done it all now, and in the presence of a man with whom she'd no intention of experiencing anything more than the basest sort of pleasure, added to her sense of degradation.

She wanted him to leave. She waved him away.

He said, 'Yeah. But you comin' as well.'

He strode to the bedroom door, which he opened. He called out, 'Joel? You hear me, blood?'

The sound on *Pumping Iron* lowered, Arnold expatiating on some topic or another, mercifully muted. Joel called out, 'Yeah?'

'How fas' you get ready? Toby too?'

'For what?'

'We going out.'

'Where?' A slight pitch in voice, which Dix took for excitement and happiness: a dad giving his boys some good news.

'Time you met my mum an' dad, bred. Toby an' your Aunt Ken 's well. You up for dat? They got a caff up the Harrow Road and my mum . . . ? She do apple pie wiv hot custard. You lot ready for dat?'

'Yeah! Hey, Tobe . . . !' The rest Dix did not hear, as he had shut the door and turned back to Kendra. He began to sort through the clothing she had strewn around the floor, wispy bits of lace that were knickers and bra, tights, a skirt that skimmed her hips, a v-necked blouse that was cream on her skin. He found a thin T-shirt in a drawer, as well, and this he used gently to blot her face.

She said, 'Oh Jesus. What d'you want wiv me, man?'

He said, 'Come on, Ken. Le's get you dressed. Time my mum and dad met th' woman I love.'

9

Any reasonable person looking upon the Blade – let alone spending one or two hours in his company – would have been able to draw a few conclusions about what entering into an extended relationship with the man would be like. First, there was the matter of his tattoo and what decorating one's face with a venom-spitting cobra suggested about his inner issues as well as about his potential for lucrative – not to mention legal – employment. Next there was his size, so suggestive of a Napoleon-in-the-making, without benefit of the designation *emperor* to give reason for the less salubrious aspects of his personality. Then, there was his place of abode and all the inconveniences offered by a squat destined for the wreckers' ball. Finally, there was his line of work, which involved nothing that promised even the semblance of longevity. But for someone to look upon the Blade and have time to consider all these facts about him and what they might imply, that person would also have to be capable of rational and extended thought. The night that Ness met the Blade she was capable of neither and, by the time she might have been able to look at him more clearly, she was too involved to be willing to do so.

So she told herself that there were elements in her relationship with the Blade that indicated she'd been *chosen* by him, although what she had been chosen for was something she wasn't able to identify. At this point in her life, she couldn't afford to be a deep thinker on the topic of male-female liaisons, so what she did was to leap to premature conclusions based on superficial information. This information was limited to three areas of her life: the sexual, the commercial, and the drug-oriented.

She and the Blade were lovers, if such a word could be applied to the Neanderthal manner in which the young man approached the sexual act. There was no pleasure involved in this for Ness, but she neither expected nor desired pleasure from it. As long as it continued to happen, she was one step closer to the baby that she claimed she wanted, at the same time as she was reassured that her place in the Blade's life was as secure as she needed it to be. Thus, his demands on her – which women with a greater sense of self might have found degrading – were transformed in her mind to the reasonable exigencies of 'a man wiv his needs', as she would have put it had someone asked her about the pounding to which she regularly acquiesced without having experienced anything resembling either foreplay or seduction. Since they were lovers and since he continued to behave in a fashion that suggested an attachment to her, she was, if not content, then at least occupied. A woman occupied has little time to question.

When he gave her the mobile phone, she had that which her girlfriends so desired, and this commercial aspect of her relationship with the Blade allowed her to believe in his romantic intentions towards her, every bit as if he'd presented her with a costly diamond. At the same time, it gave her a dominance that she liked, raising her in the eyes of her associates.

She remained there – above Six and Natasha – because of the Blade as well. For he was the source of the weed she smoked and the coke she snorted, removing her from having to depend solely upon the neighbourhood's delivery boys for a handout, as Six and Natasha had to do. To Ness, the fact that the Blade shared substance with her freely meant they were a real couple.

Having all these beliefs, then, and clinging to them because, indeed, she had nothing else to cling to, Ness tried to forget what Six had said about the Blade. She could cope with his past. Good God, he was 'a man wiv needs', after all, and she could hardly have expected him to remain celibate, waiting for her. But she found that within all the information about the Blade that Six had so cruelly passed along in Kensington High Street, there were two facts that she could not dismiss no matter how she tried. One of these was the fact of two children fathered by the Blade: a baby on Dickens Estate and another in Adair Street. The other was the fact of Arissa.

The babies constituted a terrible question Ness couldn't bring herself to form in her mind, let alone to ask outright about herself. Arissa, on the other hand, represented an easy topic for thought at the same time as she comprised every besotted young woman's nightmare: betrayal by the man she believes to be her own.

Ness couldn't extirpate the thought of Arissa from her head once Six had planted the seed. She told herself that she had to know the truth in order to know what, if anything, she could do about it. She decided, wisely, that confronting the Blade was an ill-conceived idea, so she went for information to Cal Hancock instead.

Since no one, aside from her brother Joel, had ever shown Ness the least degree of loyalty, she had no real thought that Cal might refuse to betray the man who was the source of everything that allowed Cal to keep body, soul, and mind together. Cal's own parents having departed the UK when he was sixteen – taking his siblings with them but leaving him behind to fend for himself – he had joined forces with the Blade as a teenager, first proving himself as the most dependable of the bicycle delivery boys and then rising rapidly through what ranks there were to become part major-domo and part bodyguard, a position he'd successfully held for over four years. But Ness didn't know any of this. When she saw Cal Hancock, she saw the dreadlocked graffiti artist, frequently stoned but generally close at hand unless he'd been dismissed for those few minutes of privacy the Blade required for the sexual act. Ness reckoned that if anyone knew the truth about Arissa, it would be Cal.

She waited for one of the times when the Blade was, as he called it, 'tending to t'ings'. This tending occurred sporadically, and it involved the receipt of stolen property, drugs, or other contraband. All of this came to the Blade at premises unrelated to the squat. Generally Cal accompanied the Blade to this hideaway, but once, having intentions towards Ness that he promised to fulfil upon the conclusion of his meeting, he told her to wait for him at the squat. To keep her safe in this disreputable location, he told Cal to remain with her. This gave Ness the opportunity for which she had been waiting.

Cal lit a spliff and offered it to her. Ness shook her head and gave him time to toke up. He was lazy with the way he talked when he was stoned, and she wanted him to be less than vigilant with what he said in answer to her questions.

She used an approach that presumed knowledge. 'So where's dis Arissa living, Cal?'

He was deep into his developing buzz, and he nodded, letting his eyelids droop. He got very little sleep as the Blade's bodyguard. Any chance for a catnap was a chance he took. He slid down the wall to rest on the futon. Above him a graffito featured a buxom black girl in a tiny skirt, guns drawn in the manner of a shoot-out specialist. The black girl wasn't a caricature of Ness and, as she'd been there when Ness had first come to this place, Ness hadn't really given her a second thought. Now, however, Ness looked at her more closely and saw that her scarlet top was cropped to reveal a tattoo, a miniature snake identical to the Blade's.

She said, 'Dis her, Cal? You paint Arissa on th' wall?'

Cal looked up and saw what she was referring to. He said, 'Her? No. Dat ain't Rissa. Dat's Thena.'

'Oh? So when you painting Arissa?'

'I ain't got plans . . .' He glanced her way, toking up on the spliff as he hesitated. He'd realised what she was doing, and now he was trying to decide how much hell he was going to have to pay for saying what he'd so far said.

'Where she live, mon?' Ness asked.

Cal said nothing. He removed the spliff from his lips and gazed at the little plume of smoke that was rising from the end of it. He offered it to her again, saying, 'G'on. Le's not waste it, mon.'

'I ain't a man. And I said. I don't want it.'

Cal took another hit, holding the smoke in deep. He removed his cap. He tossed it on the futon and shook his head to let his dreads fall loose.

Ness said, 'So how long the Blade been fucking her? True he doing it 'fore he fucking me?'

Cal rolled his head towards her and squinted. She was at the window with the light behind her, and he waved her over to where he could see her better. He said, 'Dere's t'ings you ain't got a need to know. I 'spect dat's one of dem.'

'Tell me.'

'Nuffink to tell. He is or he ain't. He did or he di'n't. Wha' you 'scover don't change what is.'

'An' 'xactly what is dat s'posed to mean?'

'T'ink 'bout it. But don't ask nuffink else.'

'Dat's all you going to say, den, Cal? I could make you talk. If I wanted. I could.'

He smiled. He looked as afraid of her threat as he would have looked confronted by a duckling bearing arms. 'Yeah? How you going to do it?'

'You don't tell me, I tell him you tried to fuck me, Cal. You know what he do den, I 'spect.'

Cal laughed outright before he took another hit. 'Dat wha' the big plan is? You t'ink you so special to the mon, he kill anyone else who touch you? Darlin, you ain't seeing life 's it is. I fuck you, *you* gone, innit. Cos you damn bloody easier'n me f'r the Blade to replace, and dat's the truth. You jus' lucky I ain't in'erested in you, y'unnerstan. Cos if I was, I tell the Blade and he hand you over when he finished wiv you.'

Ness had heard enough. She said, 'Dat's it, blood,' and she followed her usual pattern when she didn't get her way, which was to leave the scene. She made for the door – which had neither knob nor lock – and told herself she'd get Calvin Hancock and she'd get him where it would hurt him good.

She held true to her intentions. The next time she was alone with the Blade, she told him what Cal had said about sharing her. Into her expectation that the Blade would rise in justifiable rage and smite Cal Hancock the way he deserved, however, came the Blade's laughter instead.

He said, 'Dat blood get stoned, he say anyt'ing,' and he gave no indication that he intended to do anything to discipline the other man.

When she demanded he do something to defend her, he nuzzled her neck instead. He said, 'You t'ink I give dis to *any*one? You crazy you t'ink dat shit.'

But still there remained the question of Arissa, and the only way to get an answer to this question was to see if the Blade would lead her to one. Ness knew that she couldn't follow him, however. Cal was good at his job as the Blade's protector, and he would see her no matter what she did to escape his detection. The only alternative Ness could see was to seek information from Six. She hated to do it since it put her at Six's mercy, but there was no other way.

Since Six was not a girl to hold a grudge where a potential source of free substance was concerned, she pretended that what had happened between herself and Ness on Kensington High Street had never happened. Instead, she welcomed Ness into the disreputable flat on Mozart Estate and after insisting Ness join in a karaoke rendition of *These Boots are Made for Walking* – all the more melodious for the fact that she had drunk a bottle of her mother's mouthwash in an attempt to get high prior to singing it – she imparted the information Ness sought. Arissa lived in Portnall Road. Six didn't know the address, but there was only one block of flats in the street, mostly inhabited by old-age pensioners. Arissa lived there with her gran.

Ness took herself to Portnall Road, and there she waited. She found the building with no trouble and had little more devising a spot from which she could watch the entrance to the building unobserved. She did not have long to wait. On her second attempt to catch the Blade in what she saw as a sexual transgression, he showed up, driven by Cal as always, and let himself in to the building. For his part, Cal lounged in the entrance. He took out a pad – it looked like a sketch pad from where Ness stood – and he began to use a pencil upon it. He leaned against the wall and only occasionally looked up to make sure the area was still safe for whatever the Blade was up to.

Which could be only one thing, and Ness knew it. So she was unsurprised when the Blade reappeared half an hour later, making final adjustments to his clothes. He and Cal started down the path to the street when a window opened above them. Cal immediately thrust himself between the Blade and the building, using his body as a shield. A girl laughed from above and said, 'You t'ink I hurt dat mon, Cal Hancock? You f'rgot dis, baby,' and Ness followed the sound to see her: perfect chocolate skin and silky hair, full lips and heavy-lidded eyes. She tossed a set of keys down to the men. 'Bye bye,' she said with another laugh – this one sultry – and she closed the window.

What prompted Ness to move from her hiding space wasn't so much the knowledge of the girl as the expression on the Blade's face as he gazed up at the window. Ness could see that he was thinking of going back up to her. He wanted more of whatever it was that she could give him.

Ness was on the path before she could consider the ramifications of a public scene with the Blade. She strode up to him and made her demand.

'I want to see that cunt who's fucking my man,' she told him, for she put the blame not on the Blade but on the girl. It was the only way she could survive the moment. 'Dat cunt Arissa, you take me *to* her,' Ness said. 'I show her what happens she put her hands on my man. Take me to her, blood. I swear, you don't, I wait out here anyways an' I jump her she comes out dat door.'

Another sort of man might have sought to defuse the situation. But as the Blade did not dwell much on women as human beings but rather as a source of entertainment, he considered the amusement value of a cat fight over him between Ness and Arissa. He liked the idea and took Ness by the arm. He shoved her towards the door.

Behind her, Ness heard Cal say, 'Hey mon, I don't t'ink—' but whatever else he intended for the Blade, it was cut off when the door shut behind them.

The Blade said nothing to Ness. She kept her anger at a high pitch by picturing the two of them – the Blade and Arissa – doing what she and the Blade should have been doing instead. She kept the picture of them so clear in her mind that when the door to the flat swung open, she charged in and went for the girl's long hair. She grabbed it up in a fist and shrieked, 'You fucking stay *'way*, you hear me? I see you near dis mon again, I kill you, cunt. Y'unnerstan?' She pulled back her fist and punched Arissa solidly in the face.

What she expected then was a claw and scratch fight, but that didn't happen. The girl didn't fight back at all. Instead, she dropped to the floor in a foetal position, so Ness kicked her in the back, going for her kidneys, and then repositioned herself to kick her in the stomach as well. She connected once, and that was when Arissa screamed. She screamed far out of proportion to the violence.

'Blade! I got a baby inside!'

Before the Blade could move, Ness kicked her again. Then she fell upon her because she could see that Arissa spoke the truth. Not so much because there was a telltale bump on the girl's body but because Arissa hadn't bothered to try to take Ness on. That was indication enough that there was something more at stake for the girl than her street credentials.

Ness beat her around the face and shoulders, but what she was beating was a fact not a girl. It was a fact that she couldn't look at squarely because to do so meant to look at herself and to draw a conclusion from her past that would colour her future. Ness shrieked, 'Bitch! I kill you, slag, you don't stay 'way.'

Arissa screamed, 'Blade!'

This put an end to the entertainment, which, while it hadn't gone on long, had escalated quickly enough to sate the Blade's need for a demonstration of his desirability. He pulled Ness off the other girl. He held her, bent at the waist and panting and trying to get back to Arissa for more. Ness continued to shriek her curses at the girl, which obviated the necessity of asking her any outright questions about the true history of her relationship with the Blade, and she fought savagely as the Blade jerked her back towards the door and in two deft movements opened it and shoved her into the corridor.

He did not follow at once, instead remaining behind to assess the reliability of Arissa's declaration. To him, she looked no different from when he'd taken her upright in the kitchen a short while before, thrusting and grunting with her back against the cooker, working quickly as was his habit when he had other things waiting for his attention.

She was still on the floor, foetally arranged as before, but he didn't help her up. He merely gazed upon her and did a few mental calculations. Could be she was; on the other hand, could be she was merely a lying slag. Could be his; could be anyone's. In any case, there was a simple answer and he gave it to her.

'Get rid of it, Riss. I got two and 'nother on the way. Don't need no more.'

That said, he went out to Ness in the corridor. His plan was to sort her out in a fashion she wouldn't likely forget because the one thing a man in his position couldn't have was a woman following him around North Kensington and causing scenes whenever she felt like it. But Ness wasn't there.

The way the Blade looked at this development was: could be good; could be bad.

After that, Ness decided she was finished with the Blade. The reason she admitted to herself was the lying, cheating, two-faced nature of the man, going at Arissa like a hatchet-faced monkey at the same time he was going at her. She wasn't about to stand for that, no matter who he was or how big his reputation.

She chose her moment. The Blade had a past, as she had learned, and what she'd also learned – from careful questioning of Six on the matter – was that the other women who'd been in his life over the years had been dismissed without troubling him further. This included the two hapless souls who'd borne him children. Whatever their expectations had been of Blade's future part in the lives of his offspring, he had disabused the two women of them in very short order, although he did drop by the estates on occasion when he felt the need to point out to Cal – or to anyone else he wished to impress – the fruit of his loins as they played in their nappies among the rusting shopping trolleys.

Ness determined that she would not be one of these women, going meekly out of the Blade's life when he was tired of her. What she told herself was that she was sick and tired of *him*, and tired especially of his pathetic skill as a lover.

She waited for the right opportunity to present itself, which it did in a mere three days. Again, Six – that fount of useful information on the topic of illegal activities in North

Kensington – put her in the picture as to where the Blade took receipt of the contraband whose sale allowed him to keep his position of dominance in the community. This place was on Bravington Road, Six told Ness, where it intersected Kilburn Lane. There was a brick wall along a shop yard that backed on to an alley. The wall had a gate, but this was always locked and even if it wasn't, Ness wasn't to go inside for love or money. No one went inside except the Blade and Cal Hancock. Everyone else did business with him in the alley. This alley was in full view not only of the street but of a line of houses that backed on to it. No one would think to phone the police about the furtive business going on outside, though. Everyone knew who was conducting it.

Ness went there when she knew the Blade would be dealing with his underlings. She found him as she hoped she might: looking over the goods provided by two thugs and three boys on bicycles.

She elbowed through them. The gate in the brick wall was open, revealing the back of an abandoned building, a platform running along it and upon this platform several wooden crates that were open and others that were not. Cal Hancock was shifting goods around in one of these crates, which meant that he'd left the Blade unguarded. The Blade himself was examining an air pistol he'd been handed, the better to see how much work would be required to modify it into a useful weapon.

Ness said, 'Hey. We finished, fucker. Jus' thought I stop by and let you know.'

The Blade looked up. An indrawn breath seemed to be taken in unison by the group that surrounded him. Across the yard, Cal Hancock dropped the top of the crate back into place. He leapt from the platform. Ness knew his intention. She had to be quick, so she spoke in a rush.

'You nuffink,' she said to the Blade. 'You got dat, bred? Act like you a *real* big mon cos you know you a worm crawl round in the dirt. An' *size* of a worm, you got dat, mon?' She laughed and put her hands on her hips. 'Blood, I been *sick* of y'r face wiv dat stupid tattoo since second time I saw you, an' I even more sick of dat eight ball head an' the way it looks when you licking. Y' unnerstan me? You get what I say? You good for getting high, i's true, but, shit, it jus' ain't worth it no more, not f'r what you got to offer. So—'

Cal clamped on to her. The Blade's face was a mask. His eyes had gone opaque. No one else moved.

Cal strong-armed her away from the wall and out of the alley, through a dead silence in which Ness acknowledged her triumph by saying to the thugs and the boys on their bikes, 'You t'ink he's summick? He *nuffink*. He a worm. You 'fraid of him? You 'fraid of a *worm*?'

Then she was back in Bravington Road, and Cal was hissing, 'You one stupid cow. You one sorry, stupid, bloody-minded cow. You know who you messin wiv? You *know* what he c'n do 'f he wants? Get *out* of here now. An' stay out of his way.' He gave her a push, one that was designed to direct her reluctant feet away from the spot. Since Ness had accomplished what she'd set out to do, she didn't protest or fight to get away.

Instead, she laughed. She was finished with the Blade. She felt as light as the air. He could have Arissa and anyone else he wanted, she told herself. What he would *not* have – and could never have again – was Vanessa Campbell.

In his quest for physical perfection – which the title *Mr Universe* would affirm – Dix D'Court needed financial support, and so he had gathered sponsors. Without them, he would have been doomed to squeezing out time for his power-lifting before or after work or at the weekends, and this would be when the gym was most crowded. He'd have had little real hope of attaining his dream of the world's most magnificently sculpted male body if he had to pursue it that way so, early on, he'd gathered around him individuals who were willing to finance his endeavour. He had to meet them occasionally, to bring them up to date on the recent competitions he'd entered and won, and he inadvertently scheduled one of these meetings for the night of Toby's birthday. Once he learned of this, Dix wanted to cancel his meeting. But allowing this cancellation suggested another step towards the sort of commitment that Kendra was trying to avoid, so she told him that the birthday needed to be a private, family affair. The message in this was implicit: Dix was not family. He shot her a look that said *Have it your own way*. Privately, however, he told Joel he would be there directly after his sponsors' meeting.

From this remark, Joel knew not to tell Kendra that Dix would be turning up. There were depths between his aunt and Dix that he could not plumb, and he had other worries anyway. Primary among these was his failure to find a *Happy Birthday* sign to hang upon the kitchen window. It was bad enough not to have the family's old tin carousel any longer to set in the middle of the table, but to have no dramatic way to wish the birthday boy happiness felt to Joel like a more significant blow. Even Glory Campbell had managed to hang on to the children's birthday sign, resurrecting it – more tattered every year – from wherever she stowed it when it wasn't in use. This sign with its grommets, which allowed it to be hung with haphazard cheer any which way, had gone the way of most of Glory's non-sartorial possessions prior to her departure for Jamaica: she'd tossed it in the rubbish without Joel's knowledge and only when he looked through his own belongings did he realise it was no longer a possession of the immediate Campbell clan.

He didn't have enough cash to get another one, so he'd had to settle for making one himself, which he did by using notebook paper. He took one sheet for each letter and he coloured them with a red pencil borrowed from Mr Eastbourne. On Toby's birthday he was ready to hang them on the window, but there was nothing to use as adhesive save a book of first-class postage stamps.

He would have preferred Sellotape or Blu Tac. But he lacked the funds to purchase that as well. So he used the stamps, reckoning they could be glued to envelopes afterwards, as long as he was careful to put them on the window in such a way as to make them easy to get off later. That was how he began to explain matters to his aunt when she arrived home after work on the day in question, exclaiming 'What the hell!' as she saw the handmade sign and how it had been attached to the window. She dropped her carrier bags on the worktop and turned to Joel, who'd followed her into the kitchen with his explanation ready. But she stopped him in the midst of it by putting her arm around his shoulders.

'You did a good thing,' she said into the top of his head. Her voice was husky, and it occurred to Joel that she'd softened a bit since Dix had started coming around No 84 Edenham Way, especially since the day they'd all trooped up to the Rainbow Café to meet his dad and his mum, the latter of whom was more than generous with dollops of hot custard when it involved an order of her apple pie.

Kendra unpacked the carrier bags, which turned out to be holding takeaway curry. She said, 'Where's Ness?' and then called up the stairs, where the television sounds indicated cartoons were playing, 'Mr Toby Campbell? You get into this kitchen straightway. You hear?'

Joel shrugged, his answer to the whereabouts of Ness. She'd been around more often in the past few days, a brooding presence licking its wounds when she wasn't out and about with Six and Natasha. Joel didn't know where she'd taken herself off to. He hadn't seen her since yesterday evening.

'She knows what day this is, doesn't she?' Kendra asked.

'S'pose,' Joel said. 'I di'n't tell her. I ain't seen her.'

'Haven't,' Kendra said.

'I haven't seen her.' He added, 'Have you?' because he

couldn't help it. So much still the child, it seemed to him that, as the adult, Kendra could have done something about the problem that was Ness.

Kendra eyed him, and she read him as well as if he'd spoken. 'What?' she said. 'Tie her down? Lock her up in a room?' She removed plates from the cupboard and handed them to him, along with cutlery. He started to set the table. 'Time comes, Joel, when a person decides what her life's going to look like. Ness's decided.'

Joel said nothing because he couldn't articulate what he believed since *what* he believed rose from the history he shared with his sister as well as what he felt about her. What he felt was longing: for the Ness she had been. What he believed was that she missed who she'd been as much as he did, but had even less hope of getting her back.

Toby clattered down the stairs, his lava lamp under his arm. He set it in the middle of the table and extended its flex to plug it into a point. He climbed into a chair and rested his chin on his hands to watch the shining orange globules begin their rhythmic rising and falling.

Kendra said to him, 'Got your favourite here, Mr Campbell. *Naan* with raisins, almonds, and honey. You ready for that?'

Toby looked over at her, his eyes bright at the thought of the bread. Kendra smiled and took from her shoulder bag an envelope with three foreign stamps fixed to it. She handed this over to Toby, saying, 'Looks like your gran didn't forget your special day, either. This came all the way from Jamaica—' she made no mention of the fact that she'd phoned her mother three times about sending it and had herself included the five pound note Toby was going to find when he wrestled it open – 'so open it up and let's see what she says.'

Joel helped Toby ease the large card from its envelope. He scooped up the limp five pound note that fluttered to the floor. He said, 'Hey, lookit this, Tobe! Y'r rich,' but Toby was studying a Polaroid picture Glory had sent as well. In it, she and George stood with a string of strangers, arms slung around one another and bottles of Red Stripe hoisted in the air. Glory wore a halter top – not a wise choice for a woman her age –, a baseball cap with *Cardinals* written on it, shorts, and no shoes.

'Looks like she's found her niche,' Kendra said when she took the picture from Toby and gave it a look. 'Who're all these people? George's clan? And she sent you five pounds, Toby? Well, that was nice, wasn't it? What're you going to do with all that dosh?'

Toby smiled happily and fingered the note, which Joel handed to him. It was more money than he'd ever had at any one time in his entire life.

Ness joined them soon after that, right at the point when Joel was deciding what would do as a special plate that Toby could eat from on his special day. He'd settled for a tin tray painted with the face of Father Christmas, which he unearthed from beneath two pie tins and a baking dish. Dust grimed the edges, but a quick wash would remedy that.

Ness hadn't forgotten Toby's birthday either. She arrived bringing what she announced was a magic wand. It was made of clear plastic and filled with sparkles, which glowed brightly when someone shook it. She made no mention of where she'd got it, which was just as well since she'd pinched it from the very same shop in Portobello Road where Joel had purchased the lava lamp.

Toby grinned when Ness demonstrated how the magic wand worked. He said, 'Wicked.' He shook it happily. 'C'n I make a wish when it's shook?'

'You c'n do whatever you want,' Ness told him. 'It's your birthday innit.'

'And *since* it's his birthday,' Kendra said, 'I got something as well . . .' She disappeared up the stairs at a trot, returning with a long package that she handed to Toby. This he unwrapped to discover a snorkel and an underwater mask, perhaps as useless a gift as any child has ever received from a well-meaning relation. Kendra said helpfully, 'They go with your life-ring, Toby. Where is it anyway? Why've you not got it on?'

Joel and Toby hadn't told her, of course, about the day they'd had the confrontation with Neal Wyatt, the day on which the life-ring had taken its near fatal wound. Since that time, Joel had attempted a repair with glue, but it hadn't held well. Consequently, the life-ring was pretty much done for.

Things were not perfect, but no one dwelt on that since every one of them – including Ness – was determined to maintain an aura of good cheer. Toby himself didn't appear to notice everything that was missing from his celebration: the birthday sign, the tin carousel, and most of all the mother who'd given him birth.

The four of them tucked into the takeaway, revelling in everything from vegetable *jalfrezi* to onions *bhaji*. They drank lemonade, and they talked about what Toby could do with his birthday five pounds. All the time the lava lamp sat in the middle of the table, blurping and oozing with an eerie light.

They'd just got to the *naan* when someone banged on the front door. Three sharp raps were followed by a silence, two more raps and someone yelling, 'Give it *over*, cow. You hear me?' It was a man's voice, nasty with threat. Kendra looked up from tearing off a piece of *naan* for Toby. Joel gave his attention to the door. Toby gazed at the lava lamp. Ness kept her eyes fixed to her plate.

The banging on the door began again, more in earnest this time. Another shout accompanied it. 'Ness! You hear me? I say open or I kick this piece of shit door down wiv one foot, easy.' More banging ensued. 'Don't vex me, Ness. I break up your fucking head, you don't open when I say.'

This wasn't the sort of language that frightened Kendra Osborne. But it was the sort of language that fired the cylinders of her outrage. She began to get to her feet, saying, 'Who the hell is that? I won't have *anyone*—'

'I c'n get it.' Ness rose to stop Kendra.

'Not alone, you won't.' Kendra stalked to the door, Ness hard on her heels. Toby and Joel followed. Toby was chewing on his piece of *naan*, his eyes wide with curiosity, like someone believing that this was part of an unexpected birthday show.

'What the *hell* are you on about?' Kendra demanded as she swung open the door. 'What d'you mean, pounding on this door like a common—' Then she saw who it was, and the seeing stopped her from saying anything more. Instead, she looked from the Blade to Ness and then back to the Blade, who was dressed like a London banker but who, with a red beret covering his hairless head and a venom-spitting cobra tattooed on his cheek, would never have been mistaken for one.

Kendra knew who he was. She'd lived in North Kensington long enough to have heard about him. Even had this not been the case, Adair Street was no great distance from Edenham Way, and it was on Adair Street that the Blade's mother lived in a terrace house from which – according to gossip exchanged in the market in Golborne Road – she had evicted her eldest son when it became apparent to her that following in an older sibling's footsteps meant that her younger children would be treading one path or another which led without diversions to places like Pentonville or Dartmoor.

Kendra added everything up in the time it took her to digest the Blade's words, which was no time at all. She said to Ness, 'You've got some talking to do about this.'

In the meantime, the Blade pushed past her, uninvited and unwilling to wait for an invitation to enter, which he correctly assumed was not about to be issued. He was accompanied by Arissa, black miniskirt riding high on her thighs, black crop top plunging over her breasts, a pair of black boots soaring up her legs to her knees, the heels so high and so tapered they might have been considered lethal weapons. She was the perfect companion for this night's adventure, and her appearance at the Blade's side effected the result he'd wanted when he told her to accompany him.

Ness came forward. 'What d'you want, blood? I tol' you b'fore. I ain't having no more 'f what you got to offer, 'specially if it means I end up looking like this slag here.'

'Liked it fine last time you had it, though. Di'n't you, skank?' he asked her.

'Dat'd be summick you'd not likely notice.'

At this exchange, Arissa made a noise that could have been taken as amusement. The Blade shot her a look and her face went blank. She said, to him, 'C'mon, baby. We don't need vexing ourselves wiv dis.' She ran her hand down his arm to reach his fingers.

He shook her off. 'Fuck it, Arissa. We got business here.'

'You done y'r business wiv me,' Ness told him. 'It's over.'

'*You* don't tell *me* when t'ings's over, slag.'

'Oh, dat never happen before? No one else got the bot'le to walk away from you?'

'No one else dat stupid. I'm th' one dat say—'

'I am jus' shivering in my knickers, mon. Wha' you want anyway, bringin' dis slag to my house? 'M I s'posed to give her demonstration so she know how to give you what you want?'

'You don't know nothing 'bout what I want.'

Kendra put herself between them. The front door was still open – with Arissa standing well inside – and Kendra pointed to it. She said, 'I don't know what's gone on between you two, and I don't want to hear it just now. This is my house you're in –' this she directed at the Blade and his companion – 'and I'm telling you to leave. Not asking. Telling. Take yourselves back to whatever . . .' She hesitated and then made a wise correction since *cesspool you've crawled out of* was an expression she deemed likely to escalate matters. 'Take yourselves back to wherever you came from.'

'Best idea I heard in weeks.' Ness might have let things go

at that – indeed, she actually would have done so – had the Blade not come accompanied by Arissa and all that Arissa stood for. She couldn't let him leave without having the last word. She said with a smile that expressed a depth of insincerity and animosity that was more than evident to the others in the room, "Sides, now you an' crackbitch here c'n go do a grind. You c'n even take her up that deluxe establishment you got in Kilburn Lane an' go for it among the cockroaches, which I expect she'll like. Cos den she won't have to take notice dat you, blood, don't know more'n sticking it in and having it off when it comes to pleasing y'r partner. Like I—'

The Blade surged forward. He caught Ness's face on the jaw. He held her head in a grasp that dug into her skin. Before anyone else could move, he brought the side of his other fist into her temple. The strength behind the blow knocked Ness off her feet. The force of the fall left her out of breath.

Toby cried out. Joel pulled him away. Arissa sighed, 'Oh,' with pleasure fanning across her features.

Kendra moved. In an instant she'd shoved past Joel and Toby into the kitchen to get to the cooker. She kept her pots and pans inside the oven, and she snatched up a frying pan as a weapon. She dashed back across the room at the Blade.

'You get out of here, rabbit sucker,' she said. 'You aren't out 'f the door in the next five seconds, this pan'll be making acquaintance with your skull. And *you*,' to Arissa, who was grinning inanely at the unfolding scene, 'if this is the bes' you c'n do for a man, you're a sorrier sight than I'm looking at with my eyes.'

'Shut your ugly gob,' the Blade said to Kendra. He kicked Ness to one side. He faced Kendra down. 'Come on, den. You want t' distress me, cow? You jus' try. Come on. Come *on*. I ain't going nowhere, so you better come get me.'

'You scare me as much 's shit on a tissue,' Kendra told him. 'I been blowing off divs like you since you was in nappies. Now get out of here, *now*. You don't, you'll be trying your stuff on someone likely to serve your little prong on yesterday's toast. Y'unnerstan me, blood?'

The fact that the Blade understood Kendra perfectly was demonstrated in the very next moment. From his pocket, he brought out the flick knife that had long ago given him his sobriquet. It caught the light as it flashed open. He said to Kendra, 'Your tongue goes first,' and sprang towards her.

She hurled the frying pan at his head. The pan made contact just above his eye, splitting the skin. Arissa screamed. Toby wailed. The Blade went for Kendra who was now weaponless.

Ness grabbed the Blade's leg as Joel dashed from the kitchen, where he'd huddled in the doorway with Toby. Ness shrieked at him, 'Get summick, Joel!' and she sank her teeth into the meat of the Blade's calf. He slashed down at her. The knife sliced through her crinkly puff of hair. Ness cried out. Kendra leapt on to the Blade's back.

Joel scrambled around the brawling bodies, desperately trying to get to the only weapon he could see: the frying pan, which had skittered beneath a chair. As he did this, Kendra locked on to the Blade's slashing arm to keep him from striking at Ness again. Joel reached for the pan, but Arissa stopped him. She pulled him away. He slipped on the floor. He found himself inches from the Blade's left leg, so he did as his sister had done and bit deep. Ness was shrieking, both in pain and in fear, the blood from her scalp wound dripping down her face. Arissa was shouting and Toby was crying. The Blade grunted as he tried to dislodge Kendra. All of this whirled around the room, like suds in a washing machine.

But suddenly, there was another presence as a voice – loud and hot – came from the open front door. Someone yelled, 'What the bloody hell . . . !' and Dix was with them, Dix who was far stronger than the Blade, Dix who was taller than the Blade, Dix who saw that Kendra was in trouble and Ness was bleeding and Toby was weeping and Joel was doing his inadequate best to protect them all.

Dix flung his sports bag to the floor. He shoved Arissa to one side and threw a single punch. It snapped the Blade's head back like a dandelion puff and ended the fray in an instant. The Blade fell backwards, Kendra flew from his back, and both of them landed on the floor with Ness and Joel. The Blade's prized knife went soaring across the room and into the kitchen. It slid to a stop beneath the cooker.

Dix hauled the Blade to his feet, shouting, 'Ken, you all right? Ken? Ken!'

Kendra waved in reply and crawled over to Ness, coughing and saying, 'Too many damn fags,' and then to Ness, 'You all right, Ness? How bad're you cut?'

'You want the cops?' Dix asked her, his grip still firmly on the Blade who, like Ness, was bleeding copiously.

'He i'n't worth the cops,' was the answer. Ness gave it. She huddled in a ball, with Kendra hovering over her. 'He i'n't worth dog piss.'

'You a fucking slag, Ness.'

'Was when I did you. I should've took money for all th' good it did me.'

The Blade tried to get to her once again, but Dix had him in a grip that he couldn't break. He struggled and Dix said into his ear, 'Mess up your jacket nice, bred, you don't settle down.' He danced the other man towards the door and when he had him close enough, he flung him out on to the steps. The Blade lost his footing and tumbled, landing on one knee on the concrete path from the street. Arissa dashed to his side to help him up. He shook her off. During the scuffle, he'd lost his red beret, and the light from inside Kendra's house shone on his hairless pate. A few neighbours had come to stand outside, hearing the brawl. They faded into the shadows quickly when they saw who was in the midst of the fight.

'I'll have wha' I meant to have, y'unnerstan?' the Blade said, his breathing harsh. And then in a louder voice, 'You got me, Ness? I wan' dat phone.'

Inside, Ness staggered to her feet. She went to the kitchen where she'd hung her bag on the back of a chair. She grabbed the mobile phone from within and, at the door, she threw it at the Blade with all the force she could muster.

'Give it to her, den,' she shrieked. 'Maybe she pop 'nother kid for you. Den you drop her like poison and go t' the next. She know dat's what it all 'bout? You tell her dat? Put her up the chute but it ain't enough cos *nothing* make you big outside when your insides is so small.'

That said, she slammed the door and fell back against it, sobbing and hitting her face with her fists. Toby fled to the kitchen, where he hid under the table. Joel got to his feet and stood mute and helpless. Dix went to Kendra but Kendra went to Ness.

She spoke the question whose answer was a nightmare yet too frightening to articulate. 'Ness, Ness, what happened to you, baby?'

'I couldn't,' was all Ness said as she continued to weep and beat at her face. 'She could an' I *couldn't.*'

IO

Although Joel could hardly have been declared responsible for any of the events that had crashed down upon Toby's birthday celebration, he *felt* responsible. Toby's special evening had been ruined. Realising how little his brother asked of life, Joel determined to set out to make sure no birthday ever again would come to such an end.

The end was further chaos. Once Dix D'Court had dispatched the Blade, there was Ness to see to. The cut from the flick knife wasn't something that called for a simple plaster, so Kendra and Dix had rushed her off to the nearest casualty, using an old tea towel imprinted with the faded visage of the Princess of Wales to staunch the bleeding. This left Joel with the detritus of the meal and the detritus of the Blade's visit either to ignore or to contend with. He chose to contend with it: doing the washing up, setting the kitchen and the eating area back into order, carefully removing the *Happy Birthday* sign from the kitchen window, stowing the postage stamps in a container by the toaster, which was where he'd found them. He wanted to make up for what had happened in the house, and he felt a real urgency to do so as he set about his work. In the meantime, Toby sat at the table with his chin on his fists, watching his lava lamp and breathing through his new snorkel. Toby made no mention of what had happened. He'd taken himself into Sose.

Once Joel had the bottom floor of the house tidy, he took Toby upstairs. There, he supervised his bath – which Toby rightfully saw as a first opportunity to use his mask and snorkel

– and he set his brother down to watch the television afterwards. Both boys finally fell asleep on the sofa and did not awaken till their aunt returned with Ness. Even then it was only a shake on their shoulders that roused Joel and Toby. Ness, said Kendra, was upstairs and in bed. Her head was bandaged – the cut requiring ten stitches – but they could see her before they went to sleep if they wanted, so that they would know she was all right.

Ness was in Kendra's room with her head done up in white, like a Sikh's turban. She was wearing so many bandages that she looked like a patient after brain surgery, but Kendra told them that the turban was more a fashion statement than anything else. They'd had to shave part of her head to get to the cut, she said, and Ness had begged them to cover the resulting bare spot.

She wasn't asleep, but she also wasn't talking. Joel knew the wisdom of letting her be, so he told her he was glad she was okay. He approached her and awkwardly patted her shoulder. She looked at him but not as if she actually saw him. She didn't look at Toby at all.

That response reminded Joel of their mother and caused him to feel even more the necessity of making things better, which to him meant returning life to what it once had been for all of them. The fact that this was impossible – given their father's death and their mother's condition – only made the urgency of doing something that much more intense. Joel floundered around trying to come up with an appropriate anodyne. As a young boy with limited resources and only an imperfect understanding of what was going on in his family, he set upon the replacement of their Happy Birthday sign as an activity designed to please.

Joel conducted his search for the sign in three locations. He began in Portobello Road. Having no luck there, he continued in Golborne Road without success. He finally ended up in the Harrow Road, where there was a small Ryman's.

But it, too, offered nothing like the sign he was looking for, and it was only when he went along in the direction of Kensal Rise that he came to one of those London shops where one can find everything from phone cards to steam irons. He entered.

What he found was a plastic banner. It read *It's a Boy!* and it featured a helmet-wearing stork on a motorcycle, a nappied bundle in its beak. Dispirited at not having unearthed what he wanted, despite trudging the length of three thoroughfares in his search, Joel decided to buy the banner. He took it to the till and handed over the money. But he felt defeated by the entire enterprise.

On his way out of the shop, he saw a small poster, a bright orange paper with an advertisement on it, not dissimilar to the sort of announcement he'd taken around North Kensington for his aunt's massage business. The colour of the handout made it difficult to ignore. Joel paused to read it.

What he saw was an advertisement for a script-writing course at Paddington Arts, and there was certainly nothing unusual about this since Paddington Arts – supported in part by lottery money – had been designed to stimulate just this sort of creative activity in North Kensington. What *was* unusual, however, was the name of the instructor. *I. Weatherall* was printed beneath the title of the course, after the words *Offered by.*

It didn't seem possible that there could be more than one I. Weatherall in the area. To make certain, however, Joel dug around in his rucksack and found the card that Ivan had handed to him on the day he'd broken up the scuffle with Neal. There was a phone number on the bottom of the card, and it matched the number that followed the words *For Questions And For Further Information Please Ring* on the orange hand-out.

Ivan Weatherall lived in Sixth Avenue, a fact that Joel recalled when he looked at the card. He himself was that moment near the corner of Third. That coincidence was enough to prompt Joel into his next move.

Logic suggested that the street in question would be just a bit farther along from Third Avenue but, when Joel set off to find it, he discovered that this was not the case. Five streets separated Third from Sixth, and when Joel got there, he found a neighbourhood of terrace houses quite unlike any he'd seen since coming to live with his aunt. In contrast to the looming estates that comprised so much of North Kensington, these houses – curious remnants of the nineteenth century – were small, neat structures of only two floors, and most of them had stones imprinted with *1880* sunk into the lintels of their tiny, gabled porches. The buildings themselves were identical, differentiated from one another by their numbers, by what hung in their windows, and by their front doors and miniature gardens. No 32 had the additional feature of a trellis attached to the wall between the front door and what would be the sitting-room window. On this trellis, four of the Seven Dwarfs were climbing to reach a Snow White who sat at the apex of the woodwork. There was no actual front garden to speak of. Rather, a rectangle of paving stones held a bicycle chained to an iron railing, which surmounted a low brick wall. This wall ran along the pavement, marking the boundary of the tiny property.

Joel hesitated. All at once, it seemed absurd that he had come looking for this house. He had no idea what he would say if he knocked on the door and found Ivan Weatherall at home. It was true that he'd continued to meet with the mentor at school, but their meetings had been professional in nature, all about school itself and help with homework, with Ivan throwing in the occasional attempt at a probing life question and with Joel parrying that question as best he could. Thus, aside from 'Any further problems with Neal, my lad?' which Joel had answered truthfully with, 'Nah,' nothing personal had passed between them.

After a moment of staring at the front door and trying to decide what to do, Joel made up his mind. What his mind told him was that he really needed to get back to Toby. Joel had left him at the learning centre for his regular session, and he'd be expected there to fetch him home soon enough. He hardly had time, therefore, to pay a visit to Ivan Weatherall. It would be best to be on his way.

He turned to go, but the front door opened suddenly, and there was Ivan Weatherall himself, peering out. Without preamble, he said, 'What a godsend, quite as if I'd knelt in prayer. Come in, come in. Another pair of hands is needed.' He disappeared back inside the house, leaving the door standing open in confident expectation.

Outside, Joel shuffled his feet, trying to make up his mind. Put to the test, he couldn't have said exactly why he'd come to Sixth Avenue. But since he had come and since he knew Ivan from school and since all he had to show for his efforts on this day was a pathetic sign that announced *It's a Boy* . . . He went inside the little house.

Directly within, there was a tiny vestibule, where a red bucket lettered with the word *Sand* held four furled umbrellas and a walking stick. Above it, the smallish head of a wooden elephant with its trunk curled upward served as a coat hook and from the animal's single tusk hung a set of keys.

Joel eased the door closed and was immediately aware of two sensations: the scent of fresh mint and the pleasant ticking of clocks. He was in a place of regimentally organised clutter. Aside from the elephant, the walls of the tiny vestibule held a collection of small black and white photographs of antique vintage, but not a single one was askew in that way framed pictures become when they get knocked about by the inhabitants of a house. Beneath them on one side of the vestibule and extending into the shoe-box size sitting-room that opened off it, bookshelves acted the part of wainscoting and they held volumes that filled them to bursting. But all the books were

arranged neatly, with their unbroken spines facing outward
and right side up. Above these bookshelves, more than a dozen
clocks hung, the source of the ticking. Joel found it soothing.

'Come along. Step in.' Ivan Weatherall spoke from a table
that had been pressed into the bay window of the sitting-room,
which explained to Joel how he'd been seen hesitating at the
front of the house. He joined Ivan and saw that within the
small space of the room the man had managed to fashion a
study, a workshop, and a music room. At this moment, he was
using the space in workshop mode: he was attempting to empty
a large cardboard box into which something was packed tightly
in a block of Styrofoam.

'You've appeared at just the right moment,' Ivan told him.
'Give me a hand, please. I'm having the devil of a time getting
this out. It was, I assume, packed by sadists who even as I
speak are having a wonderful laugh at the thought of my impotent struggles. Well, I shall have the last laugh now. Come along,
Joel. Even in my own demesne, you shall find I don't bite.'

Joel approached him. As he did, the scent of mint grew
stronger, and he saw that Ivan was chewing it. It wasn't gum,
but actual mint. There was a shallow bowl of leafy sprigs at
one side of the table, and Ivan dipped into it for a stem, which
he held in his lips like a cigarette as Joel joined him.

'It appears we shall have to dance this out. If you'll be so
good as to hold the box down, I believe I can manage to jiggle
everything else loose.'

Joel did as he was asked, setting the *It's a Boy* banner on
the floor and going to Ivan's assistance. As Ivan jiggled, Joel
said, 'Wha's in here, anyway?'

'A clock.'

Joel glanced round at the time-pieces that already showed
the hour of the day – and sometimes the day itself – in numbers
large, numbers small, and numbers not at all. He said, 'What
d'you need wiv another one, then?'

Ivan followed his gaze. 'Ah. Yes. Well, it's not about telling time, if that's what you mean. It's about the adventure. It's about the delicacy, balance, and patience required to see a project through, no matter how complicated it looks. I build them, in other words. I find it relaxing. Something to think about rather than thinking about—' he smiled – 'what I would otherwise think about. And beyond that, I find the process a microcosm of the human condition.'

Joel frowned. He'd never heard anyone speak as Ivan spoke, even Kendra when she was Lady Muck. He said, 'What're you on about anyways?'

Ivan didn't reply until they had the block of Styrofoam released. He lifted the top piece off the lower three-quarters of it, and he gently laid this to one side. 'I'm on about delicacy, balance, and patience. Just as I said. The communion one has with others, the duty one must fulfil to self, and the commitment required to attain one's goals.'

He peered into the Styrofoam container, which Joel could now see held plastic packets bearing single large letters, along with small cardboard cartons with labels affixed to them. Ivan began to lift these out and he laid them lovingly on the table, along with a pamphlet that appeared to be a set of instructions. Last to come out was a packet from which Ivan drew a pair of thin white gloves. He laid these gently on his knee and twisted in his chair to go through a wooden box sitting at one side of the table. From this he unearthed a second pair of gloves, and these he passed to Joel. 'You'll be needing them,' he said. 'We can't touch the brass or we'll mark it with our fingerprints and that will be the end of it.'

Joel obediently put on the gloves as Ivan opened the pamphlet, spread it on the table, and pulled an ancient pair of wire spectacles from the breast pocket of his tattersall shirt. He looped the wires over his ears and then ran his finger down the first page of the pamphlet till he found what he wanted. He donned his own pair of white gloves and said, 'The inventory first. Crucial, you know. Others might foolishly forge ahead without making certain they have everything they need. We, however, shall not be so foolhardy as to assume we're in possession of all items necessary for completion of this journey. Let's have the bag marked A. Don't tear it, though. We shall be putting everything back inside once we've made certain all its contents are accounted for.'

Thus the two of them set to work, comparing what had been sent to what was on the list. They ticked off every screw and minuscule bolt, every gear, every column, and each piece of brass. As they did so, Ivan chatted away about time-pieces, explaining the origin of his love affair with clocks. Upon the conclusion of this expatiation, he said suddenly, 'What brings you to Sixth Avenue, Joel?'

Joel went for the easiest reply. 'Saw the advert.'

Ivan raised an eyebrow in need of trimming. 'Which would be . . . ?'

'The one for the script class. At Paddington Arts. Dat's you teaching it, innit?'

Ivan looked pleased. 'Indeed. Are you going to enrol? Have you come to ask me about it? Age is no object, if that concerns you. We always engage in a collaborative effort, from which will emerge the film itself.'

'What? You make a *real* film?'

'Yes indeed. I did tell you I once produced films, yes? Well, this is where every film begins: with a script. I've found that the more minds that engage in the process, the better the process in its initial stages. Later on as we begin to edit and polish, someone emerges as the strongest voice. Does this interest you?'

'I was getting a sign f'r birthdays,' Joel said. 'Down the Harrow Road.'

'Oh. I see. Don't fancy a career in film, then? Well, I suppose I can hardly blame you, modern films being mostly blue screens, miniatures, car chases, and explosions. Hitchcock, I tell you, Joel, is spinning in his grave. Not to *mention* what

Cecil B. de Mille is doing. So what do you have in store for yourself? Rock 'n' roll singer? Footballer? Lord Chief Justice? Scientist? Banker?'

Joel got to his feet abruptly. While other elements of the conversation might have been tough for him, he *did* know when someone was having a laugh at his expense, even if that person was not actually laughing. He said, 'I'm off, man.' He took off the gloves and picked up his banner.

'Good heavens!' Ivan jumped to his feet. 'What's wrong? Have I said . . . ? See here, I can see I've offended you in some way, but rest assured I had no intention . . . Oh. I do think I know. You've assumed . . . I say, Joel, have you assumed I was taking the mickey? But why should you not be Lord Chief Justice or Prime Minister if that's what you prefer? Why shouldn't you be an astronaut or a neurosurgeon if that's your interest?'

Joel hesitated, gauging the words, their tone, and Ivan's expression. The man stood with his hand extended, white-gloved like Mickey Mouse.

Ivan said, 'Joel. Perhaps you ought to tell me.'

Joel felt a chill. 'What?'

'Most people do find me as harmless as a box of cotton wool. I do natter on sometimes without thinking exactly how I sound. But, good Lord, you know that by now, don't you? And if we're to become friends instead of acting out the roles assigned to us at Holland Park School – and by this I mean mentor and pupil – then it seems that as friends—'

'Who says friends?' Joel felt laughed at again. He ought to have felt cautious as well, with a grown man talking about friendship between them. But he didn't feel cautious, just confused. And even then it was a confusion born of the novelty of the situation. No adult had ever asked him for friendship, if that was what Ivan was indeed doing.

'No one, actually,' Ivan said. 'But why shouldn't we be friends if that's what we mutually decide and want? Can one actually *have* enough friends when it comes down to it? I don't think so. As far as I'm concerned, if I share with someone an interest, an enthusiasm, a particular way of looking at life . . . whatever it is . . . that makes that person a kindred soul no matter who he is. Or she, for that matter. Or even *what*, because frankly, there are insects, birds, and animals with whom I have more in common sometimes than with people.'

At this Joel smiled, taken by the image of Ivan Weatherall in communion with a flock of birds. He lowered the banner to his side. He heard himself saying what he'd never expected even to whisper to another living soul. 'Psychiatrist.'

Ivan nodded thoughtfully. 'Noble work. The analysis and reconstitution of the suffering mind. Assisted brain chemistry. I'm impressed. How did you settle on psychiatry?' He returned to his seat and gestured Joel back to his side to continue their inventory of parts for the clock.

Joel didn't move. There were some things that didn't bear speaking of, even now. But he decided to try, at least in part. He said, 'Toby's birthday was las' week. When it was someone's birthday, we used to . . .' He felt a sting in his eyes, the way they would feel if smoke were seeping beneath his closed lids from someone's cigarette. But there was no cigarette languishing in an ashtray in this room. There was only Ivan, and he was reaching for another sprig of mint, which he rolled between his fingers and popped into his mouth. He kept his gaze fixed on Joel, though, and Joel continued because it felt as if the words were actually being *drawn* from him, not as if he were truly speaking. 'Dad sang on birthdays, innit. But he couldn't sing, not really, and we always had a laugh 'bout that. He had dis mad ukulele – yellow plastic, it was – an' he pretend he knew how to play. "Takin' requests now, boys and girls," he'd say. If Mum was there, she'd ask for an Elvis. An' dad say, "'Dat ol' bag, Caro? You outta step wiv the times, woman.'" But he sing it anyways. He sing so bad, it'd make your ears hurt an' everyone'd shout at him to stop.'

Ivan sat still, one hand on the pamphlet they'd been using for the inventory and the other on his thigh. 'And then?'

'He'd stop. Bring the presents in instead. I got a football once. Ness got a Ken doll.'

'Not then.' Ivan's words sounded kind. 'I meant later. I know you don't live with your parents. The school told me that, of course. But I don't know why. What happened to them?'

This was no man's land. Joel made no reply. But for the first time, he wanted to. Yet to speak was to violate a family taboo: no one talked about it; no one could cope with saying the words.

Joel tried. 'Cops said he went to the off licence. Mum told 'em no cos he was cured. He wa'n't using any more, she said. He wasn't using nuffink. He was jus' fetching Ness from her dancing lesson like he always did. 'Sides, he had me an' Toby wiv him. How'd they t'ink he meant to use if he had me an' Toby wiv him?'

But that was all he could manage. The rest of it . . . It was too sore a place. Even thinking about it hurt at a level no palliative could ever reach.

Ivan was watching him. But now Joel didn't want to be watched. There was only one option he could see at this point. Taking his banner with him, he hurried from the house.

In the aftermath of the Blade's descent upon Edenham Way, Dix made his decision. And he communicated it to Kendra in a way that brooked neither refusal nor argument. He was moving in, he informed her. He wasn't going to let her live on her own – even in the company of three children and perhaps *because* of the company of those particular three children – while some lout like the Blade was intent upon sorting them out in a fashion anyone could easily guess at. Besides, whatever the Blade's intentions had been on the night of his visit to Kendra and the Campbells, those intentions would now be fortified by the treatment he'd received at Dix's hands. And make no mistake about it, Dix told Kendra when she attempted to protest his plans, the Blade wasn't going to target Dix for payback. That was not the way his type sought revenge. Instead, he was going to go after one of the other members of the household. Dix meant to be there to stop him.

He didn't mention the fact that, by moving in, he'd be one step closer to getting what he wanted, which was a sense of permanency with Kendra. He couched the rest of his explanation in terms of his own need to get away from the Falcon, where living with two body-building flatmates had long since constituted swimming in an excess of testosterone. To his parents (who, it must be said, were not entirely delighted with his connection to a woman closer to their own age than to his) he merely said that this was something he had to do. They had little choice but to accept his decision. They could see that Kendra was not an ordinary sort of woman – and this they decided was to her credit – but still they'd always had their own dreams about what sort of life their son ought to be leading, and that life had never contained a forty-year-old woman responsible for three children. Aside from their initial murmurs of caution, however, they kept their reservations to themselves.

Joel and Toby were happy to have Dix join their household, for to them he was something of a god. Not only had he appeared out of nowhere and saved the day in the fashion of a cinematic action hero, but he was also in their eyes perfect in all ways. He talked to them as if they were equals, he clearly adored their aunt – which was a plus as they were becoming fond of her too – and if he was perhaps rather *too* single-minded on the subject of bodily perfection in general, and *his* bodily perfection in particular, that was easy enough to ignore because of the security his presence brought them.

The only problem was Ness. It soon became apparent that, as drunk as she had been on the occasion, she didn't remember Dix as the man who'd delivered her from a nasty fate at the

Falcon. She simply bore no liking for him despite his timely arrival during the Blade's attack upon her. There were several reasons for this, although she was prepared to admit to none of them.

The most obvious was her displacement. Since coming to North Kensington from East Acton, she'd shared Kendra's bed on the nights when she'd actually slept at home, and upon Dix's arrival she found herself removed from her aunt's bedroom and stationed on the sofa instead. The fact that Dix built a screen to give her privacy did not ameliorate her feelings in the matter, and these feelings were aggravated by the knowledge that Dix – a mere eight years older than she and a breathtaking specimen of man flesh – was markedly indifferent to her presence and instead besotted with her aunt. She felt like a rack of cold toast in his presence, and she translated what she felt into a renewal of surliness towards her family and a renewal of friendship with Six and Natasha.

This perplexed Kendra, who'd mistakenly assumed that Ness would be a changed young woman after the Blade's attack upon her, seeing the error of her previous ways and grateful that a man's protection was now available to all of them. In frustration at Ness's continued churlishness, she pointed out to her niece that it was down to her, anyway, that Dix D'Court was moving in with them. Had she not involved herself with the Blade, she wouldn't have found herself in the position she now was in: on the sofa at night, in the sitting-room, behind a collapsible screen.

This fruitless – albeit understandable – approach to dealing with Ness possessed the unmistakable potential to make the situation worse. Dix pointed this out to Kendra privately, telling her to go easier on the girl. If Ness didn't want to speak to him, fine. If she stalked out of the room when he came into it, fine as well. If she used his razor, dropped his body lotion in the toilet, and poured his one hundred per cent organic juices down the kitchen sink, let her. For now. Time would come when she realised that none of this was changing reality. She would have to choose a different course, then. They needed to be ready and willing to provide her with one so that she didn't choose a course that would take her into more trouble.

To Kendra, this was an overly sanguine way of looking at the problem of Ness. The girl had brought nothing but ever-increasing difficulty into Kendra's life from the moment of her arrival, and something had to be done about her. Kendra could not, however, come up with anything beyond giving orders and making threats, most of which – out of duty to her brother, Ness's father – she lacked the courage to carry out.

'You keep 'specting her to be like you,' was Dix's maddeningly reasonable assessment of the situation when he and Kendra discussed it. 'You get past that, you got a chance of 'cepting her for what she is.'

'What she is is a tart,' Kendra told him. 'A truant, a layabout, and a slag.'

'You don't mean dat,' Dix replied, laying a finger across her lips and smiling down at her. It was late. They were drowsy from their lovemaking and readying themselves for sleep. 'Dat's your frustration talking. Just like hers is talking as well. You letting her vex you 'stead of looking at the why of what she's doing.'

Mostly, they circled each other, wary as cats. Kendra walked into a room; Ness flounced out of it. Kendra assigned a chore for the girl; Ness did it only when the request became the demand and the demand became the threat and even then she did it as badly as possible. She was monosyllabic, angry, and sarcastic when what Kendra expected of her was gratitude. Not gratitude for the roof over her head – which even Kendra knew was too much to ask for, considering how it had come to pass that Ness and her brothers were living in Edenham Way – but gratitude at least for the deliverance from the Blade as effected by Dix. The second time, in fact, that Dix had delivered her from trouble, a truth that Kendra pointed out to her.

'He was *dat* bloke?' Ness responded to this news. 'From the Falcon? No way.' But after learning this, Ness eyed him differently and in a manner that would have caused concern in a woman less sure of herself than Kendra.

'Yes way,' was Kendra's reply. 'How drunk *were* you, girl, that you don't remember?'

'Too drunk to study up on his *face*,' she said. 'But wha' I *do* remember . . .' She smiled and rolled her eyes expressively. 'My, my, my, Ken*dra*. Ain't you one lucky slag.'

Her remark was a small pebble thrown into a large pond, but the ripples still made their way outward. Kendra tried to avoid attending to them. She told herself that Ness, in her present state, liked to mess with minds and didn't care how she did it.

Still, she couldn't avoid a reaction deep within her, one that eventually prompted her to say to Dix as a way of approaching the topic obliquely, 'Blood, what're you doing loving on this middle-aged body of mine? You don't like girl flesh? Is that what it is? Your age, I'd think you'd want someone young.'

'Y'are young,' he said promptly, a gratifying response. But he went on with an intuitive question. 'Wha's dis really about, Ken?'

That maddened Kendra: Dix's seeing through her indirections. She said, 'It's about nothing.'

He said, 'Don't think so.'

'All right, then. You mean me to think you don't look at girls? Young women? Down the pub, at the gym, sunning themselves in the park?'

'Course I look. Ain't a robot.'

'And when Ness walks round here with half her clothes off? You take note of that?'

'Like I said, Ken. Wha's dis really about?'

Pressed to it, however, Kendra couldn't bring herself to say more. More would have indicated a lack of trust, a lack of confidence, and a lack of esteem. Not esteem for herself but esteem for him. To take her mind off what Ness clearly wanted her mind on, Kendra redoubled her efforts to increase her list of clients for massage, telling herself that everything else was secondary to the future that she was trying to build.

She hadn't intended that future to include the Campbells, though, and as Ness continued to demonstrate how unpleasant life with an adolescent girl could be, Kendra understandably gave thought to ways in which life with an adolescent girl could be brought to an end. She considered the possibility that their mother might re-enter their world and take them off her hands. She even visited Carole Campbell privately to assess whether her maternal instincts – such as they were – might be reawakened. But Carole, having 'a faraway day' as her lapse into a fugue state was called, was mute on the subject of Ness and Joel. Toby, Kendra knew, was a topic best left unmentioned.

The fact that Dix wasn't bothered by the presence of the Campbells – and particularly by Ness – increased Kendra's sense of guilt about her own feelings. She told herself that she was 'good God, their *aunt* for heaven's sake' and she tried to shake the general sense of uneasiness that had her waiting endlessly for the worst.

As for Ness, she knew that her aunt was wary and, powerless for so long, she enjoyed the feeling of supremacy she was able to experience simply by being in the same room with her aunt and Dix D'Court. For Kendra had begun to study her like a microscopic specimen on a slide and, reading her aunt's suspicions as jealousy, Ness couldn't help trying to give her something to be jealous about.

This required Dix's cooperation. Since, to Ness, he was a man like all men – governed by base desires – she set out to seduce him. There was nothing subtle in her approach.

He was standing at the kitchen sink when she went up to him. He'd made himself one of his protein-packed juice drinks, and he was powering it down. His back was to her. They were alone in the house.

She murmured, 'Ken's got *all* the luck. You, blood, are one fine man.'

He turned to her, surprised because he thought she'd left the house. He had things to do – primary among them his daily work-out – and having a tête-à-tête with his woman's niece wasn't among them. Besides, he'd seen the way Ness had started looking at him, assessing and deciding, and he had a fairly good idea of where a private colloquy with her might lead. He drank down the rest of his smoothie and turned to rinse out the glass.

Ness joined him at the sink. She put her hand on his shoulder and ran it down his arm. It was bare, as was his chest. Ness turned his wrist and traced his vein. Her touch was light, her hands were soft, and there was no mistaking her intentions.

He was human and if he thought fleetingly of returning her touch and if his eyes dropped even more fleetingly to the rich dark nipples that, braless, pressed against her thin white T-shirt, it was owing to this humanity. Pure biology worked in him for a moment, but he mastered it.

He removed Ness's hand from his body. He said, 'Good way to get into trouble, innit.'

She caught his hand, pressed it to her waist and held it there. She fixed her eyes on his and raised his hand slowly till she had it at the swell of her breast. 'Why she got all the luck?' she repeated. ''Specially when I saw you first. Come on, mon. I know you wan' it. I know *how* you wan' it. An' I know you wan' it from me.'

Biology again and he felt himself heating in spite of his wishes. But this prompted him to jerk away from her. He said, 'You reading t'ings wrong, Ness. Dat, or you making 'em up.'

'Oh right. You was bein' *noble* at the Falcon dat night, Dix? You telling me dat? You saying you don' *remember* just before you drove me home? We got to your car. You put me inside. You make *sure* I got dat seatbelt fastened. "Here, lemme help you, lit'le lady. Lemme draw it 'cross you, make sure you're *snug.*"'

Dix held up a hand to stop her words. 'Don't go dat way,' he told her.

'What way? Way of you grazing your fingers 'cross me like you want to do now? Way of your hand sliding up my leg, high as you can, till you find what you want? Which way is it you don't want me to go?'

He narrowed his eyes. His nostrils flared when he breathed, and he took in her scent. Kendra was sexy, but this girl was sex. She was raw, she was present, and she scared him to death. He said, 'You a liar as well as a slag, den, Ness? Keep away from me. I mean it, y'unnerstan.'

He pushed past her and left the kitchen. What he left behind was the sound of her laugh. A single note of it, high and possessing neither heart nor amusement. It felt like a scalpel peeling back his flesh.

Ness was not of an age to understand what she felt. All she knew about what was going on inside her was that she was roiling. To her, this roiling was a thing demanding action, for action is always easier than thought.

Her opportunity for taking an action to express herself came soon enough. She'd imagined the action being sexual: herself and Dix entwined hotly in such a manner and in such a place that discovery by Kendra was guaranteed. But that was not how her life played out. Instead, Six and Natasha supplied the opportunity for expression, which came about because two circumstances, to which none of them were strangers, occurred simultaneously: lack of cash collided with a desire for substance on an evening when the girls had nothing to do.

This should have presented no problem. Following hand jobs, blow jobs, full penetration, or whatever else they had negotiated for, the area's bicycle delivery boys had always been happy to hand over to the girls payment in the form of cocaine, cannabis, Ecstasy, crystal meth . . . the beauty for them being that the girls weren't choosy about substance. But lately, the situation had altered. The source of dope had begun watching the boys more carefully because a wary customer along the line had complained about someone skimming. Thus, the well had run dry and no number of sexual favours appeared to be able to prime it.

There was no question that the girls needed money. But they had nothing to sell, and the idea of actually seeking employment – had any of them been employable, which they were not – didn't occur to them. They were of the instant gratification generation anyway, so they thrashed around through their options in order to decide how best to come up with cash. There seemed to be two possibilities: they could sell sexual favours to someone other than the delivery boys or they could nick the money. They chose the latter option, as it seemed quicker, and it left them with merely deciding from whom they should lift what they needed. Here again, there were further choices: they could nick money from Six's mother's purse; they could nick it from someone using a cash point machine; they could nick it from someone defenceless in the street.

Since Six's mother was rarely around, neither was her bag and she had no cache of cash in the flat that Six knew about, so that eliminated her as a possibility. The cash point machine sounded quite good until Tash, of all people, pointed out that most machines had CCTV cameras mounted nearby and the last thing they wanted was to have their faces photographed in the midst of mugging someone using the machine. That left them with a confrontation in the street. This was agreed to, and all that remained was selecting the area in which to carry out the operation and selecting the appropriate victim.

The three estates in which the girls lived were rejected at once. So were Great Western Road, Kilburn Lane, Golborne Road and the Harrow Road. These, they decided were far too crowded and a person mugged would likely send up a cry that would get them noticed if not get them stopped. They settled on an estate directly across from the Harrow Road police station. While others might have rejected this as a ludicrous spot in which to mug a London citizen, the girls liked it for two reasons: it had a locked entry gate, which would foster a false sense of security in their potential victim; and it was so close to the police station that no one would expect to be mugged there. It was, the girls decided, sheer brilliance on their part to make the estate their selection.

Getting on to the estate proved no problem. They merely hung around three wheelie bins near the gate and waited until an unwary elderly woman approached, toddling along with a shopping trolley in tow. Tash dashed forward to hold the gate open for her once she had it unlocked, saying, 'Lemme help you wiv dis, ma'am,' and the woman was so surprised to be spoken to and dealt with politely that she had no suspicions when Tash followed her inside and gestured for Six and Ness to do likewise.

Six shook her head to indicate that they'd let the woman go on her way. A pensioner, she'd be unlikely to have enough cash on her for what they wanted and, anyway, Six drew the line at mugging defenceless old ladies. They reminded her of her own gran and not mugging them was a form of deal-making with fate, guaranteeing that her gran would remain unmolested on her own estate.

So the girls began to prowl up and down the paths, watching and waiting. Neither operation took long. They hadn't been inside the walls ten minutes when they saw their target. A woman came out of one of the terrace houses and set off towards the Harrow Road, foolishly – and in direct defiance of everything the police recommended – taking a mobile phone from her handbag.

She seemed a godsend as she punched in a few numbers, oblivious of what was going on around her. Even if she had no cash, she had a mobile, and nothing had changed in the lives of Six and Natasha heretofore, so possession of a mobile phone still represented the apex of their dreams.

Three of them and one of her: the odds seemed excellent. All it would take was two girls in front of her and one behind. A confrontation without violence but with the threat of bodily harm omnipresent. Looking tough because they *were* tough. What's more, she was white and they were black. She was middle-aged and they were young. It was, in short, a match made in heaven, and the girls had no hesitation about going forward.

Six led the way. She and Tash would confront. Ness would be surprise back-up behind the lady.

'Patty? This is Sue,' the woman was saying into her mobile. 'Could you unlock the door for me? I'm running late, and the students aren't likely to wait more than ten minutes if . . .' She saw Tash and Six in front of her. She stopped on the path. From behind, Ness clamped a hand on her shoulder. The woman stiffened.

'Le's have the mobile, bitch,' Six said. She closed in quickly. Tash did the same.

'Le's have the purse 's well,' Tash said.

Sue's face was white to her lips, although the girls had no way of knowing this was her natural colour. She said, 'I don't know you girls, do I?'

'Well, ain't that true,' Six said. 'Give us the phone an' do it now. You don't, you get cut.'

'Oh yes, oh of course. Just . . .' Sue said into the phone, 'Listen, Patty, I'm being mugged. If you wouldn't mind ringing—'

Ness shoved her forward. Six shoved her back. Tash said, 'Don't play games wiv us, cunt.'

The woman, appearing flustered, said, 'Yes. Yes. I'm terribly sorry. I just . . . Here. Let me . . . My money's inside . . .' And she fumbled round to reach into her bag, which had straps and buckles all over it. She dropped it and the mobile to the ground. Six and Tash bent to get them. And in an instant the complexion of the mugging altered.

From her pocket the woman whipped out a small can, which she began spraying wildly at the girls. It was nothing more than a strong room freshener, but it did the trick. As Sue sprayed and began screaming for help, the girls fell back.

'I'm not afraid of you! I'm not afraid of anyone! You rotten little . . .' Sue shrieked and shrieked. And to prove whatever point she was attempting to make, she grabbed the girl nearest her and sprayed her directly in the face. This was Ness, who doubled over just as lights went on in nearby porches, and residents began opening their doors and blowing whistles. It was a neighbourhood watch from hell.

All this was enough for Six and Natasha, who took off in the direction of the gate. The mobile and the bag they left behind, along with Ness. Since she was already incapacitated by the spray, she was easy for Sue to deal with, and this she did summarily. She threw her to the ground and sat upon her. She reached for her phone and punched in three nines.

'Three girls have just attempted to mug me,' she said into the phone to the police after the emergency operator put her through to them. 'Two of them are heading west on the Harrow Road. The third I'm sitting on . . . No, no, I have no idea . . . Listen to me, I suggest you send someone straightaway because I don't intend to let this one go, and I won't answer for her condition if I have to spray her in the face again . . . I'm directly across the street from the Harrow Road station, you absolute ninny. You can send the janitor for all I care.'

11

Thus did Ness Campbell end up meeting her social worker. How it happened followed the rule of law. The police – in the person of a female constable with sturdy shoes and bad hair – arrived to assist Sue, who continued to sit upon Ness and occasionally spray her in the face with the room freshener. This same constable made short work of hauling Ness to her feet in the presence of the gathered estate neighbours who, mercifully and finally, stopped blowing their whistles. They formed a jeering gauntlet – from which exercise they could not be dissuaded by the constable – and Ness found herself being frog-marched through it. She was relieved when she was away from the place. She was less relieved to be inside the Harrow Road police station, where the female constable dumped her in an interview room and left her there with her eyes still running from the spray. She was shaken as well, but that was not something Ness would ever admit to.

The police knew they could not speak to Ness without a non-police adult present to monitor the conversation. Ness not being forthcoming about the responsible adult in her life, the only recourse for the Harrow Road station was to phone the Youth Offending Team. A social worker was dispatched: Fabia Bender, the very same social worker who'd been trying to contact Kendra Osborne about her for weeks.

Fabia Bender's job in this situation was not herself to question Ness. The girl wasn't in the clutches of the police because she had failed to attend school, which was the reason behind the Youth Offending Team's previous interest in her. In this situation, the social worker's job was to act as a buffer between the police and the arrested juvenile. Acting as buffer meant seeing that the rights of the juvenile being questioned were not violated.

Since Ness had been caught red-handed in an attempted mugging, the only questions the police had were to ask for the names of her accomplices in the crime. But Ness turned away instead of giving up Six and Natasha. When the policeman – his name was Sergeant Starr – asked her if she understood that she would take the fall alone should she not name her mates, Ness said, 'Whatever. Like I ackshully care,' and told him that she wanted a fag. Fabia Bender she ignored altogether. She was a white woman. The cop, at least, was black.

Sergeant Starr said, 'No cigarettes.'

Ness said, 'Whatever,' and dropped her head on to her arms, crossed on the table. They were in a room designed to be uncomfortable. The table was bolted to the floor, the chairs were bolted to the floor, the lights were blinding, and the heat was tropical. The arrested party was meant to think that cooperation in the matter of being questioned would at least get him – or her, in this case – into a more comfortable environment. That, of course, was a fairy tale only an idiot would believe.

Sergeant Starr said, 'Y'unnerstan you're facing the magistrate on this?'

Ness shrugged without raising her head.

'Y'unnerstan he can do with you what he likes? Send you to detention, take you away from your family?'

Ness laughed at this. 'Ooooh. Dat scares me shitless, innit. Look. Do wha' you want. Only I ain't talking.'

The only thing she *would* tell Sergeant Starr was where she lived and Kendra's phone numbers. Let the cow come fetch her, was how Ness thought of things. The cops ringing up her aunt would probably disrupt the woman's nasty, nightly shag, and that was absolutely fine with Ness.

But when Kendra got the call, she wasn't in bed. She was, instead, giving herself a face peel, waiting for the solution to dry. She was doing this in the relative privacy of the bathroom, the better to keep Dix from knowing what she was up to.

Dix was the one to answer the phone and the one to tell her the cops were ringing. He said, on the other side of the closed bathroom door, 'They got Ness, Ken.' He sounded worried.

Kendra felt her spirits plummet. She rinsed off her face, the treatment incomplete, looking exactly the same as when she'd begun it. She looked no different when she walked into the Harrow Road police station less than twenty minutes later. Dix had wanted to go with her, but she'd refused. Stay with the boys, she told him. Who knew what might happen if someone out there – and they both knew whom she meant – realised Joel and Toby were alone.

There was a small waiting area in reception – currently occupied by a slouching young black man nursing a swollen eye – but Kendra wasn't required to wait there very long. In a few minutes, a white woman came to fetch her. She wore blue jeans turned up at the ankles, a French beret, and a blindingly white T-shirt. She had equally white trainers on her feet. *Feisty* was what Kendra thought when she saw her. She was short, wiry, with tousled grey hair and a no-nonsense attitude that suggested the course of wisdom was not to mess her about.

When Kendra heard her name – Fabia Bender – it was everything she could do not to wince and begin making excuses for why she hadn't returned the social worker's calls, which had been numerous over the last few weeks. She managed to look at the white woman blankly, as if she'd never heard of her before. She said, 'What's Ness done?'

'Not "What's happened to her?"' Fabia Bender noted shrewdly. 'You've been expecting this, Mrs Osborne?'

Kendra disliked her at once. Partly because the white

woman had leapt to a conclusion that was utterly accurate. Partly because the white woman was simply who she was: the sort who liked to think she could tell what type of individual she was dealing with by the way they acted when she locked her milky blue eyes with theirs.

Kendra felt smaller than she was. She loathed that feeling. She said shortly, 'Cops called me to come fetch her. Where is she, then?'

'She was talking to Sergeant Starr. Or rather, he was talking to her. I expect they're waiting for me to get back to them because he's not allowed to ask her any questions unless I'm in the room. Or you're in the room. She wouldn't give your name when she was first arrested, by the way. Have you any idea why?'

'Arrested for what?' Kendra asked, for she wasn't about to give Fabia Bender chapter and verse on her relationship with her niece.

Fabia Bender related what she knew of what had happened, information she'd been given by Sergeant Starr. She concluded with the fact that Ness wouldn't give up her friends. Kendra did it for her. But all she knew was the first name of each of the girls: Six and Natasha. One of them lived on the Mozart Estate. She did not know where the other lived.

Kendra burned with shame even as she relayed this information to the social worker. It wasn't the shame of handing over details, however. It was the shame of having so few facts. She asked if she could see Ness, talk to her, take her home. Fabia Bender said, 'Presently,' and ushered Kendra into an empty interview room.

Hers was a thankless job, but Fabia Bender was a woman who did not see it that way. It was a job she'd done in North Kensington for nearly thirty years and, if she'd lost more children than she'd managed to save, it was not because she was lacking either in commitment to them or in a belief in the inherent goodness of mankind. She rose every day knowing that she was exactly where she was meant to be, doing exactly what she was supposed to be doing. Each morning was ripe with possibility. Each evening was an opportunity to reflect on how she had met the challenges of the day. She knew neither discouragement nor despair. Change, she had long ago come to understand, was not something that happened overnight.

She said to Kendra, 'I won't pretend to be happy that you've not returned my calls, Mrs Osborne. Had you done so, we might not be here now. I need to tell you in all honesty that I see this situation as a partial result of Vanessa's failure to go to school.'

This was not the sort of preliminary statement that promised an imminent meeting of minds. Kendra reacted to it as one might expect of a proud woman: she bristled. Her skin became hot, burning hot, and the sense of it melting right off her bones did not encourage her to reach out to the other woman in a show of common humanity. She said nothing.

Fabia Bender changed course. 'I'm sorry. That wasn't the proper thing to say. What you heard was my frustration speaking. Let me start again. My aim has always been to help Vanessa, and I'm a believer in education as at least one step in setting a child on the right path.'

'You think I didn't try to get her to go to school?' Kendra demanded, and if she sounded offended – which indeed she did – it was owing to what she felt at having failed as a substitute parent to Ness. 'I *did* try. But nothing worked. I told her over and over how important it was. I delivered her to the school personally once I talked to Mr Whoever He Was, the education officer. And I did what he said. I walked her to the door. I waited till she went inside. I tried to gate her when she played truant. I told her if she didn't sort herself out, she'd end up just where she's ended up. But nothing worked. She's got her own mind and she's damn well determined to—'

Fabia held up both hands. It was a story that she'd heard for so many years from so many parents – generally female and generally deserted by an unworthy male – that she could have recited it from beginning to end. Its characters were mothers who pulled at their hair in despair and children whose cries for understanding had gone too long misinterpreted as everything from defiance to depression. The real answer to what plagued their society lay in open communication. But parents, there to assist in their young people's interpretation of life's great journey, often had had no one assist in their *own* interpretation of life's great journey when they were youths. Thus, it became a case of the blind attempting, and failing, to lead the blind on a path neither of them understood.

She said, 'Again, forgive me, Mrs Osborne. I'm not here to blame. I'm here to help. May we start again? Please, sit down.'

'I want to take her—'

'Home. Yes. I know. No girl her age belongs in a police station. I quite agree. And you *will* be able to take her home presently. But I'd very much like to talk to you first.'

The interview room was exactly the same as the one in which Ness waited with Sergeant Starr. Kendra saw it as a place she wanted to escape, but since she also wanted to escape with Ness, she cooperated with the white woman. She sat in one of the plastic chairs and drove her hands into the pockets of her cardigan.

'We're on the same side of the street in this,' Fabia Bender told her when they were both positioned at the table, facing each other. 'We both want to sort Vanessa out. When a girl heads in the wrong direction as she has done, there's generally a reason. If we can develop a complete understanding of what the reason is, we have a chance of helping her learn to cope. Coping with life is the essential skill we need to give her. It's also one that schools, unfortunately, fail to teach. So if parents don't have it to pass along to their children – and be assured I'm not referring to you at this moment – then chances are the children won't learn it either.' She took a breath and smiled. She had teeth stained from coffee and nicotine, and the bad skin of a lifelong smoker.

Kendra didn't like the sensation of being lectured. She was able to see that the white woman meant well, but the nature of what Fabia Bender said merely resulted in Kendra's feeling less than. Feeling less than a white woman – and this, despite being part white herself – was something that guaranteed Kendra's back going up. Fabia Bender didn't know the first thing about the chaos and tragedy of Vanessa Campbell's childhood, and Kendra, offended, wasn't about to tell her.

She wanted to, though. Not because she believed the information would help but because she could imagine it setting the social worker straight. She wanted to stand over her and drive the story into her brain: Ness being ten years old and waiting for her dad to come and fetch her as he always did on Saturdays after her ballet lessons, standing outside and all alone and knowing that what she was *never* supposed to do was cross the A40 to get back to Old Oak Common Lane by herself, becoming frightened when he didn't turn up and finally hearing the scream of sirens, and crossing over at last because what else was there to do except try to get home. Then coming upon him where he lay, a crowd gathered round and an oozing of blood pooling round his head and Joel kneeling at one side of that pool shouting Dad! Dad! and Toby sitting there with his legs splayed out and his back against the front of the off licence and crying because he didn't understand at three years old that his father had been shot down in the street in a drug dispute, a drug dispute in which he had had no part. Who was Ness to them: the cops, the crowd, the ambulance driver and his mate, the official who finally showed up to pronounce the obvious over the body? She was just a screaming little girl in a leotard who couldn't make herself heard by any of them.

You want to know the *cause*, white lady? Kendra wanted to ask her. I can tell you the cause.

But that was only part of the story. Even Kendra didn't know the rest.

Fabia Bender said, 'We have to begin by gaining her trust, Mrs Osborne. One of us has to form a bond with the girl. It's not going to be easy, but it has to be done.'

Kendra nodded. What else was there for her to do? 'I understand,' she said. 'Can I take her home now?'

'Yes. Of course. In a moment.' Then the social worker settled more firmly into her chair, her body language making it clear that the interview was far from over. She said that she'd managed to gather a bit of information on Vanessa in the weeks since her first phone call to Mrs Osborne. The officials at East Acton's Wood Lane School, not to mention the local police in that area, had cooperatively filled in some blanks. Thus Fabia Bender had some history, but she sensed there was more to it than one dead father, an institutionalised mother, two brothers, and an aunt with no children of her own. If Kendra Osborne would be willing to fill in some additional blanks for the social worker . . .

So Kendra realised that Fabia Bender *did* have some of the family secrets, but this knowledge did nothing but make her own discomfort worse. Kendra developed a deeper loathing for the woman, especially for her accent. Fabia's well-modulated tone screamed upper middle class. Her choice of vocabulary said university graduate. Her ease of manner declared that she'd had a life of privilege. To Kendra, all of this added up to someone who could neither understand what she was dealing with nor begin to negotiate a way through it.

'Seems like you've got the blanks filled in,' Kendra told her shortly.

'Some, as I've said. But what I need to understand more clearly is the source of her anger.'

Try her gran, Kendra wanted to tell her. Try being on the receiving end of Glory Campbell's lies and desertion. But Glory Campbell and her casual disposal of her three grandkids comprised dirty linen in Kendra's cupboard, and she did not intend to air her own used knickers in this white woman's face. So she asked Fabia Bender a logical question: How much *more* than a dead father and an institutionalised mother was necessary to the understanding of Ness's fury? And what did an understanding of her fury have to do with keeping her from ruining her life? Because, Kendra told the social worker, it was becoming damn clear to her that doing some serious life ruining was what Ness Campbell had in mind. She saw her existence as destroyed already, so she'd decided to go along for the ride. To speed things up, as it were. When nothing mattered in the future, nothing mattered at all.

'You speak like someone who's been there,' Fabia Bender said kindly. 'Is there a Mr Osborne?'

'Not any longer,' Kendra told her.

'Divorced?'

'That's right. What does this have to do with Ness's trouble?'

'So there is no male in Vanessa's life? No father figure?'

'No.' Kendra made no mention of Dix, of the Blade, or of the smell of men that had, for months, clung to her niece like the trail of slime left by a legion of slugs. 'Look. I expect you mean well. But I'd like to take her home.'

'Yes,' Fabia said. 'I can see that. Well, there's only one thing left to discuss, then, and that's her appearance before the magistrate.'

'She's never been in trouble before,' Kendra pointed out.

'Except for the small matter of her failure to attend school,' Fabia said. 'That's not going to count in her favour. I'll do what I can to get her probation and not a custodial sentence—'

'A *sentence*? For a mugging that di'n't even *happen*? When we got drug dealers, car hijackers, housebreakers, and everything else running 'bout the streets? And *she* the one going to get put away?'

'I'll provide a report to the magistrate, Mrs Osborne. He'll read it in advance of her hearing. We'll hope for the best.' She stood. Kendra did likewise. At the door to the room, Fabia Bender paused. She said, 'Someone needs to form a bond with this girl. Someone besides the friends she's choosing just now. It's not going to be easy. She's got very good defences. But it must be done.'

Life in No 84 Edenham Way was tense in the aftermath of Ness's arrest, and this was one of the reasons that Joel decided not to wait until Toby's next birthday to do something with the *It's a Boy!* banner. Not only did he want to make up for how Toby's birthday had turned out, but he also believed it was important that his little brother be distracted from what was happening in Ness's life, lest he drift off and away from the family, disappearing into his own head for an extended time. So he put up the banner across the window in their bedroom and waited for Toby's reaction to it. He didn't need to use stamps this time. Instead, he asked Mr Eastbourne for several lengths of Sellotape, which he carefully brought home from school affixed to the plastic cover of a notebook and, consequently, easily removed.

Joel need not have concerned himself with any of this. Toby liked the banner well enough – although not as much as his lava lamp – but it turned out that he was maintaining an admirable degree of oblivion with regard to Ness's difficulties with the law, not so much by visiting Sose as by listening to daily messages being sent to him from there. As far as the night of his birthday went, he had virtually no memory of it. He recalled the takeaway curry and especially the almond, raisin and honey *naan*. He recalled eating his meal off the tin tray with Father Christmas's face decorating it. He even recalled that Ness had been there, bringing a magic wand for him. But he had no memory of the Blade's appearance at their house or the disruption he'd caused when he'd walked through the door.

That was the beauty of what was happening inside Toby's head. Some things he could recall with a clarity that surprised everyone. Other things were gone, like wisps of smoke against a foggy sky. This provided him with a form of contentment that his siblings were not able to match.

His parents, for example, existed for Toby within a pleasant cloud. His father was a man who took his children to the community hall next to St Aidan's church, where they waited for him in the crèche. That, Toby spoke about when pressed to do so. But the reason they were in that crèche waiting for their father, the fact of the meetings that Gavin Campbell had clung to and attended every day in another room of the hall . . . Toby had no memory of that. As for his mother, she was the person who had fondly run her fingers through his hair the last time she'd come home. The rest of it – an open window, three floors up with an asphalt car park yawning below, a train rushing by on tracks just beyond the building – he did not remember, nor could he have done so, so young had he been at the time. Toby's mind offered its curses, but it offered its blessings as well.

Joel didn't have this same situation in his own mind. On the other hand, he did have Ivan Weatherall and the unspoken promise Ivan made of escaping – if only for a few hours – from the electrical atmosphere of Kendra's home, where Kendra existed in a state of anxious anticipation regarding Ness's upcoming appearance before the magistrate, where Ness herself was lounging about and pretending she didn't care what happened to her, and where Dix was attempting to have hushed conversations with Kendra in which he tried to act the role of conciliator between aunt and niece.

'Maybe they ain't the kids you wanted, Ken,' Joel heard him murmur in the kitchen as Kendra poured herself coffee. 'An' maybe they ain't the kids you ever saw yourself having. But they sure as hell 's the kids you got.'

'Stay out of this, Dix,' was her reply. 'You don't know what you're talking about.'

He persisted. 'Y'ever t'ink about how God works?'

'Man, I tell you: no God I'm familiar with has ever lived in this part of town.'

If her reaction illustrated how impermanent was the living situation in which Joel and his siblings found themselves, Dix's was at least more heartening. And if he didn't exactly act the part of father to the Campbell children, at least he tolerated them, and this was good enough. That's why, on an afternoon when Dix was repairing the old barbecue in Kendra's back garden in anticipation of coming good weather, he let Toby watch and hand him tools, which gave Joel the chance he'd been waiting for to visit Ivan Weatherall again.

He'd been thinking about the script-writing class. More, he'd been thinking of the film that would be the result of the class's efforts. He'd never written anything before, so he didn't see himself as being able to join them in fashioning a screenplay, but he'd begun to dream that he might be chosen to do *something* that was related to the film. They'd need a crew. They'd probably need a whole gang of people. Why, he thought, shouldn't he be one of them? So, while Dix and Toby worked on the barbecue, while Ness gave herself a manicure, while Kendra went on a massage call, Joel headed in the direction of Sixth Avenue.

He chose a route that put him in the vicinity of Portnall Road. It was a fine spring day of sun and breeze and, as Joel passed along the point where Portnall and the Harrow Roads met, this same breeze carried to him the unmistakable odour of cannabis. He looked around for the source. He found it at the front of a smallish block of flats, where a figure was sitting in the doorway, knees up, his back against the wall and a pad of paper lying on the ground at his side. He was in a patch of sunlight, and he'd raised his face to it. As Joel watched, he toked up deeply, eyes closed, relaxed.

Joel slowed his pace and then stopped, observing the man from the other side of a low box hedge that defined the edge of the property. He saw that it was Calvin Hancock, the graffiti artist from the sunken football pitch, but his appearance was altered. The dreadlocks were missing. His head had been shaved, but in fits and starts. From where Joel stood, it looked as if some sort of pattern now decorated the young man's skull.

Joel called out, 'Wha' you do to your hair, mon? Ain't you a Rasta no more?'

Cal turned his head. It was a lazy movement, more like a roll than an actual turn. He removed the spliff from between his lips. He smiled. Even from where Joel was standing, he could see that Calvin's eyes looked unnaturally bright.

'Blood,' Cal drawled. 'Wha's happening wiv you, bred?'

'Goin up to see a friend on Six' Avenue.'

Cal nodded, a look on his face that suggested this information had some profound meaning for him. He extended the spliff in Joel's direction in an amiable fashion. Joel shook his head. 'Smart, dat,' Cal said in approval. 'You stay 'way from th' shit 's long as you can.' He looked down at the pad that lay next to him, as if he suddenly remembered what he'd been doing before getting high.

Joel ventured on to the property to have a look. 'What're you working on, den?'

Cal said, 'Oh, dis ain't nuffink. Just some sketching I like to do to mark the time.'

'Lemme see.' Joel looked at the pad. Cal had been sketching what appeared to be random faces, all of them dark. They were each different but, taken as a group, there was something about them that suggested a family. As indeed they were, Calvin's own: five faces together and a sixth by itself, apart from the rest and unmistakably Calvin. Joel said, 'Dis is wicked, mon. You take lessons or summick?'

'Nah.' Cal picked up the pad and tossed it to his other side, out of Joel's sight. He drew deeply on the spliff and held the smoke in his lungs. He squinted up at Joel and said, 'Bes' not hang here,' and he tilted his head towards the door of the building. Someone had tagged it in the way much of the neighbourhood was tagged. In this case, *Chiv!* made an amateur scrawl of yellow against the grey metal of the door.

'Why?' Joel asked him. 'What're you doing here, anyways?'

'Waiting.'

'For what?'

'More like for who, innit. The Blade's inside, and you just 'bout the last person he going to be happy to see if he comes walking out.'

Joel looked at the building again. Cal, he realised, was bodyguarding, no matter how strung out he seemed to be. 'Wha's he doing, den?' Joel asked the Rasta.

'Fucking Arissa,' Cal said bluntly. 'Jus' about dat time of day, innit.' He pretended to look at a non-existent watch on his wrist as he spoke, and then he added slyly, 'I can't 'xactly hear her howls of pleasure, though, so this's all speculation. Could be his parts ain't working like they ought. But hey, what I tell you, a man's got to do what a man's got to do.'

Joel smiled at this. So did Calvin. Then he began to laugh, seeing in his own words a humour that only cannabis could create. He put his head on his knees to control his chuckling, and this gave Joel a better view of his head. What Joel saw was a bizarre pattern that had been shaved on to Cal's skull: a crude striking snake's head seen in profile. By the look of the design, it was apparent that whoever had wielded the cutting shears had been an amateur. Joel had a fairly good idea who that person had been.

He asked his question without thinking. 'Why d'you hang wiv him, mon?'

Cal lifted his head, neither chuckling nor smiling. He took another long hit of the spliff before he answered, although the act of toking up was in itself a form of reply. He said, 'He need me. Who else going to guard dis door, make sure he can do Arissa in peace wivout some blood blasting in and taking him out while he's got his trousers down. Man's got enemies, innit.'

And so he did, although not one of them was an enemy without reason. They existed among the women the Blade had used and deserted, and among the men who were more than eager to take over his patch. For the Blade ran a sweet operation. He had weed, bone, and powder for cash but also for goods or, better yet, as barter. Plenty of young men on the streets had been willing to risk themselves taking on this jewellery shop at the Blade's command or that post office or the other corner grocery or some darkened house where the owners would be out on a Friday night . . . and all to get supplied with whatever it was that they used to get high. With this as his main line of business, there were any number of thugs who wanted in on the Blade's action, no matter the risks that went with it. Even Joel had to admit that there was something enticing about inspiring fear in some, jealousy in others, loathing in most, and – if the truth be told – lust in girls eighteen and younger.

Which explained – at least in part – what had happened to his own sister, who was the last female on earth whom Joel would have expected to get involved with someone like the Blade. But involved she clearly had been, a piece of information he'd gleaned the night of Toby's birthday.

He said to Calvin, 'Guess you got to protect him, innit. Di'n't do dat good when he came to see us, though.'

Cal finished the spliff and pinched the end of it, carefully depositing the quarter inch of what remained in an old tobacco tin that he took from his pocket. He said, 'I tol' him I should go wiv him, but the man wa'n't having none of dat. He wanted Arissa seeing the Blade being the Blade, y'unnerstan. Collecting what was his and making your sister wish on her stars she wa'n't alive.'

'He doesn't know Ness if he thought he'd make her wish dat,' Joel remarked.

'Das right,' Cal said. 'But it wa'n't never 'bout him knowing her. The Blade too busy to know any slag. Least too busy for anyt'ing other dan a plunge-oh-ramma-damma wiv her, y'un-nerstan.'

Joel laughed at the term. Calvin grinned in response. The door to the block of flats opened.

The Blade stood there. Calvin got quickly to his feet, a remarkable manoeuvre considering his condition. Joel didn't move, although he wanted to take a quick step back in response to the look of hostility that played across the Blade's sharp features. The man flicked a contemptuous glance at Joel, dismissed him like a bug, and went on to direct his attention to Cal.

'What you doing?' he demanded.

'I been—'

'Shut up. You call dis watching? You call it guarding? And wha' is dis shit?' With the tip of his cowboy boot, the Blade toed the pad on which Cal had been drawing. He looked at the picture. He looked back at Cal. 'Mummy, daddy, and the kids, Cal-vin? Das wha' you got here?' His lips worked around a smile remarkable for the degree of menace it managed to convey. 'Missing dem, mon? Wonderin where dey are? Ponderin why dey all jus' disappear one day? Maybe it's cos you a loser, Cal. Ever t'ink of dat?'

Joel looked from the Blade to Calvin. Even at his young age, he was able to see that the Blade was itching to do damage somewhere, and he intuitively knew he needed to be out of this place. But he also knew that he couldn't afford to look afraid.

'I had an eye out, bred.' Calvin sounded patient. 'Ain't been no one in dis street past hour, I c'n tell you dat.'

'Dat th' case?' The Blade flicked a glance at Joel. 'You call dis no one? Well, I guess it's right, innit. Half-caste bastard wiv his half-caste sister. They pretty much no one, all right.' He gave his attention to Joel. 'What d'you want, den? You got business round here? You bringing a message from dat slag you call sister?'

Joel thought of the knife, the blood, and the stitches in Ness's scalp. He also thought of who his sister once had been and who she was now. He felt an unaccountable sense of grief. It was this that made him say, 'My sister ain't no slag, mon,' and he heard Cal's breath hiss, like a warning from a snake.

'Dat what you t'ink?' the Blade asked him, and he looked like a man setting up to make the most of an unexpected opportunity. 'Want me to tell you the way she likes it, den? Going up the chute. Dat's how she wants it. Fact is, dat's the *only* way she wants it, and she wants it all the time, every day in fac'. Got to give the slag real discipline, don't I, to get her to take it any other way.'

'Maybe dat's the case,' Joel said agreeably although he wasn't at all sure he could speak past the tightness coming into his chest. 'But maybe she knew dat was best for you. You know what I mean: th' only way you could ackshully do it.'

Cal said, 'Hey bred,' in a clear tone of warning, but Joel had ventured into this river too far. He had to reach the other side. Anything less and he'd be marked as a coward, which was the last conclusion he wished someone like the Blade to reach about him.

He said, 'She nice, like dat, Ness is. See you limp no matter how you try, Ness goin do summick to help you out. Anways, taking it dat way – through the back, like you say – she don't have to look at your ugly mug. So it works out good for both of you.'

The Blade said nothing in reply. Calvin's breath went out in a whoosh. No one knew the Blade as Calvin Hancock did, so he was the one who knew exactly what the other man was capable of, pushed to the wall. He said, 'You get on 'bout seeing your mate on Sixth Ave, bred,' and he sounded quite different from the pleasantly high pothead who had been speaking to Joel prior to the Blade's appearance on the scene. 'Don't t'ink you want to get into it here.'

The Blade said, 'Oh, dat's beautiful, innit. Guarding me from *dis*? Dat what you're doing? You one useless piece 'f shit, y'unnerstan?' He spat on the path and said to Joel, 'Get out 'f my sight. Not worth th' effort to sort. Not you and not your ugly cow sister.'

Joel wanted to say more, despite the foolhardy nature of that desire. In the manner of a young cock ready to challenge his better, he wanted to take on the Blade. But he knew there was no way he could match the man and, even if he could have, he would have had to go through Cal Hancock to get to him. On the other hand, Joel knew he could not skulk off upon the Blade's order to do so. So he waited a good thirty terrifying seconds of staring the Blade down, despite the furious rushing of blood in his ears and the equally furious churning in his gut. He waited until the Blade said, 'Wha'? You *deaf* or summick?' and then he worked up enough juice in the desert that was his mouth so that he, too, could spit on the path. Once he'd done that, he turned on his heel and forced himself to walk – not run – back to the pavement and down the street.

He didn't look back. He didn't hurry either. He made himself saunter as if he were someone without a care. It wasn't easy for him to do, on rubbery legs and with a chest so constricted he could barely get enough air to remain conscious. But he did it, and he gained the end of the street before he vomited into a pool of standing water in the gutter.

12

The day of Ness Campbell's appearance before the magistrate did not begin auspiciously, nor did it develop or end that way. Traffic thwarted her timely arrival at court, which proved to be only the beginning of her undoing. This undoing was advanced by her attitude towards the entire proceedings, which was not a good one and which was worsened by the condition of what must be called her erstwhile friendship with Six and Natasha.

Six and Natasha were not unmindful of the difficulties they might face should Ness decide to name them as her accomplices in the attempted mugging for which she had been arrested. While one way of assuring that this naming did not happen might have been to encourage a meeting of the minds with Ness, neither Six nor Natasha possessed adequate language skills to effect an agreement. Nor did they possess either the ability or the imagination to see beyond the immediate moment in order to assess the consequences of any action they might take. Their way of making their feelings known – these feelings being worry over having to face the magistrate themselves, not to mention a modicum of anxiety about having to deal with their parents' wrath in the matter – was to avoid Ness as if she were a carrier of the ebola virus. When this didn't suffice to give Ness the message that their friendship was at an end, they went on to tell her directly that they didn't like the way she'd been acting, 'Like you t'ink you're better'n anyone else, when all you are is a bloody stupid cow'. And that approach worked fine.

So, when Ness went to face the magistrate, she went with the knowledge that she stood alone. She had Kendra with her, but Ness was not of a mind to seek succour from her, and her feelings for the social worker – whom she'd finally met and to whom she'd revealed nothing of value – were not of a sort to make Fabia Bender's presence good for much. Thus, when Ness faced the magistrate, she projected an attitude so far from remorse and humility that the only recourse he saw was to throw every available book at her.

The saving grace for Ness was that hers was a first offence. While another young woman evidencing the same degree of indifference to the proceedings, to her advocates, and to her life, might have found herself sentenced to what the magistrate – with an antique formality that might have been endearing in other circumstances – insisted upon referring to as 'borstal', Ness received 2,000 hours of community service: to be religiously documented, supervised, and signed off by the individual in whose charge this community service was intended to be served. And, the magistrate concluded, Miss Campbell *would* be attending school when the autumn term began. He didn't add 'or else', but that was understood.

Fabia Bender told Ness she was lucky. Kendra Osborne did the same. But Ness saw only that 2,000 hours of community service might take her the rest of her life to serve, and her displeasure was in exact proportion to what she believed were the inherent inequities of the situation. 'Ain't fair,' was how she put it.

'You don't like it, you tell them the names of your mates and where to find them, then,' was how Kendra responded.

Since Ness was not about to do that – despite Six and Natasha's rejection of her – she had no other recourse than to serve her time. This, she learned, would take place at the Meanwhile Gardens child drop-in centre, a site whose complete convenience to her home also did not garner from Ness any degree of appreciation. Instead, she was the incarnation of a

young woman put upon, and she decided to make her super-
visor at the child drop-in centre aware of this at the first opportunity.

That opportunity came quickly enough. A phone call from
Majidah Ghafoor on the same day as Ness received her
sentence informed her of the hours that she would be expected
to work. They would begin immediately, Ness was told. Since
she lived less than fifty yards from the site of her community
service, she could come round right now and hear the rules.

'Rules?' Ness asked her. 'Wha' you mean, *rules*? Dis ain't
no prison. Dis is a job.'

'A job to which you have been assigned,' Majidah told her.
'Come at once please. I shall wait ten minutes before phoning
probation.'

'Shit!' Ness said.

'Less than well-expressed,' Majidah told her in the pleasant
accent of her place of birth. 'We will be having no profanities
in the drop-in centre, miss.'

So Ness went around, still in the state in which her appearance before the magistrate had left her. She let herself in
through the gate in the chain link fence and stalked across the
play area to the cabin that housed all the indoor activities
offered to children six years old and under. There, with the
children gone for the day, Majidah was in the process of doing
the washing up after a late afternoon snack of milk, toasted
teacakes, and strawberry jam. She handed Ness a tea towel to
begin drying glasses and plates ('And see you do take care,
for you will pay for whatever it is you happen to break'), and
she started to talk.

Majidah Ghafoor turned out to be an ethnically attired
Pakistani woman of young middle age. She was a widow who,
in defiance of the traditions of her culture, refused to live with
any of her married sons. Their wives she deemed 'too English'
for her liking, despite the fact that she'd had the main hand
in choosing each of them and, while she found her eleven

grandchildren attractive, she also saw them as largely an undisciplined lot destined for lives of dissolution unless their parents reined them in.

'No, I am happier on my own,' she told Ness, who couldn't have been less interested in matters pertaining to Majidah's life. 'And you shall be as well. Happy here, that is. As long as you adhere to the rules.'

The rules consisted of a catalogue of the forbidden: no smoking, no mobile phone use, no land line use, no heavy makeup, no excessive jewellery, no music via iPod, MP3 player, Walkman or anything else, no card playing, no dancing, no tattoos, no overt piercings of the body, no visitors, no junk food ('This McDonald's is the bane of the civilised world, I do think'), no revealing clothing ('such as what you are currently wearing, which I shall not allow in this building again'), no adult or adolescent person inside the fence unless accompanied by a child of six or younger.

To all of this, Ness rolled her eyes expressively and said, 'Whatever. S'when do I start?'

'Now. Once you have finished with the dishes, you may scrub the floor. While you do that, I shall come up with a schedule for you. This I will send to your probation officer and your social worker so they will see how we intend to work on the two thousand hours you were given for your crime.'

'I di'n't commit no—'

'Please.' Majidah cut her off with a wave of the hand. 'I am not the least interested in the nature of your disreputable activities, miss. They shall have no part in our business arrangement. You are here to complete hours; I am here to document that completion. You will find a mop and bucket in the long cupboard next to the sink. I require hot water and a cup of Ajax. When you have finished the floor, you may clean the loo.'

'Where you marking down my hours, den?'

'That, miss, is not for you to concern yourself about. Now

shoo, *shoo*. Work awaits us both. The centre must be tidied and there are only you and I to do it.'

'*No* one else works here?' Ness asked, incredulous.

'Which makes the day blessedly full of activity,' Majidah said.

Ness didn't think she was going to be seeing it that way. But she found the mop, the bucket and the Ajax, and she set to work on the drop-in centre's green lino floor.

There were four rooms in all: kitchen, storage room, toilet, and activity room, with the most serious grit and grime in the two rooms to which the children were given access. Ness mopped the activity room, where pint-sized tables and chairs were scattered across a floor made sticky by various spillages. She did the same to the toilet, shuddering to think what the various spillages in there implied. Under Majidah's super-vision, she went on to scrub the kitchen. The storage room, she was told, required only a thorough sweeping out, after which she could dust the shelves and the windowsills and clean the lopsided Venetian blinds.

Ness did all of this with less than good grace, muttering and casting sidelong looks at Majidah, which the Pakistani woman ignored. At a desk to one side of the room, she instead occupied herself with two schedules: Ness's and the children's. She viewed Ness's assignment to the drop-in centre as a gift from the gods, and she intended to make use of that gift. How Ness felt about matters was not her concern. Experience had shown her that hard work killed no one, nor did accepting what life threw at you.

Kendra met up with Cordie for advice once Ness had received her sentence. She went to her house in Kensal Green, where Cordie was tolerantly taking part in her two daughters' fantasy tea party in the cramped back garden. Uncharacteristically Manda and Patia had decided upon a royal theme for this event, with Manda acting the role of monarch – ancient pillbox hat, lace gloves, and oversize handbag on her arm – and Cordie and Patia playing a grateful and decidedly non-royal public invited to partake of Fanta orange served in chipped china cups (courtesy of the charity shop), bowls of crisps (in Patia's favourite flavour, which happened to be lamb and mint), a bag of Cheddar popcorn emptied into a plastic colander and set into the middle of the rickety garden table, and a plate of Jaffa cakes looking rather crumbly.

Manda, apparently suffering some degree of confusion over the respect demanded by the papacy and that demanded by the monarchy, was imperiously directing her mother and sister to kiss her ring when Kendra joined them. The child was standing on a deckchair in lieu of sitting on a throne and, quite caught up in a role for which she was clearly born, once her ring was kissed, she went on to give instruction in the proper position of teacup in relation to one's pinkie Patia declared all of this rubbish and demanded to be monarch instead. Cordie informed her that she'd lost the cut of cards fair and square, so she'd have to play along until next time when, one hoped, her luck would improve.

'An' no pouting 'bout it,' Cordie told her. 'Fair is fair, Patia.'

When Cordie saw Kendra, admitted to the house and then to the garden by Gerald, who was watching a World Cup football match beamed live from Barbados, she asked leave of Her Majesty to speak to her friend. Leave was reluctantly given, and even then her decree was that Cordie could *not* take her teacup with her. Cordie curtseyed and backed off with a suitable degree of humility. She joined Kendra on the small patio that made a square just outside the back door. It was a fine day and, from the back gardens on either side of Cordie's, other families were enjoying the weather with outdoor meals, outdoor music, outdoor conversations, and the occasional argument. The noise of all this floated over the walls, providing an ambience that promised to remind them of where they were at all times, lest they begin to think themselves – as Manda and Patia would have them – in a palace garden.

There was no place to sit, since the girls were using all available outdoor furniture for the tea party, so Cordie and Kendra decamped to the kitchen. Ignoring Gerald's admonition that smoking could endanger the baby should Cordie be pregnant – a warning at which Cordie smiled serenely – they lit up cigarettes and relaxed.

Kendra told her friend about Ness's appearance in front of the magistrate. She also told her about Fabia Bender and about the direction she'd been given to form a bond with the girl if she didn't want to see Ness trip down the rock-strewn pathway of further trouble. She said, 'Seems like we should be doing girl t'ings together, way I see it.'

'Such as?' Cordie sent a plume of cigarette smoke towards the open back door. She cast a glance at the tea party. Her girls had moved from ring kissing to gobbling Cheddar popcorn.

'Facials at a spa?' Kendra said. 'Getting our nails done? Getting our hair done? Going out to lunch? Having a girls' night out, maybe wiv you and me? Making somet'ing together? Jewellery maybe? Taking a class?'

Cordie considered all this. She shook her head. 'I don' see Ness having no facial, Ken. An' the res' . . . ? Well, all dat's what *you* might like to do, innit. You got to t'ink what *she* like to do.'

'She like to dope up and she like to have sex,' Kendra said. 'She like to mug old ladies and she like to get drunk. She like to watch telly and lie round doing nothing. Oh, and she like to flaunt it round Dix.'

Cordie raised an eyebrow. 'Dat's trouble,' she noted.

Kendra didn't want to make that part of the conversation. She'd already done so with Dix, and it hadn't worked out. Insult to him. Frustration to her. The resulting question of 'Who d' you t'ink I bloody am, Ken?' being one she could not answer. She said, 'You and your girls, you got a relationship, Cordie.'

'Sure as hell hope. I'm their mum. Plus, they been wiv me always, so it's easier for me. I know dem. I know what they like. Ness's like dat, anyways. She got to like somet'ing.'

Kendra thought about this. She continued to think about it in the days that followed. She considered who Ness had been in childhood, before everything in her life had altered, and she came up with ballet. That, she decided, had to be it. She and her niece could begin their bonding over ballet.

To attend the Royal Ballet was wildly beyond Kendra's means, so the first step was to find a performance somewhere nearby that was simultaneously worth seeing and affordable. This didn't prove as difficult as Kendra thought it might. She tried Kensington and Chelsea College first, and while she found that there was indeed a dance department, it was modern dance which she did not think would do. Her next source was Paddington Arts, and there she was successful. In addition to the classes and the art-related events, the centre offered concerts of various types, and one of these was a performance by a small ballet company. Kendra promptly bought two tickets.

She decided that it would be a surprise. She called it a reward for Ness's putting in her community service time without major complaints. She told her niece to dress up in her finery because they were going to do a proper 'girl thing' together. She herself dressed to the nines and she made no comment about Ness's plunging neckline and six inches of cleavage, about her micro-miniskirt and her high-heeled boots. She was determined that the evening would succeed and that the necessary bonding would occur between them.

In planning all this, what she didn't understand was what ballet represented to her niece. She did not know that watching a score of thin young women *en pointe* cast Ness back where she least wanted to be. Ballet meant her father. It meant being his princess. It put her at his side walking to the dance studio every Tuesday and Thursday afternoon, every Saturday morning. It put her on stage those few times she had actually been on stage, with her dad in the audience – in the first row always – with his face shining bright and no one around him knowing that what he looked like was not who he was. Thin to the point of disease, but no longer diseased. Dissolute of face but no longer a dissolute. Shaking of hand but no longer from need. Having been to the brink, but no longer in danger of tumbling over. Just a dad who liked to vary his routine, which was why he walked on the other side of the street that day, which was why he was anywhere near the off licence, where people said he meant to go inside but he hadn't, he hadn't, he had merely been in the wrong place at a terrible time.

When Ness could stand no more of the ballet because of the memories which she could not bear, she got up and fought her way down the row to the aisle. The only thing that mattered was getting out of the place so that she could forget once more.

Kendra followed her. She hissed her name. She burned with embarrassment and anger. The anger grew out of her despair. It seemed to her that nothing she did, nothing she tried, nothing she offered . . . The girl was simply beyond her.

Ness was outside when Kendra caught up with her. She swung around on her aunt before Kendra could speak.

'Dis is my fucking reward?' she demanded. 'Dis is wha' I get for putting up wiv dat fucking Majidah every day? Don' do me any more favours, Ken-*dra*.' That said, she pushed off.

Kendra watched her go. What she saw in Ness's march up the street was not escape but lack of gratitude. She floundered around for a way to bring the girl to her senses once and for all.

It seemed to Kendra that a comparison was in order: how things were versus how they could be. Well-intentioned but ill-informed, she believed she knew how to bring that comparison about.

Dix disagreed with her plan, which Kendra found maddening. Her point of view was that Dix was hardly in a position to know how to cope with an adolescent, being little more than an adolescent himself. He didn't take this declaration well – especially since it seemed like something intended, among other things, to underscore the difference in their ages – and, with an irritating and unexpected combination of insight and maturity, he pointed out to Kendra that her flailing around and attempting to form an attachment to her niece looked more like an effort to control the girl than to have a relationship with her. Besides, he said, it seemed to him that Kendra wanted Ness to become attached to her without *herself* becoming attached to Ness. 'Like "Love me, girl, but I ain't intending to love you back",' was how he put it.

'Of *course* I love her,' Kendra said hotly. 'I love all *three* of them. I'm their *bloody* aunt.'

Dix observed her evenly. 'I ain't saying it's bad, Ken, what you feel. Hell, what you feel is jus' what you feel. Not right, not wrong. Jus' *is*, y'unnerstan? How're you *s'posed* to feel anyway, wiv three kids jus' turned over to you when you don't even know they're coming, eh? No one 'spects you to love them jus' cos they're your blood.'

'I love them. I *love* them.' She heard herself shrieking, and she hated him for bringing her to that sort of reaction.

'So accept dem,' he said. 'Accept everyone, Ken. Might as well. Can't change dem.'

To Kendra, he was himself the picture of something that she needed to accept and had succeeded in accepting. There he was, during this conversation, standing in the bathroom with his body lathered in pink depilatory cream so that the skin he showed to the body-building judges would be smooth and hairless from head to toe, looking like a fool in a dozen ways, and she was *making no comment about that, was she* because she knew how important to him was his dream of sculpting his way to a crown that meant *nothing* to most of the world and if that wasn't acceptance . . .

More than that Kendra couldn't face, however. She had too many responsibilities. The only way that she could see to handle them was to get them under control, which had been Dix's point exactly although she couldn't admit that to herself. Joel was easy, since he was so eager to please that he generally anticipated how he was meant to behave before she informed him of her wishes. Toby was simple, his lava lamp and the television kept him occupied and content, and more than that about Toby she didn't wish – and could not afford – to consider. But Ness from the first had been a nut impossible to crack. She'd gone her own way, and look what had happened. A change was called for and, with the determination that Kendra had always applied to everything else in her life, she decided that a change would occur.

Ages had passed since the children had last seen Carole Campbell, so the natural excuse for the comparison that Kendra wanted Ness to experience was right at hand. A visit to Carole meant that arrangements had to be made with Fabia Bender to get Ness released from her required appearance at the child drop-in centre for one day, but that did not prove difficult. Once release was accomplished, what remained was informing Ness that the time had arrived for the Campbell children to pay a call on their mother.

Since Kendra knew how unlikely it was that Ness would cooperate in this plan – considering how the girl had responded to the last visit they'd paid to the children's mother – she altered the arrangement slightly from what she would have preferred it to be. Instead of going with the Campbells to make certain they got themselves into Carole's presence, she assigned to Ness the responsibility of taking her little brothers from home to the hospital and back. This, she decided, would illustrate her trust in the girl at the same time as it would put Ness in the position of assessing – even subconsciously – what life would be like should she have to live it in the presence of and with the companionship of her poor mother. *This* would develop a sense of gratitude in the girl. In Kendra's mind, gratitude was part of the bonding process.

Ness, presented with the alternative of appearing for her regularly scheduled time at the child drop-in centre or travelling to the countryside hospital to see her mother, chose the latter option as any girl might have done. She carefully pocketed the forty pounds her aunt gave her for the journey and for Carole's treats, and she steered Joel and Toby on to the number 23 bus to Paddington station like a young adult determined to prove herself. She took the boys to the upper deck of the bus, and she didn't even seem to mind that Toby had insisted upon bringing his lava lamp with him and that he trailed the flex up the stairs and down the aisle, tripping over it twice as he made his way past the other passengers. This, indeed, was a brand-new Ness, one about whom a person might make positive assumptions.

Which was what Joel did. He felt himself relax. For the first time in a very long while, it seemed to him that the complicated duty of minding Toby, caring for himself, and seeing to the rest of the world had been lifted from his shoulders. He even looked out of the window for once, enjoying the spectacle of Londoners out and about in good weather: a peregrinating populace in as few clothes as possible.

The Campbells made it all the way to Paddington station and into the ticket hall before Ness's plan became apparent. She bought only two returns for the journey and handed over just part of the change to Joel, pocketing the rest.

She said, 'Get her an Aero like she likes. Get her summick cheaper 'n *Elle* or *Vogue*. Dere ain't enough for crisps dis time, so you got to do wivout, y'unnerstan.'

Joel said in futile protest, 'But, Ness, what're you—'

'You tell Aunt Ken, and I beat you shitless,' Ness informed him. 'I got a day off from dat bitch Majidah and I mean to take it. You got dat, blood?'

'You'll get in trouble.'

'Like I could fucking care,' she said. 'I meet you back here half-past four. I'm not here, you wait. You got dat, Joel? You wait cos if you go home wivout me, I beat you shitless like I said, y'unnerstan.'

That pronounced so succinctly as to leave no room for questions, she made him find the correct train on the departures board, after which she directed him to WH Smith. When he went inside, with Toby hanging on to his trouser leg, she disappeared, a girl determined not to dance to *anyone's* bloody tune, least of all to her aunt's.

Joel watched her from inside the shop until he lost her as she wove through the crowd. Then he bought a magazine and an Aero, and he took his brother to the correct platform. Once they were on the train, he gave Toby the chocolate. Their mother, he decided, would just have to suffer.

A moment after he had the thought, though, he felt nasty for having entertained it. To drive that nastiness away, he observed the graffiti-scarred brick walls on either side of the station as the train moved past them, and he tried to read individual tags. Looking at the graffiti and the tags reminded him of Cal Hancock. Cal Hancock reminded him of facing off with the Blade and being sick in the gutter afterwards. That thought took him inevitably to what had followed: his decision to pay a call upon Ivan Weatherall anyway.

Joel had found Ivan at home, and he'd been grateful for this. If Ivan smelled the scent of vomit upon him, he was good enough not to mention the matter. He was in the midst of a delicate part of the operation of clock building when Joel arrived, and he didn't stop his work when he bade Joel enter the house and help himself from a chipped bowl of grapes that sat on the edge of the table. He did, however, hand Joel a piece of green paper with *Wield Words Not Weapons* printed across the top of it. He said, 'Have a look at this, and tell me what you think,' as he gave his attention back to his clock.

'What is it?' Joel asked him.

'Read,' Ivan said.

The paper appeared to be announcing some sort of writing contest. The notice gave page lengths, line lengths, and the terms of critiquing, along with cash prizes and other awards. The big moment seemed to be something called *Walk the Word* because the largest prize of all – which was fifty pounds – went to that, whatever it was. *Wield Words Not Weapons* occurred in one of the community centres in the area: a place called the Basement Activities Centre in Oxford Gardens.

'I still don' get it,' Joel said to Ivan once he'd read the advertisement for *Wield Words Not Weapons*. ''M I s'posed to do summick wiv dis?'

'Hmm. I hope so. You're supposed to attend. It's a poetry . . . well, a poetry event, I dare say would be the best term for it. Have you been to one before? No? Well, I suggest you come and find out about it. You might be surprised to see what it's like. *Walk the Word* is a new element, by the way.'

'*Poetry*? We sit round and talk 'bout poems or summick?' Joel made a face. He pictured a circle of old ladies with sagging stockings, enthusing about the sort of dead white men one heard about at school.

'We *write* poems,' Ivan said. 'It's a chance for self-expression without censorship, although not without criticism from the audience.'

Joel looked at the paper again, and he homed in on the prize money being offered. He said, 'Wha's dis *Walk the Word* t'ing?'

'Ah. Interested in prize money, are you?'

Joel didn't reply although he did think of what he could do with fifty pounds. There was a vast gap between who he was at the present moment, a twelve-year-old reliant upon his aunt for food and for shelter, and who he wanted to be as a man, with a real career as a psychiatrist. Along with the sheer determination to succeed, which he did possess, there was the question of money for his education, which he did not. Money was going to be required to make the leap from who he was now to who he wanted to become, and while fifty pounds didn't amount to much, compared to what Joel had at the moment – nothing – it was also a fortune.

He finally said, 'Might be. What d' I got to do?'

Ivan smiled. 'Turn up.'

''M I s'posed to write summick before I get there?'

'Not for *Walk the Word.* That's done on the spot. I give you key words – everyone gets the same words – and you have a specific period of time to craft a poem that uses them. The best poem wins, with the best decided upon by a committee from the audience.'

'Oh.' Joel handed the paper back to Ivan. He knew how little chance he stood of winning anything if judges would be involved in making the decision. He said, 'I can't write poems anyways.'

Ivan said, 'Tried, have you? Well. Here's my thinking on the subject if you don't mind listening. Do you, by the way?'

Joel shook his head.

'That's a start, isn't it,' Ivan said. 'It's very good: listening. I'd call it second cousin to trying. And that's the crucial element of life experience that so many of us avoid, you know. Trying something new, taking that single leap of faith into the utterly and absolutely unknown. Into the *different.* Those who take that leap are the ones who challenge whatever fate they might otherwise have. They fly in the face of societal expectations, determining for *themselves* who and what they will be and not allowing the bonds of birth, class, and bias to make that determination for them.' Ivan folded the advertisement into eighths and tucked the square into Joel's shirt pocket. 'Basement Activities. Oxford Gardens,' he said. 'You'll recognise the building as it's one of those ghastly monstrosities from the sixties that refer to themselves as architecture. Think concrete, stucco, and painted plywood, and you'll have it right. I do hope we'll see you there, Joel. Bring your family if you'd like. The more the merrier. Coffee and cakes afterwards.'

Joel was still carrying that advertisement around, even as he and Toby rode on the train to see their mother. He hadn't yet shown up at *Wield Words Not Weapons* but the thought of those fifty pounds continued to burn in his mind. It burned so brightly that the previous idea of being involved in Ivan's script-writing class became a smaller, secondary one. Each time an evening for *Wield Words Not Weapons* arrived and passed, Joel felt one step closer to having enough courage to try his hand at writing a poem.

As for now, however, there was the hospital visit to cope with. In reception, they were sent not to the upper floor where the day room and their mother's room were located, but instead along a ground-floor corridor to what was called the conservatory, a glassed-in room on the south side of the building.

Joel joyfully took their mother's presence here as a positive sign. In the conservatory there was nothing really to restrict a patient's movements: no bars on the windows, specifically. A patient could do some serious damage to herself by breaking one of the enormous panes of glass, so the fact that Carole Campbell was allowed to spend time here suggested to Joel that progress was being made in her recovery.

Sadly, this turned out to be an overly sanguine conclusion.

So Kendra's intended effect of a visit to Carole Campbell did indeed occur. It merely occurred to the wrong sibling. Ness went her own way for that day and met Joel and Toby forty-two minutes later than the prescribed time and in a mood so surly that Joel knew her afternoon had been less successful than she'd planned it to be, while Joel was the one whose apprehension about where the Campbells might live in the future was heightened.

Ness's 'How was the bloody cow, den?' didn't make matters any better, for the question and the manner in which Ness asked didn't extend the offer of having a heartfelt conversation. Joel wanted to tell her the truth about his call upon their mother: that Carole hadn't known Toby, that she had thought their father was alive, and that she was existing on a plane so ethereal that she was far beyond his ability to reach her. But none of this could he put into words. So he just said, 'You should've gone,' to which Ness said, 'Fuck you, den,' and sashayed in the direction of the buses.

When Kendra asked how the visit had gone, Joel said Fine, good, Mum had even been doing some gardening in the hospital conservatory. He said, 'She asked 'bout you, Aunt Ken,' and he couldn't understand why his aunt didn't seem pleased to hear this lie. The way Joel thought of it, Kendra was supposed to see Carole's alleged improvement as an indication that the Campbells would not need a permanent living situation with her. But Kendra didn't seem pleased at all, which made Joel feel his insides knot up as he sought a way to soften whatever blow he'd accidentally dealt her. But before he had a chance to come up with something, Dix took him to one side. He said, 'Ain't you, bred. It's Ness. How'd she take your mum, den?', a question Joel knew better than to answer.

Dix eyed Ness, and Ness eyed him right back. Her posture, her facial expression, and even the way she breathed out with her nostrils flared, all served to challenge him. Wisely, he refused to take up the challenge. Instead, when she was likely to be around the house, he went about his own business: at the gym, meeting with his body-building sponsors, preparing for his next contest with a new determination, shopping for his special foods, cooking his special meals.

For several weeks, life lurched in the direction of what a

casual observer might have called normal. It was in the Harrow Road where the uneasy peace of the family's existence was broken. Joel was on his way to fetch Toby from the learning centre, where he still went regularly despite the summer holidays. He had just made the turn from Great Western Road when he saw that a disturbing bit of action was in process across the street, behind the iron railing that lined the pavement and prevented people from crossing. There, a neighbourhood character commonly called Drunk Bob sat in his wheelchair in what was one of his regular spots, just to the left of the doorway of an off licence and beneath the window on which a special deal for Spanish wine was being advertised. He was clutching a paper bag to his chest, his grip on the top of it curving around the unmistakable neck of a bottle. He was shouting his usual cry of 'Oy! Oy!' but this time, instead of bellowing into the traffic, he was directing the exclamation at a group of boys who were harassing him. One boy had grasped the handles of his wheelchair and was spinning him around while the others made lunges at him, attempting to grab the bag he was holding. Drunk Bob weaved from side to side in his chair as the boys spun and jerked him. Clearly, they wished him to hold on to the arms of the chair and loosen his grip on the bag, which, in addition to plaguing him, was their object. But Drunk Bob obviously knew their intention. The bag was his priority. He'd taken the better part of a day to cadge enough money from passersby to purchase his drink, and he wasn't about to hand it over to a group of boys, no matter how menacing they were.

So the boys spun him, their laughter and taunts nearly drowning out the old man's cries of 'Oy! Oy!' No one came out of any of the shops to stop them, for in the Harrow Road the course of wisdom had long suggested that one's business ought to be minded before the business of anyone else in the process of being disturbed by neighbourhood thugs. Several people passed by on the pavement as the boys vexed Drunk

Bob. But no one said a word save an elderly woman who shook a walking stick at them but who hurried on her way the moment one of the boys made a grab for her bag.

From where he stood, Joel could see that Drunk Bob was sliding down in his seat. In another few moments, the old man would be on the pavement and there was little chance he could defend himself there. Looking right and left for a policeman made no change in matters, for there was never a policeman in the vicinity when one was needed and always a policeman there when no one was doing a thing. Joel had no desire to be a hero, but nonetheless he shouted, 'Hey! You breds let dat bloke alone. He's crippled, innit,' which momentarily made one of the boys look up to see who was daring to spoil the group's fun.

Joel muttered, 'Damn,' when he saw who it was. Neal Wyatt and he met glances, and the expression that crossed Neal's face was perfectly readable despite his half-frozen features. Over his shoulder, he said something to his crew, and they halted their harassing of Drunk Bob at once.

Joel wasn't so foolish as to think this cessation of their activity had anything to do with his cry from across the street. Since, in the next moment, every one of the boys looked in his direction, he was perfectly aware of what was about to happen. He began to sprint up the Harrow Road, just as Neal and his crew began moving towards the pavement railing. Neal was leading the pack, smiling like someone who'd just had a bag of money dropped in front of him.

Joel knew it was a mistake to run, but he also knew that Neal had things to prove to his crew, not the least of which was his capacity to finish Joel off. Joel was the little worm he'd been intent upon squashing in Meanwhile Gardens when Ivan Weatherall had intervened. He was also the slug who'd been chosen by Hibah for friendship, regardless of Neal's own wishes.

Joel heard the shouts of the boys behind him as he dashed

in the direction of the learning centre. The road was only the width of two vehicles, and it would take Neal and his crew less than ten seconds to leap the railing, gain the opposite pavement, and hurtle over its railing as well. So Joel pounded furiously along, dodging a young mother with a pushchair, three chador-wearing women with shopping bags over their arms, and a white-haired gentleman who shouted 'Stop! Thief! Help!' in anticipation of whatever was to come as Joel charged by.

A quick glance over his shoulder allowed Joel to see that he'd been momentarily blessed. A bus and two lorries had swerved into view. Neal and his crew were hot to pursue him but not hot to be caught under the wheels of a vehicle, so they had to wait until all three had passed before they crossed the road and took up the chase. By that time, and despite his labouring lungs, Joel had gained fifty yards on them. The charity shop was in view, and he flung himself inside, panting like an over-heated dog as he slammed the door behind him.

Kendra was in the back, sorting through bags of new donations. She looked up when the door crashed closed, and what was on her tongue was something meant to sort Joel for the way he'd arrived. But when she saw his face, her intention altered. She said, 'What's going on? Where's Toby? Aren't you meant to fetch—'

Joel waved her off, a response so unusual that she was stunned into silence. He peered out of the window and saw Neal on his way, leading his crew like a hound on the scent. Joel glanced back at his aunt, then beyond her to the little room at the back of the shop. He knew there was a door within it and an alley behind it. He made for them both without a word.

Kendra said, 'Joel! What's going on? What're you doing? Who's out there?'

He managed 'Blokes,' as he pushed past her. His breath

was coming so hard that he was feeling light-headed, and his chest seemed branded with a red-hot iron.

Kendra walked to the window as Joel dived for the back room. Seeing the boys on their way, she said, 'Are they vexing you? *That* lot? I'll sort them out.' She reached for the door's handle.

'No!' Joel shouted. He had no time to say more, certainly no time to tell his aunt she would make things worse if she tried to deal with the other boys. No one sorted anyone in his kind of situation, and sometimes an enemy was just an enemy for reasons no one could actually fathom. Joel was Neal Wyatt's chosen death partner. That's just how it was. Joel crashed into the back room, where a dim bulb lit the way to the door.

He shoved it open. It slammed against the rear wall of the building. He threw himself out into the alley, and a moment later he was hurtling up it while Kendra shut the door behind him.

Joel pounded along for another thirty yards before he was too winded to continue. He knew he had to stop to catch his breath, but he also knew he had moments only before Neal Wyatt worked out which shop he had gone into and what he'd done when he got there. He looked for a place that was safe to hide. He found it in a skip that was sprouting rubbish from a building site just behind a block of flats.

With the last of his breath, he heaved himself inside. He had to toss out several cardboard boxes and carrier bags filled with rubbish, but this was something his pursuers were unlikely to notice, given the condition of the rest of the alley.

He ducked down and waited, breathing as shallowly as his aching lungs could manage. In less than two minutes he was rewarded. He heard the slapping of feet coming in his direction. And then their voices:

'Fucking yellow-arse got away.'

'Nah. He's round here innit.'

'Wants sorting, dat cunt.'

'Neal, you see where?'

'Real shit hole, dis.'

'Perfec' place for likes of him, den.'

Laughter and then Neal Wyatt's voice saying, 'Le's go. Dat slag is hiding him. Le's get her.'

The boys moved off, and Joel stayed where he was. Indecision and fear made his bowels pressure downward, demanding release. He concentrated on not letting anything go. Arms wrapped around himself, knees tucked up to his chest, he closed his eyes and listened harder.

He heard a door slam in the distance. He knew it was the back door to the charity shop, the boys returning there and intent upon damage. He tried to remember how many of them there were – as if this would somehow help the situation – because he knew that his aunt was more than a match for one or two boys, perhaps even three. But more than that in a confrontation would mean trouble for her.

Joel forced himself past the fear, past the rumbling at the bottom of his gut. He rose and lifted himself to the edge of the skip. He was saved by the sirens, which at that point came screaming down the Harrow Road.

When Joel heard them, he knew what his aunt had done. Anticipating the boys, she'd phoned nine-nine-nine the moment Joel had ducked into the alley and she had closed the door behind him. Her accent, her language, and the term *gang of boys* or perhaps, even better, *gang of black louts* had got the police moving, quicker than usual, bringing them on the run with lights, sirens, batons, and handcuffs. Neal Wyatt and his crew would soon know the rough justice of the Harrow Road police station if they weren't quick about clearing out of the charity shop. His aunt had won the day.

Joel dropped to the ground and scurried off. Less than five minutes later he was entering the learning centre, where Toby had his meetings with the specialist who'd been assigned to help him.

In the vestibule, Joel stopped to brush himself off. He'd got fairly dirty inside the skip, mostly from having landed on a bag of kitchen rubbish largely containing discarded baked beans and coffee grounds. His jeans bore the evidence of this, all along one leg, as did his jacket, where his shoulder and arm had ploughed into the remains of what looked like a mustard sandwich. He cleaned himself off as well as he could, pushed open the inner doors, and entered the centre.

Toby was waiting for him on the cracked vinyl sofa that comprised the furnishings of the reception area. He had his lava lamp on his lap, his hands curved around the bottom of it. He wasn't looking at anything other than the unplugged lamp, but his bottom lip was trembling and his shoulders were hunched.

Joel said cheerfully, 'Hey, Tobe. Wha's going, blood?'

Toby looked up. A bright smile eased the drawn expression on his face. He bounced off the sofa, all eagerness to leave, and it came to Joel that Toby had been frightened, thinking that no one was going to turn up, claim him, and take him home. Joel's heart grew fiery for his little brother. Toby, he decided, was not intended to feel so scared.

He said to him, 'Le's nick off, mon. You ready, or wha'? I'm sorry I'm late. You wa'n't worried or nuffink?'

Toby shook his head, everything forgotten. He said, 'Nah,' then 'Hey, c'n we get some chips 'long the road before we go home? I got fifty pee. Dix gave it me. I got dat five pounds from Gran as well.'

'You don't want to be spendin' dat money on chips,' Joel pointed out. 'It's birthday money. You got to spend it on somet'ing to remember your birthday by.'

'But if I want chips, how else I get 'em? An' the fifty pee wa'n't birthday money anyways.'

Joel was trying to come up with a reply for this, one that would explain – with kindness – that fifty pence would not be enough to buy the chips, no matter that it wasn't birthday money, when a tall black woman with close-cropped hair and golden earrings the size of hubcaps appeared from one of the centre's interior offices. This was Luce Chinaka, one of the learning specialists who worked with Toby. She smiled and said, 'I thought I heard someone out here talking to my young man. Could I have a word, please?' This last she said to Joel before she went on to Toby, 'Did you forget to tell him I wanted to see him when he came to fetch you, Mr Campbell?'

Toby ducked his head. He clutched his lava lamp closer to his chest. Luce Chinaka touched him lightly on his sparse hair and said, 'It's all right, luv. You're allowed to forget things. Wait here, won't you? We won't be long.'

Toby looked to Joel for guidance, and Joel could see the panic rise in his brother's face at the idea of being left alone so soon after being rescued. He said, 'Hang here, mate,' and he searched the room until he found a Spider-Man comic for Toby to look at. He handed it over and told him to wait, promising that he wouldn't be long. Toby took the comic under his arm and clambered back on to the sofa. He placed the lava lamp carefully next to him and laid the comic on his lap. He didn't look at it, however. Instead, he fastened his eyes on Joel. They were simultaneously trusting eyes and eyes of appeal. Only someone with a stone in his chest in place of his heart would have failed to be moved by their expression.

Joel followed Luce Chinaka to a small office crammed with a desk, table, chairs, notice boards, white boards, and bookshelves that spilled notebooks, volumes, board games, and folders. She had a name plate on her desk – brass with *Luce Chinaka* engraved upon it – and next to it stood a picture of her with her family: arm-in-arm with an equally tall, dark-skinned husband, three winsome children stair-stepped in front of them.

Luce went behind her desk, but she didn't sit. Instead, she pulled the chair out and drew it around the side. She pointed to another chair for Joel, so that they could sit facing each other. They almost touched knees since space in the room was so limited.

Luce took a folder from the top of her desk, and she glanced inside it as if to verify something. She said to Joel, 'We haven't talked before this. You're Toby's brother . . . It's Joel, isn't it?'

Joel nodded. The only reason he knew that adults called children into official places like their offices was if there was some sort of trouble. So he assumed Toby had done something he wasn't meant to do. He waited for elucidation and steeled himself to its inevitable appearance.

'He's talked about you quite a bit,' Luce Chinaka went on. 'You're very important to him, but I expect you know that.'

Joel nodded again. He sought something in his head as a response, but he could come up with nothing other than the nod.

Luce picked up a pen. It was gold and slender, and it suited her. Joel saw that a form had been fixed to the cover of the folder she was holding, and there was writing on this, which she read for a moment before she spoke. Then it was to tell Joel what he already knew: that Toby's primary school had made the recommendation that he enrol in the learning centre, that in fact the school had made it a condition of his acceptance as a pupil. She concluded with, 'Do you know this, Joel?' At his nod, she continued.

'Toby's quite behind where he should be for his age. Do you understand the nature of his problem?' Luce Chinaka's voice was kind, as were her eyes, which were deep brown although one had flecks of gold in it.

'He i'n't stupid,' Joel said.

'No. Of course not,' Luce assured him. 'But he has a serious learning disability and . . . well, there do appear to be . . .' She hesitated. Once again, she looked at the file, but this time it seemed to be a way of deciding how best to say what needed saying. 'There appear to be other . . . well, other problems as well. Our job here at the centre is to determine exactly *what* those problems are and how best someone like Toby can be taught. We then teach him in the way that he learns – as an adjunct to his regular schooling. We also offer him alternatives in . . . well, alternatives in social behaviour that he can learn to choose from. Do you understand all this?'

Joel nodded. He was concentrating hard. He had the distinct feeling that Luce Chinaka was leading up to something important and dreadful, so he felt wary.

She continued. 'Essentially, Toby has trouble both processing and retrieving information, Joel. He has a *language* disability complicated by what we call a cognitive dysfunction. But that,' Luce fluttered her fingers as if to wave the words away and make what she had to say sensible to a twelve-year-old boy for whom every word sounded like another step on the familial trail of tears he and his siblings had been treading for ages, 'is just how we label things. The real issue is that a language disability is serious because everything we're taught in school depends first and foremost upon our capacity for taking it in in the form of language: words and sentences.'

Joel could tell that the woman was making her explanation simple for him to understand because he was Toby's brother and not Toby's dad. He wasn't offended by this. Rather, it felt oddly comforting, despite the trepidation he was feeling about the entire discussion. He expected that Luce Chinaka was a very good mother. He pictured her tucking her three children into their beds at night and not leaving the room till she made sure they'd said their prayers and received her kiss.

'Good,' she said. 'But now we come to the crux of the matter. You see, there are limits to what we can do for Toby here in the learning centre. When we reach those limits, we have to consider what we're going to do next.'

Alarms went off in Joel's head. He said, 'You saying you can't help Toby or summick? You want him to leave?'

'No, no,' she said hastily. 'But I do want to develop a plan for him, which we can't do without a broader assessment. Call it . . . well, call it a study of him. Now, everyone needs to be involved in this. Toby's teacher at Middle Row School, the learning centre staff, a doctor, and your parents. I see from the records here that your father is deceased, but we'd definitely like the opportunity to have a meeting with your mum. We'll need to begin by having you give her these documents to read and after that—'

'Can't.' It was the only word Joel could manage. The thought of having his mother here, in this office, facing this woman, was too much for him, even though he knew it would never happen. She wouldn't ever be allowed out on her own and, even if Joel could fetch her from the hospital, Carole Campbell would have lasted less than five minutes in the presence of Luce Chinaka before she crumbled to bits.

Luce looked up from the paperwork she'd been removing from Toby's file. She seemed to dwell on the word *can't*, and she seemed to compare it to everything she knew about the family so far, which was very little and had been deliberately kept that way by the family itself. She made an interpretation.

'Your mum doesn't read?' she asked. 'I'm sorry. I did assume because her name's on the paperwork . . .' Luce brought it closer to her face and examined what Joel knew had to be his aunt's hasty scrawl.

He said, 'Dat's . . . That's Aunt Ken's writing. She went to Toby's school.'

'Oh, I see. Kendra Osborne is your aunt, then, not your mum? She's your legal guardian?'

Joel nodded although he had no knowledge of what made someone legal or not.

'Is your mum deceased as well, then, Joel?' Luce Chinaka asked. 'Is that what you mean when you said she couldn't read this?'

He shook his head. But he couldn't and wouldn't tell her about his mother. The truth was that Carole Campbell could read as well as any person alive. The additional truth was that it didn't make any difference if she could read or not.

He reached for the papers that Luce Chinaka held, and he said the only words that he could manage, which were the only words that told the truth of the matter as Joel saw it. 'I c'n read it,' he told her. 'I c'n take care of Toby.'

'But this isn't about . . .' Luce sought another way to explain. 'Oh my dear, there needs to be a study done and only a responsible adult can give approval for it. You see, we must have quite a . . . well, let's call it quite a *thorough* examination of Toby, and it must be done by . . .'

'I said, I c'n do it!' Joel cried. He grabbed the papers and crumpled them to his chest.

'But Joel—'

'I *can!*'

He left her watching him in a mixture of confusion and wonder as he went to fetch his little brother. He also left her reaching for the phone.

13

When Ness deserted her brothers that day in Paddington, she didn't leave the railway station at once. Instead, she paused behind a sandwich kiosk, using the excuse of lighting up a cigarette that she'd nicked from Kendra. As she dug in her bag for matches, she eased her way around the kiosk so that she had a view of WH Smith. Although it was crowded within the shop, she had no trouble picking out Joel. He was dutifully heading for the magazines, his shoulders slumped as they generally were and Toby in his wake as he always was.

Ness waited until Joel was in the queue at the till, his purchases in hand, before she went on her way. She couldn't see what his choice was from among the various magazines on offer, but she knew he'd get something appropriate for their mother because she also knew that was just who Joel was: dependable and dutiful to a fault. He was also capable of pretending whatever he needed to pretend in order to get through the day. As for herself, she was through with pretending. Pretending had got her exactly where she was at that moment, which was nowhere. Pretending changed nothing, and it especially did not change how she felt inside, which was full to bursting, as if her blood might seep through her skin.

Had she been asked to do so, Ness couldn't have put another name to that feeling of being full. She couldn't have named it simply, as a child might: full of mad, bad, sad, or glad. She couldn't have named it more complexly: full of the milk of human kindness, full of compassion, full of the love one might

have for a helpless baby or an innocent kitten, full of right-
eous anger at an injustice, full of rage at life's inequities. All
she knew was that she felt so full that she had to do something to relieve the pressure building up within her. This pressure was a constant in her life, but it was one that had been
increasing dangerously since the moment she'd sat in the audience of that ballet with the environment assaulting her and no
way of explaining why she could not remain to watch those
dancers *bourrée* across the stage.

She needed to *do* something. That was all she knew. She
needed to run, she needed to push over a rubbish bin,
she needed to snatch an infant out of its pram and trip its
mother, she needed to push an old lady into the Grand Union
Canal and watch her sink, she needed a way to get rid of the
full. She began by leaving the environs of the sandwich kiosk
and making her way to the ladies' toilet.

Twenty pence was required to get inside. This made Ness
so unaccountably angry that she kicked the turnstile and then
crawled beneath it, not because she didn't have the money but
because the railway station's demanding it of someone wanting
to have a simple wee, for God's sake, seemed suddenly out-
rageous to her, a final straw and she the camel. She didn't
even look around to make sure no one was watching her on
hands and knees effecting her marginally illegal entry. She
wanted to be *seen* doing it, in fact, so that she could allow her
indignation a physical manifestation. But no one was there to
see her, so she went inside and used the toilet.

An inspection of herself in the mirror came next, and this
told her adjustments in her appearance were called for. She
attended first to the top she was wearing, pulling it down and
tucking it more deeply into her jeans so as to reveal the swell
of her breasts dangerously close to the nipple. She followed
this with a fluffing of her hair, making it big hair, woman's
hair, woman-with-intentions hair. She scrutinised her makeup
and decided that her skin was dark enough but more lipstick

was called for. From her bag she brought out a tube long ago pinched from Boots, and this action – just the tube of lipstick coming to rest in her hand – reminded her of Six and Natasha. The thought of her erstwhile friends produced a renewed surge of that damnable fullness. This time, the pressure was such that her hands shook. When she tried to apply the lipstick, she broke it and then felt the horror of certain tears.

Tears meant a release of pressure and an end to the fullness, but Ness didn't know that. She knew tears only as a sign of defeat, as the last resort and potentially the last gasp of the terminally weak and the decidedly conquered. So, instead of weeping, she flung the ruined lipstick into the bin, and she left the ladies' toilet.

Outside the station, she made her way to the bus stop, where the vicissitudes of London Transport forced her into fifteen minutes of waiting for a number 23 bus. When one finally came along, she elbowed past two women with pushchairs who were struggling to get on to the vehicle and she told them to fuck themselves when they asked her to stand aside and let them on first. It was crowded within and hot, but she didn't climb to the upper deck as she would have done with Joel and Toby. Instead, she moved towards the back of the lower deck and placed herself near the exit doors from which position she would at least get a breath of fresh air when the doors swung open at each stop. She clung to a pole as the bus lurched back into the traffic and found herself eye to eye with an old-age pensioner, hairs bursting from his nose and his ears, like minuscule antennae.

He had a seat on the aisle. He smiled at her, what appeared to be a grandfatherly smile until he dropped his gaze to her chest. He kept it there long enough to telegraph what he was looking at, and then raised his glance once again to capture hers. His tongue came out and made the circuit of his lips: the first white with some kind of unappealing coating, the second colourless and cracked. He winked.

'Fuck *off*.' Ness made no attempt to keep her voice down. She wanted to turn away from him, but she didn't dare, as that would have left her unprotected. No, she needed her eyes on him, so she kept them there. If he made a move, she would be ready.

But nothing more happened. The old man gave her breasts one more look, said 'My goodness,' and shook out a folded tabloid. He adjusted it in such a way that the Page Three girl was well on view. Ness thought, Fucking bugger, and as soon as the bus lumbered to the stop nearest Queensway, she got off.

She didn't have far to go, and she attracted a fair amount of attention on her way. Queensway was bustling with shoppers but, even so, Ness was something different. Her revealing clothing – some of it skimpy and some of it tight – demanded notice. Her expression and her gait, the first haughty and the second confident, succeeded in creating the impression of a female set on seduction. In combination, these elements allowed her to project such an air of danger that she was safe from approach, which was what she wanted. If any approaching was to be done, *she* would be the person to do it.

When she came to a chemist's shop, she ducked inside. Like the pavement outside, it was crowded. The cosmetics were as far from the door as possible, but that provided a challenge that Ness had no difficulty in taking up. She went directly to the display of lipsticks and made a brief study of the colours. She chose a deep burgundy and, without bothering to glance around to make certain she was not being watched, she slid the lipstick into her bag at the same moment as she reached to inspect another colour. She spent a few more minutes in the shop with her heart pounding loudly in her ears before she made her way to the door. In a moment, she was outside on the pavement and moving down the street in the direction of Whiteley's, her mission accomplished.

It was a simple thing, really: the pinching of a lipstick on a day when the rest of the world was shopping and creating a diversion by their sheer numbers. By all rights, Ness shouldn't have felt particularly triumphant. But she did. She felt like singing. She felt like stamping her feet and crowing. She felt, in short, completely different from the way she'd felt when she'd entered the shop. The rush of delight that washed through her seemed to alter her very substance, as if she'd taken a drug instead of merely breaking the law. Finally, she felt released from the pressure that had been filling her.

She strutted. She giggled. She laughed aloud. She would, she decided, do it again. She'd head towards Whiteley's, where the pickings were better. She had hours before Joel and Toby would return to Paddington station.

That was when she saw Six and Natasha, just as she crossed the road. They were tripping along with their heads together and their arms entwined. There was a little stumble to their gait that suggested they'd been drinking or drugging.

High with the success of her venture, Ness decided the time had come to bury whatever hatchet the past few weeks had produced among them. She called out to them good-naturedly. 'Six! Tash! Where you *been*?'

The two girls stopped. Their faces altered from expectant to wary when they saw who'd hailed them. They gave each other a look, but they maintained their ground as Ness approached.

'Happenin?' Six said with a nod at Ness. 'You ain't been round f'r a while, Moonbeam.'

Ness read this slight rewriting of their mutual history as a peace offering. She made no attempt to correct it. She accepted it as given, and sought her cigarettes. Custom suggested she offer one to each of the girls, but she hadn't taken enough of her aunt's Benson and Hedges to make this possible so, instead of lighting up and offending them when it seemed she had an opening with them, she brought out her newly pinched lipstick

instead. She took it from its packaging and twisted the base
till the cylinder of colour was fully extended and looking
vaguely obscene. She played with it a bit, in and out and in
and out, and gave her former friends a grin before she turned
to the window of the nearest shop and used it as a mirror.
She applied the colour and inspected her lips. She said, 'Well,
shit. Dat looks like I been eating road kill, innit,' and she tossed
the new lipstick into the street. It was a more-where-that-came-
from kind of gesture. She completed it with a ritual fluffing
of her hair.

'Got dat shit off th' chemist up near Westbourne Grove. I
should've nicked 'bout five of 'em, it so easy, you know wha'
I mean? So. Wha' you two doing?'

'Not pinching shit from Boots, an' dat's for sure,' Six said.
It was a warning sign, but it was not sufficient to deflate Ness
entirely.

She said with a grin, 'Why? You changed your lyin' and
thievin' ways, den, Six? Or you got a man providing for you
now?'

'Don't need a man to get wha' I want,' Six replied, and to
demonstrate her point, she brought out a mobile phone and
examined it, as if a pressing text message had just come in.

Ness knew she was meant to admire the mobile. It was part
of the ritual. Cooperatively, she said, 'Nice, dat. Where'd you
get it, den?'

Six cocked her head and looked smug. Tash was less cool.
She said with evident pride, 'Got dat off a white girl over
Kensington Square. Six go up to her, says "Hand dat over,
cunt," an' I get behind her case she t'ink 'bout running off.
She start to cry, an' she say, "Oh *please*. My mummy going
to be *so* cheesed off I got her phone nicked," and Six jus' grab
it and we push her down. Time she get up, we halfway to the
High Street. Easy as anyt'ing, wa'n't it, Six?'

Six punched in a few numbers. She said to Tash, 'Got a
fag?' Tash obediently fished around in her bag and handed

over a packet of Dunhills. Six took one, lit up and handed the cigarettes back. When Tash began to extend them to Ness, Six said, 'Tash,' in a way that told her what she was meant to do. Tash looked from Six to Ness, then back to Six. Knowing which side her metaphorical bread was buttered, she stowed the Dunhills.

Six said into the mobile, 'Hey, baby. Wha's happening, den? You got summick for your mummy or wha'? . . . Hell no. I ain't going dat far. Wha' you 'specting to get off me I come all dat way? . . . In Queensway wiv Tash . . . Yeah, me and Tash c'n do dat, you got substance to make it worthwhile for us, y'unnerstan. Otherwise . . .' Six listened for a longer moment. She shifted her weight to one hip and tapped her foot. She finally said, 'No way, mon. Me and Tash come all dat way, we too damn knackered to . . . Hey, don't talk nasty or I sort you, baby. Me and Tash *both* set on you, and den you be sorry, innit.' She laughed and gave Natasha a wink. For her part, Natasha merely looked confused. Six listened a moment longer and said, 'Okay, but you be ready for us, mon,' before she punched the mobile off and looked at Ness with a satisfied smile.

The smile was unnecessary as Ness, unlike Natasha, was far from dim. The constant *me and Tash* of the conversation had had its desired effect. Lines had been drawn. There was no crossing over. There was also no way of going back to how things had been. For one hundred and one female adolescent reasons, Ness was anathema and she would remain that way.

She could have demanded an explanation for this. She could have accused or analysed. She was able to do none of this in the pressure of the moment, though. She was only able to make a stab at saving face for having crossed the road to talk to the two girls in the first place.

Saving face meant not caring. It meant not dignifying a slight by acknowledging it. It meant ignoring the fullness inside.

Ness locked eyes with Six and gave her a curt nod. She said, 'Whatever.'

Six said, 'Yeah.'

Tash looked as confused as she'd looked during all the *me and Tash* of Six's mobile conversation, with their implications of an equality that clearly did not exist between her and the other girl.

Six said to Tash, 'Le's go, den. We got someone waiting.' And to Ness as she stepped aside to let the other girls pass, 'You watch yourself, gash,' which put a full stop to the interaction.

Ness watched them go. She told herself they were two bloody stupid bitches and she didn't want their friendship, let alone did she need it. But, even as she assured herself of this fact – which was true enough – she felt *driven* once again. As a result, she moved towards Whiteley's. There was lipstick waiting to be pinched by someone. Ness knew she was just the girl to do it.

Kendra was loading her massage table into the Punto when Fabia Bender arrived on Edenham Estate in the company of two enormous and well-cared for dogs: a gleaming doberman and a giant schnauzer. Although Kendra, with a limited knowledge of canine breeds, would have been hard-pressed to identify the latter animal, she was impressed and intimidated by his size since his head reached above Fabia Bender's waist. Kendra stopped what she was doing. Any move – precipitate or otherwise – didn't seem wise.

Fabia Bender said, 'No worries, Mrs Osborne. They're lambs, actually. The doberman's Castor. The schnauzer's Pollux. No relation, of course, but I rashly decided that having two puppies at once would be easier than going through puppyhood twice, so I thought, Well why not. I intended from the first to have two dogs. Two large dogs. I like them big. But it took four times longer to train them, and both breeds are supposed to be easy. Pollux quite likes you, I can see. He's hoping for a pat on the head.'

She had them on extendable leads and when she told them to 'Sit, boys,' they did so obediently, and she dropped the leads to the ground. Castor remained at attention, in keeping with his breed. Pollux huffed gustily and sank down so that his great head lay upon his enormous paws. A literary person would have thought at once of the Baskervilles. Kendra thought of all the reasons why Fabia Bender was putting in an un-expected appearance at her house.

She said, 'Ness's been doing her community service, hasn't she? She's been leaving the house right on time, but I've not followed her there to make sure she's showing up. It seemed to me that I needed to . . . demonstrate trust in her?'

'And a good idea as well,' Fabia Bender said. 'Mrs Ghafoor gives us only positive reports about Ness so far. I wouldn't say she's enjoying the experience – this is Ness, not Mrs Ghafoor – but she *is* being consistent. High marks in her favour.'

Kendra nodded and waited for elucidation. She had an appointment in a posh neighbourhood of Maida Vale, with a middle-aged white American lady who intended becoming a regular client and who also had a great deal of time and money on her hands. Kendra didn't want to be late for it. She glanced at her watch and put her container of oils and lotions into the back of the car, tucked alongside the massage table.

'It's actually Ness's brother that I've come to talk to you about,' Fabia said. 'Could we have this conversation inside rather than in the street, Mrs Osborne?'

Kendra hesitated. She didn't ask which brother because it had to be Joel. She couldn't imagine a social worker from Youth Offending having a reason to talk to her about Toby, which meant that – as difficult as it was to believe, considering his personality – Joel was now in trouble. She said, 'What's he done?' and tried to sound concerned instead of what she was, which was panicked.

'If we could go inside? The boys will stay out here, of course.' She smiled. 'You needn't worry about your belongings. If I ask them to guard the car, they'll do it very nicely.' She tilted her head expectantly in the direction of the front door. 'This shouldn't take long,' she added and went on to say to the dogs, 'Guard, boys.'

These final remarks were a way of saying there was no getting around her intention to go inside the house, and Kendra recognised them as such. She lowered the boot lid and stepped past the dogs, neither of which moved. Fabia Bender followed her.

Once within, the social worker didn't reveal her mission at once. Instead she asked if Mrs Osborne would be willing to show her around. She'd never been in one of the terrace houses on Edenham Estate, she said pleasantly, and she confessed to an interest in how all buildings were laid out or converted to accommodate families.

Kendra believed this as much as she believed the moon was made of green cheese, but she saw no alternative to cooperation, considering the trouble Fabia Bender could cause if the social worker decided to do so. So, while there was little enough to see, Kendra showed it to Fabia anyway, playing along with the game at the same time as knowing how unlikely was the scenario that the white woman had come calling in order to further her knowledge of interior design.

Fabia asked questions as they went: How long had Kendra lived in this house? Was she a lucky owner or was this rented housing? How many people lived here? What were the sleeping arrangements?

Kendra couldn't see what the questions had to do with Joel or any trouble Joel might have been in, so she was suspicious. She didn't want to entrap herself should that be the social worker's intention and, because of this, she kept her answers as brief as possible and vague when vagueness appeared to be called for. Thus, on the first floor, she gave no reason for the screen that leaned against the wall near the sofa like a languishing debutante without a dance partner and, on the second floor, she made no explanation for having camp beds and sleeping bags for the boys instead of normal beds and sheets.

Above all, she didn't mention Dix. No matter that all over the city – not to mention all over the country – people lived in conditions far more irregular than this one, with the partners of parents coming and going with dizzying regularity as women searched for men and men searched for women, all in terror of having to be alone for more than five minutes. Kendra decided that the less said about Dix the better. She went so far as to mention sharing her own bedroom with Ness, a decision she regretted when Fabia Bender glanced inside the bathroom and noticed the man-sized vests that were drying on hangers above the bath. Above the basin there was further evidence of a man's occupation of the house. Dix's shaving gear was laid out neatly: safety razor, shaving soap, and brush.

Fabia Bender said nothing until they were back downstairs. There, she suggested that Kendra and she sit at the kitchen table for a moment. She explained that throughout the time that she had spent with Ness – at the police station, at the magistrate's court, and at the Youth Offending Team's office in Oxford Gardens – no mention had ever been made that there were two other Campbell children living with Mrs Osborne. This knowledge had come to her via the Westminster Learning Centre, where a woman called Luce Chinaka had become concerned when some paperwork requiring a parental signature – or the signature of a guardian, for that matter – had not been returned as requested. The request had been made of one Joel Campbell in reference to his brother Toby.

It was no coincidence that Fabia Bender had received the phone call from Luce Chinaka. Over-burdened with work, as all of the employees of the Youth Offending Team were, the secretary who routed phone calls to the social workers recognised *Campbell* as the surname of one of Fabia's clients and she passed the phone call to her. Trouble historically ran in families. When Luce Chinaka expressed her concern about one Joel Campbell, it seemed likely to the secretary that a sibling of Ness had surfaced.

'What sort of paperwork?' Kendra asked. 'Why'd he not give it to me?'

It had to do with advanced testing for Toby, with a possible placement in a situation better designed to meet his needs than was Middle Row School, Fabia told her.

'Testing?' Kendra asked cautiously. This rang bells and set off sirens. Toby was forbidden territory. Testing Toby, assessing Toby, evaluating Toby . . . It was all completely unthinkable. Nonetheless, because she had to know the exact nature of the enemy she faced, she said, 'What kind of testing? Testing done by who?'

'We're not certain yet,' Fabia Bender said. 'But that's not actually why I've come.' Because there were three children, not one, occupying Mrs Osborne's dwelling, she explained, she was there to assess the living situation. She was also there to talk about establishing permanent, official, and formal guardianship over the children.

Kendra wanted to know why this was necessary. They had a mother, they had a grandmother – although she didn't mention Glory's removal to Jamaica – and they had an aunt. One of their relations would always look out for them. Why did this need to be official? And what did *official* mean anyway?

Paperwork, as things turned out. Signatures. Carole either signing her children over or being declared incompetent so that someone else could manage their lives. Decisions had to be made about the future, and at present there was apparently no one designated to make them. Should no one be willing to take on that responsibility, then the Government—

Kendra told her there would be no going into Care for these children, if that was what Fabia Bender was alluding to. They were trouble; there was no denying it. Especially Ness, and there was virtually *no* reward in having to put up with the girl. But the children represented Kendra's last blood relatives in England and, while she would never have thought that detail an important one, with Fabia Bender sitting at her kitchen table mentioning the Government and mentioning testing for Toby, for her it became a detail writ very large.

Fabia hastened to reassure her. When there was a willing family member, the Government was *always* on the side of leaving children with their relations. Providing, of course, that the relations were suitable and could provide a stable environment in the children's best interests. That *appeared* to be the case – Kendra did not miss the emphasis on the predicate in that sentence – and Fabia would certainly make note of that in her report. In the meantime, Kendra needed to read and sign the paperwork given to Joel by Luce Chinaka at the learning centre. She also needed to speak to the children's mother about establishing permanent guardianship. As long as there was—

It was at this point that the dogs began barking. Since she knew what this meant, Fabia got to her feet at the same moment as Dix D'Court shouted from outside.

'Ken, baby! Wha's going on? I come home to love my woman, and dis is my greeting?'

Fabia strode to the door and opened it. She said, 'Boys, enough. Let him pass,' and then she added to Dix, 'I do beg your pardon. They thought you meant to touch the car and they'd been told to guard it. Do come in. They won't bother you now.'

A white woman in the house told Dix that something was going on, so he didn't continue in the vein he'd been employing outside. He entered, carrying two shopping bags. He put them on the worktop, where they spilled out vegetables, fruit, nuts, brown rice, beans, and yoghurt. He remained there, leaning against it, his arms crossed and his expression expectant. He was wearing a vest, just like those hanging above the bath, with running shorts and trainers. The ensemble did much to emphasise his body. What he'd said outside before being admitted to the house did much to emphasise the way things stood between Kendra and him.

Both he and Fabia Bender waited for Kendra to introduce them. There was no getting around it, so she made as brief a piece of work of the matter as possible. 'Dix D'Court, Fabia Bender from Youth Offending,' was how she put it. Fabia jotted down his name.

'She didn't know there were three,' Kendra added. 'She's dealt with Ness but she's come because of Joel.'

'He in trouble?' Dix asked. 'Don't sound like Joel, innit.'

Kendra was gratified by the response. It suggested Dix's positive involvement with the boy. 'He was supposed to give me some paperwork from the learning centre and he didn't.'

'Dat an offence or summick?'

'Just a point of interest,' Fabia Bender said. 'Do you live here, Mr D'Court? Or do you just visit?'

Dix looked to Kendra for an indication of how he was meant to answer, which was answer enough. When he said, 'I come an' go,' Fabia Bender wrote something in her notebook, but it seemed clear by the way her lips adjusted that either *lie* or *falsehood* was part of the information she took down. Kendra knew she would probably consider Dix's presence in the same house as a nubile fifteen-year-old girl in whatever she might ultimately recommend. Fabia, after all, had seen Ness. She would likely conclude that a delectable twenty-three-year-old man and a seductive adolescent girl amounted to something that would be labelled Potential Trouble rather than Suitable Situation.

When she'd written what she needed to write, Fabia Bender closed her notebook. She told Kendra to ask Joel for the paperwork that Luce Chinaka had given him for signature and she instructed her further to tell Ness to phone her. She went through the motions of informing Dix what a pleasure it had been to meet him, and she ended with stating her assumption that Ness had no private place for sleeping or dressing and was that the case, Mrs Osborne?

Dix said, 'I built her dat screen and—'

Kendra cut him off. 'We give her the privacy and respect she needs.'

Fabia Bender nodded. 'I see,' she said.

What she saw, however, was something upon which she did not expound.

When Kendra confronted Joel, she was both angry and worried. Despite her intentions to do nothing at all with the paperwork, she lectured the boy. If he'd only *given* her the documents in the first place, she told him, there would have been no need for Fabia Bender to turn up on Edenham Estate and consequently no report for her to have to fill out. Now there would likely be trouble in the form of hoops to jump through, explanations to give, investigations to endure, and officials to meet. Joel's reluctance to do his simple duty had put them all squarely in the jaws of the System, facing all of the System's attendant time-eating activities.

So Kendra wanted to know what the hell he was thinking of, not giving her the papers that the learning centre woman – in her agitation she'd forgotten Luce Chinaka's name – had wanted her to see. Did he understand that they were all under scrutiny now? Did he *know* what it meant when a family came to the attention of Social Services?

Of course Joel knew. It was his greatest fear. But he wouldn't articulate it since to do so would give the fear a legitimacy that might make it a reality. So he told his aunt he'd forgotten because he'd been caught up in thinking about . . . He had to consider what the subject of his thoughts might be, and he settled upon telling her he'd been caught up in thinking about *Wield Words Not Weapons* since this was at least a wholesome subject. It wasn't far from the truth anyway.

He didn't anticipate Kendra's encouraging him to go once she learned about it, but that was what she did. To her, it would be evidence of a positive influence invading Joel's life, and she knew it was likely that positive influences would be required in all the children's lives to offset the potential negative influence of their living with a forty-year-old aunt who was nightly, and at considerable volume, satisfying her baser urges with a twenty-three-year-old body-builder.

So Joel found himself going to *Wield Words Not Weapons*, leaving Toby with Dix, Kendra, pizza, and a video. He made his way over to Oxford Gardens, where a hand-lettered sign on the front door of a long, low, post-war building – home also of the Youth Offending Team's office as it happened – directed participants to the Basement Activities Centre, which proved easy enough to find. In the entry, a young black woman sat at a card table filling out stick-on name-tags as people came through the door. Joel hesitated before approaching her, until she said to him, 'First timer? Cool. How you called, speck?' at which point he felt a rush of blood to his cheeks. She'd accepted him casually. She'd given him a welcome without the blink of an eye.

He said, 'Joel,' and he watched her loop the four letters of his name across the tag.

She said, 'Don't have none of the custard creams,' as she put the tag on his shirt. 'They stale as shoe soles. Go for the fig bars,' and she gave him a wink.

He nodded solemnly, this piece of information seeming to him like the key to success at the entire affair. Then he sidled over to a refreshment table at one side of the room. There, tin plates held biscuits and cakes, and a coffee urn nearby bubbled fragrantly. He took a chocolate digestive and shot a hesitant glance around the people gathered for the event.

Joel saw that they comprised a mixed group of every race and every age. Blacks, whites, Orientals, and Asians blended together: from ancients to babies in prams and pushchairs. Most of them appeared to know each other as, after enthusiastic greetings among them, conversations began and the noise level rose.

Ivan Weatherall moved in the midst of all the people. He saw Joel and raised a hand in salute, but he did not approach although Joel decided Ivan looked happy to see him. Instead, Ivan worked his way to a dais at the front of the room where a microphone stood with a tall stool behind it. In front of the mike, yellow and orange plastic chairs fanned out, and Ivan's progress to the dais acted as a signal for the event's participants to begin filling in the rows. Ivan said, 'A record crowd this evening,' and he sounded delighted. 'Can it be the increase in prize money? Well, I always believed you lot were available for bribery.'

Laughter greeted this. It was obvious that Ivan was comfortable with the group. Joel wasn't surprised.

'I see a few new faces, and I welcome you to *Wield Words Not Weapons*,' Ivan said. 'I hope you'll find a home here for your talents. So, without further blather from me, then . . .' He was carrying a clipboard to which he then referred. 'You're first, Adam Whitburn. May I encourage you to *endeavour* to overcome your natural shyness this evening?'

Everyone chuckled as a Rasta with his dreads tucked into a massive knitted cap leapt out of the audience and on to the dais with the attitude of a prize fighter entering the ring. He tugged at the brim of his cap and shot an affable grin at the audience when someone cried out, 'You go, bred.' He perched on the stool and began to read from a dog-eared spiral notebook. He announced the piece as *Stephen G'wan Home*.

'Got him on the street, they did,' he began. 'Blood poured red, hot like blaze, but knife go cool. Stuck like no one, Dad, not a man, not a goat. Stuck just cos the way of the street.'

The room was hushed as Adam Whitburn read. Not even a baby mewled for attention. Joel dropped his gaze to his knees as the story was told: documenting the gathering crowd, the police, the investigation, the arrest, the trial, and the end. No justice and no way to put anything at rest. Ever. Merely dead in the street.

When Adam Whitburn finished, for a moment nothing happened. Then applause rose from the audience, accompanied by shouts and hoots. But what followed next came as a surprise to Joel. Members of the audience began to offer criticism about the writing, referring to it as a *poem*, which also surprised him as it hadn't rhymed and the only thing he knew about poetry was that the words were supposed to rhyme. No one mentioned the *facts* of the piece at all: specifically the death and subsequent injustice that were at the centre of it. Instead, they talked about language and metre, intention and accomplishment. They talked about scanning and figurative language, and they asked Adam Whitburn questions about form. The Rasta listened intently, replied when necessary, and took notes. Then he thanked the audience, nodded and stepped back to join them.

A girl called Sunny Drake followed him. The piece she wrote appeared to Joel to be about pregnancy and cocaine, about being born addicted to her mother's addiction, about giving birth to a baby born the same. Again, a discussion followed: criticism with no judgement offered about the facts.

In this way, ninety minutes passed. Aside from Ivan calling out names from his clipboard, no one actually ran the event after his initial comments. Instead, it appeared to run itself, with the familiarity of a ritual that everyone understood. When the time for a break arrived, Ivan returned to the microphone. He announced that *Walk the Word* would be happening at the front of the room for those who were interested, while the rest of the audience partook of refreshments. Joel watched curiously as the group dispersed and twelve people from the audience moved eagerly towards the dais. There, Ivan was handing out sheets of paper and, from this and the murmurs of conversation which included the words *fifty pounds*, Joel understood that this was the part of the event that had at first attracted his attention: the part that included prize money.

While he knew he didn't have much chance of winning – especially since he had no idea of what the event actually was – he moved forward with the rest of the people. He saw that Adam Whitburn was among them, and he almost considered leaving at that point. But Ivan called out, 'Delighted to see you, Joel Campbell. Here you are. Join in the fray,' and soon enough Joel had a piece of paper in his hand upon which were written five words: *havoc, forever, question, destruction,* and *forgiveness.*

He stared at them with absolutely no comprehension. He knew what they meant but, other than that, he was without a clue. He looked around for an indication of what he was supposed to do next, and he saw that the other participants in *Walk theWord* were setting about creating something, writing furiously, pausing for thought, chewing on their pencils, clicking the cartridges of their biros in and out. It seemed to Joel that what they were creating had to be more of the curious poetry. He knew he could wander off or he could join them. Fifty pounds seemed reason enough for him to do the latter.

For the first five minutes, he gazed at the paper he'd been given as all around him people scribbled, rubbed out, muttered, scribbled, scratched out, rubbed out, and scribbled some more. He wrote *havoc* and he waited for something miraculous to happen, something lightning-like, rendering him a poetic St Paul. He made the *o* in *havoc* into a wheel with spokes. He surrounded the word itself with shooting stars. He doodled and underlined. He sighed and crumpled the paper into a ball.

Next to him, a grandmotherly white woman in enormous spectacles was thoughtfully chewing on the end of her biro. She looked at Joel, then patted him on the knee. She whispered,

'Start with one of the other words, pet. No need to go from top to bottom or take them in any particular order.'

'You sure?'

'Been doing it since the first, I have. Take up the word you can feel right here –' she pointed to her chest '– and go from there. Let go. Your subconscious will do the rest. Give it a try.'

Joel looked at her doubtfully, but decided to have a go at doing it her way. He smoothed out the paper and read each of the words again. He seemed to feel the most for the word *forever* so he wrote it down and then something curious happened: words began to pile on top of that first one – *forever* – and he merely acted as their scribe.

'"Forever kind of place hold her close,"' he wrote. '"She asks why and the question screams. No answer, girl. You been playing too long. Ain't no forgiveness for the death inside you. What you did, how it ended with destruction. You die, slag, and havoc goes home."'

Joel dropped his pencil and stared, slack-jawed, at what he'd written. He felt as if steam were coming from his ears. He read his piece twice over, then four times more. He was about to shove it surreptitiously into the pocket of his jeans when someone flitted by and plucked the paper out of his hand. It went to a group who had volunteered to be the evening's judges. They disappeared from the room with all the entries as *Wield Words Not Weapons* continued with more readings and more reactions from the audience.

Joel couldn't attend to very much after that. Instead, he watched the door through which the judges for *Walk the Word* had passed. It seemed to him that the length of four more *Wield Words Not Weapons* events passed while he waited to hear the judges' verdict on his first literary effort. When they finally emerged, they handed the entries to Ivan Weatherall, who looked them over and nodded happily as he read them.

When the time arrived to announce the winner of *Walk the*

Word, recognition went in reverse order, with honourable mentions first. Their poems were read, and the poets identified themselves, were applauded, and were given certificates stamped in gold along with a coupon for a free video from Apollo Entertainment. Third place went to the elderly lady who'd given Joel advice, and she got a certificate, five pounds, and a coupon for a takeaway curry from Spicy Joe's. Second place went to an Asian girl in a headscarf – Joel checked to see if she was Hibah, but she was not – and then a hush fell over the group for the announcement of first place and fifty pounds.

Joel told himself that he couldn't *really* win. He didn't know poems, and he didn't know words. Still, he couldn't help thinking about the fifty pounds prize money, and what he could do with fifty pounds if a miracle happened and he turned out to be—

The winner was Adam Whitburn.

'Step up here, collect your prize, and accept the adulation of your peers, my man,' Ivan told him.

The Rasta bounded forward, all smiles. He swept off his cap and bowed, and his dreadlocks poured down around his shoulders. When the applause died down, he took the mike for the second time that evening, and he read his poem. Joel tried to listen, but he couldn't hear. He had the distinct feeling of floodwater rising around him.

He wished for a quick escape, but his seat was in the middle of the row and there was no route that did not involve stepping over people and pushchairs. Thus, he had to endure Adam Whitburn's triumph, and he agonised for the moment when the evening would come to an end and he could go home. But, as Adam returned to his seat, Ivan Weatherall went back to the mike. He had a last announcement, he said, because the judges had also made a selection of a Poet of Promise, and this was the first time such an honour had been bestowed upon anyone since Adam Whitburn had himself been so designated five years earlier. They wanted to give this individual a special nod, Ivan declared. Then he read the poem, and Joel heard his own words.

'Take a bow,' Ivan said, 'whoever wrote this one.'

14

Poet of Promise. Even after *Wield Words Not Weapons* was over, Joel was still able to summon up the pleasure he felt at the slaps on his back and the congratulations. He could still see the smiles on the faces of the audience as he faced them from the dais, and it would be a long time before the sound of their applause entirely faded from his ears.

As the crowd began to disperse, Adam Whitburn sought Joel. He said, 'How old are you, bred?' and then with a grin when Joel said his age, '*Twelve?* Shit. You not half, speck.' He slapped Joel's palm. 'I di'n't put words together like dat 'fore I was seventeen. You got summick special.'

A frisson of pleasure tingled Joel's spine. Having never been told he was special at anything, he wasn't sure how he was meant to answer, so he nodded and said, 'Cool.'

He found that he didn't want to leave the Basement Activities Centre, which would mean putting an end to the evening, so he stayed behind and helped stack the plastic chairs and bag the remaining refreshments. When these small tasks were completed, he remained by the door, prolonging the sensation of having been part of something for the first time in his life. He watched Ivan Weatherall and several other hangers-on like himself making sure the basement was put back in order. When it seemed that everything was in its proper place, someone switched off the lights and it was time to leave.

Ivan came to him then, whistling softly and looking what he was, which was extremely pleased at the end of a successful evening. He called out goodnights to those who were leaving and he turned down an offer of a post-event coffee, saying, 'Another time, perhaps? I'd like to speak to our Poet of Promise,' and shooting Joel a friendly smile.

Joel smiled back in reflex. He felt charged up with a kind of energy he could not identify. This was the energy of a creator, the rush of renewal and sheer aliveness experienced by the artist, but he did not know that yet.

Ivan locked the basement door. Together he and Joel climbed to the street. He said, 'So. You've had a triumph at your very first *Wield*. Well worth stopping in to try your hand, I'd say. This lot don't give out that title often, by the way, should you be thinking of dismissing it. And they've never given it to someone your age. I was . . . Well, to be honest, I was quite astonished although I assure you that's no reflection on you. Still and all, it should give you something to consider, and I hope you do that. But forgive me for preaching. Shall we walk home together? We're going in the same direction, aren't we?'

'Consider what?' Joel asked.

'Hmm? Oh, yes. Well, writing. Poetry. The written word in any form. You've been given the power to wield, and I suggest you wield it. At your age, to be able to put words together in such a way as to move a reader naturally . . . no manipulative devices, no clever traps . . . Just emotion that's raw and real . . . But I *am* running on. Let's get you home safely before we map out your future, shall we?'

Ivan headed them in the general direction of Portobello Road, and he chatted amiably as they walked. What Joel had, he explained, was a facility for language, and this was a gift from God. It meant that he possessed a rare but inherent talent for using words in such a way as to demonstrate their metric power.

To a boy whose knowledge of poetry was limited to what was written on the inside of sentimental birthday cards, all of this was Greek. But that didn't present a problem to Ivan, who simply went on.

By fostering this facility, he explained, Joel would have myriad options as his life unfolded. For being able to use language was a critical skill that could carry one far. One could use it professionally, as a crafter of everything from political speeches to modern novels. One could use it personally, as a tool of discovery or a means of staying connected to others. One could use it as an outlet that would feed the artistic spirit of the creator, which existed in everyone.

Joel trotted along at Ivan's side, and he tried to digest all of this. Himself as a writer. Poet, playwright, novelist, lyricist, speech-writer, journalist, giant of the biro. Most of it felt like a very large suit of clothes handed down to Joel by someone who had no idea of his proper size. The rest of it felt like forgetting the single and most important fact directly related to his responsibility to his family. He was thus silent. He was very glad that he'd been called a poet of promise, but the truth was that it didn't change anything.

'I want to help people,' he finally said, not so much because he actually did want this, but because his entire life to this moment indicated to Joel that helping people was what he was intended to do. He could hardly have been given the mother he had and the brother he had if there was another calling to which he was supposed to be drawn.

'Ah, yes. The plan. Psychiatry.' Ivan turned them up Golborne Road, where shops were closed for the night and unwashed cars crouched along the kerb. 'Even if you settle upon that permanently you must still find a creative outlet for yourself. You see, where people go wrong when they set out in life is in not exploring that part of themselves that feeds their spirit. Without that food, the spirit dies, and it's a large part of our responsibility to ourselves not to allow that to happen. In fact, consider how few psychiatric problems there might be if every individual actually knew what to do to keep alive in himself something that could affirm the very essence of who he is. That's what the creative act does, Joel. Blessed is the man or woman who knows this at a young age like yours.'

Joel thought about this, attaching the thought quite naturally to his mother. He wondered if this was the answer for her, beyond the hospital, the doctor, and the drugs. Something to do with herself to take her away from herself, something to make her spirit whole, something to make her psyche heal. It seemed unlikely.

Still, he said, 'Maybe . . .' and without realising what he was admitting to or to whom he was speaking, he mused aloud. 'I got to help my mum, though. She's in hospital.'

Ivan's steps slowed. He said, 'I see. How long has she been . . . Where is she, exactly?'

The question served to bring Joel around, depositing him in a more wakened state. He felt marked by the immensity of the betrayal he'd committed. Certainly, he could not say more about his mother: nothing about the locked doors and barred windows and the myriad failed attempts to make Carole Campbell better.

Up the street from them, then, a small group came from the direction of Portobello Bridge. They comprised three people, and Joel recognised them at once. He took a sharp breath and looked at Ivan, knowing that it would be wise for them to cross the road and hope not to be seen. For to be seen by the Blade in daylight was bad enough. To be seen by him at night was pure danger. He was accompanied by Arissa – whom he appeared to be holding by the back of her neck – with Cal Hancock trailing them like an officer from the royal protection squad.

Joel said, 'Ivan, le's cross over.'

Ivan, who'd been waiting for Joel to answer his question, took this remark as avoidance on Joel's part. He said, 'I'm being disrespectful? I do apologise for treading where I oughtn't. But if you ever wish to talk—'

'No. I mean le's cross over the street. You know.'

But it was too late; the Blade had seen them. He stopped beneath a street lamp, where the light cast long shadows on his face. He said, 'Eye-van. Eye-van the man. Wha' you doin out on y'r own? Picking up another ack-o-lite, innit?'

Ivan stopped walking as well, while Joel attempted to digest this information. He would never have considered the Blade to be someone Ivan Weatherall knew. His body went tense with anticipation as his mind sought an answer to the question of what he would do if the Blade decided to get nasty with them. The odds were even, but that didn't make them good.

'Good evening, Stanley,' Ivan said affably. He sounded like a man who'd just run into an acquaintance for whom he had high regard. 'Good gracious, my man. How long has it been?'

Stanley? Joel thought. He looked from Ivan to the Blade. The Blade's nostrils widened, but he said nothing.

'Stanley Hynds, Joel Campbell,' Ivan went on. 'I'd make further introductions, Stanley, but I've not had the honour . . .' He gave a little antique bow towards Arissa and Calvin.

'Full of it like always, Eye-van,' the Blade said.

'Indeed. It appears to be my calling. Have you finished the Nietzsche, by the way? That was intended as a loan, not a gift.'

The Blade snorted. 'You been sorted yet, mon?'

Ivan smiled. 'Stanley, I continue to walk these streets unscathed. Unarmed and unscathed as ever I was. Am I correct in assuming that's something of your doing?'

'I ain't tired of you yet.'

'Long may I continue to entertain. Should I not . . . Well, the Harrow Road gentlemen in blue always know where to find you, I assume.'

This was apparently the limit of what the Blade's companions were willing to endure. Arissa said, 'Le's go, baby,' as Calvin stepped forward, saying, 'You making threats, mon?' in a distinctly unCalvin-like voice.

Ivan smiled at this and tipped a mock hat in the Blade's direction. 'By the company he keeps, Stanley,' he said.

'Soon now, Eye-van,' the Blade returned. 'Fast losing your power to amuse me, mon.'

'I shall work on the quality of my repartee. Now, if you don't mind, I'm seeing my young friend to his doorstep. May we pass with your blessing?'

The request was designed to appease and it did so. A smile flicked around the Blade's lips and he jerked his head at Calvin, who stepped aside. 'Watch your back, Eye-van,' the Blade said as they passed him. 'Never know who's coming up on you.'

'Words I shall take to my heart and my grave,' was Ivan's reply.

All of this left Joel astonished. Every moment he'd expected disaster, and he did not know what to do with the fact that nothing resembling disaster had struck. When he looked at Ivan once they were again on their way, it was with new eyes. He didn't know what first to wonder about the man because there was simply so much to wonder about.

All Joel managed to say was 'Stanley?' That served to embody all the questions that he wanted to ask but for which he could not find the words.

Ivan glanced at him. He guided him on to Portobello Bridge.

'The Blade,' Joel said. 'I never heard someone talk to him like that. I never 'spected—'

'One to do so and live to tell the tale?' Ivan chuckled. 'Stanley and I go back a number of years, to his pre-Blade days. He's as clever a man as ever was. He could have gone far. But his curse, poor soul, has always been the need for immediate gratification, which is also, let's be frank, the curse of our times. And this is odd because the man's quite an auto-didact, which is the least immediately gratifying course of education one might ever embrace. But Stanley doesn't see it that way. What he sees is that *he* is the one in charge of his studies – whatever they might be at the moment – and that's enough to make him happy.'

Joel was silent. They'd reached Elkstone Road, and Trellick

Tower loomed over them, shining lights from its myriad flats into the dark night sky. Joel hadn't the slightest idea what his companion was going on about.

Ivan said, 'Are you familiar with the term, by the way? Autodidact? It means someone who educates himself. Our Stanley – as difficult as it may be to believe – is the true embodiment of not being able to ascertain a book's quality or its contents by examining only its cover. One would assume from his appearance – not to mention from his deliberate and rather charming mangling of our language – that he's something of an ill-bred and uneducated lout. But that would be selling Mr Hynds for far less than he's actually worth. When I met him – he must have been sixteen at the time – he was studying Latin, dabbling in Greek, and had recently turned his attention to the physical sciences and twentieth-century philosophers. Unfortunately, he'd also turned his attention to the various means of fast and easy money available to those who don't mind shimmying along on the wrong side of the law. And money is *always* a compelling mistress to boys who've never had it.'

'How'd you meet him, then?'

'In Kilburn Lane. I believe his intention was to mug me, but I noticed a suppurating sore in the corner of his mouth. Before he was able to make his demand for whatever he mistakenly thought I had on my person, I hustled him off to the chemist for medication. The poor boy never quite knew what was happening. One moment he's poised to commit a crime and the next he's facing the pharmacist with the man he's just attempted to rob, listening to a recommendation for an unguent. But it all worked out, and he learned an important lesson from it.'

'What kind of lesson?'

'The obvious one: that you mustn't ignore something strange and oozing upon your body. God only knows where it can lead if you do.'

Joel didn't know what to make of this. There appeared to be only one logical question. 'Why d'you do all this?' he asked.

'All . . . ?'

'The *Wield Words* t'ing. Talking to people like you do. Walking home wiv me, even.'

'Why wouldn't I?' Ivan enquired. They had made their way along the pavement and now they turned into Edenham Way. 'But that's not much of an answer, is it? Suffice it to say that every man needs to leave his mark upon the society into which he was born. This is mine.'

Joel wanted to ask more, but they'd come to Kendra's house, and there was no time. At the steps, Ivan tipped his fantasy hat once again, just as he had done to the Blade. He said, 'Let's meet again soon, shall we? I want to see more poetry from you,' before he vanished between two buildings, in the direction of Meanwhile Gardens.

Joel heard him whistling as he walked.

After her encounter with Six and Natasha in Queensway, Ness felt the pressure inside again. The high of managing to walk out of the chemist's with a lipstick in her bag and no one the wiser didn't so much fade as it actually deflated, punctured by the scorn of her former friends. She was left feeling worse than before, restless and experiencing a sense of irrational doom.

What she felt was heightened by what she heard. Her makeshift bed on the first-floor sofa was directly beneath Kendra's second-floor bedroom. Worse, it was directly beneath Kendra's bed, and the nightly rhythmic movement of that bed was anything but a soporific. And it *was* nightly. Sometimes it was thrice nightly, awakening Ness from whatever uneasy sleep she'd managed to fall into. Frequently, groans, moans, and throaty laughter accompanied the thumping of bed against wall and floor. Occasionally *Oh baby* comprised the coupling's full stop, punctuating orgasm on three rising notes after which a final crash of the bed indicated someone's satiated collapse. These were not noises any adolescent girl would likely appreciate hearing from the adults in her life. For Ness, they comprised auditory torture: a blatant statement about love, desire and acceptance, a form of imprimatur upon her aunt's desirability and worthiness.

The pure animal nature of what was going on between Kendra and Dix escaped Ness entirely. Male and female driven by instinct to mate when in naked proximity to each other and in possession of sufficient energy to do so as a means of propagating a species . . . Ness simply did not understand this. She heard sex. She thought love: Kendra having something that Ness had not.

In the state in which Ness found herself after her encounter with Six and Natasha in Queensway, then, Kendra's situation seemed monumentally unfair. Ness saw her aunt as practically an old lady, an ageing woman who'd had her chances with men and who by rights ought to be stepping aside in the eternal competition for male attention. Ness began to hate the very sight of Kendra when she appeared each morning, and she found herself unable to repress comments such as 'Had a *good* time las' night, innit?' which took the place of a more conventional morning greeting, as did, 'Feeling *sore* 'tween the legs today, *Ken*dra?' and 'How you managing to walk, slag?' and 'So he givin' it to you the way you *like* it, Ken?'

Kendra's response was, 'Who's giving what to whom is none of your business, Vanessa,' but she worried. She felt inextricably caught between lust and duty. She wanted the freedom implied by sex with Dix whenever she felt like sex with Dix, but she didn't want to be judged unfit to keep the Campbells with her. She finally said to him, 'I think we got to cool things off, baby,' one night as he approached her. 'Ness can hear us and she's . . . Maybe not every night, Dix. What d'you think? This is . . . well, this is bothering her.'

'Let her be bothered,' was his reply. 'She got to get used

to it, Ken.' He nuzzled her neck, then kissed her mouth, and trailed his fingers down and down until she arched, gasped, sighed, desired, and forgot Ness entirely.

So the pressure Ness felt continued to build, mitigated by nothing. She knew she would have to do something for relief. She thought she knew what that something was.

Dix was watching his pirated copy of *Pumping Iron* when she made her move. He was preparing for an upcoming competition, which generally made him less aware of his surroundings than he ordinarily was. Whenever he faced a body-building event, his concentration was on preparing to take another title or trophy. Competitive body-building was a mind game as much as it was a demonstration of one's ability to sculpt one's muscles to obscene proportions. For days before an event, Dix prepared his mind.

He was on a beanbag, his back against the sofa, his gaze on the television screen where Arnold was eternally playing mental games with Lou Ferrigno. All attention on Arnold, he noted when someone sat down on the sofa, but he didn't note who it was. He also didn't note what she was wearing: fresh from having bathed, a thin summer dressing-gown of Kendra's pulled around her naked body.

Kendra was at the charity shop. Joel and Toby were in Meanwhile Gardens, where Joel had promised to accompany Toby so that he could watch the board riders and the cyclists in the skate bowl. Ness herself was due at the child drop-in centre to work more of her community service hours, but the sight of Dix watching his video, the reality of their being alone in the house, the persistent memory of the thumping bed, and the fact that she needed to dress in this very space that he was occupying – her supposed *private* space – all urged her to approach him.

He was taking notes, chuckling at an Arnold witticism. He held a clipboard on his knees, and his legs were bare. He wore silky running shorts and a vest. He wore nothing else that Ness could see.

She noted the hand in which he held the biro. She said, 'I di'n't know you were a lefty, blood.'

He stirred, but was only partially aware. He said, 'Dat's how it is,' and continued writing. He chuckled again and said, 'Lookit him. Dat bloke . . . Never been anyone like him.'

Ness glanced at the television. At best it was a grainy film, peopled by men with pudding-bowl haircuts on heads too small for the rest of their bodies. They stood before mirrors and heaved their shoulders around. They clasped their hands this way and that with their legs poised to show off massively bulging muscles. It was all not-so-vaguely obscene. Ness shuddered but said, 'You look better'n dem.'

He said, 'No one looks better'n Arnold.'

'You do, baby,' was her reply.

She was close enough to him to feel the heat coming off his body. She moved closer. She said, 'I got to get dressed, Dix.'

He said, 'Hmm,' but did not pay attention.

She gazed at his hand. She said, 'You use that lefty for everyt'ing?'

He said, 'Dat's right,' and made a notation.

She said, 'You put it in wiv your left?'

His note-taking hesitated. She went on.

'C'n you do it wiv either hand is what I mean. Or do you have to guide it at all? Reckon not, eh. Bet you don't have to. Big enough an' hard enough to find its own way, innit.' She stood. 'Oh, I been feeling fat. What d'you t'ink, Dix? You t'ink I'm fat?' She placed herself between him and the television, her hands on her hips. 'Gimme your 'pinion.' She loosened the belt of the gown and let it fall open, presenting herself to him. 'You t'ink I'm too fat, Dix?'

Dix averted his eyes. 'Tie dat t'ing up.'

'Not till you answer,' she replied. 'You got to tell me cos you're a man. What I got . . . you t'ink it good enough make a man feel hot?'

He got to his feet. 'You dress yourself,' he told her. He looked for the video player's remote control and he switched off the film. He knew he needed to get out of the room, but Ness stood between him and the stairs. He said, 'I got to go.'

She said, 'You got to answer first. Shit. I ain't going to bite you, Dix, and you the only man round here I c'n ask. I let you go once you tell me the truth.'

'You ain't fat,' he said.

'You di'n't even have a look,' she told him. 'All it's going t' take is a little one, anyways. You c'n do dat much, can't you? I need to know.'

He could have pushed past her, but he was wary of how she would take any physical contact between them. So he co-operated to buy her cooperation. He gave her a glance and said, 'You look good.'

She said, 'You call *dat* a look? Shit, I seen blind men give once-overs better 'n dat. You going to need some help, ain't you? Here, den. Le's try dis again.' She dropped the dressing-gown and stood before him naked. She cupped her breasts towards him, and she licked her lips. 'You guide it in, Dix, or it go by itself? You got to tell me or you got to show me. I know which way I want it, mon.'

Dix would have been inhuman had he not felt aroused. He tried to look elsewhere but the very flesh of her demanded, and so he looked at her and for a terrible moment fixed on her chocolate nipples and then, even worse, on her triangle of woolly hair from which it seemed the scent of a siren rose. Her age was girl; her body was woman. It would be easy enough, but fatal as well.

He grabbed her by one arm. Her flesh burned as much as his, and her face brightened. He stooped quickly and felt her hand on his head, heard her little cry as she tried to guide his face, his mouth . . . He scooped up the dressing-gown and flung it on her, wresting himself away from her grip.

'Cover yourself,' he hissed. 'What're you *t'inking* anyways?

Life s'pose to be 'bout getting stuffed by every man come your way? An' *dis* the way you t'ink men like it? Dat what you t'ink? Strutting round displaying yourself like some ten quid slag? Hell, you got the parts of a woman, but dat's it, Ness. Rest of you, so goddamn bloody stupid I can't t'ink of a man who'd even want a piece, no matter how desperate. Y'unnerstan? Now get out of my way.'

He pushed past her. He left her in the sitting-room. She was trembling. She stumbled to the video machine and pulled out the cassette. It was a simple matter for her to yank the tape from its housing and to trample it. But it was not enough.

Fabia Bender's visit to Edenham Estate put Kendra in a position of having to reevaluate. She didn't want to do that, but she found herself doing so anyway, especially once she read through all the paperwork that Joel had been given by Luce Chinaka at the learning centre.

Kendra wasn't stupid. She'd always known that something would have to be done eventually about the problem of Toby. But she'd convinced herself that Toby's difficulties had to do with the way he learned. To dwell on anything else as the source of his oddity meant heading directly into a nightmare. So she'd told herself that he merely had to be sorted out, educated properly to the extent he could actually *be* educated, given some kind of appropriate life skills, and led into an area of employment that might allow him a modicum of adult independence, eventually. If that could not happen for him in Middle Row School and with the extra assistance of the learning centre, then another educational environment would have to be scouted out for him. But that was the extent to which Kendra had so far been willing to dwell on her little nephew, which allowed her to ignore the times Toby just faded away, the muttered conversations he had with no one present, and the frightening implications of both these behaviours. Indeed, in the months the Campbells had been in her care,

Kendra had successfully managed to use the disclaimer 'Toby's just Toby', no matter what the boy did. Anything else didn't bear consideration. So she read the paperwork and she put it away. No one would test, assess, evaluate, or study Toby Campbell while she had a say in the matter.

But that meant doing everything possible not to attract undue attention from any interfering governmental agencies. Thus, Kendra made a study of the room in which Toby and Joel slept, seeing it as Fabia Bender had likely seen it. It screamed impermanency, which was not good. The camp beds and sleeping bags were bad enough. The two suitcases in which the boys had kept their clothes for six months were even worse. Aside from the *It's a Boy!* sign that still tilted drunkenly across the window, there was no decoration. There were not even curtains to block out the night-time light from a lamp on one of the paths in Meanwhile Gardens.

This would have to change. She was going to have to sort out beds and chests, curtains, and something for the walls. She would need to haunt second-hand and charity shops to do this; she would need to ask for handouts. Cordie helped her. She provided old sheets and blankets, and she put the word out in her neighbourhood. This produced two chests in moderate disrepair, and a set of posters featuring travel destinations that neither Joel nor Toby was likely ever to see.

'Looks good, girl,' was how Cordie supportively evaluated it when they had the room set up.

'Looks like a fucking rubbish tip,' was Ness's contribution.

Kendra ignored her. Tension had been rolling off Ness for some time, but she'd been continuing with her community service, so everything else she was doing and saying was bearable.

'What's dis all about?' was Dix's reaction when he saw the changes to the boys' room.

'It's about showing that Joel and Toby have a decent place to live.'

'Who t'inks they don't?'

'That Youth Offending woman.'

'Dat woman wiv the dogs? You t'ink she means to take Joel and Toby away?'

'Don't know and don't intend to wait round to see.'

'I thought she come here 'bout Toby and th' learning centre.'

'She came because she didn't know there *was* a Toby. She came because she didn't know there was anyone besides Ness living with me till she got called by the learning centre woman and . . . Look. What does it matter, Dix? I got to get a proper environment set up for those kids in case that woman wants to give me aggravation about having them living here. As it is, they're looking too close at Toby, and can you imagine what that'll do to Joel and Ness if he gets sent away? Or if *they* get separated 's well? Or if . . . Hell, I don't know.'

Dix thought about this as he watched Kendra straighten second-hand sheets and third-hand blankets on old beds – an Oxfam find – whose pedigree was displayed in the myriad cracks and gouges upon their headboards. With all the furniture in the room, there was barely space enough to move, just a narrow opening between the beds. The house was tiny, unintended for five people. The solution seemed obvious to Dix.

He said, 'Ken, baby, you ever t'ink it's all for the best?'

'What?'

'Wha's going on.'

She straightened. 'What's that s'posed to mean?'

'I mean the fact dis woman shows up. The fact dat maybe she t'ink about changing where the kids're living. Truth is, dis place ain't proper for dem. It's too bloody small, and wiv dis woman making a report, seems to me like it's the proper time to t'ink about—'

'What the *hell* are you suggesting?' Kendra demanded. 'That I send 'em off? That I let 'em be separated? That I let 'em get taken away without trying to do something to head that off?

And then you and I can *what*, Dix? Shag like bunnies in every room in the house?'

He crossed his arms and leaned against the door jamb. He didn't reply at once, so Kendra was left listening to the emotional echo of her words.

He finally said quietly, 'I was t'inking time we got married, Kendra. I was t'inking time I showed I c'n be a proper dad to dese kids. Mum and Dad been wanting me to learn the café business, and—'

'What about Mr Universe? You give up your dreams as easy as that?'

'Sometimes t'ings come up dat make 'emselves bigger'n dreams. More important 'n dreams. You and I get married, I c'n work a proper job. We c'n get a bigger place, we c'n have rooms for—'

'I like *this* place.' Kendra was aware that she sounded shrill, unreasonable, and unnervingly Nesslike, but she didn't care. 'I worked for it, I got a mortgage for it, I'm paying for it. None of it's easy, but it's mine.'

'Sure. But if we got a bigger place an' we got married, den no social worker's ever going to even suggest th' kids need to be anywhere but wiv us, see. We'd be a proper family.'

'With you going off to work in the café every day? Coming home smelling like bacon grease? Watching your Arnold tape and eating up your insides because of what you gave up for . . . for what? And why?'

'Cos it's the right t'ing to do,' he said.

She laughed. But the laugh broke on a note that was rising hysteria, a reaction that preceded panic. She said, 'You're twenty-three years old!'

'I figger I know how old I am.'

'Then you c'n also *figger* that these're growing adolescents we're talking about, troubled ones who've had a rough go of life so far, and you're little more 'n adolescent yourself, so what makes you t'ink . . . *think* you can cope with 'em? An' what makes you think that Fabia Bender woman would ever consider you *able* to cope with 'em? C'n you answer that?'

Again, Dix didn't reply at once. He was developing an irritating habit of forcing Kendra to listen to herself, and this was maddening to her. More, his silence was demanding that she consider the reasons for her words, which was the last thing she wanted to do. She wanted to have a row with him.

Dix finally said, 'Well, I'm willing, Ken. An' Joel 'n Toby . . . They need a dad.'

She said shrewdly, 'What about Ness? What does *she* need?'

Dix met her gaze, unflinching. Whatever she might suspect, Kendra didn't know about his scene with Ness, and he had no intention of telling her. He said, 'She need to see a man and woman loving each other proper. I reckoned we could show her dat. Could be I was wrong.'

He pushed off from the door jamb. When he left her alone, Kendra threw a pillow at the door.

Dix was not a man to shrink from a challenge. Had he been, he wouldn't have joined the world of competitive body-building. As it was, he saw Kendra's evaluation of him as akin to an Arnold mind game. She didn't think he had the goods at his age to be a father to developing adolescents. He would prove to her otherwise.

He didn't start with Ness. He was wiser than that. Although he knew that his ruined copy of *Pumping Iron* was Ness's form of a gauntlet, he also knew it was a dare whose conclusion was predetermined. Take it up and he would open himself to whatever fanciful charges Ness decided to hurl at him, which would take the form of all the reasons she had destroyed his tape, doubtless screamed in the presence of her aunt and coming directly from her own imagination. He wasn't about to participate in that so, when he found the tape, he set about seeing to its repair. Could it not be fixed, so be it. Ness wanted a reaction. He would not give her one.

The boys were an easier matter. They were boys; so was he. After an outing to the gym, during which Toby and Joel watched awestruck from the sidelines as Dix bench-pressed superhuman weights, the next step seemed logical: he would take them to a competition. They would go with him to the YMCA at the Barbican, all the way across town. It wouldn't be one of the huge competitions, but it would give them the flavour of what it had been like for poor Lou when he faced Arnold, always meeting with defeat at the hands of the wily Austrian.

They went by underground. Neither of the boys had ever been to this part of town and, as they followed Dix from the station to the YMCA, they gawked at the great coiling mass of grey concrete that comprised the many buildings of the Barbican, set in an incomprehensible maze of streets with traffic whizzing by and brown location signs pointing in every direction. To them, it was a labyrinth of structures: exhibition halls, concert halls, theatres, cinemas, conference centres, schools for drama and music. They were lost within moments, and they scurried to keep up with Dix who – to their great admiration – seemed to be completely at home in this place.

The YMCA was tucked into a housing estate that appeared to be part of the Barbican itself. Dix ushered Joel and Toby inside and led the way to an auditorium redolent of dust and sweat. He sat them in the front row and fished around in the pocket of his tracksuit. He gave the boys three pounds to buy themselves treats from the vending machines in the lobby and he told them not to leave the building. He himself, he said, would be hanging between the work-out room and the locker room, psyching out the competition and mentally preparing himself to appear before the judges.

'Look good, Dix,' Joel said supportively. 'No one going to beat you, mon.'

Dix was pleased at this sign of Joel's acceptance. He touched his fist to the boy's forehead and was even more pleased to receive in return Joel's happy grin. He said, 'Hang cool here, blood,' and he added with a glance at Toby, 'He going to be okay wiv dis?'

'Sure,' Joel said.

But he was far from certain. Although Toby had followed cooperatively in Joel and Dix's wake from North Kensington to this part of town, he'd done so lethargically. Not even a rare ride on the underground had stirred him to interest. He was listless and subdued. He looked flat of feature, which was worrying. When Joel studied him, he tried to tell himself this was all due to Toby's being made to leave his lava lamp at home, but he couldn't convince himself of that. So, when Dix left them, Joel asked Toby if he was all right. Toby said that his stomach felt dead peculiar. There was just enough time before the competition began for Joel to fetch him a Coke from the vending machine, using a pound coin to do so. 'Meant to settle you,' was what he told his little brother, but after one sip, he couldn't get Toby to take any more. Soon enough, he forgot to try.

The judges for the competition took their places at a long table to the right of the stage. Lights dimmed in the auditorium and the disembodied voice of an announcer informed them that the Barbican's YMCA was proud to be staging the sixth annual Men's Competitive Body-Building Competition, with a special under-sixteen exhibition to follow. After this, music began – Beethoven's *Ode to Joy*, oddly enough – and into the spotlight upon the stage walked a man whose muscles had their own muscles. In the first round of posing, his job was to show those muscles off to their best advantage.

Joel had seen this sort of thing before, not only in *Pumping Iron* but also in his own home. He could not have lived in the same house as Dix D'Court and missed the sight of Dix oiled and practising in front of the bathroom mirror since Dix never stopped if anyone other than Ness had to use the facilities. He had to be smooth, he explained to whoever sat upon the toilet. Each pose had to flow into the next one. Your personality had to emerge as well. This was the reason that Arnold had been so much better than the rest of them. Clearly, he'd enjoyed what he was doing. He was a bloke with no self-doubt.

Joel could see that the first few competitors hadn't got that idea. They had the body in spades, even in the semi-relaxed round of posing, but they hadn't the moves. They hadn't the minds. They stood no chance in comparison to Dix.

After a few men had shown their stuff, Joel became aware of Toby getting restless. Eventually, Toby plucked at Joel's sleeve, saying, 'I got to go,' but when Joel glanced at his programme, he saw that Dix was due to come on stage quite soon, and there was consequently little enough time for him to search out a toilet for Toby.

He said, 'Can't you hold it, Tobe?'

'Ain't dat,' Toby told him. 'Joel, I gotta—'

'Hang on, okay?'

'But—'

'Look, he's coming up in a minute. He's right over there. You c'n see him waiting to the side, can't you?'

'I'm just—'

'He brought us to see him so we got to see him, Tobe.'

'Den . . . If I can . . .' But that was all Toby managed to say before he began to retch.

Joel hissed, 'Shit!' and turned to Toby just as he began to vomit. Unfortunately, it was no ordinary moment of sickness. A foul stream fairly shot out of Toby's mouth, a veritable show-stopper as things turned out.

The stench was deadly. Toby was groaning, murmurs were rising all around the boys, and someone called for the lights to go on. In very short order, the music halted, leaving a body-builder on the stage, mid-pose. After this, the lights illumin-ated the audience and several of the judges rose from their places, craning their necks to see the source of the disturbance.

Joel said, 'Sorry. Sorry. *Sorry*,' to anyone willing to listen to him.

As if in reply, Toby retched again. Vomit splashed down the front of him. Mercifully, it no longer projected although it soaked into the front of his jeans, which turned out to be worse.

'Get him out of here, lad,' someone said.

'Doesn't matter much now, does it?' someone else muttered in disgust.

And, it *was* disgusting unless one had no olfactory capability. Further comments, questions, and advice accompanied the smell of Toby's sickness, but Joel was deaf to all of it, utterly intent upon getting Toby to stand so that they could leave. Toby, however, was immobile. He clutched his stomach and began to cry.

Joel heard Dix speak into his ear, low and insistent. 'Wha's going *on*? Wha' happened, mon?'

Joel said, 'He's sick, is all. I need to get him to the toilet. I need to get him home. C'n we . . . ?' He looked and saw that Dix was oiled and ready, bare to the bone except for his tiny red Speedo. It was inconceivable to Joel that he should ask Dix if they could all leave.

But Dix knew without the request being made. He was caught and conflicted. He said, 'I'm up in five blokes. Dis whole t'ing counts towards . . .' He ran his hand back over his bare skull. He bent to Toby. He said, 'You okay, bred? You get to the toilet okay 'f Joel shows you where it is?'

Toby continued to cry. His nose had begun to run. He was nothing short of a spectacle.

The rumble of something rolling towards them heralded the arrival of one of the YMCA custodians. Someone called out 'The mess is over there, Kevin' and someone else said, 'Jaysus, git it cleaned 'fore we all sick up.' At that point, what had seemed to Joel to be a mass of looming faces dissipated, and a skinny old man with few teeth and less hair starting wielding a mop and a pungent solution around the floor.

Someone said, 'Can't you carry him out of here?'

'You want to? Little bastard's got puke all over him,' was someone else's reply.

Burning with shame, Joel said, 'S'okay. I c'n get him . . . Come on, Tobe. You c'n walk, innit. Le's go to the toilet.' And to Dix, 'Where's it at?'

He pulled Toby by the arm. Mercifully, the little boy rose, although he hung his head and continued to sob. Joel couldn't blame him.

Dix shepherded them to the doorway of the auditorium. He told Joel the gents was just down the stairs from the lobby and along the corridor. He said, 'C'n you . . . ? I mean, you need me . . . ?' with a backward look at the stage.

That look was enough to tell Joel what his answer was supposed to be. He said, 'Nah. We c'n cope. I got to take him home, though.'

'Okay,' Dix said. 'You good to do dat on y'r own?' When Joel nodded, Dix squatted in front of Toby. He said, 'Blood, you don't worry 'bout dis. Shit happens to ever'one. You jus' go on home. I'll bring you summick on my way back.' Then he rose and said to Joel, 'I got to go. I'm up in a couple minutes.'

'Dat's cool,' Joel told him, and Dix left them at the auditorium door.

Joel led Toby out and down the stairs. Thankfully, they had the men's toilet to themselves. There, Joel managed his first truly good look at his brother, and it wasn't a pretty sight. Mucus and vomit dirtied his face, and his T-shirt was streaked with sick, smelling like the floor of an upside-down, tumbling, funfair ride. Toby's jeans were little better. He'd even managed to get vomit on his shoes.

If ever the ministrations of a consoling mother were called for, this was that moment. Joel took Toby to the basin and turned on the tap. He looked around for paper towels, but there was only a grimy pull-down roller of blue cotton that looped inextricably through a dispenser and hung wetly to the floor. Joel saw, then, that his efforts would have to be limited to washing Toby's face and hands. The rest of him would have to wait until their return to Edenham Estate.

Toby stood mutely through the application of a sliver of soap to his face and his hands. He accepted the toilet tissue pressed to his skin, and he didn't say anything until Joel had done the best he could do with the soiled T-shirt and jeans. Then what he said would have surprised anyone who knew him less well than Joel, anyone who made assumptions about the world that he felt safe to inhabit. He said, 'Joel, why i'n't Mum coming home? Cos she i'n't, eh?'

'Don't say dat. You don't know an' neither do I.'

'She t'inks Dad's at home.'

'Yeah.'

'Why?'

'Cos she can't cope wiv t'inking anything else.'

Toby considered this, his nose still dripping. Joel wiped it with another bit of tissue and took him by the hand. He led him back along the corridor and up the stairs, surrounded by the foul sick smell of him, so strong an odour that it seemed like a palpable presence. Joel told himself it would be better when he got Toby outside. The air – even laden with the fumes of vehicles zipping by – would make the stench less foetid, surely.

They were out of the YMCA and heading vaguely in the direction from which Joel remembered them coming when he realised two things simultaneously. The first was that he didn't know where the underground station was and the brown directional signs pointing every which way were not helping matters. The second was that finding the station was of no account anyway since he didn't have enough money to buy them tickets. Dix had bought returns when they'd left Westbourne Park station, but he'd held on to them throughout the journey, and they were in his gym bag inside the YMCA locker room. It was inconceivable to Joel that he should go back there, taking

Toby into that auditorium again and seeking out Dix to get
to the tickets. It was also inconceivable to him that he should
leave Toby alone outside while he did it. So there was nothing
for it but to return to North Kensington by bus since he did
have enough money to pay for a single ride for each of them.

The problem he faced with this plan, however, was that
there was no single ride that would take them from the Barbican
all the way across town. When, after twenty-two minutes of
wandering around the maze of buildings, Joel finally found a
bus stop that was more than a pole sticking up from the pavement, he studied the plan and saw that no less than three
different bus routes were going to be necessary to get them
home. He knew he could manage it. He would recognise
Oxford Street where the first change had to be made. The real
problem was that they didn't have enough money to make the
necessary changes after the first ride. That meant for the
second two rides he and Toby were going to have to sneak on
and pray they weren't noticed. Their best hope for that would
be if two of the three buses they needed were of the old, open-
backed double-decker type: utterly unsafe, completely convenient, and quintessentially London. These types offered entrance
from the rear, a driver and a conductor, and crowded conditions. They also offered Joel the best chance of sneaking on
unnoticed and getting home on the meagre funds they had.

As things turned out for the boys, this operation took more
than five hours. This was not because they got lost because
they didn't. Rather, the journey stretched and stretched
because the first change at Oxford Street resulted in their being
thrown off the bus without tickets, and four more buses
lumbered past in the mass congestion of the shopping district
before one suitably packed with passengers suggested that the
conductor might be too preoccupied to notice them. This
indeed proved to be the case, but they had the same trouble
with the next change at Queensway. From there it took six
buses – leaping on, riding one or two stops, getting thrown

off – just to make it to Chepstow Road, where they were thrown off once again. Joel finally decided that they'd walk the rest of the way as Toby hadn't been sick since the YMCA. He smelled no better and he was obviously tired, but Joel reckoned the air – as fresh as it could ever be in London – would do him some good.

It was after seven in the evening when they finally reached Edenham Estate. Kendra met them at the door. By this time she had become quite frantic with worrying about what had happened to them as Dix had arrived hours earlier – his trophy in hand – asking how Toby was feeling and setting off at once to search for the boys when he learned they hadn't returned. Kendra's mental state was evidenced by the state of her language. She cried out, 'Where you been? Where you *been*? Dix's out there . . . Ness even went out 's well. What happened? Toby, baby, you sick? Dix said . . . Joel, goddamn. Why di'n't you give me a bloody bell? I would've . . . Oh God!' She swept them both into her arms.

Joel was surprised to find she was crying. No astute student of the human psyche at his age, he had no way of understanding that his aunt was reacting to what she'd been seeing as the incarnation of her own unspoken dream to be relieved of the burden of responsibility. For Kendra, it was a real case of be-careful-what-you-subconsciously-wish-for.

As she ran the bath for Toby and stripped the ruined clothes from his body, she talked like a woman on amphetamines. Dix, she said, had been home for hours. He'd walked in with his bloody stupid trophy – 'Oh yeah, he won, di'n't he just' – and he looked round and said Boys make it all right? like he di'n't have no worry at all dat you lot'd find your way 'cross the whole bloody stupid town though you never even been there before. I say to him, What you raving 'bout, mon? Dem boys wiv you, innit? He say Toby sicked up down the front of himself and *he* made you come on home.

Here, in all fairness, Joel interrupted. He'd been sitting on the toilet watching his aunt wash Toby with a soapy flannel and shampoo, and he knew it was only just that he set his aunt straight in the matter of Dix. He said, 'He di'n't make us, Aunt Ken. I told him—'

'Don't tell me who tol' who what,' Kendra said. 'Oh, I 'spect he di'n't tell you to disappear, but he made his bloody *feelings* known, di'n't he? Don't lie to me, Joel.'

'It wasn't like dat,' Joel protested. 'He was near up before the judges. He'd've had to leave. And look, anyways he won, di'n't he? Dat's what's important.'

Kendra turned from the bath where she was rinsing Toby. 'Holy God in heaven. You thinking like *him* now, Joel?' She didn't wait for an answer before she turned back. She wrapped Toby in a towel and helped him out of the bath. She used her dryer on his crinkly hair, roughed him up with the towel, and patted him with powder. Toby glowed under all the attention.

She took him to the bedroom and tucked him in, telling him she was going to make him Ovaltine and soldiers with butter and sugar, so 'Just rest there, baby, till Auntie gets back'. Toby blinked at her, all awe at this unexpected maternal outpouring. He settled into bed and became expectant. Ovaltine and soldiers constituted more nurturing than he'd had so far in his brief life.

A jerk of Kendra's head told Joel he was meant to follow her down to the kitchen. There, his aunt had him tell her the story start to finish, and she managed to listen more calmly this time. Once he had completed the tale of their trip across town, the Ovaltine and the soldiers were ready. She handed them over to Joel and gave a nod to the stairs. She poured herself a glass of wine from the fridge, lit a cigarette, and sat at the kitchen table.

She tried to sort out her feelings. She was an amalgamation of the physical and emotional in a pitched battle with the psychological. It was all too much for her to cope with. She sought out a focus just as focus walked through the front door.

Dix said, 'Ken, I been all over in th' car. All I got was dat Joel set off like he said he was going to do. A bloke busking near the bus stop at the Barbican tol' me—'

'He's here,' Kendra said. 'They're both here. Thank God.'

Thank God also meant No thanks to you. Dix understood that from the tone and from the look Kendra cast him. In concert, that look and that tone stopped him in his tracks. He knew he was being blamed for what had happened, and he accepted that. What he couldn't sort out was Kendra's state of mind. It seemed more logical to Dix that she would be feeling relief at this juncture and not whatever it was that she *was* feeling, which read like hostility.

He approached their encounter cautiously. 'Dat's good. But what th' hell happened? Why di'n't they come straight home like Joel said?'

''Cause they didn't have the means,' Kendra told him. 'Which you apparently didn't consider. You got the damn tickets in your gym bag, Dix. They didn't want to disturb your concentration, so they tried to come home on the bus. Which of course they couldn't.'

Dix's gym bag was where he'd left it earlier, near the doorway to the stairs. His gaze went to it and his mind's eye saw the tickets where he'd stuffed them – indeed where he'd actually seen them when he dug out his own to return home after the competition. He said, 'Damn. I'm dead sorry 'bout this whole t'ing, Ken.'

'Sorry.' Kendra was a missile, seeking culpability. 'You let an eight-year-old boy wander round London—'

'He's wiv Joel, Ken.'

'– without the means to even get home. You let a boy been sick all down the front of him try to find his way out of the middle of a city he never been into before . . .' Kendra paused to breathe, not so much to dismiss her anger but to organise her thoughts and to express them from a position of power. 'You talk a good talk about being a father to these kids,' she pointed out. 'But at th' end of the day, it all comes down to you, not to them. What you want and not what they need. That sort of thinking has nothing to do with being anyone's dad, y'unnerstand?'

'Now that ain't fair,' he protested.

'You got . . . You have your competition to attend and that's what the whole day's about to you. Nothing's going to distract you from that. Not another lifter – cause you got to be like bloody Arnold, 'f course, and *he'd* never be distracted by anything, not even a nuclear bomb – and surely not a little boy being sick. Concen*tra*tion is the name of the game. And God knows you a man who can concentrate.'

'Joel said he could cope. I trusted him. You got someone you want to rave at, Ken, you rave at Joel.'

'You blaming *him*? He's bloody twelve years old, Dix. He thinks your competition counts more 'n anything he might need from you. You di'n't see that? You don't see that?'

'Joel said he'd bring him straight home. 'F I can't trust Joel to tell the truth of the matter—'

'Don't you blame him! Don't you *bloody* blame him.'

'I'm not *blaming* anyone. Seems to me you the one doing the blaming here. Makes me wonder why, Ken. Joel's back home. Toby's back home. I 'spect they're both upstairs, listening in on dis if it comes down to it. Everyt'ing's okay. So question is: wha's going on wiv you?'

'This is not 'bout me.'

'I'n't it? Den why you casting blame? Why you *looking* for someone to blame when what you should be doing is being relieved Joel 'n Toby got back here wivout trouble.'

'You call five hours of wand'ring round London like two lost mongrels "without trouble"? Shit. What're you thinking?'

'I di'n't *know* . . . Oh hell, I already said.' He waved her off. He headed in the direction of the stairs.

She said, 'Where you going?'

'Taking a shower. Which, by th' way, I di'n't do at the end

of the competition cos I meant to get home quick an' see how Toby was doing, Ken.'

'An' that was your bow to being a dad? Not taking a bloody shower at the end of a competition you refuse to leave when your boy gets sick down the front of him? You want you and me to get married so we c'n keep the kids safe from Social Services, but this is what I c'n expect in the way of fathering?'

He raised a hand. 'You vex just now. We talk 'bout this later.'

'We talk about it *bloody* now,' she said. 'Don't you climb those stairs. Don't you walk out of this room.'

'An' if I do?'

'Then pack up and get out.'

He cocked his head. He hesitated, not from indecision but from surprise. He did not see how they'd come to this point, let alone why they had come to this point. All he knew was that for a moment Kendra was playing a game whose rules he did not understand. He said, 'I'm taking a shower, Ken. We c'n talk 'bout this when you ain't so vex.'

'I want you out 'f here, then,' she said. 'I got no time for selfish bastards in my life. I been there before and I'm not going there again. If your bloody shower is more important to you than—'

'You comparing me? To which one of dem?'

'I 'spect you know which one.'

'So? Dat it?' He shook his head. He looked around. He made his move but this time it was towards the front door and not towards the stairs. He said regretfully, 'Got your wish, Ken. I give you 'sactly what you want.'

15

Dix's absence from Edenham Estate affected everyone differently. Ness began to swagger around the house as if she had successfully brought about a change that she had long desired. Kendra threw herself into work and didn't mention the fact that Dix was gone. Toby explained Dix's absence to someone unseen whom he began openly and daily referring to as Maydarc. And, for the first time, Joel experienced a creative outpouring of poetry.

He couldn't have told anyone what any of his poems were actually about. Nor could he have traced his surge of artistic energy to their source: Dix's leaving them. All he could have said about his verse was that it was what it was, and that it came from a place he could not identify.

He showed none of these poems to anyone, save a single piece that he selected after much thought – and an equal amount of screwing up his courage – to pass to Adam Whitburn one night at *Wield Words Not Weapons*. He lingered near the basement door, waiting till the young Rasta was heading out. He handed it over and then stood there mute, in an agony of anticipation, while the Rasta read it. When he'd done so, Adam looked at Joel curiously, then returned his gaze to the page and re-read. He handed the paper back to Joel, saying, 'You show dis to Ivan?' to which Joel shook his head. Adam said, 'Mon, you got to show dis shit to Ivan, y'unnerstan? And why'n't you reading at the mike? You *got* summick, blood. Ever'one want to see it.'

But that was unthinkable to Joel. He felt the pleasure of

Adam Whitburn's approval, which was enough. Only Ivan's approval would have meant more to him and, as for the rest – the public reading, the analysing and critiquing, the opportunity to win money or certificates or acknowledgement in some form during *Walk the Word* – it had become less important as his pleasure in the process grew.

Something about all of the scribbling, the scratching out and staring upward without seeing what he was looking at, followed by further scribbling, took him to an altered state. It wasn't one that he could have described, but he grew to look forward to being in it. It offered him a sanctuary but, more than that, it offered him a sense of completion that he'd never felt before. He reckoned how he felt was something akin to how Toby felt when he faded into Sose or when he watched his lava lamp or even carried it around in his arms. It just made things different, less important that their father was gone and their mother was locked up within padded walls.

So, naturally, he sought this refuge when, where, and as often as he could. He was able to block out the world as he wrote so, even when he walked over to Meanwhile Gardens when Toby wanted to watch the riders and cyclists in the skate bowl, he himself could sit on one of the benches with his tattered notebook on his knees and he could pull words out of the air and put them together, much as he'd done on the night he'd been named a Poet of Promise.

He was doing just this, with Toby perched on the rim of the deepest skate bowl nearby, when someone sat next to him and a girl's voice said, 'So what're you doing? Can't be homework, this time 'f year. And where you *been*, Joel? You go on holiday or summick?'

Joel looked up to see Hibah trying to get a glimpse of what he was writing. She was, she said, just returning from taking her dad his lunch over at the bus depot. Her mum was expecting her home and would probably phone her dad on his mobile if she didn't turn up when she was supposed to, which was in about fifteen minutes.

'Said they saw me out an' about, they did,' Hibah confided. 'An' said they di'n't much like *what* they saw. But I know tha' cow who works Kensal Library was one tha' ackshully saw me. Cos if it'd really been my mum and dad tha' saw me, I wouldn't be getting out of tha' damn flat on my own till I was married, no matter how bad Dad wanted his lunch. So, see, they want me to *think* they saw me while they still giving me the benefit of the doubt wivout telling me they're doing it. It's all cos they can't be sure that ol' library cow knows what she's talking about cos she doesn't like us anyways.'

From all of this, Joel assumed that Hibah had been seen in improper company. He knew who that improper company was likely to be, so he glanced around uneasily, not eager for another encounter with Neal Wyatt. The coast seemed clear. It was a pleasant day, and there were other people in the park, but Neal wasn't among them.

Hibah said, 'So what're you doing? Lemme see.'

'Just poems,' Joel said. 'But they ain't ready to be shown cos I'm still writing 'em.'

Hibah smiled. 'Di'n't know you was a poet, Joel Campbell. Like you writing rhymes? Rap songs or summick? C'mon. Lemme see. I never read a poem in person before.' She made a grab for the notebook, but he held it away. She laughed and said, 'Come *on*. Don't be like that. You go to that poet event over Oxford Gardens? I know a lady goes there. Tha' Ivan bloke from school goes 's well.'

'He runs it,' Joel said.

'So you been? Well, lemme *see*. I don't know much 'bout poems but I c'n tell if they rhyme.'

'Ain't s'posed to rhyme, these,' Joel told her. 'Ain't dat kind 'f poem.'

'What kind, then?' She looked thoughtful and gave a glance

towards one of the immature oak trees that dotted the little hills of the garden. Under several, young men and women lay: dozing, embracing, or more seriously entwined. Hibah grinned. 'Love poems!' she crowed. 'Joel Campbell, you got a girlfriend now? She round here somewheres? Hmm. I c'n tell you ain't saying, so lemme see I c'n make her come running. I bet I know how.'

She inched over mischievously till she was touching thighs with Joel. She put her arm around his waist and tilted her head to his shoulder. There they remained for several minutes, as Joel wrote and Hibah giggled.

But 'Wha' the fuck . . . !' was the response to Hibah's gesture of affection, and Joel wasn't the person who said it. Instead, it came from the towpath beside the Grand Union Canal. No glance in that direction was required to see who the speaker was. Neal Wyatt came storming across the lawn.

Behind Neal, three members of his crew remained on the towpath. They'd all been slouching in the direction of Great Western Road. They evidently felt that whatever Neal wished to handle at that moment could be handled by Neal alone, a fact that became quickly evident when he homed in on Hibah rather than on Joel.

He said to the girl, 'What the *fuck* you doing? I tell you where we meet and you bring *dis* wiv you? Wha's dat all about?'

Hibah didn't drop her arm from around Joel's waist as another girl might have done. Instead, she stared at Neal and tightened her grip on Joel. She wasn't intimidated. She was, however, shocked and confused. She said, 'What? Neal, who're you talking to like that? Wha's going on?'

'Disre*spec's* what's going on,' he said. 'You hang wiv dis shit, you shit yourself. An' my woman ain't displaying herself like shit. Y'unnerstand?'

'Hey! I said. Who're you talking to like that? I come here like you want and I see a friend. We talk, him and me. You can't cope or summick?'

'You listen. *I* tell *you* who's right f'r you to speak wiv. You don't tell me. An' dis yellow-arse—'

'Wha's *wrong* wiv you, Neal Wyatt?' Hibah demanded. 'You los' your mind? This's Joel an' he's not even—'

Neal advanced on her. 'I show you wha's wrong wiv me.' He grabbed her arm and pulled her to her feet. He yanked her towards his mates on the towpath.

Joel had no choice. He stood. He said, 'Hey! Leave her 'lone. She ain't done nuffink to disrespeck you.'

Neal glanced his way contemptuously. 'You telling me . . . ?'

'Yeah. I telling you. Wha' kind of lowlife go after a girl? I guess same kind dat vex cripples up the Harrow Road.'

This reference to their last encounter and the intrusion of the police was enough to make Neal release the hold he had on Hibah. He turned to Joel.

'Dis bitch's mine,' he said. 'An' you got nuffink to say 'bout dat.'

Hibah cried, 'Neal, what're you going *on* like that for? You *never* talk like that. *Ever.* You and me—'

'Shut up!'

'I won't!'

'You do what I say, an' 'f you don't, you feel the palm.'

She squared off at him. Her headscarf had loosened, and now it fell back altogether, revealing her hair. This was not the Neal Wyatt she knew, nor was this the Neal Wyatt for whom she was risking everything, from the goodwill of her parents to her reputation. She cried, 'You keep talking to me like tha', I make *bloody* well sure—'

He slapped her. She fell back in surprise.

Joel latched on to him. He said to the girl, 'Hibah, you get home.'

The idea that Joel would tell Hibah – Neal's designated woman – what to do would have been enough to encourage a collective gasp from onlookers, had any of them been interested. As it was, no members of the community enjoying the bright fine day made a move to stop what happened next.

Neal swung on Joel. His face blazed absolute joy, which should have told Joel that forces far greater than those he understood were at work in this place and on this day. But he had no time to consider that. Neal set upon him. He gripped Joel around the neck and Joel went down, with Neal falling upon him with a grunt of pleasure.

Neal said, 'Fucking little . . .' but that was all. The rest was pounding, administered with his fists to Joel's face. Hibah shrieked Neal's name, but Neal was not to be thwarted in this encounter.

Joel flailed around beneath him, trying and failing to connect with Neal's face. He kicked and squirmed to get away. He felt Neal's blows on the sides of his head. He felt Neal's spittle on his cheeks. Above the *thwapping* of the other boy's fists, he heard the wind-rush noise of the skateboarders. He heard the dim shouting of Hibah.

Then Neal's hands were around Joel's neck. He grunted, 'Stupid . . . I'll kill . . .' as he tightened them. Joel's knee sought his groin, but didn't connect. Hibah screamed and Joel heard Toby crying out his name.

And then, just as suddenly as the encounter had begun, it was over. It hadn't been ended by Ivan Weatherall this time, nor by Hibah's entreaties, by Toby's fearful tears, or by the intervention of the police. Rather, one of Neal's crew had finally come down from the towpath and pulled Neal off. He said tersely, 'Blood, blood. You ain't *s'posed* to . . .' And then in a clear correction of course, 'You take it far 'nough f'r now. You got dat?'

Neal shook him off and, in doing so, he also shook off this apparent incursion into his rank as head of the crew. This left Joel on the ground, bleeding from a cut near his left eye and gasping for breath.

Hibah had crumpled on to the bench where she rocked herself

in shock and dismay. She shook her head at this Neal whom she had never seen and did not know, her fist to her mouth.

Toby had come running from the skate bowl. He'd brought his lava lamp along with him for the outing, and he trailed its flex over the grass. He'd begun to cry. Joel heaved himself to his knees in an attempt to reassure him.

He muttered, 'S'all right, Tobe. S'all right, mon.'

Toby stumbled to him. 'He bunged you up,' he cried. 'You got cut on your face. He wanted to—'

'S'okay.' Joel staggered to his feet. For a moment Meanwhile Gardens whirled round him like images seen from a merry-go-round. When the dizziness passed, he pressed his arm to his face. It came away bloody. He looked at Neal.

Neal was breathing hard from his exertions, but he no longer looked as if he wanted to leap upon Joel. Instead, he made a move in Hibah's direction. She jumped to her feet.

'You,' she said to him.

He said, 'Listen.' He looked at his crew. Two of them shook their heads. He said urgently, 'We *talk*, Hibah.'

To which she responded, 'I die before I talk to you again.'

'You don't unnerstan how t'ings going down.'

'I unnerstan all I need, Neal Wyatt.'

She swept off, leaving Neal and everyone else watching her. Joel said nothing, but he didn't need to. Neal took his presence as both cause and blame, and he jerked his head with a look that went from Joel to his brother.

He said, 'You fucked. You and weirdshit. You got dat?'

Joel said, 'I ain't—'

'You *fucked*, yellowskin. Both of you. Next time.'

He tilted his chin in the direction of the towpath. His companion took it as it was meant and led the way so that Neal and he could rejoin the rest of the crew.

Ness enjoyed the absence of Dix initially. But the long-term delight that she thought she would feel with him gone did not materialise. She liked not having to listen nightly to her aunt's bed thumping and she liked the fact that the ground seemed more or less even between herself and Kendra once Dix was gone. Beyond that, though, there was no permanent joy for her in Dix's removal. She hated him for his rejection of her, yet she still wanted the chance to prove she was dozens of times the woman her aunt could ever be.

Having the opportunity to move into Kendra's bedroom to share her aunt's bed, and thus achieve a modicum of privacy in the household, did not appeal to her, nor did it give her a sense of pleasure or power. Kendra made the offer, but Ness refused it. She couldn't imagine sleeping in the same bed that Dix D'Court had so recently vacated and, even if that hadn't been the case, sleeping in Kendra's room with Kendra there was hardly going to give Ness the sort of privacy she preferred. She knew she didn't belong in her aunt's bedroom; she knew – although she never would have admitted it to anyone – that Dix did. She also knew her aunt didn't really want her there.

The outcome of all this was that she felt bad when she wanted to feel good. She needed a way back to the good again, and she felt fairly certain of what would work.

She chose Kensington High Street this time. She went by bus and disembarked not far from St Mary Abbots church. From there, she sauntered down the slope to the flower stall in front of the churchyard. She surveyed her options from this vantage point while, behind her, tuberoses, lilies, ferns, and babies' breath were fashioned into fine bouquets.

She decided first on H & M, where the crowded conditions and the racks of garments from the subcontinent promised her the camouflage of other adolescents as well as excellent pickings. She wandered from one floor to the next, seeking something that would challenge her as well as delight her, but she could find nothing that she did not deem b-o-r-i-n-g when she evaluated it. So she meandered up the street to Accessorize, where the challenge to pocket something was much greater since the shop was so small and her photograph was still sell-otaped next to the till as someone who wasn't allowed inside. But conditions were crowded and she gained entry, only to discover that, on this day, the merchandise wasn't significant enough to provide her with the pleasure she wanted to feel upon successfully stealing it.

After trying Top Shop and Monsoon, she finally walked into in a large department store, and this was the location she settled upon. A wiser girl with malefaction on her mind might have chosen otherwise, for there were no big crowds in which to hide and, as a mixed-race adolescent in revealing clothes and big hair, Ness stood out like a sunflower in a strawberry patch. But the merchandise looked higher class, and she liked that. She quickly spied a sequinned headband that she coveted.

This headband was in a serendipitous location, as far as Ness was concerned. On a rack just a half-dozen steps from the exit, it fairly announced its desire to be pocketed. Checking it out and deciding it was worthy of her efforts, Ness made a recce of the immediate area to make sure she was if not safe from notice then close enough to the doorway to dash out of the store once the headband was in her pocket.

There didn't seem to be anyone watching her. There didn't seem to be anyone of note nearby at all. There *was* an old pensioner giving her the eye from a rack of socks, but she could tell from his expression that the fact he was watching her had nothing at *all* to do with making sure she didn't walk off with something she hadn't paid for and everything to do with the décolletáge supplied by her choice of T-shirt. She dismissed him with contempt.

In anticipation of pinching the desired item, Ness felt the nervous energy begin to tingle up her arms. It promised her that the rush of delight she wanted was already on its way. All she had to do was reach out, take two headbands from the rack, drop them to the floor, bend, pick them up, and return only one of them as the other was safely tucked in her bag. It was easy, simple, quick, and sure. It was sweets from an infant, food from a kitten, tripping a blind man, whatever you will.

With the sequinned band in her possession, she made for the door. She walked as casually as she'd done when she'd first entered the store, and she felt suffused with a combination of warmth and excitement as she mixed with a group of shoppers outside.

She didn't get far. Lit with success, she'd decided on Tower Records next, and she was about to cross the road when she was blocked by the pensioner she'd seen inside the department store.

He said, 'I don't think so, dearie,' as he took her by the arm.

She said, 'What the *hell* you think you're doing, mon?'

'Nothing at all, as long as you can provide a receipt for the merchandise you've got inside that bag of yours. Come with me.'

He was far stronger than he appeared. In fact, upon a closer look at him, Ness saw that he wasn't a pensioner at all. He wasn't stooped as he'd appeared to be in the store, and his face wasn't lined to match his thin, grey hair. Still, she didn't realise how he fitted into the scheme of things, and she continued to protest – loudly – as he led her back towards the door of the department store.

Once inside, he marched her along an aisle and towards the back of the store. There, a swing door led to the bowels of the building. Soon enough she was through it and being ushered down a flight of stairs.

Hotly, she said, 'Where the *fuck* do you think you're taking me?'

His answer was, 'Where I take all shoplifters, dearie.'

Thus she understood that the man she'd thought was a pensioner was a security guard for the infernal department store. So she didn't willingly go a step farther. She put up as much of a fight as his grip upon her arm would allow. For she knew that she'd just caused herself a fair amount of trouble. Already on probation, already doing community service, she had no wish to put in another appearance in front of a magistrate, where she'd be risking more this time than merely having to show up at the child drop-in centre.

Once down the stairs, she found herself in a narrow lino-floored corridor, where she could see that she wasn't going to get away easily. She assumed they were on their way to wherever it was that they took shoplifters while they waited for a constable to show up from the Earl's Court Road police station, and she began to prepare a tale to spin when the constable got there. She'd have time to do this in whatever lock-up they provided for her. It would be, she reckoned, at best a small and windowless room and at worst a real cell.

It was neither. Instead, the security guard opened a door and pushed her into a locker room. It smelled of perspiration and disinfectant. Rows of grey lockers lined it on either side, and a narrow, unpainted wooden bench went down its middle.

Ness said, 'I di'n't do nothing, mon. Why're you bringing me to dis place?'

'I expect you know. I expect we can open that bag of yours and see.' The guard turned from her, and locked the door behind them. The deadbolt clicked into place like a pistol cocking. He held out his hand. 'Give me the bag,' he told her. 'And let me say that things tend to go easier with your lot if I can tell the cops you've been cooperative from the first.'

Ness hated the idea of handing over her bag, but she did it because *cooperative* was indeed how she wanted to seem. She watched as the guard opened the bag as any man might: clumsily and unsure how the thing was meant to be handled. He dumped out its contents and there was the offending article, sequins glittering in the overhead lights. He picked it up and held it dangling from one finger. He looked from her to it, and he said, 'Worth it, then?'

'What're you talking 'bout?'

'I'm asking is it worth it to nick something like this when the consequences might be a lock-up?'

'You saying I nicked it. I ain't.'

'How'd it get in your bag if you didn't nick it?'

'Don't know,' she said. 'I never saw it before.'

'And who d'you expect to believe that? Especially when I give chapter and verse of your picking up two, dropping them both, and returning only one of them to the rack. There was this one – with the silver sequins – and there was the other one – with the red and blue. Who d'you think will be believed? D'you have any priors, by the way?'

'What're you yammering—'

'I think you know. And I think you have them. Priors, that is. Problems with the cops. The last thing you want is for me to phone them. I can see that in your face as plain as anything, and don't deny it.'

'You don't know nuffink.'

'Don't I now? Then you won't mind when the coppers come along, when I tell 'em my tale and you tell 'em yours. Who do you expect they're likely to believe, a girl with priors – kitted out like a tart – or an upstanding member of the public who happens to be on staff at this establishment?'

Ness said nothing. She attempted to seem indifferent but the truth of the matter was that she was not. She didn't want to face the police another time, and the fact that she was eyeball-to-eyeball with doing just that infuriated her. The fact that she was in the hands of someone who was clearly going to play cat and mouse with her till he turned her over to the authorities only made matters worse. She felt tears of futility come into her eyes and this enraged her more. The security guard saw them, and carried on in accordance with what he believed about them.

'Not so tough when it comes down to it, are you, now?' he asked her. 'Dress tough, act tough, talk tough, all of it. But at the end of the day, you want to go home like the rest of 'em, I expect. That it? You want to go home? Forget about this?'

Ness said nothing. She waited. She sensed more was to come, and she was not wrong in this. The guard was watching her, waiting for a reaction of some kind. She finally said, with a degree of caution, 'What? You saying you mean to let me go home?'

'If certain conditions are met,' he said. 'I being the only one who knows about this—' He swung the headband from his finger again. 'I let you leave and I return this to where it belongs. Nothing further said between us.'

Ness thought about this and knew there was no alternative. She said, 'What, then?'

He smiled. 'Take off your T-shirt. Bra as well, if you're wearing one, which I doubt, considering how much I can already see.'

Ness swallowed. 'What for? What're you going—'

'You want to leave? No questions asked? No further cause for interaction between us? Take off your T-shirt and let me look at them. That's what I want. I want to look at them. I want to see what you have.'

'That's all? Then you let me—'

'Take *off* your T-shirt.'

It wasn't, she told herself, any worse than opening the dressing-gown in front of Dix D'Court. And it surely wasn't worse than everything else she'd already seen and done and experienced . . . *And* it meant that she would walk out of this place without a cop in attendance, which meant everything there was.

She clenched her teeth. It *didn't* matter. Nothing mattered. In one quick movement, she pulled the T-shirt up, over her head, and off.

'Face me square,' he said. 'Don't cover yourself cause I don't expect you do that for all the younger blokes, do you? Drop the T-shirt as well. Put your arms at your sides.'

She did it. She stood there. He drank her in. His eyes were greedy. His breathing was loud. He swallowed so hard she could hear the sound of it from where she stood some ten feet away. Too many feet away, as things turned out. He said to her, 'One thing more.'

'You said—'

'Well, that was before I saw, wasn't it? Come over here, then.'

'I don't—'

'Just ask yourself if you want all this—' again the headband – 'to go away, dearie.'

He waited then. He was sure of himself, as a man who'd stood in this spot many times before and made the most of it.

Ness approached him, without any other option that she could see. She steeled herself to what would happen next and when he put his hand over one of her breasts, she did her best not to shudder although she felt a prickling sensation inside her nose: harbinger of the most useless of tears. His entire hand covered her breast, her nipple cushioned in the centre of his palm. His fingers tightened. He pulled her forward.

When she was inches from him he looked at her squarely. 'This,' he said, 'can all go away. You out of here and home to your mummy. No one the wiser about nicking this and that from the store. That what you want?'

A tear escaped her eye.

'You got to say,' he said. 'That's what you want. Say it.'

She managed to mutter. 'Yeah.'

'No. You must *say* it, dear.'

'Tha's what I want.'

He smiled. 'I guessed as much,' he said. 'Girls like you, they always want it. You hold still now, and I give you what you asked for, dearie. Will you do that for me? Answer me now.'

Ness steeled herself. 'I do that for you.'

'Willingly?'

'Yeah. I do it.'

'How nice,' he said. 'You're a good girl, aren't you?' He bent to her, then, and he began to suck.

She was late to the child drop-in centre. She made the trip from Kensington High Street north to Meanwhile Gardens without thinking about the locker room, but the effort to do this made her rage inside. Rage brought tears and tears brought more rage. She told herself she would return, she would wait outside the employees' door – the very door he'd taken her to at last, releasing her into a side street with a pleasant 'Now get along with you, dearie' – and when he came out at the end of the day, she'd kill him. She would shoot him between the eyes, and what they did to her afterwards would be of no account because he would be dead as he deserved to be.

She didn't wait for the bus that would take her up Kensington Church Street and then on to Ladbroke Grove. She told herself she couldn't be bothered, but the truth was that she didn't want to be seen, and on foot she felt somehow invisible.

Humiliation – which she would not admit as even existing – was washing over her. The only way to avoid feeling it was to stalk furiously in the general direction of the drop-in centre, savagely pushing her way through the crowds while she remained in the shopping district, seeking something she could damage when those crowds thinned and she was left on the wider pavements of Holland Park Avenue where there was no one close by to smash into and snarl at and nothing to do save keep walking and trying to avoid her own thoughts.

She finally boarded a bus in Notting Hill because it happened to pull up just as she reached the stop and there would be no need for her to wait and think. But this did little to get her to the drop-in centre so that her arrival would be timely. She was ninety minutes late as she went through the gate in the cyclone fence. In the play area three children toddled about in the paddling pool under the watchful eyes of their mothers.

The sight of them – children and mothers – was something that Ness couldn't bear to look at but *had* to look at, so what she felt was even more anger. The effect was like air being forced into an over-full balloon.

She shoved open the door of the drop-in centre. It banged against the wall. Several children were applying white glue to an art project that involved poster board, seashells, and beads. Majidah was the kitchen. The children looked up with wide eyes, and Majidah came into the main room. Ness readied herself for what the Muslim woman would say, thinking Just let her, just *let* the bloody bitch.

Majidah looked her over, her eyes narrowing in evaluation. She didn't like Ness because she didn't like Ness's attitude, not to mention her dress sense and the reason she was working at the centre. But she was also a woman who'd gone through much in her forty-six years, not the least of which was to come to terms with profound suffering: in herself and in others. While her philosophy in life could best be described as *Work hard, don't whinge, and just get on with it*, she was not devoid of compassion for people who had not yet found the way to do any of these things.

So she said, with a meaningful glance at the Felix the Cat clock that hung above a rank of storage blocks containing toys, 'You must try to be on time, Vanessa. Please do assist those children with their gluing. You and I will speak once we close for the day.'

Joel's confrontation with Neal Wyatt turned out to be a two-edged sword. One edge had Joel watching his back from that moment forward. The other edge had him writing. More words than he would ever have thought possible prompted more verse than he would ever have thought possible, the oddest feature about this process being the fact that the words coming out of his head weren't the sort that Joel would have thought could produce a poem. They were ordinary. Words like *bridge* or *kneel*, like *float* or *dismay*, had him diving for his notebook. He did it so often that Kendra became curious and asked Joel what he was up to with his nose bent over a notebook all the time. She assumed he was writing letters to someone and asked him if the intended recipient was his mother. When he told her it wasn't letters but rather poems, Kendra – like Hibah – jumped to love poems and she began to tease him about being stuck on a girl. But there was a half-hearted nature to her teasing that even Joel – with all his focus on verse – could not fail to notice. He said wisely, 'You seen Dix, then, Aunt Ken?' to which her response of '*Have* you seen,' took their conversation towards the importance of proper English and away from the importance of love.

Kendra told herself it wasn't love anyway and how could it have been with those nearly twenty years forming a yawning chasm between them. She told herself Good riddance, time for both of them to move on, but that message was prevented from working its way from her mind to her heart *because* of her heart. She altered the message after a time, to one of 'It was just lust, girl,' and she adhered to that because it seemed reasonable.

With Kendra's thoughts caught up in all this and with Joel's concentration on his poetry, there was only Toby left to notice a change in Ness in the following days. But since the change constituted doing what she had been ordered to do by the magistrate – and suddenly without complaint – the subtlety of the situation was beyond Toby. He soothed himself with his lava lamp, watched the television, and kept mum about Joel's run-in with Neal Wyatt.

This was at Joel's request. He explained away his cuts and bruises by telling his aunt that – daft as it was since he had no skill – he'd borrowed a skateboard and tried out the skate bowl. She accepted this story and talked about safety helmets.

For his part, Joel took the word *safety* and began to fashion another poem. When it was complete, he put it in the suitcase beneath his bed. Before he shut the lid, though, he counted the number of poems that he'd written. He was amazed to see he'd crafted twenty-seven, and the logical question arose in his mind: what was he going to do with them?

He continued to go to *Wield Words Not Weapons*, but he did not join the others at the microphone and he never participated in *Walk the Word*. Rather, he became an observer of the proceedings and a sponge for the criticism that was offered to the other poets who were willing to read.

Throughout all this, Ivan Weatherall didn't bother with him much, just saying hello, expressing his pleasure at seeing Joel at *Wield Words Not Weapons*, asking whether Joel was writing, and not making anything of it when Joel ducked his head, too embarrassed to answer directly. He merely said, 'You've got a gift, my friend. Mustn't turn away from it.' Otherwise, Ivan concentrated on the delight he felt at the growing attendance at his poetry events. He added a poetry-writing course to the script-writing course he offered at Paddington Arts, but Joel couldn't imagine taking it. He couldn't imagine *having* to write a poem. The creative act didn't work that way for him.

He had thirty-five pieces when he decided that he would let Ivan see some of his work. He picked out four that he liked and, on a day when he had to fetch Toby from the learning centre, he left Edenham Estate earlier than usual, and he went up to Sixth Avenue.

He found Ivan, white-gloved, working on another clock. This time, though, he wasn't building it. Rather, he was cleaning an old one which, he explained, had taken to striking the half hour whenever the fancy came upon it.

'Completely unacceptable behaviour in a time-piece,' Ivan confided as he ushered Joel into the little sitting-room. There, on the table beneath the window, the parts of a clock lay spread out on a white towel in a neat arrangement along with a small squeeze tin of oil, a pair of tweezers, and several sizes of minute screwdrivers. Ivan waved Joel in the direction of an armchair next to the fireplace. Coal had once burned there, but now an electric fire sat askew and unlit upon the grate. 'This is damn tedious work, and your presence brings me a distraction from total concentration on it for which I thank you,' Ivan said.

At first, Joel's thinking was that Ivan meant the four poems in his pocket, so he took them out and unfolded them, not questioning how the older man knew he'd come with a purpose. But Ivan merely went back to his clock work after reaching for a sprig of mint and popping it into his mouth. He began to talk of an art show that he'd seen on the south bank of the Thames. He said it was 'the emperor's whatevers' because one of the exhibits had been a urinal encased in plexiglass and signed by the artist, and another had been a glass of water on a shelf mounted high on the wall with the title *Oak Tree* tacked beneath it. Then, he went on, there was an entire room 'dedicated to an angry lesbian who made sofas into acts of sexual congress, don't ask. I can't say what her message was meant to be, but her rage came through remarkably. Do you like art, Joel?'

Ivan's question came so suddenly at the end of his chatter that Joel didn't take it in at first, and he didn't realise that his opinion was being solicited. But then Ivan looked up from his work, and his face appeared so friendly and expectant that Joel responded spontaneously for once, giving his answer without censoring himself.

'Cal draws good,' he said. 'I seen his stuff.'

Ivan frowned for a moment. Then he held up a finger and said, 'Ah. Calvin Hancock. At the right hand of Stanley. Yes. He's got something, hasn't he? Untutored, which is a shame, and unwilling to *become* tutored, which is worse. But masses of raw talent. You've an eye for it, then. What about the rest? Have you been to any of our city's great galleries?'

Joel hadn't, but he didn't want to say so. He didn't want to lie, either, so he murmured, 'Dad took us to Trafalgar Square once.'

'Ah. The National Gallery. What did you think? Bit stuffy, isn't it? Or did they have something special on?'

Joel pulled at a thread on the hem of his T-shirt. He knew there was some sort of museum in Trafalgar Square, but they'd only gone to see the enormous flocks of pigeons. They'd sat on the edge of one of the fountains and watched the birds, and Toby had wanted to climb on one of the lions at the base of the tall column at the square's centre. They'd listened to a busker entertaining with an accordion and they'd studied a girl painted gold and posing as a statue for donations that could be dropped into a bucket at her feet. They'd had Cornettos bought from a vendor at the side of the square, but they'd melted too fast because the day was hot. Toby had got ice-cream down the front of him and all over his hands. Their father had dipped his handkerchief into the fountain and had cleaned him up after he'd finished with the cone.

Joel hadn't thought of any of this in ages. The sudden memory made his eyes tingle.

Unaccountably as far as Joel was concerned, Ivan said, 'Ah. If we knew what the hand of cards was going to be, we'd develop a plan to play them in advance, I dare say. But the devilment of life is that we don't. We're caught out, most often with our trousers round our knees.'

Joel wanted to say, 'What're you *on* about?' but he didn't because he knew *exactly* what Ivan was on about: there one moment and gone the next, walking to the dancing school to fetch Ness from her Saturday lesson, Toby's hand in their dad's and Joel pausing some thirty yards back because in front of the discount store a container of footballs caught his attention, so much so that at first he didn't realise what the four loud pops were that he heard in advance of the shouting.

Joel said in a rush, 'I brought these,' and he thrust his poems at Ivan.

Ivan took them, mercifully saying nothing further about hands of cards or how one could play them. Instead, he placed the papers on the towel, and he bent over them exactly as he would bend over a clock. He read and as he did so, he chewed on his mint leaves.

At first, he said nothing. He merely went from one poem to the next, setting each aside after he had read it. Joel found that his ankles had begun to itch and the ticking of the clocks seemed louder than usual. He thought he'd been foolish to bring the poems to Ivan and he silently said Stupid, stupid, dumb shit, thick head, die die die.

Ivan's reaction was quite unlike Joel's, however. He finally turned in his seat and said, 'The greatest sin is letting riches go to waste once you know they're riches. The difficulty is that most people *don't* know. They define riches only by what they can see because that's what they've been taught to do: to look at the *end* of things, the destination. What they never recognise is that riches are in the process, the journey, in what one does with what one has. Not in what one manages to amass.'

This was all a bit much for Joel, so he said nothing. He did wonder, though, if Ivan was merely coming up with something to say because he'd read the poems and he'd found them as stupid as Joel himself was beginning to suspect they truly were.

Before he could voice this, Ivan opened a wooden box on his table and took out a pencil. He said, 'You've a natural flair for metre and language, but occasionally the rawness is just too raw, and that's where shading comes in. If we scan this verse . . . Here. Let me show you what I mean.'

He motioned Joel to come to the table, and there he explained. He used terms Joel had never heard of, but he made marks on the paper to illustrate what he meant. He took his explanation slowly, and there was an honest friendliness to the recitation that made Joel easy with listening to it. There was also an eagerness behind the words that Joel could see was directed at the poems themselves.

So completely involved did he become in listening to Ivan talk about his verse and in watching the way Ivan was able to improve each piece that, when Joel finally heard the clocks chiming around him, he looked up to see he'd been there for nearly two hours. This was one hour longer than he'd meant to be there, and one hour later than the conclusion of Toby's summertime appointment at the learning centre.

Joel jumped to his feet, crying out, 'Holy hell!'

Ivan said, 'What . . . ?' but Joel heard nothing more of the question. The only sound he heard from that moment was the slapping of his trainers on the pavement as he ran in the direction of the Harrow Road.

16

Joel fairly threw himself at the doors of the learning centre. He was out of breath, but he managed to burst into reception, panting, 'Tobe . . . *Sorry*,' only to find himself being stared at by the sole occupants of the room: a young mother breast-feeding her infant, a toddler at her side with a dummy plugged into his mouth.

Still, Joel looked for Toby, as if he might be hiding under one of the vinyl sofas or behind the two artificial aspidistras. He next went in search of Luce Chinaka, and he found her in her office. She said, 'He's not waiting for you, Joel?' as she looked down at her wrist-watch. She then said, 'Oh, but weren't you meant to be here at . . .' but her voice drifted off mercifully when she saw the expression on Joel's panicked face. She got to her feet and said kindly enough, 'Let's just have a quick look round.'

But Toby was nowhere in the learning centre: not at the pint-sized tables where games were spread out, not at one of the keyboards in the computer room, not working in one of the smaller rooms with a teacher bent over him, not among the toys or the art materials. All this resulted in Joel's reaching the last conclusion he wished to reach: somehow Toby had slipped through a crack in the system and set off into the streets alone.

Luce Chinaka was saying, 'Come with me. Let's phone –' when Joel tore out of the centre. His mouth had gone dry. He couldn't think straight. He couldn't, in fact, even remember the route he usually followed when taking Toby home. Since he rarely used the same route anyway – someone unfamiliar up ahead and he'd abruptly change course without telling Toby why – virtually any direction that ultimately took one to Edenham Way was possible.

He looked up and down the pavement, hoping against unreasonable hope that he might catch a glimpse of Toby. But there was no familiar form in sight, tripping along on his tiptoes and trailing the flex of his lava lamp, which left Joel in an agony of indecision. He was finally roused from this by the thought of Kendra. The charity shop was just along the Harrow Road.

Resolutely, Joel set off. He walked at a fast clip, peering into each place of business on the route. At a William Hill betting shop, he even paused to ask Drunk Bob if Toby had somehow got inside, but all Drunk Bob said in reply was his usual – 'Oy! Oy!' – and he shook the arms of his wheelchair as if he meant to tell Joel more.

Kendra was helping a Chinese lady when Joel entered the charity shop. She automatically looked up when the bell rang and, seeing Joel, she glanced to each side of him for Toby. Then she looked at an old clock that was mounted above a display of worn-out shoes and she said, 'Where's your brother?'

This told Joel all he wanted to know. He turned on his heel and left, with his aunt's cry of 'Joel! What's going on?' following him.

Outside the learning centre once more, Joel bit the side of his thumb and tried to think things through. He doubted his brother would have crossed the road and headed into West Kilburn since he himself had never taken Toby there. This reduced the options to going right towards Great Western Road and ducking down one of the streets leading off it or going left in the direction of Kensal Town.

Joel chose right and tried to think like his brother. He decided it was likely that Toby would trip along the pavement, turning aimlessly when it turned into a side street. Joel would thus do that as well and, with luck, he would find that Toby had got distracted by something along the way and was, perhaps, staring meditatively at it with his mind elsewhere. Or, failing that, he had become tired and sat down to wait until someone found him. Or, what would be even more likely, perhaps he'd got hungry and wandered into a sweet shop or a newsagent's where there'd be a display of snacks.

Bearing all this in mind and trying to think of nothing else – certainly nothing sinister – Joel turned right at the first street he came to. A line of terrace houses stood in a rank along it, all of them identical London brick. All along the way, cars were parked nose to tail at the kerb, and the occasional bicycle was chained to a railing or a street lamp, frequently with one of its tyres removed. Midway down the street, the road curved to the left, and it was at this spot that Joel saw someone alighting from a van. It was a man dressed in a navy blue boilersuit and likely returning home from work but, instead of proceeding into one of the nearby houses, he stood looking beyond the curve of the street to a point which Joel himself could not see. He shouted something and then dug in his pocket to bring out a mobile phone, into which he punched a few numbers. He waited, spoke, and then shouted down the street again.

Joel watched all this as he hurriedly advanced. By the time he reached the van, the man had gone inside one of the houses. What he'd been shouting at remained outside, however. Joel took it in and knew what he was looking at: some ten or twelve houses further along, a group of boys circled like a pack of hounds around a figure huddled on the pavement, quite small against the wall of a property, like a hedgehog protecting its vital parts.

Joel took off running and shouted as he ran. 'Fuck you, Wyatt! Leave him alone!'

But Neal Wyatt had no intention of leaving Toby alone, intent as he was upon keeping several promises. This time he had his full crew of henchmen to lend a hand in the proceedings and, by the time Joel reached them, Neal had already done his worst: Toby was weeping, he'd wet himself, and his treasured lava lamp lay stamped to bits on the pavement, all plastic and glass and liquid, its flex lying like a splattered snake among the debris.

Joel's vision went black, then clear. He chose the most foolhardy of the alternatives open to him, and he threw himself at Neal Wyatt. But he got no further than a single blow, which barely connected anyway, when one of Neal's crew grabbed him by the arms and another drove a fist into his stomach. Neal himself shouted, 'Fucker's *mine*,' and everything happened quickly after that. Joel felt a rain of blows. He tasted blood as his lip split open. The breath left him with an *oof* as he sank to the pavement. There, heavy boots and trainers connected with his ribs.

Finally, someone shouted, 'Shit! Clear it!' and the boys began to run in every direction. Neal was the last to leave. He took a moment to bend to Joel, twist his hand in Joel's hair, and say into his face with the rank breath of someone whose teeth are going bad, 'It'll be his arm next time, wanker.' Then he too was gone. What replaced him was what the boys had apparently seen cruising down from the Harrow Road.

The panda car pulled to a stop and a constable got out while his partner remained in the vehicle. From where he lay on the pavement, Joel watched the policeman's polished shoes approaching.

Trouble here? he wanted to know. S'going on? Live round here? Hurt? Cut? Shot? What?

The radio in the car squawked. Joel looked up from the polished shoes, and saw the blank face watching him, a white man whose lips twisted in a movement of distaste as his opaque blue eyes moved from Joel to Toby and took in the urine that had spread in a widening stain on the child's trousers. Toby's eyes were squeezed shut so tight that his face was nothing more than a mass of creases.

Joel reached for his brother. He said, 'S'okay, mon. Le's go home. You okay, Tobe? Here. Look. They're gone. Cops's shown up. You okay, Tobe?'

The driver of the panda car barked out, 'Bernard, what's the brief? Anyone hurt?'

Bernard said that it was business as usual and what the hell else did they expect since this lot were going to kill each other eventually and sooner was better than later.

'D'they want a ride? Get 'em in the car. We c'n take 'em home.'

Hell no, Bernard told him. One of them's pissed his panties and no way was that smell going to foul up *their* car.

The driver cursed. He stamped so hard on the brakes of the vehicle that the sound was like chains dragging on concrete. He got out of the car and joined Bernard on the pavement, where he looked down at Joel and Toby. Joel had, by this time, got himself into a kneeling position and was trying to ease Toby out of his protective curl. The driver said, 'Get the hell into the car,' and it took a moment before Joel realised that he was talking not to him and his brother but to his partner. Bernard responded with, 'See for yourself, you love it so much,' as he complied.

The driver then squatted next to Joel. He said, 'Let me see your face, lad. Want to tell me who did this?'

Both of them knew what naming and shaming meant in a boy's life, so both of them knew Joel would not point a finger at anyone. He said, 'Don't know. I jus' found 'em 'rassing my brother.'

The constable said to Toby, 'D'you know who they were?'

But Joel knew they would get nothing from Toby. His brother was as good as done for this day. Joel just needed to get him home.

He said, 'We're okay. Tobe doesn't know 'em, either. Just some bloods not liking the look of us, is all.'

'Let's get him into the car, then. We'll take you home.'

This was the last thing Joel wanted: drawing attention to themselves by arriving in Edenham Way in a panda car. He said, 'We'll be okay now. We just got to walk over to Elkstone Road.' He got to his feet and hauled Toby to his.

Toby's head flopped forward on his chest like a rag doll's. 'They broke it,' he cried. 'They grabbed it and it fell and they stamped it up and down.'

'What's he on about, then?' the constable asked.

'Jus' something he was carrying home.' Joel indicated the remains of the lava lamp. He said to Toby, 'S'okay, bred. We'll get 'nother,' although the truth of the matter was that Joel had no idea how, where, or when he'd ever be able to get another sixteen pounds to replace what his little brother had lost. He kicked the remains of the lava lamp to the kerb and deposited them in the gutter.

Inside the panda car, the radio squawked another time. Bernard spoke into it and then to his partner, 'Hugh, we're wanted.'

Hugh said to Joel. 'You set off home, if you don't want a ride. Here, use this on your mouth as you go.' He handed over his handkerchief, which he pressed on Joel's lip until Joel himself held it properly. He said, 'Go on, lad. We'll keep you in sight to the end of the street,' and he returned to the car and climbed inside.

Joel took Toby by the hand and began to pull him in the direction of Great Western Road, which was where the street they were walking along terminated. As good as his word, Hugh kept the panda car crawling along just behind them, leaving them only when they came to the corner and headed towards the bridge over the Grand Union Canal. Then they were on their own once more, descending the steps and crossing Meanwhile Gardens.

Joel urged Toby along as fast as he could, which wasn't as fast as he would have liked. Toby babbled about the destruction of his lava lamp, but Joel had far greater worries to keep him occupied. He knew that Neal Wyatt would bide his time until he got the chance to make good his threat. He meant to go after Toby, and he wouldn't rest until he dealt with Joel by dealing with Joel's little brother.

It was impossible for Joel to pretend that he'd taken a fall riding a skateboard this time. Even if his aunt had not known he'd been looking for Toby, even if consequently she *might* have been led into believing both of the boys had been in Meanwhile Gardens all along, the condition of Joel's face and the bruises across his body did not suggest a simple tumble. While Joel managed to get Toby cleaned up prior to Kendra's return from the charity shop, he couldn't do much about himself. He washed off the blood, but the cuts on his face were still there, and his right eye was swelling and would soon go black. Then there was the matter of the lava lamp, about which Toby was inconsolable, so when Kendra walked in, it was only moments before she learned the truth.

She whisked both boys to Casualty. Toby didn't need attending to, but she insisted that he be looked over as well although Joel was her real concern. She was furious that this had happened to her nephews and insistent upon knowing who had set upon them.

Toby didn't know their names and Joel wouldn't say their names. Kendra could tell that Joel knew them, however, and the fact that he wouldn't tell her infuriated her more. The conclusion she reached was that these were the same nasty little pieces of business who'd been after Joel the day he'd stormed through the charity shop and burst out of the back door into the alley. She'd heard one of them call their obvious leader Neal. It would, she decided, be no difficult task to ask around, find out his surname, and sort him out.

The only problem with this plan was the sorting out part of it. Kendra remembered the boy, and he seemed a hateful creature. A talking-to wasn't going to make any difference to him. He was the kind of yob who only understood the threat of bodily harm.

This called for Dix. Kendra knew she had no choice in the matter. She was going to have to be humble and throw herself upon his essential good nature in order to ask for his help, but she became willing to do that once she saw that Toby was afraid to leave the house and Joel was watching his back at all times, like a millionaire strolling through Peckham.

The question for her was where to approach Dix so that her approach would not be open to misinterpretation. She couldn't go the Falcon where, she assumed correctly, he had taken up residence once again with the two other power lifters. She couldn't ring him and ask him to come to Edenham Estate lest he think she wanted him to move back in. A chance encounter in the street somewhere seemed the best, but she couldn't rely upon that. This seemed to leave the gym, where he did his lifting.

So that was where she went, as soon as she was able to manage it. She made her way to Caird Street, where the Jubilee Sports Centre stretched in a low-slung brick mass just south of the Mozart Estate. She was taking her chances with regard to Dix's being there, but as it was around lunchtime and as he put in a good six hours at his work-out each day, it seemed reasonable to conclude he'd be power lifting.

He was. In a snowy vest and navy shorts, he was bench pressing what looked to Kendra to be a mind-boggling amount of weight. He was being spotted by a fellow lifter taking a casual approach to his job by discussing low reps versus singles with third lifter who was standing nearby with an upended water bottle, pouring its contents into his mouth.

These two men saw Kendra before Dix. Aside from the fact that she was a woman entering a largely male world, in her pencil skirt, her ivory blouse, and her heels, she was hardly dressed for the place. Beyond that, she did not have the look of a female body-builder or of anyone wishing to become a female body-builder. Dix's companions ceased their conversation when it became clear that she was approaching them.

Kendra waited until Dix had completed his reps and his spotter had guided the barbell back into position on the stand. The spotter said to him quietly, 'Dis yours, mon?' which directed his attention to Kendra. Dix reached for a white towel and used it as he rose from the bench.

They faced each other. Kendra would have had to be blind not to see that Dix looked good. She would have had to be insensate not to feel the same stirring for him that she'd felt when they were together. More, she would have had to be demented not to *remember* how they were together when they'd been together. All of this caused her to hesitate before she spoke.

So he spoke first, saying, 'Ken. Looking good. How you been?'

She said, 'C'n I have a word?'

He glanced at the other two men. One shrugged and the other flipped his hand as if to say, Whatever.

Kendra added hastily, 'Or later, if you're in the middle of something.'

He clearly *was* in the middle of something, but he said, ''S okay. I'm good.' He came to join her. 'Happening?' he asked. 'Kids okay?'

'C'n we go . . . ? Not leave here or anything, but is there some place . . . ?' She felt shy with him, on the wrong foot. This had to do with the reason for her visit; nonetheless, she wished she felt more in control of the situation.

He nodded towards the door through which she'd come, where a vending machine sold bottled water and energy drinks. Four small tables with chairs ran along a window opposite the machine. This was where Dix took her.

She looked at the machine. She was parched. It was a warm day, and her nerves were in the process of drying out her mouth. She opened her bag and fished out some coins.

He said, 'I c'n get you—'

She used his own, previous words. 'I'm good. I don't expect you're carrying any money in those shorts,' and then she felt hot again because it seemed to her that what she'd said was rife with connotations.

He chose to ignore them. He said, 'Dat would be the truth.'

'You want something?'

He shook his head. He waited till she had her water. They sat and faced each other. He said again, 'Looking good, Ken.'

She said, 'Ta. Yourself. But that's no surprise.'

He looked confused by this. He felt judged, her remark reminding him of obsession and of everything that had been off-kilter in their relationship.

Kendra saw this and hastened to add, 'I mean, you always work hard. So it's no surprise to me you look good. Any more competitions coming up?'

He thought about this before saying, 'Dat's not why you're here, innit.'

She swallowed. 'True.'

She had no real idea how to make her request of him, so she plunged in without prefatory remarks. She told him what had happened to Joel and Toby – she'd put two and two together on the earlier 'fall' from a skateboard as well – and once she'd concluded with the casualty department and Joel's refusal to name their tormentor, she named him herself and asked for Dix's help in the matter.

'Ugly little mixed-race kid with his face half-frozen. He's called Neal. Ask round and you should be able to find him without much trouble. He runs with a crew in the Harrow Road. All I'm asking is that you have a word with him, Dix. A *serious* word. Let him see Joel and Toby have a friend who's willing to do something if they get hurt.'

Dix didn't reply. He reached for the bottle from which Kendra had been drinking her water and he took a swig of it. He held on to it afterwards, rolling it between his palms.

Kendra said, 'These boys . . . They've been vexing Joel for a while, evidently, but they didn't know about Toby till recently. Joel's afraid they'll go after him again – go after Toby—'

'He saying that?'

'No. But I can tell. He hovers. He . . . he gives *instructions* to Toby. Stay inside the learning centre and don't go out on the steps. Don't wander down to the charity shop. Don't visit the skate bowl unless I'm with you. That kind of thing. I know why he's saying it. I'd talk to those boys myself—'

'*Can't* do that.'

'I know. They wouldn't care if a woman—'

'Ken, that ain't it.'

'– was the one trying to sort them. But if it was a man, if it was a man like you, someone they could *see* would take them on if he had to and would give them a dose of what they give to helpless little boys, then they'd leave Joel and Toby alone.'

Dix looked at the bottle in his hands and he kept his eyes on it as he replied. 'Ken, 'f I sort dis for the boys, t'ings'll go worse. Joel and Toby end up having more trouble'n ever. You don't want dat and neither do I. You know how t'ings on the street work out.'

'Yeah, I do know,' Kendra said curtly. 'People die is how things in the street work out.'

He winced. 'Not always,' he said. 'And we're not talking 'bout a drug ring, Ken. We're talking about a group of boys.'

'A group of boys going after Toby. *Toby.* You should see him now, how scared he is. He's had nightmares about it and his days aren't much better.'

'It'll pass. Boy like dis Neal, he's into posturing, innit. His street creds're not going to grow 'f he does some job on an eight-year-old. What he's doing right now – making threats 'n' all dat – you'll see dat's the limit of wha' he's going to do an' he's doing it to unnerve you lot.'

'Well, he's damn well succeeding.'

'Don't have to be dat way. He's a limp-dick, innit. 'F he's

talking 'bout seeing to Toby, it means he just dat – all talk and nuffink else.'

Kendra looked away from him as she realised what the outcome of this conversation was going to be. She said, 'You aren't willing to help.'

'Not what I'm saying.'

'Then what?'

'Kids got to learn survival round here. Kids got to learn how to get along or get away.'

'What you're saying . . . That's not a whole lot different than saying you won't help me out.'

'I *am* helping you out. I'm tellin' you how it is and how it has to be.' He took another drink of the water and he handed the bottle back as he went on. His voice was not unkind. 'Ken, you got to think . . .' He chewed on the inside of his lip for a moment. He made a study of her till she stirred uncomfortably beneath it. He finally sighed and said, 'Maybe you got more 'n you can handle. You ever t'ink dat?'

Her backbone stiffened. She said, 'So I should get rid of 'em? That what you're saying? I should ring up Miss Fabulous Bender and tell her to come fetch 'em?'

'Dat's not what I meant.'

'And I'm supposed to live with myself afterwards? Maybe by telling myself they're *safe* now? Away from this place an' all its troubles?'

'Ken. *Ken.* I said it wrong.'

'Then what?'

'I just meant maybe you got too much to handle alone.'

'Like what?'

'Why're you asking dat? What d'you mean "like what?" You know what I'm talking about. Like Toby 'n' whatever's wrong wiv him dat no one ever like to talk about. Like Ness an'—'

'Ness is doing *fine*.'

'Fine? Ken, she came on to me. More 'n once while I was living wiv you. Last time, she presented herself wivout no clothes on, and I'm telling you somet'ing's *wrong* wiv her.'

'She's over-sexed like three-quarters of the girls her age.'

'Yeah. Sure. Dat I unnerstan. But she knew I was your man, and dat makes a diff'rence, or at least it should. But nuffink makes a difference to Ness, and you got to see that makes somet'ing wrong.'

Kendra couldn't go to the subject of Ness. Staying with the subject of Joel, Toby, and the street thugs seemed to give her the moral high ground. She said, 'If you don't want to help, jus' say it. Don't make this a judgement on me, all right?'

'I *ain't* judging . . .'

She got to her feet.

He said, 'God damn it, Kendra. I'm willing to make it so you don't have to handle dis shit alone. Those kids got needs an' you don't have to be the only one tryin' to meet 'em.'

'Seems to me that I *am* the only one meeting a need here,' she said. She headed for the doorway, leaving him sitting at the table with her bottle of water.

When the autumn term began, Joel knew that dodging the occasion of a run-in with Neal and his crew was not going to be enough, especially since Neal and his crew knew exactly where to find him. He tried to vary the route he and Toby took to Middle Row School in the morning, but there was no way to vary the *fact* of Middle Row School or of Holland Park School either. He knew that he needed to deal with the issue of Neal Wyatt, not only for himself but for Toby.

For himself, he came up with the knife.

In the long aftermath of the visit paid by the Blade to Edenham Way, everyone but Joel had forgotten about the flick knife that had been sent flying during the mêlée. Too many things had happened all at once for the household to remember that knife: Toby's hysterics, Ness bleeding from the head, the Blade being thrown out on his arse, Kendra coping with Ness's injury . . . In the midst of all this, the flick knife had gone the way of bad dreams.

Even Joel didn't remember the knife at first. It was only when he was rescuing a piece of cutlery from beneath the cooker where he'd accidentally dropped and kicked it while laying the table that he saw the glint of silver against the wall. He knew at once what it was. He said nothing about it, but when the coast was clear, he went back and, using a long-handled wooden spoon, he scooped it forward. When he had his hands on it, he saw a thin line of his sister's blood along the blade. So he washed it carefully and, when it was dry, he put it under his mattress – right in the middle – where no one was likely to find it.

He had no thought of using it for anything until he over-heard his aunt in conversation with Cordie, telling her about her visit with Dix, her umbrage high. 'He say let 'em sort t'ings out 'emselves,' she was saying, her voice low but the hiss of it unmistakable. 'Like I'm s'posed to wait till one of 'em gets beat bad enough to go into hospital wiv a broken skull.'

Joel understood this to mean he and Toby were on their own. He, too, had considered going to Dix for help – as unwise as he knew that would have been – but hearing Kendra and making the correct interpretation, he realised he would need a different plan.

So, for himself, the plan was the knife. He fetched it from beneath his mattress and he put it in the rucksack that he carried to school. He'd get into serious trouble if he was caught with it, but he had no intention of showing it around like someone in need of impressing his schoolmates. He only intended to bring it out if an emergency called for it, and this would be a Neal Wyatt emergency, one in which Neal needed to know what was in store for him if he crossed Joel another time.

That left Joel with the problem of what to do for Toby. He meant to keep a sharp eye on his brother, and he especially meant never again to be late to the Westminster Learning Centre when it was time to fetch him. He meant to hand Toby over to Ness at the child drop-in centre – begging and bargaining for her help if necessary – should there be any occasion when he needed to leave Toby supervised. But on the chance that anything wreaked havoc with these carefully laid plans, he needed to have a carefully laid additional plan for Toby as well, one that would kick in automatically should Neal Wyatt appear anywhere near his horizon if he inadvertently found himself alone.

Joel knew Toby would not be able to remember anything complicated. He understood also that, in a moment of fear, Toby might well freeze up altogether, curling into a ball and hoping he might go unnoticed. So he tried to make the plan sound like a game and the game involved hiding like an explorer in a jungle the moment he saw . . . What? The dinosaurs coming after him? The lions getting ready to pounce on him? Gorillas? Rhinos? Pygmies with poisoned spears? Cannibals?

Joel finally settled on head-hunters, which seemed gruesome enough for Toby to remember. He made a shrunken head from a dismembered and unsaleable troll doll that he got from the charity shop. He plaited its bright orange hair and drew stitches on its face. He said in reference to it, 'This's what they do, Tobe, and you got to remember,' and he put the severed doll head into his brother's school rucksack. There were head-hunters out there, he told him, and he had to find places to hide from them.

After school, after the learning centre, at the weekends, whenever there was time, Joel took Toby out into the streets and together they found useful shelters. These would be the places Toby would run to if he saw *anyone* approaching him. The thing about head-hunters, Joel told him, was that they looked just like everyone else. They wore disguises. Like those blokes who broke his lava lamp. Did Toby understand that? Yes? Truly?

On Edenham Estate, they practised dashing for the rubbish area where there was just enough space behind two wheelie bins for Toby to squeeze himself till he heard Joel call out that the coast was clear. Depending upon where he was in Meanwhile Gardens, he could slip down to the pond and hide in the reeds or – what was better – he could run for the abandoned barge beneath the canal bridge and there he could hole up under a crisscrossed pile of rotting timbers. On the Harrow Road, he could dash to the charity shop and hide in the back room where their aunt kept bins for the clothing that was still to be sorted.

Joel took his brother to each location time and time again. He said, 'I'm the head-hunter. Run!' and he gave Toby a shove in the correct direction. He kept this up until the sheer repetition of the exercise took Toby's legs to the correct hiding places.

During all of this, Neal Wyatt and his crew kept their distance. They gave no trouble to either Joel or Toby, and Joel was beginning to think that they'd actually moved on to tormenting someone else when they resurfaced, like hungry sharks returning to their feeding area.

What they did was follow. They took this up one day as Joel walked Toby to the learning centre. They emerged from a video shop across the road and, when Joel first saw them, he was certain they would vault the railing, dash through the traffic as they'd done before, and chase him and Toby down. But instead, they kept their distance across the street, stalking along the pavement and making soft hooting noises, as if they were signalling someone to jump out of one of the shops that Toby and Joel passed.

When he saw them, Toby grabbed the leg of Joel's trousers, saying, 'There's dem blokes't broke my lava lamp,' and he sounded frightened, which he was.

For his part, Joel stayed as calm as he could and merely reminded his brother about jungle explorers and head-hunters, asking him, 'Where'd you run, Tobe, if I wasn't here?'

Toby responded correctly: to the charity shop, to the back room, into those bins, and no stopping to tell Aunt Ken what he was doing.

But Neal and his crew didn't do anything more than follow and hoot on that day. On subsequent days they merely followed, doing their best to unnerve their quarry. Surprise was well and good for some kinds of contests. But for others, psychological warfare worked better to soften up the foe.

That was exactly what it did to Toby. After four days of being trailed by the silent crowd of boys, Toby wet his trousers again. It happened right on the steps of Middle Row School where he was obediently waiting for Joel. As Joel came round the corner from the bus, he saw Neal and his crew directly across the street from the school, gathered around a pub called the Chilled Eskimo, their eyes fastened on Toby.

Nothing in Joel's experience had prepared him for such a degree of extended cleverness on the part of these boys. This type of individual he'd previously seen as the type to jump, to clobber, and then to run. But now he understood that Neal was quite clever. There was a reason, then, why he was the one to run the crew.

Additional wisdom was called for: another way to handle the situation. Kendra could not be spoken to about it lest she worry even more. Ness – a peculiar change having come over her – was too involved with the drop-in centre. Dix was out of the question as was Carole Campbell. That left Ivan Weatherall.

Joel went at it through verse, which he gave to Ivan the next time he saw him.

Walking out he is, his poem began, *blood and hurting heavy on his mind.*

Ivan read it during their mentoring session at Holland Park School, where they still met as they'd done during the previous term. After he'd read the poem, Ivan spoke for a few minutes about emotive language and artistic intentions – as if he and Joel were at *Wield Words Not Weapons* or at the poetry class Ivan offered at Paddington Arts – and after a bit, Joel thought he meant to ignore the subject of the poem altogether.

Finally, though, Ivan said, 'This is it, I dare say.'

'What?'

'Why you've not taken the microphone at *Wield Words*. Why you don't participate in *Walk the Word* either.'

'I still been doing poems.'

'Hmm. Yes. And that's to the good.' Ivan read Joel's piece another time before he said, 'So exactly who is he? Are we speaking of Stanley? This is a fairly apt description of what appears to be his frame of mind.'

'The Blade? Nah.'

'Then . . . ?'

Joel reached down and retied his shoe, which didn't need retying. 'Neal Wyatt. You know.'

'Ah. Neal. That altercation in Meanwhile Gardens.'

'There's been more stuff. He's vexing Toby. I been trying to think what to do to stop him.'

Ivan set the poem on the table. He lined it up with the edge precisely, which allowed Joel to notice for the first time that Ivan's hands were manicured, with trimmed and buffed nails. In that moment, the vast difference between them became emphasised. Joel saw those hands as extensions of the world in which they lived, one where Ivan Weatherall – for all his good intentions – had never known labour in the way that Joel's own father had known it. This lack of knowledge created a chasm, not only between them but between Ivan and the entire community. No poetry event could span that chasm, no classes at Paddington Arts, no visits to Ivan's home. Thus, before the white man responded, Joel had a good idea what he would say.

'Neal's abandoned his art, Joel. Piano would have fed his

soul, but he wasn't patient enough to find that out. This is the difference between you. You have a greater means of expression now, but he does not. So what's in here –' this, with a fist to his heart – 'is experienced here' – the same fist lowered to the paper on the table. 'This gives you no reason to strike out against others. And you'll never *have* a reason while you have your verse.'

'But Toby,' Joel said. 'I got to stop them vexing Toby.'

'To do that is to engage in the circle,' Ivan said. 'You do see that, don't you?'

'What?'

'"Stopping them." How do you propose to do it?'

'They need sorting.'

'People always need "sorting" if you insist upon thinking within the box.'

Circles. Boxes. None of it made sense. Joel said, 'Wha's that s'posed to mean? Toby can't defend himself 'gainst those blokes. Neal's crew's waiting for a moment to get him, and if dat happens . . .' Joel squeezed his eyes shut. There was nothing more to say if Ivan could not imagine what it would be like for Toby should Neal's crew put their hands on him.

Ivan said, 'That's not what I meant.' They were seated side by side, and he pulled his chair closer to Joel's and put his arm around Joel's shoulders. This was the first time he'd ever touched the boy, and Joel felt the embrace with some surprise. But it seemed like a gesture meant to comfort him and he tried to take comfort from it although nothing would truly be able to soothe him until the problem of Neal Wyatt was seen to.

'What appears to be the answer is always the same when it comes to dealing with someone like Neal. Sort him out, have a dust-up, give him a taste of his own medicine, do unto him exactly what has been done to you. But that perpetuates the problem, Joel. Thinking within the box of doing what's always been done does nothing more than keep you going round the circle. He strikes, you strike, he strikes, you strike. Nothing gets resolved and the matter escalates to the point of no return. And you know what that means. I know you do.'

'He's set to hurt Toby,' Joel managed to say although his neck and his throat were stiff with holding back everything else that wanted to come out of him. 'I got to protect—'

'You can do that only up to a point. After that, you've got to protect yourself: who you are at this moment and who you can be. The very things Neal himself can't bear to think of because they don't gratify what he wants right now. Strike out at Neal for whatever reason, Joel, and you become Neal. I know you understand what I'm talking about. You have the words inside you and the talent to use them. That's what you're meant to do.'

He picked the poem up and read it aloud. When he was done, he said, 'Not even Adam Whitburn wrote like this at your age. Believe me, that's saying a lot.'

'Poems ain't nuffink,' Joel protested.

'Poems,' Ivan said, 'are the only thing.'

Joel wanted to believe that, but day after day in the street proved otherwise and Toby's retreating into Sose – communing with Maydarc and afraid to leave the house – proved even more. Joel found himself ultimately at the place he never thought he'd be: wishing that his little brother could be sent away to a special school or a special place where, at least, he would be safe. But when he asked his aunt about the paperwork that Luce Chinaka had sent home to have filled out and what this paperwork might mean for Toby's future, Kendra made it clear that no one was going to scrutinise Toby for love or money or anything else.

'And I expect you can work out why,' she said.

So the long and short of it was that Toby was going nowhere and now he was afraid to go anywhere. In Joel's world, then, something had to give.

There turned out to be only one solution that Joel could see if he wanted to act in a way that existed outside the box, which Ivan had described. He was going to have to get Neal Wyatt alone. They were going to have to talk.

17

While all of this was going on with Joel, Ness's experiences were taking an unexpected turn, beginning on the very day of her humiliation at the hands of the security guard. Had anyone told her that the result of this degrading situation would be friendship, had anyone told her that the person with whom she would come to form that friendship would be a middle-aged Pakistani woman, Ness would have called the person making that prognostication exceedingly stupid, although she probably would have phrased it in a far more colourful fashion. But that was exactly what occurred, like a slowly budding flower.

This unlikely friendship began with Majidah's invitation to Ness – or perhaps, better said, her order to Ness – to accompany her home on the day she'd shown up at the child drop-in centre, late from Kensington High Street. They did not go directly there, however. Instead, they began with some necessary shopping in Golborne Road.

Ness went along with trepidation hanging over her. She understood perfectly that Majidah held her future in her hands. One phone call from the Asian woman to the Youth Offending Team – in the person of Fabia Bender – would be sufficient to toast her properly. In the market area, she felt that Majidah was toying with her, prolonging the moment before she let the axe fall, and this provoked a very Nesslike reaction. But she managed to hold in her fury as Majidah did her shopping, knowing that it was better to wait to display it until they were not in a public forum.

Majidah went first to E. Price & Sons, where the two antique gentlemen helped her with her selection of fruit and veg. They knew her well and treated her respectfully. She was a shrewd buyer and took nothing from them that she did not inspect from every angle. She went next to the butcher. This was not any butcher, but one which sold only *halal* meats. There, she placed her order and turned to Ness as the butcher was weighing and wrapping. She said, 'Do you know what *halal* meat is, Vanessa?' And when Ness said, 'Summick Asians eat,' she said, 'This is the limit of what you know, is it? What an ignorant girl you are! What is it that they teach in school these days? But of course, you have not gone to school, have you? Sometimes I do forget how foolish you English girls can be.'

'Hey, I'm taking a course now,' Ness told her, 'over the college an' the magistrate even approved it.'

'Oh, yes indeed. A course in what? Tattoo drawing? Rolling one's own cigarettes?' She scrupulously counted out a collection of coins to pay for the *halal* meat, and they left the shop with Majidah waxing on the topic, which was obviously dear to her heart. She said, 'Do you know what I would have made of my life, had I had the opportunities for education that you have, you foolish girl? Aeronautical engineering, that is what I would have learned. Do you know what that is? Never mind. Do not further display your appalling ignorance to me. I would have made planes fly. I would have *designed* flying planes. That is what I would have done with my life had I the opportunity to be properly educated as you have. But you English girls, you are given everything so you appreciate nothing. This is your trouble. What you aspire to is shopping on the high street and purchasing those ridiculous high heels and pointy-toed boots that look like witch shoes. *And* silver eyebrow rings. What a waste of money all of that is.' She paused. Not for breath but because they'd come to a flower seller, where Majidah inspected the blooms on offer and selected three pounds worth.

As they were being wrapped, Ness said, 'An' these i'n't a waste of money? Why'd 'at be, exackly?'

'Because these are things of beauty made by the Creator. High heels and eyebrow rings are not. Come along please. Here, then. Be useful. Carry the flowers.'

She led the way into Wornington Road. They passed the sunken football pitch, which Majidah looked at in some disgust, saying, 'This graffiti . . . Men do this, you know. Men and boys who ought to have better things to do with their time. But they have not been brought up to be useful. And why? Because of their mothers, this is why. Girls like you, who pop out babies and care for nothing but purchasing high heels and eyebrow rings.'

'You got any other conversation?' Ness asked.

'I know what I speak of. Do not show the mouth to me, young lady.'

She marched on, Ness in tow. They passed Kensington and Chelsea College and finally turned into the southern part of Wornington Green Estate. This was one of the less disreputable housing estates in the area. It offered the same kind of vistas as the other estates: blocks of flats looking out upon other blocks of flats. But there was less rubbish strewn about, and a sense of the house-proud was evident in the lack of discarded objects like rusting bicycles and burnt-out armchairs sitting on balconies. Majidah took Ness to Watts House where her departed husband had purchased a flat during one of the Tory periods of government. 'The one decent thing he did,' she informed Ness. 'I confess that when the man died, it was truly one of the happiest days of my life.'

She went up the stairs beyond the entry door, leading Ness to the second floor. Some twenty paces along a lino corridor, where someone had scrawled *Eatme Eatme Eatme Fuckers* in marking pen, Majidah's front door was an oddity. It was done up in steel like the vault of a bank, with a spyhole in the centre.

'What you got in here?' Ness asked her as the Asian woman

inserted the first of four keys in the same number of locks. 'Gold bars or summick?'

'In here, I have peace of mind,' Majidah said, 'which, as you will learn eventually, one can only hope, is more valuable than gold or silver.' She opened the door and ushered Ness inside.

There was little to surprise within. The flat was tidy and redolent of furniture polish. The decorations were sparse; the furniture was old. The carpet squares were covered by a worn Persian rug, and – here was the first discordant note – on the walls hung coloured pencil sketches of a variety of headdresses. There were photographs as well, a collection of them in wooden frames. They were grouped together on a table by the sofa. Men, women, and children. A great number of children.

The second discordant note in the flat consisted of a collection of pottery. This was of a particularly whimsical nature: jugs, planters, posy holders and vases, all characterised by the presence of a cartoon-like forest creature. Rabbits and fauns predominated, although there was the occasional mouse, frog, or squirrel. Shelves on either side of the entrance to the kitchen displayed this unusual collection. When Ness looked from it to Majidah – the Asian woman seeming the person least likely to be collecting such things – Majidah spoke.

'Everyone must have something that makes them smile, Vanessa. Can you look upon them and fail to smile yourself? Ah, perhaps. But then, you are a serious young lady in possession of serious problems. Come set the kettle to boil. We shall have tea.'

The kitchen was much like the sitting-room in its neatness. The electric kettle sat on a worktop perfectly free of clutter, and Ness filled it at a spotless sink as Majidah put her meat in the fridge, her fruit and veg in a basket on the little kitchen table, and her flowers in a vase. This vase she set lovingly next to a photograph on the window-sill. When Ness had the kettle plugged in and Majidah was bringing teapot and cups out of a cupboard, Ness went to examine the picture. It seemed out of place in here.

A very young Majidah was the subject of the photo, standing next to a grey-haired man with a deeply lined face. She looked ten or twelve years old, solemn and decked out in any number of gold chains and gold bracelets. She was wearing a blue and gold *shalwar kamis*. The old man wore a white one.

'Dis your granddad?' Ness asked, picking up the picture. 'You ain't looking so happy to be wiv him, innit.'

'Please ask before you remove an object from its place,' Majidah said. 'That is my first husband.'

Ness widened her eyes. 'How *old* was you? Shit, you must've been—'

'Vanessa, profanity ceases at my front door, please. Put the photograph down and make yourself useful. Take these things to the table. Do you wish to have a teacake or are you able to consume something more interesting than you English generally eat at this hour?'

'Teacake's good,' Ness said. She wasn't about to try anything else. She replaced the photo, but she continued to eye Majidah the way one might look at a species of animal one has never seen before. She said, 'So how old was you? What're you doing marrying some granddad, anyways?'

'I was twelve years old when I first married. Rakin was fifty-eight.'

'*Twelve* years old? Twelve years old an' hooked up permanent to some old man? What in hell're you *t'inking*? Did he . . . Did you . . . I mean . . . Wiv *him*?'

Majidah used hot water from the tap to heat the teapot. She took a brown paper packet of loose tea from a cupboard. She went for the milk and poured this into a small white jug. Only then did she answer. 'My goodness, isn't your questioning rude. This cannot be the way you've been brought up to speak to an older person. But—' she held up her hand to prevent Ness saying anything – 'I have learned to understand that you

English do not always mean to be as disrespectful of other cultures as you seem to be. Rakin was my father's cousin. He came to Pakistan – from England – when his first wife died because he believed himself in need of another one. He had, at the time, four children in their twenties so one would think he might have proceeded throughout the rest of his life in the company of one or all of them. But this was not Rakin's way. He came to our house and looked us over. I'm the youngest, and as I have five sisters, it was naturally assumed that Rakin would select one of them. He did not. He wished to have me. I was introduced to him, and we were married. Nothing more was said of the matter.'

'Shit,' Ness said. And then she added hastily, 'Sorry. Sorry. Slipped out, innit.'

Majidah pressed her lips together to quell a smile. 'We married in my village and then he brought me to England, a little girl who spoke no English and knew not a single thing of life, not even how to cook. But Rakin was a gentle man in all ways and a gentle man is a patient teacher. So I learned to cook. And I learned other things. I had my first child two days before my thirteenth birthday.'

'You d'i'nt,' Ness said in disbelief.

'Oh yes. Indeed I did.' The kettle clicked off and Majidah made the tea. She toasted a teacake for Ness and took it to the table with a square of butter, but for herself she brought forth poppadums and chutney, both of which she declared to be homemade. When she had everything assembled, she sat and said, 'My Rakin died when he was sixty-one. A sudden heart attack and he was gone. And there I was, fifteen years old, with a small child and four stepchildren approaching thirty. I could, of course, have lived with them, but they would not have that: an adolescent stepmother with a toddler who would have become their responsibility. So another husband was found for me. This was my unfortunate second husband, who remained alive for twenty-seven interminable years of marriage before he had the good sense to pass on from liver failure. I have no pictures of him.'

'You get kids from him?'

'Oh my goodness, yes. Five more children. They are all adults now with children of their own.' She smiled. 'And how they disapprove of a mother who will not live with any one of them. They inherited, alas, their father's traditional nature.'

'Wha' 'bout the rest of your fam'ly?'

'The rest . . . ?'

'Your mum and dad. Your sisters.'

'Ah. They remain in Pakistan. My sisters married, of course, and raised families there.'

'You get to see 'em?'

Majidah spread a bit of chutney on a sliver of poppadum, which she had broken off from the larger piece. She said, 'Once. I attended my father's funeral. You are not eating your teacake, Vanessa. Do not waste my food or we shall not have tea together again.'

That didn't seem like an altogether bad idea, but Ness was sufficiently intrigued by the Asian woman's history to butter her teacake and begin to consume it. Majidah watched her disapprovingly. Ness's table manners were in need of adjustment as far as she was concerned, but she said nothing until Ness took up her tea and slurped it.

'This *will* not do,' Majidah told her. 'Has no one taught you how to drink a hot beverage? Where is your mother? Who are the responsible adults in your life? Do they slurp as well? This is common, Vanessa, this noisy drinking. This is vulgar. Watch me and listen . . . Do you hear my lips flap against the tea? No, you do not. And why is this? Because I have learned the method to drink, which has nothing to do with sucking and everything to do with—' Majidah stopped because Ness had put her cup down so abruptly that tea sloshed into her saucer, which was an even greater offence. 'What is the matter with you, you foolish girl? Do you wish to break my china?'

It was the word. Sucking. Ness had not expected it. Nor had she expected it to produce a series of images in her mind: mental mementoes that she preferred to forget. She said, 'C'n I go now?' Her voice was sullen.

'What do you mean with this "Can I go now?" This is not a gaol. You are not my prisoner. You may go whenever you wish to go. But I can see that I have hurt you in some way—'

'I ain't hurt.'

'– and if it has to do with your tea drinking I must tell you that I meant no harm. My intention was to educate you. If no one bothers to inform you when your manners are not what they should be, how are you to learn? Does your mother never—'

'She ain't . . . She's in hospital, innit. We don't live wiv her. Haven't done since I was little, okay?'

Majidah sat back in her chair. She looked thoughtful. She said, 'I apologise to you. I did not know this, Vanessa. She is ill, your mum?'

'Whatever,' Ness said. 'Look, c'n I go?'

'Again I say: you are not a prisoner here. You may come and go as you like.'

At this second expression of liberation, Ness might have got to her feet and departed. But she did not, because of that photo on the window-sill. Little Majidah in gold and blue on the arm of a man the age of her granddad kept Ness in her chair. She looked long at that picture before she finally said, 'You scared?'

'Of what?' Majidah said. 'Of you? Oh my goodness, I hope not. You do not frighten me in the least.'

'Not me. Him.'

'Whom?'

'Dat bloke.' She nodded at the photo. 'Rakin. He scare you?'

'What an odd question you ask me.' Majidah looked at the picture and then back at Ness. She took a reading off her, making an assessment that grew from having brought up six children, three of whom were female. She said quietly, 'Ah. I was not prepared. This was a sin against me, committed by my parents. By my mother, especially. She said to me, "Obey your husband," but she said nothing else. Naturally, I had seen animals . . . One cannot live in a village and escape the sight of copulation among the beasts of the field. The dogs and the cats as well. But I did not think men and women did such strange things together, and no one told me otherwise. So I wept at first but Rakin, as I have told you, was kind. He did not force anything upon me, which made me far luckier than I knew at the time. Things were very different when I married again.'

Ness pulled on her upper lip, listening. Within her was a tremendous stirring, a begging to be spoken. She did not know if she could manage the words, but she also did not know if she could hold them back. She said, 'Yeah. I 'spect . . .' but that was all she could say.

Majidah took the leap. She said quietly, 'This has happened to you, has it not? At what age, Vanessa?'

Ness blinked. 'Summick like . . . I dunno . . . ten maybe.'

'This is . . . I am very very sorry. It was not, of course, a husband chosen for you.'

'Course not.'

'This is very bad,' Majidah said quietly. 'This is very wrong and bad indeed. This dreadful thing should not have happened. But happen it did, and I am sorry.'

'Yeah. Well.'

'Sorry for you, however, will not change things. Only how you view the past can alter the present and the future.'

'How'm I s'posed to view it?' Ness asked.

'As something terrible that happened but was not your fault. As something that was part of a larger plan that you do not yet see. I have learned in this life not to question or fight the ways of Allah – of God, Vanessa. I have learned to wait in quiet to see what will come next.'

'Nuffink,' Ness said. 'Tha's what comes next.'

'This is hardly the truth. That very terrible thing that was done to you led to this moment, to this conversation, to you sitting in my kitchen having a lesson on how to drink tea like a lady.'

Ness rolled her eyes. But she also smiled. Just a curve of her lips, but that was the last thing she would have expected, having just told Majidah part of her darkest secret. Still, the smile meant her armour had been pierced, which she didn't want. So she said roughly, 'Look. C'n I go now?'

Majidah didn't correct her this time. Instead she said, 'Not until you taste my poppadums. And my chutney, which is far superior, you will find, than anything a supermarket will sell you.' She broke a piece off her large poppadum and passed it to Ness with a scoop of chutney. 'Eat,' she instructed.

Which was what Ness did.

Joel's opportunity to have a talk with Neal Wyatt came sooner than he expected, on a day when Toby required Joel's guidance to complete an assignment for school. London had wildlife – in the form of urban foxes, feral cats, squirrels, pigeons and other assorted birds – and the children in Toby's new year at Middle Row School were asked to document the close sighting of one of them. They were to make a sketch, create a report and, to prevent their fanciful manufacture of either, they were to do this in the company of a parent or guardian. Kendra's schedule precluded her doing this duty, and Ness wasn't around to be asked. So it fell to Joel.

Toby was all afire for foxes. It took some work for Joel to talk him out of that. Foxes, he explained, weren't going to be just swanning around Edenham Estate in convenient packs. They'd probably be solo and they'd be skulking around at night. Toby needed to choose something else.

Joel's brother wasn't willing to take the easy way out and document the sighting of a pigeon, so he switched to waiting for a swan to appear on the pond in Meanwhile Gardens. Joel knew that seeing a swan on the pond was about as likely as seeing a pack of foxes goose-stepping in an orderly formation along Edenham Way, so he suggested a squirrel instead. It was no infrequent sight to see one climbing the concrete face of Trellick Tower in search of food on the balconies. It shouldn't be the least bit difficult to come across one elsewhere. Squirrels and birds being the tamest of London's wild creatures – likely to alight on one's shoulder in the hope of finding food on offer – this seemed a decent plan. What a fine report it would turn out to be, Joel enthused, if they had a close encounter with a squirrel. They could go into the nature walk just above and beyond the pond. They could make themselves a spot off the path that wound beneath the trees and through the shrubbery. If they sat quite still, there was every chance a squirrel would come right up to them.

The time of year was propitious. Autumn and instinct demanded that squirrels begin foraging and storing food for the winter. When Joel and Toby settled themselves in a clump of blue bean not quite ready to produce its distinctive and eponymous pods, they had to wait less than ten minutes before they were joined by an inquisitive and hopeful squirrel. Seeing the animal was the easy part for Toby. Sketching both him and where he saw him – snuffling on the ground right next to Joel's foot – was rather more difficult. Toby got through it by means of plenty of encouragement, but he was nearly defeated by having to fashion a report about the sighting. *Just write how it happened* was not a direction that Toby found even moderately helpful, so it took forty-five minutes of laborious printing and rubbing out before he had something that resembled a report. By that time, both of the boys needed a break and the skate bowl seemed the perfect diversion.

There was generally action in one of three bowls and on this day, seven riders and two cyclists were doing their stuff when Joel and Toby came up the slope from the duck pond and out on to the towpath just above the gardens. Spectators sat on a couple of the hillocks watching the action, while a few others gathered on the benches nearby. Toby, of course. wanted to get as close as possible, and he was set upon doing so when Joel saw that among the spectators were Hibah and Neal Wyatt.

He said to Toby, 'Head-hunters, Tobe! You 'member what to do?'

To his credit and because of the many times they'd practised for just this moment, Toby stopped in his tracks. But he was overly used to rehearsals by now, so he said, 'For reals? Cos I want to watch—'

'Dis is for real,' Joel said. 'We'll watch 'em later. Meantime, what're you going to—'

Toby was, gratifyingly, on his way before Joel could finish the question. He trotted along the towpath and made for the abandoned barge beneath the bridge. In a moment he had hopped upon it. It bobbed in the water, then he was gone from sight. He was gone specifically from Neal Wyatt's sight. Hibah there or not, Joel didn't want Neal to get close to his brother until they had a satisfactory truce.

Joel took in a breath. It was a public place. There were others present. It was daylight. All of this should have reassured him, but when it came to dealing with Neal, nothing was a certainty. He approached the bench on which the boy and Hibah were sitting. He saw they were holding hands, and from this he understood that they'd somehow – and unwisely on Hibah's part as far as Joel was concerned – arrived at a rapprochement after their altercation in the gardens. He was clever enough to realise he wasn't going to be welcome – especially from Neal's point of view – but he couldn't see any help for the matter. Besides, he had the flick knife with him if things became dicey, and he doubted even Neal would take on a flick knife.

Hibah was saying, 'But it i'n't as easy as you think,' when Joel came upon them from the rear. 'Mum keeps me pract'cally locked up 'n tha' place. 'S not like your situation, innit. I make a wrong move and I'm gated f'rever.'

Joel said, 'Neal, c'n I have a word?'

Neal whirled around. Hibah jumped to her feet. Joel said quickly, 'S'okay. I don't mean no harm. I ain't ramping you.'

Neal stood but, unlike Hibah, he did it slowly. He made the movement like that of a 1930s' film gangster, which was indeed where he got most of his moves: from ancient Hollywood character actors with beaten-up faces. He said, 'Piss off.'

'I got to talk to you.'

'You deaf or summick? I say piss off 'fore I take care of you good.'

'Down to you if we fight, bred,' Joel said calmly, although he didn't feel calm. What he felt like was clutching the flick knife as a form of security. 'All's I want is a word, but you c'n have more off me, dat how you want it.'

'Neal,' Hibah said. 'You can talk to him, innit.' And to Joel with a smile, 'How's it going, Joel? Where you been at lunchtimes cos I look for you by the guard shack a bunch.'

Neal scowled at this. He said to Joel, 'I ain't your bred. Go suck yuh muddah's pussy.'

It was a deliberate provocation, a begging of Joel to fling himself at the other boy. But he didn't do it. He didn't even need to reply because Hibah did it for him.

'Tha's just the *most* disgusting thing I ever heard,' she said to Neal. 'He's asking to *talk* to you, nuffink else. Wha's the matter wiv you? I swear, Neal, sometimes I wonder 'f your head's on right. You talk to him or I'm out 'f here. Why'd I want to take a risk like this – meeting out here which is *expressly* what my mum tol' me I wasn't to do – for someone wiv no brains to speak of?'

'Take five minutes,' Joel said, 'maybe less, if we get down to it.'

'I ain't getting down to nuffink wiv you,' Neal said. ''F you t'ink I'm about—'

'Neal.' Hibah spoke again. But it sounded like a warning this time. For a moment Joel thought the Muslim girl had lost her mind and was going to take his side in the matter even more overtly – such as with a threat – but then he saw she was looking over at the bridge. Two uniformed constables stood there, and they were looking down at the gardens, their gaze directed at the three adolescents themselves. One of the constables spoke into the radio fixed to his shoulder. The other merely waited.

It didn't take a long leap to know what they were doing. Two mixed-race boys in conversation with a Muslim girl. They were waiting for trouble.

Neal said, 'Fuck it.'

Hibah said, 'I got to go. 'F they come down here . . . 'F they ask our names . . . Las' thing I c'n cope wiv is having my mum get a call from the cops.'

'Jus' sit and be cool,' Joel told her. 'They won't do nothing 'f we don't give 'em reason.'

Neal gave Hibah a look. 'Be cool,' he told her.

Joel took this as a form of agreement with what he'd said. He thought it might presage further agreement, so he spoke openly as Hibah sat down again. 'I been thinking,' he said to Neal. 'Why we vexing each other? 'S not getting us anywheres 'cept—'

'You ain't vexing me,' Neal cut in as he joined Hibah on the bench. 'You basic'ly an arse-wipe needing tossed in the bin. Dat's all I'm trying to do wiv you. Put you where you need to be put.'

Joel wouldn't let this remark boil inside him. He could see how Neal was going to take advantage of the presence of the police. Sitting, he'd made himself a target. If Joel launched himself at Neal with the cops as witnesses, Joel would take the fall for it. He said, 'I don't want to fight wiv you. Dis shit going on, it's been happening too long. We keep it up, summick bad's coming down. You want dat? I don't.'

Neal smirked. 'Dat's cos you ain't got the bottle for a war 'tween you and me. But you know it's coming. You c'n feel it, eh? Dat's good. Keep you on your toes.'

'Damn it, Neal Wyatt,' Hibah said.

'Shut up!' Neal turned to her. 'Shut your *mouf* for once, Hibah. You don't know what you're talking about so jus' stop talking, y'unnerstan?'

Surprise stopped her. But something in his words also caused a dawn to break over her. She said slowly and thoughtfully, with a growing awareness, 'Hey, this right here . . . This stuff going on between you an' Joel . . . Hey, this ain't about you, is it? Cos—'

'I said *shut up!*' Neal glanced at the bridge. The cops were gone. He gave Hibah a shove to indicate his desire that she leave them. 'Your mum's wanting you at home,' he told her. 'You can't keep it plugged, you go back and do wha'ever she tell you. Say your prayers or wha'ever.'

'You can't tell me—'

'You do like I say. Or you want summick help you make up your mind?'

Her eyes widened. He'd said enough. She looked at Joel. 'You keep clear,' she said. 'Y'unnerstan?' But that was all she said before she rose from the bench and headed out of the gardens, leaving Joel alone with Neal.

'You listen good, yellow,' Neal said to Joel when Hibah was out of earshot. 'You in my face, and dat's exactly where I don't want to see you, y'unnerstan? Piss off and be glad wha's coming ain't come yet. Maybe you still sucking on your muddah's tit, but I ain't. Got it?'

Joel felt the full weight of the flick knife then. Bring it out, press the button, thrust it at the other boy, and who's sucking on whose tit where? But he did nothing.

He tried a final time, for Toby's sake. 'Dis ain't the way to solve nuffink. You got to know dat. We got to put t'ings to rest between us cos there ain't no point in it otherwise.'

Neal stood in a rush. Joel took a step backwards.

'*I* tell *you* what gets put at rest,' Neal said. 'Don't work th'other way round no way. I mark you and you stay marked. 'F you t'ink any different, you end up—'

'Joel! Joel Joel!' The cry came from the direction of the bridge, from beneath where Toby had emerged from his hiding place. He was clutching his crotch, his knees pressed together. He could not have been more specific about his needs. Nonetheless, with the disturbing honesty that was typical of him, he called out, 'I got to use the toilet. There's no head-hunters round any more, is there?'

Joel felt something akin to a stab entering his heart. He heard Neal's short abrasive laugh. 'Stupid shit,' he said in a voice that sounded like wonder. 'Wha's wrong wiv dat dumb cunt?' He looked at Joel who'd turned back to him. 'Head-hunters, innit? Got yourself a spot to bolt for, eh? Mon, you got one stupid fuck of a—'

'Leave him alone.' Joel heard himself give the directive in a voice that was not quite his own. 'You touch my brother again an' I swear you die an' die bloody. You got dat, mon? You got a problem wiv me, you leave it wiv me. Leave Toby out of it.'

He walked away, knowing the risk of turning his back on Neal but reckoning that if a brawl should start, he still had the knife. He was, at this point, more than itching to use it.

But Neal didn't attack. Instead he said, 'Next time, mon. We take care of business, you an' me. Meantime, you keep an eye on dat brother twenty-four seven. Cos you ain't first on the list no more, Jo-oell. No more no way, y'unnerstan?'

Kendra felt increasingly miserable as the weeks went by. While she had more time for building her business and even enough time to take a class in Thai massage for modest clients wishing to remain loosely clothed when she worked upon them, she was acutely aware of the hole in her life.

She tried to fill it at first with a new concentration on the Campbells. But the problem with her approach to giving the children attention was that she failed to see on the horizon a different sort of danger from the dangers she'd seen before. Most of those had involved Ness, who was – for reasons remaining mysterious to Kendra – suddenly doing what she was supposed to do, which was community service, seeing her probation officer, and attempting to get herself sorted out with regard to school by taking a course at the college. Kendra's worries about Toby she put on the back burner, along with the paperwork that she was meant to fill out to allow someone – and she didn't want to know *who* that someone was – to engage in studies of the little boy. *That*, she swore, was not going to happen. And Joel, from what she could see on the surface, seemed to have dealt with his problems with the neighbourhood louts by himself. Thus, there seemed nothing for her to do for the children aside from giving them food, shelter, and the occasional outing that did not require paying an admission charge.

This mistaken idea of there being nothing left for Kendra to do took her thoughts ineluctably to Dix D'Court. It had been exactly as Dix had said it would be, she decided. Joel and Neal Wyatt, left to their own devices, had come to an agreement allowing both of them to live in peace.

Thus, having no idea what was really going on, Kendra possessed ample opportunity to look at her life and find it wanting. She spoke to Cordie about this, taking the opportunity over a lunch hour to catch her girlfriend in the midst of painting a set of talon-like nails on the hands of a middle-aged overweight white lady with fuchsia hair and sunglasses that she didn't remove despite being inside the shop. She was called Isis, Cordie informed Kendra, without a hint that she might be conscious that the name – attached to this particular female – was in no small way ironic.

Kendra nodded to Isis and spent approximately one minute

watching the work being done on her nails. Cordie was something of a legend in the Harrow Road, possessing a talent for
decorating artificial fingernails in such a way as to leave
absolutely no doubt that they were entirely false from cuticle
to tip. In this case and in keeping with the time of year, she
was going for an autumn motif on top of the acrylic. The base
colour was purple and she was painting golden sheaves of
wheat on top of it.

Kendra said to Cordie, 'Nice, that.' And to Isis, 'Colour's
real good with your skin.' This was not actually true, but
anything directing attention away from Isis's hair was an
improvement.

Isis said frankly, 'She's a fucking genius,' with a nod at
Cordie. 'I been telling her no way's she going on leave of
absence *this* time round and making me find someone else to
do my nails.'

Kendra drew her eyebrows together and looked at her
friend. She said, 'Leave of absence?'

Cordie shrugged, nail varnish brush in hand. She looked
embarrassed.

Her embarrassment told the tale. 'Cordie! You *pregnant*?
What happened?'

Isis said to Kendra, 'You look damn well old enough to
know the fac's of life, luv.'

Kendra waved her off. 'Cordie?'

Cordie drew her mouth to one side, her way of screwing
up her courage to speak. She said, 'First off, he found the pills.
F'r a week he rant 'bout betrayal. I c'n handle dat, but den he
talk 'bout leaving us. An' I c'n tell he mean it.'

'*That's* blackmail.'

'Di'n't I tell her,' Isis intoned.

'It c'n be whatever it want to be,' Cordie said. 'Fac is, I
don't want dat mon leavin or looking nowhere else. I love the
blood. He good to me and he good to our girls. He the bes'
dad I know and all's he asking is one more chance at a son.

So I give it him. Dis here's the result.' She as yet had no bump but she gestured to her stomach. 'All's I c'n say's I hope dis time it's got a dick. Cos nuffink else will satisfy Gerald, lemme tell you.'

In that way in which misery loves company, Cordie's pregnancy suggested to Kendra that she should in some way give in to her desire to have Dix back in her life. It also gave her permission to speak of this desire, which she did in short order. Cordie listened – as did Isis, unashamedly – and at the end of Kendra's story of her last encounter with Dix and how she'd filled the time since then, the other two women weighed in with identical advice, albeit voiced differently.

Cordie said, 'You, girl, jus' need to get laid and dat'll put an end to the matter.'

Isis said, somewhat more colourfully, 'Someone needs to see to your plumbing straightaway.'

'Le's have a girls' night out,' Cordie said. 'We ain't done that in months, and we're both due. Now I've done wha' Gerald want, he be happy to mind the girls for an evening. You name the day, we put our dancin' shoes on. We find you some nice fresh man flesh, Ken. Dat take your mind off Dix D'Court.'

So that was what they did. They chose the gastropub on Great Western Road, sitting along the side of the canal. This was a cut above their usual choice for an outing, and they had their dinner on an Indian summer night, on the patio next to the water. During their meal, they were entertained by a classical guitarist whom Cordie earmarked as up for the job that needed doing. But to Kendra he looked like a student, and she declared herself one hundred per cent through with younger men.

This left the young man for Cordie, who had no compunction whatsoever about reeling him in. When he took his break, she bought him a drink. Walking her fingers up his arm was enough to telegraph the message about her interests, which were not musical. As Kendra watched from the outdoor table at which she was having the last of the bottle of wine they'd ordered – when it came to her habits and her lifestyle, it must be said that Cordie had never been overly concerned about altering either when she was pregnant – Cordie and the guitarist sauntered out of the front door of the pub and round the corner. This street led to Paddington Arts. Cordie, obviously, was not intent upon that. Just a dark spot for a little snog.

Left alone, Kendra looked around to see if there were any pickings. As luck or fate would have it, at that same moment a middle-aged white man – later revealing his name as 'just Geoff' – was checking out the pickings himself. He was of the ilk who harboured what he liked to call secret fantasies about sex with black women, having the notion that they were inherently more sexual – not to mention more sexually active and consequently more willing to bed a perfect stranger – than their white counterparts. He'd been encouraged in this fantasy by certain pornographic websites dedicated to men with such notions, and on this evening he'd spent a few hours entertaining himself with these sites in the basement of his home before finally deciding the time was right to make his dreams a reality.

Going for a woman on the game would have made sense at this point, but Just Geoff was not a man who would ever consider paying. He had looks, he had money, he had the moves, he had conversation. He believed in mutual pleasure for both parties. He was married but that was a minor detail. The wife travelled for her work as an architect. They were a modern couple. They had an understanding.

He revealed most of this to Kendra – with a few variations here and there – when he came out of the pub to join her on the patio. They'd locked eyes. Neither had broken the gaze. She'd picked up her wine glass and touched her tongue to its rim. Message received. He wasted no time.

He said nothing out of the norm for the situation. She was

a beautiful woman so what was she doing here alone? (This, naturally, was a question requiring him to overlook the second wine glass out of which Cordie had been drinking before she bunked off with her guitarist.) Was she a regular here? He'd been watching her for a while and he'd finally thought What the hell? when he'd caught her eye. It wasn't, she was to understand, the kind of thing he generally did. But his wife was out of town and he'd been at a loose end for the evening and . . . Did she want to go some quiet place for a drink?

This last was all form. Both of them knew it since the patio of the gastropub was perfectly quiet, romantically lit and licensed to serve alcoholic beverages. But she agreed. She liked the look of him, all squeaky clean with nice teeth, well-cut hair, and fingernails looking as if they'd been buffed. He wore a signet ring and a white shirt and tie. He had slip-on shoes with tassels, and his socks did not droop. She knew he wouldn't be able to hold a match to Dix in the breathtaking body department, but she needed a man. He would do.

Outside, she made the suggestion that both of them knew she would make. She lived close by and it was quiet, she said. She had kids there, but they'd be in bed.

She didn't know this about Ness, but she hoped for the best. Even if Ness were still up, there was no need to see her as they climbed the stairs to the second floor. They could pass the doorway to the sitting-room and keep climbing. There would be no problem.

The idea of kids gave Just Geoff pause. Kendra could see his dilemma: what he thought and what he clearly did not want. She said, 'They're not mine and I'm not on the game. This, tonight. It's just what I want. It's not what I do regularly.'

Just Geoff allowed this to be sufficient reassurance. He had only one rationale for doing this: she was a gorgeous woman with a gorgeous body. He didn't want her but he wanted it.

He put his hand on the small of her back and said, 'Then let's go' with a smile.

The walk was a short one but Just Geoff knew the importance of build-up, so it took them a while to cross Meanwhile Gardens. He was very good at the business of making women ready for him, so Kendra was throbbing in all the right places and thanking her stars she'd chosen him by the time they reached her front door, a walk of five minutes that took twenty-five.

She was glad she'd worn a clingy dress that evening, held in place with a simple sash tied at the side. Aside from wisps of underwear and a pair of strappy high heels, she had nothing else on. And she had nothing on at all by the time they reached the top of the stairs.

She worked on Just Geoff's clothes while he worked on her body, all hands and tongue and mouth. She got him naked in a trail of clothes leading from the stairs to her bed, whereupon they fell upon it and coupled ferociously. Just Geoff did the job he'd set out to do on her before he positioned her legs over his shoulders, which was the way he liked to have his women in his own final moments. He then carried his fantasy to its logical conclusion. He withdrew at once and collapsed next to her.

He said, '*Christ*, what a fuck. I was actually seeing stars,' and he laughed weakly in the direction of the ceiling. He was panting, and his body was slick with sweat.

Kendra said nothing. She'd had pleasure from him. Truth be told, she'd had more pleasure from him than she'd ever had with anyone else, Dix included. She, too, was breathless, dripping sweat and fluid, and by any other definition she was a woman fulfilled. But it had been the wrong prescription for the state she'd been in, and it didn't take long for her to work that out from the emptiness she felt, beyond the lovely contractions she was still experiencing from her orgasm.

She wanted him to leave and in this she was lucky, as Just

Geoff had no intention of staying. He scooped up his clothing and came to the side of the bed, where he rested the tips of his fingers on her nipple.

'Good for you?' he asked.

Good depended on the definition, but she accommodated him saying, 'Jesus, yeah,' and rolling on her side to reach for her cigarettes.

She didn't see his look of distaste – women who smoked after sex were not part of his fantasy – as he turned his back to put on his clothes. She watched him dress and he asked if she had a comb or brush. She said, 'The bathroom,' and still watched him as he opened the door.

He walked directly into Ness.

There were no lights on, but lights weren't needed as Kendra's bedroom curtains were open. The tableau was an unmistakable one: Kendra on the bed, naked and uncovered in the warm night, lazily smoking, with the bedcovers in wild disarray around her and the man still not entirely dressed but carrying his shoes and his jacket with the clear intention of decamping at the conclusion of a successful conquest. And the scent in the air – clinging to him, to her, to the very walls, it seemed – was one that Ness could not fail to recognise.

Startled, Just Geoff said, 'Holy shit!' He retreated into Kendra's room and shut the door.

Kendra said, 'Damn,' and stubbed her cigarette out in the ashtray on her bedside table. It had always been a risk that one of the kids would see, but she would have preferred the seeing child to be one of the boys for reasons she could not have articulated at the moment. She said unnecessarily to Just Geoff, 'That's my niece. She sleeps in the sitting-room. Down below.'

'Beneath . . . ?' he gestured at the bed.

'She must've heard.' Which was hardly a surprise, considering how they had gone at each other. Kendra pressed her fingers to her forehead and sighed. She'd got what she wanted but not what she needed. And now this, she thought. Life was not fair.

They heard a door shut. They listened for more. In a moment, the toilet flushed. Water ran. The door opened and footsteps receded down the stairs. They waited four interminable minutes before Just Geoff returned to what he'd been doing. At this point, he decided that he didn't need to comb his hair; he just needed to leave. He slipped on his shoes, donned his jacket, pocketed his tie. He looked at Kendra, who'd pulled the sheet up over her, and he nodded. Some sort of leave-taking was called for, obviously, but nothing seemed appropriate. He could hardly say, 'See you later' since he had no intention of doing that. 'Thanks' seemed ghastly, and any reference to the act itself seemed untimely post Ness's arrival on the scene. So he fell back on a combination of public school manners and Edwardian costume dramas. 'I'll see myself out,' was what he said, and he quickly did just that.

Alone, Kendra sat up in the bed and stared at the wall. She lit another cigarette, with the hope that smoke could obliterate sight. For what she saw was Ness's face. There hadn't been judgement upon it. Nor had there been caustic knowledge. Rather, there had been surprise, quickly replaced by a world-weary acceptance that no fifteen-year-old girl was ever meant to possess. This prompted in Kendra a feeling she had not expected when she'd invited Just Geoff into her bed. She felt ashamed.

She finally roused herself and went into the bathroom, where she filled the bath with water as hot as she could stand it. She stepped inside and scalded her skin. She sank back and raised her face to the ceiling. She wept.

18

Kendra was being far harder on herself than was necessary when it came to Ness, who had more pressing concerns than reacting to her aunt's inviting some strange white man into her bed. True, finding him there had been something of a surprise. Ness had heard the commotion and had assumed that Dix was back. But, to her wonder, she didn't feel what she'd earlier felt when listening to the rousing creak, bounce, and slam of Kendra's bed from the floor above her. Instead, she'd awakened, heard the noise, grimaced, and realised she needed to use the toilet. Reckoning it was Dix with her aunt – which meant he'd stay the night and she'd run little risk of encountering him when she used the facility – she'd climbed the stairs, only to find a stranger emerging from Kendra's bedroom.

At one time the sight of any man coming out of Kendra's bedroom would have filled Ness with jealousy only thinly disguised as disgust. But that was before she'd shared a poppadum with a Pakistani woman she'd thought she didn't like. It was also before what sharing a poppadum with that Pakistani woman had led to.

When Majidah informed her they'd be closing the drop-in centre early one day, not long after Ness's visit to her flat, Ness thought it meant she was free from further obligation for the rest of the afternoon. But Majidah disabused her of that notion in short order, telling her that they were meant to be picking up supplies in Covent Garden. Ness was to assist.

At this Ness felt completely ill-used. Doing community

service surely didn't mean she was intended to traipse all round London like a servant, did it?

Majidah informed Ness that she was not the one whom the magistrate allowed to determine what constituted community service. 'We will leave at precisely two o'clock,' she told Ness. 'We shall take the tube.'

'Hey, I ain't got—'

'Please. *Ain't got?* What sort of language is this, Vanessa? How can you hope to make something of your life if you speak in this way?'

'Wha'? Like I'm *s'posed* to make "summick of myself"? Dat it?'

'Good gracious, yes. What else are you thinking? Do you believe that you are *entitled* to whatever it is that you want and that you need do nothing to achieve it? And what *is* it that you want, precisely? Fame, fortune, additional pairs of silly high-heeled shoes? Or are you one of these foolish young girls who have ambitions solely of celebrity? Famous actress, famous model, famous pop star? Is that it, Vanessa? Celebrity alone when you could do whatever you want, a young woman like you with no man determining your fate as if you were a farm animal, mind you. There is no question that you could choose a career right out of the sky, and yet you have no gratitude for this. Only the wish to be a pop star.'

'Did I say dat?' Ness demanded when Majidah was finally forced to take a breath. 'Did I f'r one minute say any of dat? Hell, Majidah, you got a one-track mind, anyone ever tell you? An' how'd we get on dis anyways? I ain't got money—' She saw Majidah's thunderous face and she relented. 'I haven't got money in my possession to purchase a ticket,' she said primly.

Majidah held back her smile at Ness's posh accent. She said, 'That is all? Good gracious, Vanessa, I do not intend you to pay for the journey. This is work, and work shall recompense me for supplying you with the ticket you require.'

That detail established, two o'clock saw them setting off

from the drop-in centre, whose cabin Majidah locked and then checked three times before Ness took her by the arm and dragged her through the chain link gate. They walked the short distance to Westbourne Park underground station. Majidah made much of studying the map to determine the best route to their destination, clucking and tutting and counting stops while Ness stood by and tapped her foot. The decision made, they embarked for the journey, alighting at Covent Garden from where Majidah led the way not to the market – where one might assume some sort of supplies could be purchased, albeit hardly economically – but north to Shelton Street. There, a doorway between a minuscule bookshop and a coffee bar opened on to a stairway. This in turn took them up four flights – 'The cursed lift in this wretched building does not work and never has,' Majidah informed Ness – and, breathless when they finally got there, into a loft where bolts of colourful linen, silk, cotton, velvet and felt lay across wide worktables. Four individuals worked in silence while Kiri Te Kanawa went through Mimi's death throes on a CD player that sat atop a bank of containers holding everything from sequins to seed pearls.

Two of the workers were women dressed in *shalwar kamis*; one of them was a woman in a *chador*; the fourth was a man. He wore blue jeans, trainers, and a white cotton shirt. The women were sewing and gluing. He was fitting a headpiece on to the fifth person in the room: a sloe-eyed Mediterranean beauty who read from a magazine and muttered, 'Bloody stupid warmongering *idiots*,' to which the man said, 'Truer words and all that. But mind the position of your head, please, Miss Rivelle. The fit's not right.' He, like the women at work, was Asian.

Miss Rivelle raised her hand to feel what he was affixing to her heavy dark hair. She said, 'Really, Sayf, this *is* impossible. Can you not make it weigh less? It's extraordinary you should expect me to be able to make an entrance, do the aria, and die dramatically, and all of it without this . . . this *thing* dropping to the floor. Who approved the design, for God's sake?'

'Mr Peterson-Hayes.'

'The director doesn't have to *wear* it. No, no, this absolutely will *not* do.' She took the headpiece off, handed it to Sayf al Din, and saw Majidah and Ness across the room. As did Sayf, at that precise moment.

He said, 'Ma! Bloody hell if I didn't forget.' And to Ness, 'Hullo. You must be the convict.'

'Sayf al Din,' Majidah said sternly. 'What sort of greeting is this? And you, Rand,' to the woman in the *chador*, 'do you not stifle beneath that ridiculous counterpane you're wearing? When will your husband come to his senses? This is outdoor clothing you happen to have on. It is not meant to be worn within.'

'Your son's presence . . .' Rand murmured.

'Oh yes, my dear, my goodness me, but he will surely ravish you if your face is exposed. Is that not the truth, Sayf al Din? Have you not ravished two hundred women and counting? Where is your dance card, my son?'

'Score card,' Sayf al Din corrected her. He took up the headpiece he'd been fashioning for Miss Rivelle and placed it carefully on a wooden form. He said to the singer, 'I'll try to reduce the weight, but it'll be up to Peterson-Hayes, so you'll want to have a word with him.' He went to a monstrously cluttered desk beneath one of the room's windows and there he unearthed a diary. He said, 'Thursday? Four o'clock?'

'If I must,' she replied languidly. She gathered her belongings – shopping bags and a handbag the size of a picnic basket – and approached Sayf al Din for a formal farewell. This consisted of air kisses, three of them in the Italian fashion, after which she patted his cheek and he kissed her hand. Then she was gone, fluttering her fingers at the rest of them. One of the *shalwar kamis* women murmured, 'Divas,' with some scorn.

'They are our bread and butter,' Sayf al Din reminded her, 'despite sometimes being caricatures of themselves.' He smiled at his mother. 'And I am, beyond that, *quite* used to divas.'

Majidah tutted, but Ness could tell she took no offence. Indeed, she sounded pleased as she said to Ness, 'This piece of nonsense is my Sayf al Din, Vanessa, the eldest of my children,' which made him the child of her first husband, less than thirteen years younger than his own mother. He was quite handsome – olive-skinned and dark-eyed – and he had about him an air of perpetual amusement.

'And how is that wife of yours, Sayf al Din?' his mother asked him. 'Is she still scraping away at the teeth of the unfortunate rather than having more babies? This son of mine has wed a dentist, Vanessa. She produces two children and returns to her work when they are six weeks old. I cannot comprehend this lunacy: to wish to be looking into the mouths of strangers instead of gazing upon the faces of your infants. She should be like your sisters and like your brothers' wives, Sayf al Din. Nine children among *them* so far and not one of them placed into the hands of a child-minder.'

Sayf al Din had obviously heard this recitation before as he said the last sentence of it in concert with his mother. He went on with, 'What a scandal it is, this woman using her education as it was meant to be used when she could be at home making *murghi makhani* for her husband's dinner, Vanessa.' He did such an accurate imitation of his mother that Ness laughed, as did the others in the room.

'Oh, you may find him amusing,' Majidah told them. 'But he will be laughing out of his posterior should that woman walk off with—'

'An orthodontist,' he finished. 'Ah, what dangers there are when one's wife is a dentist. Beware. Beware.' He kissed his mother loudly on the cheek. 'Let me look at you,' he said. 'Why have you not come for Sunday dinner all this month?'

'And eat her dried-out *murghi makhani*? You must be mad, Sayf al Din. That wife of yours needs to learn how to cook.'

He looked at Ness, 'She's a record playing a single song, my mum.'

'I got that 'bout her,' Ness agreed. 'Only the song's diff'rent for everyone she knows.'

'She's clever that way,' Sayf al Din said. 'It makes one think she actually possesses conversation.' He put his arm around his mother's shoulders and squeezed. 'You're losing weight again,' he told her. 'Are you skipping meals, Ma? If you keep doing that, you know, I shall be forced to strap you down and feed you May's *samosas* till you burst.'

'You might go ahead and just poison me instead,' Majidah said. 'This is Vanessa Campbell, as you have guessed, Sayf al Din. She has come to assist me, but you might show her your studio first.'

Sayf al Din accommodated his mother with pleasure, like any man might who enjoys his work. He showed off a loft of organised chaos, where he designed and fashioned headwear for the Royal Opera Company, for West End theatrical productions, for television and for film. He explained the process and brought out sketches. Ness recognised the finished hand-coloured drawings and their pencilled notes as similar to the framed pictures that hung on Majidah's sitting-room walls. She said, 'Oh yeah, I seen these at your mum's. I wondered 'bout them.'

'What did you wonder?' he asked.

'Who did 'em, I s'pose. An' why they was on the wall. Not that they ain't—'

'"Are not," Vanessa,' Majidah said patiently.

'*Aren't* pretty cos they are. Just not what you 'spect to see . . .'

'Ah. Yes. But she's proud of me, aren't you, Ma? You wouldn't think so, considering how she goes on, but she'd not have it any other way. Is that not the truth, Ma?'

'Have no misconception about it,' Majidah said. 'You are the most troublesome of my children.'

He smiled, as did she. He said, 'As that will be. Rand, of whom you so disapprove, will help you gather up the materials you want. And while you do that, I'll show your companion how the drawings get themselves made into the headgear.'

Sayf al Din was as much of a talker as his mother. He gave Ness not only explanations of what he did but demonstrations as well. He offered not only demonstrations but gossip, too. He was as amusing a companion as he looked, and part of his pleasure in his work was to try his millinery on others. He beckoned Ness to put on everything from turbans to tiaras. He perched hats and headdresses on his workers, who chuckled and continued with their sewing. He put a sequinned Stetson on Rand's veiled head, and for himself he chose the hat and plume of a musketeer.

His enthusiasm got directly into Ness's blood and filled her with what she had least expected upon setting out on this jaunt with Majidah: pleasure, interest, and curiosity.

After several days reliving in her mind the experience in Sayf al Din's studio, Ness took action. She went to the offices of the Youth Offending Team on a day when Fabia Bender was not expecting her.

Ness was different from how she'd been at their last meeting, and Fabia Bender had no trouble seeing this, although she couldn't put a name to what had altered the girl. She learned soon enough when Ness introduced the reason for her call. She finally had a plan for her education, she said, and she needed the approval of the magistrate.

So far the matter of Ness's schooling had been a dicey one for Fabia Bender. Holland Park School had refused to take the girl back, using as their excuse the lack of places for the autumn term. Every comprehensive nearby had told the same tale, and it was only on the south bank of the Thames that the social worker had finally found a school willing to take her. But an inspection of it had given Fabia pause. Not only was it in Peckham, which would have necessitated more than an hour's commute by bus in each direction, but it was also in the worst part of Peckham, acting as a blatant invitation for Vanessa Campbell to fall in with the sort of young people easiest available to a troubled adolescent, which is to say the wrong sort of young people altogether.

So Fabia had made a plea to the magistrate for more time. She *would* find something suitable, she told him, and in the meantime Vanessa Campbell was taking a simple course in music appreciation at the college and fulfilling her community service sentence without a complaint from the Meanwhile Gardens child drop-in centre. *Surely* that had to count in her favour . . . ? It had done, and a reprieve was given. But, she was told, something permanent had to be arranged before the winter term.

'Millinery?' Fabia Bender said when Ness told her what she wanted to pursue. 'Making *hats*?' It wasn't that she thought Ness had no ability to do this. It was just that out of every possible line of work that the girl might have come up with to define her future, millinery seemed the least likely. 'Do you fancy designing for Royal Ascot or something?'

Ness heard the astonishment in the social worker's voice, and she did not take it well. She shifted her weight on to one hip, that belligerent pose so common to girls her age. 'Wha' if I do?' she asked, although designing the huge and often nonsensical pieces of headgear worn by posh white ladies during that annual period of horse-racing was the last thing on her mind. Indeed, she hadn't even considered it and barely knew what Royal Ascot was, aside from a source of tabloid pictures of champagne-drinking, skinny females with titles in front of their names.

Fabia Bender was hasty in her reply. She said, 'Forgive me. That was completely inappropriate of me. Tell me how you arrived at millinery and what plan you have to pursue it.' She examined Ness and took the measure of her determination. 'Because you *have* a plan, don't you? Something tells me that you wouldn't have come here without a plan.'

In this she was correct, and the fact that she'd acknowledged Ness's far-sightedness pleased the girl. Assisted by Majidah and Sayf al Din, she'd done her homework. While she didn't answer the first part of Fabia Bender's query – her pride prevented her from admitting that something *good* might actually be coming out of her stint of community service – she did tell her about courses offered at Kensington and Chelsea College. Indeed, she'd discovered a veritable treasure trove of opportunities at the college to explore her newfound interest in millinery, even a year-long national certificate course which she pronounced herself 'dead keen' on taking.

Fabia Bender was pleased, but cautious. This change in Ness was sudden enough to give her pause and to remind her not to count her chickens. But since hers was a difficult and often thankless job, to have one of her troubled clients actually taking steps to alter what would otherwise have been the unswerving course of a life heading towards perdition did make her feel that her own career choice had perhaps not been in vain. Ness needed encouragement. Fabia would provide it.

She said, 'This is outstanding, Vanessa. Let's see where you need to begin.'

After his futile confrontation with Neal Wyatt, Joel found himself at what he believed was at the point of no alternatives. He heard the clock ticking, and he needed to do something to stop it.

The irony of his situation was that the one change in his life that he had once so feared was now the one change he most desired. If Toby could be sent away to a special school, he would be safe. But that possibility did not seem likely, which meant that Toby would not be leaving the near clutches of Neal Wyatt.

That put Joel on constant alert. It also necessitated never letting his brother out of his sight unless someone else was with him or he was at Middle Row School. As the weeks wore on – weeks in which Neal and his crew went back to following, hooting, sniggering, and making low-voiced threats – this constant vigilance took its toll. His schoolwork suffered, and his poetry dwindled. He knew things could not go on like this without his aunt finding out and taking steps to deal with the situation in a way that would only make it worse.

So he had to deal with it himself, and there appeared to be only one avenue left open. He could feel it in the weight of the flick knife that he carried in his rucksack or in his pocket. Neal Wyatt, he decided, wasn't going to listen to reason. But he would very likely listen to the Blade.

Daily, then, after Joel took Toby to the learning centre, he sought out the Blade. He began by asking Ness where he could find her erstwhile lover, but her reply was unhelpful. 'Wha' d'you want wiv *dat* blood?' she asked him shrewdly. 'You getting up to trouble or summick?' And then more pointedly, 'You smoking weed? Shit, you *snorting*?'

To his protestations that it was 'nuffink like dat', she said, 'Better not be,' but that was all she said. She wasn't about to tell him how to locate the Blade. No good had come out of *her* knowing him, so how could good come out of her brother's having anything to do with the man?

Thus, Joel was on his own. Hibah was no help. She knew who the Blade was – who, with eyes and ears in North Kensington, didn't know who the Blade was? – but as to where he might be found . . . It was more a case of the Blade finding you than you finding the Blade.

Joel knew of only one place that the Blade actually went, so he went there too: to the block of flats on Portnall Road, where Arissa lived. Having found him there once, it seemed reasonable to conclude that it was only a matter of time before he might find him there again.

Cal Hancock would be the sign. Joel would not have to knock on doors. He would merely have to wait until he saw Cal lounging at the entrance of that building, doing guard duty.

Once Joel made this decision, it was three more days before he had a pay-off. On an afternoon that blustered with the promise of an autumn rainfall, he finally saw Calvin in position, toking up on a spliff the size of a small banana, the knitted cap he'd abandoned earlier pulled low on his brow. He was stretched across the red and black tiles, his legs the only thing preventing anyone's entrance to the building. A closer look, though, showed Joel that Cal meant business after his own fashion. A length of chain was wrapped around his wrist and the butt of what appeared to be a pistol stuck out from the waistband of his jeans. Joel's eyes widened when he saw this last item. He could not believe it was real.

Joel said to him, 'Happenin, mon?' He spoke from a few feet away, having come up the path from the pavement without Cal's knowledge. So much for guarding, was what Joel thought.

Cal came around from his meditative state. Dreamily, he nodded at Joel. 'Bred,' he said. He toked up again.

'You s'posed to be guardin him like dis? I could've jumped you, blood. He see you . . .' Joel let his voice drop meaningfully.

''S cool man, innit,' Cal replied. 'Ain't no one vexing the Blade while Calvin's watching. 'Sides, he ain't in a mood to cause me aggro, he don't like wha' I do.'

'Why's 'at?'

'Know V'ronica over Mozart Estate?' And when Joel shook his head, 'She popped out a kid f'r him dis morning. A boy. His third, dis is. He tol' her to get rid 'f it months ago, but she wouldn't an' now he's pleased as punch. Three sons make him the *mon*, innit. He celebratin with Rissa.'

'She know about V'ronica, den?'

Cal laughed. 'You mad all th' way? Course she don't know.

Dumb bitch prob'ly t'inks he jus' happy to see her. Well, I 'spect he's happy enough. She got rid 'f hers like he told her.' Cal took another hit and held it in. 'So what you want?'

'I got to talk to the Blade. I got summick for him.'

Calvin shook his head. 'Bred, dat ain't a good idea. He don't like reminding 'bout you and yours.'

'Cos Ness—?'

'Le's not go there. Less said 'bout your sister, better it is. Bu' I tell you dis,' Cal leaned forward, drawing up his legs and resting his elbows on his knees as if to emphasise his next words. 'No one throws the Blade over, bred. He the one does the throwing when he feels like the throwing time's come, y'unnerstan what I say? 'F some woe-man makes a move on her own, *an'* turns out there's another swack involved and she lie about it . . .' Cal tilted his head to Joel, a movement that said *Finish the thought for yourself.* 'You jus' keep distance 'tween you and the Blade. Like I say, dis ain't a good place for you to be.'

'Ness di'n't have no other bloke,' Joel protested. 'The Blade t'ink she did?'

Cal flicked ash off the spliff. 'Don't know, don't want to, don't mean to ask. And don't you neither.'

'But he *got* Arissa,' Joel pointed out. 'Can't she take Ness's place?'

'Ain't *'bout* taking nobody's place. Dis's about respeck.'

'Dat's how he sees it?'

'No other way.' Cal played with the chain wrapped around his wrist, moving it to wrap around his knuckles. He flexed his fingers to see how they worked thus bound. 'So right now . . . ?' he said. 'Best not to break up the party. Long as he's doing Arissa, he's getting b'yond Ness Campbell, and dat's a very good place for him to be.'

'But dat was *months* ago!'

Cal sucked his teeth. There was nothing more to say.

Joel's shoulders dropped. The Blade was the only real hope

he had. Without his help, Joel didn't see how he could manage to keep Toby safe. If Neal had been after him alone, he would have trudged back where he'd come from, knowing that a serious battle with the other boy was inevitable. But the fact was that Neal knew his real weakness: it had nothing to do with his fear for his own safety and everything to do with Toby.

Joel thought about his alternatives. They came down to one thing. He said, 'Okay, but I got summick for him. You give it him from me? He's gonna want it and I want him to know it come from me. You promise dat, I hand it over and bunk off.'

'What you got he want?' Cal said with a smile. 'You write him a pome? And yeah, we know you going to dat word t'ing Ivan put on. The Blade know everyt'ing go down in dis place. Dat's why he's the Blade. And listen –' he showed off the pistol tucked into his waistband – 'you wonder why I carry dis piece wivout worry bout the cops hauling me into the Harrow Road station? T'ink bout dat one, too, m'friend. It ain't rocket science, innit.'

This point seemed irrelevant to Joel. He chose to bypass it, which would not be the first of his mistakes. He said, 'It ain't a poem I got for him. I ain't stupid, y'know.' He dug the flick knife out of his rucksack. He clicked it open, then closed it on his thigh.

Cal looked impressed enough. 'Where'd you get dat?'

'He used it on Ness. Cut up her head and lost it in a bangabout wiv Dix D'Court right after. You give him dis, okay? You tell him I need his help wiv summick.'

Cal didn't take the knife, which Joel held out to him. He said with a sigh instead, 'Blood, wha' c'n I tell you? You *got* to keep the Blade out of your life. Dat's it.'

'Didn't hurt you none to have him in yours.'

Cal gave a soft laugh. 'Lemme tell you summick. You got Ness, right? You got your bruv. You got Auntie an'Mum an' I know 'bout her being in the nuthouse, but still she's Mum.

You don't *need* dis blood here. Trust me, you don't need him. An' if you want him, mon, he's gonna name a price.'

Joel said, 'Jus' give him the knife for me, Cal. Tell him I give it back cos I need his help wiv summick. Tell him I could've kept it and that *means* summick. I di'n't set up no trade wiv the knife. I handed it over. Take it and tell him, Cal. Please.'

While Cal thought this over, Joel considered yet another approach to his problems – that Cal himself might help him – but he dismissed this quickly. Cal without the Blade nearby would intimidate no one. He was just Cal: right-hand man and graffiti artist, spaced on weed. If he had to fight, he probably would, but going at Neal Wyatt wasn't about fighting. It was about drawing a line in the sand. Cal couldn't do that for Neal Wyatt or for anyone. The Blade, on the other hand, could do it for everyone.

Joel thrust the knife at Cal once more. 'Take it,' he said. 'One way or 'nother, you know the Blade want it back.'

Reluctantly, then, Cal took the flick knife. 'I ain't promising—'

'Jus' talk to him. Dat's all I'm asking.'

Cal put the knife in his pocket. 'Be in touch 'f he want to help out,' he said. And as Joel prepared to walk off, he went on. 'You know the Blade do nothing wivout there being a price attached to it.'

'I got dat,' Joel said. 'You tell him I'm willing to pay.'

19

The seed of Ness's millinery idea did not bear immediate fruit. Things were not easily arranged, and she'd not anticipated facing difficulties. She wanted the courses; they would be hers for the taking. Anything else was inconceivable to her. Thus, at the first stumbling block – a considerably sized monetary one – she did just that: she stumbled. She shimmered with hostility towards life, but she directed it at the children with whom she was supposed to be making jewellery at the drop-in centre.

Making jewellery was an umbrella term, a euphemism for stringing brightly coloured wooden beads on equally brightly coloured plastic cords. Since the children engaged in this activity were all under four years old with the limited eye-hand coordination that one might expect of this age, making jewellery consisted largely of spilling more beads than stringing them and an expression of frustration at such spillage consisted largely of throwing beads rather than replacing them in their containers.

Ness didn't handle any of this well. She grumbled at first as she scrambled around the floor, rescuing beads. Next, she smacked her hand on the table when the uplifted arm of a child called Maya indicated another palmful of beads was about to be launched. Finally, she resorted to swearing. She snapped, '*Fuck* it all, you lot. 'F you can't hold on to 'em beads, you c'n just *forget* 'bout stringing 'em at all cos I ain't playing dis stupid game wiv you,' and she began to gather up containers, cords, and round-nosed scissors.

The children reacted with shouts of protest, which attracted Majidah from the kitchen. She observed for a moment and picked up on some of the more colourful mutterings emanating from Ness. She strode across the room and put an end to the jewellery-making herself, but not in the way Ness intended. She demanded to know what Miss Vanessa Campbell thought she was doing: swearing in front of innocent children. She didn't wait for an answer. She told Ness to get herself outside, where she would deal with her directly.

Ness took the opportunity outdoors to light up a cigarette, which she did with no little pleasure. She wasn't supposed to smoke anywhere near the child drop-in centre. She'd protested this rule more than once, telling Majidah that these kids' parents smoked in their presence – not to mention whatever the hell else they got up to in front of them – so why couldn't she smoke if she wanted to? Majidah had refused to engage her in this discussion. The rule was the rule. There would be no bending, breaking, adjusting, or ignoring it.

Ness didn't care at this point, on this day. She hated working at the drop-in centre, she hated rules, she hated Majidah, she hated life. She was thrilled to bits when Majidah – having re-established the four-year-olds at their activity with larger beads this time – joined her outdoors, pulling a coat around herself and narrowing her eyes at the spectacle of Ness outrageously inhaling from the forbidden Benson and Hedges. Good for you, was what Ness thought. See what aggravation feels like, bitch.

Majidah had not raised six children to find Ness's behaviour off-putting. She also had no intention of addressing it at the moment, which she saw as something that Ness clearly wanted. Instead, she told Ness that, as she was unable to work in peace with the children on this particular day, she could instead wash all the windows of the centre, which were sadly in need of attention.

Ness repeated the order, incredulous. She was to wash

windows? In this bloody weather? First off it was fucking too cold and second off it was probably going to fucking rain before the bloody end of the fucking day, so what the hell was Majidah thinking because no way was Ness going to fucking wash any fucking windows.

In reply, Majidah calmly assembled the equipment required for the job. She then gave detailed instructions, as if she'd heard nothing of what Ness had said. Three steps were involved, she informed her. So were water, detergent, a hose-pipe, newspapers, and white vinegar. Wash the windows inside and out, and afterwards they would talk about Ness's future at the drop-in centre.

'I don't want no future at dis fucking place,' Ness shrieked as Majidah headed back inside the building. 'Don't you got nuffink else to *say*?'

Of course, Majidah had plenty to say, but she wasn't about to engage Ness when the girl was in such a state. She said to her, 'We shall speak once the windows are clean, Vanessa,' and when Ness said, 'I c'n walk straight out 'f here, you know,' Majidah said serenely, 'As is always your choice.'

That very serenity was a slap in the face. Ness decided to give Majidah what for when she had the chance. She told herself she could hardly *wait* to do it, and in the meantime, she'd rehearse her comments *and* show the maddening woman some window washing that she would *never* forget.

She hosed, she scrubbed, she polished. And she smoked. Outside the centre. She did not have the courage to do so when she began seeing to the windows inside. By the time the day was at its end – with the windows sparkling, the children gone, and the first drops of rain beginning to fall just as Ness had thought they would – she had been in mental conversation with the Asian woman for a good four hours and she was burning to take her on in person, given the opportunity.

This opportunity grew from Majidah's inspection of the windows. She took her time about it. She looked over each one, ignoring the rain that was spotting them. She said, 'Well done, Vanessa. Your anger, you see, was put to good use.'

Ness wasn't about to admit to anything resembling anger. She said, with a meaningful curl of the lip, 'Yeah. Well, I 'spect I got a *real* exceptional career in front of me, eh: window washing.'

Majidah glanced her way. 'And of course there are worse careers to have, when one considers the number of windows in this city that want to be washed, yes?'

Ness blew out a frustrated breath. She demanded to know if there was *anything* Majidah could not turn around and make into something positive because it was getting damn irritating having to be around such a merry ray of bloody flaming fucking sunshine every day.

Majidah thought a moment before speaking, for she too had been awaiting an opportunity for a conversation with Ness, although not a conversation of the sort Ness wished to have with her. She said, 'My gracious, is this not an important life skill? Is this not additionally the most basic skill an individual can develop in order to survive life's disappointments in a healthy manner?'

Ness spluttered, her form of pooh-poohing the Asian woman's words.

Majidah sat at one of the pint-sized tables, waved Ness into the chair opposite hers, and said kindly, 'Do you wish now to tell me what has gone wrong?'

Ness's lips began to form the word *nuffink*. But at the end, she couldn't say it. Instead, the gentle expression on Majidah's face, still present despite everything Ness had done to wipe it off, prompted her to tell the truth although she managed to do it with an attitude of spurious indifference that would have fooled no one. She'd met with Fabia Bender at the Youth Offending Team's office, Ness revealed. She wanted to take a certificate course at Kensington and Chelsea College, a course that would lead to a real career in a field besides window washing or bead stringing. But the course had turned out to cost over six hundred pounds and where the hell was Ness supposed to come up with that kind of money, short of going on the game or robbing a bank?

'What sort of course is it that you wish to take?' Majidah asked her.

Ness wouldn't say. She felt she would have to admit too much if she revealed it was millinery that interested her. She believed she would be admitting to everything that had altered in her life but remained unacknowledged and needed to stay that way.

'Wa'n't I s'posed to be coming up wiv a career?' Ness demanded instead. 'Wa'n't I s'posed to be trying to *make* something of myself?'

'This is bitterness I hear,' Majidah said. 'So you must tell me what good bitterness offers you. You see life as a series of disappointments. Seeing this, you fail also to see that if one door closes, another opens.'

'Right. Wha'ever.' Ness stood. 'C'n I go?'

'Listen to me before you leave, Vanessa,' Majidah said, 'for what I tell you is meant in friendship. If, as many others do, you thrash about in the wilderness of anger and disappointment, you will fail to see the opportunities that God will lay in front of you. Anger and disappointment blind us, my dear. If not that, they distract us. They make it impossible to keep our eyes open since when we rage, we squint and thus we cannot see all that surrounds us. If we instead accept what the present moment is offering, if we simply move forward through it, doing whatever task is in front of us, we then have the serenity necessary to be an observer. Observation is our way of recognising the next thing we are meant to do.'

'Yeah?' Ness asked, and her tone presaged the next words she spoke. 'Dat work good for you, Maji*dah*? Life say you can't be an aeronautical engineer, so you keep your eyes open, you jus' keep moving forward ever'day and you end up *here*?'

'I end up with you,' Majidah said. 'This, to me, was part of God's plan.'

'Thought you lot called him Allah,' Ness sneered.

'Allah. God. Lord. Fate. Karma. Whoever. Whatever. It is all the same, Vanessa.'

Majidah was silent for a moment, observing, much as she'd done over the months that Vanessa Campbell had been working at the drop-in centre. She wanted to impart the lessons she herself had learned from a difficult life. She wanted to tell Ness that it is not the circumstance of one's life but what one *does* with the circumstance that is important: choices, outcomes, and knowledge gained from outcomes. But she did not say this, knowing that Ness's present state would prevent her from hearing. So, instead she said to her, 'You are at the turning point, my dear. What is it that you intend to do with all of this bitterness, I ask you?'

After handing the flick knife over to Cal, there was nothing for Joel to do but wait to hear from the Blade. Days melted into weeks as he did so, watching his back and watching Toby's back as well. They sought places of safety from Neal Wyatt when they were out and about. They walked quickly, and they continued to practise hiding from head-hunters upon Joel's command.

They were standing on the bridge that carries Great Western Road over the canal when things changed. They'd gone there to observe a gaily coloured narrow boat that was motoring eastward in the direction of Regent's Park. Toby was chattering about the possibility of the boat's containing pirates – to which his brother was listening only dimly – when Joel caught sight of a figure coming towards them along the pavement, sauntering from the direction of the Harrow Road.

Joel recognised him: it was Greve, number one henchman of Neal Wyatt. Joel automatically looked around for Neal and for other members of Neal's crew. None of them were nearby, which made the hair on the back of Joel's neck tingle. He said to Toby, 'Get down to that barge. Do it now Tobe. Don't come out no matter what, till you hear me call you, y'unnerstan?'

Toby didn't. He thought, considering what they'd been discussing, that Joel meant the narrow boat, which was at that moment precisely beneath them with a bearded man at the helm and a woman watering lush pot plants in the stern. He said, 'But where they going? Cos I don't want to go 'nless you—'

'The barge,' Joel said. 'Head-hunters, Tobe. Y'unnerstan? Don't come out till I tell you time's right. You hear?'

Toby got it the second time. He scurried to the metal steps and quickly descended. By the time Greve had reached the bridge, Toby was scampering on to the abandoned barge. It bobbed in the water as he went to his hiding place among the discarded timbers.

Greve joined Joel at the railing. He glanced down at the water and then back at Joel with a smirk. Joel thought he intended to give him aggro, but when Greve spoke, he merely relayed a message. Neal Wyatt wanted to have a counsel. If Joel was interested, he could meet Neal at the sunken football pitch in ten minutes. If Joel wasn't interested, then things could continue just as they were.

'Don't matter to him,' was how Greve put it, with an indifference implying that the counsel hadn't been Neal's idea.

That spoke volumes. It seemed to Joel that the Blade had anticipated the request he'd intended to make of him, and this was no surprise. The man had demonstrated more than once that he knew what was going on in the neighborhood. This was, in part, the source of his power.

Joel thought about the time – ten minutes – and then the meeting between them which would take perhaps ten more. He wondered about Toby being on the barge for that length of time. He didn't want to take his little brother with him to talk to Neal, but he also didn't want to risk Toby's revealing himself to their enemies if this was a trick. He looked around to see if anyone was lingering in a doorway nearby. There was only Greve, though, who said impatiently, 'Wha's it going to be, mon?'

Joel said he'd meet Neal. Ten minutes. He'd be there at the football pitch, and Neal had better turn up.

Greve smirked. He left the bridge and went back the way he'd come.

When he was out of sight, Joel hurried down the steps and approached the abandoned barge. He said quietly, 'Tobe. Don't come out. C'n you hear me?' He waited till the disembodied voice whispered in reply. Then he said, 'I'll be back. *Don't* come out till you hear me call you. Don't be scared neither. I jus' got to go talk to someone. Okay?'

''Kay,' was the whispered reply, releasing Joel from the obligation of standing guard. With another look around to make sure he hadn't been seen talking to the barge, he went on his way.

He crossed Meanwhile Gardens and trotted up Elkstone Road. When he reached the pitch, he saw that the town council had painted over the work of the local graffiti artists – something that the town council did on a yearly basis – inadvertently giving them a fresh canvas on which to work. A sign had been put up, threatening prosecution for the defacement of public property. This sign had already been tagged in red and black paint with the balloon-like moniker *ARK*. Joel circled around to the gated opening at the pitch's far side. He descended the steps. Neal was not yet there.

Joel was nervous about meeting the other boy in such a place. Once inside, with the playing area some eight feet below the level of the pavement that passed it, a person couldn't be seen unless he stood in the middle or unless a pedestrian walking by – of whom there were few enough in the rainy autumn weather – made the effort to peer through the surrounding chain link fence.

It seemed to Joel abnormally cold. When he walked to the middle of the pitch, it felt as if a damp fog rose from the ground and settled around his legs. He stamped his feet and tucked his hands into his armpits. At this time of year, there was far less daylight, and what there was was fast fading. The shadows cast by the retaining walls oozed farther and farther into the pitch, creeping among the weeds, which grew from cracks in the tarmac.

As the minutes passed, the first thing Joel wondered was whether he'd come to the correct place. There was indeed another football pitch – tucked behind Trellick Tower – but it wasn't sunk below the level of the street as this one was, and Greve *had* said the sunken football pitch. Hadn't he?

Joel began to doubt. Twice he heard someone approaching, and his muscles grew tight in readiness. But both times the footsteps passed by, leaving behind their echo and the acrid scent of cigarette smoke.

Joel paced. He bit the side of his thumb. He tried to think what he was meant to do.

What he wanted was peace: both of mind and of body. That, in conjunction with his message to the Blade and Neal's recent lack of interest in him, was why he'd been willing to latch on to the word *counsel* and to do something that he now began to think of as stupid. The truth of the matter was that he'd exposed himself to danger in this place. He was alone, weaponless, and unprotected, so if he remained in this spot and something happened to him, he'd have only himself to blame. All Neal and his crew had to do, really, was to hop the fence and to corner him. There'd be no quick escape, and he'd be finished as they doubtless wanted him to be.

Joel's bowels turned to liquid. The sound of rough footsteps made things worse. The lid of a dustbin, rattling in the nearby mews, nearly did him in, and he understood that Neal would want him like this: nervous, waiting, and wondering. He saw that having Joel a mass of anxiety would make Neal feel big and in control. It would offer him the opportunity he wanted to—

Opportunity. That was the thought that did it for Joel. That single word flashed in his mind, brightening his situation until he saw it in an entirely new light. When that occurred, he was out of the pitch like a fox bolting from the hounds. He knew that he'd been worse than stupid. He'd been inattentive. That was how people died.

He shot to the corner and tore around the turn, making for the railway tracks. With Goldfinger's great tower looming as his landmark, he pounded in the direction of Edenham Estate. He knew at that point what was going on, but he didn't want to believe it.

He heard the sirens when he was in Elkstone Road, before he actually saw anything. When at last he did see, it was the lights first, those twirling rooftop lights that told vehicles to clear the way for the fire brigade. The fire engine itself stood on the bridge above the canal. A hose snaked down the steps, but no water yet cannoned out to douse the fire which was merrily consuming the abandoned barge. Someone had untied it as well as ignited it, for now it floated in the middle of the canal, and smoke billowed thickly from it, a foetid cloud like a renegade belch.

There were watchers everywhere, lining the bridge above the water and crowding the towpath alongside it. They peered from the skate bowl and even from behind the fence that protected the child drop-in centre.

Even as he *knew* the truth and continued his approach, Joel looked for Toby. He shouted his brother's name and pushed through the crowd. He then saw why no fire-fighter had begun shooting water on to the flames that were consuming the barge.

One fireman held the nozzle of the hose poised while another was up to his chest in the greasy water of the canal. This second man – his protective jacket discarded on the towpath – was working his way over to the barge, a rope coiled over his shoulder. He was making for the end of the barge not yet burning. There, a small form cowered.

'Toby!' Joel shouted. 'Toby! Tobe!'

But there was too much going on for Toby to hear Joel's cry. Flames crackled old dry wood, people called out encouragement to the fireman, a loud radio on the engine above them spasmodically spat out information, and all around was a babble of voices into which broke the hooting of a police vehicle pulling on to the bridge.

Joel cursed himself for having given Neal Wyatt the opening he'd been looking for: Toby had run to his hiding place as commanded, and it had been transformed by Neal and his crew into a trap. End of story. Joel looked around fruitlessly for his nemesis, even as he knew that Neal and everyone else associated with Neal would be gone by now, their worst already done. And not done to Joel, who could at least fight back, but done to his brother who didn't and never would understand what marked him out for this treatment.

In the canal, the fireman reached the barge and heaved himself on to it. From where he cowered, Toby looked up at this apparition rising from the depths. He might have taken him for one of the head-hunters he'd been told to fear – or even the incarnation of Maydarc, come to him from the land of Sose – but he sensed that the real danger was from the fire not from the man with the rope. So he worked his way on his hands and knees towards his rescuer. The fireman fixed a line to the barge to keep it from floating in a fiery mass along the canal, then he grabbed Toby as the child reached him. Once he had him out of danger, a shout to his fellows above with the engine started the water flowing. A gratified cheer went up from the crowd as water spewed from the hose in a fierce cascade.

All could have been well at this point had life been a fade-to-black celluloid fantasy. The presence of the police prevented this. They reached Toby before Joel was able to. One of them had him by the collar of his jacket the moment his rescuer had deposited him on the ground. It was fairly obvious that this was the intimidating moment that presaged interrogation, and Joel shoved his way over to intercede.

'. . . set that fire, boy?' one of the constables was saying. 'Best answer directly and be truthful about it.'

Joel cried, 'He di'n't!' and reached Toby's side. 'He was hiding,' he said to the police. 'I tol' him to hide there.'

Toby, wide-eyed and shaking but relieved that Joel was with him at last, gave his reply to his brother instead of to the constable. 'I did like you said. I waited to hear you say to come out.'

'"Like you *said*"?' The constable grabbed Joel now, so that he had both boys in his grip. 'This is down to you, then. What's your name?'

'I heard 'em, Joel,' Toby told him. 'They squirted summick on the barge. I could smell it.'

'Accelerant,' a man's voice said. Then it barked towards the canal. 'See if these two've left a starter on the barge.'

'Hey,' Joel cried. 'I di'n't do this. My brother di'n't neither. He doesn't even know how to light a match.'

The cop answered this with an ominous directive. 'Come along with me,' and he turned both boys towards the spiral stairs.

Toby began to cry. Joel said, 'Hey! We di'n't . . . I wasn't even here an' you c'n ask . . . You c'n ask those blokes in the skate bowl, innit. They would've seen—'

'Save it for the station,' the cop said.

'Joel, I was hiding,' Toby wailed. 'Just like you said.'

They reached the panda car. Its back door was open. There, however, an elderly Asian man was speaking insistently to a second constable who was climbing into the driving seat. As Joel and Toby were placed inside, he said, 'This boy did not set that fire, do you hear me? From my window over there – you see? It is just above the canal? – I watched these boys.

There were five of them, and they sprayed the boat first with something from a tin. They lit it and untied it. I was witness to all this. My good man, you must listen. These two boys here, they had nothing to do with it.'

'Make your statement at the station, Gandhi,' was the driver's reply. He closed his door on the old man's protests and put the car into gear as the other constable climbed in and slapped his hand on the roof to indicate they were ready to roll.

Joel's thought was that these two men had seen far too many American cop programmes on the television. He said in a low voice to his weeping brother, 'Don't cry, Tobe. We'll get it sorted.' He was aware of dozens of faces watching, but he forced himself to hold his head up, not because he wanted to evidence pride but because he wanted to look among the watchers for the only watcher who mattered. But Neal Wyatt was not among them.

At the Harrow Road police station, Joel and Toby were ushered into an over-heated interview room, where four chairs fixed permanently to the floor sat two on a side at a table. There, a large tape recorder and a pad of paper stood waiting. The boys were told to sit, so that was what they did. The door closed, but it did not lock. Joel decided to take hope from this.

Toby had stopped crying, but it was not going to take much to set him off again. His eyes were the size of teacakes, and his fingers clutched the leg of Joel's jeans.

'I was hid,' Toby whispered. 'But they found me anyways. Joel, how you 'spect they found me if I was hid?'

Joel couldn't think of a way to explain things to his brother. He said, 'You did what I tol' you, Tobe. That was real good.'

When the next thing happened, it happened in the person of Fabia Bender. She entered the room, accompanied by a hefty black man in a business suit. She introduced herself first and then the man, saying he was DS August Starr. They'd begin by taking the boys' names, she said. They would need to contact their parents.

Having never met the other two Campbells, Fabia Bender drew the pad of paper towards her once she and DS Starr were seated. She picked up the pen and waited to use it, but when Joel told her their names, she didn't write. Instead she said, 'Are you Vanessa's brothers?' and when Joel nodded, she said, 'I see.'

She was thoughtful. She looked down at her pad and tapped the pen against it. DS Starr, glancing at her curiously because this was generally not a moment in which Fabia Bender hesitated, said to the boys, 'Who're your parents? Where are they?'

'Mum's in hospital,' Toby offered, encouraged by the pleasant tone that both of the adults had taken and not understanding that this pleasant tone was designed to wrest information from children and not to befriend them, no matter how needy for friendship they were. 'She pots plants sometimes. She talks to Joel but not to me. I ate her Aero once.'

'We live with—'

Fabia Bender interrupted Joel. 'They live with their aunt, August. I've been working with the sister for some months.'

'Trouble?'

'Community service. The girl who did that mugging directly across the street . . . ?'

August Starr sighed. 'You lot got no dad?' he asked the boys.

'Dad got killt outside the off licence,' Toby said. 'I was little. We lived wiv Gran for a while but now she's in Jamaica.'

Joel said, 'Tobe,' by way of a warning. The law of survival that he knew was a simple one. Nothing about it involved talking to cops. They didn't mean well because they'd crossed over, and what they'd left behind was their understanding of how life really was. Joel could tell by looking at DS Starr – by looking at Fabia Bender as well – that to them the story was a simple one. The death of Gavin Campbell was a case of black men doing what black men always did: shooting, knifing, beating and killing each other over drugs in the street.

Joel had successfully silenced Toby, and he intended to say nothing more himself. As for Fabia Bender, she had the information she needed since she knew Ness. So she settled back in her seat to do her job, which was to monitor the interview that August Starr would conduct.

Although Joel and Toby could not know it, they were lucky in their assigned interlocutor. Joel might have thought August Starr was a turncoat with preconceived notions about his own people, but the truth was that DS Starr saw before him two boys who needed his help. He knew their physical appearance – not to mention Toby's manner – made life difficult for them. But he also knew that a life made difficult sometimes led boys into trouble. He needed to get to the bottom of what was going on before he could come up with a plan to help them. This, unfortunately, was not something that Joel was conditioned to understand.

DS Starr flicked on the tape recorder, reciting the time, the date, and the names of the people in the room. Then he turned to Joel and asked him what had happened out there. Don't fib, he added. He could always tell when people were fibbing.

Joel told him a sanitised version of the story, one that conveniently mentioned no names. He'd gone to the football pitch in Wornington Road to meet a bloke, but the arranged time had got bollocksed-up or something because the boy never showed up. So he returned to Meanwhile Gardens and that was when he saw the barge on fire.

To the question of what Toby was doing on the barge, he told the truth. He'd instructed Toby to wait for him there. Sometimes he got aggro from older kids in the area, and Joel wanted to keep him safe. He added the fact that an Asian man had tried to tell the cops all this right there on the bridge above the canal, but those cops weren't having anything off him. All they wanted to do was hustle Joel and Toby over to the Harrow Road station. Here they now were. That was it.

Unfortunately, Joel did not anticipate what DS Starr would next ask: the names of the boys he was intending to meet at the football pitch.

'Why d'you want to know?' Joel asked. 'I just tol' you—'

Fabia Bender interrupted to explain the procedure: they'd be wanting someone to confirm Joel's story. It wasn't that Sergeant Starr didn't believe Joel's claims, by the way. This was just procedure when a crime had been committed. Joel understood that, didn't he?

Naturally, Joel more than understood. Like other boys his age, he'd grown up on a diet of films and television shows in which cops were always trying to get the bad guys. But he also understood a much more pressing concept than the apprehension of whoever had set fire to an abandoned barge: grass on Neal Wyatt and he'd make thing worse.

So Joel said nothing. He knew he was safe from Toby's saying anything either, for Toby didn't know the boys' names.

'Do you want to think about this for a while?' August Starr asked pleasantly. 'You understand that private property has been destroyed, don't you?'

'Barge was a wreck,' Joel said. ''S been there f'rever, innit.'

'That's of no account. It belongs to someone. We can't have people setting fire to other people's belongings, no matter their condition.'

Joel looked at his hands, which he'd folded on the table. 'I wa'n't there. I di'n't see,' he said.

'That,' Starr said, 'won't buy you a bag of crisps, Joel.' He recited the time once again for the tape recorder and he switched it off. He told Joel he'd give him a little while to sit here and think about things, and he told Fabia Bender that he'd leave her with the boys while he made some phone calls. When he got back, he said, perhaps Joel would have something more to tell him.

Next to Joel, Toby whimpered as the detective sergeant left the room. Joel said, 'Don't worry, mon. He can't keep us here. He don't even want to.'

Fabia said, 'But he can hand you over to me, Joel.' She paused and let *Hand you over to me* sink in. 'Do you want to tell me anything else about what happened? It'll be between us. You can trust me, and the tape recorder's not running, as you can see.'

Classic good cop, bad cop was how Joel saw this. Sergeant Starr was the tough guy. Fabia Bender was the marshmallow. Together they would do the scare-and-soften routine. It might work with other kids caught in this sort of circumstance, but Joel was determined it would not work with him.

'I tol' you what happened,' he said.

'Joel, if you boys are being bullied—'

'What?' he asked. 'What're you 'tending to do if we are? *Sort* someone? Have a *word* somewhere? Anyways, we ain't being bullied. I tol' you what happened. So'd that Asian man. Go ask him if you don't believe me.'

Fabia Bender studied him, all too aware of the truths he spoke. There were so few resources and so many people in need of them. What *could* she do? She said, 'I'd really rather have this matter put at rest straightaway. Here and now.'

Joel shrugged. There was, he knew, only one way to put matters at rest and that way had nothing to do with a white woman inside a police station.

Fabia Bender got up as Sergeant Starr had done. She said, 'I'll need to make a few phone calls as well. You're to wait here. Do you want something in the meantime? A sandwich? A Coke?'

'C'n I have—'

Joel cut into Toby's eager reply. 'We don't want nuffink.'

Fabia Bender left them. She left the thought of phone calls behind her. Phone calls in the plural suggested plans and arrangements. Joel avoided even thinking about that. This, he told himself, was going to work out. All he had to do was not break.

When the door opened again, it was Sergeant Starr who entered, his words a surprise: he told the boys that they were free to leave. Ms Bender would take them to their aunt. A man called Ubayy Mochi had shown up at the station. He had seen the occurrence from his window along the canal. He told the same tale as Toby.

'I don't want to see you here again,' Sergeant Starr told Joel.

Joel thought, Whatever, but he said only, 'C'mon, Tobe. We c'n go innit.'

Fabia Bender was waiting for them in reception, bundled into a tweed jacket and scarf, with a French beret on her head. She offered the boys an understanding smile before leading them outside where her two dogs lounged at the base of the steps leading into the station. She said their names, 'Castor, Pollux. Rise. Come.' The dogs did as they were told.

Toby hung back. He'd never seen such monstrous canines. Fabia said to him, 'No worries, my dear. They're gentle as lambs when it comes down to it. Let them smell your hands. You too, Joel. See? Aren't they lovely?'

'You keep 'em wiv you for protection?' Toby asked.

'I keep them with me because they'll tear up the garden if I leave them at home. They're terribly spoiled.'

The way she talked indicated to Joel that there were no hard feelings about the way things had gone inside the station. In this, Fabia Bender was wise. She knew when to withdraw, and she was grateful, in fact, that Mr Ubayy Mochi had turned up and given her the opportunity to do so. She had the two Campbell boys on the back burner of her mind now, and she assumed this was not the last time she would see them.

Although Joel told her they could find their way to the charity shop, Fabia wasn't having that. Despite what they had tried to pass off as an explanation for what had happened with the barge, what Fabia saw in Joel and Toby was two children in jeopardy. Their aunt needed to be brought into the picture about this, which was what Fabia did when they got to the shop.

Kendra had a choice at the end of Fabia Bender's visit, and she chose Joel. She told herself it was because he was family, but the truth was that choosing Joel was easier. To choose the social worker would have meant doing something sooner rather than later, and while Kendra was not unwilling, unable, or unloving, she *was* at a loss.

Joel told one story about the barge. Fabia Bender – in confidence and as an aside while the boys petted the dogs – told another. While it was true that an Asian man called Ubayy Mochi had corroborated much of what Toby and Joel had told the police, Fabia felt there was more to the story than that.

What sort of more? Kendra asked.

Joel wasn't involved with a gang, was he? was Fabia Bender's careful reply. She hastened to add that she wondered if he'd been threatened by a gang, harassed by a gang, bullied by a gang? Had there been any other signs of trouble? Any difficulties? Anything at all that Mrs Osborne had noticed?

Kendra knew the laws of the street as well as did Joel, but she called him over anyway. She told him to tell her again what had happened and to be straight about it this time. Did this have to do with those boys who'd been giving him aggro?

Joel lied as he knew he was intended to do. That situation had already been sorted, he said.

Kendra chose to believe him, which put Fabia Bender in the position of having nothing more to do, at least for the moment. She departed, which left Kendra alone with her nephews and even more alone with her thoughts. First Ness, now this. She wasn't a fool. Like Fabia Bender, she knew things had the potential to get worse.

She sighed, then cursed. She cursed Glory Campbell for

having left. She cursed Dix D'Court for being gone from their lives. She cursed the solitude she craved and the complications she did not want. She told Joel to tell her the real truth about what had happened now they were alone. He lied again, and again she grasped that lie.

She knew she was grasping, and she felt wretched. To assuage this feeling, she searched the shop. In the last load of donations, there had been a skateboard with a wonky wheel. She made an offering of it to Toby, her way of apologising to him for the growing list of life's difficulties, fears, and disappointments.

For Toby, the skateboard was heaven made concrete. He wanted to use it at once. This necessitated the wonky wheel's repair, which involved Joel and Kendra in a remediation, which in turn put both of them one step farther away from the stuff of life waiting to be dealt with. But that was how both of them wanted things: Joel choosing the lie, Kendra choosing Joel.

She relayed a version of all this when she next saw Cordie. Caught up in a conflict of emotions, desires, and duties, she needed someone to affirm the choices she was making. In exchange for a maternity massage performed in her minuscule sitting-room while her daughters demonstrated their skill with crayons on an old colouring book featuring the Little Mermaid, Cordie listened to the tale of the barge and everything that had followed its burning. But what she said at the end wasn't what Kendra expected to hear.

She told Kendra to hang on with the massage, and she sat up, wrapping the sheet around herself. She looked at Kendra shrewdly but not without sympathy. She said, 'Ken, I got to ask you a question: you ever t'ink you in over your head?'

'What makes you ask that?'

''S obvious, innit. First Ness, now Joel. Ken, it ain't easy trying to bring up kids in dis place when they *already* your kids an' they been wiv you all their lives. It's worse trying to do it wiv kids got dropped on you by their gran. I guess what

I'm saying 's . . .' She stalled. She slid off the massage table and fetched a packet of cigarettes. She lit one up, told her elder daughter to hush her mouth and 'Do *not* be telling your dad 'bout dis cos it's only one fag and it ain't hurting no one and especially no baby to have one fag,' and then she returned to Kendra and the topic, fortified to explore it. 'Th' boys don't need a skateboard,' she said. 'Nice you give it, but nice as it is, it ain't what's important, and I 'spect you know dat. You're wanting to make it up to them, but it's not what they need.'

Kendra felt deflated. Cordie, who otherwise seemed so frivolous with her girls' nights out and her snogging sessions with twenty-year-old boys in dark corridors and alleys, had got to the heart of the matter. And the heart of the matter went beyond Ness's attempted mugging, her community service, and Joel's entanglement with the local yobs and now with the police.

'Kids need a parent,' Cordie went on. 'Best of all worlds which's near impossible these days, kids need *two* parents.'

'I'm trying—'

'You know,' Cordie cut in, 'point is, Ken, you don't got to try. No sin in unnerstanning you got too much on your plate wiv no cutlery at hand, you know wha' I mean? Not ever' one's meant to do dis sort of t'ing, and no sin in admitting it neither. Way I've always seen it is dis: jus' cos a woman's got th' parts, don't mean she got to use 'em.'

That smarted for reasons having nothing to do with the Campbell children. Kendra reminded her friend, 'I don't even have the parts.'

'Could be, Ken, there's a reason.'

This was, it must be said, something that Kendra had thought on more than one occasion since the Campbells had been foisted upon her. She had never given it actual voice, however. Had she done so, she believed she would have been committing a betrayal so enormous there would be no way to make recompense for it in her natural lifetime. She would become another Glory to the children. She'd be worse than Glory, in fact.

She said, 'I got to do this, Cordie. I got to find a way. What I ain't *ever* doing is putting—'

Cordie showed mercy when she interrupted. 'No one asking you to. But you got to do summick and what you got to do ain't got nuffink to do wiv skateboards.'

Her options were limited. Indeed, they seemed virtually non-existent. So she went to the Falcon. She made a deliberate choice of this place, rather than the gym. She wanted privacy this time. She knew she was being devious, but she told herself that there were things to discuss and she needed a quiet place in which to do it. The gym certainly wasn't that. The Falcon – or at least the bed-sit above it – was.

Dix wasn't there. One of his two flatmates was, though. He directed Kendra to the Rainbow Café. Dix was working there, helping out his mum. Had been for the last three weeks, she was told. Had to give the body-building a rest.

Kendra thought in terms of Dix's doing damage to himself from which he had to recover. But when she got to the Rainbow Café, she discovered that this was not the case. His dad had suffered a heart attack on the premises, serious enough to frighten his wife and his children into insisting that he follow doctor's orders: five months of rest and no messing about with those instructions, Mr D'Court. The man – only fifty-two years old – was himself frightened enough to obey. But that meant someone had to step up to the cooktop and take his place.

The Rainbow Café comprised an L of tables that ran across the front window and along the wall, as well as a counter with old swivel stools in front of it. When Kendra entered, she went to that counter. It wasn't a mealtime so, behind the counter, Dix was engaged in cleaning the cooking surface with a metal scraper while his mother put paper napkins into dispensers, which she had removed from the tables. She had the salt and pepper cellars ranked in front of her on a tray as well.

The only customer present was an elderly woman with grey hairs sprouting from her chin. Despite the warmth of the café, she hadn't removed her tweed coat. Her stockings bunched around her ankles and she wore thick-soled brogues on her feet. She was nodding over a cup of tea and a plate of beans on toast. To Kendra, she seemed the complete embodiment of the What Could Be's, a chilling sight.

When Dix's mother saw Kendra, she recognised her immediately. She assessed the situation as any shrewd mother might have done in similar circumstances, and what she saw she didn't like.

She said, 'Dix,' and when he looked up, she nodded in the direction of Kendra. Dix thought he was meant to take an order from someone, and turned to do so but let out a breath when he saw who'd come calling.

The estrangement from Kendra hadn't been easy for him. She was in his blood. He hated this but he'd come to accept it. He didn't know what to call it: love, lust, or something in between. She was just there.

As for Kendra, Dix still looked good. She'd known that she missed him but not how much.

Dix wasn't a man to lie. He said, 'Still looking good, Ken.'

'You,' Kendra said, returning the compliment. She gave a glance to his mother and nodded hello. The woman nodded back. Her acknowledgement was pro forma. A tightening of the rest of Mariama D'Court's face spoke much more.

Dix looked to his mother and they communicated wordlessly. She disappeared into a storeroom, taking the tray of salt and pepper cellars with her, leaving the napkin dispensers behind.

When Kendra asked when Dix had started working at the café, he brought her into the picture about his dad. When she asked about his training, he said some things had to wait. He got in two hours a day just now. That had to be enough until his dad was well. Kendra wanted to know how was he coping, what with competitions coming and not having enough time to prepare for them. He said there were more important things than competitions. Besides, his sister came around to help out every day as well.

Kendra felt a rush of embarrassment. She hadn't even known Dix D'Court had a sister. She was too awkward in that moment to ask a single thing about her: older, younger, married, single, etc. She just nodded and waited for him to ask in turn about life on Edenham Estate.

He did, and just the way she'd hoped because that was his good-hearted nature. He wanted to know about the kids. How were they doing? He turned to continue cleaning the stove. He seemed to give his complete attention to the task.

She said Good, the kids were good. Ness was doing her community service without complaint and Toby was still topping up his education at the learning centre. She'd decided no further testing was going to be necessary for Toby, by the way. He was doing that well.

And Joel? Dix asked.

Kendra didn't answer until Dix turned back to her. She asked him if he minded if she smoked, adding that she remembered how he didn't like it much.

He told her to suit herself so she did. She lit a cigarette and said, 'Missing you.'

'Joel?'

She smiled. 'S'pose. But I'm talking about me. I see you here and it all goes away, you know?'

'Wha's 'at?'

'Whatever made us split apart. I can't remember what it was, just what we had. Who're you seeing now?'

Dix breathed out a laugh. 'You t'ink I got time to see anyone?'

'What about wanting to see someone? You know what I mean.'

'Don't work like dat for me, Ken.'

'You're a good man.'

'Dat's right.'

'Okay. So I say it straight out: I was wrong and I want you back. I need you back. I don't like life without you.'

'T''ings're different now.'

'Cos you're working here? Cos of your dad? What? You said there's no one—'

'You di'n't answer me 'bout Joel.'

And she wasn't about to. Not just yet. She said, 'We're the same, you and me. We got dreams and we fight to keep the dreams alive. People c'n fight better together than alone. There's that and everything we feel for each other. Or am I wrong? You not feeling wiv me what I'm feeling wiv you? You not wanting to leave this caff straightaway and be wiv me the way we c'n be together?'

'I di'n't say dat, Ken.'

'Then let's talk about it. Let's see. Let's try. I was in the wrong about everything, Dix.'

'Yeah. Well. I can't give you what you want.'

'You gave me what I wanted before.'

'Now,' he said. 'I can't give you what you want now. I ain't a security service, Kendra. I know what you want, and I can't give it.'

'What I . . . ?'

'You ain't mentioning Joel. The cops. The barge burning. You t'ink I don't know wha's going on in your life? Wha' I'm saying's t'ings no different'n the last time we talked except you got more reason to be worried now you got two kids under the eye of the cops instead of just one. An' I can't make a diff'rence in all dat. I can't make it go away the way you want. I can't make the *reason* for it go away. Like I said, I ain't a security service.'

Kendra wanted to tell herself that he was being deliberately cruel to her instead of merely honest. She also wanted to lie to him, telling him that her request had nothing to do with

Joel and everything to do with love and the future they might have together. But she was, at the moment, too stricken by his knowledge of her that was far superior to her knowledge of him. She was additionally stricken by the fact that his mother had heard their conversation, as the satisfied expression on her face indicated when she emerged from the storage room with her salt and pepper cellars filled and ready to be replaced on the tables.

Kendra said to Dix, 'I was thinking family. What we could be.'

'More to family 'n dat,' was his reply.

20

Kendra told herself that things weren't as bad as they seemed. Since there were parts of Joel's story that she knew were true and supported by the statement of one Ubayy Mochi, there was also a slim chance that the burning of the barge was a one-off situation having nothing to do with the boys who'd been tormenting Joel and Toby. In order to believe this, however, there were other parts of the tale that she had to ignore – such as Joel's having a confabulation scheduled with a boy who'd earlier been in several nasty fights with him – but she was willing to do that. She largely had no choice in the matter. Joel was saying nothing else.

Kendra thought life might smooth out a bit. Fabia Bender's return to the charity shop disabused her of that notion. She came on foot, accompanied by her two monstrous dogs. As always, they dropped to the ground upon hearing her command of 'Down, dogs.' They remained there like sentinels on either side of the doorway, a position that Kendra found intensely irritating.

'They're going to scare away customers,' she said to Fabia as the social worker closed the door behind her. Rain was falling, and she wore a bright yellow raincoat and a matching hat, of the sort one might see on a fisherman facing a raging southwester. It was an odd get-up for London, but not, somehow, for Fabia Bender. She took off the hat but not the coat. She brought a brochure out of its pocket.

'I won't be a moment,' she said to Kendra. 'Are you expecting a throng? For a sale or something?'

She said it without irony as she looked around the shop for an indication that at any moment Kendra was going to be fighting off two dozen customers vying for old shoes and third-hand blue jeans. She didn't wait for a reply as she came to the counter where Kendra had been standing at the till, flipping through an old copy of *Vogue* from the magazine rack. She said she had been thinking of Joel. Of Ness as well, but mostly of Joel.

Kendra fastened on her niece. 'Ness's not missed the drop-in centre, has she?'

'No, no.' Fabia hastened to reassure her. 'She actually appears to be doing quite well there.' She didn't tell Kendra about the effort she was making on Ness's behalf with regard to her recently revealed and somewhat surprising desire for a millinery certificate. That wasn't going as well as she'd hoped: so many young people in need and so few financial resources to meet that need. She placed the brochure on the counter. She said, 'There's something . . . Mrs Osborne, there may be something more we can do for Joel. I've come across this . . . Well, not quite come *across* it . . . I've had it for a while but I've been reluctant because of the distance. But as there's nothing like it on this side of the river . . . It's an outreach programme for adolescents. Here, you can see for yourself . . .'

It turned out she'd come to tell Kendra about a special programme for adolescents who'd shown the potential for getting into trouble. It was called Colossus, she explained, and it was run by a privately funded group in South London. South London was, of course, an enormous commuting stretch for a troubled child this far north of the river but, as there was no programme like it in North Kensington, it might be worthwhile to introduce Joel to it. They evidently had a high quotient of success with boys like him.

Kendra jumped on the final part of Fabia Bender's statement. ' "Boys like him"? What's that mean?'

Fabia didn't want to give offence. She knew the woman

standing on the other side of the counter was doing her best with the three children she'd taken into her home, but it was a difficult situation to begin with. She had no experience with children, and the children themselves had needs that appeared to be far greater than those which one busy and inexperienced adult could meet. That, and not some bad seed planted deeply within them and lying dormant until an appropriate moment arose in which to germinate, was why many children ended up in trouble. If Fabia saw a way to head off trouble, she liked to pursue it.

'I have a feeling that there's more going on with Joel than what we're seeing, Mrs Osborne. This group –' she tapped her finger on the brochure, which Kendra had left on the counter – 'provides outlets, counselling, job training, activities . . . I'd like you to consider it. I'm willing to go over there with you – with Joel as well – to speak to them.'

Kendra looked at the brochure more closely. She read the location. She said, 'Elephant and Castle? He can't be trekking over there every day. He's got school. He's got helping me out with Toby. He's got . . .' She shook her head and slid the brochure back to the social worker.

Fabia had thought Joel's aunt would respond in this fashion, so she went on to her second suggestion. This was that Joel should have a male role model, a mentor, a friend, someone older and steady who could involve the boy in an interest beyond what could be found in the streets. Dix immediately sprang to Kendra's mind: Dix, lifting weights, the gym, and body-building. But she couldn't go back to Dix with this suggestion after she'd humiliated herself with an indirect and less than honest approach to get him back into their lives. That left the only other male whom Kendra knew about, the man who'd been flitting on the periphery of Joel's life since he'd started attending Holland Park School.

She said, 'He used to see a white man over Holland Park School.'

'Ah. Yes. Through their mentoring programme? I know about the set-up. Who was this man?'

'He's called Ivan—' Kendra struggled to remember the surname.

'Mr Weatherall? Joel knows him?'

'He was going to his poetry nights for a time. He was writing poetry himself. Seemed like he was always putting something in a notebook. Poems for Ivan, he'd say. I think he liked it.'

Fabia thought this might be just the ticket. She knew Ivan Weatherall by reputation: an eccentric white man in his fifties with an advanced sense of social responsibility rare in people of his background. He came from a landed family in Shropshire whose landed condition could have nurtured within him the sense of entitlement one frequently found in wealthy people whose riches allowed them to lead marginally – or entirely – meaningless lives. But perhaps because the family's wealth had grown out of a nineteenth-century glove-making business, they had a different attitude towards their money and what was meant to be done with it.

If Joel could be encouraged to strengthen ties to Ivan Weatherall, Fabia said, 'I'll phone the school and see if they still have Mr Weatherall mentoring Joel. In the meantime, will you encourage him with his poetry from your end? I'll be frank with you. It's little enough – this writing of poetry – but it might be something. And he needs something, Mrs Osborne. All children do.'

Kendra was raw on the subject of what children needed. She wanted Fabia Bender to be gone, so she said she'd do what she could to get Joel back into Ivan Weatherall's poetry nights. But when the social worker left the charity shop, squashing her fisherman's hat on her head and saying 'Come, dogs' as she stepped out on to the pavement, Kendra was faced with an additional reality about Joel's attending *Wield Words Not Weapons*. If he went back to that poetry event, he'd be out on the streets at night once again. Out on the streets at night put him in danger. Something had to be done to head off that danger. It seemed to Kendra that there remained only one way to do this. If Dix would not help her sort out the boys who were after Joel and Toby, she would have to do so herself.

When Kendra asked Joel the full name of the boy who was giving him trouble in the street, Joel knew what she intended to do but he didn't associate this with *Wield Words Not Weapons*. She would not believe him when he claimed ignorance of the name of the very boy he'd earlier declared he was scheduled to meet at the football pitch, so he was forced to tell her that he was called Neal Wyatt. He asked her to stay away from him, though. Talk to Neal, you make things worse for me and Tobe, he told her. Things were fine at the present, anyway. Neal had had his fun with the burning of the barge. Joel hadn't seen him in weeks. This latter was a lie, but she wouldn't know that. Neal had been keeping his distance, but he'd been making sure Joel knew he was not far away.

Kendra asked if Joel was lying to her, and Joel managed to sound outraged at the question. He wasn't about to lie in a circumstance involving Toby's safety, he told her. Didn't she know *that* about him, at least, if she didn't believe anything he said? This was an excellent ploy: Kendra studied him and was momentarily appeased. But Joel knew he could not let matters rest there. He had only a reprieve. He still had to stop his aunt in her quest. He also had to make Neal back off.

Obviously, the return of the flick knife hadn't made a sufficient impression on the Blade regarding Joel's worthiness of the man's notice. He would have to talk to him personally.

He knew better than to ask Ness again, lest she raise a ruckus that Kendra might overhear. Instead, he moved on to a different source.

He found Hibah at school, having lunch with a mixed group of girls, sitting in a circle in one of the corridors to keep out

of the rain. They were talking about 'dat bitch Mrs Jackson' –
this was a maths teacher – when Joel caught Hibah's eye and
signalled to her that he wanted to talk. She got to her feet and
ignored the girls' tee-heeing about her having a conversation
with a younger man.

Joel didn't obfuscate. He needed to find the Blade, he told
her. Did she know where he was?

Like his sister, Hibah wanted to know what the bloody hell
Joel wanted with the Blade, of all people. She didn't wait for
an answer, though. She merely went on to tell him that she
didn't know where he was and neither did anyone else who
wasn't meant to know. And that meant *everyone* in her acquaintance.

Then she asked him what this was all about anyway, and
she went on shrewdly to answer her own question. 'Neal,' she
said. 'He vexing you. Tha' barge an' everyt'ing, innit.'

This prompted Joel to ask Hibah something he'd wanted
to know from the first. What was she *doing* hooked up with a
lout like Neal Wyatt?

'He ain't all bad,' she replied.

What she didn't say and couldn't have said was what Neal
Wyatt represented to her: a modern-day version of Heathcliff,
Rochester, and a hundred other dark heroes of literature,
although in Hibah's world he was more representative of the
mysterious, elusive, and misunderstood hero found in modern
romance novels, on the television, and in films. She was, in
short, a victim of the myth that has been foisted upon women
since the time of the troubadours: love conquers all; love saves;
love endures.

She said, 'I know you two been trouble for each other, Joel,
but this is summick comes down to respect.'

Joel made a sound of derision. Hibah didn't take offence,
but she did take it as an invitation to continue.

She said, 'Neal's clever, you know. He could be a good
learner in this place here –' she indicated the corridor in which

they stood – 'if he wanted to. He could be anything, innit. He could go to university. He could be a scientist, a doctor, a solicitor. Anyt'ing he wanted to be. But you ain't been able to see that, innit. An' he knows that, y'unnerstan.'

'He wants to run a crew in the street,' Joel said. 'Dat's what he wants.'

'He doesn't,' she said. 'He's only mixing wiv the other boys cos he wants respect. Tha's what he wants from you as well.'

'People want respect, they got to earn it.'

'Yeah. Tha's what he's been trying to—'

'He tries the wrong way,' Joel told her. 'An' you c'n tell him dat, if you want. Anyways, I di'n't ask to talk to you 'bout Neal. I ask you 'bout the Blade.'

He began to walk off, leaving her to her mates, but Hibah didn't like people being at odds with each other, and she didn't like being at odds with Joel. She said, 'I can't tell you where tha' bloke is. But girl called Six . . . ? She prob'ly knows cos she involved wiv a blood called Greve an' he knows the Blade good enough.'

Joel looked back at her. He knew of Six. He didn't know where she lived, though, or how to find her. Hibah told him. Mozart Estate, she said. Just ask around. Someone would know her. She had a reputation.

That turned out to be the case. When Joel went to the Mozart Estate, it was a matter of questioning only a few people before he rooted out the flat in which Six lived with her mother and some of her siblings. Six recognised Joel's name, looked him over, assessed his potential to do her benefit or harm, and gave him the information he wanted. She told him about a squat on the edge of the Mozart Estate, tucked into a crook of Lancefield Road where it led to Kilburn Lane.

Joel chose darkness when he went there, not because he wanted the safety of shadows but because he thought it was probable that the Blade would be in the squat at night rather than in the daytime when he'd more likely be cruising the streets, doing whatever he did to maintain his credentials with the lower level thugs in the area.

Joel knew he was correct in his assumption when he saw Cal Hancock. The graffiti artist was at the foot of some stairs, behind a chain link fence whose gate had enough of a gap in it for people to slip through with a minimum of trouble. And people had done that, Joel could see. The flickering lights from candles or lanterns came from three derelict flats, two of which were at the top of the three-floor building and as far away as possible from the first-floor flat in which the Blade was apparently doing some sort of business. The stairs leading up to this flat were concrete, as was the building itself.

Cal was definitely on guard this time. He sat, alert, on the fourth step from the bottom and when Joel slipped through the gate in the fence, he stood at ease but intimidating to someone who didn't know him, legs spread and arms crossed.

'Happenin',' he said as Joel approached. He gave a nod. He sounded official. Something, then, was going on above him in the Blade's presence.

'I got to see him.' Joel attempted to sound as formal as Cal but also insistent. He wasn't to be put off this time. 'You give him dat flick knife?'

'Did.'

'He chuck it or keep it?'

'Likes the knife, mon. He got it wiv him.'

'He know where it come from?'

'I tell him.'

'Good. Now you tell him I need to talk. And don't mess me about, Cal. Dis is business.'

Cal came down the steps and looked Joel over. 'How you come to have business wiv the Blade?'

'You jus' tell him I got to talk.'

'Dis about dat sister of yours? She got a wanker boyfriend or summick? You come wiv a message from her?'

Joel frowned. 'I said before. Ness's moved on.'

'Dat ain't summick the Blade likes, mon.'

'Look. I can't help what Ness's doing. You jus' tell the Blade I want to talk. I'll keep watch here and put up a shout 'f someone wants to go up. Dis is important, Cal. I ain't leave dis time till I see him.'

Cal drew in a breath and glanced above at the dimly lit flat. He started to say something but changed his mind. He climbed the stairs.

While Joel waited, he listened for sounds: voices, music, anything. But the only noise came from Kilburn Lane, where the occasional car passed by.

A soft footfall brought Cal back to him. He said that Joel was to go on up. The Blade was willing to have a chat. He added that there were people above, but Joel wasn't to look at them.

'I'm cool,' Joel told him, although he didn't feel it.

Since the stairs were not lit, Joel felt his way upwards by means of the handrail. He came out on a landing off which opened a door to the external first-floor corridor. He went out and found the light was better since it came from a street lamp on Lancefield Court not too far away. He made his way towards a partially opened door from which more light flickered. As he approached, he smelled burning weed.

He pushed the door farther open. It gave on to a short corridor at the end of which a battery lantern burned. This illuminated soiled walls and lino ripped from the floor. It also exposed part of a room, stacked with old mattresses and damaged futons, in which shadowy forms were engaged in transactions with the Blade.

Joel thought at first that he'd come to a crack house and he understood why Cal Hancock had been hesitant about allowing him to climb the stairs. But he soon realised that what he was looking at was a different sort of business being conducted. Instead of men and women on the mattresses and futons, nodding off on substances supplied by the Blade, these were boys being handed plastic bags of powder, of rock, and of weed, and being given addresses to make deliveries. The Blade was doing the portioning out of substances from a card table, speaking occasionally to callers who rang his mobile.

The scent of weed was coming from a far corner of the room. There, Arissa was sitting, her eyes half-closed and a stupefied smile on her face. She had a half-burnt spliff between her fingers, but she was obviously high on something more than weed.

The Blade ignored Joel until all the delivery boys had been supplied and had shuffled out of the squat. Following Cal's instructions, Joel hadn't made a study of any of them, so he didn't know who they were or who was among them, and he was clever enough to realise that this was all for the best. The Blade closed up shop – putting goods into a large satchel and locking it – and glanced at Joel. He didn't speak, though. Instead, he crossed over to Arissa, bent to her and kissed her deeply. He slid his hand down the front of her jumper and caressed her breasts.

She moaned and made a stab at working his jeans zip, but she lacked the coordination to get it down. She said, 'You wan' it, babe? No shit I do you in front 'f the Queen if you want, innit.'

The Blade looked around at Joel, then, and it came to Joel that this was a performance for his benefit, something from which he was supposed to take a message. But what it was didn't compute because of what Joel knew of the man in front of him.

Ivan had said Stanley Hynds was intelligent and self-educated. He'd studied Latin and Greek and the sciences. He had a part to him that was not a part of what people saw when they had a run-in with him. But what all that meant in light of the man who was looking at him from across the room as a strung-out teenager tried to massage his member . . . This was something Joel did not understand, and he did not struggle to understand it. All he knew was that he needed the Blade's help, and he meant to have it before he left the squat.

So he waited for the Blade to decide whether he'd allow Arissa to service him in front of Joel, and he did his best to look unconcerned. He crossed his arms as he'd seen Cal do, and he leaned against the wall. He said nothing and he kept his face without expression, hoping this reaction was the key to proving whatever he needed to prove to the Blade.

The Blade laughed outright and disengaged from Arissa's ineffectual fingers. He crossed over to Joel and, as he did so, he took a spliff from the breast pocket of the suit jacket he was wearing and he lit it with a silver lighter. He took a toke and offered it to Joel. Joel shook his head. 'Cal give you the knife?' he asked.

The Blade observed him long enough to let Joel know he wasn't meant to speak before being told it was appropriate to do so. Then he said, 'He give it. You lookin' for summick in return, I 'spect. Dat what dis is?'

'I ain't lying,' Joel said.

'So what you need from the Blade, Jo-ell?' He drew in a lungful of smoke that seemed to go on for ever. He held it there. In the corner, Arissa fumbled around on her futon, apparently looking for something. He said to her sharply, 'No more, Riss.'

She said, 'I comin' down, baby.'

'Dat's where I want it,' he told her. And then to Joel, 'So what you need?'

Joel told him in as few words as possible. They amounted to safety. Not for him but for his brother. One word on the street that Toby had the Blade's protection and Toby wouldn't have anyone vexing him any longer.

'Whyn't you get what you need from someone else?' the Blade enquired.

Joel, hardly an idiot in these matters, knew the Blade was asking so that he would have to say what the Blade believed about himself: there was no one else with his power in North Kensington; he could sort people out with a single word and, if that didn't work, he could pay them a visit.

Joel made the recitation. He saw the gratified gleam come into the Blade's dark eyes. Obeisance given, Joel went on to make specific his request.

This required a history of his encounters with Neal Wyatt, and he gave it, beginning with his first run-in with the other boy and concluding with the fire on the barge. He crossed the final line when he said Neal's name in advance of any agreement he might garner from the Blade to help him. He could think of no other way to demonstrate how willing he was to trust the older man.

What he hadn't considered was that the Blade might not reciprocate that trust. He hadn't considered that the return of a flick knife might not serve as an adequate expression of his good intentions. Because of this, he waited for the Blade's reply in mistaken confidence, assuming that now all would be well. He wasn't prepared, therefore, to receive a response that was noncommittal.

'Ain't my man, Jo-ell,' the Blade said, knocking ash from his spliff on to the floor. 'Spitting on me, 's I recall. Outside Rissa's, you remember?'

Joel was hardly likely to forget. But he'd also been pushed because the Blade had spoken badly about his family, which was unacceptable. He told the Blade something of this, saying, 'M' family, mon. You can't be talking bad 'bout them and 'spect me to do nuffink. Dat ain't right. You would've done the same 's I did, I reckon.'

'Did and have done,' the Blade noted with a smile. 'Dat mean you want dis patch someday, bred?'

'What?' Joel asked.

'You take on the Blade cos you want to run his patch someday yourself?' In the corner, Arissa laughed at this notion. The Blade silenced her with a look.

Joel blinked. That idea had been so far from his consideration that it hadn't even made it on to his radar screen. He told the Blade that what he wanted was help with his brother. He said he didn't want Toby vexed any longer. Neal Wyatt and his crew could take on Joel as much as they wanted, he explained, but they were meant to leave Toby alone. 'He can't do nuffink to defend himself,' Joel said. 'It's like going after a kitten wiv a hammer.'

The Blade took all this in and looked thoughtful. After a moment, he said, 'You willing to owe me?'

Joel had thought about this in advance. He knew the Blade would extract a payment of some sort. It was inconceivable that the king pin of North Kensington would do something out of the milk of human kindness since whatever he might have once had of that substance had long ago curdled in his veins. From what he'd seen tonight, Joel assumed it would have to do with drugs: joining the Blade's delivery team. He didn't want to do it – the risks of getting caught were great – but he was down to his last hope.

The Blade knew that. His expression said that Joel was caught in a seller's market. He could walk away and hope Neal Wyatt had done the most he intended to do to Toby, or he could strike a bargain in which he knew he was going to end up paying more than the product was actually worth.

Joel saw no other choice. He couldn't go to Cal, who would do nothing without the Blade's permission. He couldn't go to Dix, who was out of the picture. If he asked Ivan to intervene, what would likely come of that was a poetry duel between conflicting parties. If he waited for his aunt to track down and speak to Neal, that would make life infinitely worse.

There was simply no alternative that Joel could see. There was only this moment, and during it he felt a stabbing that he knew was regret. Nonetheless he said, 'Yeah. I owe. You do this for me, I owe.'

The Blade took a toke of his spliff, and his face showed

satisfaction and the kind of enjoyment that Joel suspected he otherwise got from a woman on her knees in front of him. He told himself that it didn't matter. He said, 'So we got a deal or what?' and he tried to sound as rough as he could. 'Cos if we don't, I got other business to conduct.'

The Blade lifted an eyebrow. 'You like to take th' piss, eh? You got to stop dat, bred. It'll buy you trouble.'

Joel made no reply. Arissa stirred in her corner. She curled into a foetal position on the dirty futon and said, 'Baby, come *on,*' extending one hand to the Blade.

He ignored her. He nodded at Joel, the message implicit: I know who you are and don't forget it. He stubbed out the rest of his spliff on the wall, and he motioned Joel to approach him. When Joel did so, the Blade dropped a hand to his shoulder and spoke into his face.

'Your family vex me,' he said. 'I get dissed by dem. You recall dis, mon? I t'ink you setting me up for more just now and dat being the case—'

'Dis ain't no set-up!' Joel protested. 'You t'ink any diff'rent, you talk to the cops. They tell you what happened. They tell you—'

The Blade's hand clamped down brutally. So tight and hard was the grasp he had on Joel that it cut off the rest of what the boy wanted to say. 'Do not in'errupt me, blood. You listen good. You want help from me, you got to prove yourself first. You prove dis situation here ain't 'bout dissing me more, y'unnerstan? You do the job I give you – in advance, eh? – then I do the job you want done as well. And then you owe me. An' *dat's* the deal if you want it. Dis ain't no negotiation we doing.'

'Prove myself how?' Joel asked.

'Dat's the deal,' the Blade said. 'You ain't need to worry 'bout the hows. They come to you when they come to you.' He walked back to Arissa, who'd begun to snore slightly, her lips parted and her tongue lolling between them. He looked down at her and shook his head. 'Shit, I hate a cow dat does drugs. It's so p'thetic. You popped your cherry yet, Jo-ell?' He looked over his shoulder. 'No? We got to take care of dat.'

We. Joel clung on to that word. What it meant, what it promised, what it said in answer. He said, 'Deal,' to the Blade. 'What d'you want me to do, Stanley?'

When Joel received the call that he was to go to the small mentoring office, he knew that Ivan Weatherall would be waiting for him. He trudged off – excused from his religious studies class, which was a relief since the teacher never spoke in anything but a monotone as if afraid to offend God through a show of enthusiasm about the subject matter – and dreaded what was to come. He thought feverishly about what he would say as an excuse to the mentor who would no doubt want to know what had happened to his attendance at *Wield Words Not Weapons*. He settled on telling him that his courses this term were far more difficult than they'd been in the previous school year. He had to devote more time to them, he'd say. He had to keep his marks up. He had to prepare for the future. Ivan, he thought, would like preparation for the future as an excuse.

Unfortunately, Ivan had done what Joel had not done: his homework. When Joel walked into the conference room, he could see as much. The mentor had a file spread out, which Joel correctly concluded boded ill. In this file were his current marks from every course he was taking.

'Mon,' Joel said to him in a greeting notable for its degree of factitious pleasure. 'Hey. Ain't seen you in a while.'

'We've missed you at *Wield Words*,' Ivan replied. He sounded friendly enough as he looked up from the file. 'I thought at first you'd been cracking the school books, but that doesn't appear to be the case. You've slipped. Want to tell me about that?' He pulled out a chair at an angle to his own. He had a takeaway coffee in his right hand, and he sipped from this as he waited for a reply, keeping his eyes on Joel over the rim.

The last thing Joel wanted was to tell Ivan anything. He didn't actually want to talk at all. Least of all did he want to talk about his marks at school, but as he hadn't written a poem since before the barge fire, he couldn't talk to Ivan about verse either. He kicked his toe against the shiny blue lino. He said, 'Classes're rough dis term. An' I got t'ings on my mind, innit. An' I been busy wiv Toby an' stuff.'

'What sort of stuff would this be?' Ivan asked.

Joel looked at him, thinking about traps. Ivan looked at Joel, thinking about lies. He knew about the fire on the barge through community gossip that had taken a more concrete form when he'd received a phone call from Fabia Bender. Was he still meeting with Joel Campbell? she'd wanted to know. The boy was teetering on the edge of serious trouble, and a male role model was urgently called for. The aunt had her hands full and was in over her head – if you'll pardon the metaphor mixing, Fabia Bender had said – but if Mr Weatherall would once again engage with Joel, he and Fabia might together be able to turn the boy from the direction in which he appeared to be heading. Had Mr Weatherall heard about the barge . . . ?

Ivan had let things slide a bit with Joel. He was spread rather thin – what with the poetry course, the script-writing course, the film project he hoped to get off the ground, and his brother's ill health in Shropshire where he was paying the price for forty-eight years of nonstop cigarette smoking – but he wasn't a man to make excuses. He told Fabia Bender he'd been remiss, for which he apologised since he generally kept commitments once he made them. It hadn't been lack of interest in Joel but lack of time, he said, a situation that he would remedy at once.

Joel shrugged: the adolescent boy's answer to every question he didn't want to answer, a bodily expression of the eternal *whatever* voiced by teenagers in hundreds of languages. Mostly it was Toby, he said. He had a skateboard now and Joel was teaching him to ride it so he could take it to the skate bowl in Meanwhile Gardens.

'You're a good brother to him,' Ivan said. 'He means a lot to you, doesn't he?'

Joel gave no reply, merely kicking at the lino again.

Ivan went in an unexpected direction. He said, 'This isn't the sort of thing I generally do, Joel. But perhaps it needs to be done.'

'What?' Joel looked up. He didn't like Ivan's tone, which sounded like something caught between regret and indecision.

'This burning of the barge and your run-in with the Harrow Road police . . . ? Would you like me to tell them about Neal Wyatt? I have a feeling about Neal, and I believe there's a very good chance that a single visit to the station – a few hours being interviewed by a detective, with a social worker in attendance – might be just what Neal needs to turn him around. It might be meant, you see, that he should speak to the police.'

It also, Joel wanted to say, might be suicide on a stick. He cursed the fact that he'd ever mentioned Neal Wyatt's name to anyone. He said hotly, 'Why's ever'one t'ink Neal Wyatt burnt dat barge? I don't *know* who burnt it. I di'n't see who burnt it. Neither did Tobe. So giving Neal over to th' cops i'n't going to do nuffink but—'

'Joel, don't take me for a fool. I can see you're angry. And I'm guessing you're angry because you're anxious. Anxiety-ridden. Frightened as well. I know your history with Neal – good God, didn't I break up the first fight you two had? – and I'm suggesting we take a step to alter that history before someone gets seriously hurt.'

''F I'm anxious, it's cos everyone want to pull Neal into a situation where he don't belong,' Joel said. 'I got no proof he lit up dat barge, and I ain't claiming he did if I got no proof. You name him to th' cops, they drag him in . . . an' *what*, Ivan?

He ain't naming no one else, he back out on the street in two hours, and he start looking for who grassed him up.' Joel heard the degree to which his language had disintegrated, and he knew what it revealed about his state. But he also saw a way to use those things – his language and his state of mind – to turn the present moment to his advantage. He shoved his hand through his hair in a gesture meant to be interpreted as frustration. He said, 'Shit. You're right. I got anxiety climbing up to my eyeballs. Me and Tobe in the police station. Aunt Ken t'inking *she* going to sort Neal 'f she ever find him. Me watching my back and jus' waiting to get jumped. Yeah. I'm anxious, innit. I ain't writing no poems cos I can't even t'ink about poems, wiv t'ings like they are.'

Ivan nodded. This was something he understood. It was also a subject dear to his heart, an attractor to which his brain automatically veered, dismissing anything else on his mind, whenever the topic came up. He said, 'That's called being blocked. Anxiety is nearly always a block to creativity. No wonder you've not been writing poetry. How could you be expected to?'

'Yeah, well I *liked* writing poems.'

'There's an answer to that.'

'Which's what?'

Ivan shut the folder. Joel felt a modicum of relief. He felt even more when Ivan warmed to his topic. 'You have to work *during* the anxiety to overcome the anxiety, Joel. It's a catch twenty-two situation. Do you know what that means? No? A contradiction in terms or available fact. Anxiety prevents you from working, but the only way to relieve the anxiety is by doing what it prevents you from doing: working. In your case, writing. Anxiety is thus always a signpost, telling a person he ought to be engaged in his creative act. In your case, writing. Wise people recognise this and use the signpost to get back to the work. Others avoid, seeking an external relief to the anxiety, which tempers it only moderately well. Alcohol, for example, or drugs. Something to make them forget they're anxious.'

This was so convoluted a concept that all Joel managed to do was nod as if in eager acceptance of its precepts. Ivan, enthused by his own attraction to the subject, took this as comprehension. He said, 'You have a real talent, Joel. Turning away from that is like turning away from God. This is essentially what happened to Neal when he turned away from the piano. To be frank, I don't want that to happen to you, and I'm afraid it will if you don't get back to your creative source.'

This was cold mashed potatoes, as far as Joel was concerned, but again he nodded and tried to look thoughtful. If he was anxious – which he agreed that he was – it had very little to do with putting words on paper. No, he was anxious about the Blade and what the Blade would ask of him as proof of his respect. Joel hadn't yet heard, and the waiting was torture since Neal Wyatt still lurked, waiting as well.

As for Ivan, well-meaning but innocent, he saw what he wanted to believe was a solution to Joel's problems. He said, 'Will you come back to *Wield Words*, Joel? We miss you there and I think it will do you a world of good.'

'Don't know if Aunt Ken'll let me out, what wiv my marks in school once she sees 'em.'

'It's a simple matter for me to speak to her.'

Joel considered this. He saw a way that returning to *Wield Words* might work to his benefit, ultimately. He said, 'Okay. I like to do it.'

Ivan smiled. 'Brilliant. And before our next meeting, perhaps you'll write a bit of verse to share with us? As a way to work through the anxiety, you see. Will you try that for me?'

He would try, Joel told him.

So he used *Wield Words Not Weapons* as a red herring. It was essential that life appear normal while he waited for what the Blade would tell him to do. He found the practice excruciatingly difficult because his mind was so much on other things and he lacked the discipline to focus his thoughts on the creative act while the very antithesis of that act perched on his shoulder, waiting to happen. But the sight of him sitting at the kitchen table jotting words in a notebook was enough to alter his aunt's way of thinking about sorting out Neal Wyatt and, as long as that continued to work, Joel was willing to do it. And *she* was willing to let him go to *Wield Words Not Weapons* when the next occasion of the gathering of poets came along.

Joel saw the people differently this time. He saw the place differently. The Basement Activities Centre in Oxford Gardens seemed over-heated, ill-lit, and malodorous. The attendees at the event seemed impotent: men and women of all ages who were inadequate to the challenge of effecting change in their lives. They were what Joel had determined he would never be: victims of the circumstances into which they had been born. Sitting on the sidelines of their own lives, they were passive observers. Things happened to passive observers, and Joel told himself he wasn't about to become one.

He had brought three poems, all of which he knew were perfect examples of the wretched depths to which his pre-occupation with the Blade had taken him. He didn't dare take the microphone and read them to the gathering, especially since he'd been once been named a Poet of Promise. So he sat and watched others offer their work: Adam Whitburn – embraced, as before, enthusiastically by the crowd; the Chinese girl with blonde-streaked hair and purple-framed sparkly glasses: a spotty-faced adolescent girl obviously writing about her passion for a pop singer.

In his nervous state of mind, it was something akin to agony for Joel to sit through this first part of the evening. He had nothing to offer the poets in the way of helpful criticism, and the fact that he could not attune himself to the rhythms of the meeting did not help his restlessness. He began to think this restless state would squeeze his heart to a stop if he didn't do something to quell it.

That something appeared to be *Walk the Word*, as nothing else was on offer. When Ivan took the microphone to introduce that portion of the evening's activities, Joel borrowed a pencil from a toothless old man. He thought What the bloody hell, and he jotted down the words that Ivan read: *soldier, foundling, anarchy, crimson, whip* and *ash*. He asked the old man what *foundling* meant and, while he knew his ignorance didn't exactly presage success at the contest, he decided to go at it in the manner he'd first been taught, letting the words come from that mysterious place inside, not worrying about how anyone else happened to be putting them together. He wrote:

> *Foundling learns fast the crimson*
> *Way of the street.*
> *Anarchy marks the whip*
> *That the soldier holds,*
> *Where the gun reduces*
> *All to ash.*

Then he stared at what he'd written, and he wondered at the message contained in his own interpretation of the words. From the mouths of babes, Ivan had said in an earlier time when he'd bent to one of Joel's poems with his green pencil in hand. You've a sagacity beyond your years, my friend. But looking at his latest poem and swallowing hard, Joel knew it wasn't anything close to innate wisdom that had prompted it. It was his past; it was his present; it was the Blade.

When the time came for the poems to be collected, he shoved his in with the rest. He went to the back of the room where the refreshment table stood, and he took two pieces of ginger-flavoured shortbread and a cup of coffee, which he'd never drunk before. After a sip, he loaded it with milk and sugar. He stood to one side and he nodded when Ivan came up to him.

'I saw you engaging in *Walk the Word*,' Ivan said, placing a friendly hand on Joel's shoulder. 'How did it feel? More at ease with the process than you were before?'

'Bit,' Joel said although he couldn't tell if this was the truth since what he'd written at home was suitable only for lining the rubbish bin and the piece he'd just created for *Walk the Word* represented the first time he'd felt spontaneous with language in ages.

'Excellent,' Ivan said. 'Good luck to you. And I'm glad you're back with us. Perhaps next time, you'll be willing to take the microphone. Give Adam some competition before his head gets too big for his body.'

Joel offered the chuckle that was the expected response. 'I ain't likely to do better'n him.'

'Don't,' Ivan said, 'be so sure of that.' He excused himself with a smile and wandered off, to engage the Chinese girl in conversation.

Joel remained near the refreshment table until the judges returned with their decision on the *Walk the Word* offerings. He reckoned the winner would be the Chinese girl since she'd come equipped with a thesaurus and she'd begun jotting frantically in her notebook the moment Ivan had called out the first word. But when Ivan took from the judges the paper on which the winning entry had been written, Joel recognised a diagonal tear he'd created in it when he'd ripped it from his spiral book. His heart began slamming before Ivan read even the first line.

It came to Joel that he'd defeated Adam Whitburn. He'd defeated everyone who'd made an attempt to *Walk the Word*. He'd shown himself not only as a Poet of Promise but as the real thing as well.

At the end of the reading, there was a moment of silence before the crowd began to applaud. It was as if they'd had to pause and take in the passion of the words, in order to feel that passion themselves before they could react to it. And, truth be told, the words *did* constitute passion this time for Joel. They were fully felt, part of the fabric of who he was.

When the applause ended, Ivan said, 'If the poet will stand and allow us to celebrate with him or with her . . . ?'

Joel, still by the refreshment table, had no need to stand. He moved forward. He heard the applause once again. All he was able to think was that just for a moment, he'd been a poet.

When he reached the dais, he felt Ivan take his hand in congratulation. The man's expression was one of 'You *see?*' and Joel accepted it for what it was: affection and affirmation of what Ivan had long declared to be his talent. Then his prizes were pressed upon him. These comprised a leather-bound journal for future poetic endeavours, a winner's certificate, and fifty pounds.

Joel stared at the note when it was in his hands. He turned it over and examined both sides, stunned by his sudden fortune. Suddenly, it seemed to him that his world had altered on the edge of a coin.

Adam Whitburn had no apparent difficulty accepting the situation. He was the first to congratulate Joel when the evening came to an end. There were other congratulations as well, but those that came from Adam Whitburn meant the most to Joel. So did the invitation that Adam extended to him directly after the basement had been cleared and cleaned.

He said, 'Bred, we're going for coffee. Ivan's coming. You join us?'

'Did Ivan say—'

'Ivan ain't told me to invite you, blood,' Adam cut in. 'I'm asking cos I'm asking.'

'Cool.' It was the only word that Joel could think of, and when he said it, he felt idiotic. But if Adam Whitburn wanted to tell him how *un*cool it was to say something was cool, he didn't do so. He merely said, 'Le's go, den. It ain't far. Just over Portobello Road.'

The coffee house was called Caffeine Messiah, less than a ten-minute walk from Oxford Gardens. Its furnishings were entirely religious, mostly given to statues of Jesus and rosary beads hanging from old chandeliers. A group of rickety tables had been pushed together at one end of a room lined with holy cards, which had been enlarged to poster size, featuring the sombre images of martyred saints. At battered chairs around these tables sat ten of the poets from *Wield Words Not Weapons*, along with Ivan. They were speaking to each other over the coffee house's choice of music, a Gregorian chant played at a non-heavenly volume.

They were served by a nun, or so she seemed until she came to get Joel's order and he saw that she had a pierced eyebrow, a ring through her lip, and tears tattooed down her cheek. She was called Map, and everyone appeared to know her and she them since she said, 'What's it to be? Th' regular or you changing your ways?' to several of them. Coins got tossed into the centre of the table to pay for drinks, and Joel wasn't sure if he was meant to toss his fifty pound note into the midst of the money since he had no other means to pay for whatever he ordered. As he made a move to do this, though, Adam Whitburn stopped him. He said, 'Winner don't pay, bred,' and he gave Joel a wink, adding, 'Don't make no habit of it, though, y'unnerstan? I wipe the floor wiv you next time.'

When Map had returned with their drinks and distributed them, a dark-skinned boy called Damon called them all to order. It turned out that this was no ordinary post-poetry gathering.

Joel listened and put it all together: The group were not only members of *Wield Words Not Weapons*, but also pupils of Ivan's screen-writing class. Their meeting was about the film they were attempting to develop and, as Joel took all of this in, he saw how they'd divided the labour. Adam and two others – Charlie and Daph – had completed a fifth revision of the screenplay. Mark and Vincent had spent several weeks scouting out locations. Penny, Astarte, and Tam had sorted out equipment suppliers. Kayla had contacted the talent agents. Then Ivan made a report on funding, to which everyone listened in earnest as he spoke of the potential investors he'd managed to unearth. From all of this, Joel began to see that making a film was no pipedream to them. They were actually going to do it, with Ivan organising the experience for them and none of them wondering why a white man with no apparent need to find himself suitable employment would want to spend his time offering them options for a different kind of life than the one to which their circumstances otherwise propelled them.

Joel sipped his hot chocolate and listened in wonder. He was used to the people around Edenham Estate and other estates. He was used to his grandmother and her hopeless relationship with George Gilbert. These people had always spoken of what they intended to do on a someday that never came: fantastic holidays spent in villas in Bermuda or the south of France; cruising around the Mediterranean on a rich man's yacht; buying a brand new home on a sparkling housing estate where everything worked and the windows all had double glazing; zooming a fast car through the countryside. Even the youngest of them had impossible dreams of becoming rap singers with mountains of cash, of being cast on a night-time soap. Everyone talked this sort of rubbish, but no one ever expected to do it. No one even knew where to begin.

But that was not the case with this group. Joel could see they intended to make things happen, and he could not sit there and not want to be part of that.

They didn't ask him. Indeed, once their meeting began, they forgot all about his presence. But he didn't mind this as it seemed to indicate a dedication to their cause. This dedication to cause instilled in him a dedication to his own cause. He would join their team and help make the dream become real.

He determined that he would talk to Ivan about this the next time they met. It would mean more time away from home, more time away from Toby. It would mean relying on Ness to help him care for their little brother. But Joel was confident he could talk her into it. On this night, his life became filled with dreams.

21

Joel was not the only person in the Campbell clan to have sudden hope visited upon him. Ness, too, was blessed with it although she did not recognise it at first. Fabia Bender brought it to her at the child drop-in centre, accompanied as always by Castor and Pollux. When the social worker came through the chain link gate, two separate reactions emanated from Ness and from Majidah. The former felt her back go up, assuming that Fabia was checking up on her. The latter – having never actually met the social worker but only having spoken to her on the phone – took one look at the dogs and raced out into the play area, coatless in the cold, damp weather and waving her arms.

'No, no, no!' she cried. 'These beastly creatures have no place within these confines, madam. Aside from the danger they present to small children, there is the not small matter of defecation and urination, which cannot be tolerated. No, no, no, no.'

Fabia was surprised at the strength and volume of Majidah's protest. She said, 'Down, dogs,' and turned to reassure the Asian woman. 'Castor and Pollux only do their business on command,' she said. 'And neither of them will move from this spot until they're instructed to do so. You must be Majidah, if I may call you by your first name? I'm Fabia Bender.'

'*You?*' Majidah clucked in disapproval. She'd had another picture of the social worker, and it had to do with twin sets, pearls, tweed skirts, brogues, and very thick tights. It certainly had nothing to do with blue jeans turned up at the ankles and pristinely white trainers. Not to mention berets, polo-necked sweaters, donkey jackets, and cheeks red from the cold.

'Yes,' Fabia said. 'I've come to see Ness. She's here, isn't she?'

'Where else would that girl be? Come in, come in. But if those animals move so much as an inch, I must ask you to tie them to the fence. This is a very dangerous business, you know, dogs like that running wild like so many wolves in the street.'

'I'm afraid they're far too lazy for running wild,' Fabia said and to the animals, 'Stay, dogs, or you'll become this lady's dinner. Does this satisfy, Majidah?'

The irony was lost. 'I do not eat meat that is not *halal*,' she said.

From inside the drop-in centre's cabin, Ness had watched the exchange. Behind her, a group of three-year-olds and their mothers were playing a game of catch-and-fall-over with brightly coloured inflatable balls. Much laughter and squealing accompanied this. Across from them several five-year-olds were building a stronghold from cardboard boxes painted to look like blocks of stone. Ness's job was to supervise and to fetch whatever the players required: more balls, more cardboard boxes, rubber mats to prevent excited children from smacking their heads on the lino. They were coming up to a snack time as well so, as Fabia Bender came into the cabin, Ness retreated to the kitchen where she began assembling biscuits and milk on large metal trays.

Fabia joined her, looking pleased. Ness assumed her expression had to do with finding a subject of probation doing exactly what she was supposed to be doing while on probation. But when Fabia spoke, it was on another subject.

She said, 'Hullo, Ness. I have some news. Some *very* good news, I might add. I think we've come up with a solution that's going to allow you to attend that course at the college.'

Ness had given up hope of this. Anything other than her dismal music appreciation course during the autumn term was a long-ago impossibility at this point, and, when that had become apparent to her, she'd dismissed the thought of millinery altogether, bitterly concluding that anything Fabia Bender had said about looking into matters in order to help her finance her dream was just an example of the social worker blowing smoke to placate her.

But Fabia was there to prove her wrong. She said, 'We've got the money. It took some doing because most funding had already been allocated for the year, but I did manage to find a rather obscure programme based in Lambeth and . . .' Fabia brushed aside the rest of the explanation. 'Oh, the details don't matter. What does matter is the course itself and getting you into it for the winter term.'

Ness could hardly believe things had fallen into place since the rest of her life had never given her an indication that such could possibly happen. But now . . . The certificate course would mean that she had the opportunity for a real career, not merely a job at which she worked day after day just waiting for something to happen to alter her circumstances.

Still, life had taught her to be cautious about excitement. She said, 'They going to accept me? Dat course started in September, innit. How'd I catch up wiv the rest of the girls if I missed the opening? They give the same courses in the winter term? Cos they ain't letting me join up if I missed the first part, are they?'

Fabia drew her eyebrows together. It took her a moment to unravel what Ness was talking about. Then she realised. They were going at two slightly different subjects. She said, 'Oh. No, no. Not the *certificate* course, Ness. Wouldn't it be lovely if I'd managed to find full funding for that? But alas, I haven't. What I do have is one hundred pounds for a single course. I've had a look at the college catalogue and there *are* single courses available.'

'Jus' one . . . ? Oh. Yeah. Well. Figgers.' Ness didn't attempt to hide her disappointment.

Fabia was used to this sort of reaction. She said, 'Hang on, Ness. You can only take one course at a time anyway. You've got your work to do here, and I can assure you that the magistrate has bent as far as he's going to bend when it comes to you. He isn't going to rescind the requirement for community service. That's something we can't even think about, my dear.'

Ness said in less than gracious fashion, 'So wha' course is it, den?'

'There are three actually, so you have your choice. But there's one small problem, although it's hardly insurmountable. None of the courses – and this includes the entire certification programme, by the way – are offered here at the Wornington Road college site.'

'Then where the hell're they offered?'

'At a place called the Hortensia Centre. Near Fulham Broadway.'

'Fulham *Broad*way?' It might as well have been the moon. 'How'm I s'posed to get down to Fulham Broadway, wivout money for transport? Like you say, I got to do community service here. I can't do dat an' get a job 's well to pay for transport – if there was any jobs, which there ain't. And anyways, what's one bloody course at some Hortensia Centre going to do f'r me? Nuffink, far 's I c'n see.'

'I did think your aunt might be able to—'

'She works in a *charity* shop, Fabia. Wha' d'you t'ink she makes for doing dat? I ain't asking her for money. Forget dat shit.'

Majidah had come to the kitchen door, having heard the agitation in Ness's voice, not to mention the volume, her grammar and her choice of language. She said, 'What is this, Vanessa? Have you forgotten there are small and impressionable children in the very next room? They are ears and sponges. Have I not told you this more than once? Profanity is an unacceptable form of expression in this building. If you cannot find another means of sharing your displeasure, then you must leave.'

Ness said nothing in reply. She merely slammed the biscuit containers back into the cupboards. She took the trays through to the playroom as a means of ending her conversation with Fabia Bender, which gave Majidah time to learn what it was that had caused her agitation. By the time Ness was back in the kitchen, the Asian woman knew it all. Particularly she'd concluded that Ness's interest in millinery had been the result of her visit to Sayf al Din's studio in Covent Garden. Majidah was secretly thrilled by this. Ness was openly embarrassed. Ness hated the thought of fulfilling anyone's expectations of her and, while she could not know what Majidah's expectations were, the fact that her interest in millinery had arisen from her visit to the Covent Garden studio was enough to suggest that Majidah was somehow responsible. In Ness's mind that gave the Asian woman power, and power was the last thing Ness wanted her to have.

'So,' Majidah said when Ness set the trays down on the worktop. 'This is how you react to a small setback, is it? Miss Bender brings you news – which any other human being of reasonable intellect would be forced to consider good, is this not the case? – and because it is not *precisely* the news you wish to hear, you throw the apples out with the bathwater, do you not?'

'What're you on about?' Ness asked irritably.

'You know very well what I'm "on" about. Girls like you, they are all the same. They want what they want in an instant. They want it tomorrow. They want it yesterday. They want the result without being capable of sustaining the effort to get to the result. They want to be . . . I do not know . . . some skinny sickly catwalk model, an astronaut, the archbishop of Canterbury. What does it matter? They always approach it the same way, do they not? And this is to say they have no plan. But even if they *did* have a plan, what would it matter since they cannot attain what they wish to attain by dinner-time? This is the problem with you girls. And boys as well. Everything must happen to you at once. You have an idea. You want the result. Now, now, now. What nonsense this is.'

Ness said, 'You finished? Cos I don't got to stand here and listen to you rave, Majidah.'

'Oh, but that is exactly what you *do* have to do, Miss Vanessa Campbell. Fabia Bender has found you an opportunity, and you bloody well will take it. And *if* you do not, then I shall have to ask her to find you another community service placement, for I cannot be expected to put up with an adolescent girl without any brains, which is what you will be indicating you seriously lack if you do not accept the money to take the millinery course.'

Ness was struck dumb by Majidah's use of the word *bloody*. So she made no immediate reply.

For her part, Fabia Bender was less unrelenting than the Asian woman. She told Ness to think about her offer. One hundred pounds was the best she could do. There might be more money available in the spring and summer, setting students up for the autumn term. But, as for now, it was a take it or leave it proposition. Ness could think it over, but since the enrolment period was fast coming upon them, perhaps she didn't want to think it over for too long . . . ?

Ness would not need to think it over at all, Majidah said, if *she* had anything to say about it. She would accept, she would be grateful, she would attend, she would work hard.

Well and good, Fabia told the Asian woman kindly, but Ness would have to be the one to answer.

Majidah was determined what Ness's answer would be, so the very next day she ordered her over to her flat for late afternoon tea once the child drop-in centre was locked tight as a drum with its security lights switched on for the night. She made her usual stops in Golborne Road, purchasing courgettes from E. Price & Son, haddock from the corner fish-monger, and a loaf of bread and carton of milk from the grocery. Then she marched her charge on to Wornington Green Estate and up to her flat where she put on the kettle. She instructed Ness to get the tea things ready, telling her that a third cup, saucer, and spoon would be required but not telling her who the additional tea-drinker would be.

That became apparent soon enough. As if the boiling water were a herald, the sound of a key sliding into the door of the flat announced the arrival of Sayf al Din. He did not imme-diately enter, though. Rather, he cracked open the door and called out, 'Ma? Are you decent?'

'What else would I be, you foolish boy?'

'Lovemaking with a rugby player? Dancing in the nude like Isadora Duncan?'

'And who might that be? Some nasty English girl you've met? A replacement for that dentist of yours? And why might she need a replacement, I ask you? Has she at last run off with the orthodontist? This is what comes of marrying a woman who looks into other people's mouths, Sayf al Din. It should not surprise you. I told you from the first it would happen.'

Sayf al Din came into the kitchen as his mother was speaking. He leaned against the door jamb and tolerantly listened to her expound on her favourite topic. He was carrying a covered dish, which he extended to her when she had concluded her remarks.

'May has sent you lamb *rogan josh*,' he said. 'Apparently, she had time to spend in the kitchen between her trysts with the orthodontist.'

'Am I not able to cook my own meals, Sayf al Din? What does she think? That her mother-in-law has lost her wits?'

'I think she's trying to win you over, although I don't know why. All things being equal, you're an utter monster, and she shouldn't bother.' He came to her side and kissed her soundly, setting the covered dish on the worktop.

'Hmmph,' was his mother's response. She looked pleased, however, and she peeked beneath the foil covering and sniffed suspiciously.

Sayf al Din said hello to Ness as he poured boiling water into the teapot and gave it a few swishes to heat the porcelain. He and his mother fell into a rhythm of making tea together and, as they did so, they talked family matters quite as if Ness were not in the room. His brothers, their wives, his sisters, their husbands, their children, their jobs, a new automobile purchase, an upcoming family dinner to celebrate a first birthday, someone's pregnancy, someone else's DIY remodelling project. They brought tea to the table, accompanied by Majidah's poppadums. They sliced a fruitcake and toasted bread as well. They sat, they poured, they used milk and sugar.

Ness wondered what she was to make of all this: mother and son in harmony together. It left her with a raw feeling inside. She wanted to leave this place, but she knew Majidah would not permit it because she also knew Majidah's ways by now and one of them was to do nothing without a purpose. She would have to wait to see what that purpose was.

This became clear when the Asian woman took an envelope from the window-sill where it stood propped behind the treasured photo of herself and her first husband, the father of Sayf al Din. She slid this across the table to Ness and told her to open it. They would, she said, then speak further on a topic most important to all of them.

Inside the envelope, Ness found sixty pounds in ten pound notes. This, Majidah told her, was the money she needed for transport. It was not a gift – Majidah did not believe in giving gifts of cash to adolescent girls who were not only not relatives but also quasi-criminals in the midst of fulfilling their sentences to community service – but rather a loan. It was meant to be repaid with interest, and it *would* be repaid if Ness knew what was good for her.

Ness made a not illogical assumption about the use to which this money was to be put. She said, 'How'm I s'posed to pay dis back if I'm going to dat class and working in the drop-in centre and I got no job?'

'Oh, this is not money for your transport to Fulham Broadway, Vanessa,' Majidah then informed her. 'This is to be used to travel to Covent Garden, where you will *earn* the money for transport to Fulham Broadway as well as the money to repay this loan.' To Sayf al Din, she said, 'Tell her, my son.'

Sayf al Din did so. Rand was no longer in his employ. Her husband, alas, had put a stop to her working in the same room as another man, even draped in her claustrophobic *chador*.

'Foolish idiot,' Majidah interjected redundantly.

Sayf al Din thus had to hire a replacement for her. His mother had told him that Ness was interested in millinery so, if she wished for employment, he would be happy to take her on. She wouldn't earn a fortune, but she would be able save enough – after repaying Majidah, his mother put in – to finance her transport to Fulham Broadway.

But hadn't Rand worked for Sayf al Din full-time? Ness wanted to know. And how could she do Rand's work – or even a small part of her work – when she still had to do her community service?

That, Majidah informed her, would not be a problem. First of all, Rand at work had all the speed of a tortoise under anaesthetic, her vision being occluded by that foolish black sheet she insisted upon wearing as if Sayf al Din would ravish her on the spot had he the opportunity to lay his eyes upon her. It would hardly take a full-time employee to replace her. Indeed, a one-armed monkey could probably do the job. Secondly, Ness would divide her day into two equal parts, spending half the time fulfilling her sentence of community service and the other half working for Sayf al Din. That, by the way, had already been arranged, cleared, signed, sealed, and delivered by Fabia Bender.

But, Ness said, when was she supposed to take the millinery course? How was she supposed to do all three things: work for Sayf al Din, fulfil her obligations to community service, and take the millinery course as well? She *couldn't* do all three.

Of course she could not, Majidah agreed. Not at first. But once she became used to working instead of lolling about like most adolescent girls, she would find she had time for many more things than she thought she had time for. At first, she would merely work for Sayf al Din and do her community service hours. By the time she had the rhythm and endurance to take on more, another school term would have arrived and she could take her first millinery course then.

'So I'm s'posed to do all three t'ings?' Ness asked, incredulous. 'Take the course, work in the millinery studio, do community service? When am I s'posed to eat an' sleep?'

'Nothing is perfect, you foolish girl,' Majidah said. 'And nothing happens by magic in the real world. Did it happen to you by magic, my son?'

Sayf al Din assured his mother that it had not.

'Hard work, Vanessa,' Majidah told her. 'Hard work is what follows opportunity. It is time you learned that, so make up your mind.'

Ness was not so intent upon instantly being gratified in her desires that she failed to see a door opening for her. Because it wasn't *exactly* the door she wanted, though, she didn't embrace the idea with full-hearted gratitude. Nonetheless, she agreed to the scheme, at which point Majidah – always a woman to think ahead – produced an entirely unenforceable contract for her to sign. This included specific hours of community service, specific hours of work for Sayf al Din, and the schedule of repayment of the sixty-pound loan, with interest of course. Ness signed it, Majidah signed it, and Sayf al Din witnessed it. The deal was concluded. Majidah toasted Ness in typical fashion:

'See that you do not fail, you foolish girl,' she said.

* * *

Ness began her work with Sayf al Din at once, after her morning hours at the child drop-in centre had been completed. He set her to menial tasks at first but, when he was engaged in something that he believed would advance her education, he told her to join him and to watch. He explained what he was doing, with all the fire of a man engaged in work that he was meant by God to do. During this, Ness's brittle carapace of self-preservation began to fall away. She didn't know what to make of this, although someone with a bit more wisdom might have called it the needful death of anomie.

Kendra, it must be said, felt such relief at the change in Ness that she let down her guard when it came to Joel. When he talked with enthusiasm about the screen-writing class that Ivan Weatherall offered, and in particular about the film in development by Ivan's band of street kids, she gave her blessing to his involvement in this project as long as his marks in school improved. Yes, he could be gone on the occasional evening, she told him. She would mind Toby and Ness would mind Toby when Kendra could not. Even Ness agreed to the plan, not with good grace but then anything other than marginally intolerant compliance would have been out of character.

Had Joel not been a marked man in the street, things might have proceeded smoothly. But there were forces at work far greater than the Campbell children and their aunt, making North Kensington a place unsafe for harbouring or advancing dreams. Neal Wyatt still existed on the periphery of their lives and, while some circumstances had altered for the Campbells, this was not the case for Neal. He continued to be a lurking presence. There were scores to settle.

Respect remained the key for sweetening the bad blood between Neal and Joel. For his part, Joel intended to develop that in one way or another. It just wasn't going to happen in the way that Hibah had intimated it should happen: with Joel submitting to the other boy like a dog flipping on to its back. For Joel knew what Hibah gave no evidence of knowing about life in a place like North Kensington: there were only two ways to be entirely safe. One was to be invisible or of no interest to anyone. The other was to have everyone's respect. Not to *give* respect away like so much discarded clothing, but to garner it. To give it away, as Hibah suggested, meant to seal your fate, making you a lackey, a whipping boy, and a fool. To garner it, on the other hand, meant that you and your family would be able to survive.

Joel's route was still the Blade. His safety and the safety of his brother rested in his alliance with the Blade. Joel could raise his marks in school; he could write bullet-proof poetry that brought tears to the eyes of everyone in *Wield Words Not Weapons*; he could take part in a film project that put his name in lights. But those accomplishments would gain him nothing in the world through which he had to walk every day because none of them were capable of reducing anyone else to fear. Fear came in the person of the Blade. To forge an alliance with him, Joel knew he would have to prove himself in whatever way the Blade ordered him to do so.

Cal Hancock brought Joel the assignment weeks later. He did it with two words, 'Time, mon,' as he created a roll-up for himself, leaning against the window of a launderette on Joel's route to Middle Row School from the bus stop in the late afternoon.

'F'r what?' Joel asked.

'What you wanted, depending on if you still wan' it.' Cal looked away from him, down the street where two old ladies walked arm in arm, each supporting the other. Cal's breath steamed in the icy air. When Joel didn't reply, he turned back to look at him. 'Well? You in or out 'f dis business?'

Joel was in, but he hesitated, not because he was worried about what the Blade would ask of him but rather because there was Toby to consider. He was meant to take his brother from school to the learning centre, and that was going to occupy another hour. Joel explained this to Cal.

Cal shook his head. He told Joel in short order that he couldn't pass that information along to the Blade. It would disrespect the man by indicating something else was more important than fulfilling his wishes.

'I don't mean to disrepeck him,' Joel said. 'It's only dat Toby . . . Cal, he knows Toby i'n't right in the head.'

'Wha' the Blade wants, he wants tonight.'

'I c'n do what he wants. But I can't let Toby try to get home on his own from school. It's already getting dark, and only time he tried to get home alone, he got set on.'

Joel would have to solve the problem, Cal said. If he couldn't solve this one, he wasn't going to be able to solve any others. He would have to go his way; the Blade would have to go his. Perhaps that was all for the best.

Joel tried to think what he could do. His only option seemed to be the age-old excuse used by every child who doesn't want to do what he is meant to do. He decided he would feign illness. He would phone his aunt, tell her he'd sicked up at school, and ask her if she thought he should still fetch Toby. She would say no, naturally. She would tell him to go straight home. She would lock up the charity shop for a while and herself dash out to take Toby from school to the learning centre. She would then keep Toby with her till it was time for them both to go home for the evening. All things being equal, by the time she returned to Edenham Estate, Joel himself would be there as well, having demonstrated loyalty and respect to the Blade.

He told Cal to wait and he went to a phone box. In a few minutes, his plan was in motion. Cal asked him if he'd thought things through.

'I ain't stupid,' was Joel's reply. 'I know how t'ings go. The Blade does summick for me, I owe him. I got dat, Cal.' He hiked up his trousers as a means of emphasising his readiness.

It was a let's go gesture: ready for anything, ready for it all, time to show the Blade his mettle, time to show commitment.

Cal examined him sombrely before he said, 'Come wiv me, den' and began striding towards the north, in the direction of Kensal Green.

He walked without conversation and without pause to see if Joel was still with him. He didn't stop walking until they came to the high brick wall that enclosed the crumbling overgrown ruins of Kensal Green Cemetery. Here, at the large gates leading into the place, he finally looked at Joel. Joel couldn't imagine what he was going to be asked to do, but robbing a grave came to mind and it didn't hold much appeal.

An arch comprised the entrance. It gave way to a square of tarmac and a keeper's lodge where light shone through a curtained window. The tarmac itself marked the starting point of the cemetery's main road. This veered off towards the west, strewn with the decomposing leaves of the many trees that grew, scattered and untrimmed, in the grounds.

Cal set off down this lane. Joel tried to see the delicious adventure of it all. He told himself it was going to be a bloody good laugh, carrying out an assignment in this creepy place. He and Cal would attack some grave in the fast-coming darkness, and they'd jump behind a lopsided tombstone should a guard stroll by. They'd take care not to tumble into one of the collapsing gravesites that signs along the lane warned them about and, when they were done, they'd hop the wall and be on their way with whatever prize the Blade wished them to unearth. It was, he decided, like a scavenger hunt.

In the growing early darkness of winter, however, the cemetery was a grim location, not conducive to the sense of adventure Joel wished to feel. With enormous wing-spread angels praying on monuments, mausoleums shrouded by swathes of ivy and every inch of space overgrown with shrubbery and weeds, the cemetery was more like a ghoul town than it was a resting place for souls. Joel half-expected to see ethereal spirits emerging from broken-down tombs and headless ghosts flitting above the undergrowth.

Unpaved muddy tracks led off the main lane and, in the dying light, Cal took one of these. Some fifty yards along, he disappeared altogether through a thick stand of Italian cypresses and, when Joel ducked through them a moment later, he found himself facing a large and lichenous tomb. This had long ago been fashioned to resemble a chapel, but there was masonry where its three stained-glass windows had been, and the door that once gave access to the little structure was buried by junipers so densely planted that only a machete could have hacked through them.

Cal was nowhere to be seen, and the idea of ambush came upon Joel with a rush. His previous consternation grew in proportion to his realisation that no one knew where he was. He thought of Cal's words of warning, of his own bravado. He muttered 'Shit' and listened as hard as a frightened boy can listen. If someone was going to jump him now, he reckoned that he could at least try to sort out from what direction the danger would come.

It would come from above, it seemed. Joel heard a rustling that appeared to emanate from the cypresses, and he backed away. An old wooden bench stood some three yards from the chapel-shaped tomb, and he made for this and climbed upon it, as if this action would somehow protect him. But there he noticed what he could not see when he stood at the base of the chapel itself. Although its gabled roof had at one time been fashioned from large rectangles of slate, a number of them were missing, leaving a gaping hole that opened the tomb's interior to the elements.

The noise Joel heard was coming from inside the tomb and, as he watched, a shadowy form rose from within. It lifted head and shoulders above the wall and then a leg followed. All of it was black except the feet, which were dingy white and dressed in trainers.

Joel said, 'What the hell you *doing*, blood?'

Cal heaved himself over and dropped lightly from the chapel wall to the ground, a distance of some ten feet. He said, 'You ready, mon?'

'Yeah, but what're you *doing* in there?'

'Seeing.'

'What?'

'Dat t'ings all right. C'mere, den. You're inside.' Cal jerked his thumb at the tomb.

Joel looked from him to the opening in the roof. 'Doing what?'

'Waiting.'

'For what? How long?'

'Well, dat's it, innit. Dat's wha' you don't know. The Blade wants to know do you trust him, spee. You don't trust him, he don't trust you. You stay till I fetch you, blood. You not here when I fetch you, the Blade knows who you are.'

Despite his youth, Joel saw the ingenious nature of the game. It was contained in the simplicity of not knowing. An hour, a day, one night, a week. One rule only: put yourself into someone else's hands entirely. Prove yourself to the Blade before the Blade was willing to prove himself to you.

Joel's mouth was drier than he would have liked. 'What 'f I'm caught?' he said. 'Ain't my fault 'f some guard comes by and hauls me out, innit.'

'What guards you t'ink stick their heads in tombs if they don't got reason to do it? You quiet, blood, no one comes looking. You in or out?'

What choice was there? 'In,' Joel said.

Cal made a stirrup of his hand and Joel mounted. He felt himself hoisted on to the wall, where he straddled the top and looked down into the well of darkness below. He could see dim shapes only, one of them looking like a ghostly body under a pall of decomposing leaves. He felt a tremor at the sight of this and he glanced back at Cal, who was watching him, silent.

Joel drew a deep breath, closed his eyes and, with a shudder, dropped into the tomb.

He landed on leaves. One of his shoes sank through to a sodden depression and the cold rose around him as his foot hit water. He cried out and jumped back, half-expecting a skeletal hand to reach up, begging for rescue from a liquid grave. He could see virtually nothing inside the rectangular chamber, and he only hoped his eyes would adjust quickly from the muted light of the graveyard to the darkness in here so that he might know with whom – or with what – he would be spending his time.

Cal's voice came like a whisper from the distance. 'All right, bred? You in?'

'S'okay,' Joel said although he hardly felt that way.

'You hang till I come.' Then Cal was gone, in a rustle of branches that indicated he was making his way back through the Italian cypresses.

Joel smothered the protest that he wanted to give. This was nothing, he told himself. This was just proving to the Blade that he had the bottle to gut something out.

His hands felt clammy, so he rubbed them along the sides of his trousers. He remembered what he'd made out from the wall of the tomb just before he dropped down to its interior base. He steeled himself to the sight of a body, telling himself it was dead, long gone, improperly buried, and that was all. But he'd never really seen a body before, not one that was out in the open, exposed to the elements, decomposing, with rotting flesh, grinning teeth, and worms eating out its eyeballs.

The thought of that body just behind him somewhere made Joel's lips quiver. He became aware that his own body was shivering from head to toe, and he understood that in this place the cold of the night intensified because of the damp stone walls around him. Like Dorothy in Oz, he thought of home. He thought of his aunt, his brother, his sister, his bed, eating dinner around the table in the kitchen and watching a cartoon video with Toby afterwards. But then he made himself stop such thoughts because his eyes were filling. He was acting like someone who couldn't bloody even *cope*, he thought. He remembered how easily Cal had appeared to climb out of the tomb and he understood that he wasn't trapped. He didn't have to do something for which he might get into trouble with the law. All he had to do was wait, and he surely had the bottle to do that.

Thus reassured, he made himself take action. Since he couldn't stand there for ever with his face to the wall simply because he shared space with a body, he forced himself to turn and confront it. He pivoted with his eyes squeezed shut. He balled his fists and slowly raised his eyelids.

Adjusted to the darkness, his eyes picked out what they hadn't been able to see earlier. The body was missing a nose; part of its cheek was caved in. It was dressed in some sort of flowing gown whose folds surged through the fallen leaves. All of it was white: the body itself, the head of hair upon it, the hands folded on the abdomen, the gown that clothed it. It was stone, Joel realised, an internal effigy that decorated the tomb.

He saw that a tartan blanket was folded over the effigy's feet. It bore no leaves, which meant it had been placed there recently, and probably for him. He picked it up and beneath it found two bottles of water and two packaged sandwiches. He'd be there for a while.

He unfolded the blanket and wound it around his shoulders. He boosted himself up to the legs of the effigy and settled in for a lengthy stay.

Cal didn't return for Joel that night. Nor did he return the next day. The hours crawled by and the low winter sun never once warmed the inside of Joel's place of waiting. Still, he remained. He was committed. While it was true that he was cold and – despite the sandwiches – growing hungrier by the minute, that more than once he'd had to relieve himself in a corner beneath a pile of rotting leaves, that he'd barely dozed off during the night and every sound had startled him into wakefulness, he told himself that a pay-off was coming and the pay-off would make this waiting worthwhile.

He started to doubt this on the second night. He began to think that the Blade meant him to die in Kensal Green Cemetery. He understood how easily that could happen. He was in a tomb already; it hadn't been opened in years and probably *wouldn't* be opened again. He and Cal had come to the spot in near darkness and if anyone had seen them sauntering along in the direction of the entrance to the cemetery, what would they have thought of it? There were many places they could have been heading: the underground station, a superstore across the canal, even all the way to Wormwood Scrubs.

He considered climbing out at this point. When he examined the interior walls of the tomb, he saw that it would be easy enough for him to scale the ten feet. But the list of what ifs that accompanied the idea of departure stopped him. What if he climbed out just at the moment Cal was coming for him? What if the Blade was nearby, watching and waiting, and saw his disgrace? What if he was seen by a groundsman or a security man? What if he was collared and hauled into the Harrow Road police station again?

As to his family and the what ifs they were conjuring up as this second night approached, he did not think of that. His aunt, his brother, and his sister were merely blips on the screen of his consciousness.

The second night passed slowly. It was terribly cold, and a soft rain fell. It became a long and windy fall of rain that soaked his blanket, which in turn soaked his school trousers. He had only his anorak as protection from the weather, but it would be useless by morning if the rain did not cease, and Joel knew that.

The sky was turning light when he finally heard the sounds

he'd been waiting for: the swooshing of cypress branches and the sucking noise of trainers falling on saturated ground. Then Cal's voice came softly. 'You there, blood?'

Joel, crouching in the inadequate shelter of the damaged slate roof, got to his feet with a grunt. 'Here, bred,' he said.

'Have it knocked good, den. You make it out okay?'

Joel wasn't sure, but he said that he could. Hunger made him dizzy, and cold made him clumsy. It would, he thought, be a sodding hell of a thing if he broke his neck trying to get out of this place.

He tried several times. He had success on his fourth attempt. By that time, Cal had climbed the wall and was straddling the top, extending a hand to him. But Joel wouldn't take it, so close was he to passing the Blade's test completely. He wanted Cal Hancock to carry a message back to Mr Stanley Hynds: he did it all, and he did it by himself.

He lifted his leg over the wall and straddled it, mimicking Cal's posture although, unlike Cal, he was forced to cling to the stones like a shipwreck survivor. He said, 'You tell him, mon,' before he was out of strength. He toppled to the ground.

Cal hopped down and helped him to his feet. 'Okay?' he asked earnestly. 'Noise going down 'bout where you been.'

Joel squinted at Cal, his head feeling weak. He said, 'You rampin', mon?'

'Hell no. I been by your drum and there's been cops wiv your aunt. I 'spect you in for it when you get home.'

'Shit.' Of all things, Joel hadn't thought of this. Like most of their people, his aunt was no fan of the police, and he found it difficult to believe that she'd phoned them. He said, 'I got to get home. When c'n I talk to the Blade, den?'

'He ain't taking your part wiv the cops. On your own f'r dat, blood.'

''S not what I meant. I got to talk to him 'bout dis bloke needs sorting.'

'He'll sort him when he's ready,' Cal said.

'Hey!' Joel protested. 'Di'n't I just—'

'Don't work like dat.' Cal led Joel through the cypresses, and along the muddy path towards the cemetery's central lane. There, he took a moment to clean the bottom of his trainers on a spot in the tarmac where the fallen leaves had blown away during the night. He looked around – in the manner of a man searching for eavesdroppers – and said in a low voice and without looking up from his shoes, 'You c'n stop dis, bred. You got dat power.'

'Stop what?' Joel asked.

'Blood, he mean you *harm*. Y'unnerstan? No way he means to end it wiv dis.'

'Who? The Blade? Cal, I gave him the flick knife. And you weren't there when we talked. We got t'ings sorted between us. We're cool.'

'He don't sort t'ings, spee. He i'n't like dat.'

'He was straight wiv me. Like I said, you weren't there. And anyways, I done what he asked. He c'n see I'm straight wiv him. We c'n go on.'

Cal, whose eyes had been cast on his shoes during this, raised his head. He said, 'Where 'sactly you t'ink you're going? The Blade sort dis bloke, you *owe* him, y'unnerstan? You got family, bred. Whyn't you t'ink 'bout dem?'

'Dat's what I *am* doing,' Joel protested. 'Wha' you t'ink I'm doing dis for?'

'Dat's a question you best start asking,' Cal returned. 'What you t'ink *he* doing dis for?'

22

When he made the turn into Edenham Way, Joel saw that Dix D'Court's car was parked in front of his aunt's house. He was cold, wet, tired, and hungry, and all he wanted was to fall into bed, which sadly reduced his ability to fast-talk his way through the coming encounters. He ducked behind a wheelie bin and there he stayed for several minutes, trying to work out what he was going to say to his aunt when he finally faced her. The truth would hardly do.

He thought at first that he might stay behind the bin until Kendra left the house to go to work for the day, which would be sooner rather than later. She'd have to get Toby off to school and Ness would be off as well, which would leave the house empty at that point, since Dix surely wouldn't hang about once Kendra was gone. Joel would have the day, then, to cook up something . . . if only he managed to wait.

But waiting was exactly what Joel was not able to do. Seven minutes behind the wheelie bin was enough time to tell him he could remain outside in the cold no longer. He eased his way out and trudged to the front door. He hauled himself up the four steps like a dead man walking.

He put his key in the lock, but this was enough noise to alert his family. The door jerked open. He expected to see his aunt there, furious and ready to pounce, but it was Ness who had her hand on the knob and Ness whose body blocked his path. She took one look at him and said over her shoulder, 'Aunt Ken, the lit'l sod's home.' And then to Joel, 'You in for it, mon. We got cops calling round, we got school on the phone,

we got Social Services involved. Where you *been*, 'sactly?' And
then in a lower voice, 'Joel, you doping up or summick?'

He didn't answer, and there was no need, for the door was
jerked wide open and there stood Kendra. She was still dressed
in the clothing she'd had on two days ago. Red rimmed her
eyes, and bruised flesh half-mooned beneath them. Like Ness,
she cried out, 'Where you *been*? What's been . . . Who've you
been . . .' and then she simply wept. It was a release of pent-
up stress, but as Joel had never seen his aunt cry before this,
he did not know what to make of it. She grabbed him and
hugged him fiercely, but the hug turned into fists beating
against his back, although with all the force of a humming-
bird's heartbeat.

Over her shoulder, Joel saw Toby come out of the kitchen
in his cowboy pyjamas, clattering across the lino in his cowboy
boots. Beyond him, Dix D'Court stood in the centre of that
room, his face expressionless. He watched for a moment before
he came to the door and gently disengaged Kendra from Joel.
He turned her to him and took her into his arms, giving Joel
a disgusted shake of the head before he led Kendra in the
direction of the stairs. Before he mounted them, he said to
Ness, 'Best phone the cops and tell 'em he's back.'

Ness shut the front door and went to make the call. She
left Joel where he was, experiencing a form of solitary confine-
ment that he hadn't expected, one that he found far worse
than being left in a tomb for two nights. It felt unfair to him
that he was being treated like some sort of pariah instead of
being welcomed home with celebration and relief. He wanted
to say, D'you lot *know* what I been through for you?

Toby inadvertently added to Joel's sense of indignation. He
said unnecessarily, 'Dix come back, Joel. Aunt Ken phoned
him up to help when you di'n't come home cos she thought
you might've been wiv him at the gym or summick. Ivan said
he di'n't know where you were—'

'What? She rang Ivan?'

'She rang ever'one. It was late when she phoned Ivan. She thought he took you to a film or summick but he say no. Den she thought you got in trouble wiv the cops, so she phoned dem. Af'er dat, she thought maybe dat bloke Neal set 'pon you an'—'

'Okay. Shut up,' Joel said.

'But I wanted—'

'Hey. I said shut up. I don't care. Shut up.'

Toby's eyes filled. This was a Joel he did not know. He came to him and tugged on the sleeve of his anorak, saying, 'You got wet. You wan' to change your clothes, innit. I got a jersey from the charity shop when Aunt Ken come to school to fetch me an' you c'n borrow—'

'Shut up shut up shut *up*!' Joel pushed Toby to one side. He went through to the kitchen. Toby ran for the stairs with a sob. Joel hated himself for having hurt his brother's feelings, but he also hated Toby for being so dim that he couldn't take an order without having to be shouted at.

Ness was completing her phone call as Joel went to the kitchen table and slumped into a chair, pillowing his head into his crossed arms, which he folded upon a mass of tabloids that lay open on the table's surface. He wanted only to be left alone. He didn't understand why everyone was reacting so much, as if he'd committed the crime of the century when Ness had been out all night more than once without coming home to a scene like this. He told himself that the lot of them were acting like he'd faked his own suicide or something.

Ness said to his bowed head, 'You really done it, blood.' She lit a cigarette, and the acrid scent of sulphur from the match and then from the burning tobacco came to Joel and made his stomach churn. 'Fabia Bender stopped by, talking 'bout time to send you some place to be sorted out 'fore you *really* get into trouble. Cops went crawling through ev'ry room like we murdered you. Some detective even went and tried to get some sense out of Mum, innit. I say dis: When you shit, mon, you do it like an elephant. So where you been?'

Joel shook his head but he didn't raise it. He said, 'Why'd she go off her nut?'

'You ain't *heard*?'

At this Joel wearily raised his head. Ness came to the table, cigarette dangling from her lips, and gestured him to move his arms from the tabloids. She closed one of them – it was the *Mirror* – and she flipped it so that its front page faced him. 'Have a look at dis,' she said. 'Aunt Ken thought . . . Well, I 'spect you got brains enough to sort it out.'

Joel dropped his gaze from his sister to the tabloid. **ANOTHER BODY** blazed across the top of the page. Beneath the headline, three photographs showed a railway arch obstructed by sawhorses and crime scene tape, a clutch of people in earnest conversation, and a lone blond man in an overcoat, talking on a mobile and identified as a Scotland Yard detective superintendent. Joel looked up from this to his sister, saying, 'I don't get it. You saying Aunt Ken was t'inking . . . ?'

''*Course* she t'inking,' Ness declared. 'What else you 'spect? You i'n't home when you say you home being sick. She rings dat bloke Ivan and *he* says he ain't seen you, but dat's after she been trying to get him on the line for hours and she t'inks he did summick to you cos of these newspaper stories, innit. So she gives the cops a bell, and *they* drag dis Ivan to the station and grill him—'

'*Ivan?*' Joel groaned. 'Cops talked to Ivan?'

'Hell yes, what else you t'ink? So they give him aggro and all the time you're . . . where?'

Joel stared at the tabloid. He couldn't believe so much had happened simply because he was gone for two nights. And what had happened couldn't have been worse: the involvement of the local police, Ivan being harassed, the Youth Offending Team alerted through the person of Fabia Bender, upon whose radar Joel already had a position. He felt light-headed with all of the information. He brought the tabloid back into focus.

'Boys been getting taken all over London,' Ness was saying. 'Dis one here in th' paper, he's like number five or six or whatever. They been just round your age. So when you don't come home and Aunt Ken sees dis story in th' paper – Cordie brought it over, di'n't she – she t'inks dis body's you, innit. So you cocked t'ings up proper, y'unnerstan. You in f'r it, and I'm glad I ain't you.'

'She's right in dat.' It was Dix speaking. He'd come back down the stairs. He looked at Joel with the same expression of disgust he'd had on his face when Joel had come through the door. He carried a glass in his hand, and he took it to the sink and rinsed it out. 'Where you been, Joel? What you been doing?'

'Why'n't you stop her fr'm calling the cops?' Joel directed his question to both of them, and he asked it in despair. His aunt had complicated his entire situation more wildly than he ever would have expected, and right on the brink of his sorting out everything on his own. She was, he concluded, making a dog's dinner out of all his efforts.

Dix said, 'Mon, I asked you a question. I want an answer.'

This sent Joel's back up. It was the tone of it, the daddy tone. Whatever Dix was in their lives, the one thing he wasn't was their father. Joel said, 'Hey. Bugger off. I don't got to tell you—'

'You,' Dix cut in, 'best watch your mouth.'

'I c'n say what I want. You don't run my life.'

Ness said, 'Joel,' in a tone that blended warning with appeal, and this in itself was something unusual. For Joel, it put his sister directly into the enemy camp. He shoved himself away from the table and made for the stairs.

'Don't t'ink dis conversation i'n't going to be picked up later on,' Dix told him.

Joel said, 'Whatever,' and began to climb.

He heard Dix following, and he thought that the body-builder meant to force him to cooperate by resorting to a physical confrontation. But rather than trail Joel into his room, Dix went into Kendra's and shut the door.

She was on the bed with one arm over her eyes, but she removed it when he sat down next to her, his hand coming to rest on her thigh. She said, 'He say anything?'

Dix shook his head. 'Dis i'n't good,' he told her. 'How it start when boys go bad, Ken.'

'I know,' she said wearily. 'I know, I know. I got a ex-husband in Wandsworth, you recall, and I c'n see him all over Joel just now. He's involved in something – running drugs? breaking into houses? car jacking? mugging half-crippled pensioners? – and tha's how it starts, don't think I don't know cause I do, Dix. I *do*.'

'You got to cut dis off.'

'You think I'm blind to that? I already got him wiv a mentor in school only now I called the cops on the man, so I can't 'spect him to want to go on mentoring, can I? Meantime, the social service woman mentions a place across the river where boys like Joel go to get sorted but it's all the way in Elephant and Castle and I can't have him trekking there every day after school cause I need his help wiv Toby . . .' She plucked at the chenille counterpane on the bed. Since her head was aching and she hadn't slept in two days, there were no answers for Kendra.

So Dix supplied the only answer he knew. 'Needs a dad,' he said.

'Well, he doesn' *have* a dad.'

'Needs someone to stand in place of his dad.'

'I figured that bloke Ivan—'

'Ken. Come on. White man? Dat partic'lar white man? You see him as someone Joel likely to become? Cos dat's wha' he needs: someone standing in front 'f him in place of his dad and dat someone being someone he might like to become.'

'Joel's part white.'

'So're you. But dis ain't *about* being white, innit. It's 'bout being practical and figgering what the boy's likely to admire.'

'So what d'you suggest?'

To Dix it was evident. He would move back in, he told her. He missed her and he knew she missed him. They would make things work this time. The only reason they hadn't worked before was that he'd been too consumed with his body-building to pay sufficient attention to her and to the kids. But that didn't have to be the case now. He would change his ways. He had to, hadn't he?

Kendra pointed out to him that the case just now was even worse than it had been before, since his own dad was still recovering from a heart attack and Dix was, as a result, spread even more thinly. But Dix argued that the situation was actually improved and that it offered them possibilities they hadn't yet discussed. Kendra wanted to know what these possibilities were. Dix told her that Joel could work at the Rainbow Café, earning himself some honest money and staying out of trouble at the same time. He could also go to the gym with Dix. He could otherwise go to school, help out with Toby, and continue with his poetry events. He wouldn't have the leisure necessary to get into trouble. And he'd also have a man of colour to act as a role model, which he badly needed.

'An' you want nothing in return?' Kendra asked him. 'You do all this out of the goodness of your heart? Why is it I don't believe that much?'

'I ain't 'bout to lie. I want you like I always want you, Ken.'

'You say that today, but in five years . . .' Kendra sighed. 'Dix. Baby. I can't *give* you what you want. You got to know that at some level, man.'

'How c'n you say dat,' he asked her, touching her cheek fondly, 'when you're giving me th' only t'ing I want right now?'

So Dix returned to them and to the outside world they resembled a family. Dix proceeded with caution, but at twenty-three

– albeit soon to be twenty-four – he was out of his depth with a teenaged girl, a soon-to-be teenaged boy, and an eight-year-old with needs vastly outweighing Dix D'Court's ability to meet them. Had these been ordinary children in ordinary circumstances, he might have stood a chance as foster-father to them – despite his youth – because it was clear, even to them, that he did actually mean well.

But Ness wasn't having any part of a father-figure seven years her senior and Joel wasn't interested. Instead he was confident that, having proved his worthiness to the Blade, matters with Neal Wyatt would soon be taken care of. And, once matters with Neal were taken care of, life could go on and they all would be reasonably secure. So Joel rebuffed Dix's well-intentioned attempts at what might be called male bonding. Too little too late, was what he thought of Dix's invitations to the gym and his offer of after-school employment at the Rainbow Café. Besides, he didn't take the invitations or the offer seriously since he could nightly hear the enthusiastic resumption of sexual relations between Dix and his aunt. This, he believed, was the real reason for the body-builder's return to Edenham Way, and he knew it had nothing to do with any of the Campbells or Dix's interest in practising his paternal skills.

Dix was patient with Joel's reluctance. Kendra was not. She put up with Joel's indifference to Dix's overtures for only a few days before she decided to intervene. She did so once he'd gone to bed, on a night that Dix was at the gym. She went to the boys' bedroom and found them in pyjamas, Joel on his side with his eyes closed and Toby sitting with his back against the battered headboard, skateboard across his knees, disconsolately spinning its wheels.

She said to the little boy, 'He asleep?'

Toby shook his head. 'He breathes funny when he's asleep and he ain't.'

Kendra sat on the edge of Joel's bed. She touched the side

of his head and his crinkly hair depressed like candyfloss beneath her fingers. She said, 'Sit up, Joel. We got to talk.'

Joel continued with his pretence of sleep. Whatever she wanted with talking to him, he decided it couldn't be good. He'd so far managed to keep her in the dark about what he'd been doing out all night, and that was the way he wanted to keep it.

She put her hand on his rump and gave it a tap. 'Come on now,' she said. 'I know you're not sleeping. It's time for a talk.'

But what she wanted to talk about was precisely what Joel wanted to keep hidden. He told himself that he couldn't talk to her for the simple reason that she would not understand. Despite the fact that they were blood relations, her life was too different from his. She'd always had people she could depend upon, so she would never understand what it meant to be completely on her own: reliant but with no one reliable on the horizon. She didn't know how that felt.

He mumbled, 'Wan' to sleep, Aunt Ken.'

'Later. You c'n talk to me now.'

He scrunched his body into a ball. He held on to the blankets so she could not pull them off had she a mind to do so.

She sighed. 'Right,' she said and her voice altered to full Lady Muck, causing Joel to steel himself to what was to come. 'You're making a decision, Joel, and that's a fine and adult thing to do as long as you're willing to live with the consequences. D'you want to think about that? D'you want to hang on to your decision or alter it?'

Joel said nothing. She said his name, less patiently now, less a reasonable woman making a reasonable request. She said, 'We've been trying to help you out, but you've not met us halfway. Either me or Dix. You want to play your cards close, I s'pose that's your right. But since I don't know what's going on with you, I got to do my duty to keep you safe. So home, school, home again. Fetch Toby from his school and that's all. That's your life.'

Joel's eyes opened, then. 'That ain't fair.'

'No poetry events, no visits to Ivan. No trips to see your mum unless I take you out there and bring you back. We'll see how you cope with all that for the next two months, and then we'll renegotiate things.'

'But I *di'n't* do—'

'Don't take your auntie for a fool,' she said. 'I know this whole situation goes back to that little lout you've been having run-ins with. So I'm taking care of that as well.'

Joel squirmed around then. He sat up. Her tone suggested what was coming next, and he sought a way to head her off. 'It ain't nuffink,' he told her. '*He* ain't nuffink. Dis is all jus' summick I had to do, okay? I di'n't break no laws. No one got hurt.'

'We'll be working on your English as well,' she said. 'No more street talk.'

'But Dix talk—'

'And that brings us to Dix. He's trying his best with you lot. You meet him halfway.' She stood. 'I held off before, but I'm not holding off any longer. It's time the police—'

'You *ain't*—'

'English.'

'You can't get *into* this, Aunt Ken. Please. Just let it go.'

'Too late for that. Two nights away from home that you're not talking about, Joel . . . They make it too late.'

'Don't do it. Don't *do* it,' Joel pleaded with her.

His very protest told Kendra that Neal Wyatt was indeed the source of what was going wrong in Joel's life. Burning the barge, assaulting Toby in the street, threatening her in the charity shop . . . She was going to phone the police and *something* was going to stick to this boy. If nothing did at this point, at least he'd be warned.

Hibah was the one who broke the news to Joel. She found him waiting for the bus after school, but she didn't say anything until he'd made his way inside, where the crowded conditions forced both of them to stand, swaying with the bus and clinging to the poles.

She said to him in a low fierce voice, 'Why'd you grass, Joel? Don't you *know* how bloody stupid tha' was? You know what he want to do to you now?'

Joel saw that her face was pinched beneath her headscarf. He said, 'I di'n't grass no one. What're you talking 'bout?'

'Oh, you di'n't bloody grass,' she scoffed. 'How'd Neal end up wiv the cops 'f you di'n't grass, Joel? They had him down the station 'bout that stupid barge. *And* 'bout shaking up people in the street, your bruvver included. If you di'n't do that, who bloody did?'

Joel felt air whoosh out of his lungs. 'My aunt. She must've cos she said she would.'

'Your aunt, oh yeah,' Hibah said in derision. 'An' she know Neal's name wivout you telling her? You are such a damn fool stupid idiot, Joel Campbell. I tell you how to cope wiv Neal and dis is what you decide. You vex him, and he set for you now. An' don't think I can help you cos I can't. Y'unnerstan' dat, mon? You got no brains.'

Having never heard Hibah express herself with such passion, Joel saw the further jeopardy he was in. And not only him, because he knew that Neal Wyatt was clever enough and determined enough to get to him through his relations as well, as he'd already proved through Toby. He cursed his aunt for her failure to see what her interference in his affairs might bring about.

Joel decided something had to be done. Even if the Blade *had* done his part and sorted out Neal Wyatt, the fact that Neal's name had been given to the cops cancelled out everything and fired up Neal's enmity once again. The long and short of it was that Kendra couldn't have done more to make matters worse.

After thinking through his options, Joel came to believe Ivan

Weatherall was the answer to at least part of his problem. Ivan, poetry, and *Wield Words Not Weapons* constituted the door through which he would walk in order to make things right.

Joel hadn't seen Ivan since a week before the cemetery fiasco and what had followed it when Kendra had given the white man's name to the Harrow Road police. But Joel knew the days on which Ivan came to Holland Park School, so he put in a request to see the mentor and waited to be called into his presence. Despite what had occurred, he was confident Ivan would see him, Ivan being Ivan after all, optimistic about young people to the point of foolishness. So Joel prepared himself by writing five poems. They were little more than doggerel, but they would have to do. Then he waited.

He felt a rush of relief when he was called to meet his mentor. He took his five poems with him, and he did some Machiavellian mental gymnastics in order to convince himself that using a friend was not such a terrible thing to do if the use to which that friend was put was in a good cause.

He found Ivan not seated at their regular table but rather standing at the window looking out at the grey January day: trees leafless, ground sodden, shrubbery skeletal, sky sombre. He turned when Joel came into the room.

Something was required of Joel at this moment, a bridge that would take them from Kendra's phoning the police about Ivan to where they were now. It seemed that only an apology would suffice, so Joel made that apology, which Ivan accepted as was his nature. It was, he confessed, more embarrassing than anything else. He'd had a script-writing class on the first night Joel had been gone and a dinner with his brother on the second night, so he was 'thick with a sufficiency of alibis', as he put it wryly. But he would not lie to Joel about matters. It was embarrassing to have to account for his whereabouts and distressing to have the police insist upon searching his property for signs that Joel had been held hostage . . . or worse. 'That didn't go down well with my neighbours, I'm afraid,'

Ivan said, 'although I suppose I ought to consider it a mark of distinction, being taken for a serial killer.'

Joel winced. 'Sorry. I should've . . . I di'n't think, see . . . Aunt Ken had a conniption, Ivan. She saw the news 'bout those kids being killed, those boys the same age 's me, and she thought . . .'

'Of me. Logical, I suppose, all things considered.'

'Ain't logical at all. Mon, I am sorry dis happened, y'un-nerstan?'

'I'm quite recovered from it,' Ivan said. 'Do you want to talk about where you were those two nights?'

Joel definitely did not. It was nothing, he said. Ivan could take his word. It had nothing to do with anything illegal like drugs, weapons, crimes against fellow citizens or the like. As he spoke, he brought out his poems. He said he'd been writing as he knew this would divert Ivan from conversation about Joel's two nights away from home. He had poems, he said. He could tell they weren't very good, he confessed, and he wondered if Ivan would take a look . . . ?

This was raw meat to a starving lion. The fact that Joel had been writing poetry indicated to Ivan – however falsely – that all was not lost when it came to his young friend. He sat at the table, drew the poetry to him, and read. The room was hushed and expectant, as was Joel.

He'd come up with a way to explain why the poetry was so wretched. No quiet place to write, he'd say, if Ivan wanted to talk about the general deterioration of his work. Toby watching the telly, Ness talking on the phone, radio playing, Aunt Ken and Dix going at it like monkeys up above in the bedroom . . . This did not make for the solitude required for inspiration to translate itself into words. But until things changed at home – which meant until the restrictions on his movements were somewhat lifted – this was probably the best he'd be able to do.

Ivan looked up. 'These are very bad, my friend.'

Joel let his shoulders sink, a motion of spurious defeat. 'I been trying to sort how to fix 'em, but maybe they're just ready for the bin.'

'Well, let's not throw out the baby,' Ivan said, and he read them another time. But when he'd done so, he looked even less hopeful. He asked the question Joel was waiting to hear. What did Joel think had altered his writing so very much?

Joel went through his list of prepared excuses. He made no suggestions for rectifying the situation, but he did not need to do so when Ivan's entire conditioning programmed him to make the suggestion himself. Would Joel's aunt consider lifting part of the restrictions she had in place, in order to let Joel attend *Wield Words Not Weapons* once again? What did Joel think?

Joel shook his head. 'No way c'n I ask her. She's dat cheesed off wiv me.'

'What if I phoned her? Or stopped by the charity shop to talk?'

This was exactly what Joel hoped for, but he didn't want to seem overly enthusiastic. He said that Ivan could certainly try. Aunt Kendra felt dead bad about having put the cops on to Ivan in the first place, so she might want to do something to make up for that.

All that remained was waiting for the inevitable, which didn't take long to happen. Ivan paid a call upon Kendra that afternoon, taking with him Joel's five poems. They had never met so when Ivan introduced himself, Kendra felt a rush of chagrin. She dismissed this quickly, however, telling herself that she'd done what the situation called for when Joel had gone missing. When a white man involves himself with black kids, she reckoned, he has only himself to blame if something happens to one of them and he gets suspected of malfeasance in the aftermath.

The fact that Ivan was so ready to let the issue go melted any resistance to his ideas that Kendra might have had. The ideas were simple enough anyway: Ivan explained that Joel's writing, which was surely the best representation of his future, was suffering under the restrictions his aunt had placed upon him. While he – Ivan – had no doubt these restrictions were absolutely well-deserved, he wondered if Mrs Osborne might lift them just enough to allow Joel to return to *Wield Words Not Weapons*, where he would be once again exposed to other poets whose criticism and support would not only improve his verse but also allow him to mix with people of all ages – young people included – who were engaged in a creative act which kept them off the streets and out of trouble.

As Dix's efforts with Joel – taking him daily to the Rainbow Café – had not paid off, as Fabia Bender was still suggesting an outside influence to keep Joel on the straight and narrow, as *Wield Words Not Weapons* was at least convenient, and Joel's attendance there did not involve a long bus ride to the other side of the river to some programme about which Kendra knew nothing, as she could wrest from Joel his word of honour that he would attend the poetry meetings and then return home . . . Kendra agreed. But if she found out he'd gone anywhere besides *Wield Words Not Weapons* on a night on which the poetry meeting took place, she would sort Joel in ways that currently defied his imagination.

'We clear on that?' she asked her nephew.

'Yes, Aunt Ken,' he told her solemnly.

Inside, Joel was clicking along, making plans. Neal had resurfaced, which was hardly a surprise. He kept his distance, but still he watched and Joel never knew where he would see him next. The other boy seemed capable of simply materialising, as if some force scrambled the atoms of his being, transported him, and reassembled him wherever he wished to be. He also seemed to have contacts everywhere – boys whom Joel had not associated with Neal – and these contacts shoved into Joel hard when crowds were about, murmured Neal's name at bus stops or in Meanwhile Gardens, shouted out a greeting to a Neal who could not even be seen just outside Toby's school. Neal Wyatt became like an undercurrent, and Joel knew that he was merely biding his time as he waited for the moment when he'd be able to settle the score that Kendra had built up when she'd given his name to the cops.

All of this told Joel that he had to return to the Blade. *Wield Words Not Weapons* gave him the opportunity. When the regular night for the meeting came around, he set off with his aunt's warning in his ears. She'd be ringing Ivan to make sure he went to *Wield Words* and nowhere else. Did he understand? He said that he did.

He didn't have so much a plan as knowledge, which he intended to use. He'd been to enough poetry evenings to know how Ivan organised them. When it came time for *Walk the Word*, those who weren't up for the challenge afforded themselves of the refreshments, mingled, talked poetry, and sought out Ivan and each other for private help with their work. What they didn't do was keep an eye out for what one twelve-year-old boy was up to. That, Joel decided, would be his moment, but he needed a bad poem to make it work.

He made certain that everyone knew he was in the Basement Activities Centre. He mounted the dais and read out one of his worst pieces. At the end of his reading, he gamely suffered the silence until from the back of the room a throat cleared and someone offered a bit of criticism meant to be constructive. More careful criticism followed and a discussion ensued. Through it all, Joel did his best to act like the serious student of verse that they supposed him to be, taking notes, nodding, saying ruefully, 'Oooh. Ouch. I knew it was bad, but you lot are starting to vex me,' and going through the rest of the motions. These included a conversation afterwards with Adam Whitburn, one in which he was forced to listen to encouragement about a creative act that no longer held any importance to him.

After Adam clapped him on the shoulder and said, 'Ballsy of you to read it, mon,' it was time for *Walk the Word*, and Joel eased his way to the exit. He reckoned that anyone who noticed would conclude – as he intended – that he was slinking off in embarrassment.

He jogged the distance from Oxford Gardens to the Mozart Estate. There, he wound his way through the narrow streets to the squat that stood in Lancefield Court. It was completely dark this time, however, with no Cal Hancock at the foot of the stairs, guarding the Blade from whoever might want in on the business he was conducting.

Joel muttered, 'Damn,' and considered his next move. He hustled back through the estate and, in the dim light, he looked at the housing plan, a large metal map in Lancefield Street. This gave him nothing useful at all. The place was a sprawl and, although he knew that a girl called Veronica lived within – mother to the Blade's most recent son – he had to wonder how likely it was that he could find her and, even if he found her, how likely it was that the Blade would be there. She'd served her purpose; he'd moved on. The block of flats in Portnall Road where Arissa lived was a more likely place to find him.

Joel trotted to this location next, arriving out of breath at the building halfway down the street. But again, no Cal Hancock lounged in the doorway, which meant no Blade upstairs.

Joel felt thwarted. Time was running out. He was due home at the end of *Wield Words Not Weapons* and, if he wasn't there, there would be a hell designed by his aunt to pay. He felt defeated, and that feeling made him want to punch his hand into a dirty brick wall. There was nothing for it that he could see but to head for home.

He chose a route that would take him down Great Western Road. He began to think of another plan to find the Blade, and he was so deeply into his thoughts that he didn't notice when a car slid up beside him. He only realised it was there when his nose caught an unmistakable whiff of weed. He looked up then and saw the Blade behind the wheel of the car with Cal Hancock in the passenger seat and Arissa in the back, leaning forward to lick her man's tattooed neck.

'Blood,' the Blade said. He braked the car and jerked his head at Cal, who got out, took a hit of weed, and nodded at Joel. He said, 'Happenin', bred,' but Joel made no reply. Instead, he said to the Blade, 'Neal Wyatt ain't acting like he sorted, mon.'

The Blade smiled, without amusement or pleasure. 'Listen to him,' he said. 'Spite of everyt'ing, you are the mon. So. You ready for Rissa, den? She likes 'em young.'

Arissa's tongue came out and ran along the edge of the Blade's ear.

'You sort dat bloke?' Joel demanded. 'Cos you and me, we had a deal.'

The Blade's eyes narrowed. In the car's overhead light, the serpent on his cheek moved as the muscle in his jaw clenched. He said, 'Get in, blood,' and jerked his head towards the back seat. 'We got plans to make now you such a big *mon*.'

Cal flipped the seat forward. Joel looked at him to see if there was a sign on his face that would tell him what was going to happen next. But Cal was unreadable, and the weed he'd smoked hadn't loosened his features.

Joel got into the car. A large dog-eared *A to Z* lay open face-down on the seat. When he moved it to one side, he saw that it covered a ragged burn in the seat's upholstery. Someone had been plucking at this, and stuffing leaked out from inside.

When Cal got back into the car, the Blade took off before the door was closed. Tyres squealed like something from a bad Hollywood film, and Joel was thrown back against the seat. Arissa cried, 'Baby, *do* it.' She draped her arms over her man's chest and resumed licking his neck.

Joel kept his gaze away from her. He couldn't help thinking about his sister. She'd been the Blade's, before Arissa. He couldn't imagine her in this girl's place.

'How old're you, blood?'

Joel met the Blade's gaze in the mirror. They took a turn too fast, and Arissa slammed to one side. She giggled, rose up, and hung over the front seat to ease her hands down the front of the Blade's black sweater.

Cal glanced back at Joel and offered him a toke of his spliff. Joel shook his head. Cal jerked the spliff towards him more insistently. There was something in his eyes, a message he was meant to understand.

Joel took the spliff. He'd never smoked weed, but he'd seen it done. He sucked in shallowly and managed not to cough. Cal nodded.

'Twelve,' Joel said in answer to the Blade's question.

'Twelve. T-welve. You a tough little shit. You di'n't tell me before when I ask. You still got your cherry?'

Joel said, 'Neal Wyatt ain't acting like he sorted, Stanley. I did what you tol' me. When you doing your part?'

The Blade said to Cal, 'He still got his cherry. Dat's cool, ain't it.' With a look at Joel through the rear-view mirror, he went on with, 'Rissa likes to take boys' cherries, blood. Don' you, Riss? You wan' to take Jo-ell's?'

Arissa disengaged from the Blade and looked Joel over. She said, 'Wouldn't last long 'nough for me to get my knickers down. Wan' me to suck him 'nstead?' She reached for Joel's crotch.

Joel shoved her away before she made contact with him. He said, 'Get your bitch 'way from me, mon. We had a 'range-ment, you 'n' me. Dat's what I want to talk about.'

The Blade pulled abruptly to the kerb. Joel looked out, but he didn't know where they were. Just that it was a street some-where with tall bare trees, fancy houses, and clean pavements. It was not a part of town he recognised. The Blade said to

Cal, 'Take her home. Me and the *man* here have t'ings to discuss.' He turned in his seat and grabbed Arissa under one arm. He lifted her over – her legs flailing so that her knickers were on view – and he kissed her hard, his mouth descending on hers like a punch. He handed her over to Cal and said, 'Don't let her have any more tonight.'

Cal took Arissa by the arm. She protested, rubbing at her bruised mouth. 'Mon,' she said, 'I don' want to walk.'

'Clear your head,' he told her and when Cal shut the door, he took off again, veering into the street.

He drove rapidly and made many turns. Joel tried to memorise the route, but he soon realised there was little point. He had no idea where they'd begun this stage of the journey, so to know the path to their destination wasn't particularly useful.

The Blade said nothing to him until he parked the car. Then it was only, 'Get out,' which Joel did, to find himself standing on a street corner in front of a derelict building. It had a brick exterior that was dingy even in the night-time illumination from a street lamp some twenty yards away. It possessed peeling green woodwork and a chipped and fading sign above a garage-sized door. This said *A.Q.W. Motors*, but whatever business had been done in the building was long since finished. Boards and metal plates covered the ground-floor windows while, up above, ragged curtains indicated that someone had once occupied a first-floor flat.

Joel expected the Blade to head for this flat: yet another drum from which he could deal on the occasions when the Lancefield Court squat became too hot. But, instead, the Blade took him around the side and towards the back. There, an alley gaped, shadows broken only by a single bulb of light burning on the back of a building some distance away.

Behind A.Q.W. Motors, a brick wall enclosed a yard of some sort. A metal gate gave access to this yard and while it bore a lock which looked both official and impenetrable, this was not the case. The Blade took a key from his pocket and used it. The gate swung open soundlessly, and the Blade jerked his thumb to indicate Joel was meant to go inside.

Joel stood his ground. There was little point to anything else since, if the Blade intended to finish him off, he was going to do so no matter how Joel responded to the situation. He said, 'We talking about Neal Wyatt or what?'

'How much mon is mon?' the Blade replied.

'I ain't playing riddles wiv you. Fuck it, blood. It's cold as hell 'n' I got to get home. 'F dis is just some sort 'f bullshit game—'

'You t'ink everyone stupid just cos you are, bred?'

'I ain't—'

'Get inside. We'll talk when we talk. You don't like dat, you find your way home. Nice warm bed, cup of Ovaltine, bedtime story. Whatever it takes.'

Joel cursed for effect and went through the gate. The Blade followed him inside.

It was dark as pitch within the yard, a place of shapes. Only by waiting for his eyes to adjust would Joel see anything. At that point, the shapes became old wheelie bins, packing crates, a trunk, a discarded ladder, and weeds. At the back of the building, bricked-up doors gave access from the interior to a concrete platform. This extended the entire length of the building, raised four feet above the ground. Joel understood from this that they were at the back of an abandoned underground station – which was above the ground in this part of town – one of many in London that had come and gone with the adjustment of the population and the alteration of various lines throughout the city. The arched doorways into the building gave mute testimony to that fact.

The Blade made his way across the yard and across the broken remains of two railway lines. He leapt on to the platform and went across it to a secondary door. This was also metal and of the kind to keep out squatters and other vagrants, but it provided no problem for the Blade. He unlocked the padlock as before and went inside. Joel followed him.

The old underground station had been altered in its use: from a transport centre to a car repair shop. The icy air within still smelled of petrol and oil, and when the Blade clicked on a lantern he'd picked up near the door, it was to reveal that the old ticket window remained in place and an ancient map overhung with dust still displayed routes that were eighty years old. The rest of the place bore signs of different use: shelving for tools, a hydraulic lift, hoses dangling from the ceiling. Beneath these, someone had stacked wooden crates of a recent vintage. The Blade went to these and used a screwdriver to lift the top of one of them.

From what he knew of the Blade, Joel expected the contents of the crates to be drugs. He expected to be told that he was to make bicycle deliveries like so many other boys his age in North Kensington. This conclusion not only vexed him, but it put swagger into his voice. He said, 'Look. We talking or what, blood? Cos if we ain't, I'm out 'f here. I got more to do 'n stand round and watch you massage your goodies.'

The Blade didn't even glance his way. His shook his head fondly and said, 'You the mon, spee, ain't you? Lord, I got to watch my back round you.'

'You c'n watch whatever you wan' to watch,' Joel said. 'You helping me or not?'

'Did I say not?' the Blade asked him quietly. 'You want him sorted, he gonna be sorted. But all t'ings considered dat been happening lately, he jus' ain't being sorted like you had in mind.'

That said, the Blade straightened and turned to Joel. He held something in the flat of his hand, but it wasn't a bag of cocaine that he extended. It was a gun.

'Jus' how much mon is mon?' he said.

23

The Blade drove Joel back to Edenham Estate, and all the way the weapon lay in Joel's lap like a cobra coiled. He had no intention of using it. Touching it had been unnerving enough. The Blade had thrust it at him – handle first – and told him to get used to it: the heft and the feel, cold metal and power, and everyone in the street from now on looking at him and seeing a real man. A real man was capable of violence, so no one messed a real man about. Respect was the order of the day when someone had a decent skeng upon him.

There were no bullets for the piece, and Joel was glad of that. He could only imagine what the future might have held had the weapon actually been loaded: Toby coming upon it no matter how well he had stowed it away; Toby thinking it was a toy and firing it without knowing it could kill; Toby shooting Joel by accident, shooting Ness, shooting Kendra, shooting himself.

The Blade reached across him and opened the door. He said, 'We straight on dis, mon? Y'unnerstan how t'ings go down?'

Joel looked at him. 'Dis is all? You sort out Neal after? Cos I ain't—'

'You calling the Blade a liar?' His tone was hard. 'Seems to me you do what the Blade wants doing, not th'other way round.'

Joel said, 'I did Kensal Green Cemetery like you wanted. How d'I know you ain't just going to ask for summick else, I do dis?'

'You don't know, bred,' the Blade replied. 'You just show you trust. Trust and obey. Dat's how it works. You don't trust the Blade, the Blade got no reason to trust you back.'

'Yeah. But if I get caught—'

'Well, dat's th' point, Jo-ell. 'F you get caught, wha' you going to do? You grass the Blade or you play dumb? Wha'll it be? Anyway, see you don't get caught. You c'n run, innit. You got a piece. What d'you 'spect to happen you take some care?' He smiled, taking out a spliff and lighting it, watching Joel over a flame that made his eyes look as if sparks danced in them. 'You a clever little sod, Jo-ell. Dat's your whole family. Clever as hell. So I see you doing dis job jus' fine. An' look at it like another step, blood. Bring you one bit closer to who you meant to be. So take that piece now, and get going, mon. Cal'll let you know when you meant to act.'

Joel looked from the Blade to Edenham Estate. He couldn't see his aunt's house from this spot, but he knew what awaited him when he climbed the steps to her front door: what went for family in his world, as well as his responsibilities to them.

He had his rucksack with him from *Wield Words Not Weapons*, and he unbuckled it, shoving the pistol as far down as it would go. He got out of the car and bent to have a final word with the Blade.

'Safe, mon,' he said with a nod.

The Blade offered him a smile made lazy by weed. 'Safe, bred,' he said. 'And tell that cunt sister of yours hello.'

Joel shut the door smartly on the Blade's laughter. He said to no one, 'Yeah, I'll do that, Stanley. Fuck you,' as the car shot off along the road in the direction of Meanwhile Gardens.

Joel trudged to his aunt's house. He was deep in thought and most of those thoughts involved telling himself that he could do what the Blade was asking him to do. There was little enough risk. With Cal there to help him choose the victim – because Joel knew that Cal would not stand by idly and let him make the choice on his own without advice – how much time and effort and risk were involved in performing a street mugging? He could even make it easier on himself by simply snatching someone's bag. The Blade hadn't said he had to stand there while some Asian woman pawed through her belongings with shaking hands, looking for her purse to hand over. He'd just said he wanted Joel to take cash from an Asian bitch in the street. That was the limit of what his instructions had been. Certainly, Joel thought, he could interpret them in whatever way he wanted to.

For Joel, everything in that evening seemed to point to the ease with which he'd be able to accomplish this task for the Blade. He'd gone looking for the man, but the Blade had found him. Their entire encounter had ended just about the time that *Wield Words Not Weapons* ended as well. He was back at home unmolested and he even had notes from the critique to which he'd exposed his miserable poetry. All this could do nothing save improve his position in the eyes of his aunt. And if all that was not a sign of what he was meant to do next, what was?

Joel expected Kendra to be sitting at the kitchen table with her eyes fixed on the clock, testing the veracity of his announced plans for the evening. But when he got inside, he found the ground floor empty and dark. Sounds came from above, so he climbed the stairs. In the sitting-room, a video was playing: a gang of train robbers on horseback galloping away from a blown-up boxcar as money flew everywhere and a posse pursued them. But no one was there. Joel hesitated, listening and worrying, with his rucksack feeling heavier than it ought. He climbed the second set of stairs, where he saw a strip of light beneath his bedroom door and heard the sound of rhythmically creaking bedsprings from behind his aunt's. The latter was enough to tell him why Kendra hadn't been waiting for him. He opened his own bedroom door and found Toby awake, sitting up in bed, using marking pens to decorate his skateboard.

'Dix give 'em to me,' Toby told Joel without preamble. He was referring to the pens. 'He bring 'em home from the caff wiv a colouring book 's well. Colouring book's for babies, but I like the pens good enough. He brought a video dat I was meant to watch cos he want to do Aunt Ken.'

'Why di'n't you watch the video?' Joel asked.

Toby examined his artwork closely, squinting at it as if this would alter its merit in some way. 'Di'n't like to watch it by myself,' he said.

'Where's Ness?'

'Wiv dat lady an' her son.'

'What lady and her son?'

'From the drop-in centre. They went for dinner some place. Ness even phoned and asked Aunt Ken could she go.'

This was a startling development, which caused Joel no little wonder. It marked change in Ness and while the courtesy of a phone call to her aunt wasn't an earth-shattering event, it gave Joel pause.

Toby held up the skateboard for his inspection. Joel saw that he'd drawn a lightning bolt upon it, making it multicoloured and most of the time staying within the original lines he'd sketched out. Joel said, 'Nice, Tobe,' and he set his rucksack on his bed, all too aware of what it contained and determined to put it somewhere safe – like in his old suitcase under a pile of summer clothes – as soon as Toby fell asleep.

'Yeah,' Toby said, 'but I'm t'inking, Joel.'

''Bout what?'

'Dis board. If I do it up nice and we take it to Mum, d'you t'ink it might make her better? I like it a lot and I wan' to keep it, but if Mum had it from me an' if you told her what it was an' all dat . . .'

Toby looked so hopeful that Joel didn't know what to tell him. He understood what his brother was thinking. If he made the ultimate sacrifice for their mother, wouldn't that somehow mean *something* to God or to whoever decided which person fell ill, which person stayed ill, and which person recovered? For Toby, giving Carole Campbell the skateboard would be akin to giving her the lava lamp. It would be a case of hand over something you love above all else and surely the recipient of this object would see that she counted so greatly in your life that she would want to be part of it.

Joel doubted it would work, but he was willing to give it a try. He said, 'Next time we go, Tobe, we take that skateboard. But you got to learn to ride it first. You get good on it, you c'n show Mum. That'll take her mind off what's bothering her and maybe she c'n come home.'

'You t'ink?' Toby asked, his face bright.

'Yeah. Dat's what I think,' Joel lied.

The hope of Carole Campbell's improvement existed in varying degrees within her children. Its presence was greatest within Toby, whose limited experience had not yet taught him to be leery of having expectations. In Joel it was a fleeting thought whenever he had to make a decision that involved the care and protection of his family. In Ness, however, Carole was a passing and summarily rejected thought. The girl was too busy to entertain fantasies in which her mother returned to their lives as the whole and functioning human being she had never been.

Majidah and Sayf al Din were largely responsible for this. As were having a plan for the future and a route to follow in achieving that plan.

Ness first paid a call upon Fabia Bender at the Youth Offending Team's offices in Oxford Gardens. She told the social worker that she would be pleased and *extremely* grateful – these last two words, including the emphasis, were spoken at Majidah's insistence – to accept the scholarship or grant or charity money or whatever it was that would allow her to take a single millinery course during the next term at college. Fabia declared herself delighted with this information, although she'd been brought into the picture by Majidah every step of the way to this destination. She allowed Ness to lay out the entire plan and she expressed interest, encouragement, and delight as Sayf al Din's offer of employment was explained to her, along with Majidah's loan, the manner of repayment, the schedule of work, the reduced hours at the child drop-in centre, and everything else remotely related to Ness's circumstances. Everything, Fabia Bender told her, would be approved by the magistrate.

Fabia used Ness's visit to ask about Joel. But on this topic, Ness was not forthcoming. She didn't trust the social worker *that* far and, beyond that, she didn't really know what was going on with her brother. Joel had become far more watchful and secretive than he'd been in the past.

Naturally, working for Sayf al Din didn't unfold the way Ness would have liked it to. In her imagination, she descended upon his studio ablaze with ideas that he embraced, allowing her access to all his supplies and equipment. Her fantasy had it that he accepted a commission from the Royal Opera House – or perhaps from a film company producing an enormous costume drama – and that commission proved far too large for one man to design by himself. Casting about for a partner, he chose Ness the way the prince eternally chooses Cinderella. She expressed a suitable amount of humble doubt about her capabilities, all of which he brushed aside. She rose to the occasion, created one masterwork after another in rapid succession, earning herself a reputation, Sayf al Din's gratitude, and a permanent creative partnership with him.

The reality was that she began her tenure in the Asian man's studio with broom in hand, far more like Cinderella's earlier life than her later days post fairy godmother's appearance on the scene. She was a one-person clean-up crew, assigned to keep the studio in order via dustpan, cleaning rags, mops, and the like. She chafed under this assignment, but she gritted her teeth and did it.

The day Sayf al Din finally allowed her to use a glue gun was thus one of celebration. The assignment was simple enough, involving beads fixed to a band that was a small part of the overall headpiece being fashioned. But even though the job was virtually insignificant, it signalled a step forward. So intent was Ness upon doing it perfectly and thus proving her superiority over the other workers that it took her far longer than it should have done and it kept her in the studio far later than she should have been. There was no danger in her being there, since Sayf al Din was working as well. He even walked her to the underground station when she was finally ready to go home for the day, to make certain she arrived there unmolested. They chatted as they walked; he promised her more work of a more advanced nature. She was doing well, she was catching on, she was responsible and she was the kind of person he wanted working with him. *With* him, he said, not *for* him. Ness burned a little more brightly at the thought of the partnership that *with* implied.

Once he'd seen her through the turnstile in the Covent Garden underground station, Sayf al Din returned to his studio to finish his own work. He had no worries about Ness getting home, since she had only to change lines at King's Cross station – which could be accomplished in the light of the underground tunnels – and afterwards, the walk to Edenham Estate from Westbourne Park station was less than ten minutes and closer to five if she was brisk about it. Sayf al Din had done his duty as prescribed by his mother, whose interest in the troublesome teenager was a source of mystification for him.

Because the delights of the day had been just that – delightful – Ness was full of future imaginings as she walked home from the underground station. Thus, she crossed over Elkstone Road with her mind somewhat fogged by her success. She walked along the edge of Meanwhile Gardens without the full consciousness required for a winter stroll along a dimly lit park in a questionable part of town.

She saw nothing. But she was seen. From halfway down the spiral stairs – and consequently sheltered from view – a group of watchers had long waited for just such a moment. They saw Ness cross over Elkstone Road and a nod was all they needed to tell them this was the girl they'd been looking for.

They moved with the silence and grace of cats, down the stairs and along the path. They hurried over the rise of land that marked one of the hillocks inside the garden, and by the time Ness reached the entrance to the place – never locked, for there were no gates – they were there as well.

'Yellow-skin bitch gonna give us some or wha'?' was the question Ness heard coming from behind her. Because she was feeling good, capable, and equal to anything, she broke the rule that might have ensured her safety. Rather than call out for help, run, blow a whistle, scream, or otherwise draw attention to her potential danger – which behaviour, it must be admitted, had only a limited possibility of success – she turned. She could tell the voice was young. She thought herself evenly matched to youth.

What she had not counted on was the number of them. What she did not realise was that this was no fortuitous encounter. There were eight boys behind her, and by the time she understood the extent to which she was outnumbered, they were upon her. One face emerged from the pack, genetically odd and further contorted by design and by loathing. Before she could put a name to that face, a blow on her back caused her to fall forward. Her arms were grabbed. She was dragged from the pavement into the park. She screamed. A hand clamped over her mouth.

'You gonna like wha' we give you, bitch,' Neal Wyatt said.

Neither Kendra nor Dix was at home when three sharp raps sounded on the front door, followed by an accented male Asian voice. Had it not been for that voice, Joel wouldn't have answered. As it was, he still hesi-tated until he heard the man say, 'You please must open the door at once, as I fear this poor young lady may be seriously injured.'

Joel fumbled with the deadbolt and jerked the door open. A familiar looking older Asian with heavy rimmed glasses, wearing *shalwar kameez* topped by an overcoat, had both arms around Ness. She was sagging against him, clinging to his coat's lapel. Her jacket and scarf were missing, and her jersey was torn at the right shoulder and otherwise splattered with filth and blood. Her proud hair was flattened. Round her jaw were ugly marks, the sort that came from trying to hold someone's mouth closed or fully open.

'Where are your parents, young man?' the man asked. He introduced himself as Ubayy Mochi. 'This poor girl was set upon in the gardens, I'm afraid.'

'Ness?' was the only thing Joel could say. 'Nessa? Ness?' He was afraid to touch her. He stepped back from the door and heard Toby coming down the stairs He called over his shoulder, 'Tobe, you stay upstairs, okay? You watch the telly? 'S only Ness, okay?'

This was as good as an invitation. Toby descended the rest of the way and came through the kitchen. He stopped short, hugging his skateboard to his chest. He looked at Ness, then at Joel. He began to cry, caught between fear and confusion.

'Shit,' Joel muttered. He himself was trapped between soothing Toby and doing something to care for their sister. He didn't know how to accomplish either. He stood like a statue and waited for something to happen.

'Where are your parents?' Ubayy Mochi asked again, more insistently this time. He urged Ness across the threshold. 'Something must be done about this girl.'

'We ain't got parents,' Joel responded, and this seemed to produce a further wail from Toby.

'Surely you do not live here alone?'

'We got an auntie.'

'You must then fetch her, boy.'

That was impossible as Kendra was out for the evening with Cordie. But she had her mobile with her, so Joel stumbled to the kitchen to phone her. Mochi followed with Ness, passing Toby, who reached out to touch his sister's thigh. He sobbed only louder when Ness flinched.

Ubayy Mochi sat Ness in one of the kitchen chairs, and this revealed more of what had happened to her. She'd worn a short skirt that day, which was now ripped to the waist. Her tights were missing. So were her knickers.

Joel said, 'Ness. Nessa. Wha' happened? Who hurt you? Who did . . . ?' But he knew who had done it, he knew why, and he knew what it meant. When he heard his aunt's voice on her mobile, he told her only that she had to come home. He said, 'It's Ness.'

'What's she done?' Kendra asked.

The unexpected impact of the question made Joel gasp for a breath that did not come easily. He disconnected the call. He remained at one side of the kitchen by the phone. Toby came to him, wanting comfort. Joel had nothing to offer his little brother.

Ubayy Mochi put on the kettle for want of something to do. Joel told him that their aunt was coming – although he didn't know this to be the fact – and he waited for the Asian man to leave. But it became quite clear that Mochi had no intention of doing that. He said, 'Fetch the tea, young man. And the milk and the sugar. And can you do nothing about that poor little boy?'

Joel said, 'Toby, you got to shut up.'

Toby sobbed, 'Someone bunged up Ness. She i'n't talking. Why i'n't she talking?'

Ness's silence was unnerving Joel as well. His sister in a rage he could cope with, but he had no resources to deal with this. He said, 'Toby. Shut up, okay?'

'But Ness . . .'

'I said shut the fuck up!' Joel cried. 'Get out 'f here. Go upstairs. Get out! You ain't stupid, so do it 'fore I kick your arse.'

Toby clattered out of the room like an animal in flight. His broken howls echoed down the stairway. He went up the next flight, and a slamming door told Joel he'd hidden himself away in their bedroom. That left only Ness, Ubayy Mochi, and the injunction to make tea. Joel set about this although in the end, no one drank a single cup of it, and they found it the next morning still brewing, a cold foul mess that was poured down the drain.

When Kendra arrived, it was to discover a tableau comprising a complete stranger, her niece, and Joel: two of them at the old pine table and the other standing in front of the sink. She came into the house, calling Joel's name. She said, 'What's going on?' before she saw them. She understood without needing to be told. She went to the phone. She punched the three nines and spoke tersely. When she had completed the phone call, she went to Ness.

'They'll meet us in Casualty,' she said. 'Can you walk, Nessa?' And to the Asian man, 'Where'd it happen? Who was it? What'd you see?'

Ubayy Mochi explained in a low voice, casting a look at Joel. He sought to protect him from disturbing knowledge, but Joel heard anyway, not that hearing was necessary at that point.

A gang of boys had set upon the young lady. Ubayy Mochi did not know where they had found her, but it was inconceivable to him that any young girl would be walking through Meanwhile Gardens by herself after dark. So they must have fetched her from somewhere else. But they'd taken her to where the footpath next to the Grand Union Canal passed beneath the bridge carrying Great Western Road over the water. There, thinking themselves safe from sight, they assaulted her and would no doubt have done even worse than they'd done but Mochi – roused from his nightly meditation practice by a single scream – had gone to the window of his small flat and had seen what was going on.

'I possess a powerful torch,' he said, 'which I find quite useful for just such moments. This I shone upon them. I shouted that I recognised them – although I fear this is not the truth – and I told them I would name them to the police. They ran off. I went to this young lady's assistance.'

'You ring the cops?'

'There was no time. Had I done so . . . Considering the length of time between a phone call and their arrival on the scene . . .' The man looked from Kendra to Ness. He said delicately, 'I believe those boys had not yet . . . I felt it imperative to see to her safety first.'

'Thank God,' Kendra said. 'They di'n't rape you then, Ness? Those boys di'n't rape you?'

Ness stirred at this, for the first time focusing on someone. She said, 'Wha'?'

'I asked did those boys rape you, Ness?'

'Like tha's the *worst* c'n happen or summick?'

'Nessa, I'm asking because we got to tell the cops—'

'No. Lemme set you straight. Rape ain't the worst. Just the *end* of the worst. Y'unnerstan me? Just the end, okay? Just the end, the . . .' And she began to cry. But on the subject of what had happened to her, she would say no more.

This continued to be the case in Casualty, where her injuries were seen to. Physically, they were superficial, requiring only ointments and plasters. In other ways, they were profound. When questioned by a youthful white constable with beads of sweat shining on his upper lip, she declared herself without memory of what had happened after the time she'd left the underground station and until she'd found herself sitting at the table in her aunt's kitchen. She didn't know who had set upon her. She didn't know how many of them there were. The constable didn't ask any whys of her, such as why she might have been targeted for assault. People were targeted for assault all the time, by virtue of being out by themselves, foolishly, after dark. He told her to take some care next time, and he handed over a pamphlet called 'Awareness and Defence'. She should read it, he told her. Half the battle against thugs was knowing what they were likely to do and when they were likely to do it. He closed his notebook and told them to come down to the Harrow Road station in the next day or two when Ness was able. There would be a statement for her to sign and, if she wished, she could look through their collection of mugshots and old e-fits – for whatever good it might do, he added unhelpfully – to see if she could pick out one or more of her attackers.

'Yeah. Right. I'll do that,' was Ness's reply.

She knew the dance. Everyone knew the dance. Nothing would be done because nothing could be done. But as things happened, that suited Ness fine.

She said no more on the matter. She acted as if the attack upon her was moving water under the bridge of her life. But that armour of indifference that she'd worn for so long prior to her acquaintance with Majidah and Sayf al Din began to cover her once again, an insentient insulation that held the world at bay.

Everyone reacted differently to Ness's unreal calm, depending upon their understanding of human nature and the level of energy they possessed. Kendra lied to herself, believing she was giving Ness 'time to recover' when in reality she was embracing the opportunity to pretend that life was returning to normal. Dix kept a wary distance from Ness, unequal to the task of being a father to her in these circumstances. Toby developed a neediness that had him clinging to all who would allow it. Joel watched, waited, and knew not only the truth but what had to be done in response.

Only Majidah took Ness on directly. 'You must not allow this matter to cloud your vision,' she said to her. 'What happened to you was terrible. Do not think I do not know that. But to give up on yourself, to abjure your plans . . . This hands triumph over to evil, and that you must never do, Vanessa.'

'Wha'ever,' was Ness's response. She went through the motions of getting on with what she'd been doing so as not to arouse anyone's suspicions, but she too watched and waited.

Joel saw Toby to Middle Row School and then himself went truant. He sought out Cal Hancock, and he found the graffiti artist in Meanwhile Gardens, generously handing over a spliff to three girls who'd rolled over their school uniform skirts at the waist to make them shorter and themselves appear sexier, a questionable manoeuvre considering the general dowdiness of the rest of their apparel. They were standing on the spiral steps, with Cal sitting below them. He saw Joel and said, 'Happenin', mon?' and then to the girls, 'Have it 'f you want,' with a nod at the spliff. They took the hint and disappeared up the stairs, passing the weed among them.

'Early for toking up,' Joel noted.

Cal gave him a lazy, drug-induced salute. 'Never too early for dat, mon. You lookin' for me or for him?'

'Here to do what the Blade wants doing,' Joel said. 'Neal Wyatt went after my sister, mon. I want him sorted.'

'Yeah? You got the means, I unnerstan'. So whyn't you sort him yourself?'

'I ain't killing him, Cal,' Joel said. 'And I ain't 'sactly got bullets for the piece.'

'So use it to scare th' fuck out 'f him.'

'Then he comes back strong 'nother time. Him and his crew. Going after Toby. Or Aunt Ken. Look. I want the Blade to do what needs being done to sort this bloke. So who's the bitch I'm meant to mug?'

Cal studied Joel before he got to his feet. He said, 'You bring the piece?'

'In my rucksack here.'

'Okay, den. Le's go.'

Cal led him out of the gardens and beneath the Westway Flyover. They passed the tube station and began to crisscross streets until they arrived at the northern section of Portobello Road, not far from where – in what felt to Joel like the far distant past – he had bought the lava lamp for Toby. There, Cal pointed out a newsagent's shop. He said, 'Turns out dis is perfec' timing, mon. She comes out reg'lar every day round dis time. You hang till I tell you who she is.'

Joel didn't know if this was the truth or a lie, but he found it didn't much matter. He just wanted to get the job done. So he positioned himself in a doorway next to Cal, the entrance to an abandoned bakery whose windows were covered in plywood. Cal lit up yet another spliff – the man had an endless supply of them, it seemed – and he handed it over. Joel took a hit and breathed in more deeply this time. He took another and then a third. He would have gone on toking up had Cal not taken the weed from him with a low laugh, saying, 'Hang on wiv dat, bred. You wan' to be able to stand, speck.'

Joel's brain felt larger. He felt more relaxed, more capable, less frightened, even rather amused by what was to happen in the next few minutes to what he thought of as some poor dumb cow. He said, 'Whatever,' and he dug around in his ruck-sack till he found his pistol. He slipped it into the pocket of his anorak, where it felt heavy and secure against his thigh.

'There she is, blood,' Cal murmured.

Joel looked around the corner of the old bakery's entrance. He saw that an Asian woman had come out of the newagent's. She wore a man's overcoat, and she limped along with the aid of a stick. A leather bag dangled from her shoulder. She was, according to Cal, 'Easy money, mon. She don't even look round to see 'f she safe. She *waiting* to be mugged. Go 'head. Take you less 'n a minute.'

It was clear that the woman didn't stand a chance, but suddenly Joel wasn't so sure how he was meant to accomplish the Blade's wishes in this matter. He said, 'C'n I jus' snatch her bag, den? Stead of making her hand over her money?'

'No way, mon. The Blade wants you face to face wiv the bitch.'

'We wait till later, den. We do it af'er dark. Try 'nother woman. Cos I run by her and grab the bag, she doesn' see me. But 'f I go face to face in daytime—'

'Shit, we look the same to 'em, mon. Go on wiv you. You going to do it, you got to do it now.'

'But I don' look the same to 'em. Let me snatch the bag on the run, Cal. We c'n tell the Blade I stuck her up. How's he gonna know—'

'I ain't lying to the Blade. He find out the truth, you don't want to be round him, b'lieve it. So go ahead. Stick her up. We running out of time on dis, mon.'

That much was true. For across the street, the targeted woman was hobbling along at a relatively steady pace, approaching the street corner. If she turned there and disappeared from view, the opportunity Joel had could easily be gone.

He ducked out of the entrance to the derelict bakery. He crossed over the road and jogged to catch up with the hobbling woman. He kept his hand curled around the gun in his pocket, sincerely hoping he would not have to take it out. The pistol scared him as much as it would likely scare the woman whose money and credit cards he meant to have.

He came upon her and grabbed her arm. He said, ridiculously, ''Scuse me,' driven by years of instruction about common courtesy. Then he altered his tone, roughing it up as the woman turned to face him. 'Give us your money,' he said. 'Hand it over. I'll have credit cards 's well.'

The woman's face was lined and sad. She seemed not all present. In this, she reminded Joel of his mother.

'I *said*,' Joel told her roughly, 'give us the money. The *money*, bitch.'

She did nothing.

There was no alternative. Joel pulled out the gun. '*Money,*' he said. 'Y'unnerstan me now?'

She screamed then. She screamed twice, three times. Joel grabbed her bag and jerked it from her. She toppled to her knees. Even as she fell, she continued to scream.

Joel shoved the gun back into his pocket. He began to run. He didn't think of the Asian woman, the shopkeepers, people in the street, or Cal Hancock. All he thought of was getting out of the area. He tore down Portobello Road. He veered around the first corner he came to. He did this again and again, going left and going right, until he found himself finally on Westbourne Park Road, where the traffic was heavier, a bus was trundling to the kerb, and a panda car was five yards away and coming steadily in his direction.

Joel halted on the edge of a hair. He looked frantically for a way to escape. He hopped over the low wall to a housing estate. He set off across a winter-pruned rose garden. Behind him, he heard someone yell, 'Stop!' Two car doors slammed in rapid succession. He kept going, for he was running for his life, for the lives of his siblings, for his entire future. But he wasn't fast enough.

Near the second building he came to, a hand clamped on to the back of his anorak. An arm went around his waist and threw him to the ground, and a foot stamped on the small of his back. A voice said, 'So what've we got here, then?' and the question itself told Joel the tale:

The cops hadn't been after him. Their presence was not the result of an Asian woman screaming on Portobello Road. How could it have been? The police got around to responding to crimes committed in the street when they got *around* to responding to crimes committed in the street. How long had it taken them to get to the scene when Joel's own father had been shot? Fifteen minutes? More? And that had been a shooting while this was simply a woman screaming in

Portobello Road. Cops didn't respond to that with their tails on fire.

Joel swore. He struggled to get free. He was hauled up till he was eye to eye with a uniformed constable possessing a face like the underside of a mushroom. The man pushed Joel back towards the street where he flung him against the side of the panda car next to which his partner was standing. The gun in Joel's pocket clanged against the metal of the car, and as the first constable cried, 'Pat! This bugger's got a weapon!' that brought the other to assist him.

A crowd began to gather and Joel looked frantically around to find Cal. He'd not had the presence of mind to toss away the Asian woman's shoulder bag, so he was caught and he knew very well he was done for. He didn't know what they did to muggers. Less did he knew what they did to boys who were caught with pistols, whether they were loaded or not. It wouldn't be good, though. He understood that much.

One of the constables took the gun from his pocket as the other put his hand on Joel's head and lowered him to the back seat of the car. The shoulder bag was thrown into the front of the car, after which the two constables climbed inside. The driver turned on the roof lights to get the gathering crowd to disperse. Joel saw faces he did not recognise as the car pulled from the kerb. None of them were friendly. Heads shook, eyes looked sorrowful, fists clenched. Joel was unsure whether all this was directed towards him or towards the cops. What he was sure of was that Cal Hancock's head, eyes, and fists were not among them.

Back at the Harrow Road police station, Joel found himself in the same interview room he'd been in before. The same individuals danced attendance on him. Fabia Bender sat opposite him in the unmoving chair at the unmoving table. At her side was DS Starr, whose black skin shone like satin beneath the room's otherwise unforgiving light. A duty solicitor had joined

Joel on his side of the table. This was a new development. The presence of a lawyer – a stringy-haired blonde girl in shoes with foolishly elongated points and a wrinkled black trouser suit – informed Joel how serious his present situation was.

August Starr wanted to know about the gun. The Asian woman was a closed book to him. She'd been scraped up around the knees, but was otherwise unharmed, aside from the fact that a few years had been taken off her life by the terror of what she'd gone through. Nonetheless, she'd had her bag returned to her, along with her money and her credit cards, so her part of the equation was solved once she identified Joel as the boy who'd mugged her. She was a signed, sealed, and delivered matter in August Starr's mind. The gun, however, was not.

In a society in which handguns had once been virtually non-existent among the thieving and murdering classes, they were now becoming disturbingly prevalent. That this was a direct result of the easing of borders that came along with European unification – which was, to some, just another term for opening one's arms to smuggling into the country every-thing from cigarettes to explosives – could have been mooted forever, and Sergeant Starr had no time for such mooting. The fact was that guns were here, in Sergeant Starr's community. All he wanted to know was how a twelve-year-old boy had got his hands on one.

Joel told Starr that he'd found the gun. Back of the charity shop where his aunt worked, he said. There was an alley there with skips and wheelie bins, all over the place. He'd found the gun inside one of them while doing some bin diving one after-noon. He didn't remember which.

Where, exactly? Starr wanted to know. He was taking notes as well as recording Joel's every word.

Just in one of the bins, Joel told him. Like he said, he didn't remember which one. It was wrapped up in someone's rubbish, in a plastic carrier bag.

What kind of carrier bag? Starr asked him, and he wrote those words – *carrier* and *bag* – in a well-schooled script on a new page in his notebook, signalling the expectation that they were at last getting somewhere and triggering in Joel the determination to lead them nowhere at all.

Joel said he didn't know what sort of bag the gun had been in. It could have been a Sainsbury bag. It could have been a Boots bag.

Boots *or* Sainsbury? August Starr made this sound like a fascinating detail. He wrote *Boots* and *Sainsbury* in his notebook. He pointed out that this was quite an odd detail since those bags were so very different from each other. They weren't even the same colour and, even if that were not the case, you wouldn't expect to find rubbish inside of a Boots bag, would you?

Joel sensed a trick. He looked at the duty solicitor in the hope she would intervene as lawyers did on the television when they talked assertively about 'my client' and 'the law'. But the solicitor said nothing. Her concerns revolved around the pregnancy test she'd administered to herself that morning, right there in the police station in the women's lavatory.

Fabia Bender was the one to speak. Boots bags were too flimsy to pack rubbish into, she explained to Joel. A gun would likely burst right through a Boots bag. So didn't Joel prefer to tell Sergeant Starr the truth? It would be far easier if he did that, dear.

Joel said nothing. He would tough it out, he decided. The best thing to do was to keep his mouth shut. He was twelve years old, after all. What were they going to do to him?

Into his extended silence, Fabia Bender asked if she might have a private word with Joel. Finally, his solicitor spoke. She said that no one was going to speak to her client – Joel was gratified to hear her use that term – without his solicitor being present. Starr pointed out that there was no cause for anyone to be unreasonable about anything since all they were trying to do at the moment was sort out the truth. The solicitor said, 'Nonetheless,' but was interrupted by Fabia Bender who declared that all anyone wanted was the best for the boy, whereupon August Starr cut in on them both but was unable to make a complete statement since the door to the interview room opened before he could say anything more than, 'Let's hang on and consider—'

A female constable said, 'C'n I have a word, Sergeant?' and Starr stepped out of the room. During the two minutes that he was gone, the solicitor gave Fabia Bender a short lecture on what she referred to as 'the rights of the accused under British law, madam, when the accused is a juvenile'. She said that she'd expected Miss Bender to know all this, considering her line of employment, a remark that set Fabia Bender off. But before Fabia could complete a reply that put the solicitor into her place, the sergeant returned. He slapped his notebook on to the table and said without looking at anyone but Joel, 'You're free to go.'

All three of them stared at the policeman in various stages of what could only be called being gobsmacked. Then the solicitor stood. She smiled triumphantly, as if she'd somehow managed to effect this development, and said, 'Come along, Joel.'

As the door closed behind them, leaving the other two within the room, Joel heard Fabia Bender say, 'But, August, what's happened?'

He also heard Starr's terse reply. 'I don't God damn bloody know, do I.'

In very short order, with a hasty goodbye from the duty solicitor and an unfriendly look from the special constable behind the reception counter, Joel was released from custody. He found himself on the pavement in front of the station: no phone call made to his aunt or to anyone else, no request for someone to fetch the wayward youth home, to school, or to a remand centre.

Joel couldn't work out what had happened. One moment he'd been seeing his freedom and his life going up in smoke. The next moment it had all been a dream. Without a slap on the wrist. Without a lecture. Without a word. It didn't make sense.

He headed up the road towards the Prince of Wales pub on the corner. He walked on psychological tiptoes, all the way expecting a cop to leap out of a doorway, laughing at the trick that had just been played on a very foolish boy. But in that, too, Joel found his anticipation went unfulfilled. Instead, he made it to the corner before a car pulled up along the kerb. Its passenger door opened. Cal Hancock got out.

Joel didn't need to look to know who the driver was. He got into the back without question when Cal nodded at him. The car shot into the street. Joel wasn't so foolish as to believe the Blade intended to drive him home.

No one spoke, and Joel found this unnerving, far more unnerving than if the Blade had railed at him. He'd failed in his mission to mug the Asian woman, and that was bad. What was worse was that he'd lost the gun. But what was worst of all was that he'd lost the gun to the cops. They'd try to trace it. It probably had the Blade's fingerprints on it. If the cops had the Blade's prints on file for some reason, there would be enormous trouble for the man. And this didn't even begin to address the money that was lost now that the gun could not be sold in the street.

The tension in the car felt to Joel like a windless, tropical day. He couldn't bear what it was doing to his stomach, so he said, 'How'd I get out, mon?' and he directed the question to the two men in the front seat.

Neither answered. The Blade turned a corner too quickly and had to swerve to avoid a colourfully garbed African woman who was using a zebra crossing. He swore and called her a fucking freakshow.

Joel said, 'Cheers, then,' referring to whatever the Blade had done to get him out of trouble. He knew that such assistance had to have come from the Blade, as there was simply no way he could have walked out of the Harrow Road police station otherwise. It was one thing to be caught trying to snatch a bag or trying to mug someone out on the pavement somewhere. That sort of thing resulted in an appearance in front of the magistrate followed by a spate of counselling with someone like Fabia Bender or a period of community service at a place similar to the child drop-in centre in Meanwhile Gardens. But it was quite another thing to have been caught with a weapon. Knives were bad enough. But guns . . . ? Guns meant more than a talking to by a well-meaning but essentially weary adult.

So Joel couldn't imagine what the Blade had done to get him out of the clutches of the police. More, he couldn't imagine *why* he'd done it unless he thought Joel was on the verge of grassing him up, in which case Joel would be in need of the kind of sorting out he'd hoped the Blade would use upon Neal Wyatt.

They headed nowhere near Edenham Estate. This reinforced in Joel's mind the thought that he was indeed going to be dealt with. Not far away lay the stretch of land that was Wormwood Scrubs. Joel knew it would be an easy matter for the Blade to march him out there – broad daylight or not – and put a bullet through his head, leaving his body for someone to find in a few hours, a few days, even a few weeks. The Blade would know where to leave his body so that it would be found when he wanted it found. And if he didn't want it found at all, the Blade would know how to manage that, too.

Joel said, 'I di'n't say *nuffink*, mon. No way.'

Cal cast him a look from the passenger seat, but there was no degree of reassurance to it. This was a different Cal entirely, a man who moved his upper lip in a way that told Joel he was meant to keep his mouth shut. Joel, though, didn't see how he would be able to do that, with his life on the line.

The Blade changed down gears, and they turned another

corner. They passed a newsagent's shop, where an advertising placard for the *Evening Standard* announced **ANOTHER SERIAL KILLING!** in boldly scrawled blue letters. That seemed to Joel like a definite portent, and he felt a resulting weight on his chest. He struggled against his desire to cry.

He dropped his gaze to his lap. He knew exactly how badly he'd cocked up. He'd forced the Blade to pull in a marker – or perhaps to pay off someone in a very big way – and there was simply no walking off with a 'Cheers, mon,' for such a favour. It wasn't, in fact, a favour at all. It was an inconceivable inconvenience, and when someone caused the Blade an inconceivable inconvenience, someone was inconceivably inconvenienced in return.

Cal had certainly tried to warn him. But Joel had assumed he had nothing to fear from the Blade as long as he didn't cross him. And he hadn't *expected* to cross him, least of all when he was in the act of doing what he'd been instructed to do.

The car finally jerked to a stop. Joel raised his head to see the *A.Q.W. Motors* sign that he'd seen before. Despite it being broad daylight, albeit a grey and rain-threatening broad daylight, they'd come to the Blade's special secret place. They climbed out of the car and went wordlessly into the deserted alley.

The Blade led the way. Cal and Joel followed. Joel tried to get a muttered word from Cal about what was going to happen next, but the graffiti artist didn't look his way as the Blade unlocked the gate in the old brick wall and jerked his head for them enter the yard of the abandoned underground station. There he unlocked the door to the erstwhile garage. As if he knew that Joel was considering making a futile run for it, the Blade jerked his chin at Cal. Cal took Joel firmly by the arm, in a grip that was neither warm nor friendly.

Inside the old garage, it was pitch dark once the Blade shut the door behind them. Joel heard the sound of a lock clicking into place and he spoke hastily into the gloom. 'I di'n't 'spect her to scream, mon. Who would've, y'unnerstan? She walked wiv a stick and she acted like she di'n't even know where she was going. You c'n ask Cal. He picked her for me to mug.'

'You blaming Cal?' The Blade's voice was close. Joel started. The man had moved near him in perfect silence, like the striking snake tattooed on his cheek.

'I ain't saying dat,' Joel protested. 'I just telling you anyone could've done like I did. When she start screaming, I had to get out of there, di'n't I?'

The Blade said nothing. A moment passed. Joel could hear himself breathing. It was a wheezy sound which he tried and failed to stop. He strained to hear something besides himself, but there didn't seem to be anything to hear. It was as if they'd all fallen down a great dark hole.

Then a *click* sounded, followed by a pool of light which formed on top of one of the wooden crates from which the Blade had taken the pistol the last time Joel had been in this place. Joel saw that the Blade had moved away from him in silence again, that he'd lit the same electric lantern that he'd used before. It cast elongated shadows against the walls.

Behind Joel, Cal *snicked* a match against something. The smell of tobacco joined the other scents – motor oil, mould, dust, and wood rot – in the icy air.

Joel said, 'Look, mon—'

'Shut the fuck up.' The Blade turned to a second crate. He prised open the top. He removed a mixture of crumpled news-papers, straw, and Styrofoam pellets, tossing all this to the floor.

Despite his fear, Joel noticed that there were many more crates in this dismal place than there had been before. He gave himself a moment to hope that their newness and number might indicate different contents, but in this he would soon be disappointed. The Blade removed an object thickly wrapped in plastic bubbles.

Joel knew how unlikely it was that, after his wretched performance in Portobello Road, the Blade was unpacking a gun to give him another try at having it taken by the cops. That meant he had another use for it, and Joel didn't want to consider what that use might be.

His tumbling thoughts led directly to the loosening of his bowels. He told himself in the roughest language he could manage that he would *not* shit his pants. If he was meant to pay with his life for his inept performance, then pay he would. But he wouldn't do it like a snivelling little wanker. He wouldn't give the Blade that pleasure.

'Cal,' the Blade said, 'you got lead wiv you?'

'Got it.' Cal brought forth from his pocket a small box, which he handed over. The Blade loaded the bullets into the weapon with the sureness of movement that indicated long practice.

Joel, seeing what he concluded his limited future would be, said, 'Hey, mon, hang on.'

'Shut the fuck up,' the Blade told him. 'Or can't you hear?'

'I only want you to unnerstan'—'

The Blade slammed home the top of the crate with such force that dust rose around it. 'You are one damn stubborn cocksucker motherfucker, ain't you, Jo-ell?' He advanced on Joel, the gun in his hand. In three steps he was there, and he jabbed the pistol beneath Joel's chin. 'This enough to get you to plug it, mon?'

Joel squashed his eyes closed. He tried to believe that Cal Hancock possessed enough humanity to not simply stand there and watch Joel be blown away to kingdom come. But Cal said nothing, and Joel couldn't hear him move. He could, on the other hand, smell the Blade's rank sweat and he could feel the simultaneously cold and fiery metal of the gun barrel shaping a coin beneath his chin.

'You know what they gen'rally do with wankers your age get caught wiv weapons?' the Blade said into Joel's ear. 'They send 'em away. Couple years in youth de*ten*tion start if off. How'd you like it in there, Jo-ell? Tossing off in the toilet for the entertainment of the sixteen-year-olds? Bending over when they tell you to afterwards cos you got yours and now they want theirs. Think you'd like that, mon?'

Joel couldn't answer. He was trying not to pee, trying not to cry, trying not to lose control of his bowels, trying not to pass out because he couldn't get enough air to fill his lungs.

'Answer me, fucker! And you best tell me wha' I want to hear.'

'No.' Joel made his lips form the word, although no sound actually came out of him. 'I wouldn' like dat.'

'Well, dat's what happens, I leave you to the cops.'

'Cheers, mon,' Joel whispered. 'I mean it.'

'Oh, fuck you mean it. I oughta blast your bloody face—'

'Please.' Joel despised himself for saying that word. It came out of his mouth before he was able to stop it.

'You know what it took, getting you out 'f there, fucker?' The gun dug deeply into Joel's chin. 'You t'ink the Blade just picks up the phone and has a word wiv Mr Chief Constable or summick? You got *any* idea what dis cost me?'

'I pay you back,' Joel said. 'I got fifty pounds and I can—'

'Oh, you pay me back. You pay me back.' With each word the Blade thrust the gun upward, harder.

Joel went with it, rising on his toes. 'I will. Jus' tell me.'

'I'll tell you, fucker. I'll God *damn* tell you.'

The Blade dropped the gun to his side as quickly as he'd raised it. Joel nearly sank to his knees: both with the sudden movement and with his own relief. Cal came up behind him. He led Joel to a crate and pushed him down upon it. Cal's hands held him there, by the shoulders. They weren't harsh hands, but they were far from friendly.

'You,' the Blade said, 'are going to do *exactly* like I tell you to do. And if you don't, Jo-ell, I find you and I deal wiv you. I deal wiv you one way or th' other. Before the cops get to you or after. Don't make no difference. You get me, mon?'

Joel nodded. 'I get you.'

'An' I deal wiv your family next. You get dat as well?'

Joel swallowed. 'I get you.'

He watched, then, and saw the Blade wipe every vestige of his fingerprints from the pistol. He extended it in Joel's direction. He said, 'You take this piece and you listen good, then. You cock dis one up, and there's going to be real hell to pay.'

24

Ness remained alone: secretive and sullen. She fulfilled her obligation to community service, but she ceased journeying to Covent Garden.

This seemed reasonable at first. She'd been attacked upon her return from Covent Garden. It wasn't out of the question that she'd harbour certain fears about travelling on her own to and from the place. But when she refused to join Sayf al Din and his helpers even during the height of business hours – when anyone's comings and goings on the underground would have been made in the company of millions of other commuters and even the walk home from the Westbourne Park station would not have been made in solitude – then it seemed that the girl's fears needed to be addressed.

Majidah tried. 'Do you not see you let them win, Vanessa, when you give in in such a manner?'

To which Ness replied, 'F'rget it, okay? I'm doing my community service, innit. I got one stupid course at college, an' I don't got to do nuffink more 'n dat.'

This was true. The fact of it tied everyone's hands. But the additional fact was that Ness was bound by order of the magistrate to attend school full-time as well, so if she didn't enrol in some programme or another at the college – which working for Sayf al Din was preparing her to do – then she was going to find herself standing in front of the magistrate once again, and this time there would be no leniency. There had been enough exceptions made for her.

Fabia Bender held the whip hand in this matter. When she

called upon Kendra, she had done some preparation for their meeting. She had separate files on each of the children. Her possession of them and the fact she laid them out on the kitchen table were designed to impress upon the children's aunt the gravity of the situation.

Kendra certainly needed no metaphor for this. Both the social worker and Sergeant Starr had put her in the picture about Joel's attempt at mugging a woman on Portobello Road as well as his possession of a weapon and his subsequent and mysterious release from custody. Although she told herself it had likely been a case of mistaken identity – for how else could he have been released so summarily? – in her heart she wasn't so sure. This, then, in combination with the change in Ness was sufficient to fix her full attention on all three of the children.

'Social worker's coming to the house to talk to me,' she told Cordie after Fabia Bender's phone call to the charity shop. 'She wants it to be just the two of us, 'cept Dix c'n be there if he's round just then.'

Cordie nodded in sympathetic silence, listening to the sound of her two girls peacefully playing with paper dolls in the lounge while the rain beat on the windows outside. She thanked God: for her daughters' innocence, for her husband's solid presence despite his maddening desire for a son, and for her own good luck. She had a gainfully employed man in the house, a fully functioning family, and a job she enjoyed with colleagues who shared her passion.

'Did I do wrong phoning up the cops wiv dis Neal Wyatt's name?' Kendra asked her.

Cordie couldn't say. In her experience nothing good *ever* came of involving the police in any aspect of one's life, but she was willing to make an exception to that belief. So she said, ''S all gonna work out, Ken,' which was the truth although whether it was going to work out well or work out disastrously was something she didn't predict. To Cordie, life was better if

it was lived off the radar screens of the myriad arms of governmental institutions. Since Kendra and her relations had placed
themselves firmly *on* these radar screens, it was hardly likely
that there was going to be a happily ever after involved. She
said, 'You t'ink 'bout options here, Ken?'

'What sort of options?'

'Whatever you c'n propose if dis woman has her *own* ideas
dat you don't like.'

But there seemed only three options when Kendra thought
everything over: going on as they had been for the last year;
creating a radical intervention to effect an immediate change
that would shake up Ness and Joel and bring them to their
senses – provided Joel even *needed* that, which she still didn't
want to admit to; or hoping for a miracle in the person of
Carole Campbell and her sudden, complete, and permanent
recovery. The first was clearly not working out, the second
seemed to involve a governmental agency and was thus
unthinkable, and the third was unlikely. A final and potentially efficacious option was marriage to Dix and the
semblance of permanence and family that such a marriage
might offer. But marriage to Dix was precisely what Kendra
did not want; indeed, she wanted marriage to no one at all.
Marriage was a form of giving up and giving in, and she
could not face this, even as she knew it might be the only
solution.

Fabia Bender had no intention of making things easy on
the children's aunt. This was a runaway train she was
attempting to halt, and she intended to use whatever means
were available to put on the brakes. She could tell that Kendra
Osborne wasn't a bad woman. She knew the children's aunt
meant well by all of them. But with Joel in possession of a
firearm – not to mention identified as a mugger and *still*
somehow escaping prosecution for these offences – and with
Ness the victim of a street assault and the street assault's aftermath, the children's jeopardy was fast reaching what could

only be described as a critical mass. An explosion was imminent. Years of experience told the social worker that.

She began with Ness, whose folder she opened and studied
with an apparent need to refresh her memory on the details,
although she knew them well enough and did this only for
effect. Across from her sat Kendra, joined by Dix, who'd turned
up smelling of oil and fried fish from his parents' café, anxious
to get to the gym for his work-out but eager to be of support
to Kendra, and thus a bundle of warring energies.

Ness was doing her community service, which was good,
Fabia told them. But she'd ceased her work for Sayf al Din,
which was substituting for her required full-time schooling.
Fabia was – at this time – interceding with the magistrate in
respect of Vanessa Campbell's meeting her obligations under
the terms of her probation. But, if something didn't change
quickly, Ness was going to face the magistrate and things were
not going to go smoothly when she did.

'He knows about the assault, however, and he's agreed to
counselling in place of full-time school for now,' Fabia told
Kendra. 'We have someone in Oxford Gardens she can see,
if you can guarantee she gets there. As to Joel—'

'I got him sorted,' Kendra said quickly, not because this
was the truth, but because she hadn't told Dix about the
mugging and the gun. Why should she? she asked herself. It
was all a mistake, wasn't it? 'He hasn't gone truant since that
one time—'

Dix looked at her sharply and frowned.

'– and he knows he was lucky with the way things turned
out.'

'But there's more involved here than meets the eye,' Fabia
said. 'That he was released so quickly—'

'*Released?* Wha's going down wiv Joel?' Dix asked abruptly.
'Joel in trouble? Ken, *damn* it . . .' He ran his hand over his
pate. It was an act of frustration and disappointment, with Dix
not realising what his ignorance in this matter revealed to the

social worker, who glanced between woman and man and made an evaluation of their relationship that Kendra could not afford to have made.

'Cops had him down the Harrow Road station,' she told him. 'I di'n't like to trouble you with this cos you been busy and it got sorted. It di'n't seem—'

'How we make dis work if you keep secrets, Ken?' He asked the question in a fierce whisper.

Kendra answered, 'C'n we talk 'bout this later?'

'Shit.' He crossed his arms and leaned back in his chair, and Fabia Bender read the movements for what they were. She made a mental note. No father figure. Another tick in the column towards the children's removal from this home.

She said, 'Under other circumstances, I'd insist on Joel's placement in that programme I mentioned to you earlier, the one across the river at Elephant and Castle. In fact, I'd advise it for Ness as well. But I agree with you, Mrs Osborne. There's the distance and the fact that there's no one to ensure either their attendance or their safety in making the journey to South London . . .'

She lifted her hand and dropped it on the folder containing Joel's information. 'Joel needs counselling, just like Ness, but he needs more than that. He needs supervision, a direction in life, an interest to focus on, an outlet for his concerns, and a male role model. We have to provide him with those or we have to consider other options for him.'

'Dis is down to me,' Dix interceded, believing he bore a certain amount of responsibility for what had happened to Joel even if he wasn't quite sure what *what had happened* meant. 'I c'n do more wiv Joel than I been doing. I ain't tried hard enough cos . . .' He blew out a breath as he thought about all the reasons he'd failed to be the father figure he'd *sought* to be: his responsibilities to his own family, his desire for success in his chosen field, his insatiable lust for Kendra's body, his inadequacy in the face of the children's troubles, his lack of experience and history with the children, the image he possessed of what a family was supposed to be. He could name some of these as reasons for his failure; the rest he could see in his mind. In any case, what he felt was guilt for all of them, and he ended up expressing them with, 'Cos of life. I meant to do better wiv the kids, an' I will from now on.'

Fabia Bender wasn't in the business of breaking up families, and she wanted to believe that commitment on the part of the two people sitting with her at what was an inadequately sized kitchen table meant that a possibility existed that Joel's trouble would serve as a wake-up call to everyone. Still, she was bound by duty to finish what she had come to say, so that was what she did.

'We need to think carefully about the children's future. Sometimes a removal from the environment – even for a brief time – is all that's necessary to bring about change. I'd like you to think about this. Care is an option. Boarding school is another: a special school to meet Toby's needs—'

'Toby's fine where he is,' Kendra put in. She made the declaration sound firm, not panicked.

'– and another school to give Joel new direction,' Fabia continued as if Kendra hadn't spoken. 'With them taken care of in this way, we can concentrate on Ness.'

'I don't got . . .' Kendra stopped. 'I don't need to think about it. I can't send them away. They won't understand. They been through too much. They . . .' She gestured futilely. Tears in front of this woman were unthinkable. She said nothing more.

Dix said it for her. 'Jus' now ever'one's doing what they're s'posed to be doing, innit?'

'Yes,' Fabia Bender said. 'Technically. But Ness is going to have to—'

'Den you let us be fam'ly. We see to Ness. We see to the boys. We stop doing dat, you free to come back.'

Fabia agreed to this, but anyone could see how insurmountable was the task that faced the two adults. There were too many needs to be met and most of them were not the simple ones of food, shelter, and clothing, which required money for their procurement and time for their purchase and nothing else. As to the deeper needs of assuaging fears, quelling daily anxieties, reconciling past pain with present reality and future possibility . . . These required the participation of a professional or a group of professionals. Fabia could tell that the aunt and her lover didn't see this; she was wise enough to know that people had to reach conclusions on their own.

She told them she would return in two weeks to see how all of them were doing. But, in the meantime, they were going to have to get Ness to Oxford Gardens for counselling. The magistrate would accept nothing less.

'I don't need fucking counselling,' was how Ness responded to this information.

'You need a lock-up instead?' was how Kendra replied. 'You need being sent away? Having Toby put away in a special school and Joel going off to board somewhere? Or worse? That what you need, Vanessa Campbell?'

Dix said, 'Ken. Ken. Go easy,' and he tried to sound sympathetic towards Ness. Just as he tried to be a father to Joel and Toby: checking on school work, watching the skateboarding in Meanwhile Gardens when the winter weather permitted, carving out two hours to go to the cinema for an action-hero film, coaxing the boys to the gym to participate in a work-out in which neither of them was interested. But all of this was a street upon which Dix was the only driver: Ness scorned his attempts to intervene; Joel's cooperation was given in a silence that indicated no cooperation at all; Toby went the way of Joel as always, utterly confused by the entire situation in which he was now living.

'You best understand this,' Kendra hissed at Joel when she surveyed Dix's well-meaning attempts and the children's indifference towards them. 'We don't sort everything out to her liking, this Fabia Bender's taking the lot of you. Y'understand me, Joel? You know what that means?'

Joel knew, but he was caught in ways that he could not afford to explain to his aunt. For his escape from the Harrow Road police station, he owed the Blade and he knew that if he did not pay when the account came due, the trouble they would face would make their current trouble seem like a spring-time stroll along the towpath by the Grand Union Canal.

For, somehow, everything had gone wrong. What had started out for Joel as a simple and primeval struggle to gain respect in the street had turned into an exercise in sheer survival. The existence of Neal Wyatt receded into the back-ground once Joel found himself a central figure of the Blade's attention. In comparison to the Blade, Neal Wyatt was as irri-tating as an ant crawling up the inside of a trouser leg. He was nothing at all set against the knowledge that Joel had at this point in his life. He'd come up against the hardest and most unforgiving place of all in North Kensington. He'd come up against the wishes of Stanley Hynds.

As unrealistic as it might seem to a rational person in posses-sion of even a small amount of history of the woman, to Joel Carole Campbell seemed the only answer that could lead to escape.

He had the money – that blessed fifty pounds from *Walk the Word* – so there was no need to involve anyone in knowing that he intended to visit his mother. Joel chose a frigid day when his aunt was working, when Dix was at the Rainbow Café, and when Ness was at the child drop-in centre. That left him with Toby to look after, with sufficient time to put his plan for rescue into motion.

He knew the routine. The bus appeared to be waiting just for them at the appointed stop along Elkstone Road, and it trundled over to Paddington station with so few passengers on board that the journey seemed designed to symbolise the ease with which Joel's plans were going to come to fruition. He bought their tickets for the train ride and took Toby, as always, to WH Smith. He kept a firm grip on his brother, but he needn't have worried. Toby was determined to stick to Joel like a burr in a fox's tail. With his skateboard tucked under his arm, he tripped along and asked if he would be allowed to have a bar of chocolate or a bag of crisps.

'Bag of crisps,' Joel told him. The last thing he needed to contend with was Toby smeared with chocolate when they went to see their mother.

Toby selected prawn crisps with a surprising alacrity that also suggested how well Joel's mental scenario was developing. He purchased a magazine for their mother – choosing *Harper's Bazaar* because it was the thickest on offer – and, on impulse, he bought her a tin of sweets as well.

Soon enough they were rolling out of Paddington station, past the dismal and dingy brick walls that separated the railway tracks from the even more dismal and dingy houses that backed directly on to them. Toby kicked his feet against the bottom of the seat and happily munched his crisps. Joel watched the scenery and tried to think how to bring their mother home.

They got out of the train into bitter cold, much colder than in London. Frost rimed hedgerows whose bare branches sheltered shivering sparrows, and the fields beyond them bore a gauzy cover of frozen fog. Crusts of ice skinned over standing pools of rainwater and where there were sheep, they chuffed gustily and huddled together in a woollen mass against stone walls.

At the hospital and through the guard gate, the boys hustled up the drive. The lawns, like the fields, were white with fog that had frozen and fallen, and more fog was descending as Joel and Toby dashed towards the main building. This hovered in the mist, an object that might disappear before they reached it.

Inside, a blast of hot air hit them. The contrast felt like

going from the North Pole into the tropics with no stop at an intermediate climate. They stumbled through the heat that blasted from radiators, and Joel gave their names at Reception. He learned that Carole Campbell was in the mobile beauty caravan. They could wait for her right here in the lobby or they could look for her in the caravan, which they could find in the employees' car park at the back of the building. Did they know where that was?

Joel said they would find it. Going back outside was, to him, infinitely preferable than having to wilt among the plastic greenery that decorated the lobby. He got Toby back into his anorak, which the little boy had already shed and dropped to the floor, and they went back outside. They slipped and slid along a concrete path. They followed it down one long wing of the hospital, where it branched at the back towards the infirmary in one direction and the employees' car park in the other.

The caravan in question was a small hump-backed mobile holiday home of the type once seen widely in the English countryside prior to the days of inexpensive flights to the coast of Spain. It had been named Hair and There, a tediously self-amused pun that was painted on the caravan's side in great chunky letters along with a rainbow which led not to a pot of gold but to a hair-drying chair next to a cartoon woman all done up in curlers and dashing through puffs of clouds to sit down. Over the door was yet another rainbow. Joel led Toby to this and up two slick steps.

Inside, it was warm but nothing like the hospital's insufferable heat. There were three hair stations, where women sat in various stages of beautification at the hands of a single hairdresser, and at the far end there was a manicure and pedicure area. That was where Joel and Toby found their mother, who was being worked upon by a girl with tri-coloured hair erupting from the top of her head. Red, blue, and deep purple, her locks were like the proud flag of a newly born nation.

Carole Campbell didn't see them at first. She and the

manicurist were intent upon an examination of Carole's hands. The manicurist was saying to her, 'I dunno how else to 'splain it to you, luv. You just not got a big enough base. They won't last. First time you knock 'em about, that's it.'

'I don't care, do I?' Carole's voice was gay. 'I won't hold you responsible if they fall off. It's coming up to Valentine's Day, so I want the jewellery as well. I want the prettiest you have.' She looked up then and smiled when her gaze fell upon Joel. She said, 'Oh my goodness, look who's come to call, Serena. Right behind you. Tell me I'm not hallucinating. I didn't forget to take my pills, did I?'

'You will have your joke, Caro.' The hairdresser called this out as she painted something thick and gooey into a client's head of thin hair.

But Serena humoured Carole, since she'd been taught to humour the patients lest they become agitated. She gave a glance in Joel and Toby's direction, nodded a hello to them, and said to her client. 'Right, then, luv. You're not hallucinating. These little blokes belong to you?'

'This is my Joel,' Carole said. 'My great *big* Joel. Look how he's *grown*, Serena. Darling, come see what Serena's doing to Mummy's fingernails.'

Joel waited for her to acknowledge Toby and to introduce him to the manicurist. Toby hung back shyly, so Joel drew him forward. Carole had gone back to studying her hands. ''S'okay,' Joel murmured to his brother. 'She got summick on her mind and she c'n never do two things at once.'

'I brought my skateboard,' Toby said helpfully. 'I c'n ride it, Joel. I c'n show her.'

'Af'er she's done wiv dis,' Joel said.

He and Toby sidled up to the manicure table. There, Carole had spread her hands upon a white towel less clean than it might have been. They lay like inert specimens under the bright light of an anglepoise lamp. Row upon row of nail varnish bottles stood by, ready to be used upon them.

The only problem with Carole's plan for her beautification was that she had no nails to speak of. She'd bitten them down so far that mere slivers remained. To these unappealing stubs she was requesting a set of false nails be attached. These sat neatly in plastic boxes that the manicurist tapped her own nails against as she tried, with no success, to explain to Joel and Toby's mother that her plan for instant nail beauty was not going to work. In this, she was an honest – albeit impractical – expositor. For Carole wanted what Carole wanted: the false nails, painted and then gaily decorated with tiny seasonal gold hearts, which waited on a cardboard card propped against one of the bottles of nail varnish.

Serena finally gave a mighty sigh and said, ''F that's what you want,' although she shook her head in an unmistakable don't-blame-me sort of motion as she set to work. 'These're gonna last all of five minutes,' she said darkly.

'The five happiest minutes of my life.' Carole settled back into her chair and looked at Joel. She drew her eyebrows together, her face clouding. Then she brightened. 'How's Auntie Ken?' she asked.

This caused Joel's heart to bump hopefully. Over the years, his mother had rarely even acknowledged that there *was* an Auntie Ken.

Joel said, 'She's good. Dix's back. Dat's her boyfriend. He's keeping her happy 'nough.'

'Auntie Ken and her men.' Carole gave a shake to her coppery head. 'She always had a soft spot for the hard spot, didn't she?'

Serena guffawed and lightly slapped Carole's hand. 'You mind your mouth, Miss Caro, or I got to report you.'

'But it's true,' Carole said. 'When Joel's gran followed her man to Jamaica and the kids' aunt Kendra started minding them, the first thing I thought was *Now* they're going to get some real sex education. I even said it as well, didn't I, Joel?'

Joel couldn't help grinning. She'd never said such a thing,

but the fact that she was pretending she had, the fact that she was even aware that his grandmother had decamped for Jamaica, the fact that she *knew* very well where the children were living and with whom and why . . . Before this moment, Carole Campbell had not spoken of Kendra, of Glory, of Jamaica, or of anything else that indicated she knew what period of time she was living through. So all of this – off-colour or not, true or not, imagined or not – was so new to Joel, so unexpected, so welcome . . . He felt like someone at the gates of heaven.

Carole said, 'And Ness? Joel, why doesn't she come to see me? I know how much she hurts from your dad's death: with *how* he died, with all of it. I understand how she feels. But if she'd just come to talk to me, I can't help but think how much better she'd feel in the long run. I miss her. Will you tell her I miss her?'

Joel hardly dared to reply, so difficult was it for him to believe what he was hearing. He said, 'I'll tell her, Mum. She's . . . she's going through a bad patch jus' now, but I'll tell her what you say.' He didn't add more. He didn't want their mother to know about the attack upon Ness and how Ness was reacting to that and to everything else. To give Carole anything that resembled bad news felt like too risky a proposition. It might send her back to the Nowhere Land she'd inhabited for so long.

Thus, Joel cringed when Toby spoke unexpectedly. 'Ness got in a bad fight, Mum. Some blokes bunged her up. Aunt Ken had to take her to Casualty, innit.'

Serena looked over her shoulder at them, an eyebrow raised and a tube of nailglue suspended in her fingers. 'She okay now?' she asked before she applied the glue to a false nail, which she pressed uselessly on to one of Carole's stubs.

Carole was quiet. Joel waited, breath held, for what she would say. She cocked her head and looked thoughtful, her gaze on Joel. When she finally spoke, her voice was as before.

'You are looking more like your father every day,' she said although the remark was odd because all of them knew that nothing could have been further from the truth. She clarified her statement with, 'Something about your eyes. How is your schoolwork? Have you brought me some to see?'

Joel let the breath go. He felt uneasy with the remark about his father, but he brushed it off. 'Forgot,' he said. 'But we brought you these.' He handed over the WH Smith bag.

'I love Harper's,' Carole said. 'And what's this? Oh, are there sweets inside this tin? How lovely. Thank you, Joel.'

'I'll open 'em for you.' Joel took the tin and removed its plastic covering. This he tossed into a swing bin, where it became caught up in someone's shorn, damp hair. He prised open the lid and handed the boiled sweets back to his mother.

She said mischievously, 'Let's each have one, shall we?'

'They're meant to be only f'r you,' Joel told her. He knew to be cautious with sweets around Toby. Offer him one and he'd likely eat the lot.

'C'n I have one?' Toby asked on cue.

Carole said, 'For me alone? Oh darling, I can't eat them all. Have one, do. No? No one wants . . . ? Not even you, Serena?'

'Mum . . .' Toby said.

'Well, right then. We'll set them aside for another time. Do you like my hearts?' She nodded at the card to which the nail jewellery was fixed. 'They're silly, I know, but as we're to have a little Valentine party . . . I wanted something festive. It's a dreary time of year anyway – February. One wonders if the sun is gone for ever. Although April can be worse except it's the rain then and not this infernal eternal fog.'

'*Mum*, I want a sweet. Why can't I have one? Joel . . .'

'Anything that serves to cheer us up at this time of year is something I want to participate in,' Carole went on. 'I always wonder, though, why February seems so long when it's actually the shortest month of the year, even during Leap Year.

But it just seems to go on and on, doesn't it? Or perhaps the truth is I *want* it to be long. I want all the months that precede it to go on and on as well. I don't want the anniversary to come round. Your dad's death, you see. I don't want to look that anniversary in the eyes another time.'

'Joel!' Toby grabbed Joel's arm. 'Why won't Mum let me have one of dem sweets?'

Joel said, 'Shh. I get you one later. They got a machine somewheres round here, and I get you some chocolate.'

'But Joel, she won't—'

'Jus' hang on, Tobe.'

'But Joel, I *want*—'

'Hang *on*.' Joel loosened Toby's grip. 'Whyn't you take your skateboard outside? You c'n use it in the car park a bit.'

'It's *cold* in the car park.'

'We'll have a hot chocolate after you practise round here and when Mum's done wiv her nails, you c'n show her how good you ride it, okay?'

'But I *want*—'

Joel turned Toby by the shoulders and propelled him towards the caravan door. He was in a terror that something might set their mother off, and to him Toby was looking more and more like a human detonator.

He opened the door and took his brother down the steps. He looked around and saw a vacant patch of car park where Toby would be safe with his skateboard. He made sure his brother's anorak was zipped, and he pulled his knitted cap tightly over his hair. He said, 'You stay here, Tobe, and I'll get you some sweets af'er. Hot chocolate as well. I got the money. You know Mum's not right up here.' He pointed to his head. 'I meant the sweets for her and she pro'lly misunnerstood when I said I di'n't want one. She pro'lly thought you di'n't want one either.'

'But I kept *saying* . . .' Toby looked as bleak as the day and bleaker than the car park, which was bumpy and no place to practise with his board. He sniffed loudly and wiped his nose on the sleeve of his anorak. He said, 'I don't want to ride the skateboard. It's stupid, innit.'

Joel put his arm around his brother. 'You want to show Mum, don't you? You want her to see how good you are on it. Soon's she gets her hands done, she going to want to see you, so you got to be ready. It won't take long.'

Toby looked from Joel to the caravan to Joel. 'Promise?' he said.

'I ain't never lied to you, mon.'

That was enough. Toby trudged off in the direction of the open space, his skateboard dangling from his hand. Joel watched until he dropped the board to the lumpy tarmac and scooted a few yards forward, one foot on the board and the other on the ground. That was as well as he rode it anywhere, so it didn't matter much what kind of surface was beneath its wheels.

Joel returned to their mother. She was in the midst of examining the false nails that Serena had so far managed to glue to her fingers. They were overlong and pointed, and the manicurist was trying to explain that they needed to be shortened considerably in order to stay put for even a day. But Carole wasn't having any of this. She wanted them long, painted red, and decorated with gold hearts. Anything less would not be acceptable. Even Joel, lacking all knowledge of plastic nails, glue, and fingernail jewellery, understood that Carole had a bad idea. You couldn't glue something to nothing and hope to make it stick.

He said, 'Mum, maybe S'rena's right. If you shortened 'em a bit—'

Carole looked at him. 'You're being intrusive,' she said.

He felt slapped. 'Sorry.'

'Thank you. Go ahead, Serena. Do the rest of them.'

Serena pursed her lips and went back to business. The truth was that it was no skin off her nose if some nuthouse woman insisted on having nails glued to wherever she said she wanted them glued. The end product was just the same: money in Serena's pocket.

Carole watched and nodded in approval as the second set of useless nails went on. She gave her attention to Joel and indicated a small padded stool that sat nearby. 'Come and sit,' she said. 'Tell me everything that's happened since the last time I saw you. Why've you stayed away so long? Oh, I'm so *happy* to see you. And thank you so much for the gifts.'

'They're from all 'f us, Mum,' Joel told her.

'But *you* bought them, didn't you? You chose them, Joel.'

'Yeah, but—'

'I *knew* it. Your name was written all over everything. Your sensitivity. You. It was very thoughtful, and I wanted to say . . . Well, this is a bit more difficult, I'm afraid.'

'What?' he asked.

She looked left and right. She smiled slyly. 'Joel, thank you so much for not bringing that grubby little boy with you this time. You know the one I mean. Your little friend with the runny nose. I don't mean to be cruel, but I'm glad not to see him. He was beginning to get on my nerves.'

'You mean Tobe?' Joel asked. 'Mum, tha' was Toby.'

'Is that what he's called?' Carole Campbell asked with a smile. 'Well, whatever, darling. I'm just thrilled to bits you came alone today.'

25

W hat Joel had not considered in his careful planning was that he and his siblings had ceased to be part of London's anonymous mass of children and adolescents who daily go about their lives: in and out of school, taking part in sports, doing homework, flirting, gossiping, shopping, hanging about, mobile phones pressed to their ears or gazed upon raptly as text messages appear, blasting music into their heads via various intriguing electronic devices . . . In an ordinary London world, Joel would have been a fellow among them. But he did not live in an ordinary London world. So when he took the decision to travel out to see his mother, he was not able to do it surreptitiously.

In part, this was because he went to the hospital in the company of Toby, whose absence from school was reported at once. But in part it was also because, having come under closer scrutiny since his brief encounter with the Harrow Road police and owing to a message from Fabia Bender, his own absence from school was duly noted. Both notations triggered a phone call to his aunt.

With Toby missing as well as Joel, Kendra did not leap to the conclusion that Joel was involved in anything risky or illegal. She knew her elder nephew would never jeopardise Toby's safety. But a serial killer had been stalking young boys just Joel's age, and since the most recent two boys had been from North London, Kendra could not stop her thoughts from heading ineluctably in that direction, just as they'd done when Joel had gone missing for two nights.

She didn't arrive at that mental destination immediately. Instead, she did what any woman might have done, informed that her boys were not where they were supposed to be. She phoned home to see if they'd bunked off school to watch videos; she phoned the child drop-in centre in the unlikely event they'd gone there; she phoned the Rainbow Café to check with Dix on the chance he'd taken them to work with him for some reason; ultimately, she panicked. She closed the charity shop and went on the hunt. After driving up streets and through housing estates, she remembered Ivan Weatherall and phoned him as well, to no avail. This sent her into further panic, which was her state when she went into the Rainbow Café.

Dix didn't join her in full-blown anxiety. He sat her down with a cup of tea and, not as sanguine as Kendra about the probability of Joel's keeping his brother out of trouble at all costs, he phoned the Harrow Road police. Two boys were missing, he told them when he learned Joel was not in custody for some heretofore unknown malefaction. What with the serial killings . . .

The constable on the other end of the line cut him off: the boys had not been missing even twenty-four hours, had they? Put quite simply, there was nothing the police could do until they'd been missing for a longer period.

So Dix phoned New Scotland Yard next, where the investigation into the serial killings was headquartered. But there again, he had no luck. They were being inundated with phone calls from parents whose boys had been missing far longer than a mere few hours, sir. New Scotland Yard was not equipped to send up a hue and cry over two boys who'd merely played truant from school.

There was nothing for it but for Dix to follow Kendra's example. He turned his job over to his harried mother and changed out of his cook's garb. He had to be part of the search, he explained, handing over his apron.

His mother made no comment. She glanced at Kendra, tried to keep her face impassive, rued the day her son had fallen into the clutches of a woman with whom he could build no conventional future, and donned his large apron. Go, she told him.

Dix was the one to suggest the hospital where Carole Campbell was housed. Could the boys have gone there?

Kendra didn't see how. They had no money for the bus and the train. But she phoned anyway, and that was how Dix D'Court came to be waiting at Paddington station when Toby and Joel debarked some hours later.

He'd been meeting every train. He'd missed his work-out. By the time the boys showed up, he was devilishly hungry but unwilling to pollute his body with anything sold within the station. He was, as a result, tightly coiled with frustration and annoyance. It wasn't going to take much to set him off, no matter his earlier intentions.

When Joel saw Dix on the other side of the barrier, he could tell the man was coiled like a wound-up spring. He knew he was in trouble, but he didn't care. He saw himself as someone out of every option, so the fact that Dix D'Court was cheesed off at him was a minor wrinkle in the altogether permanently crumpled linen that was his present life.

Toby was tripping along at Joel's heels, mostly involved in a conversation with a spider transfer that a previous owner had applied to his skateboard. He didn't see Dix until Dix was upon them, until Joel said, 'Hey! Let go my arm, mon.' Then he looked up and said, ''Lo, Dix. Mum wanted fingernails. I got a bag of crisps. It looked like snow ever'where, only it wasn't.'

Dix marched Joel out of the station. Toby followed. Joel continued to protest. Dix said nothing. Toby grabbed Joel's arm, needing the reassurance of something solid that represented something he understood.

At his car, Dix stuffed both boys into the back seat. Looking into the rear-view mirror, he said to Joel, 'You *know* the state you put your aunt into? How much more you 'spect she's going to take off you?'

Joel turned his head away and looked out of the window. Hopes dashed, he was in no state to accept blame for anything. He mouthed *Fuck you*.

Dix read the words. They were a match to tinder. He got out of the car and jerked open the back door. He pulled Joel out. He shoved him against the wing and barked, 'You want to take me on? Dat's wha' you looking to happen just now?'

'Hey,' Joel said. 'Lemme alone.'

'How long you t'ink you last wiv me, mon?'

'Lemme the fuck *alone*,' Joel said. 'I di'n't do nuffink.'

'Dat's how you see it? Your aunt out searching, phoning the cops, getting told there's no help, falling into a state . . . And you di'n't do nuffink?' In a disgust that was only in part directed at Joel, Dix shoved him back inside.

The drive to North Kensington was not a long one. They made it in silence, with Dix incapable of seeing past Joel's external animus and Joel incapable of seeing past Dix's re-action to what lay at the core of it.

In Edenham Way, Joel flung himself up the steps to his aunt's house. Toby rapidly followed. He clutched his skate-board to his chest like a life-ring. When, inside the house, Dix snatched it from him and tossed it to one side, he began to cry.

It was too much for Joel. He said, 'You fucking leave Toby alone, mon! You got summick to say or summick to do, you do it to me. You got dat, blood?'

Dix might have responded but Kendra came from the kitchen. So, instead of speaking, he pushed the boy towards his aunt, saying, 'Here he is, den. He's a big mon now, hear him talk. Cause of all th' trouble and him wivout a care in th' world dat he worried anyone.'

'Shut up,' Joel said. He said it in exhaustion and despair.

Dix took a step towards him. Kendra said, 'Don't.' And then to Joel, 'What's going on? Why'd you go out there without telling me? You know the school phoned? Yours? Toby's?'

'I wanted to see Mum,' Joel said. 'I don't get what the big deal's all 'bout.'

'We had rules. School. Toby. Home.' Kendra ticked off these items on her fingers. 'Those're your limits. That's what I told you. The hospital isn't among them.'

'Whatever,' Joel said.

'And where'd you get the money for tickets?'

'It was mine.'

'Where'd you get it, Joel?'

'I tol' you. It was mine, and if you don't believe me—'

'That's right. I don't. Give me a reason to.'

'I fucking don't have to.'

'Joel . . .' Toby cried. All of this was beyond his ability to comprehend. One moment they had been on the train, gazing out at a landscape shrouded in mystery through the means of freezing fog, and the next moment they were in trouble. So much trouble that Joel was cursing, Dix was angry and ready to bang people about, and Kendra's face was looking like a mask. The burden of all this was too heavy to carry in his mind. Toby said, 'Mum wanted hearts on her fingernails, Auntie. Tell her, Joel. 'Bout them gold hearts.'

Kendra said thinly, 'Right,' ignoring Toby's fruitless attempt to alter the course of what was happening. She said, 'Let's just have a check of things, then,' and she headed up the stairs. Joel followed her. Toby tagged along, and Dix trailed Toby.

It was obvious what Kendra's intentions were. Joel didn't protest. Indeed, he found he didn't much care. There was nothing for her to discover in his room because he was telling her the truth, and he knew she wouldn't find the gun he'd been given by the Blade. This was tucked in the space beneath the floor and the bottom drawer of the clothes chest. The only way to get it out was to tilt the chest up, and his aunt was unlikely to go to that extreme once she realised there was nothing to find elsewhere in the room.

Kendra dumped out his rucksack and pawed through it, a woman on an undefined mission. She was looking for something without knowing what she was looking for: evidence that he'd mugged someone successfully, gobs of cash to indicate he was selling some kind of contraband, weapons, drugs, cigarettes, alcohol . . . It didn't matter. She just wanted to find something that would give her a sign of what she was meant to do next because, just like Joel but with different cause, she was finding herself running out of options.

There was nothing: in the rucksack, under or in the bed, inside books, behind posters on the walls, in the chest of drawers. She went from all this to shaking Joel down, and he removed his clothes for her in an indifferent cooperation that infuriated her.

The only answer was Toby, she thought, and she wondered why she hadn't considered it before. So he was made to undress as well, and this in turn infuriated Joel.

He said, 'I *told* you! He don't have nuffink to do wiv . . .' He said nothing else.

'What?' Kendra demanded. 'With what? *What?*'

Joel would have liked to stalk from the room, but Dix was in the doorway, an impassable object. Toby was, if anything, crying harder than ever. He fell on to his bed in his underwear.

Joel was inflamed, but he did nothing. There was nothing *to* do, and he knew it. So he told his aunt the truth. 'I won it, okay? I won the fucking money at *Wield Words*. Fifty pounds. Dat's it. You happy now?'

She said, 'We'll see about that,' and she left him, crossing the corridor to her own bedroom where she placed a phone call that she made certain her nephews could hear.

She told Ivan Weatherall Joel's claim. She even used the word *claim* to indicate her incredulity. Governed more by anger than by wisdom, she told him more than he needed to know.

Joel had to be watched, she said. He had fractured her trust in him. He'd sneaked off without permission, he was responding to her questions with insolence and defiance, and now he was claiming he'd got some unaccounted for money off the poetry evening. What did Ivan know about that?

Ivan, naturally, knew quite a lot about it. He confirmed Joel's story.

But more than one seed in more than one breast was planted through this conversation. It would not take long for that seed to sprout.

With a clear understanding of what would happen should she fail to cooperate, Ness went to counselling in Oxford Gardens. She sat through three appointments but, since she was there under duress, that was the extent of her participation in recovering from the assault made upon her: sitting in a chair that was faced towards the counsellor.

The counsellor in question was twenty-five years old, in possession of a first-class degree from a third-class university, and of a solid middle-class background – clearly evident in her choice of clothing and her careful use of words like *loo* instead of *toilet* – which put her in the unfortunate position of believing she had most of the answers required to navigate encounters with recalcitrant adolescent girls. She was white, blonde, and squeaky clean. These were not faults, but they were disadvantages. She saw herself as a role model instead of what she appeared to be to those who were supposed to be her clients: an adversary incapable of relating to a single element of their lives.

After those three meetings with Ness, she decided group counselling might be an efficacious approach to achieve what she termed 'a breakthrough'. To her credit, she did a considerable amount of homework on her client, and it was on this subject that she approached Fabia Bender, a manila folder in her hand.

'No luck?' Fabia said to her. They were in the copy room, where an antique Mr Coffee was delivering a viscous-looking brew into a glass carafe.

The counsellor – whose name for reasons her parents would never reveal was Ruma, which the well-travelled Fabia knew very well meant 'queen of the apes' – recounted what her sessions with Ness had been like so far. Tough, she said. Indeed, Vanessa Campbell was a very tough nut to crack.

Fabia waited for more. So far, Ruma was telling her nothing that she didn't know.

Ruma drew a breath. The truth of the matter was that they were getting absolutely nowhere, she said. 'I was thinking about a different approach, like a group,' she offered. 'Other girls who've gone through the same thing. God knows we've got them by the dozens.'

'But . . . ?' Fabia prompted her. She could tell there was more to come. Ruma had not yet learned to obscure her intent through the use of careful intonation.

'But I've done some digging around, and there's information here . . .' Ruma tapped her fingernails – well-groomed, French manicured, uniformly shaped – against the folder. 'I'm thinking there's a lot more than meets the eye. D'you have the time . . . ?'

There was never enough time, but Fabia was intrigued. She liked Ruma, she knew the young woman meant well, and she admired the tireless way Ruma pursued every avenue for her clients, no matter how ineffective her efforts might prove to be. Where there was breath, there was life. Where there was life, there was hope. There were worse philosophies for someone who'd chosen the profession of counselling the unfortunate, Fabia thought.

They repaired to Fabia's office once the coffee was brewed and Fabia had filled herself a cup. There, Ruma shared the information she'd come up with.

'You know Mum's in a psychiatric hospital, right?' Ruma

began. To Fabia's nod, she added, 'How much d'you know about why she's there?'

'Unresolved postnatal blues is what I've got,' Fabia told her. 'She's been in and out for years, as I understand things.'

'Try psychosis,' Ruma said. 'Try severe psychotic postnatal depression. Try attempted murder.'

Fabia sipped her coffee, watching Ruma over the rim of her cup. She evaluated the young woman, heard no excitement in her voice, and approved of the level of her professionalism in the matter. She said, 'When? Who?'

'Twice. Once she was prevented – evidently in the nick of time – from chucking her youngest out of a third-floor window towards a railway track. This is from a flat they lived in, in Du Cane Road. East Acton. Neighbour was there and she phoned the cops once she got the kid away from her. Another time she parked the same kid's pram in the path of an oncoming bus and did a runner. Clearly out of her head.'

'How was that determined?'

'History and examination.'

'What sort of history?'

'You said she's been in and out for years. Did you know it's been since she was thirteen?'

Fabia didn't know this. She considered the fact. 'Any precipitating event?'

'And then some. Her mum committed suicide just three weeks after being released from a facility herself. Paranoid schizophrenic. Carole was with her when she took the leap in front of a train in Baker Street underground station. This would have been when Carole was twelve.'

Fabia set down her cup. 'I should have known this,' she said. 'I should have found out.'

Ruma said quickly, 'No. That's not why I'm telling you. And anyway, how much digging are you supposed to do? It's not your job.'

'Is it yours?'

'I'm the one trying to make the breakthrough here. You're just trying to hold things together.'

'I'm putting on plasters where surgery's called for.'

'No one knows till it's time to know,' Ruma said. 'Anyway, here's my point.'

Fabia didn't need to be told. 'Ness slipping into psychosis? Like her mum?'

'It's possible, isn't it? And here's what's interesting: Carole Campbell tried to kill the youngest because she believed he'd inherited the affliction. I don't know why, because he was a baby, but she singled him out. Like a mother dog who won't nurse a newborn pup because she knows something's wrong with it. Her instincts tell her.'

'Are you saying this *is* inherited, then?'

'It's the old nature and nurture thing. The predisposition is inherited. Look. This is a brain disorder: proteins not doing what they're supposed to be doing. A genetic mutation. That sets someone up for psychosis. The person's environment does the rest.'

Fabia thought about Toby, what she'd seen and heard, and how the family attempted to shield him, about everything they'd done from the first to see to it that he would not be evaluated by someone who might pinpoint an illness that could spell misery for him. She said, 'There's clearly something wrong with the youngest. That's evident enough.'

'They *all* need to be tested. Evaluated by a psychiatrist. Have a genetic history taken. What I'm saying is that my idea for Ness to enter group counselling is a load of bollocks. If she's heading for a psychotic breakdown—'

'If she's *in* one already,' Fabia offered.

'Or if she's in the midst of one, then we need to get onto this before something else happens.'

Fabia agreed. But she wondered how Ness – both uncommunicative and uncooperative in sessions with a counsellor –

was going to take having her mind probed in one way or another by a psychiatrist. Not well, she decided.

A visit to the magistrate was in order, then. What Fabia and Ruma could not effect in the girl would surely come about if the magistrate's court gave her the word. And more than the word: the option between cooperation or incarceration. The mere threat of an increase in her community service hours would hardly make an impression upon her.

'Let me talk to some people,' Fabia said.

Ivan Weatherall, being neither an idiot nor a fool, had quickly put together a number of pieces to the puzzle of Joel Campbell once he'd taken that phone call from Kendra. Most of these pieces had to do with Joel's talent and with *Wield Words Not Weapons*, but some of them related to the attempted mugging in Portobello Road. This, he'd earlier concluded, was so far out of character in the boy that only a case of mistaken identity could possibly explain it. In conjunction with Joel's quick release from custody, there seemed to be no other answer.

But Kendra's call had forced him to consider the possibility that there was a Joel he didn't know. Since there were two sides to every coin – a ghastly cliché, but one that had an apparent application in this particular case as far as Ivan was concerned – it stood to reason that Joel had kept part of himself hidden from Ivan, and the truth was that the facts supported this conclusion.

Ivan didn't know about Joel's dealings with the Blade. As far as the less wholesome individuals who populated parts of North Kensington went, Ivan knew only that Joel had rubbed metaphorical elbows with Neal Wyatt. And Neal was someone whom Ivan mistakenly saw as troubled, but not essentially dangerous. So while Ivan understood that something worrisome was brewing within Joel, he thought in terms of the home itself instead of the streets.

What Ivan knew was this: the aunt's boyfriend was a live-in.

The father was dead. The mother was gone. The sister had been sentenced to community service. The younger brother was . . . well, rather odd. Change in the form of a new home, new school, and new associates was difficult for anyone to endure. Was there any wonder that Joel occasionally lost his grip on the ability to cope? The way Ivan saw things, Joel was a perfectly good lad. Surely, then, any potential for serious trouble could be nipped in the bud if the adults in his life all agreed on how to deal with him.

Ivan himself had grown up under the firm but loving thumbs of his parents. Thus, firmness was what was called for, he decided. Firmness, fairness, and honesty.

When he next met Joel, he went directly to the home. Seeing Joel *in situ*, as he described it to himself, would gain him further information on how best to help the boy.

As it turned out, all three of the Campbell children were there when Ivan knocked on the door. Joel admitted him – obviously surprised but quickly altering his face to mask whatever else was going on within him – and cartoon noise from upstairs suggested that the little brother was present as well. Beyond the entrance and in the kitchen, Ivan could see Joel's sister. She was at the table, one foot propped up on the edge as she painted her toenails metallic blue. An ashtray sat next to the bottle of varnish. Cigarette smoke plumed upward in a lazy spiral. A radio playing on the worktop added to the general cacophony of the household. Rap music issued forth, most of it grunted indecipherably by a singer later identified by the DJ as someone calling himself Big R Balz.

Ivan said, 'Could I have a word, Joel?'

'I ain't written nuffink lately.' Joel glanced beyond Ivan as if wishing him to leave.

Ivan wasn't about to be dismissed. 'This isn't about your poetry, actually. Your aunt phoned me.'

'Yeah. Know.'

'I'd like to talk about that.'

Joel led him into the kitchen, where Ness looked Ivan over. She didn't say anything, but she didn't have to. Lately, as she'd managed in the past, all Ness had to do was to fix her great dark eyes upon people to discomfit them. She was scornful on the surface but something else beneath it. That *something else* made people uneasy.

Ivan nodded a hello. Ness's full lips curved in a smile. She gave him a head-to-toe and made an evaluation of him that she didn't bother to hide, taking in his lank grey hair, his bad teeth, his worn and countrified tweed jacket, his scuffed shoes. She nodded but not in an exchange of greeting. Rather her nod said, Man I know your kind, and she lit another cigarette from the dying end of the one in the ashtray. She held it between her fingers with the smoke coiling around her head. She said to her brother, 'Dis's Ivan, eh? Di'n't t'ink I'd ever see him over here. 'Spect he i'n't round dis part of town very often innit. So how you like it, mon, seeing how us ethnic types live?'

'He ain't like dat,' Joel said.

'Right,' was her laconic response.

But Ivan wasn't put off by Ness. He said, 'Good heavens, I've seen you before, but I'd no idea you were Joel's sister. You're in the drop-in centre, aren't you? Playing with the children? You've obviously got a real gift for working with them.'

This was hardly the response Ness expected to get from the man. Her expression fixed itself into place. She drew in on her cigarette and barked a harsh laugh. She said, 'Yeah. Make a *proper* little mummy, wouldn't I?' She pushed away from the table and sauntered from the room, up the stairs and out of sight.

Ivan said to Joel, 'Did I say—'

'Dat's just Ness,' Joel said.

'Bruised soul,' Ivan murmured.

Joel looked at him sharply. Ivan met his gaze. His own was open and too difficult to look at, so Joel glanced away.

Ivan sat at the table. He carefully screwed the top back on to Ness's abandoned nail varnish. He nodded at a chair, meaning Joel was to sit as well. When Joel had done so, moments ticked by. Rap music continued to blare from the radio. Joel got up from the table and snapped it off. They were left with the sound of explosions upstairs: a cartoon character meeting his fate with Toby crowing with laughter as he watched.

In keeping with his determination that firmness, fairness, and honesty were called for, Ivan brought up the topic of *Wield Words Not Weapons*. More specifically, he brought up the topic of Joel's use of the poetry event to serve his own interests. Ivan began by saying, 'I'd thought we were friends, Joel. But I must say that your aunt's phone call has forced me to reevaluate.'

Joel – having taken the opportunity presented by turning off the radio to remain standing – leaned against the worktop but said nothing. He wasn't sure what Ivan was talking about anyway, although at this point he knew adults well enough to understand that clarification was not far off.

Ivan said, 'I don't like being used. Even less do I like *Wield Words* being used. This is because using *Wield Words* for a purpose other than the creation of poetry runs in the face of what I've created the event to be. Do you understand?'

Joel didn't. He knew he was supposed to, however. That knowledge and the knowledge of his failure acted in concert to encourage his silence.

Ivan read this silence as indifference, and he was affronted. He tried not to go in the direction of *After all I've done* and, in this, he was fairly successful. He knew enough about boys like Joel to understand that their behaviour was not about him. Still, he'd thought Joel different, more sensitive to nuances, and Ivan didn't like considering he might have been wrong.

He clarified. 'You came to *Wield Words*, but you left. During *Walk the Word*. You thought I didn't see and I might not have done, but for the phone call from your aunt. Oh, not the one asking about the money, not the one you heard. There was another.'

Joel's eyebrows rose in spite of himself. He drew his lip in between his teeth.

'Yes. That very night, she phoned. In the midst of *Walk the Word*, so that was how I knew you weren't there. But I couldn't be certain, could I? You might've gone to the lavatory at the very moment when my mobile went off, so I couldn't tell her you weren't there, could I? I said, Of course he's here. He's even read to us a rather abysmal poem, Mrs Osborne. Not to worry, I said. I'll see he goes home straightaway, when we're finished here.'

Joel looked down. What he saw were his trainers, one of them untied. He bent and redid the laces.

Ivan repeated his theme. 'I don't like being used.'

'You di'n't have to tell her—'

'That you were there? I realise that. But you *were* there, weren't you? You were careful that way. You were there, you made sure I knew it, and then you left. Would you like to tell me about it?'

'Nuffink *to* tell, mon.'

'Where did you go?'

Joel said nothing.

'Joel, don't you see? If I'm to help you, there has to be an element of trust between us. I thought we had that. Now to see that I've been mistaken . . . What is it you don't want to talk about? Has it do with Neal Wyatt?'

It had and it hadn't, but how was Joel to explain this to Ivan? To Ivan the solution to everything was to write a poem, to read it to strangers, to listen to them and pretend that what they said made a difference in life when it made no difference at all save in that moment of sitting in front of them on the dais and engaging them in conversation. It was play-acting, really, just a useless bit of salve on a sore that would not heal.

He said, 'It's nuffink, innit. I jus' di'n't want to be there.

You c'n see I ain't writing, not like I was. It ain't working for me, Ivan. Dat's all there is.'

Ivan attempted to use this, as he saw no other way to proceed. 'So you've hit a dry patch. That happens to everyone. What's best is to divert your attention to another area of creative endeavour, related to the written word or not.' He was silent as he looked for an anodyne for what he saw as the boy's situation: a not unreasonable creative blockage rising from his home circumstances. Ludicrous to suggest he take up painting, sculpture, dance, music, or anything else requiring his presence some place where his aunt was entirely unlikely to let him go. But there was one outlet . . .

'Join us on the film,' he said. 'You went to that one meeting. You saw what we're about. We need input on the script, and yours would be most welcome. If your aunt will agree to your coming to our meetings . . . perhaps once a week at first? . . . then chances are the act of working with words once again will stimulate your ideas and get them rolling.'

Joel could see this playing out, and how it played out wasn't helpful. He would go to the meetings if his aunt agreed, and she would ring up Ivan in the midst of them to make certain he was where he said he'd be. He would have nothing to offer the script-writing team because he could no longer think about anything as unimportant as a dream of film that would never come true.

Ivan waited and read Joel's hesitation as despair, which in part it was. He merely applied Joel's sense of desolation to the wrong source. He said, 'You're struggling now, but it won't be that way for ever, Joel. Sometimes you have to grasp on to a lifeline that's being offered, even if that lifeline doesn't look like something that will pull you out of the troubles you have.'

Joel went back to looking at his feet. Above them, calliope music played. Joel recognised it as the theme song to yet another cartoon show. He couldn't have known how otherwise appropriate it was to the conversation they were having.

Ivan did and he smiled. 'Ah. The Muse,' he said. And then because the very sound of a calliope told him things were truly meant to be as they were in this moment – the two of them in the neat little kitchen with Ivan proposing a cure for what ailed his much younger friend – he said, 'Know that I'm not the enemy, Joel. I never have been and I never will be.'

But what Joel thought upon hearing this was that everyone in his world was the enemy. That being the case, there was danger everywhere. Danger to himself and danger to anyone who, against all odds, decided to be his friend.

Joel was on his way to fetch Toby from the learning centre when Cal Hancock appeared. He seemed to come out of nowhere, materialising at Joel's side as he passed a William Hill betting shop. Joel smelled him first as Cal fell into step beside him. The odour of weed clung to his clothing.

Cal said to him, 'Nex' week, blood.'

Joel said, startled, 'What?'

Cal said, 'Wha' you mean *what*? There is no *what*, mon. There's nuffink but wha' you got arranged.'

'I don't got nuffink—'

'You clear on wha' happens, you don't do like the Blade wants you to do? He got you *out*. Jus' as easy he can put you back in. A word from him an' the cops gonna move. On you, y'unnerstan. You got dat now?'

It would have been impossible not to have got it. But Joel stopped walking and made no reply. More and more, words had no meaning for him. Mostly he heard them but they did not compute. They were background noise while in the foreground was a symphony playing the notes of his fear.

Cal said, 'You *owe* him, and he a man dat collects. You cock dis up like dat Asian cow over Portobello Road, you got more trouble 'n anyone c'n help you wiv.'

Joel looked over at a school playground that they were passing. He found he wasn't sure where they were. He felt like someone caught in a maze: too far in, too many turns, no way to the centre, and no way out. But still there was something he didn't understand. He said, 'How's he *do* all dis, Cal?'

'Do all wha', mon?'

'Make t'ings happen like he does. Getting me out. Putting me back in. He bribing the cops? He got *dat* much cash?'

Cal blew out a breath that hovered like fog in the frigid air. He'd come to Joel wearing the uniform of the streets – grey sweatshirt with the hood drawn up over a baseball cap, black windbreaker, black jeans, white trainers. It wasn't Cal's usual garb, and Joel wondered about this, just as he wondered how the graffiti artist was managing to stay warm without a heavier anorak.

'Shit, mon.' Cal kept his voice low and he looked around as if searching for eavesdroppers. 'T'ings more important to cops 'an money. Don't you know dat yet? Ain't you figgered out how t'ings *happen* round here? Why no one ever bust into dat squat waving submachine guns?' He dug into a pocket of his windbreaker, and Joel thought he meant to bring out a pertinent piece of evidence that would show him once and for all who the Blade was and what Joel was dealing with. But he brought forth a spliff. He lit up without even a glance around, which should have illuminated for Joel what he'd been saying, but it did not.

'I don't get—'

'You don't *need* to get. You jus' need to do. It happens nex' week and you be ready. You carrying?'

'What?'

'Don' *what* me no more. You got dat gun wiv you?'

'Course not. I get caught wiv dat—'

'You carry it ever'day, now. Y'unnerstan? I give you th' word 'bout dis going down and you ain't carrying, consider dat's it. Cops get the word. You go back for a visit.'

'Wha's he gonna make me—'

'Mon, you know when you know.' Cal took a hit from his

joint and studied Joel. He shook his head as he let the smoke ease its way from his lungs. 'Tried,' he said. He sounded defeated.

That said, Cal left him. Joel was free to go on his way. But he knew that was the extent of his freedom.

What Joel didn't know as he fetched his brother was that he'd been seen. Dix D'Court, in transit from the Rainbow Café to the Jubilee Sports Centre, had caught sight of Joel in conversation with Cal. While he was not aware of the name of Joel's companion, he recognised the signature garments as anyone might have done. He read them as *gang* and his thoughts moved in a logical direction. He knew he could not let this go. He had a duty, both to the kids and to Kendra.

His mind was on this as he completed his work-out, a rushed and abbreviated affair. He arrived home having planned an approach, but also rather feverish in his anticipation of the conversation he intended to have. Kendra wasn't there – a massage in progress somewhere in Holland Park, according to a note she'd left on the fridge, with suitable exclamation marks to illustrate her happiness about the destination – but, to Dix, this was just as well. If he was to be a father-figure to the Campbells, there were times when he'd have to be that father-figure alone.

No one was on the ground floor of the house. Television noise – that perennial background motif to every waking moment – drifted down from above. That meant Toby was at home, which meant Joel was at home. Ness's shoulder bag dangled over a kitchen chair, but there was no other evidence of her.

Dix strode to the stairs at the back of the house and yelled Joel's name. Doing it, he heard the sound of his own father's voice issuing forth, and he recalled how both he and his sister had jumped to at the bellow. He added, 'Get down here, mon,' when Joel replied with, 'What?' from somewhere above. To that he went on with, 'We got to talk,' and when Joel said, ''Bout what?' he replied, 'Hey! Get your arse down the stairs.'

Joel came, but he did it without haste. On his tail came Toby, ever Joel's shadow. To Dix, Joel seemed to slouch down the stairs and into the kitchen and when Dix told him to sit at the table, he did so but without the alacrity that might have otherwise telegraphed respect.

Joel was in another world, and it wasn't a pleasant one. He'd tipped up the chest of drawers in his room. He'd found the gun where he'd left it. He'd buried it in his rucksack. After that, he'd sat on his bed, feeling sick at heart and sick in stomach. He tried to tell himself he could do as the Blade had ordered him. He added that, after he did it, he could go back to being who he was.

Dix said, 'What're you doing wiv dat lout, Joel?'

Joel blinked. 'Huh?'

'Don't *huh* me, blood. I seen you wiv him in the street. Him toking up an' you standin' there waiting for a hit yourself. What're you doing wiv him? You sellin now or you just smokin? How your aunt goin to react to dis, I tell her what I see you up to.'

'What?' Joel said. 'Wiv Cal, you mean? We were talking, mon. Dat's it.'

'How you come to be talkin' to some candyman, Joel?'

'I jus' know him, okay? An' he don't—'

'Wha'? Sell? Use? Offer it round? You t'ink I'm stupid?'

'I tol' you, it was Cal. Dat's all.'

'An' wha' you talkin' about, if it ain't dope?'

Joel didn't reply.

'Asked you a question. I mean to have it answered.'

Joel's back went up at Dix's tone. 'None of your business,' he replied. 'Bugger off. I don't got to tell you nuffink.'

Dix crossed the kitchen in one long bound and jerked Joel out of his chair like an unstrung marionette. 'Watch your mouf,' he ordered.

Toby, lurking in the doorway to the stairs where he'd been all along, cried, 'Dix! Dat's Joel! Don't!'

'You shut up. Let me get on wiv my business, okay?' He tightened his grip on Joel.

Joel cried, 'Lemme go! I don't got to talk to you or anyone.'

Dix shook him, hard. 'Oh yeah, you do. Start 'splaining yourself and do it now. And lemme tell you, mon, it better be good.'

'Fuck you!' Joel squirmed to get away. He kicked out and missed. 'Lemme go! Lemme go, you fucking cocksucker.'

The slap came quickly: Dix's open hand squarely meeting the flesh of Joel's face. It sounded like wet meat coming down on a board, and it flipped Joel's head backwards and upset his balance. Another slap followed, harder this time. Then Dix began to drag him towards the sink.

He grunted, 'So. Like dirty words? Like dem better'n answerin questions? Le's see if dis makes you like dem words less.' He bent Joel back against the worktop and stretched out to reach for the Fairy Liquid.

Toby shot across the kitchen to stop him. He grabbed Dix by the leg. He cried, 'Get 'way from my bruvver! He ain't done *nuffink*. Get 'way from my bruvver! Joel! Joel!'

Dix shoved him away, too hard. Toby weighed next to nothing and the force sent him crashing into the table, where he began to wail. Dix had the Fairy Liquid in his hand and he squirted the detergent into Joel's face. He aimed for his mouth but got it everywhere else. He said, 'Someone's mouf needs dis'nfectin,' as he tried to drive the spout between Joel's lips.

But a clatter from the stairs brought Ness into the room. She flung herself upon Dix and her brother. The force of her flying body threw Dix hard against Joel and Joel just as hard against the edge of the worktop. His feet scrambled for purchase against the lino and he slipped in some of the Fairy Liquid. He went down. Dix went with him. Ness landed on top of them both.

She shrieked a string of curses as she clawed at Dix's head. His grip loosened on Joel as he tried to protect his face from her nails. Joel rolled away and against the table, where he reached for a chair and staggered to his feet.

Ness was screaming, 'Damn you! Fuck you! Don't you never touch one of my brothers!' as she went after the body-builder with her hands, her feet, her elbows, her teeth.

Dix managed to catch her arms. He flipped her over and himself with her. He was on top now, and he pinned her to the floor. They writhed there in the Fairy Liquid, a desperate coupling that he tried to still by covering the length of her body with his.

She screamed then. She gave one, long horrifying cry, sounding like someone just entering hell.

It was into this scene that Kendra came: Toby in a ball under the table, Joel trying to pull Dix off his sister, Dix doing what he could to quell her, Ness far gone to another place.

'*Get off her.* Get *off* her!' Ness shrieked. She flung her head back and arched her spine with such strength that she managed to lift both of them off the floor. 'You leave her be! No! Mummy . . . *Mum*my . . .' And on that final fruitless appeal to a woman not there, never there, and never to be there, she began to howl. It was like the sound of an animal shot, doomed to dying by degrees.

Kendra rushed forward. 'Dix! Stop this!'

Dix rolled off the girl. He was bleeding from the face and panting like a runner. He shook his head, incapable of speech.

Which didn't matter, because Ness was doing all the speaking: on the floor, spread-eagled, but kicking now and beating her fists against the air and then against her own body.

'You get off. You bloody get *off.* Get *off*!'

Kendra knelt at her side.

'He did it to me. He did it. He *did.*'

'Ness!' Kendra cried.

'An' no one there.'

'Ness. *Ness!* What's—'

'An' you go off to the fruit machines. You say watch 'em and he say fine. And you jus' go and leave us wiv *him*. But it ain't him. It's all of dem. Pressing up 'gainst me an' I c'n feel it's hard. An' he says I like 'em young, he says, I like em like dis cos dey still firm mmm mmmm an' I don't know wha' to do, innit, cos I don't 'spect . . .'

Kendra yanked her fiercely into her arms. She cried, 'Jesus *God.*'

The others watched, like statues, turned to salt not by what they saw but what they heard.

'An' *you* been there for a visit,' Ness cried, clinging to Kendra and pounding at her back. 'You come round 'fore you going out to dis club, dat club, anywheres, innit, pulling dis man, dat man. An' ever'one *sees* what you mean to do cos you got dat look an' how you dress. But only a certain age you want and you make dat clear cos dey got to be young cos if they old like sixty, sixty-five, seventy, you don't want 'em. But they *hot* now, see? All of 'em hot. They hot an' they hard and they know what they want. So you leave, she leaves cos she *always* go to the fruit machines and dat's when they take it. They bloody fucking *take* it. George an' his mates on the bed in Gran's room. They all got their cocks out . . . They climb on . . . And I can't . . . I *can't* . . .'

'Ness! Ness!' Kendra cried. She held her, she rocked her. And to Joel, 'Did you know?'

He shook his head. He'd bitten into his fist as his sister was talking, and he could taste the coppery flavour of his blood. Whatever had happened to Ness had happened in silence and behind closed doors. But he could recall how often they'd come to his gran's – those friends of George, there to play cards, sometimes as many as eight of them. He could remember Glory saying as she pulled on her coat, 'George, you be able to mind the kids wiv all your mates here like dis?'

And George saying happily in reply, 'Don't you worry, Glor.

Don't you worry 'bout nuffink. I got 'nough help here to man a ocean liner or two, so three kids ain't a problem. Sides, Ness old enough to help out 'f the boys get out 'f hand. Ain't you Nessa?' with a wink at her.

And Ness saying only, 'Don't go, Gran.'

And Gran saying, 'You make your bruvs some Bournvita, darlin. Time you got it drunk up, your gran be home.'

But not home soon enough.

So when Ness sharpened a paring knife, it seemed the logical outcome of what she'd revealed and what had happened in the kitchen. Joel saw her do it, but he said nothing. He could see that Ness was, in this, just like him. If the paring knife made her feel secure, what of it? he thought.

In the aftermath of what happened with the children, Dix questioned everything. His dream had always centred around the romantic ideal of family, for his dream of the future was grounded in the past, which had as its most notable characteristic the warm kinship he'd always experienced with his own relations. To him, *family* meant paterfamilias sitting at the head of the table, carving a joint of beef at Sunday lunch. It meant fairy lights strung from the ceiling at Christmas-time and daytrips to Brighton on the odd bank holiday when there was money enough for candy floss, a bag of rock, and fish and chips by the sea. It meant parents keeping a watchful eye over children's school work, their afternoon activities, their mates, their dress, their manners, and their growth. Dentist for their teeth. Doctor for their inoculations. Thermometer thrust beneath their tongues, soup and soldiers when they were ill. Children spoke respectfully to their parents in this sort of family, and parents responded with firm but loving guidance, disciplining when necessary and making sure the lines of communication were open. If any family can be described as *normal*, it was the family in which Dix D'Court had grown up. This had provided him with an image of what life should look like when it came to his own future with a wife and offspring, but nothing about it prepared him for dealing with children who were plagued by trouble and horror.

The Campbells, he believed, needed help. More help than either Kendra or he would be able to give them in a hundred thousand lifetimes. Dix broached this subject with her, but she did not take it well. 'You want me to get rid of them?' she demanded.

'Ain't saying dat,' he told her quietly. 'Jus' dat they been through too much and we ain't got the skills to lead 'em away from where they are.'

'Ness's *in* counselling. Toby's in his learning centre. Joel's doing what he's meant to do. What more do you want?'

'Ken, dis is bigger 'n you and it's bigger 'n me. You got to see that.'

But Kendra could not. She told herself that if she had not been so bloody-minded about keeping her life exactly as it was when Glory dropped the children upon her like three sacks of grain, she might have built an adequate life for *them*. So anything that even smacked of abandoning them to their fate at this point was something she would not consider. She would do what she had to do to save them, even if it meant doing so on her own.

'Even if it means giving up everyt'ing you been working for?' Cordie asked when they saw each other next. 'The massage business? The someday spa? You letting dat go?'

'Isn't that what you've done?' Kendra countered. 'Didn't you give in to Gerald and give up on your dreams?'

'What? Cos he wants 'nother baby and I'm making him one? How's dat giving up on dreams? An' *what* dreams, anyways? I was doing fingernails, f'r God's sake, Ken.'

'You were going to be part of the spa.'

'Yeah. True. But bottom line is dis: I gonna choose Gerald if I got to make a choice. I always gonna choose Gerald. Spa come along and if it fit in wiv what I got going at th' moment, I join dat dream. If it don't fit in, I choose Gerald.'

'What about the others?'

'Wha' others?'

'Men you pull. You know what I mean.'

Cordie looked at her blankly. 'You mistaken,' she said. 'I don't pull men.'

'Cordie, you been snogging wiv nineteen-year-old boys—'

'I know wha' I got here,' Cordie said firmly, always a woman capable of turning a blind eye to her own weaknesses of the flesh. 'An' I choose Gerald. You best look at what you got and make a choice you c'n live wiv as well.'

That was the issue: making a choice and living with it afterwards. Kendra didn't want to do either.

The only answer seemed to be to make a move that would communicate a willingness to deal with the children's difficulties.

'We must file charges,' was how Fabia Bender reacted when Kendra revealed the information. They met by prior arrangement at Lisboa Patisserie in Golborne Road, with Castor and Pollux waiting patiently outside as their mistress indulged in *café au lait*, along with a prawn mayonnaise sandwich, which she brought forth from her briefcase. Fabia set her sandwich on a napkin and took out a day planner in which she kept everything from her diary to coupons for her grocery shopping. She began to flip through it.

'File charges against whom?' Kendra asked. 'George's gone. As for his mates . . . Ness doesn't know their names and my mum's not likely to know them either. And what do we gain, putting her in the hands of cops for questioning or the CPS for examining? She's not about to talk to cops about this. She's barely even talking to me.'

Fabia looked thoughtful. 'It explains a great deal, doesn't it? Especially about why she won't talk to Ruma. Or cooperate with testing. Or anything, really. Most girls have deep shame about being molested. They believe they said something, did something, encouraged something. That's how the molesters condition them to think. And, in Ness's case, no one prepared her as a young child to think anything else: her mum mental, her dad dead, her gran consumed with other things. As she was developing into a woman, there was no one present to talk to her about the right she had to protect her own body.' Fabia was mostly thinking aloud, gazing out towards the street where a light rain was falling. When she moved her eyes to take in Kendra, Fabia read her expression. She added, 'This *isn't* your fault, Mrs Osborne. You weren't in the home. Your mother was. If there's blame to be handed out—'

'What does it matter?' Kendra asked. 'I feel what I feel.'

Fabia nodded. She said, 'Well, Ruma is going to have to be told. And . . .' She hesitated, lost in thought. She observed Kendra and knew she meant well. But the aunt's attempts at parenting had been indescribably inadequate, so there was no real hope that Kendra could reach into her niece's psyche and soothe it. Still, there were other ports to turn to. Fabia Bender said, 'I'm going to talk to Majidah Ghafoor. There's something good there between her and Ness. A field to plough if not to plant. Let me see what I can do.'

With the new-found knowledge she'd been given, Ruma suggested a new course of action, one that Fabia would not have expected. Support groups were all well and good, she said, and a psychiatric evaluation might give them information about the state of Ness's brain chemistry vis à vis everything from schizophrenia to depression, but now they were talking about the state of her psyche and her mind, and with a client unwilling to touch upon the subject of molestation and certainly too old for something as obvious as anatomical dolls to play with . . . 'Hippotherapy,' Ruma concluded. 'There've been some excellent results with that.'

'*Hippo?*' Naturally, Fabia thought of the lumbering, rotund

African mammals, of their huge gaping mouths and tiny twitching ears.

Ruma said, 'Horses,' to correct her vision. 'Treatment for the mind with the help of a horse.' When Fabia's expression registered scepticism, Ruma explained how it was meant to work, this form of tactile therapy in which the horse-to-human and human-to-horse interaction not only served as metaphor for subjects too painful for the patient to discuss but also as a high-speed means of making progress in someone's recovery. 'It's about coming to terms with issues of control, power, and fear,' Ruma said. 'I know it sounds mad, Fabia, but we've got to try it. Without some sort of breakthrough with Ness . . .' She let the rest hang, and Fabia finished it for her mentally. Without a breakthrough now, things would only get worse.

'Can we dig round for funding?' Ruma asked.

Fabia sighed. 'I don't bloody know.' It was so unlikely. This was one girl among many in a system stressed and over-burdened. There might be a special fund somewhere, but it could take ages of research to find it. Fabia could look and she was willing to do so. But in the meantime, Ness's wounds would fester.

Fabia went to Majidah. She would, she decided, leave no stone unturned in this project of Vanessa Campbell. Majidah, Ruma, Fabia, Kendra . . . All the women in Ness's life had to present a united front. The message they would pass to Ness was one of concern, love, and support.

'Ah, that these terrible things must happen,' was Majidah's quiet reaction to the story Fabia told her. She herself told Fabia what little she knew about Ness's past from the girl's earlier partial admissions.

'*Eleven* years old?' Fabia repeated in horror.

'It makes one question the ways of God.'

Fabia was not a believer in God. Mankind, she'd long ago decided, was an accident of atoms colliding in an ancient atmosphere: without design, without plan, and without a single hope of a positive result unless a huge effort was put into getting one. She said, 'We're trying to arrange a special therapy for her. In the meantime, should she decide to speak to you about what's happened to her . . . I thought it best that you be brought into the picture.'

'And indeed I am glad that you have done so,' Majidah said. 'I too shall try to talk to the girl.'

'It's unlikely she's going to speak about—'

'Oh my gracious, I shall not speak about this,' Majidah said. 'But there are many things to talk about besides the past, as you must know.'

So that was the course that Majidah pursued. To her, terrible incidents could try one's soul, but lack of acceptance and lack of forgiveness led to a rotting of the spirit.

She had a plan. In the child drop-in centre she set out magazines, pots of glue, posterboard, and round-tipped scissors. She set the children to the task of collage making, and she insisted Ness join in. They would, she said, create a picture representation of their families and their world.

'Why've I got to do it?' Ness demanded. 'I can't help them, innit, 'f I got to make one of these t'ings myself.'

'You will act as their model,' Majidah told her placidly.

'But I don't—'

'Vanessa, this is what we're going to do just now. I cannot see a problem in this. If you do, then we must discuss it privately.'

This was fine with Ness, a private discussion. It was better than sitting at a table that didn't even come up to her knees, crammed alongside a four-year-old wielding scissors, no matter how dull were the blades. She followed Majidah to the side of the room, to a bank of windows looking out on the playing area and into Meanwhile Gardens. But Majidah was only able to say, 'Vanessa, Sayf al Din and I are wondering why you will not return to him,' before Ness's attention shifted from the Pakistani woman. A movement in her peripheral vision caused her to see what she'd been waiting for days upon days to see.

After that, everything happened quickly. Ness grabbed her bag and flew out of the door. She hurtled into the play area. She dashed towards the gate in the chain link fence, and she pulled from her bag the paring knife she'd been carrying. Her face was set.

Just beyond the fence, Neal Wyatt was talking to Hibah. No member of his crew was with them, and surprise was the advantage Ness had at last.

She launched herself. Through the gate and on top of Neal. Before Hibah or the boy himself could do a thing to stop her – and certainly before Majidah could go after her – Ness had used the speed, the surprise, and the weight of her attack to topple Neal Wyatt to the ground. She went down with him. The blade of her paring knife flashed grey against the grey winter sky. It disappeared. It came up red. It disappeared again. Again. Again.

Hibah screamed. She couldn't get close. Ness flailed the knife when she made the attempt. Neal fought back, but he could not match Ness for revenge and hate. Blood flecked her cheeks and her chest.

She started to shriek, 'You wan' it, baby? You wan' it like dis?' and she raised the knife in such a way that it was clear she intended to plunge it directly into Neal Wyatt's heart.

Majidah dashed outside and the children followed. She screamed, 'No!' at them and they huddled in a mass near the fence. Blood seemed to be everywhere. On Ness, on the boy she'd attacked, on the Asian girl who'd been his companion. Majidah said to this girl, 'You must help. *Now*,' and she grabbed Ness's upraised arm, pulling her back as the other young girl – incoherently shrieking – did the same.

All three of them fell. Neal rolled away. And then he was up on his feet, bleeding but not so wounded that he couldn't still kick. Grunts and curses accompanied these kicks. His feet met heads, arms, legs.

Then footsteps pounded from the direction of Elkstone Road. A young man carrying his mother's walking stick used it to drive Neal back. On the pavement, his mother stood with an elderly companion, who spoke into a mobile:

'Blood everywhere . . . three women . . . a boy . . . a dozen children . . .' The words bridged the distance from the pavement to where the attack had occurred. They were hardly accurate but they did the trick. The police and the ambulance were not long in arriving.

But they were long enough for Ness to run off, and no one was in any condition to go after her.

26

Joel saw the dogs before Toby did: the enormous schnauzer, the smaller but more menacing doberman. They were doing what they'd always done when he'd seen them in the past, lounging with their heads on their paws, awaiting instructions from their mistress. But *where* they were – on either side of the steps leading up into his aunt's house – told him something was wrong. If Fabia Bender was inside the house, that meant Kendra was inside the house. At this time of day, she was supposed to be at the charity shop.

Toby murmured, 'Lookit 'em dogs,' as he and Joel edged by them carefully.

'Don't be touchin 'em or anyt'ing,' Joel warned his brother.

''Kay,' Toby said.

Inside, they were safe, but only from the dogs. For in the kitchen, the boys' aunt and the social worker sat at the table with three manila folders fanned out in front of them and an ashtray planted with cigarette stubs next to Kendra's elbow. A notebook spilling out paperwork lay on the floor next to Fabia Bender's feet.

Joel zeroed in on the manila folders. Three of them. Three Campbell children. The suggestion was transparent.

He looked to his aunt. He looked from his aunt to Fabia Bender. 'Where's Ness?' he asked.

'Dix is looking for her,' Kendra said. For a frantic phone call from Majidah had taken Kendra out into the streets to hunt for her niece, just as a phone call from Fabia Bender had brought her home, leaving Dix to continue the frenzied search.

'Take Toby up to your room, Joel. Take a snack up with you. There's some ginger biscuits, if you'd like them.'

Food in the bedroom did the trick. Food in the bedroom was a violation, so Joel knew that whatever had happened was bad. He didn't want to leave, but he knew there was no point staying. So he got the biscuits, climbed to their room, established Toby on the bed with his skateboard and the food, and returned to the stairs. He eased down and sat, straining to hear the worst.

'. . . realistically look at your ability to cope . . .' was what he heard Fabia Bender saying.

'These are my niece and nephews,' Kendra responded dully. 'They are not cats and dogs, Miss Bender.'

'Mrs Osborne, I know you've been doing your best.'

'You don't know. How can you? You *don't*. What you see—'

'Please. Don't do this to yourself, and don't do it to me. This is no failed mugging we're talking about. This is assault with intent. They don't have her yet but they will soon enough. And when they have her in custody, she'll go directly to a juvenile detention centre, and that's the end of it. They don't give community service hours for what amounts to attempted murder, and they don't let children go home to wait for the magistrate to deal with them. I don't mean to be cruel by saying all this. You must know the reality of her situation.'

Kendra's voice went low. 'Where'll they take her?'

'As I said, there are juvenile detention centres . . . She won't be mixed in with adults.'

'But you've got to see and they've got to see, there's a reason. She'd been attacked by that boy. He's got to be the one who went after her that night. He and his mates. She wouldn't say, but he did it. I *know* this. He's been after all three of the kids from the first. And then there's what happened to her before. At her grandmother's house. There are *reasons*.'

Joel had never heard his aunt sound so broken. Her tone

made his eyes prickle. He put his chin on his knees to stop its trembling.

The front door buzzer went. Below, Kendra and Fabia turned as one to the sound. Kendra scraped back her chair, and she hesitated only a moment – a woman gathering courage for the next terrible event – before she crossed over to open the door.

Three people stood crowded on the top step, with Castor and Pollux still motionless on the ground, sentinels marking the changing circumstances in Edenham Way. Two of the people were uniformed constables: a black woman and a white man. Between them was Ness: coatless, shivering, her jersey stained with blood.

When Kendra said, 'Ness!' Joel clattered down the stairs and into the kitchen. He stopped short at the sight of the police. They said, 'Mrs Osborne?' Kendra said, 'Yes. Yes.'

It was a moment of tableau: Fabia Bender still at the kitchen table, but half-risen; Kendra with both hands extended to take Ness into her arms; the constables openly evaluating the situation; Joel afraid to make a move lest he be told to return to his room; and Ness with her face a hard mask.

The female constable was the one to alter the hesitation among them. She put her hand on Ness's back. Ness flinched. The constable didn't react. She merely increased the pressure till Ness moved inside the house. The police moved with her. All of them lifted their feet at once as if they'd rehearsed this moment of reunion.

'This young lady had some trouble with a bloke in Queensway,' the female constable said. She introduced herself as PC Cassandra Anyworth and her partner as PC Michael King. 'Big black bloke. Strong man type. He was attempting to get her inside a car. She put up a good fight. Marked him up, which is to her credit. I'd say that's why she's standing here right now. The blood's not hers. Not to worry about that.'

It came to everyone simultaneously that these constables

had no idea what had happened between Ness and Neal Wyatt in Meanwhile Gardens, which meant they were not local police. That alone would have been evident when they said they'd found Ness in altercation with a black man in Queensway. For Queensway was not in the borough monitored by the Harrow Road police. Instead, it was monitored by the Ladbroke Grove station, but this was not happy news.

The Ladbroke Grove station had a rough reputation. Someone taken there was not likely to be received with dispassion, especially someone of a minority race. *Black man* seemed to echo in the room.

'Dix found you?' Kendra asked Ness. 'Dix found you?' When she didn't answer, Kendra asked the constables, 'Was the black man called Dix D'Court?'

PC King spoke. 'Didn't get his name, madam. That would've been handled at the station. He's in custody, though, so there's no worry he'll be coming after her again.' He smiled but it was a smile without warmth. 'They'll know who he is soon enough. They'll have his details and everything he's done for the last twenty years. No worries on that score.'

'He lives here,' Kendra said. 'With me. With us. He went looking for her. I asked him. I was looking for her as well, but Fabia wanted to see me, so I came home. Ness, didn't you tell them it was Dix?'

'She wasn't in condition to tell anyone anything,' PC Anyworth said.

'But you can't hold Dix. Not for doing what I asked him—'

'If that's the case, madam, it'll all be sorted out in due course.'

'Due course? He's in *gaol*, though? He's locked up? Being questioned?' Getting banged about if he didn't answer to their liking was what she didn't say but thought, as did the rest of them. Such was the reputation of the station. Rough treatment followed by the ritualised excuse: walked into a door, he did.

Slipped on the tiles. Knocked his damn head into the cell door for reasons unknown but he's probably claustrophobic. Kendra said, 'My God.' And then, 'Oh, Ness,' and nothing more.

Fabia intervened. She introduced herself and offered her card to the PCs. She was working with the family. She would take Vanessa off the constables' hands. Mrs Osborne had told them the truth, by the way. The man who appeared to be assaulting Vanessa was merely trying to bring her home to her aunt. The situation was rather complex, you see. If the constables wished to talk further about it . . . ? Fabia gestured to the table to indicate they were welcome to sit. There, the folders containing the children's pasts, presents, and futures, were laid out and one of them was open. Fabia's notebook was still on the floor with its paperwork scattered. It was all so official.

PC King turned the business card over in his hands. He was over-worked and tired and just as happy to hand the silent teenager over to other responsible adults. He gave PC Anyworth a glance in which they communicated wordlessly. She nodded. He nodded. Further talk would not be necessary, he said. They'd leave the girl with her aunt and the social worker, and if someone wanted to go down to Ladbroke Grove to identify the man who'd been trying to force Ness into his car, that *should* take care of matters.

For Kendra, the emphasis on *should* underscored the urgency of getting Dix out of the clutches of the police. She said Thank you, thank you, to the constables. They left, and the matter seemed finished.

Except it wasn't. The Ladbroke Grove police station may not have received word of the assault upon an adolescent boy in Meanwhile Gardens and the search for the girl who'd carried out the assault, but they would eventually. Even if that had not been the case, and even if no one in Ladbroke Grove ever connected the dots in this matter, Fabia Bender now had a duty that went beyond calming the troubled waters of this household.

She said, 'I'll have to phone the Harrow Road station,' and she took out her mobile.

Kendra said, 'No. Why? You can't.'

Fabia said, the mobile pressed to her ear, 'Mrs Osborne, you know there's no alternative. Harrow Road know who they're looking for. They have her name, her address, and her past offences in their records. If I leave her here with you – which I can't do and you know it – the only result is prolonging the inevitable. My job is to see that Ness moves through the system smoothly at this point. Yours is to get Dix D'Court out of the Ladbroke Grove station.'

Joel gave an involuntary cry at this, which was when the two women noticed him. Kendra, feeling broken, told him harshly to go back to his room and to stay there until further notice. He gave his sister an agonised glance and fled back up the stairs.

Kendra said to Fabia, 'At least give me time to get her cleaned up.'

'I can't . . . Mrs Osborne . . . Kendra.' Fabia cleared her throat. Involvement with the families of her clients was inevitable, but it always cost her in the end. She hated to say what she had to say. But she pushed forward. 'Evidence,' was the word she used, and she hoped that her gesture towards Ness and the blood upon her would be enough for Kendra to understand.

As for Ness, she merely stood there. Drained, spent, scheming, wondering . . . It was impossible for the other two women to tell. What they both knew – in fact what they all knew – was that matters were finished for the foreseeable future when it came to possibilities for Ness.

Getting Dix out of the Ladbroke Grove police station was no easy matter. It involved several hours of waiting, consultations with a duty solicitor who was none too happy to have to assist, conversations with Fabia Bender via phone, and communication with the Harrow Road police. His impounded car would take several more days to disentangle from the bureaucracy. But at least Dix himself walked out of the custody area, free to go.

He'd never before had an interaction with the police. He'd never even been stopped for a traffic offence. He was shaken and trying not to be governed by hate and the need for vengeance. This required him to breathe calmly and to try to remember who he'd been before he'd seen a drunken girl in the Falcon pub and had decided to drive her home for her own safety. That had begun things: concern for Ness. It was an irony to him that concern for Ness had ended things.

What he said to Kendra, he waited to say until they were back in Edenham Way. Inside the house, he climbed the stairs to her bedroom. She followed him and shut the door. She said, 'Dix, baby,' in a tender voice. But it was also a voice that had always acted as a prelude to sex between them, and he couldn't face sex, he didn't want sex, and he was sure Kendra didn't want it either. He went to the bedroom door and propped it open.

'Boys?' he asked.

'In their room,' she said. Which meant they'd hear if they were listening, but that didn't seem to matter any longer.

Two of the drawers in the bedroom chest were his, and Dix eased them out and dumped their contents on to the bed. He went to the wardrobe and removed his clothes. He said, although the saying of this was entirely unnecessary, 'Can't do it, Ken.'

She watched him pull a duffel bag from beneath the bed, the same duffel bag that he'd brought into her house, hanging over his shoulder, and smiling smiling smiling with hope about what it meant – or rather, really, what he wanted it to mean – that he was taking up residence with the woman he loved. Then, he'd carried it up to this room and flung it into a corner because there were more important things than unpacking and making the requisite spaces in drawers and wardrobe. Those things were his woman, loving his woman, showing her, having her, and knowing the way only a twenty-three-year-old boy-man can know that *this* was so right, so meant to be, so here and now.

But too much had happened and among that *too much* were Queensway, Ness, and the Ladbroke Grove police and how a man could even *feel* their thoughts wash over him in a cesspool tide whose waters left a stench upon him that a hundred thousand steaming showers could not wash away.

Kendra said, as he began to stuff his belongings into the duffel bag, 'Dix, it wasn't you. Your fault. Anything. Things happened to her. She's been that angry. She's felt betrayed. Abandoned. You got to look at it Dix. Please.' She was still Lady Muck, her language fixed in place by everything that had happened in the last few hours. She couldn't hear herself but it did not matter. Dix could not hear her, either. 'Her dad gets murdered in the street, Dix. Her mum goes into the crazy house. My mum fails her and I fail her next. Dix, she was little. My mum's bloody boyfriend and his filthy mates, they took her. They did things to her. It was over and over, they did things to her and she didn't tell because she was afraid. So she's got to be forgiven for finally snapping like she did. In Queensway. With you. Whatever she might have said to the cops about you. There's a reason and it's horrible and I *know* you know that. I *know* you understand. Please.'

She was pleading with him, but she was beyond feeling the humiliation of having to plead. She was like one of those gypsy women one saw occasionally on the pavement, a baby at the breast, a paper cup extended for coins from strangers. Part of her – a proud woman who'd coped with a difficult life on her own – was insisting that she'd said enough, that they didn't need Dix, that if he wanted to leave, he had to be released with a quick surgical incision directly through the heart. But the other part – frightened and out of her depth for so long that drowning seemed like the only future she had – knew that she needed him, if only to act the part of man of the house in a family that had been cobbled together by death, madness, and misfortune.

Dix finally said, 'Ain't wha' I want, Ken, y'unnerstan? Ain't wha' I set out to have. I tried for a while – you got to know dat – but I can't do it.'

'You can. This only happened because—'

'Ain't listening to me, Ken. I don't want it no more.'

'You mean me, don't you? You don't want me.'

'This,' he said. 'Can't do it, won't do it, don't want to do it. Thought I could. Thought I did. Found out I was wrong.'

Desperation made her say, 'If the kids weren't here—'

'Don't. You i'n't like dat. And anyways, it ain't the kids. It's everyt'ing. Cos I want kids. Family. Kids. You always known dat.'

'Then—'

'But not like it is, Ken. Not kids I got to backtrack wiv, fixing 'em up where someone went wrong. It ain't wha' I want. Not like dis, anyways.'

Which meant, it seemed, that with another woman, with different children, with circumstances in which there appeared to be even a modicum of hope, the situation and his feelings about that situation would be different. He'd be what that woman wanted, what the children needed, and what Kendra herself had sworn she did not need, desire, or wish to have in her life.

And if she wanted all of that now – the package represented by Man Presence in her home – was the truth that the desire grew more from panic and fear than real love? It was not a question she could either ask herself or answer in that moment. She was reduced to watching him thrust his belongings helter-skelter into his duffel bag. She was transformed into the sort of hand-wringing woman she would have otherwise despised, one who followed her man from bedroom to bathroom and watched – as one might watch emergency workers wrest a dead body from a twisted vehicle – while he scooped up his shaving gear and all the lotions and oils that he used to keep his body smooth and glistening for his competitions.

When he turned back to face her, he looked beyond her. Joel had come out of the second bedroom, Toby standing just behind him. Dix met the boys' gazes, but then he dropped his because there was the duffel bag to be seen to. He zipped it, and the sound it made was different from the earlier sound of unzipping because it was full now, stuffed right to its seams, heavy but not so much so that a man of his strength would have trouble carrying it. He raised it to his shoulder.

He said to Joel, 'You take care round here, mon. Y'unnerstan? Mind you watch out for Ken.'

'Yeah,' Joel said. His voice was dull.

'Dis ain't down to you, blood,' Dix told him. 'You got dat straight? It's everyt'ing, mon. Lots 'f shit you don't unnerstan. You remember dat. It ain't down to you. It's just everyt'ing.'

Which was what landed on Joel's shoulders once Dix D'Court left them: everything. Households needed to be headed by a man in order to function, and he was the only man available to keep Toby safe and to get Ness out of the trouble she was in.

That this latter challenge was insurmountable was something Joel did not intend to face. 'She tried to *kill* him,' Hibah told him fiercely when their paths crossed near Trellick Tower. 'I was *there*, innit. So was that lady from the drop-in centre. So were maybe twenty little kids. A bigger knife and she *would've* killed him. She's mad, tha' girl. She's going to *get* it. They got her locked up and I hope they throw 'way the key.'

Hope lay in the fact that Ness *was* locked up. For locked up meant the police, the police meant the Harrow Road station, and the Harrow Road station meant a chance still existed that what seemed to be part of Ness's future didn't necessarily *have* to happen. There was still a means of extricating Ness from the quagmire, and Joel had access to that means.

Thus he saw the road he had to take, and this road was the one that led to becoming the Blade's man completely. No more temporary arrangement to acquire a favour but the real thing: proving himself as signed, sealed, and delivered to the Blade in such a way as to leave no doubt in anyone's mind where Joel Campbell's loyalties lay. This meant he had to wait to be called to action, which was not easy.

When the day arrived, he came out of school and found Cal Hancock waiting for him at the end of Airlie Gardens, on the route he would take to catch his bus. Cal was leaning against the seat of a black-as-death Triumph motorcycle that Joel thought for a moment belonged to him. He was heavily bundled against the damp February cold; his garb was head-to-toe a match for the Triumph: black knitted hat, black donkey jacket closed to the throat, black gloves, black jeans, heavy-soled black boots. His expression was sombre, not mellowed by weed and not tanked up by anything else. That and the clothes – so head-to-foot different, so head-to-foot hidden – told Joel the moment had finally arrived.

'Le's get going, mon,' was what Cal said. Not 'It's time', and certainly not 'Fetch the piece' because Joel had been instructed to have the gun on him at all times, and he'd obeyed that instruction in spite of the risk.

Joel said automatically, 'I got to fetch Toby from his school first, Cal.'

'No you ain't. Wha' you got to do is come wiv me.'

'He can't get home on his own, mon.'

'Dat ain't my problem, and it sure ain't yours. He can wait there, innit. Wha' you're doing ain't going to take long anyways.'

Joel said, 'Okay,' and he tried to sound collected. But fear came to him in the palms of his hands where he had the sensation of ice chips being deposited.

Cal said to him, 'Give us the piece,' and Joel set his rucksack on the pavement. He looked around to make sure there were no watchers to the exchange that was about to be made, and when he saw there were none, he unfastened buckles and rooted to the bottom of the bag where the pistol lay, wrapped in a towel. He handed over the entire package. Cal unwrapped it, checked out the gun, and then put it into the pocket of his jacket. He dropped the towel to the ground and said, 'Le's go.' He moved away from the motorcycle and set off, in the direction of Holland Park Avenue.

Joel said, 'Where?'

Cal said over his shoulder, 'You ain't got to worry 'bout where.'

He led Joel up the street and, when they got to Holland Park Avenue, he headed east. This was the direction of Portobello Road but, instead of turning at the corner, he went straight, and Joel followed him to the Notting Hill underground station, where Cal descended the stairs and walked along the tunnel to where the tickets were sold. He bought two from a machine. They were returns. Without glancing Joel's way, Cal headed for the turnstiles that would take them to the trains.

Joel said, 'Hey, mon. Hang on.' And when Cal did not, merely moving forward relentlessly, Joel caught him up and said tersely, 'I ain't doing anything on an underground train. No fuckin way, mon.'

Cal said, 'You doing it where you get told, blood,' and he thrust a ticket into the turnstile's slot, pushed Joel through, and then followed him.

Had he not deduced it before this moment, Joel would have understood that he was with a Calvin Hancock whom he did not know. This was no longer the easy, doped-up bloke standing casual guard while the Blade did his business on Arissa. This was the blood that other bloods saw when they overstepped themselves in some way. Clearly, Cal too had been sorted out by the Blade after the fiasco with the Asian woman in

Portobello Road. 'He does it right dis time, or I deal wiv *you,* Cal-vin,' was how the Blade would have likely put it.

Joel said, 'Mon, why you stick wiv him?'

Cal said nothing. He merely led the way down the tunnels until they emerged on to a platform crowded with commuters and shoppers, and schoolchildren on their way home for the day.

Joel had no idea in which direction they were travelling when at last they boarded a train. He hadn't paid attention to the signs at the entrance to the platform, and he hadn't looked to read the destination that flickered on the front of the train as it roared into the station, disgorged passengers, and waited for other passengers to board.

They sat opposite a pregnant teenage mother with a baby in a pushchair and a toddler who kept trying to clamber up one of the carriage's poles. The girl looked no older than Ness, and her face was dully without expression. Joel said to Cal, 'You ain't like him, mon. You c'n go your own way if you want, innit.'

Cal said, 'Shut up.'

Joel watched the toddler try to climb the pole. The train pulled out of the station with a jerk, the child fell and howled, and his mother ignored him. Joel persisted. He said, 'Shit, bred. I don't get you, Cal. Dis go off bad – wha'ever it is – and we both go down. You got to know dat, so why di'n't you ever tell Mr Stanley Hynds to do his own fucking dirty work?'

Cal said, 'You know what *shut up* means? You stupid or summick?'

'You been an artist f'rever. You're better'n dis. You c'n get serious if you want and even try—'

'Shut the bloody fuck up!'

The toddler looked at them, wide-eyed. The young mother gazed at them, her face wearing an expression caught somewhere between boredom and despair. They made a tableau of living consequences: wrong decisions made stubbornly, again and again.

Cal turned to Joel and said in a low fierce voice, 'You got warned, y'unnerstan? What you had you threw away.'

Something in Cal gave way then, despite the ferocity of his words. Joel could see this in the way a muscle moved in Cal's cheek, as if he chewed on additional words to hold them back. In that moment Joel could have sworn that the graffiti artist wanted to be the Cal he really was, but he was afraid to go there.

Concluding this, Joel decided that in this situation he and Cal were compatriots, and this gave him a modicum of comfort as they hurtled towards an unknown destination while people boarded and disembarked the train when it came into stations and while Joel waited for Cal to rise and to move towards the doors. Or to give him a sign that this or that person who boarded and rode with them was the person Joel was meant to mug. Not on the train – he could see that now – but following carefully at a distance when a station was reached and their unknowing target got out and began the short or the long walk home.

He tried to sort out who it would be: the turbanned bloke in patent leather shoes, his orange beard with its long grey roots making him difficult not to stare at; the two Goths with multiple piercings on their faces, who boarded at High Street Kensington, sat, and immediately began to suck hungrily upon each other's tongue; the old lady in the dingy pink coat, easing her swollen feet from broken-down shoes. And there were others, many others, whom Joel studied and wondered, Him? Her? Here? Where?

At last Cal stood when the train began to slow. He grasped the rail running along just inches beneath the ceiling of the carriage, and he excused himself politely and worked his way along to the door. Joel followed.

On the platform, they could have been anywhere in London. For here on the walls were the same enormous advertisements for films, the same announcements for gallery exhibitions, the same posters beckoning one to take a sunny holiday on a sunny beach. A set of stairs marked the route to the exit farther along the platform, and above it – indeed, spaced at intervals along the entire length of the platform – hung London's ubiquitous CCTV cameras, documenting all action within the station.

Cal moved out of the way of the other commuters. He took something from his pocket. For a crazy sweat-inducing moment, Joel thought Cal meant him to do the deed right on the platform, in full view of the cameras. But instead, Cal pressed something soft into Joel's hand, saying, 'Put dis on. Keep your head down good.' It was a black knitted cap, similar to his own.

Joel saw the wisdom of this headgear. He pulled it down over his steel wool mop of ginger hair. He was grateful for it and grateful that the time of year had him wearing a dark anorak that obscured his school uniform as well. Once the job was done and they were running off, it wouldn't be likely that their mark would be able to identify them to the police.

They moved along the platform and, when they got to the stairs, Joel could not resist a look upward, despite Cal's injunction to keep his head low. He saw there were additional cameras on the ceiling here, catching the image of anyone climbing towards the street. Yet another camera was doing its business above the turnstiles going into and out of the station. There were, indeed, so many security cameras around that it came to Joel that he and Cal had journeyed to a place decidedly important. He thought of Buckingham Palace – although he didn't know if there was a tube station anywhere near the royal residence – and he thought of the Houses of Parliament and he thought of wherever it was that they kept the crown jewels. That seemed the only explanation for the cameras.

He and Cal emerged from the station into everywhere bustle, before them a tree-lined square where, at the distant end, Joel could see the backside of a statue of a naked woman, pouring water from an urn into a fountain below her. The

winter-bare trees were like a procession leading up to this fountain, and between them black iron street lamps with perfectly
clean glass shades stood next to benches of wood that were
decorated with green wrought iron. Around the square, black
taxis waited in ranks so gleaming that they reflected the late
sun while buses and cars navigated the many streets that
poured into it.

Outside of programmes on the television, Joel had never
seen anything like this place. This was a London he did not
know and, if Cal Hancock decided to desert him anywhere in
this vicinity, Joel realised that he would be done for. Thus, he
took no time to gawk or even to wonder what two blokes such
as they were doing in this part of town where they both stood
out like raisins in rice pudding. Instead, he hurried to keep up
with Cal.

The graffiti artist was striding off to the right along a pavement more crowded than any Joel had ever seen in North
Kensington save on market days. Everywhere, shoppers
hurried by with fancy carrier bags, some ducking into the
underground station and others entering a large-windowed
café where a burgundy awning bore a scroll of gold letters.
Oriel, they spelled. *Grande Brasserie de la Place*. As Joel passed,
he saw through the windows a trolley piled high with pastries.
White-coated waiters carried silver trays. They moved among
tables where men and women in fine clothing smoked, talked,
and drank from tiny cups. Some of them were alone, but they
spoke into their mobiles, their heads bent low to protect their
private conversations.

Joel was about to say, 'Fuck! Wha' we *doing* here, blood?'
when Cal came to a corner and made a turn.

Here, suddenly, the atmosphere altered. A few shops operated near the square – Joel saw the gleam of cutlery in one
window, modern furniture in another, elaborate arrangements
of flowers in a third – but in less than twenty yards from the
corner, a row of fine terrace houses sprang up. They were

nothing like the dismal terraces Joel was used to. These were sparkling from their roofs to their basement windows and beyond them a block of flats stretched out, filled with window boxes that were bright with pansies and green with great thriving swags of ivy.

Although this place, too, was altogether different from what Joel was used to, he breathed more easily, out of sight of so many people. While none of them had appeared to notice him, it remained true that he and Cal were an anomaly in this place.

After a short distance, Cal crossed the road. More terrace houses followed a long block of flats, all of them painted white – pure white and absolutely unblemished – with black front doors. These buildings all had basements with windows visible from the pavement, and Joel glanced inside as they passed. He saw spotless kitchens with worktops that were covered in stone. He saw the glint of chrome and open racks of colourful crockery. Outside, he also saw well-made security grilles, barring entrance to burglars.

Another corner loomed and Cal turned yet again. Here they entered a street that was as quiet as death itself. It came to Joel that this place was like a film set waiting for the actors to appear. Unlike North Kensington, here there were no boom boxes pounding out music, and no voices raised in argument. On a distant street, a car *whooshed* by, but that was it.

They passed a pub, the only commercial enterprise in the street, and even it was a picture like everything else. Forest etching covered its windows. Amber lights glowed. Its heavy front door stood closed against the cold.

Beyond the pub, the rest of the street was lined with fine houses: another terrace but cream instead of white. Another set of perfect, gleaming black doors gave entrance to these places, though, and wrought iron railings ran along the front, marking basements below and balconies above. These held urns, pots of plants, ivy spilling down towards the street while, overhead, security alarms on the buildings warned off intruders.

At yet another corner, Cal turned again, leaving Joel wondering how they would ever find their way out of this maze when they'd done what they'd come to do. But this corner led to a passage that was just the width of a single car, a tunnel that dipped between two buildings, blinding white and surgically clean like everything else in the area. Joel saw a sign that said *Grosvenor Cottages*, and he noticed that beyond the tunnel a row of little houses lined a narrow, cobbled street. But the street quickly trickled into a twisting path, and the path went absolutely nowhere but to a tiny garden in which only a fool would try to hide. At the end of that garden, a brick wall loomed some eight feet high. There was nowhere else. There was nothing else. There was one way in. There was one way out.

Joel panicked at the thought that Cal meant him to confront someone here. With only a single means of escape should things go badly, it came to him that he might as well turn the pistol on himself and shoot off his feet because it would be highly unlikely that he'd be going anywhere after he'd done the deed that he was intended to do.

Cal, however, didn't venture more than five feet into this tunnel. What he said to Joel was, 'Now.'

Joel, confused, said in turn, 'Now what, mon?'

'Now we wait.'

'Cal, I ain't doing nuffink in dis alley here.'

Cal shot him a look. 'The point, mon,' he said, 'is you do wha' I tell you when I tell you. Ain't you got dat yet?'

That said, he leaned against the tunnel wall, just beyond a set of iron gates that hung open to admit cars and pedestrians into the vicinity of the cottages. Then, though, his face softened a bit and he said to Joel, 'Safe here, bred. No one's on guard dis part of town. First person comes 'long . . . ?' He patted his pocket where the gun resided. That gesture – and the gun – completed his thought.

Despite Cal's words of reassurance, Joel began to feel light-headed. Without wanting to, he thought of Toby patiently waiting to be fetched from school, confident that Joel would turn up in good time because Joel always turned up in good time. He thought about Kendra, dusting off the shelves in the charity shop or straightening up the merchandise, believing that no matter what else happened to turn the world upside down, she was going to be able to depend on Joel now to be the man every household needed. He thought of Ness locked up, and his mother locked up, and his father dead and gone for ever. But those thoughts resulted in his vision swimming, so he tried to stop thinking altogether, which made him think of Ivan, think of Neal Wyatt, think of the Blade.

Joel wondered what the Blade might do to him if he just walked off, saying to Cal, 'No way, mon,' and made his way back to the underground station where he'd cadge enough money to get himself a ticket and get himself home. What would the Blade do? Kill him? That hardly seemed likely since even the Blade would surely draw the line at killing a twelve-year-old, wouldn't he? The problem, though, was that defying the Blade now meant disrespecting him as well, and that made Joel fair game for some sort of discipline administered by the Blade himself, by Cal, or by anyone wishing to get into the good graces of Mr Stanley Hynds. And *that*, Joel concluded grimly, was exactly what he didn't need at the moment: a crew of wannabe gangstas on the look-out for a chance to sort him or his family with guns, with knives, with coshes, or with fists.

Any way Joel turned the matter in his head, he was caught. His only hope was to run off permanently, never to return to North Kensington, never to be present for his brother, never to be around for his aunt. He could do that, he thought, or he could stay where he was and wait for Cal to give him the nod to perform.

Cal said suddenly, 'Here, mon.'

Joel roused himself. He could see nothing near the tunnel,

and no one had come out from one of the cottages along the little cobbled street. Nonetheless, Cal had taken the gun from his jacket pocket. He pressed it firmly into Joel's hand and curved his fingers around it. It felt to Joel like one of Dix's twenty-kilo weights. He desperately wanted to let it fall to the ground.

Joel said, 'What—?' and then heard the brisk slam of a car door somewhere beyond them, out in the street. He heard a woman say, 'What on earth was I thinking, wearing these ghastly shoes? And for *shopping* of all things. Why didn't you stop me, Deborah? A decent friend would have saved me from my worst inclinations, you know.'

Another woman laughed. 'Shall I take the car to the garage for you? You do look done in.'

'You've read my mind. Thank you. But first let's unload . . .' Her voice grew fainter for a moment and then, 'Heavens, do you have any idea how to open the boot, Deborah? I pushed one of these gizmo things, but . . . *Is* it open? Unlocked? Lord, I'm hopeless when it comes to Tommy's car. Ah yes. It appears we have success.'

Joel risked a look. He saw two white women, perhaps three houses along the street, lifting what looked like four dozen fancy carrier bags from the boot of a fine silver car. They carried them several at a time up the front steps of one of the houses and then returned for more. When they'd emptied the boot, one of the women – a redhead wearing an olive coat and a matching beret – opened the driver's door. Before she climbed inside, she said, 'I'll take it to the garage, then. You go inside and take off your shoes.'

'Cup of tea?'

'Lovely. I'll be right back.'

'Mind Tommy's car, won't you? You know how he is.'

'Don't I just.'

She started the engine – it was very nearly soundless – and she drove the car slowly past the tunnel where Joel and Cal were waiting. Unfamiliar with the vehicle, she was completely focused on the street before her, her hands high on the steering wheel in the manner of someone intent upon getting from Point A to Point B without damage. She didn't look once in the direction of Joel and Cal. A short distance down the street, she turned left into a mews and disappeared from view.

Cal said, 'Now, mon,' and he jerked Joel's arm. He made for the pavement and for the other woman, who was still standing on the steps of the house. She was surrounded by her shopping bags, and she was rooting around in a leather shoulder bag for the keys to her front door. A curtain of her smooth, jaw-length dark hair hid one half of her face and, as Joel and Cal approached, she whisked this hair back behind her ear to reveal her earrings. They were gold hoops, delicately engraved. She wore a large diamond on her wedding finger.

She looked up, hearing something and perhaps that something was the approach of strangers, although she obviously didn't know it was strangers and danger because she said, 'I *can*not find my blasted keys. I am, as always, utterly hopeless of remedy. We'll have to use Tommy's if you—' She saw Joel and Cal, and she started. She followed this with a light, self-conscious laugh. She said, 'Lord. I *am* sorry. You gave me a fright.' And then with a smile, 'Hullo. May I help you? Are you lost? Do you need—'

'Now,' Cal said.

Joel froze. He couldn't. Do anything. Say anything. Move. Talk. Whisper. Shout. She was so pretty. She had dark warm eyes. She had a kind face. She had a tender smile. She had smooth skin and soft-looking lips. She looked from Cal to him to Cal to him, and she didn't even see what he was holding. So she didn't know what was about to happen. So he couldn't. Not here, not now, and not ever, no matter what happened to him or his family as a consequence.

Cal muttered, 'Fuck. *Fuck*,' and then, 'Bloody fucking *do* it, mon.'

That was when the woman saw the gun. She looked from it to Joel. She looked from Joel to Cal. She blanched as the gun exchanged hands when Cal grabbed it. She said, 'Oh my God,' and she began to turn for the door.

That was when Cal fired.

Fired, Joel thought. Shot the gun. Not a word about handing over her bag. Not a word about money, her earrings, her diamond. Just the single sound of a single shot, which cannoned between the tall houses on either side of the street as the lady crumpled among her shopping, saying, 'Oh,' and then fell silent.

Joel himself gave a strangled cry but that was all because Cal grabbed him and they both took off running. They didn't set off in the direction they'd come from because, without speaking, discussing, or making a plan, they both knew that the red-headed woman had taken the car that way and would doubtless emerge from the mews on foot at any second and see them. So they ran towards the point where the street curved into another street, and they took this turn. But Cal said, 'Shit! Fuck! Shit!' because coming towards them at a distance was an old lady walking a doddering corgi.

Cal dashed into an opening on their left. It turned out to be a mews. He followed it as it made a dogleg to the right, where a line of houses stood. But this formed a cul-de-sac at the end. They were trapped, blind men caught in the maze.

Joel said in panic, 'What're we—?' but that was all he got out. For Cal shoved him back the way they'd just come.

Just before the dogleg in the mews, a high brick wall marked the boundary of the garden of a house in another street. Even at full speed and spurred by the terror of being seen or being caught, they couldn't have hoped to leap over this. But a Range Rover – so common in this part of town – parked next to the wall blessedly gave Cal and Joel what they needed. Cal leaped on to the bonnet and from there he scrambled to the top of the wall. Joel followed as Cal dropped to the other side.

They found themselves in a pleasantly overgrown garden, and they made for the far side. They crashed through a low hedge and knocked over an empty copper bird-bath. They came face to face with another brick wall.

This one wasn't as tall as the first, and Cal was able to make it up easily. Joel had more trouble. He flung himself at it once, then twice. He said, 'Cal! Cal!' and the artist reached down, grabbed him by his anorak, and hoisted him over.

A second garden that was much like the first. A house to the left with windows that were covered. A brick path leading to a wall across a patch of lawn. A table and chairs beneath a gazebo. A tricycle lying on its side.

Cal leaped for the far wall. He gripped the top. He lost it. He leaped another time. Joel grabbed his legs and shoved him upward. Cal reached back and pulled Joel along. Joel's feet scrabbled against the wall and could gain no purchase. A ripping sound came from his anorak and he cried once in panic. He began to slide back. Cal grabbed him again, anywhere he could. Arm, shoulders, head. He knocked off Joel's knitted cap and it fell, back into the garden from which they'd come.

Joel cried, 'Cal!'

Cal heaved him over. 'Don't matter,' he grunted. They left the cap behind.

They said nothing more because they did not need to. All they needed was to escape. There was no time for Joel to question what had happened. He thought only, Gun went off, just went *off*, and he tried not to think of anything else. Not the woman's face, not her single 'Oh,' not the sight and the sound and certainly not the knowledge. Her expression had gone from startled, to kind, to friendly, to terrified, all in the space of less than fifteen seconds, all in the time it took her to see, to realise, and to try to escape.

And then there was the gun. The bullet from the gun. The smell and the sound. The flash from the pistol and the falling body. She'd hit her head on the wrought iron rail that ran along the chessboard top step as she'd crumpled among her carrier bags. She was rich, very rich. She had to be rich. She had a posh car in a posh neighbourhood that was filled with posh houses and they'd shot her, shot her, shot a rich white lady – posh to her bones – next to her own front door.

Another garden loomed before them, this one like a miniature orchard. They charged across it, towards the opposite side where another garden was a torment of bushes, hedges, shrubs, and trees, all of it left to grow completely wild. Ahead of him, Joel saw Cal mounting the next wall. At the top he waved frantically for Joel to come more quickly. Joel was breathing heavily, and his chest was tight. He was soaked about the face. He wiped his arm across his forehead.

He said, 'Can't go—'

'Fuck dat shit. Come *on*, blood. We got to get out 'f here.'

So they fell to the ground and stumbled across garden number five, where they rested for a moment, panting. Joel listened for the sound of sirens, shouting, screams, or anything else back the way they had come, but all was silent, which seemed a good sign.

'Cops?' he asked, gasping for breath.

'Oh, they coming.' Cal pushed off from the wall. He took a step back. He hurtled up it. One leg on one side and one on the other. Then he looked into the garden beyond and breathed a single word. 'Fuck.'

'What?' Joel asked.

Cal hoisted him up. Joel straddled the wall. He saw that they'd come to the end of the line. This was a final garden, but it had no wall that gave on to a street or a mews on the other side of it. Instead, the vast expanse of an external wall from a large old building – brick like everything else they'd come to – served as this final garden's boundary. The only way in or out of the patch of lawn and shrubbery was through the house that it served.

Joel and Cal tumbled to the ground. They took a moment to assess their whereabouts. The windows had security bars, but one set was pushed to the side, suggesting negligence or the fact that someone was at home. It didn't matter. They had no choice. Cal went first and Joel followed him.

On a terrace outside the back door, a group of plants stood, thickly growing sculpted shrubs from lichenous clay pots. Cal grabbed one of these and advanced on the unbarred window. He heaved the pot through it, reached inside past the broken glass, and unfastened a bolt that was insignificant. He leaped through, and Joel followed. They found themselves in some sort of home office, and they landed on its desk, where they upended a computer terminal that was already covered by earth, broken glass, and most of the shrub, which had fallen from the pot.

Cal made for the door, and they were in a corridor. He headed towards the front of the house. It wasn't a large building, and they could see the door that led to the street – a small oval window in it promising them blessed escape – but before they reached it, someone came clattering down the stairs to their left.

It was a young woman, the household *au pair*. She looked Spanish, Italian, Greek. She carried a toilet plunger as a weapon and she charged them, screaming like a heat-seeking missile, with the plunger raised.

Cal cried, 'Fuck!' He ducked the blow and shoved her to one side. He made for the door. She dropped the plunger but regained her footing. She grabbed Joel as he tried to get past. She was shrieking unintelligible words, but she made her meaning perfectly clear. She attached herself to Joel like a leech. She reached for his face, her fingers like claws.

Joel struggled with her. He kicked at her legs, her ankles, her shins. He jerked his head to avoid the fingernails with which she intended to mark him. She went for his hair. She grabbed a handful: hair that was like a beacon and hair that no one would ever forget.

Joel's eyes met hers. He thought – and it was a terror to him – Got to die, cunt. He waited for Cal to shoot her as he'd shot the dark-haired woman. But instead he heard the bang of the front door as it sprang open and hit the wall. The girl released her grip on him at the same moment. Joel dashed after Cal, out into the street.

He panted, 'Cal. Gotta get her, mon. She saw . . . She c'n—'

'Can't, blood,' Cal said. 'Don't have the gun. Le's go.' He started walking rapidly up the street. He was not running now, not wanting to draw attention to themselves.

Joel caught him up. He said, 'What? *What?* Where . . . ?'

Cal strode quickly. 'Dropped it, mon. One 'f the gardens.'

'But they gonna *know* . . . You touched . . .'

'We cool. Don't worry 'bout dat shit.' Cal held up his hands. He still had on the gloves he'd worn when he'd fetched Joel from Holland Park School in what seemed to the boy like another lifetime.

'But the Blade's gonna . . . And anyways, I . . .' Joel stared at Cal. His mind worked like a dervish because the last thing he was was a stupid child. 'Oh shit,' he whispered. 'Oh shit, oh shit.'

Cal's gloved hand pushed him along the street. There was no pavement here, just cobbles and roadway. 'Wha'?' Cal said. 'We can't go back. Jus' walk and be cool. We gonna get out. Ten minutes and this place be crawling with the bill, y'unnerstan me? Now le's fuckin *go*.'

'But . . .'

Cal kept walking, head low, chin tucked into his chest, Joel stumbled after him, his head pounding with images. They were like still shots in the middle of a film. They played back and forth in no particular order: the lady smiling as she said 'Are you lost?' Her little laugh before she understood. Cal's arm lifted. The corgi's waddle. The copper bird-bath. A holly bush snagging his anorak.

He hardly knew where they were. He saw that they were on a street narrower than the others they'd been in and, had he understood architecture in this part of town, Joel would have recognised it as an old mews whose stables had long since been converted to houses, which were tucked behind the much grander residences whose horses and carriages they once had protected. To his left stood plain-fronted buildings of brick, owners of the back gardens through which they'd just crashed. They were three storeys tall and identical: a single step up to a wooden front door with a simple stone pediment making a V above it. An inch of granite served as a front step. Garage doors were wooden, painted white. To his right, the picture was much the same, but there were also businesses planted along the way: a doctor's surgery, a solicitor's office, a car repair shop. And then more houses.

Cal said tersely, 'Keep your head down, blood,' but in unfortunate confusion, Joel did just the opposite. He saw that they were walking past the biggest house along the route, marked by black bollards with great swags of iron chains to keep cars away from the front of the building. But there was something more and he raised his face to it. A CCTV camera was mounted just above a window on the first floor.

He gasped and ducked his head. Cal caught him by the anorak once and pulled him forward. They fast-walked to the end of the street.

The first siren sounded then, wailing somewhere off in the distance just at the moment Joel saw that in front of them two more streets branched off from the one they were in. The buildings here loomed like vedettes, unlike any others they'd passed. Outside of the tower blocks of North Kensington, they were the biggest structures Joel had ever seen, but they were nothing like the dour blocks of flats that he was used to. Umber brick created them – no dingy yellow London brick here – and leaded windows with pearl-white moulding decorated them. Hundreds upon hundreds of fancifully shaped chimneys sprouted across their rooftops. Joel and Cal were ant-like here, caught in a canyon of these structures.

Cal said, 'Dis way, blood,' and, astoundingly to Joel, began to walk in the direction of the sirens.

Joel cried, 'Cal! No! We can't! They been . . . They gonna . . . If they see . . .' and he remained rooted to the spot.

Cal said over his shoulder, 'Mon, come *on*. Or stay there and end up 'splaining to the bill wha' you been doing in dis neighbourhood.'

Another siren howled its two-note warning, then, sounding from several streets away. It came to Joel that if they walked . . . if they looked like two blokes having business in the area . . . if they seemed like tourists – ludicrous though the idea was – or dopers with the *Big Issue* for sale . . . or foreign students . . . or anything . . . or what . . . ?

But there remained the fact of that *au pair*, she of the toilet plunger. She'd have gone for the telephone, Joel realised, and her shaking hands would already have punched in the nines, which was all it took to bring on the police. She would have shouted out her address. She would have explained and the cops would arrive. For this was a posh part of town where the cops came running when something went down.

So where were they? Joel asked himself. Where were they?

Wrought iron balconies seemed to loom everywhere above him. No rusting bikes on them, no burnt-out furniture shoved out of doors and left to rot in the weather. No sagging line of grimy laundry. Just winter flowers. Just pot shrubs trimmed into the shape of animals. Just thick posh curtains hanging low on the windows. And those chimneys lining up like soldiers, rank upon rank of them along the rooftops, etching their shapes against the grey sky: balloons and shields, pots and dragons. Whoever thought there could be so many chimneys?

Cal had paused at the corner of yet another street. He looked right and left, an act that assessed where they were and where they might go. Across from him was a building different from every other they'd seen so far. It was grey steel and concrete, interrupted by glass. It was more like what they were used to seeing in their own part of town, albeit newer, fresher, cleaner.

When Joel joined him, it was clear there was no safety here. People with carrier bags were emerging from shops, and the shops offered coats with fur collars, crisp bed linens, bottles of perfume, fancy bars of soap. A grocery displayed oranges resting individually in nests of green foil, and a flower seller nearby offered buckets of blooms in every imaginable colour.

It was posh. It was money. Joel wanted to run in the opposite direction. But Cal paused and looked at the display in the bakery window. He adjusted his knitted cap, pulling it low, and he turned up the collar of his donkey jacket.

Two more sirens sounded up ahead. A heavy white man came out of the bakery, cake box in his hands. He said, 'What's going on?'

Cal turned to Joel. 'Le's check it out, mon,' he said and he passed the white man with a polite, ''Scuse me,' as they headed onward.

To Joel, this seemed a lunatic activity since Cal was walking directly towards the sirens now. He said fiercely as he strode by the young man's side, 'We can't. We *can't*! Cal, we got to—'

'Mon, we got no choice 'less you see one.' Cal jerked his head in the direction of the noise. 'Dat's the way to the tube and we got to get out 'f here, y'unnerstan wha' I say? Jus' be cool. Look curious. Like ever' one else.'

Joel's gaze automatically followed the way Cal had indicated with his head. He saw, then, that Cal was correct. For, in the distance, he made out the shape of the naked lady pouring water into that fountain, seeing her from a different angle this time. So he realised that they were coming up to the square where they'd emerged from the underground. They were five minutes or less from escaping the area.

He took a few deep breaths. He needed to look like someone

curious about what was happening, but nothing more. He said to Cal, 'Right. Le's go, then.'

'Jus' be cool,' was Cal's reply.

They walked at a normal pace. As they reached the corner, yet another siren sounded, and a panda car passed. They entered the square. It seemed to them as if hundreds of people milled around on the pavements that marked the perimeter. They'd come out of cafés. They hesitated in the doorways of banks, of bookshops, and of department stores. They stood as statue-like as the bronze woman in the middle of the fountain: Venus gazing tenderly down upon a life-sustaining substance that she eternally poured from her urn.

A fire engine roared into the square. Another panda car followed. Voices buzzed. Bomb? Terrorists? Riot? Armed robbery? Street demonstration getting out of control?

Joel heard all this as he and Cal wove through the crowd. No one spoke of murder, of crime, of a mugging gone bad. No one at all.

As they crossed over into the centre of the square and made diagonally for the tube station, an ambulance shrieked up from the south, siren blasting and roof lights twirling. The ambulance was what finally gave Joel some hope, for an ambulance meant that Cal hadn't actually killed the lady when the gun went off.

Joel only hoped that she hadn't hurt her head too badly when she banged it on the wrought iron railing as she fell.

27

The worst was Toby, which was certainly something that Joel did not expect. But when he finally arrived at Middle Row School to take Toby home for the day, it was to find him huddled in the February darkness just outside the locked gates, having somehow escaped the notice of the school's administrators and teachers, carefully hidden in the deeper shadows cast by a pillar-box. He was staring at a jagged crack in the pavement, his skateboard clutched to his chest.

Joel crouched by his brother and said, 'Hey, mon. Sorry, Tobe. I di'n't forget you or nuffink. Did you think I forgot? Tobe? Hey, Tobe?'

Toby roused himself. 'Meant to go to the learning centre today,' he mumbled.

Joel said, 'Tobe, I'm sorry. I had to do summick . . . Look it's important you don't grass me up on this. It won't happen again. I swear. You c'n promise me, Tobe?'

Toby gazed at him blankly. 'I waited like I was s'posed to, Joel. I di'n't know what else to do.'

'You did good, mon. Waiting here like dis. Come on now. Le's go. When I take you to the learning centre next, I'll talk to them. I'll 'splain wha' happened. They won't be vex at you or nuffink.'

Joel urged his little brother to his feet, and they set off towards their home. Joel said to him, 'Tobe, you can't tell Aunt Ken 'bout dis. Y'unnerstan wha' I say? She find out I di'n't take you to the learning centre . . . She got 'nough vexing her already, innit. Wiv Ness. Wiv Dix gone. And dat

Fabia Bender woman jus' waiting for a reason to take you and me away . . .'

'Joel, I don't *want*—'

'Hey. Dat ain't going to happen, bred. Which is why you got to keep quiet 'bout me being late. C'n you pretend?'

'Pretend what?'

'You went to the learning centre. C'n you pretend you went today like always?'

''Kay,' Toby said.

Joel looked at his brother. Toby's brief lifetime rose up to declare how unlikely it was that he would be able to pretend anything, but Joel had to believe it would be possible to carry off a deception about the afternoon, for it was crucial to him that life should look to his aunt the way it always looked to his aunt. The slightest deviation and Kendra would be suspicious, and suspicion felt to Joel like the last thing that he could endure.

But in all his planning, Joel failed to take into account the concern of Luce Chinaka. He failed to realise that she might have been told by Fabia Bender to keep a closer watch on Toby, that she might take matters into her own hands when Toby did not turn up as scheduled, phoning Kendra at the charity shop and asking if Toby was ill and unable to keep his regular appointment. So when Kendra arrived home for the day, she first deposited a bag of Chinese takeaway in the kitchen and she then demanded to know why Joel had failed in his duty to see to Toby.

Here, however, a modicum of luck was on Joel's side. He'd taken an unsettled stomach and a growing weakness in his arms and his legs up to his bedroom, and he'd deposited them upon his bed. There he curled in the darkness, and he stared at the wall on which he found – no matter what he did to try to get it out of his mind – the image of the dark-haired lady's face floated, smiling at him and saying hello and asking if he and Cal were lost. Thus, when Kendra flipped on the light and said, 'Joel! Why didn't you take your brother to the learning centre?' Joel spoke the truth. 'Being sick,' he said.

This altered things. Kendra sat on the edge of the bed and, motherlike, felt his forehead. She said in an altogether altered tone, 'You coming down with something, baby? You're a bit hot. You should've phoned me at the shop.'

'I thought Tobe could miss—'

'I don't mean for Toby. I mean for you. If you're sick and you need me . . .' She smoothed his hair. 'We're going through bad times round here, aren't we, luv? But I want you to know something: you don't have to take care of yourself alone.'

For Joel this was actually the worst thing she could have said, for the kindness in her words caused tears to well in his eyes. He closed them, but the tears leaked out.

Kendra said, 'I'm going to make you something to settle your stomach. Why don't you come down to the lounge and wait on the settee? Have a lie-down and I'll fix you up a tray. You can watch the telly while you eat. How 'bout that?'

Joel kept his eyes closed because he felt stung by her tone. It was a voice she'd never used before. Tears dripped across the bridge of his nose and on to his pillow. He did what he could not to sob, which meant he said nothing in reply.

Kendra said, 'You come when you're ready. Toby's got a video on the telly, but I'll tell him to let you watch what you want.'

It was the thought of Toby – and the thought of what Toby might say if Kendra questioned him – that got Joel up once his aunt left the bedroom. This, it turned out, was all to the good, for when he arrived in the sitting-room, it was to find Toby blithely lying to their aunt about a supposed afternoon in the learning centre, just as Joel had instructed him to do but without the knowledge of Luce Chinaka's phone call.

'. . . reading today,' Toby was saying. 'Only I don't 'member the book.'

Joel said, 'Wa'n't today, mon. What're you on about, Tobe?'

He joined Toby on the settee, his pillow in his hands and a blanket from his bed dragging along on the floor. 'Today we came straight here from school cos I was sick. Remember?'

Toby looked at him, his expression puzzled. 'But I thought—'

'Yeah. But you tol' me all 'bout dat yesterday.'

'"That",' Kendra corrected him patiently. And then, miraculously, she dismissed the topic, saying, 'Toby, move over and let Joel have a lie-down. Let him watch the telly. You can help me in the kitchen if you've a mind to.'

Toby moved over on the sofa, but his expression remained confused. He said to Joel, 'But, Joel, you tol' me—'

'You're getting all your days mixed up,' Joel cut in. 'I tol' you we wouldn't be going to the centre when I fetched you from school jus' dis af'ernoon. How c'n you not *remember*, Tobe? Ain't they been working on your memory an' stuff?'

'"Haven't they been working",' came the automatic correction from Kendra. 'Joel, don't be so hard on him.' She went to the television and removed the video from the old recorder beneath it. She turned to a channel arbitrarily and once the picture flickered on, she gave a nod and descended to the kitchen. In a moment she was banging about down there, fixing the promised meal for Joel.

Toby's gaze hadn't moved from Joel's face, and what it showed was utter confusion. He said, 'You said I was meant to say—'

'I'm sorry, Tobe,' Joel murmured. He moved his own gaze to the stairway's door and kept it there. 'She found out, see. They phoned her up and asked where you were, so I had to tell her . . . Look, jus' say we came straight here and we been here ever since. If she asks or summick, okay?'

'But you tol' me—'

'Tobe!' Joel's whisper was fierce. 'Things change, y'unnerstan wha' I say? Things change all the time. Like Ness not being here and Dix being gone. Y'unnerstan? Things *change*.'

But things didn't easily change for Toby, not without some attempt at removing the fog from his brain. He said again, 'But—'

Joel grabbed his wrist tightly and turned to him. 'Don't be so fucking *stupid*,' he hissed. 'Jus' this once act like you got a brain.'

Toby recoiled. Joel dropped his wrist. Toby's chin dimpled, and his eyelids lowered. The skin showed the delicate tracing of blue veins across a freckled, almond surface. Joel felt a tug at his heart at the sight, but he hardened it and he hardened himself because as far as he was concerned Toby had to learn and he had to learn *now*. It was imperative that he memorise a story and get that story straight.

'Joel,' Kendra called from the kitchen, 'I've brought Chinese, but I'm making you boiled eggs and toast. D'you want jam?'

Joel didn't see how he'd be able to eat anything at all, but he called back weakly that jam was good, jam was fine, and whatever kind they had would be excellent. Then for the first time he looked at the television and saw what Kendra had switched on for him to watch. It looked like some channel's nightly news because a female reporter stood in front of the entrance to a hospital, speaking into a microphone. Joel paid attention.

'. . . footage from the vicinity of Sloane Square is being examined by Belgravia detectives who have pulled out all the stops to apprehend the shooter. There was, apparently, at least one witness – and possibly two – to the incident, which took place in broad daylight in Eaton Terrace. We've learned that the victim had just returned from a shopping trip, but that's actually the extent of what we know about the incident itself. As far as we've been able to find out, the victim – thirty-four-year-old Helen Lynley, Countess of Asherton – is under twenty-four-hour guard here at St Thomas' Hospital. But what, exactly, her condition is, we do not know.'

A man's voice said, 'Andrea, is anyone drawing a connection

between this shooting and the serial killings currently under investigation?'

The reporter adjusted her earpiece and said, 'Well, it's a bit difficult to avoid making the connection, isn't it? Or at least assuming there might be one. When the wife of the head of an investigation that's the size and scope of this one is shot . . . Inevitably, there are going to be questions.'

Behind her, the hospital doors swung open. Camera lights began to flash. A man in doctor's garb walked over to a bouquet of microphones while a number of other people in his company – a grim-faced group of individuals with *plainclothes detectives* written all over them – pushed through the reporters on their way to the car park.

'. . . life support,' were the two words that came to Joel from the man in hospital garb. 'The situation is very grave.'

There was more – questions fired from all directions and answers given hesitantly and with a desire to protect the privacy of the victim and her family – but Joel could hear nothing of it. All he could hear was the windstorm in his ears as the picture on the television finally changed to show a montage of images with which he was only too familiar: the street in which he and Cal had found their mark; the crime scene tape defining a rectangle around the front of the chessboard front steps; a photograph of the lady herself with a name beneath it identifying her as Helen Lynley. What followed this were other shots of St Thomas' Hospital on the south bank of the Thames, with a dozen panda cars flashing their lights outside; of a blond man and a dumpy-looking woman speaking into a mobile as they stood outside a grimy railway tunnel; of a bloke in the uniform of a high-ranking cop talking into a bank of microphones. And then a series of CCTV cameras pointing this way and that, on this building and under those eaves, and each of them – Joel knew this and could swear to it – in the act of filming two blokes on their way to shoot the wife of a cop from New Scotland Yard.

Joel's aunt was ascending the stairs. She brought with her a tray on which were boiled eggs and toast that gave off what should have been a comforting smell. But not for Joel. He flung himself from the settee and charged towards the stairs and the bathroom. He didn't make it.

Cal disappeared. Joel sought him out the very next day and the day after that in all the regular places where he ought to have been: the sunken football pitch, where an incomplete piece of art in Cal's style suggested he'd decamped in a hurry; Meanwhile Gardens near the spiral steps and beneath the bridge and atop the knolls, where he smoked and occasionally dealt dope to the adolescents in the neighbourhood; the abandoned flat in Lancefield Court, where the drug runners went to pick up their wares; the building that housed Arissa's flat in Portnall Road. Joel even paced through Kensal Green cemetery in an attempt to find him, but Cal was nowhere. He might as well have evaporated, so decidedly was the Rasta gone.

To Joel, this made no sense. For who was to guard the Blade if not Cal Hancock?

Except, when Joel looked for the Blade, he couldn't find him either. At least, not at first.

On the third afternoon, Joel saw him. He was on his way down the steps of the Westminster Learning Centre, having dropped Toby there for his appointment with Luce Chinaka. Across the street and some thirty yards away, he saw the Blade's car, recognising it from a stripe of black painted on its light blue surface, from the piece of cardboard taped in place in lieu of one of the back windows. The car was parked on double yellow lines at the kerb, and it was occupied, with someone bending from the pavement to speak to the two male figures inside.

The speaker straightened as Joel watched. It was Ivan Weatherall, and he placed his hand on the roof of the car, gave it a friendly tap, and then spied Joel. He smiled and waved him over, then bent back to the car once again to listen to something someone was saying from inside.

Had Ivan been alone, Joel would have made an excuse, for the last person he wanted to face was his mentor and his mentor's good intentions. But the fact of the Blade's being there and the fact of his needing to talk to the Blade about everything from Eaton Terrace to Ness . . . and the blessed fact that Cal was with him, which was going to make it safer to talk to the Blade in the first place . . . These considerations propelled Joel across the street.

He came at the car from the rear. Through the back windows he could see yet another person within, and he recognised the shape of her head. He fervently wished Arissa wasn't with the Blade and Cal – they could hardly talk frankly with a snow freak around, he thought, trying to put her hand down everyone's trousers – but Joel knew he could remain with the three of them until the Blade got tired of Arissa's presence and threw her out of the car somewhere to find her way home. Then they could speak: about what had happened in Eaton Terrace and what they were going to do next. And about Ness as well because there was still and always Ness and her trouble and the fact that *what* Joel had done he had done as a first step to getting her out of trouble.

None of this took care of the problem of Ivan's presence on the scene, however. Ivan would certainly wonder what Joel was doing, climbing into a car that belonged to the Blade, and he would definitely not forget it.

Ivan said, 'Joel, how excellent to see you. I was just bringing Stanley into the picture about the project.'

So much had crowded into Joel's mind over the weeks that he didn't know at first what Ivan was talking about until he added, 'The film. I've had an extraordinary meeting with a man called Mr Rubbish – which, of course, isn't his real name but rather the name he goes by professionally, but I'll explain all that to you later – and, at last, the final piece of pre-production work is in place. We've the funding now. We've actually got the bloody *funding*.' Ivan grinned and made an uncharacteristic gesture of jubilation, thrusting one arm into the air. This allowed Joel to see that he was holding a tabloid, and that meant one thing only: coverage of the shooting in Belgravia, which meant bringing discussion of it into North Kensington, which was the last place on earth that Joel and Cal needed such a discussion.

Joel looked towards the car and Cal. Dimly, he heard Ivan say, 'I knew we would get it if we made the right connection with someone whose background . . .' but the rest went the way of the wind. For in the car were indeed the Blade and indeed Arissa, but not Cal Hancock. Instead, riding in the front passenger seat, where Cal always sat, was Neal Wyatt, and he appeared to Joel to be someone who was perfectly comfortable there.

Joel looked from Neal to the Blade. Vaguely behind him, he heard Ivan saying, 'You're acquainted with Neal. I was just telling him what we're up to. I'd like both you boys to be involved in the project because – and you simply must listen to me on this – it's time you set aside your dislike of each other. You have far more in common than you realise, and working on the film will show you that.'

Joel barely heard any of this. For he was sorting through matters in his mind, and he was trying to work out what everything in front of him actually meant.

He arrived at the conclusion that the Blade – informed by Cal that Joel was decidedly *his* man now – was finally keeping his end of the Neal Wyatt bargain. He'd fetched the boy from wherever Neal hung about when he wasn't vexing people in the area, and he'd told Neal he was meant to come with him. Neal wouldn't say no – no one would – so he'd climbed into the car. The Blade had shared a spliff with him, which was why Neal seemed so much at ease, his guard lowered, his humour good. Now that the Blade had Neal where he wanted him, he was going to sort the lout out once and for all. Joel made an attempt to feel good about all this, trying to apply it to his own situation. Sorting out Neal as promised, he decided, had to mean also protecting Joel from the aftermath of shooting the policeman's wife.

What Joel didn't go near was the *why* of that shooting. He didn't touch upon why a mugging had transformed into a bullet entering a woman's body. Whenever he got close to that thought, he forced it away with the word *accident*. In his mind, it had to have been a terrible mistake, the gun exploding the world into violence by inadvertently discharging when Cal grabbed it from Joel, when Joel – seeing the white woman's kind face – couldn't bring himself to demand her money.

'. . . go over it with you,' Ivan was saying, sounding as if he'd reached the conclusion of his remarks. He bent back to the car, 'And, Stanley, think about what I've offered you as well, won't you, my man?'

The Blade gave Ivan a smile, his eyelids lowered. 'Eye-van,' he murmured, 'you are one lucky bugger, y'unnerstan wha' I say? You been able to keep me 'mused for so long, I don't 'spect I ever feel like killing you.'

'Why, Stanley,' Ivan said, stepping away from the car as the Blade started it up and revved its engine, 'I'm deeply touched. Have you read the Descartes yet, by the way?'

The Blade chuckled. 'Eye-van, Eye-van. Why don't you get it? More'n thinking's involved in order to get to being, mon.'

'Ah, but that's precisely where you've gone wrong.'

'Is it?' The Blade put his hand on the back of Neal Wyatt's neck and gave it a friendly tug. 'Later, Eye-van. Me and the mon here got some serious business to conduct.'

Neal sniggered. He wiped his upper lip with the back of his hand, as if this would smear the snigger away. He glanced at Joel. He mouthed the word *fucker*.

The Blade said, 'Nice to see you, Jo-ell. And tell that cunt sister of yours the Blade says hello. Wherever she is.'

He stepped on the accelerator and the car slashed into the traffic heading towards Maida Vale. Joel watched it go. An arm – Neal's arm – came out of the passenger's window, and Neal's fist appeared. It altered into a two-fingered salute. No one inside the car tried to prevent him from making it.

Ivan insisted that they go for a coffee. They had matters to discuss, now that Mr Rubbish had stepped forward to put up the funding for the film that Ivan and his following of hopeful screen-writers had been working upon. Ivan said to Joel, 'Come with me. I've a proposal for you,' and when Joel demurred, muttering vaguely about his aunt, his brother, homework to be done, Ivan promised they wouldn't be long.

Joel saw that Ivan wasn't going to accept a refusal. He would compromise again and again until he had what he wanted, which was to be of assistance. This was something that he could never be, not now at least, but as he didn't know that, he was likely to keep cajoling Joel into having a cup of coffee or a walk or a seat on a bench, unwilling to let up. So Joel agreed to accompany him. Whatever Ivan wanted to say, it wouldn't take long, and Joel didn't intend to respond, which would only prolong an unwanted conversation.

Ivan led the way to a café not far along the Harrow Road, a grimy place of sticky-topped tables with a menu that bowed its head to an England that hadn't existed in a good thirty years: beans or mushrooms on toast, fried eggs with rashers of bacon, fried bread, baked beans and eggs, sausage rolls, mixed grills. The scent of grease in the place was overpowering, but Ivan – happily oblivious of this – gestured Joel to a table in the corner and asked him what he wanted, heading to the counter to place the order. Joel chose orange juice. It would come from a tin and taste like something that had come from a tin, but he didn't intend to drink it.

Mercifully, there was no one else in the place besides Drunk Bob, who was nodding off in his wheelchair at a table in the corner. Ivan placed their order and unfolded the paper he'd been carrying to have a look at its front page. Joel could see part of the headline of the *Evening Standard*. He was able to read **CCTV** and the word **CRIMEWATCH** beneath it. From this, he concluded that the police had come up with the video footage they'd been looking for from the CCTV cameras around the square as well as from the cameras in the neighbourhood near the shooting. They intended to show that footage on *Crimewatch*.

There could be little to surprise in this. Any film that dealt with the shooting of a white woman standing on her front porch in a posh London neighbourhood was likely to find its way on to the television. The shooting of a white woman married to a New Scotland Yard detective working on a major case was guaranteed to get there.

The only hope for Joel lay in two possibilities when it came to the video from those cameras: that the quality of the CCTV footage was poor and too distant to be of any use in identifying anyone: or that the television programme itself held little or no interest in a community like his own North Kensington neighbourhood.

Ivan brought their drinks to the table. He had the paper secured under his arm. As he sat, he tossed it on to a chair. He doctored his coffee and began to speak. 'Who would have thought it possible to make a fortune on rubbish? And then to be willing to share that fortune . . . ?' Ivan curved his hands around his mug and went on to make it clear he wasn't speaking about journalism. 'When a man remembers his roots, my friend, he can do a world of good. If he doesn't turn his back on those people he left behind . . . That's what Mr Rubbish has done for us, Joel.'

Joel tried not to look at the paper on the nearby chair but, folded in half, the *Standard* had landed upside down, with its headline now hidden and the rest of the front page in clear view, and this acted like the call of a siren, utterly compelling and there Joel sat, without a ship's mast to tie himself to. What he could see was a photograph now, with the beginning of a story beneath it. He was too far away to read any part of the story, but the picture was visible. In it, a man and a woman leaned against a railing, smiling at the camera, champagne glasses in their raised hands. The man was handsome and blond; the woman was attractive and brunette. They looked like an advertisement for Perfect Couple, and behind them the placid water of a bay sparkled beneath a cloudless blue sky. Joel turned his head. He tried to attend to Ivan's words.

'. . . call himself Mr Rubbish,' Ivan was saying. 'Apparently, it's a simple design that's been snapped up by metropolitan areas all over the world. It's operated by computerised conveyors or some such device that separates everything, so the entire populace doesn't have to be educated about re-cycling. He's made a fortune on it and now he's willing to funnel some of it back into the community he came from. We're one of his beneficiaries. We've got a renewable grant. What do you say to that?'

Joel had the presence of mind to nod and say, 'Wicked.'

Ivan cocked his head. 'That's *all* you can say to two hundred and fifty thousand pounds? *Wicked?*'

'It's cool, Ivan. Adam an' that lot're gonna be raving for sure.'

'But not you? You're part of it. We'll need everyone we can find to be involved in the project if we're to carry it off.'

'I can't make no film.'

'What nonsense. You can write. You can use language in ways that other people . . . Listen to me.' Ivan brought his chair closer to Joel's and spoke earnestly, the way he gener-ally spoke when he believed that something needed to be conveyed with great urgency. 'I don't expect you to act in the film or stand behind the camera or do anything that you're not already used to doing. But we're going to need you on the script . . . No, don't argue. *Listen*. Right now, the dialogue leans too heavily towards the vernacular, and I need an advocate for broadening its appeal. Now, vernacular's fine if all we want is a local release. But, frankly, now that we've got this backing behind us, I think we ought to be aiming for more. Film festivals and the like. This is not the moment for keeping our aspirations humble. I believe you can make the others see that, Joel.'

Joel knew that this was rubbish, and he wanted to laugh at the irony of it: that he would not be sitting in this place at this moment having this conversation with Ivan had not rubbish on a very large scale made it possible. But he didn't want to argue with Ivan. He wanted to get his hands on a newspaper so that he could see what the police were up to. And he wanted to have a word with the Blade.

Abruptly he shoved himself away from the table. He stood and said, 'Ivan, I got to go.'

Ivan stood as well, his expression altered. He said, 'Joel, what's happened? I can tell something's . . . I've heard about your sister. I've not wanted to mention it. I suppose I was hoping that news of this film would allow you to think of other things for a while. Look. Forgive me. I hope you know I'm your friend. I'm ready to—'

'Later,' Joel cut in. He said this past his need to fight off the useless kindness, to fight it off physically and not only with words. 'Great news you got, Ivan. Got to go.'

He departed in a rush. It was ages before Toby would be done with his work at the learning centre, so Joel knew he had the time to get up to Lancefield Court, which was where he went once the café was behind him. He slipped through the opening in the chain link fence, and he climbed to the first floor. No one was standing guard at the foot of the stairs, which should have told him that the flat from which the Blade distributed his wares to his runners was going to be empty.

But he was desperate and his desperation compelled him to make his useless search anyway.

Joel decided then that the Blade had taken Neal Wyatt somewhere quite safe in order to deal with him. He thought of the abandoned underground station, of a tucked-away corner of Kensal Green cemetery. He thought of large car parks, of lock-up garages, of warehouses, of buildings about to be torn down. It seemed to him that London was teeming with places that the Blade might have taken Neal Wyatt, and he attempted to comfort himself with the thought that there – in any one of these thousand places – Neal Wyatt was currently being informed that his days of shadowing, bullying, assaulting, and tormenting the Campbell children were at an end.

Because *that*, Joel assured himself, was what was going on. Today. Right now. And once Neal Wyatt was finally and permanently sorted, they could get on to extricating Ness and bringing her home to her family.

Thinking about all this went a small distance towards comforting Joel. It also gave him something else to dwell upon so that he didn't have to consider what he couldn't bear to consider: what it actually might mean that Cal Hancock was nowhere to be found, that a white lady was shot, and that Belgravia, New Scotland Yard, and everyone else in the world intended to find the person responsible.

But despite his determination to keep his thoughts away from the unbearable, Joel couldn't blind himself as well. On the route back from Lancefield Court to the Harrow Road, he passed a tobacconist, and outside on the pavement stood the sort of placards that advertise newspapers all over London. The words leaped out, bleeding black ink into the porous paper on which they were written: **BELGRAVIA KILLER ON CRIMEWATCH!** one declared while another announced **COUNTESS KILLER TV PIX**.

Joel's vision went to a pinprick in which the only thing visible was **KILLER**. And then even that disappeared, leaving behind a field of black. Killer, Belgravia, Pix, Crimewatch. Joel held out his arm and felt for the side of the building he'd been passing when he'd seen the placards. He remained there until his vision cleared. He bit at his thumbnail. He tried to think.

But all he could come up with was the Blade.

He walked on. He was only vaguely aware of where he was, and he ended up in front of the charity shop without knowing how he'd got there. He went inside. It smelled of steam hitting musty clothes.

He saw that his aunt had an ironing board set up at the back of the shop. She was dealing with wrinkles on a lavender blouse, and a pile of other clothing lay waiting for her attention on a chair to her left.

'There's no sense in not giving people an idea of what things are *meant* to look like when they're taken care of,' Kendra said when she saw him. 'No one's going to buy a wrinkled mess of a thing.' She pulled the blouse off the ironing board and hung it neatly on a plastic hanger. 'Better,' she said. 'I can't say I'm wild about the colour, but someone will be. Did you decide not to wait for Toby at the centre?'

Joel came up with an explanation. 'Went for a walk instead.'

'Bit cold for that.'

'Yeah. Well.' He didn't know why he'd entered the shop. He could put it down to a vague desire for comfort, but that was the extent of his ability to explain things to himself. He wanted *something* to alter how he felt inside. He wanted his aunt to be that something or, failing that, to provide it somehow.

She went on ironing. She laid a pair of black trousers on the ironing board and examined them top to bottom. She shook her head and held them up for Joel to see. A greasy stain dripped down the front of them, elongated into the shape of Italy. She tossed them to the floor, saying, 'Why do people think *poor* equals *desperate* when what it really means is wanting something to make you *forget* you're poor, not something to remind you you're poor every time you put it on?' She went back to the pile of clothes and snatched up a skirt.

Joel watched her and had an overpowering desire to tell her everything: the Blade, Cal Hancock, the gun, the lady. Indeed, he had an overpowering need just to talk. But when she looked up, the words wouldn't come to him, and he moved away from her, restlessly prowling the length of the shop. He paused to examine a toaster that was shaped like a sausage in a bun and next to it a cowboy boot that had been fashioned into a lamp. It was odd, he thought, the objects that people bought for themselves. They wanted something and then they *un*wanted it once they saw its effect on themselves and the rest of their possessions, once they knew how it actually made everything else look, once they realised how it eventually made them feel. But if they'd known in advance, if they'd only known, there would have been no waste. There'd have been no rejection.

Kendra spoke. 'Did you know about them, Joel? I've wanted to ask you, but I didn't know how.'

For a moment, Joel thought she was talking about the toaster and the cowboy boot lamp. He couldn't imagine what sort of answer he was meant to give.

His aunt went on. 'Afterwards . . . Could you tell something was different with her? And if you could tell, did you not think of going to someone?'

Joel looked from the lamp to the toaster. He said, 'What?' He felt hot and queasy.

'Your sister.' Kendra applied pressure to the iron and it sizzled as some of the hot water within it came out upon the garment she was working on. 'Those men and what they did to her and Ness never telling. Did you know?'

Joel shook his head, but he heard more than his aunt was actually saying to him. He heard the *should* of it all. His sister had been messed with by their gran's boyfriend and all of his mates and Joel should have known, he should have seen, he should have recognised, he should have done something. Even as a seven-year-old or whatever he'd been when those terrible things had begun happening to his sister, he should have done *something*, no matter that the men always looked like giants to him and more than giants: potential granddads, potential dads, even. They looked like anything but what they were.

Joel felt his aunt's eyes fixed on him. She was waiting for something seen, something heard, something felt, anything. He wanted to give that to her, but he couldn't. He dropped his gaze.

Kendra said, 'Miss her?'

He nodded. He said, 'What'd they do . . . ?'

'She in the remand centre now. She's . . . Joel, she'll likely be going away for a while. Fabia Bender thinks—'

'She ain't going *nowhere*.' The declaration came out more fiercely than he'd intended.

Kendra set the iron to one side. She said kindly, 'I don't want her sent away, either. But Miss Bender's trying to work things so she gets placed somewhere they can help her instead of punish her. Some place like . . .' She paused.

He looked up. Their glances met. They both knew where that explanation had been heading, and it brought no comfort. *Some place like where your mum is, Joel. She's got the family curse. Wave goodbye to her.* The edges of Joel's world kept furling up, like a drying leaf detached from a tree.

He said, 'Ain't gonna happen, dat.'

'"Isn't",' his aunt patiently corrected.

She picked up the iron again, applying it to the skirt spread out on the board. She said, 'I've not done right by any of you. I didn't see that what I had was more important than what I wanted.' She spoke with great care. She ironed with great care. The task did not require the concentration and attention she was giving to it.

Joel said, 'You miss Dix, innit.'

'"Course,' she replied. 'But Dix's something separate from

what I'm talking about here. For me, this is how it was, Joel: Glory dropped you on me, and I decided okay I'll cope cos you're my family, but isn't *anything* going to change the way I'm leading my life. Because if I change the way I'm leading my life, I'll end up hating these kids for making me change things round, and I don't want to hate my brother's children 'cause none of this is their fault. They didn't want their dad getting shot and they sure as hell didn't ask to have their mum flitting in and out of the nuthouse all their lives. But we all still got to – *have* to – follow our separate paths. So I'll get 'em in school, I'll feed 'em and put a roof over their heads, and when I do that, I'll be doing my duty. But there was more 'n duty that needed to be involved. I jus' didn't want to see it.'

Joel realised at the end of all this that his aunt was apologising to him, to all of them, really, through the person of him. He wanted to tell her that she didn't need to. Had he been able to put it into words, he would have told her that none of them had asked for what they'd had handed to them, and if they bollocksed things up as they tried to cope, whose fault was it, really? His aunt had done what she'd thought was right at the time.

He said, 'S'okay, Aunt Ken.' He ran his finger the length of the cowboy boot lamp and he brought it away. Like everything else in the charity shop, it was clean and dustless, ready to be purchased and taken home by someone who wanted something quirky to act as a distraction from the rest of their lives. Toby, he thought, would have loved the lamp. Simple quirky things were enough for him.

Kendra came to his side. She put her arm around his shoulders and she kissed him on the temple. She said, 'All of this is going to pass. We'll get through it. You and Toby and I. Even Ness. We're *going* to get through it. And when we do, we'll be a family to each other the way we're meant to be. We'll be a proper family, Joel.'

'Okay,' Joel said in a voice so low that he knew his aunt couldn't possibly hear it. 'That'll be real nice, Aunt Ken.'

Joel felt drawn to *Crimewatch* like a spectator to the scene of a roadside disaster. He had to watch but he didn't know how to watch without drawing attention to what he meant to do.

As the time for the programme drew near, Joel tried hard to think how to wrest control of the television from his little brother. Toby was watching a video – a young Tom Hanks involved with a mermaid – and he knew that he could not switch off that film without Toby raising the roof in protest. Minutes trickled by. Ten, then fifteen, with Joel racking his brains to come up with a way to separate Toby from his video. It was Kendra's commitment to improved parenting that finally gave him the opening he needed. She decided that Toby's bath needed supervising and she told the little boy he could watch the rest of the film once he was bathed and in his pyjamas. When she took his brother off to the bathroom, Joel dashed to the television and found the proper channel.

Crimewatch was nearing its conclusion. The host was saying '. . . a look at that footage a final time. As a reminder, it was taken in Cadogan Lane, and the individuals in it are suspected to have been involved in the shooting that occurred in Eaton Terrace a short time earlier.'

What followed – just as Joel had hoped – was some five seconds of very grainy footage, typical of the kind from a CCTV camera that loops the same film through its system every twenty-four hours. This depicted the narrow street that Joel and Cal had burst upon when they'd crashed through the house attached to the last garden on their escape route. Two figures approached, one of them made featureless by virtue of what he wore: knitted hat, gloves, markless donkey jacket with its collar turned up. The other figure, however, was more memorable, a function of the hair that sprang around his face as he walked.

When he watched this, Joel felt a moment of blessed relief. He could see that the hair – even uncovered as it was – would not be enough, considering the quality of the film. His anorak was like a hundred thousand other anoraks in the streets of London, and his school uniform, which would have narrowed the field considerably, was not visible aside from the trousers and the shoes. And these told no tale at all. So since Cal's face was completely hidden from the CCTV camera, it stood to reason that—

Even as Joel was thinking all this, his world tilted violently on its axis. At the moment they passed beneath the camera, the head lifted and Joel's face was framed in the picture. It was still grainy and he was still several yards away from the camera, but as Joel sat transfixed in front of the television, he learned that 'the miracle of computer enhancement' was at that very moment being brought to bear upon the image, and within a few days the video film should be greatly improved by specialists at the Met, at which time *Crimewatch* would present it once again to the public. Until that moment, if anyone recognised either of the individuals shown on the film that evening, they were to phone the hotline printed on the bottom of their television screen. They could depend upon the fact that their call and their identity would be held in the strictest confidence.

In the meantime, the host said in a solemn voice, the victim of the shooting remained on life support, pending the weighty decision that her husband and family had to make about the fate of their unborn child.

Joel heard these last words like something spoken under-water. *Unborn child.* The woman had been wearing a coat. He hadn't seen – *they* hadn't seen or known – that she was preg-nant. If they had known, if they had even guessed . . . None of this would have happened. Joel swore this to himself. He clung to the thought of it as he had nothing else to cling to.

He pushed himself off the settee and went to the television.

He switched it off. He wanted to ask someone what was happening to him and to the world as he knew it. But there was no one to ask and at the moment what constituted his consciousness was what he could hear, which was the noise of Toby splashing about in the bath.

Joel played truant from school to find Cal Hancock. He began his search for the Rasta by lurking around the block of flats in which Arissa lived, certain that Cal would turn up there eventually, standing guard for the Blade as always. As Joel did this, he tried not to think of the CCTV pictures. He also tried to drive from his mind other relevant details that boded ill for him: the flood of newspaper stories with that CCTV picture of him on their front pages; the *au pair* who'd seen him up close; the gun that was lying in someone's garden along the way from Eaton Terrace to Cadogan Lane; his discarded cap at the base of one of those garden walls; a lady languishing on life support; a baby whose fate had to be decided. He did, on the other hand, think of Neal Wyatt who, along with his entire crew, was certainly making no attempt to harass Joel, Toby, or anything remotely Campbell.

From this, Joel took evidence that Neal indeed had been sorted by the Blade. No longer a supposition, this, no longer a belief he tried to cling to. There would now, he told himself, never again be trouble from Neal. The Blade had performed as promised because he'd been informed by Cal that Joel had performed as promised, and the Blade had no need ever to know that Cal Hancock, and not Joel, had been the one to pull the trigger on the lady in Eaton Terrace. Cal's fingerprints weren't even on the gun should the gun be found, so unless Cal told the Blade the truth, no one on earth would have a suspicion that Cal, and not Joel, had carried the mission to its conclusion. While there was no cash, handbag, or jewellery to show for it, there was enough notoriety to prove that the Blade's instruction had been followed to the letter.

'*Real* mugging dis time, Jo-ell,' the Blade had told him when he'd handed over the gun. 'You mon enough to do it right? Cos it better be right, and then you 'n me, we'll be done. You scratch my back, I scratch yours. An' one t'ing more, Jo-ell, listen good. Th' gun got to be used. I want to hear it been fired. More exciting dat way, y'unnerstan? More like you mean business when you tell some bitch to hand over her money.'

At first, Joel had thought the target would be a local woman, like the Asian woman he'd tried to mug in Portobello Road. Then he thought – considering the instruction that the gun was to be fired – that the mark was a female who needed sorting. It would be, perhaps, a crackhead fleabag who was turning tricks for a fingernail's measure of powder. Or perhaps it would be the tart belonging to a dealer who was trying to take over some of the Blade's patch. It would, in short, be someone who would see the gun and cooperate instantly, and it would happen in a part of town and at a time of day where a gunshot would mean business as usual among the drug dealers, the gangsters, and the general flotsam and jetsam of the population and, consequently, probably go unreported at the most and uninvestigated at the least. In any case, it would just be a gun shot, the weapon fired into the air, fired into the wooden frame of a window, fired into a door, fired anywhere but at a real person. Just fired. That was all.

This ill-founded belief was what Joel had clung to, even as they'd boarded the underground train, even as they'd trotted along through a part of town that, with every step he had taken, declared itself to be some place quite different from the world that he was used to. What he hadn't expected was what he'd been presented with for the mugging and the weapon firing: a white lady coming home with her shopping, one who smiled at them and asked if they were lost and looked like someone who believed that there was nothing to fear as long as she stood at her own front door and showed strangers kindness.

Despite what he did to reassure himself, Joel's thoughts went feverishly among three points as he lurked about and waited for Cal. The first was the actual shooting of the woman who'd turned out to be not only a countess but also the wife of a Scotland Yard detective. The second was that he'd done what he'd been *told* to do – even if Cal was ultimately the one to fire the weapon – and no matter the means to get to this end, the end had been reached and that meant Joel had proved himself. The third was that there was a film of him in Cadogan Lane, there was an *au pair* who'd seen him up close, and there was a gun with his fingerprints on it, and all of that meant something which was not good.

Ultimately, Joel saw that his only hope lay in the Blade. If Cal did not show up the next time that the Blade chose to do his business on Arissa in her flat, it would mean that Cal was well and truly gone. And if Cal was well and truly gone, it would mean that Cal had been spirited off because it made no sense that the Blade might actually do *away* with Cal instead of just easing him out of London for as long as it took for the heat of the shooting and its aftermath to run its course. The way Joel looked at the situation – indeed, the only way he *could* look at the situation – was to decide that if the Blade could do all that for Cal, he could do it for Joel, and with a photo-graph of Joel in the process of being enhanced, that was some-thing which had to be done, and soon. He wanted shelter and he needed shelter. As things turned out, he didn't have to wait long for the moment during which his request for sanctuary went answered . . . before he even made it.

On Portnall Road, he'd hidden himself on the porch of a building near Arissa's, safely away from view. He'd been there an hour, hoping the Blade would show up to pay a call on his woman. He was shivering in the cold and had cramp in his legs when the Blade's car finally pulled up. The man himself got out, and Joel stood, preparatory to making his approach. But then Neal Wyatt removed himself from the car as well and, as Joel watched, the Blade disappeared into the building and Neal established himself in what could only be called the Cal Position: bouncing a small rubber ball against one wall of the entrance to the building as he himself lounged against the other.

Joel ducked. He thought *How . . . ?* And then *Why . . . ?* He stared at nothing as he tried to puzzle out what he'd seen, and when he next ventured a look at the entrance to Arissa's building, it was to see that he'd been noticed despite his efforts: Neal was gazing right back at him. Neal pocketed the ball he'd been bouncing. He sauntered down the path, crossed the road, and came along the pavement. He stood there, observing Joel in his inadequate place of hiding. He said nothing, but he looked quite different, and it came to Joel that *what* he looked like didn't have much to do with having been sorted by anyone for anything.

Joel remembered in that moment what Hibah had said to him: Neal wants respect. Can't you show him respect?

Clearly, Joel saw, Neal had done something to get it. Joel expected the outcome to be an attack – blows, kicks, knives, whatever – delivered by Neal to his own pathetic person. But no attack came.

Instead, Neal spoke, and it was only a single statement that he made, tinged with weary sarcasm. 'You are one stupid red-skin fuck.' Having said this, he turned and walked back to the entry to Arissa's building, and there he remained.

Joel himself was Lot's wife: the desire to flee but eternally absent the ability to do so. Ten minutes passed, and the Blade came outside, Arissa following, dog to master. The Blade said something to Neal, and the three of them moved in the direc-tion of the Blade's car. He opened the driver's door as Neal got in on the other side. Arissa remained on the pavement, waiting for something that was soon in coming. The Blade turned to her, jerked her over, cupped one of her buttocks to hold her in place, and kissed her. He released her abruptly.

He pinched her breast and said something to her and the girl stood before him, looking devoted, looking like someone who would never cross him, who would wait right there till he came for her again, who would be exactly what he wanted her to be. Precisely, Joel realised with a jolt of understanding, like someone who was *not* his sister, who did not act or think like Ness. Someone, in short, who gazed upon the Blade in a way that Ness had never once looked at any man.

Joel thought, then, about how many times he had heard Blade mouth that unpleasant imperative about his sister, and a glimmer of light began to illuminate the darkness around him. But that glimmer of light was like ice against his heart and its incandescence radiated on the simple *confluence* of events as they had occurred in his life. Joel saw that they'd all led to this precise moment: Neal Wyatt waiting in the car like someone who knew very well that he belonged there, the Blade showing Arissa what was what, and Joel himself watching the action, receiving a message he'd been meant to receive from the very first.

Cal didn't matter. Joel didn't matter. In the final accounting, Neal and Arissa didn't matter. They themselves didn't know this yet, but they too would learn once their purpose had been served.

What Joel did next, he did to acknowledge all the times that Cal Hancock had tried to warn him to keep clear of the Blade. He emerged from his useless hiding place, and he approached the car, the Blade, and Arissa.

He said, 'Where's Cal?'

The Blade glanced his way. 'Jo-ell,' he said. 'Looks like t'ings're getting real hot for you, bred.'

'Where's Cal?' Joel repeated. 'What've you done to Cal, Stanley?'

Neal got out of the car in a liquid movement, but the Blade waved him back. He said, 'Long time Cal's been wanting to see his fam'ly, innit. Out there in Jah-may-ca land, wiv steel bands, ganja, and reggae all night. Uncle Bob Marley looking down from heaven. Cal scratch my back, so I scratch his.' He jerked his head at Neal, who obediently got back into the car. Then he kissed Arissa once again, and he pushed her towards her building. He said, 'Anything else, Jo-ell?'

There was no hope, but Joel said it anyway. 'That lady . . . I di'n't . . .' But he didn't know how to finish what he'd started, so he said nothing further. He merely waited.

'Didn't what?' the Blade asked him blandly, without curiosity.

A moment for decision, and Joel made the only one he could. 'Didn't nuffink,' he said.

The Blade smiled. 'Mind you keep it that way.'

The e-fit came next, supplied courtesy of the *au pair* who'd wielded the toilet plunger. Typical of the London tabloids, she became the heroine of the moment, and her past and present were explored thoroughly as next to her own picture was featured the e-fit of the ginger-haired young lout with whom she'd struggled.

IS THIS THE FACE OF A KILLER? was the headline that accom-panied the e-fit in the *Daily Mail*, the front page of which Joel saw fluttering on the pavement outside Westbourne Park station. Like most e-fits, it didn't look much like him, but the news story that accompanied it revealed that the enhancement of the video image was complete. Additional footage from Sloane Square underground station had been analysed, the paper reported. The police had isolated more images. Scotland Yard indicated an arrest was imminent as tips flooded the lines dedicated to the cause of tracking down the killer of the wife of one of their own.

Joel had taken Toby to Meanwhile Gardens when it finally occurred. They were in the skate bowl, in the topmost and simplest of the arenas, and Toby was delighting in the fact that he'd managed to balance long enough to glide from one side to the other without falling off his board. He was crowing, 'Lookit! Lookit, Joel,' when the first of the panda cars slowed and then stopped on the bridge over the Grand Union Canal. A second panda car took up a position in Elkstone Road, just beyond the corner of the child drop-in centre, but visible enough that Majidah looked up from what she was doing inside the centre, frowned, and decided to walk outside into the play area to make certain the children were safe. A third car parked at the turn from Elkstone into Great Western Road. Out of each of these cars, a uniformed constable climbed. The drivers remained inside.

They converged on the skate bowl. It came to Joel as he watched their approach that, clearly, he'd been under observation by someone from somewhere – perhaps he'd even been followed for the past days since he'd seen the Blade – and when the moment had seemed appropriate, that person had placed a phone call to the Harrow Road police. And here they were.

The constable from the car nearest the drop-in centre was the first to get to Joel. He said, 'Joel Campbell?' and Joel said to his brother, 'Tobe, you got to go home, okay?'

True to form, Toby said 'But you said I could ride my skateboard and you said you watch me. Don't you 'member?'

'We got to do it later.'

'Come with me, lad,' the constable said to Joel.

Joel said, 'Tobe? C'n you get home by yourself? If you can't, I 'spect one of the cops'll take you.'

'I want to skateboard. You said, Joel. You promised.'

'They ain't letting me stay here,' Joel said. 'You go home.'

The constable from the bridge arrived next. He said that Toby was to come with him. When he heard this, Joel thought the constable meant that he would take Toby home so that the little boy wouldn't have to go on his own, despite how close it was to the skate bowl, and he said Cheers. He began to follow the first constable to his car at the kerb near the child drop-in centre – his head averted so that he didn't have to look at the Pakistani woman watching from behind the chain link fence – but then he saw that Toby wasn't being led towards Edenham Estate at all, but rather towards the bridge.

Joel stopped. The day's cold seeped up his neck and closed around it like a fist. He said, 'Where're they taking my brother?'

'He'll be looked after,' the constable told him.

'But—'

'You'll have to come along. You'll have to get into the car.'

Joel took a useless step towards the spiral steps. 'But Tobe's meant to go—'

'Don't fight us, lad.' The constable attached himself to Joel's arm.

'But my auntie'll wonder—'

'Come along.'

At this point, the driver of the panda car parked in front of the drop-in centre came to them at a jog. He attached himself to Joel's other arm and shoved that arm behind Joel's back. He brought out a set of handcuffs and, wordlessly, snapped them on his wrists. He hissed in Joel's ear, 'Fucking little half-breed *bastard*,' and he pushed him towards the car.

'Steady on, Jer,' the other constable said.

'Don't bloody tell *me*,' the first replied. 'Open the door.'

'Jer—'

'Fucking *open* it.'

The first cooperated. In front of Joel, the car door swung open, making an invitation that he could not refuse. He felt a sharp blow on his back, and a hand crushed down on his head, propelling him inside the vehicle. When he was inside, the door slammed shut. As the two policemen climbed into the front seat of the car, Joel peered out of the window, trying to see what had happened to Toby.

The panda car on the bridge was gone. In Meanwhile Gardens, board riders in the skate bowl had stopped to watch the police interact with Joel. They lined the lowest lip of the bowl now – their skateboards balanced against their hips – and they talked among themselves as the panda car pulled away from the kerb to make the turn into Great Western Road for the short drive to the Harrow Road station. Joel craned his neck to search for a face in the park that would tell him – by its expression – what would happen from here. But there was no face. There was only his inevitable future that had begun playing out the moment the first constable had taken him by the arm.

Beyond Meanwhile Gardens – and this was what Joel could see as the car crossed the bridge over the canal – the back of Kendra's house was visible. Joel fixed his gaze on it as long as he could, but it was only a moment before the first building on Great Western Road obscured his view.

Kendra received the word from Majidah. The Pakistani woman was brief enough in her message to the charity shop, where Kendra was in the midst of making a sale to a refugee African woman in the company of an elderly man. Three cars had come from the police, Majidah informed her. Two of them had taken Ness's brothers away. Separately, this was. And, Mrs Osborne, the disturbing part comes now: one of the constables put the older boy in handcuffs.

Kendra heard this in silence because it seemed terribly important at the moment that she conclude the sale of table lamps, shoes, and yellow crockery to her customers. She said, 'Thank you. I see. I do appreciate the call' in her best formal voice and left Majidah on the other end of the line thinking Good gracious, it was hardly any wonder when children went so terribly wrong if the adults in their lives were able to receive deadly news without a single wail of horror. As westernised as she had become over the years that she had lived in London, Majidah knew that *she* would never have greeted terrible news such as this without taking at least a few minutes to tear at her hair and rip at her clothing before marshalling her forces to do something about it. So Majidah went on to phone Fabia Bender as well, but her message to the social worker was altogether unnecessary since the wheels of British jurisprudence were already turning, and Fabia was at the Harrow Road station in advance of Joel's arrival.

Kendra felt herself floundering after the refugees left the charity shop and she was free to absorb Majidah's message. She did not associate the message with murder. Naturally, she'd seen the story of the shooting in the paper since, in the constant pursuit of the ever-more-sensational, the editors of all London's tabloids and most of its broadsheets had made the quick decision that the murder of a cop's-wife-who-was-also-a-countess easily trumped every other story. So she'd read the papers and she'd seen the e-fit. But like any other e-fit, the one of Joel came only moderately close to his real appearance, and his aunt had had no reason to connect the drawing to her nephew. Besides, her mind had been crammed with other concerns, most of which involved Ness: what had happened to her in years past and what was going to become of her now.

And now . . . Joel. Kendra closed up the charity shop and walked to the Harrow Road police station, which was not far. In her haste, she went without her coat and without her bag. She had with her only demands, and she made them to the special constable working in the tiny reception area where a bulletin board offered easy answers to life's problems with announcements about Crimestoppers, Neighbourhood Watch programmes, Whistlestop Crime, and rules for Out and About at Night.

'Police picked up my nephews,' she said. 'Where are they? What's going on?'

The special constable – a police wannabe forever doomed to be just that – looked Kendra over and what he saw was a mixed race lady looking more black than white, shapely in a narrow navy skirt, with something of an attitude about her. He felt that she was making demands of him in a way that suggested she'd climbed too far above herself, when she ought to be speaking respectfully. He told her to sit. He'd be with her presently.

She said, 'This is a twelve-year-old boy we're talking about. And an eight-year-old. You've brought at least one of them here. I want to know why.'

He said nothing.

She said, 'I want to see my nephew. And where's his brother been taken if he's not here? You can't snatch children off the street and—'

'Sit *down*, madam,' the special constable said. 'I will be with you presently and what *is* it about this that you don't understand? Do I need to call someone out to explain this all to you? I can do that. You can be invited to step inside an interview room yourself.'

It was the *yourself* that told her what she needed to know. 'What's he done?' she asked hoarsely. 'Tell me what he's done.'

The special constable knew, of course. Everyone in the Harrow Road station knew because to them this was a crime of such enormity that no punishment was sufficient to mete out to the perpetrator. One of their extended fraternity had been struck down through the person of his wife, and a payment would be extracted for this crime. Thinking of what had happened in Belgravia caused blood to boil in the veins of individual policemen and women. Boiling blood produced the need to strike.

The special constable had in his possession the sharpened photo, which had at last been produced from CCTV footage in Cadogan Lane. Duplicates of this picture were up now in every police station in every borough of the city. He took this picture and he shoved it at Kendra for what he thought of as her viewing pleasure.

'Talking to the sod about this little matter,' he told her. 'Sit down, shut your mug, or get out of here.'

Kendra saw that the picture was unmistakably Joel. The

dandelion puff of hair around his head and the teacake blotches on his face said it all. As did his expression, which was of an animal caught in the lights of an oncoming car. Kendra didn't need to ask where the picture had been taken. Suddenly, she knew. She crumpled the photo to her chest and she bowed her head.

28

In the interview room, things were different this time, and Joel understood he was at a crossroads. No one questioned him at first. He sat for hours, sometimes with Sergeant Starr, sometimes with Fabia Bender, sometimes with a female constable who was called Sherry by the other two adults. The stringy-haired blonde duty solicitor was not present now – 'I'll be taking your part when the time comes,' Fabia had said to Joel – but the very large and very official-looking tape recorder was always right there, waiting to be switched on. No one pushed the relevant button on it, however, and no one said anything. Not a single word. Instead, they came and went and sat in silence. Joel told himself they were waiting for something or for someone to join them, but their silence unnerved him, making his bones feel rubbery.

He'd already realised that the position he was in – sitting there in the interview room – was likely to play itself out far differently from his earlier visit to the Harrow Road station. He'd drawn that conclusion from his last exchange with the Blade. Then, he'd finally put the pieces together, and he'd seen himself as what he'd long and unknowingly been: an actor in a drama of revenge. It was a drama whose plot he hadn't understood until that moment of conversation with Stanley Hynds while Neal Wyatt lurked nearby, doubtless waiting for more rewards to flow in his direction; remuneration for what he'd managed to accomplish at the behest of the Blade.

At this precise moment, Joel saw the details only imperfectly. Some things he knew for certain; others he only intuited.

A large mirror hung on the wall opposite the table where he was sitting. Joel deduced quickly and correctly that it was a two-way mirror because he'd seen that sort of thing in police dramas on the television. He expected that people had come and gone on the other side, studying him and waiting for him to give a sign that would mark him as guilty, so he tried very hard not to give that sign, although he wasn't sure what it was.

He reckoned that people were trying to unsettle him with the wait and the silence. This wasn't exactly what he'd expected, so he used the time to study his hands. They were out of the handcuffs, and he rubbed his wrists because, although there was no mark upon them from the restraints, he could still feel the pressure and the chafing, through his skin to his bones. He'd been made the promise of a sandwich and he'd been given a can of Coke. He curved his fingers around this and tried to think of something pleasant, of anything but where he was and what was likely to happen next. But he couldn't manage it. So he dwelt instead on questions and answers.

What did they have on him? he asked himself. A video image and nothing else. An e-fit that didn't fit at all.

And what did a video image and an e-fit mean? That someone looking vaguely like Joel Campbell had been walking down a street not far from the spot in Belgravia where a white lady had been shot.

That was it. The long and the short of it. The alpha and omega. The black and white.

But at heart Joel knew that there was more. There was the *au pair* who'd come face to face with him inside the house in Cadogan Lane. There was the old woman who'd been walking her corgi around the corner from where the countess had been shot. There was his knitted cap, left behind in one of the gardens through which they had escaped. There was the gun, lost in one of the gardens. Once the police had the gun in their possession – which really was only a matter of time, if they didn't have it already – there would also be the small problem of fingerprints. For Joel's prints were the only ones on that gun, and this had been the case from the moment that the Blade had wiped the pistol clean and handed it over, fresh as a baby newly born and newly bathed.

The thought of babies newly born and newly bathed brought unbidden into Joel's mind the thought of the lady's baby. They hadn't known because if they'd known, they'd never have . . . They *wouldn't.* All they'd done, he told himself, was just wait for someone to show up in that posh polished street of posh polished houses. That was it. And Joel had not intended her to die. He hadn't intended her to be shot at all.

This was the point. The shooting of that woman – wife of a Scotland Yard detective, pregnant, returning from a shopping excursion, in hospital now, on life support – was the fulcrum on which Joel's life was balanced. He was in a precarious and dangerous position, ready to slide in either direction. For Cal Hancock, and not Joel, had done the shooting and all Joel really had to do was to say the name and not only that name but another name, and this was what he sat there considering in the interview room.

He thought about what they did to twelve-year-old boys who found themselves in the wrong place, with the wrong companion, at the worst possible time. Surely, they didn't put them in gaol. They sent them somewhere, to some detention centre for boys, where they were held for a while before they were released back into their communities. If their crimes were heinous enough, the authorities released them elsewhere, with new identities and the possibility of a future before them. This, then, was what Joel saw as an option he could choose if he wanted to do so. For he'd had no knowledge of what was going to happen that day in Belgravia, and he could tell them that as well. He could say that he was just hanging with one Cal Hancock on that afternoon, and they'd got on the tube and ridden around on the Circle line and got off where it seemed that they could . . . what? he wondered. Mug someone was the obvious answer, and Joel knew he would have to offer that much in whatever statement he finally made.

So he would tell them, he decided, that they'd intended to mug a rich white lady if they could find one, and things went bad in the midst of the mugging. Cal Hancock pulled out the gun to frighten her, and the gun went off. But none of it had been *meant* to happen, none of it was planned, none of it had been thought out.

Thus it seemed to Joel as he sat in the interview room, with the waiting and the silence growing heavier by the moment, that naming Cal Hancock would ensure his own release, sooner rather than later. *I was wiv a blood called Cal Hancock.* Eight words and that would be it. The true guilty party would be named, someone old enough to be thrown into prison for a life sentence that would rob him of at least twenty years. Eight words. Eight words only. That was all.

But, despite his thoughts, which were bouncing around his skull like rubber balls, Joel knew that he could not grass. He also knew that everyone in the Harrow Road police station understood this as well, as did the Blade. There was simply no way. Grass and you were finished; grass and everyone whose life touched yours would suffer for your grassing as well.

That meant Toby. For Ness – and this was something that Joel had been a long and terrible time understanding – had already been dealt with.

Joel felt a hard bubble rising within him, one that grew as it climbed from his guts and worked its inevitable way to his throat. There, it wanted to burst from him in a sob, but he wouldn't let it and he couldn't let it and he had to avoid it no matter what. He put his arms on the table and his head in his arms.

He said, 'Where's Toby?'

'He's safe,' the constable called Sherry told him.

'Wha's that mean?' Joel asked. 'Where's Aunt Ken?'

There was no answer to this. The silence allowed Joel to

work out the answers for himself, which he was quick to do. Toby had been hustled off to Care – that nightmare place in which children entered the maw of a system that seemed fashioned to house them and then forget them – because with one Campbell locked up for a knife assault and another Campbell involved in a deadly shooting, the police, social services, and everyone else with a working brain had proof positive that the home of Kendra Osborne was no place for a juvenile to reside.

Joel wanted to demand to see Fabia Bender, in order to tell her that things weren't like that. He wanted her to know that *nothing* that happened was down to his aunt. He wanted to tell her it was down to someone and something else. But he couldn't say.

Everything within his mind became a series of images. They played against his eyelids when he closed his eyes; they seemed present when he held his eyes open. There was his father getting shot in the street one day . . . There was his mother holding infant Toby out of the third-floor window while a train roared by . . . There was Neal Wyatt coming after him in Meanwhile Gardens . . . There was Glory flying off to Jamaica and the night-time cold in Kensal Green cemetery, and Cal trying to tell him not to get involved with the Blade, and George Gilbert and his mates doing Ness behind closed doors, and Toby on the barge with the barge in flames . . .

There was too much to think about and not enough words in the world to explain things in such a way that he would not end up grassing. Say nothing and you had a chance to live. Name a name and you died by degrees.

So Joel told himself that the Blade would come for him. He'd done it before. He'd made that phone call when Joel had been brought in for attempting to mug the Asian woman in Portobello Road. It stood to reason that there was hope he would make a similar phone call now. But the thought of phone calls took Joel straight to the phone call that had brought the police to Meanwhile Gardens to pick him up. You scratch my back, I scratch yours.

Joel squeezed his eyes shut so hard that he should have seen stars, but all he saw were more images. He swallowed hard, and the noise he made sounded to him like a sonic boom that sent shock waves through the room. The constable put her hand on his back. He tried to take meagre comfort from this.

But she intended no comfort. She said his name. He realised he was meant to look up.

He raised his head and he saw that, while his thoughts had done cartwheels through his head, three more individuals had entered the interview room. Fabia Bender was one of them. The others were a tall black man in a business suit, a knife scar tracing a route down the side of his face, and a dumpy-looking woman in a donkey jacket that looked like something from the charity shop. These two stared at Joel. Their faces showed nothing. He took them to be plainclothes detectives like Sergeant Starr, which indeed they were: Winston Nkata and Barbara Havers from New Scotland Yard.

Fabia Bender said, 'Thank you, Sherry,' to the constable, and the woman left them. Fabia took her place next to Joel while the tall black man and the dumpy woman sat at the other two places at the table. Sergeant Starr, Fabia Bender told Joel, was fetching him a sandwich. They knew he was hungry. They knew he was tired. Things could, if he wanted, be over soon.

The black man spoke then, and while he did so, his companion kept her stony gaze fixed on Joel. He could feel the antipathy running off her. She frightened him, although she wasn't very large.

The man had a voice that blended Africa, South London, and the Caribbean. He sounded firm and sure. He said, 'Joel, you killed a cop's wife. You know that? We found a gun nearby. Fingerprints on it that'll turn out to be yours. Ballistics'll show the gun did the killing. CCTV film places you on the scene. You and 'nother bloke. What d'you got to say then, blood?'

There seemed no answer he could give to this. Joel thought of the sandwich, of Seargeant Starr. He was hungrier than they even knew.

'We want a name,' Winston Nkata said.

'We know you weren't alone,' Havers added.

Joel's reply to this was a nod. A single nod only, and nothing else. He gave it not because he agreed with anything the two detectives were saying but because he knew that what would happen next had been long determined by the unchanging world through which he moved.

Acknowledgments

Enormous thanks go to my fellow writer Courttia Newland in London, whose introduction to Ladbroke Grove, West Kilburn, North Kensington and the housing estates therein proved invaluable to my work both on this novel and on its predecessor *With No One as Witness*. I thank Betty Armstrong-Rossner for sharing her time with me at Holland Park School as well as for answering questions via email after my visit there. As always I am so indebted to Swati Gamble of Hodder & Stoughton that I can't hope to repay her kindness and generosity.

In the US, I must express my appreciation this final time – alas – to my wonderful assistant Dannielle Azoulay who could not be prevailed upon to move to the Pacific Northwest with me; to my husband Thomas McCabe for ceaselessly supporting the enormous effort that goes into completing a project of this nature; to my longtime cold reader Susan Berner for her early comments on the second draft of this novel; to my editor at HarperCollins, Carolyn Marino, and my editor at Hodder & Stoughton, Sue Fletcher, for their enthusiasm for the idea of turning the prism of Helen Lynley's murder and looking at it from a different angle; and to my literary agent Robert Gottlieb, for doing his part so well so that I can do mine.

As an American writing a novel set in London, I will have made unintended errors in these pages. The errors are mine alone and not the product of anyone who assisted me.

Seattle, Washington
December 12, 2005

Do you wish this wasn't the end?

Join us at www.hodder.co.uk, or follow us on
Twitter @hodderbooks to be a part of our community
of people who love the very best in books and reading.

Whether you want to discover more about a book
or an author, watch trailers and interviews, have the
chance to win early limited editions, or simply browse
our expert readers' selection of the very best books,
we think you'll find what you're looking for.

And if you don't,
that's the place to tell us what's missing.

We love what we do, and we'd love you to be part of it.

www.hodder.co.uk

@hodderbooks

HodderBooks

HodderBooks

Do you wish this wasn't the end?